IN BAD COMPANY

The Company Novels

In the Garden of Iden (1998)
Sky Coyote (1999)
   (collected as **On Company Time**, SFBC 1999)

Mendoza in Hollywood (2000)
The Graveyard Game (2001)
   (collected as **In Bad Company**, SFBC 2001)

IN BAD COMPANY

MENDOZA IN HOLLYWOOD
THE GRAVEYARD GAME

KAGE BAKER

FANTASY

MENDOZA IN HOLLYWOOD Copyright © 2000 by Kage Baker
    Originally published in hardcover by Harcourt, Inc. February 2000
THE GRAVEYARD GAME Copyright © 2001 by
Kage Baker
    Originally published in hardcover by Harcourt, Inc. February 2001

First SFBC Science Fiction Printing: February 2001

Published by arrangement with:
Harcourt, Inc.
15 East 26th Street
New York, NY 10010

Visit The SFBC online at *http://www.sfbc.com*
Visit Harcourt's website at *http://www.harcourtbooks.com/*
Visit Kage Baker's website at *http://members.tripod.com/MrsCheckerfield/*

ISBN 0-7394-1663-4

PRINTED IN THE UNITED STATES OF AMERICA

CONTENTS

Mendoza in Hollywood

This book is dedicated to Phyllis Patterson,
Instigator, with respect and affection;
And to the village she founded under the oak trees
And to its people. *Et in Arcadia ego.*

Prologue

*I*N THE TWENTY-FOURTH *century, about halfway through, it was said there was a fabulously powerful Company that could obtain virtually anything, if one had enough money.*

A Shakespeare first folio for your library? A live dodo for your aviary? An original sketch by da Vinci for your bedroom wall? Recordings of every performance Mick Jagger ever gave?

What about a necklace once worn by Cleopatra?

Have you a favorite historical figure? Would you like to have his baby? Or have your wife have his baby? Guaranteed authentic offspring of Julius Caesar, Napoleon Bonaparte, Elvis Presley.

As it happened, the Company actually existed, and it called itself Dr. Zeus Incorporated.

It began with two goals: to render human beings immortal and to develop time travel. Success in either goal was incomplete, though with all the money Dr. Zeus was making, it hardly mattered.

Time travel, for example, seems to be possible only backward, and then forward again to your point of departure in your present. Nor can you bring anything forward out of its own time into yours. And, by the way, history cannot be changed.

You can get around this somewhat by establishing indestructible warehouses in the past, where you stash all the loot you acquire there, to be retrieved in your present time. But you will need a workforce to maintain these sites, and run your errands through time . . .

Immortality is another matter. It's absolutely possible to confer it on a human being. Problem is, what you have when you've finished won't be a human being any longer, it'll be a cyborg, and how many people want to pay millions to become one of those things?

Somebody clever at Dr. Zeus came up with an idea that solved both problems at a stroke: Make your workforce immortal.

Since they'll live forever, there's no need to ship them back and forth through time: look at the costs you'll cut if you just create them at the beginning of time and let them work their way through it, day by day, like everybody else. Transmit your orders to your cyborgs using that subatomic particle you've discovered that exists everywhere and in all times at once. You're in business.

Every epoch has its abandoned children, its orphans of war or famine. Won't they be grateful to be rescued and gifted with immortality and lifetime jobs? And what jobs: rescuing precious things from the relentless sweep of oblivion. Of course they'll be grateful . . .

This is the third volume in the unofficial history of Dr. Zeus Incorporated.

In the Garden of Iden *introduced Botanist Mendoza, rescued as a child from the dungeons of the Inquisition in sixteenth-century Spain by a Company operative, Facilitator Joseph. In exchange for being gifted with immortality and a fantastically augmented body and mind, she would work in the past for the future, saving plants from extinction.*

On her first mission as an adult, Mendoza was sent with Joseph to England, at that time under the repressive Catholic rule of Bloody Mary. Disguised as mortals, she and other operatives were to loot the private gardens of an eccentric collector, Sir Walter Iden. Her goal: obtain samples of Ilex tormentosum, *a species that contained a powerful anticancer drug and that would be extinct in the future.*

Superior and snide as only a teenaged immortal can be, Mendoza looked down on the mortals among whom she had to labor—until she met Sir Walter's secretary, Nicholas Harpole, a Protestant heretic.

Mendoza and Nicholas engaged in a contest of wits that led them into bed. Passionately in love despite Joseph's warnings about the folly of becoming attached to a mortal, Mendoza attempted to juggle her heart, her mission, and her secret. She failed spectacularly.

Nicholas ended up being led to the stake. Mendoza was heartbroken, numb. Joseph came to her rescue again and got her transferred to the Company research base in South America: New World One.

Sky Coyote *opened 144 years later, as Joseph arrived at New World One for a brief holiday before going on to his next mission in Alta California. The project—persuading a village of Chumash to let the Company relocate them to one of its research bases—would be immense, requiring the services of operatives of all disciplines. Mendoza was also drafted for the mission.*

Unpleasant surprises awaited them in California. The immortal operatives met a number of their mortal masters from the future. They were appalled to find them ignorant and bigoted, fearful of their cyborg servants. Joseph learned unsettling facts about the Company that brought to mind a warning given him centuries earlier by Budu, the immortal who recruited him.

Why was it that, though the immortals were provided with information and entertainment from the future, nothing they received was ever dated later than the year 2355? The Company's official answer was that in 2355 Dr. Zeus would be able to go public with its great work and reward its operatives for their ages of service. But could the Company be believed?

Mendoza, back in contact again with the mortal world, found that her heart had not recovered from Nicholas. Despising the mortals and uncomfortable even with her own kind, she found comfort only in the vast wilderness of Alta California. In its forests she was able to leave her painful humanity and focus on the only reliable consolation: her work as a botanist.

Then, after 160 years, . . .

1

TRANSCRIPT ACNW032063 PRIVATE HEARING
Subject: Botanist Mendoza. March 20, 1863.
Five kilograms Theobromos administered.
Auditors magisterial: Labienus, Aethelstan, Gamaliel

Y OU WANT THE truth from me? It's a subjective thing, truth, you know, and you could easily get all the damning evidence you need from the datafeed transcripts. Oh, but you wouldn't understand my *motive*, would you? I see the point.

Will it help if I freely confess? I killed six—no, seven—mortal men, though I must say it was under provocation. I acted in direct violation of the laws that govern us, of the principles instilled in me when I was at school. I betrayed those principles by becoming involved in a mortal quarrel, supporting a cause I knew must fail in the end. Worst of all, I stole Company property—myself, when I deserted the post to which I had been assigned. I don't expect mercy, señors.

But it might help you to know that what I did, I did for love.

I had an unfortunate experience when I was a young operative, you see; I was baptized in the blood of a martyr. No, really. Did you know those things work, baptisms? I didn't. I was given the same education we all get, sanity and science and reasonable explanations for everything that happens in the world. Faith and its attendant rituals sound like a good deal, the whole eternal salvation thing, but inevitably they lead to fear, oppression, the rack and flames. I knew that much was true firsthand.

I was blindsided, as I'm sure you would have been, by the discovery that the experience actually left some kind of psychic mark on me. The mortal man smeared his blood and shouted his incantation, and there I stood like an animal that's been collared and let go, to wander bewildered among my own kind wondering what had happened. I was never right again after that. For a long time I thought I'd shaken off his spell. I was almost happy there in the mountains all alone. But you wouldn't let well enough alone. You sent me back into mortal places, and he found me again, tracked me by the mark he'd put on me for that purpose.

He will never let me rest.

Thank you, I certainly will have some more Theobromos. This is excellent stuff, by the way. Keep it coming, and no doubt you'll find out everything you want to know, with me a weepy mess at the end of it.

Okay, señors, are those tapes rolling?

2

Aɴʏ ᴏꜰ ʏᴏᴜ gentlemen ever served in Los Angeles? No? Rough place. Murders and fighting all the time since the Yankees came. No good reason to put a city there, on that clay bluff above the river; but Spain was so certain the Russians were going to invade Alta California, they had to go stick little pretend towns along its coast, like pins on a map. That way they could claim white settlement, because the mission Indians didn't count.

White! That was a laugh. What happened was that Felipe De Neve sent his goons riding up from Sinaloa with anybody he could bribe, threaten, or deceive into coming along as prospective settlers. There were maybe one or two Spaniards in that bunch, but the rest were mestizo and mulatto ex-soldiers, the mingled blood of New Spain and Africa with their wives and little children. De Neve's men dragged them up through the desert and over the mountains and set them down by that dry wash of a river, with its big sycamore trees. And after a mass was duly celebrated, they left them there, rode away and left them staring out into that night, and what an empty, empty night it must have been. No neighbors but the local Indians, and nothing to shelter them from the bears but brush huts. The settlers, huddled together listening to the coyotes howl, must have wondered what on God's earth they had got themselves into.

But they made the best of things, built a little adobe village, got some Indians to be their slaves, and in a generation or two they were gentlemen rancheros, with thousands of head of cattle on estates the size of small kingdoms, estates that would have made the threadbare gentry of the Old World sick with envy.

Of course, if one wanted a chamberpot or a carving knife or a bolt of cotton cloth, one had to wait for the supply ship from Mexico, which put in an appearance once every five years or so. This situation did not improve after the Revolution, either; a free and democratic bureaucracy moves even more slowly than a viceregal one. So in came the Yankee traders, smuggling consumer goods in their trading brigs, and the Californio rancheros were only too glad to do business with them. You know where *that* led. Richard Henry Dana wrote home about the fortune waiting to made by anybody with the ambition to build mills and factories here. Emigrants from the United States came struggling over the Rockies to see if it was true, some lady found a gold nugget in a sluice, and in no time at all we were all Americans, thanks to a little strong-arm work by John C. Fremont.

Not a bad thing, entirely, at first. It was the making of San Francisco. Los Angeles, though, sort of festered. It filled up with drunks and outlaws, white trash from the States who'd failed at gold prospecting, men on the run from civilization generally. There was nothing down there, you see, except dry brown hills and cattle, plenty of space to get lost in. Soon there were lots of saloons to get lost in too, and drunken shoot-outs in the streets. There were so many murders, people began calling Los Angeles the City of Devils rather than the City of Angels. *Los Diablos.* The old ranchero families huddled in their fine haciendas, listened to the gunfire, and wondered what in hell had happened to their town.

So you can see, señors, why I wasn't exactly thrilled to be posted down there. Monterey, green and gracious, that was where I preferred to be when I had to work near mortals; better still, the wild coastal mountains, the Ventana and Big Sur.

When you're coming down from the north, Los Angeles looks horrible at first: all brown rolling monotony. Hasn't got the redwoods, hasn't got the green mountains or the air like wine. It's a sad, trampled place. But let me put it on the record that my distaste at my assignment played no part in what happened. I went where I was told and did my job. I always have. We all do.

Weren't you briefed on this part? All right, I was sent to the HQ in Cahuenga Pass, close by La Nopalera. The cover is that it's a stagecoach stop. It's far enough out from Los Angeles to give us privacy, but being on the stage line, it's convenient for getting agents in and out. Agents and other things.

But that's all beside the point. Give me more of that—it's Guatemalan, isn't it?—and I'll try to stick to the story. You know, it's amazing, señors, but you bear a striking resemblance to certain inquisitors I knew in Old Spain. All of you. It's your eyes, I think. They're too patient.

PART ONE

Establishing Shot

CAHUENGA PASS, 1862

3

I ARRIVED DURING a miserable winter. It had rained most amazingly; the locals had never seen such rain. The canyons flooded. The new sewers down at the pueblo were a total loss. Roads washed out, and the stages were late or never arrived at all. There was, I understand, a little mining town up in the San Gabriels that was washed away completely—whole thing wound up down on the plain in scattered soggy bits. Only the rancheros were happy, because of the good grazing there was going to be from the rain. They thought. Little did they know that that was the last rain they were going to see for years. Before it rained again, Señor Drought and Señorita Smallpox and a few shrewd Yankee moneylenders would pretty well end the days of the *gentes de razón.* Ah, Los Angeles. One disaster after another, always has been.

Those particular disasters were still somewhat in the future on the day I finally walked into HQ. I'd followed the coast down as far as Buenaventura and then swung inland to follow El Camino Real through the hills and along the valley floor, traveling mostly by night to avoid the mortal population. The rain never let up the whole way, and I was soaked through. I crossed innumerable creeks swollen with white anger, roaring their way out to sea and taking willow snags with them. I saw smooth green hillsides so saturated, their grassy turf slid, like a half-taken scalp or a toupee, and left bare holes that the rain widened.

So much for Sunny California. All I saw of it that dark morning was water, brown water and creamy mud, and black twigs bobbing along in the hope of someday washing up on a white beach. You can imagine how grateful I was to see a plume of smoke going up between one foothill and the next. I checked my coordinates. *Cahuenga Pass HQ?* I broadcast tentatively.

Receiving, someone responded.

Botanist Mendoza reporting in.

Okay. You see the smoke? Follow it in.

And in another minute I'd come around the edge of a rockslide, and there it was, back under some oak trees, a long low adobe building and stable thatched with tules. A couple of cowhides had been stitched end to end and strung up in the trees like a tarpaulin, and under this nominal shelter an immortal crouched, attempting to build up a small fire with what looked like fairly damp wood. Arranged on the ground beside him were a blue graniteware coffeepot and a couple of skillets. The idea of grilled beef and frijoles drew me like a magnet.

"Hola." I jumped the last brown torrent and made my way up the sandy bank to the inn.

" 'Morning." The immortal looked up from under the brim of his dripping hat. "Welcome to the Hollywood Canteen."

"This *is* where Hollywood's going to be, isn't it?" I asked. I dropped my bag and held my hands down to the little fire. "Funny thought."

My informant stretched out an arm to point, trailing the fringe of his serape through dead leaves. "Chinese Theater and Hollywood Bowl right down there. Paramount Studios out in that direction. If you've got eighty years to hang around, we can go for breakfast at the Warner Brothers' commissary."

"I'll settle for what you've got." I eyed the skillets: last night's leftovers, cold and congealed. I looked around for something dry to add to the fire.

"So you're Mendoza?" inquired my host. He was lean and dark, with a thin black mustache and a sad, villainous face villainously scarred. The scars were all appliance makeup, of course, but they gave him the look that sends liquor store owners diving behind counters for their shotguns. I nodded in reply.

"Porfirio." He reached across the fire and shook hands with me. "I'm your case officer, subfacilitator, and security tech. Nice to meet you."

"Thanks. Is it dangerous here?"

"Oh, yeah," he said. He took up an oak log and tried stripping the wet cork layer off. "We don't get much trouble over this way, but you want to be careful when you ride out." He broke the log between his hands and fed it carefully into the coals. "Especially where you'll be working. Your temperate belt passes through some nasty bandit nests."

He was referring to the climate anomaly that was my present assignment, a long terrace roughly following the future route of Sunset Boulevard, where an unusual weather pattern had evolved some plants unique to the area, several of which had potentially remarkable commercial properties. Unfortunately they were all scheduled to go extinct in the next big drought, grazed out of existence by starving cattle.

"Bandits?" I was profoundly annoyed. "They told me I was going to be working in Beverly Hills!"

He was really amused by that. "Oh, you will be! It just isn't *there* yet. What, were you planning on having a cocktail in the Polo Lounge? You've got a while to wait if you want to see the mansions and the swimming pools." The fire blazed up at last, and he edged the skillets in toward its heart. "Come on, little fire, come on, we want some breakfast. Where's your horse, by the way?" He looked up in surprise as it occurred to him that I'd walked in.

"I don't have one."

"You're kidding me! *Nobody* walks down here. We've got a good stable you can choose from," he said firmly.

"That's okay. I don't care for horses, actually."

"I don't myself, but I ride them here. Trust me. You may need to get out of certain situations in a hurry. This is Los Diablos, after all." He put up a hand to stop my objections. "And don't think you can deal with the situation by just winking out at a speed mortals can't see. That may have been all right in the old days, but there are a lot of people out here now. It's too conspicuous. You'll need a horse. Everyone rides them. You'll need a gun, too."

"A gun?" I said, sitting back on my heels. "I've never carried a gun! You mean you've actually had to shoot people?"

He nodded somberly.

"But we were always trained—"

"I know," he said as he pushed the coffeepot over wavering flames. "The rules are different down here. You'll see."

"Who are you talking to?" Another operative emerged from the adobe, stooping below the wooden lintel of the door. He stood, sleepily scratching himself through a suit of long underwear worn under blue jeans. He gave a yawn that turned into a shiver.

"The botanist's here." Porfirio gestured with the skillet. "Mendoza, this is Einar. Einar, this is Mendoza."

"Zoologist grade 5." He came forward and shook my hand, then crouched down beside us. "Fire's not doing so good, is it?"

It wasn't. It had sunk away from the coffeepot and was smoking out.

"Wood's wet," he said.

"No kidding," we told him. He was tall for one of us, with white-blond hair and eyes like ice caves. Spectral coloring aside, he was a nice-enough-looking fellow.

"I was just giving her the safety lecture," Porfirio explained, handing him an oak log to break.

"Uh-huh." Einar snapped it into fragments. "Hey, chief, did you tell her about where we are? The movie studios and everything?"

"Yes. I thought you could issue her one of the Navy pistols and give her a short training session with it." Porfirio took the kindling from him and fed it into the coals, where it caught.

"No problem." Einar poked up the fire and coaxed a few tongues of flame to rise. "Come on, I need some coffee. There. Yeah, and I can show you where all the neat stuff will be. A lot of early cinema is shot in these very canyons. DeMille, D. W. Griffith, Hal Roach. Tinseltown!"

"But there's nothing there to actually see yet, is there?" I said.

"Well, no. Except the familiar landscapes, you know. I just enjoy the atmosphere of it all." Einar waved another oak branch in the air. "I mean, here we are in the mundane West, as far west as you can go, if you think about it, and everywhere around us the West of the cinema—the true West, if you will—is just sort of immanent. Hovering in these canyons like a spirit, waiting to be born. Ghosts of the future. All this greatness just about to happen, but not yet. We are the actors on a stage where the curtain hasn't risen!" His eyes were alight with enthusiasm.

"We're behind the scenes, you mean." Porfirio watched the fire doubtfully. A little thread of steam was rising from the mouth of the coffeepot, but the grease on the beefsteaks was still cold and waxy.

"Good morning, gentlemen," said yet another of my kind, stepping out into the courtyard. This one looked like a little Yankee lawyer or congressman, in a black suit and polished boots, with a cosmetically induced receding hairline that featured a sharp widow's peak. His eyes bulged slightly when he saw me. "*And* lady. Why, you must be our new botanist. Pleased to meet you, ma'am, I'm sure. Mendoza, isn't it? Yes. Oscar, grade 2 anthropologist, at your service."

I nodded at him. He put his hands in his pockets and came over to stand looking down at the fire. "Say, you know—"

"The wood's wet," said Porfirio.

"It is, isn't it? No, I was just thinking, wouldn't some of my corn bread go good with those steaks and beans? I'll just go fetch it out."

He ran back indoors, and Porfirio and Einar exchanged a disgruntled look.

"What?" I said.

"He tried making corn bread out of masa," Porfirio said. "He's very proud of it."

There was a gloomy silence. The trees dripped. There was a distant rumble of thunder; from the sound of it, the storm front was approaching the future site of the Whiskey a' Gogo.

"This is Raymond Chandler country too, isn't it?" I said.

"Yeah." Einar brightened. "Laurel Canyon, Hollywood Boulevard. I could show you—"

"Here it is." Oscar came bustling out with a pan. He dropped the bread beside the guttering fire—there was an audible thud—hitched up his trousers, and crouched down to cut slices. "Miss?" He offered me a slab of solid gray cake.

"My, isn't this substantial" was all I could think to say.

He beamed. "Real stick-to-your-ribs food for a chilly morning, yes indeed." He stood again with his hands in his pockets, rocking back and forth in his shiny shoes. "So, Miss. You're in botanicals? What are you going out for, if I may presume to ask?"

"Um—rarities. I was told there's a lot of good specimens of *Striata pulchra* I need to collect, as well as some mutations of common plants. Snowberry, Artemesias, that kind of thing. Creosote bush," I said. My job always sounds unbelievably boring to anyone but another botanist, so I didn't take offense when he blinked and forged on:

"You don't say so? I'm in notions, myself. Of course that's just my cover, ha ha! Actually I'm here to report on the impact of Yankee settlement on the local inhabitants—the decent ones, I mean—and document early Anglo-Californian culture."

"I see."

"I've got the sweetest little cart back there you ever saw." He nodded in the direction of the stables. "Just a wonder of clever design. Only requires the work of one mule—seats two—sides unfold for display of anything the locals could want to buy, from threepenny nails to dancing pumps, plus a complete photographer's apparatus, *plus* I can sleep in it, if I'm benighted somewhere and the weather's foul. I have but to fold down the seats and slide out the patented Collapsi-Cot!"

"Gosh, how clever."

"And, you know something? It's not Company issue! Not at all! The whole thing was made by a firm in Boston, Massachusetts!"

"Speaking of cots," said Einar, grinning. A female operative ap-

peared in the door of the house and yawned expansively, stretching
up her arms like a dancer. All I could see was a flowing wave of white
ruffles on a fancy nightdress, of the kind I hadn't owned in years.
When she brought her arms down in a slow dramatic gesture, I saw
that the bosom was cut low enough to make her look like the heroine
of a romantic novel. She gave a little toss of her head—lots of dark-
ringlet hair whooshed from side to side—and raised startling green
eyes to regard us.

"Imarte." I placed her.

"Would that be Mendoza?" She paced forward, pretending to peer
at me through the gloom. "It *is* the botanist Mendoza, isn't it? I believe
we worked together on the Humashup mission?"

"Yeah," I said.

"You were a friend of, ah, Joseph's." The corners of her lovely
mouth turned down.

"That's right." I grinned with all my teeth. "And you're an anthropologist." She hadn't got on very well with my old pal and erstwhile mentor, as I recalled. In fact, there'd been a truly nasty incident,
hadn't there? Well, this was going to be a fun posting.

"An insertion anthropologist," she corrected me, and Einar fell
over in helpless giggles. Even Porfirio smiled under his mustache.
Oscar turned red and looked at his shiny shoes. "I'm stationed in this
culture on a semipermanent basis, interacting with the mortal element
in Los Angeles in order to observe them more closely, as opposed to
an anthropologist like Oscar, who merely interviews," she said primly.

"She, uh, her cover identity is as a sort of a—" began Einar, but
Imarte finished:

"A whore. And there's really no need to make a dirty joke out of
it. I've been a temple prostitute on numerous occasions during my
career. Men speak the truth in bed, as the proverb goes, and what
better place to gain valuable insights into the *real* life of a culture?
And this is an astonishingly rich era for study. In one night I might
have a conversation with a Yankee from New York who came west
to pan for gold, followed by a Mexican outlaw whose family were
massacred by Indians, followed by an Australian ex-convict who failed
at piracy, followed by—well, followed by *anybody*." She tossed her
head. "Why, during this period in history the whole world is passing
through the Golden Gate!"

I don't think she meant the one in San Francisco. I blinked.

"You actually go to bed with all these people?" I asked.

She lifted her chin at me. "What, I should feel degraded? Should
we not consider it, rather, as a way for me to experience their lives

more fully, more meaningfully? Particularly in view of the fascinating material I'm compiling on mid-nineteenth-century mores and sexuality in California."

"Besides, any good stagecoach inn has at least one hooker," argued Porfirio. "It makes our cover more authentic, and contributes to our operating budget too."

This was more than I cared think about. I turned to Porfirio. "So, okay . . . I'd like to see my quarters after breakfast, if I could. I'm pretty tired."

"I'll bet you are, after walking all that way," Porfirio said.

"She walked here?" Oscar asked, staring. Imarte looked appalled.

Then there was another person standing beside our almost-fire, so silent in his approach, he seemed to have materialized there. He too was an immortal, but a young one; if you knew where to look, you could still see the scars of his augmentations. Remarkably enough, he had been made from an Indian. I hadn't seen many of these. My guess was he'd been among the few survivors of the Channel Island tribes, because he had their silver hair. It used to be a fairly common color for Native Americans, but smallpox was swiftly winnowing it out of their gene pool, the way the Black Death had rendered extinct similar exotic strains in Europeans.

"Hi," he said.

"Where've you been this morning? You were out early," said Porfirio.

"I heard him crying," the boy said, and held up in his cupped hands a tiny writhing monster from outer space. "It's a baby condor. *Gymnogyps californianus.* The mother hadn't come back to the nest in a while. I guess somebody shot her. I had to climb way, way back up the canyon to find him. Are you the new botanist?" He looked at me.

I nodded. "Mendoza. And you're—?"

"Juan Bautista." He came closer to the fire and peered down at it. "We need some dry wood or something, huh?"

"Wait, I have an idea," said Einar, and jumped up and ran inside. A moment later he emerged with a case bottle of a clear liquid. "Home-brewed aguardiente." He strode toward us, uncorking it. "We tried it on a plum pudding, and the damned thing burned for two hours. This'll do the job."

"Careful how you—" said Porfirio.

I threw myself flat and rolled. I heard Imarte scream. The fireball took out the cowhide tarp, but when I looked around cautiously, there was certainly a merry blaze going, all right, flames five feet high. And breakfast was cooking at last: in fact, the frijoles were on fire.

"SORRY ABOUT THAT," called Einar from where he had retreated about thirty yards up the hillside.

"Couldn't you have been more careful?" complained Oscar, squelching up from the mouth of the canyon. "Now my shoes are wet."

Later Porfirio showed me to my quarters. I had a cot all to myself in a board-and-batten lean-to next to the adobe stable. It smelled of horses, it had a dirt floor, and water was seeping up the wooden legs of my cot; but the stretched cow skin over the frame was dry, and so was the woolen blanket, and there was a dry ledge on which to put my bag. As field accommodations went, not too bad. I sat down and pulled off my wet boots.

Now, señors, I think some of the reason for my subsequent lamentable behavior is evident right here in the next scene. I hung up my oilskins and shrugged into dry clothes, meditating smugly to myself that it didn't take much to make me happy nowadays. I was an old hand now, wasn't I? A couple of tamales and a dry place to put up my feet and read a novel were enough. I could make my own space anywhere they posted me, as a good operative should. Wisdom at last. Perhaps I'd attained enlightenment after tramping through that beautiful desolation all these years collecting specimens alone. Certainly I had equilibrium.

Well. Where pride flaunts such scarlet banners, blares such brazen trumpets, you know what follows.

I had turned in early, after walking up on the ridge above the house to get a feel for the land, making friends with the oak trees, exploring the rooms of the coaching inn, chatting a little more with my fellow operatives (the male ones anyway) most amiably and normally. I had endured a few hands of gin rummy with Juan Bautista and an hour or so of anecdotes from Oscar about his mortal customers before I excused myself on the grounds that I'd been conscious for forty-eight hours and needed some alpha waves badly. And so I retired to my spartan room, pleased with myself. I'd done well for my first day back among people, I thought. I ought to be able to handle this posting just fine.

Maybe it was having an actual bed to lie down in that did it. See, I'd got out of the habit of sleeping like mortals, all those years in the mountains. I know, we're not supposed to do it—but it's so convenient just to lean into a tree limb or an angle of rock and fugue out for a couple of days, especially when you're on your own schedule. You have no idea how restful it can be. You just sort of tune in to the patterns moving in the tree or the rock, and you forget you even exist. One feels so vulnerable, undressing and getting into a bed. It summons up memories. The memory that it summoned was not one I wanted. I lay in the dark listening to the rain drip, to the wind sigh in the oak leaves. Because of the downpour, there were no coyotes howling, so you didn't necessarily know you were in California. With just the wind and the rain, it might have been anywhere. It might have been England.

Then I thought it had to be England, because my door was opening and there was green and sunlight beyond, that wet sunlight and drowningly intense green of an English garden. And *he* was there, standing in the doorway and looking at me. So tall, he had to bend to look into my narrow little room, and his black scholar's robe trailed in the lush summer grass. He was smiling, smiling at me in the old way, and held out his hand to me.

"*Talitha koum,*" he said, in that voice I'd have leaped out of a grave for. "Up and haste my love, my dove, my beautiful and come, for now is winter gone and rain departed and past!"

Who was he, señors? My martyr, who do you think? Nicholas Harpole, the mortal man with whom I fell in love when I was a young operative who should have known better. He died on April 1, 1555. This was either a dream or a haunting.

A haunting, I think.

I was so glad to get up and run to him where he waited in that doorway, to quit my dark cold room and run into the summer garden. Time must have turned backward, because there I was in my peach-colored gown with all the petticoats and my placketed bodice and stiff sleeves, and my hair falling loose. I never braided it back then, I was too vain. I leaped into his arms, and he made a little pleased chortling noise in his throat, and we were kissing, staggering backward and bumping into the orange tree, so his scholar's biretta was knocked forward over his eyes. I pushed it back, and we kissed and kissed, and oh the taste of his mouth and the scrape of stubble under his jaw and the hungry noises he made, I hadn't forgotten one detail in three centuries of trying desperately to forget.

We kissed until we were blind and gasping and his breeches needed to be unfastened, so I did it for him, and he pulled his long shirt up and out and freed himself, and I hadn't forgotten one detail about *that* either. Nor had I forgotten what to do next: one didn't just grab the front of one's skirt and haul it up, no, that was sluttish, one gathered it at the two sides as though one were going to sit down, and one lifted it in a discreet and genteel manner just far enough for the purpose. No bloomers, no underwear at all, only my fine-woven stockings gartered at the knee, and he was bending down to gather me up in his big fine hands and lift me against him.

Every detail was perfect and exact, the rustle of my gathered petticoats, the texture of his clean linen shirt and woolen doublet under my cheek, and how they smelled with the full hot sun on them releasing the scent of washing soap, and the green feverish privet-fragrance of the garden at high summer. I had my arms around his shoulders, my face pressed into the side of his neck, and a trickle of his sweat came coursing down as he labored, and I kissed the sweat away. And how we strove there together, in our mutual delight, as he growled his pleasure and I felt the vibration of it in his throat, and how soundly we knocked the trunk of the orange tree, until golden fruit fell all around us in a shower.

Oh, I thought, jackpot, surely that's a favorable omen. And as we rested, sobbing for breath, I felt a little stab. We both looked down, surprised. Protruding from my heart was the haft of a bodkin, and my heart's blood was welling out around it like a cut pomegranate. I laughed, joyous, incredulous, and he laughed with me. We both knew what this meant: I was free of the world now, I could stay in that garden with him eternally. Impossibly, wonderfully, my weary heart had stopped beating.

But I was slipping somehow, he was losing his hold, and the pain became terrible as I opened my eyes into darkness and felt the chill, heard the rain.

I hadn't gone through the doorway to him after all.

It took a long moment of struggling for air to be able to voice my agony. I wasn't loud, even so; but within seconds I heard hurrying feet crunching through the oak leaves.

Mendoza?

Go away!

He wouldn't go away. The door opened, and Porfirio looked in on me, all concern, a black silhouette against blacker night. Good God, I thought, what's he got that gun for?

You okay?

Yes! Don't you ever have bad dreams? I transmitted. He looked at me in irresolution a moment before nodding and shutting the door.

I guess, señors, if I were somebody else, I might have called him back and begged some kind of physical comfort as a favor, that I might not lie alone there in the dark. But I was and regretfully am myself, and I was not alone. The dark thundered around me like a palpable presence, and I belonged to it.

Next morning, Porfirio didn't mention the disturbance, and neither did I. I ran a diagnostic on myself, but everything tested out normal.

For the first couple of weeks that I lived at that stagecoach inn, there were no stagecoaches at all, and precious few travelers, because the roads were in no condition for going anywhere. This situation didn't improve much the whole time I was there, in part because Butterfield had decided to cancel its stage lines to California for the duration of the American Civil War, which left its rival Phineas Banning with a lot of territory to cover all by himself.

At about the point where there were no dead trees left to float down the canyons and you thought all the topsoil had washed out to sea, the rain stopped. The sun came out! And abruptly we were living in a paradise. The hills were green and purple and silver with sagebrush, the grazing land was brilliant lime-green with good grass, and everywhere there were banks of wildflowers. I stepped out under the dripping oak trees and looked up at the puffy white clouds in the blue sky. What a fine place, I thought. What a *beautiful* place. Murder? Robbery? Social dysfunction? Surely not in sunny southern California.

I was humming Rodrigo's *Concierto de Aranjuez* (first movement) as I went indoors to collect my field kit. Temperate belt, here I come! My ghost had not returned to haunt me, and my work was waiting. Who knew what botanic anomalies lay there waiting to be discovered?

But when I shouldered my pack and emerged from my quarters, Porfirio looked up from the cookfire he had just got going. "Where are you off to?" he asked with a frown.

"I thought I'd go get some work done at last, now that the rain's let up." I gestured at the enchanting sky.

"Not alone, you're not. Not over in that neck of the woods." He shook his head decisively. "Too many damn bandits. Wait until Einar gets up. He'll go with you."

"Oh, come on," I said, almost too surprised to be annoyed. "I've been on my own in California for years. I've outrun bears, Indians, and every one of the Joaquins. I worked in San Luis Obispo, where they hang so many outlaws, there's a gallows at the end of every street. I don't need an escort, thank you very much."

"It's different down here," he said, and something about his tone made me slip off my pack and find a dry place to wait as he got a pot of coffee brewing. Presently Einar came out, hopping on one booted foot as he pulled the other boot on.

"Hey, folks," he said. "Sunlight, huh? I guess I'll go out looking for a coyote or two today."

"You can go out with Mendoza," Porfirio said.

"Sure." He grinned at me. "You want the Grand Hollywood tour? Show you where the homes of the stars will be."

"I hope there's something useful growing there," I said grumpily. "And did I hear you say you were collecting *coyotes?*"

"Uh-huh." He poured a mug of coffee and handed it to me. "Don't laugh. The particular subspecies in this area will disappear after a couple of centuries. First they'll crossbreed with settlers' dogs. Then they'll crossbreed with wolves that escape from the zoo during a riot— that's during the dark ages of L.A.—and they'll get so huge and vicious, they'll start eating street beggars when the winters are bad."

"Jesus." I shivered, looking up at the sky. It was such an innocent shade of blue.

"But these little guys we have now are real sweet," he told me seriously, sipping his own coffee. "Sort of foxy. Nothing to worry about. Not like when I go after a bear."

"Bears?"

"California brown bears, like the one ·on the flag," he said. "They're already on the way out. Last known survivor in California will be shot right here, or actually out there"—he pointed down the canyon—"in 1912. Then they're extincto. Supposedly. They take some catching!"

"I can imagine." I looked into the bottom of my graniteware cup. "Tell me, are we likely to encounter any bears today?"

"Only if we're lucky," Einar said. "Since you have other work to do, I thought we'd keep things simple for now."

"Wonderful."

After a breakfast of velvety frijoles and steak rolled in tortillas, we saddled up and went to explore. Einar wore fearsome-looking bandoliers and a pair of shotguns, one behind either shoulder, like samurai swords. He showed me a trail that led through the back of the canyon and up a series of switchbacks to the top of the ridge. We followed the rimrock above the foothills, and down below us the plains swept out to the east, where there were big white snowy mountains, and south and west, where beyond the sprawl of adobes that was Los Angeles the land terminated in the blue line of the sea. Paler blue and farther out, lay a floating mountain.

"Is that an island?" I asked, squinting at it.

"Catalina," Einar said. "Location shots for *Mutiny on the Bounty, Treasure Island*, and a couple of versions of *Rain*, to name but a few.

And check this out." He leaned over in his saddle, pointing into a steep valley to our left. "Know what that is, down there? Hollywood Bowl! Imagine a big white half shell right there, with a reflecting pool in front of it, and a fan of seats sweeping up and up, rows and rows of pearly gray wooden benches, and thousands of screaming girls filling the amphitheater. Right down there is where the Beatles will perform. I've been up here at night, alone, and I swear to God I can hear them."

I stared down, impressed, though all I could see was a wilderness of sagebrush and toyon holly. "That's when, the 1960s? Only a century off. Where's the Hollywood sign?"

"Look across there." He pointed east, where a red mountain thrust up against the sky like a rippled wall. "Under the crest. It'll say *Holly-woodland* first, for the real estate park below it, and then when the last four letters fall off, they won't be replaced. There'll be two sister signs as well, for a couple of other developments, one down on that lower ridge that'll say *Bryn Mawr* and one over here that says *Outpost*, but they won't last long, and nobody will remember they were ever there. Neat, huh?"

"You certainly know the area," I said. We urged our horses on, and they continued to pick their way down the trail. "What are you going to do when it finally starts to happen, though? You're a zoologist. Dr. Z isn't likely to keep you here once the bears and the coyotes are gone."

"I have a double discipline," he said. "Programmed for zoology *and* cinema. I can stabilize a silver-nitrate print with one hand and do a genetic assay on a musk ox with the other. I've been in the field for millennia, though, so all my experience is with animals. Reindeer, caribou, wolves, those guys. The wheels of time roll swift around, though! When this assignment's up, I'm off to Menlo Park and then on to Melies in France. I'll be in on film from the beginning. I just hope Dr. Zeus sends me back here once the industry's up and running. Wouldn't that be swell?"

We both heard the shot, a little *pow* from somewhere down in the canyon to our right, and in a tiny fragment of time the bullet came zipping up through the bushes at us. We were off our horses and flat on the earth by then, however.

"Aw, shit," Einar said. He unslung one of the rifles and pointed it in the direction of our assailant; then he went into hyperfunction, firing and reloading faster than a mortal eye could have followed, sending a volley into the canyon below that cut a swath through the pretty purple sage. The echo boomed off the opposite ridge like thunder on Judgment Day. The mortal must have wondered what war zone he'd stumbled into, but he didn't wonder it for long; as I scanned, I felt his vital signs flutter and fade out.

"You killed the guy!" I gasped, rising shakily to my knees. The horses stood calmly cropping scrub, as though nothing had happened.

"Gee, I wish he hadn't done that." Einar stood and peered down the hill. "I thought he was going to leave me alone this time."

"You mean he's taken shots at you before?" I was incredulous. "And we rode up here anyway? Into *danger?*"

"What danger?" Einar loaded another couple of shells. "Stupid bastard knew he couldn't hit me, after all the times he's tried it. I'd shown him what I had to throw at him, too. When you're too dumb to learn, you're out of the gene pool, man. Down here, anyway."

I stood staring into the silent canyon. Cool air currents brought up a smell of cut sage and fresh blood. I half-expected sirens or shouting, but all I heard was the wind. "Shouldn't we go down and do something?" I suggested.

"Nope." Einar slung his gun back over his shoulder. "That's what buzzards are for. Turkey vultures, actually, according to J. B." He bent and offered me his cupped hands to climb back into the saddle. I vaulted up and sat there, bent forward nervously as he got back on his own horse.

"Let's get off the skyline, shall we?" I said. He nodded, and we moved on, descending the gentle ridges through the aromatic brush. After a moment I asked, "But who was he? He had to have had some family or somebody, someone we should notify."

Einar shook his head. "He killed 'em. That was why he was hiding out up here. Thirty-year-old Caucasian male psychopath from St. Louis, Missouri. Also killed two Mexican hookers and three Chinese guys of assorted vocations. I don't know why."

"Oh," I said. We rode on.

After a while, I ventured, "Are there many like him down here?"

"Some," Einar said. He got a loopy grin on his face. "But mostly lions and tigers and the California brown bear!"

"Oh my," I responded faintly. What sort of crazy place was this?

"Come on." He turned in his saddle to look at me, all alight with an idea. "I know that was a pretty grim scene up there. I'll show you something nice. You want to see? Come on." And he spurred his horse down the trail in front of me, and I followed while he chanted about the lions and tigers and bears all the way. Nobody else shot at us.

Below the foothills we came upon a sandy wagon track that ran east and west, in a fairly straight line through clumps of wild buckwheat and chaparral. We took it east, as I stared around in cautious expectation.

"Road to nowhere in particular," Einar said, "at the present time. But in a couple more decades, it'll be Prospect Avenue, when the genteel folks from back east build a little community here. Shortly thereafter they'll change the name to Hollywood Boulevard. Right here, to the left and right, the Walk of Stars will run. The neatest part, though, the *really* neat part, most people will never know about."

"And that would be?"

"This way." He urged his mount forward, counting off nonexistent cross streets on his interior map: "Highland, McCadden, Las Palmas, Cherokee . . ." Abruptly he turned his horse's head, and we left the trail a few yards north into the trackless thicket. "Here." He looped up the reins, slid from the saddle, and stood beaming at me, as though the Holy Grail was pulsing over the nearest cactus clump.

"Okay, señor." I looked from side to side. "What am I supposed to be seeing?"

"You're seeing the nice little streets laid out just like back east, with shady trees and picket fences and charming rose-covered cottages. Okay? All the white latticework and clapboard and gingerbread that relocated Yankees gotta have. It'll all be here. And right here, on this very spot, will stand the very nicest house with the very nicest garden, and you know whose house it'll be?" He held out his hands, as if framing a picture for me. "L. Frank Baum's. Ozcot, he'll call the place. This is where he'll settle down, this is where he'll write most of his books about the Tin Man and the Scarecrow and the rest of 'em. How many generations of children will read every word he wrote? How many kids will dream about escaping to Oz, and keep on dreaming about it when they're sick and old?"

"You're kidding." I dismounted and stared around, trying to see the fairy-tale house and its flowers in the midst of this wild place.

"I'm not. He'll even build a movie studio out there and produce his own Oz movies, years before MGM even exists. But then he dies, eventually, and guess what his wife does? *She burns his original manuscripts.* She doesn't think they're worth anything, so she piles them into the backyard incinerator, and they're reduced to ashes. All that magic, all those winkies and witches sift down in a fine silver dust through the grate and lie there forgotten, under an incinerator in a neglected garden behind a house that eventually gets sold and bulldozed." He made a leveling gesture with his hands.

"Neighborhood changes. Little houses get torn down, one by one. Gardens are paved over. A cheesy apartment building is built on this site. Right over there, the limousines zoom by, stars go to dinner at Musso & Frank's Grill, tourists wander the Walk of Stars and see the names of Judy Garland and Ray Bolger and everybody, and all the time this powder of dreams is buried and forgotten."

I stared at him, almost hearing the blaring horns of the traffic, almost breathing in the smell of expensive cigars and auto exhaust.

Smiling, Einar raised an index finger. *"Until,"* he said, "a young artist named Lincoln Copeland—"

"Oh, come on, not *the* Lincoln Copeland."

"Yes, *the* Lincoln Copeland comes out to Hollywood in 2076 to sketch the ruins. His timing's real bad. The Billy Tahiti riot breaks out while he's there. Bombs are going off all around him. He finds a bomb crater and dives for cover under a tipped-up piece of concrete that used to be a garage floor. He finds he's sitting in the middle of all this amazing gray dust.

"Now, by an incredible coincidence, L. Frank Baum is his favorite author, and luckily there's a street sign still standing. Copeland *knows* where he is, he knows this bomb crater was a magician's garden once, and he knows the story about the burnt manuscripts. What does he do? *He fills his pockets with dust.* With bullets whizzing and souvenir stands burning all around him, the guy crams all the gray dust he can carry into his pockets. And as soon as it's dark, he makes his way to Sunset Boulevard and follows it all the way to the beach, where he manages to thumb a ride out of the riot zone."

"I don't believe this."

"I swear to God! And as soon as he's out of harm's way, he finds a glass jar and shakes out his pockets, takes off every stitch he's got on and beats out the gray dust, and fills the jar. He takes it home with him. It's after that that his career takes off, that he suddenly begins painting those fantastic landscapes and allegorical murals that make him so amazingly rich. He doesn't know why he sees the things he sees when he picks up a brush, but he suspects it's because he dabs a tiny pinch of that gray dust on his palette every time he starts a new piece. He says so in his autobiography, written in 2140."

Einar bent and scooped up a double handful of sand, and let it sift through his fingers. "Right here. It's all right here, waiting to happen, man. Immanent. The air is on fire with it. Jesus, I love this town."

I started and stared, because for just a second I had seen it all: the pretty houses, the ruined city in flames, the Yellow Brick Road curving away up the wall of a soundstage.

"You are nuts," I said. "But I'll bet the Company brings you back here."

"Gotta hope." He grinned. Suddenly his gaze focused on a point in the distance behind me. He reached up for one of his shotguns. I dove for the dirt. "No, it's okay!" he said. "This is the trank gun." He aimed and fired. There was a dull bang and a plaintive little yip, and destiny had found another coyote.

We returned to the inn as darkness was falling. I had a couple of specimens of rare members of the artemisia family in my collecting kit, and Einar had a neatly trussed coyote sleeping peacefully in a wicker creel behind him. There was a loud argument going on around the cooking fire. The principal raised voice was female.

"That man had actually participated in the Bear Flag Rebellion!" Imarte was wailing. "Do you realize what a unique opportunity has been lost? Have you any idea of the insights he could have given us into the mind-set of the Anglo-American rebels?"

"I said I was sorry." Juan Bautista sounded as though he would have liked to crawl into a hole in the sand. "But Erich will die if he doesn't get the right food. It's not like I was chewing it up and vomiting it for him, anyway."

"Oh, my goddess." Imarte flung up her arms in disgust.

"The thing stinks, Juan. You're going to have to feed your bird someplace else, okay?" Porfirio said. As we rode into the clearing under the trees, it became obvious what he meant: someone, presumably Juan Bautista, had dragged a carcass into the clearing. It had been either a large dog or a small deer. I wasn't a zoologist, so I didn't know which. It had been worked over by coyotes already, so I doubted whether anyone else could have told either. Erich von Stroheim (that was what the baby condor had been christened) was sitting on it, looking bewildered. When Imarte raised her voice again, the bird ducked his head and shook his wings desperately, squeaking.

"I don't care what the little horror needs, he doesn't have to have it here when I'm bringing home a client," she said.

"Oh dear." Einar swung out of the saddle. "You lose another john?"

It seemed that the stagecoach had made a stop, and while the horses were being changed and the drivers were refreshing themselves, Imarte had sallied down and offered refreshment to the passengers. One gentleman had felt confident enough in his appetite to be able to do justice to her offer in the comparatively brief time allotted, and so she'd led him up to the adobe. Unfortunately the first sight that met his eye was Erich von Stroheim pecking at his supper, watched fondly by Juan Bautista. Not only had the gentleman been unable to avail

himself of the refreshment offered, he'd lost the lunch he'd partaken
of earlier in the day, and departed hastily.

"This *cannot* happen again," raged Imarte. "That creature *cannot*
be allowed to interfere with my work, do you understand? It's not
even as though he can be trained to live in the wild. He's nothing but
a pet."

"That's enough." Porfirio held up his hand. "Juan, take the carcass
away now. Downwind, please. We can work out a supplement with ,
chopped beef and an enzyme formula, okay? He'll be fine."

"Okay." Dejectedly Juan picked up the little condor and buttoned
him inside his shirt. The bird made happy sounds. Juan took the dead
thing by one leg and dragged it away into the darkness. Imarte went
flouncing off to her room.

"Ay-ay-ay." Porfirio put his face in his hands. "And was your day
good? Tell me your day was good."

"It was good," I said. Einar took down the creel—the coyote
twitched and growled in its sleep—and unsaddled our horses. He led
them off to the stable, whistling a little tune.

"Hell-oooo, everybody, I'm home," said Oscar as he strode into
the circle of firelight, leading his mule. Behind them the patent peddler's cart lurched from side to side, catching its roof on the lower
branches of the oak trees.

"And you had a good day too," Porfirio said.

"Oh, first-rate. Finally persuaded Mr. Cielo over at the walnut
orchard that he absolutely required the civilizing influence of music in
his home. He took a flageolet and six pieces of sheet music. Any day
now his neighbors (when he gets them) can expect to hear the strains
of popular selections from *The Bohemian Girl* wafting through the
walnut trees."

"Nice going." Porfirio poked up the fire. "Get any good material
on him?"

"Oh, certainly." Oscar set the hand brake on his cart and let the
mule out from between the traces. "Got a fair holo of his kitchen and
a splendid one of the parlor, all furnishings in situ. Extensive vocal
recordings, too. Got him to tell me half the story of his life. The
archivists will be pleased with yours truly, I shouldn't wonder." He
patted his mule fondly.

"So that's what you do?" I asked. "You go around pretending to
peddle stuff, and while people are talking to you, you record details
of historical interest about them?"

"Yes indeed! Though I hasten to add that no pretending is involved. I am a true and bona fide salesman of the first water. It's more

than a matter of personal pride with me, you see, that I can play the golden-tongued orator with the best of them when it comes to persuading a reluctant dweller in adobe that he or she wants—nay, *must* have—a patent cherry-pitting device superior to all previous models." Oscar was completely serious.

"Yeah, you are one nickel-plated Demosthenes, all right," Einar said, emerging from the stable to take charge of the mule. "Hey, Amelia, sweetie! How we doing, babe? How's our little hooves today?"

"No trace of lameness, I'm pleased to report," Oscar said. "She appears to have regained her customary surefootedness."

"Great." Einar led her away, and Oscar strutted up to the fire, hands in pockets.

"Yes, a most successful day. Might I inquire what's for supper this evening?"

"Grilled beef, tortillas, and frijoles," Porfirio said. "I just haven't had time to put it on yet."

"H'm." Oscar stood there in the light of the fire, rocking back and forth, a small frown on his bland face. "No chance of any cabbage, I suppose."

"What do you want, man? It's February."

"Oh, quite, quite, I see your point. You know what I'd like to do, though, when we can get a little more garden produce? I'd like to serve you folks a real authentic New England boiled supper. Yes, *sir*. You'd enjoy it no end. I daresay I could make the brown bread to go with it, too. I've got cans of molasses and a cake of raisins in my cart. Just the thing for a nippy night."

"Sure," Porfirio said without enthusiasm. He gave a narrow-eyed smile. "I meant to ask you: have you managed to sell that Criterion Patented Brassbound Pie Safe yet?"

Oscar's face lost some of its aplomb. "Well, no, not yet."

"Aw, that's a shame." Porfirio's grin of sympathy was very white under his mustache. "I can't think why nobody's interested in that thing."

"Neither can I," Oscar said. "You'd think, in this wild country overrun with mice and insects, that the natives would fight for a chance to possess such a marvel of guaranteed safe storage for all manner of comestibles, whether fresh-baked or fried, complete with buttermilk well and yeast compartment!"

I leaned forward, genuinely intrigued. "What is this thing, señor?"

"Ah! Let me show you," said Oscar, running to his cart. Porfirio rolled his eyes at me, but I got up and went to look anyway. Oscar unfastened a couple of latches and opened out one whole side of his cart. Glass jars glinted, and various hanging utensils and tools swung and shone in the firelight; but Oscar gestured past them to a big cabinet kind of thing that took up the entire back wall.

"There you have it. Positively the last word in preservation of fine baked goods. All drawers lined with plated tin to prevent the unwelcome attentions of minor pests such as mice, rats, or voles. And! Regard the patented securing latches designed to foil the marauding efforts of coons, polecats, or possums! Why, given the superb solid-oak construction and high-quality brass reinforcement, I daresay the Criterion Patented Brassbound Pie Safe could withstand even the predations of our friend the bruin."

He didn't know bears very well. Still, I had to admit the thing was impressive. It gleamed with fanciful brass trim all etched and inscribed with curlicue patterns of dizzying complexity. The various locks and latches looked formidable, and in addition to the drawers and cabinets were features at whose purpose I could only begin to guess: weird upswept or recessed sections.

"Gee, Oscar, that's really something," I said.

"Isn't it? And yet—can I interest even one member of the native populace of Los Angeles in this modern marvel? You'd think any one of them would jump at the chance to call it his or her own. Yet here it remains, unpurchased, unowned." Oscar shook his head in bewilderment.

"Well . . ." I hunted for the words. "You know, Oscar, I've been in California for a hundred and sixty-two years now, and in all that time I don't think I've ever seen a pie. Maybe that's part of the problem? I mean, nobody even grew much wheat here until recently. And this safe was designed for real Yankee-style pies, right? Two crusts, blueberry or rhubarb filling, that kind of thing?"

"True." Oscar looked wistful. "I could go for some rhubarb pie myself this very moment."

"San Francisco," Porfirio remarked from where he was stirring the frijoles. "That's where he could sell it. Not in El Pueblo de la Reina de Los Angeles."

"I beg to differ," Oscar said hotly. "I have sold these people maple syrup, quilting frames, and birch beer extract. I *will* sell this fine item. I simply haven't found the right customer yet."

"There must be plenty of gringos in Los Angeles," I said.

Porfirio grinned. "They don't make many pies. Too busy shooting one another."

"I'll sell it, I say, and not to a fellow Yankee," vowed Oscar. "Do you hear me, sir?"

"What, is this a bet?" said Porfirio, sitting back on his heels. "You want to wager on this?"

"By the goddess of consumer goods, yes! Name the stakes."

"Okay." Porfirio looked thoughtful. "Let's say . . . I get one of those snappy patent pearl-handled shaving razors you carry, if you don't sell that pie safe before you're transferred out of here. If you *do* sell it to a nongringo, I'll personally prepare that New England boiled supper for you. I'll even eat it with you."

"Then dig yourself a root cellar and lay in the rutabagas and parsnips," said Oscar, eyes flashing. "For I'm at my best when given a challenge, sir, I warn you."

Porfirio turned his attention back to the grilling beef. "Go for it, man" was his reply.

Personally I thought Porfirio would lose the bet. Los Angeles was becoming more of a Yankee city with every passing year. I learned from our copies of the bilingual *Los Angeles Star* that bullfights had at last been outlawed, to be replaced with the more humane pastimes of baseball, Presbyterian prayer services, and debating the outcome of the Civil War.

That Civil War raged on, over on the other end of the continent, at Mill Springs, Pea Ridge, and similar quaint-sounding places. Los Angeles was a world away from that, mired in its own problems. (Literally mired: the new brick sewers were proving a slightly more complicated engineering feat than had been expected.) To my amazement, though, the local Yankees—I must get out of the habit of calling them that, now that about half of them take it as a deadly insult—the *Americans* among us actually staked out sides and fought the war here in their own way, right in front of their bemused Hispanic neighbors. The older Yankee element, the sober sea captains and shopkeepers, were staunchly pro-Union. Banning, the stagecoach fellow, actually took time out from building his fine new house to donate land at San Pedro for a Union army barracks, so his side would have a military presence in California. The trash, the white boys from the States who'd failed at gold prospecting and trapping, were ramping stamping secessionists, so I guess Banning was wise.

Maybe I'll go on calling them Yankees anyway. The Union will win the war, after all. And it's less offensive than calling them Americans, to the people of South America, who have a claim to that word too; and less offensive to the Yankees than calling them Anglos, when so many of them were shipped into this country as Irish bond slaves. Come to think of it, I guess most Latinos don't like being called Hispanic, after the way the conquistadors treated their grandmothers. You can't win, can you?

To me, the whole issue seemed irrelevant, living back in that canyon as I was with the stagecoaches arriving and departing as time and mud permitted. I was more amused by the fact that Mexico was now in danger of becoming French. It should have warned me that I was out of touch, that I'd been in the hills too long. But for three hundred years now, the only political reality had been the long slow ruin of Old Spain's fortunes in the New World. These Kentuckians, these Narragansettians, these absurd Cape Codders, I knew they too were destined for their part on the world stage. But I was perhaps too slow in realizing that the curtain had already risen on their act. How could it affect me, after all? Nothing in the pageant of mortal fools had been able to affect me since the English Reformation, and I'd sworn never to let anything else get to me again.

4

Oᴜᴛ ᴏꜰ ᴍᴀsᴀ," announced Einar, rummaging through the store-room. "Out of brown sugar. Out of coffee. Half a bag of pinto beans. You want me to go to the store, chief?"

"Good idea. You can take those damn coyotes to the transport depot too, how about it?" Porfirio said.

"Okay, okay. I didn't think they'd make that much noise. The last batch didn't."

"You're going into town?" Imarte stuck her head out of her room. "Will you wait until I'm dressed? I'd like to go down to the Bella Union."

"I wasn't planning on staying overnight," Einar said.

"Don't worry. I'll catch the next stagecoach home." She ducked back into her room, and there was a great rustling of silks and creaking of whalebone. I was wondering why she didn't walk back—I would have, because the pueblo didn't look that far away from up on the ridge—when Einar turned to me and asked:

"How about it? You want to come?"

I blinked at him in surprise. "Okay," I said, deciding to continue my program of readaptation to human company, though it did seem a bit reckless. If there were bloodthirsty crazies hiding out in the chaparral, how many more of them would be in the infamous saloons and gambling dens? On the other hand, I'd have to visit the place some-time, and Einar seemed able enough with a gun.

I went to put on my best shawl and pin up my hair. By the time I came out, Einar had hitched a pair of horses to our wagon. Imarte came sashaying from the adobe, complete with painted face, scarlet satins, and feather boa.

"Wow, you really do look like a whore," I complimented her, with my most naive expression.

"Thank you. You won't mind riding in the back with the coyotes, will you, dear?" She vaulted into the seat beside Einar. "This satin crushes so terribly, the least little thing makes wrinkles that simply won't come out. I envy you that plain broadcloth. And how lucky you are to be able to wear that color. Dirt and stains are almost invisible on that particular shade of—what would you call it? Olive drab?"

"Matches your eyes, doesn't it?" I said, clambering up into the back, where the month's catch of *Canis latrans* slept soundly in their crates.

"Break it up, ladies," Porfirio snapped at us. I shelved my next remark, which had to do with the bitches I was riding with. You know, in the twenty-second century the feminist Ephesian Party will bid for political power on the grounds that if women ran the world, there would be less senseless aggression. Strangely, they'll never be able to get a consensus within their own party. Can you imagine why not?

"Let's have a nice happy little drive into town, shall we?" Einar said. He clucked to the horses, and we bumped and rolled away down the canyon, to turn right on the dirt road that was El Camino Real and would one day be the Hollywood Freeway.

"Check it out!" Einar pointed with his whip as we rumbled along. "Hollywood Bowl, back up in there. *Symphonies under the Stars*. That hill over there? Whitley Heights, where all the movie stars live before Beverly Hills is fashionable. Rudolph Valentino will have a house right *there*."

"I've never seen one of his films," I said. "I really ought to, sometime."

Einar half-turned in his seat as an idea hit him. "We should have a film festival! We can show them after dark. All the great Golden Age of Cinema stuff. I wonder if I can get films that were shot right here in town."

"Probably." Imarte sniffed. "You could try to find the interesting ones. There are only a few with any historical value, in my opinion."

"We'll do it," said Einar, bouncing on his seat. "We'll have the first film festival in Hollywood, how about it? I'll see what I can order from Central HQ."

We emerged from Cahuenga Pass and swung left down the track of the future Hollywood Boulevard, where Einar gave us a running commentary on the famous sights we couldn't see yet. I remember the corner of Hollywood and Vine, not for any precognitive vision of Clara Bow zooming around it in a fast car but because we had to bump through a particularly vicious seasonal creek that cut across it, and mud splattered Imarte's scarlet finery. I was proud of myself for not smiling.

As we entered the plain below the foothills, the land opened out more and changed: low green hills gently rolling as far as the eye could see, dotted with oak trees and starred everywhere with golden poppies. Here and there wandered herds of longhorn cattle, grazing and growing fat.

"See those guys?" Einar's voice was sober. "This is their last hurrah. Nobody knows it yet, of course, but this drought will pretty much wipe them out. And when they go, the old Mexican gentry go too; they'll lose their revenue, get into debt to the Yankees, and sell off their estates. Boom, whole way of life gone. The Yankees will run cattle after the drought, but not these longhorns: they'll bring in their own stock, Jerseys and Holsteins—Eurocows. All kinds of useful genetic traits scheduled to disappear from the bovine gene pool when these longhorns nearly go extinct. It'll be a bitch collecting specimens—expensive, too—but I really should get started on it."

"Why expensive?" Imarte asked. "I should imagine the rancheros will be desperate to sell, once the drought is in progress."

"Yeah, but by then the specimens will be weak and stressed out. The Company wants healthy, happy cows." Einar shook his head.

I sat up and stared at the gentle landscape, so pastoral, such an idyll. Cracked earth and skeletons soon, to be followed by another Eden, this time of prosperous little Yankee orange groves, to be followed by a gray wasteland of diesel exhaust, concrete, and steel. Paradise and hell, boom and bust, together forever in Los Angeles. I shivered and wished I was back in Big Sur.

We followed the Hollywood Freeway route all the way into the city, creaked gradually uphill, and paused at the top of a long low ridge. Einar pointed at the vista below us, a wide gesture taking in the whole horizon. "There you go, Mendoza. The original wretched hive of villainy and scum."

It didn't look particularly dangerous. What surprised me was the space it took up. It sprawled and sprawled, out to the edges of the sky, and yet you could count the number of two-story buildings on the fingers of one hand. Right below us was a squat brick thing like an armory in a weedy central plaza crisscrossed with dirt paths. I found out later that it was a cistern for dry years. There was a solid-looking church with its back to us—recently repaired, to judge from the two-tone plaster. There were a couple of stately adobes with pink tile roofs and peeling whitewash. But the vast majority of structures were little

flat-topped shacks with tarred roofs, rows of them leaning on one another and single ones peeping out from orchards or ranged across
fields. I couldn't see a single living soul moving in that vast panorama.
You could have fit every other city in California into the space Los
Angeles took up, and yet it looked like nothing so much as somebody's
big cow pasture, with an unusual number of cowsheds. A dark line of
willows and cottonwoods snaked through it, and one particularly big
sycamore: the trees must have marked the bed of the Los Angeles
River, which actually had water in it this year.

Crack! A bullet tore up weeds a few yards down the hill from
where we were parked. Oh, there was somebody. We looked down
into the belligerent stare of a man who had come out to the edge of
his little orchard. He was lowering a long rifle.

"Thass a *wahnin'*!" he called hoarsely. "Y'all stay *outa* mah orchard. Come down some *otha* place!"

Einar grinned and signed tipping his hat. "You bet, Davy Crockett!" He shook the reins and turned us around, and we followed the
trail along the ridge and down into town. Well, it was clear where all
the people must be: hiding. My knuckles were white as I clenched the
sides of the wagon.

"Does everybody shoot at perfect strangers here?" I asked between
clenched teeth.

"If they think you're going to trespass on their property, yeah,"
said Einar. He began to sing a ballad about Davy Crockett, waving
one arm for dramatic emphasis.

"Oh, shut up," said Imarte, and for once I agreed with her.

There actually was a business district, with some Yankee-style
stores of brick and of timber, and a couple of adobes Yankeefied with
false fronts. Here was where all the people had got to. There were
wagons like ours rumbling to and fro, driven by Mexicans or Yankees.
There were white boys leaning in the doorways of saloons, looking
out at the world through painfully narrowed Clint Eastwood eyes.
There were Mexican dons on elegantly caparisoned horses pacing
along, and some of these were distinctly African in appearance: dignified old gentlemen whose great-grandfathers had bought their way
out of slavery by joining the Spanish army and exploring the New
World. And here was a genuine Indian begging in the gutter, with
eerily empty eyes. Imarte leaned over and said a few words to him as
we passed. His gaze snapped into focus for a moment and locked on
her. He shouted something in a desperate voice and stumbled after the
wagon, dragging one foot. Imarte made a face and tossed him a coin.

He fell flat, covering it with his body. I looked away. Imarte shook her head.

"That man's race once conquered all their neighbors, for hundreds of miles to the north and east. They had a sophisticated monotheistic religion the equal of Christianity or Islam. Look at him now." *Sic transit Chinigchinix*, I thought.

In the next block, we passed another prostrate beggar, drunk and wailing out "Flow Gently, Sweet Afton" in ghastly Southend Cockney. Two gutters over, an obvious native of Georgia was murdering "Sweet Betsy from Pike." And a Mexican crawling along on hands and knees implored his little white dove to return to his embrace. The mud is a democratic place, at least.

And here were *señoritas de mala vida*, dressed like our Imarte, liberally represented by the assorted races, swinging along with the set smiles, upper-arm bruises, and blank eyes of the true professional. And a Chinese fellow going somewhere in quiet, self-effacing haste. And an august old shopkeeper standing just inside the door of his emporium and jingling his keys as he watched the passing scene: a Jew, to judge from the name painted on his sign. He looked exactly like Uncle Sam. Put him in a striped top hat and long tailcoat, and he could have posed for a twentieth-century war bond poster.

On Calle Principal we pulled up in front of a little place whose sign read BELLA UNION. It was dark and dirty. Imarte jumped down from her seat with the grace of a cat and made straight for the door, a gleam in her eye.

"Wait a minute," Einar said, sliding down. "Marcus has something in his hoof. Whats'a matter, boy?"

I climbed down while he coaxed the horse to put its foot up for him. Was the hotel as bad inside as it looked from the street? I ventured close enough to peer inside. God, it was worse. That couldn't be a dirt floor, could it?

There at the long bar was Imarte, advancing on the British tar who had just been served a local beer and was now staring at his glass with horrified wonder.

"Hello there, sailor. In town long?" she said, flexing a tit at him. "Got time to tell me your life story?"

He turned to meet her eyes. "It's like piss, for Chrissake!" he complained.

Silly me, to stand in the doorway of a lesser class of hotel looking amused. A regular customer mistook my smile and was suddenly in front of me, breathing rye whiskey through the fringe of his mustache.

"Well, now, señorita, you looking for someone to dance with? You want me to show you how we dance the fandango out Durango way, huh? Nice earrings. They real gold, Chiquita?" He reached for my face.

I took two hasty steps backward and summoned up my best Katherine Hepburn imitation. "Sir, if you *ever* presume to lay hands upon me, I assure you legal action will follow! Do I make myself clear, you palsied, imbecilic, and alcoholic cretin?"

He staggered back, very surprised. "Lady, I'm sorry," he gasped. "I thought you was Spanish."

Mental note: Leave the gold hoops at home next time you visit sunny downtown Los Angeles. And ditch the rebozo, too. I turned on my heel and stalked out. Einar was just releasing Marcus's hoof. He stared at me openmouthed. "You went in there?"

"Stupid, wasn't it?" I agreed, climbing up on the seat. "Let's get the hell out of here, shall we?" I didn't like mortals, I *really* didn't like mortals. In fact, I hated the sight and the smell of them.

"Come on, I'll buy you a drink," he said.

"Not in there, you won't."

He got his crazy smile again. "How about a cocktail in the Lost City of the Lizard People?"

It turned out that if you went to a drab-looking little adobe on Calle Primavera and knocked, a mortal man would let you in and obligingly help you unload your crates of tranquilized coyotes. He would then slide back a section of the floor, revealing a service elevator, on which the coyotes descended toward a new life following air transport to a Company zoo. The man would then bow you to an ornate wardrobe, which, when opened, proved to be a passenger elevator. Once you entered it, it dropped with unnerving speed thirty stories to a short length of tunnel tiled in gold enamel. At the end of the tunnel was a first-rate Company cocktail lounge, beyond which was a Company transport terminal, also tiled in gold enamel.

"There's miles of tunnel, running all the way to the undersea base in the Catalina Channel," Einar told me over a couple of margaritas. "And one long tunnel runs out to the Mojave base under the sand."

"Nice." I bit into my wedge of lime. "But what's with the lizard motif?" I waved a hand at the decor. There were lizard patterns on everything, woven into the carpet, tooled into the booth leather, printed on the cocktail napkins.

"Joke," he said. "In 1934, this guy will claim that an old Indian told him about a highly advanced race of lizard people who retreated underground following a global catastrophe in 3000 B.C.E. They built a city in the shape of a giant lizard and a maze of gold-filled tunnels right here under Los Angeles, supposedly, using magic chemicals that melted through bedrock. Rooms crammed with gold and sacred tablets, all kinds of weird shit. So anyway, this guy claims he's found out where the gold chambers are, using an invention he calls the Radio X-Ray, and he actually gets permission from the city authorities to drill. Tells them he's located a treasure room a thousand feet down. He only goes about three hundred fifty feet before the shaft starts to collapse. Tells the city he's putting the dig on hold until he can solve the technical problems, which he expects to do in no time. Then he vanishes. Drops out of sight. Never heard from again. Obviously the lizard people got him."

"Obviously."

"It gets weirder. This'll be in 1934, right? But by 1932 the Company will have abandoned this base and filled in the tunnels. Earthquake in Long Beach the next year, remember? By the time the guy claims to detect the tunnels, *they won't be there anymore*. Last call at the old Lizard Bar was months beforehand. Nuts, huh?"

"Nuts. Unless maybe the man is an undiagnosed remote viewer."

"Could be." Einar tilted his glass. "Want another cocktail?"

5

AFTER THAT VISIT I was content to stay close to Hollywood, venturing out to collect specimens when Einar's schedule allowed him to go with me. No more argument on my part that I didn't need an escort. Hot lead seemed to be the language of social encounter down there, and I felt squeamish about becoming fluent in it, though I dutifully practiced hyperfunction with a Navy pistol.

We were by no means so isolated as I had thought. We got mail; we got magazines. We subscribed to the *Los Angeles Estrella/Star*, to a couple of back-east papers so we could follow the Civil War news, and Porfirio had a subscription to *Punch*, of all things. I read it for the humor, though the British slant on the war was strange. They played both sides of the diplomatic fence with a prissy hypocrisy that I took to be Victorian. I wasn't impressed. I had known the brilliant savages of the Tudor period firsthand, and, though I'd never thought I'd say it, I preferred them to their smug descendants.

Yes, we really had our window onto the world, despite the lack of radio for the local Company news—no reception back in our canyon, because those granite hills kept the feeble broadcast out. And we made our own nightlife; we even had movies. Not holos, you understand, movies.

I woke from uneasy dreams one bright morning to find a card stuck in my boots. Yawning, I examined it, sitting on the edge of my cot. It was cream-colored pasteboard, inscribed by hand in purple ink, with nice calligraphy, and it told me that I was invited to the Cahuenga Pass Film Festival, which was to take place tonight at 2000 hours sharp. This evening's featured film: Hollywood's first premiere of the director's cut of *Greed*, based on Frank Norris's classic novel *Mc-*

Teague, a tale of mortal doom. Approximate screening time nine hours, so refreshments would be provided. Formal dress optional. (Good; the closest thing I had to evening wear was a black rebozo.) Location: suite B of the Cahuenga Pass Hilton. (Yuck yuck.) My host: Einar.

I pulled on my boots and wandered out to the fire, where Porfirio was frying breakfast. "Did you get one of these?" I held the card out to him. "What's it all about?"

"Didn't you hear him chortling when the afternoon stage left yesterday?" Porfirio said, handing me a mug of coffee, which I accepted gratefully. "He got a big box he'd ordered from Central HQ. He was fussing around in his room all last night. He's in there now, as a matter of fact. This should be some party."

"I guess." I looked at the card doubtfully. "Will we all fit in his room? I'm not much for parties, really."

"It's not a party party, it's a film screening. He's working like a dog to create a sense of occasion. I'm going, and you should too." Porfirio looked at me sternly. "What else have you got to do tonight? Sit in your room and look at plant DNA? This will be good for you."

Actually I enjoyed sitting in my room in front of a cozily glowing credenza, but I didn't want to disappoint Einar. Accordingly, at 2000 hours that evening I wrapped my black shawl around me and ventured into the adobe. I could see lamplight coming from Einar's room; and was that music? It sounded like a selection of famous film themes by Hollywood composers, tinnily played on a battery-powered portable, and that in fact was what it was. But I barely noticed the music once I crossed the threshold of Einar's room.

He *had* worked to create a sense of occasion. It was a small square room with bare adobe walls and rough furniture of peeled logs and cowhide; but he had borrowed Imarte's red velveteen bedspread and tacked it up in hanging swags against one wall, and a dusty oriental carpet had been rolled out on the floor, and a fairly clean sheet had been tacked up on another wall. That had to have come from Imarte's bed, too. In fact, there was a lot of her finery draped around to give the room a film palace look. She was being an awfully good sport about this, wasn't she? And there she stood in a ballgown of Arrest Me Red, holding forth sententiously to Oscar:

". . . outrageous what they did to von Stroheim, but it's a classic case of the fate of great literature in Hollywood. Of course it was bound to happen, given the incredible social significance of Norris's work. Audiences simply weren't ready for the grim realism, the pitiless examination of hopelessness among the uneducated working classes, the dwindling of the American Dream to despair, the ugly realities of passion."

"You don't say?" Oscar raised a graniteware coffee mug to his lips and took a cautious sip of the contents. He looked startled. "Good Lord, Einar, is this gin we're drinking?"

"Sure is," Einar said, welcoming me with a bow and handing me my libation for the evening. He was resplendent in a black tailcoat, stiff collar, and flowing foulard tie. He'd greased and combed his hair back, and so had Porfirio, also dressed to the nines. They looked like a couple of cast members from a melodrama. "It's a martini, complete with olive. Don't worry, the gin hasn't been anywhere near a bathtub. Mendoza, you look lovely this evening; pray be seated. A space has been reserved for you in the balcony." He gestured grandly at his cowhide bed, which had been dressed up with needlepoint cushions. "You too, Imarte; and as highest-ranking cyborg here, Porfirio, you have the seat of honor between the ladies, okay? The rest of us gentlemen will be seated in the loge. Well, we're only waiting for J. B. to make his fashionably late entrance—"

"Here I am. Sorry," murmured Juan Bautista from the doorway. Apparently he had no shirts that weren't plain calico, but he'd made a pasteboard shirtfront, inked a bow tie and little buttons on it, and pinned it to his chest. He'd made a little shirtfront for Erich von Stroheim too, and tied it around the bird's repulsive neck with string. Erich huddled in his arms, looking at us doubtfully.

"Cool! The director himself, here to attend his first Hollywood premiere!" Einar welcomed them in. "Have a seat, gentlemen, down in the loge—or maybe that's the mezzanine." It amounted to a row of pillows on the floor in front of the bed. Juan Bautista settled down comfortably crosslegged, and Oscar lowered into place beside him, grumbling about having to press his trousers tomorrow. Erich von Stroheim took an experimental peck at his own shirtfront, but Juan Bautista reproved him gently, closing his fingers around the nasty-looking beak. The bird lowered his head to be scratched, making a little pleading noise.

"Well, the appointed hour is upon us," said Einar, stepping to the front of the room, before the white sheet. He took his six-gun from his holster, and I half-expected him to shoot out the lamps, but he reversed it and held the butt to his face, pretending he was speaking into a microphone. "Ladies and gentlemen . . ." He altered his voice to sound as though he were speaking into a twentieth-century PA system, complete with the boom and squeal of badly adjusted speakers. "Ladies and gentlemen and, uh, condor, welcome to the first installment of the first-ever Cahuenga Pass Film Festival. And what a glittering turnout we have here tonight. We're pleased to present, as our first offering, Director Erich von Stroheim's immortal classic *Greed*, starring Jean Hersholt and Zasu Pitts. Do I see the director in the audience? Stand up and take a bow, Mr. von Stroheim!" Juan Bautista held up the bird and dipped him forward in a little bow. Erich gronked querulously and pecked to have his head scratched again. We all applauded.

"Thank you, Mr. von Stroheim. All right. Now, tonight's offering is one of the truly great films cinema has produced. Unlike most of our future offerings, it was *not* filmed primarily in Hollywood, mostly because the director was a raving fanatic about location shots. Notable examples are the authentic San Francisco sequences shot on Polk Street and the climactic scene in Death Valley, which nearly killed the cast and crew as temperatures soared to 120 degrees Fahrenheit and the camera equipment had to be iced down.

"The location shots were necessary, because von Stroheim insisted on a literal interpretation of the book, which meant he filmed *every single scene*. Unfortunately, the age of the miniseries had not yet arrived, and the resulting nine-hour spectacle was edited down by Universal executives to a much smaller masterpiece. Von Stroheim never forgave the studio, and they never forgave him either, which was why the rest of his cinematic career was pretty much limited to his role as Gloria Swanson's butler in *Sunset Boulevard*.

"Anyhow, Doctor Zeus will have a quick-fingered operative in the cutting room, with the result that we are able to present tonight the full-length director's cut, made from the original silver nitrate print, complete with the Variety Theater scene in its original version and the subplot involving the crazed Mexican cleaning woman and her Jewish pawnbroker boyfriend. I should warn the more sensitive in our audience that some of the material is really, *really* racially offensive, okay? So I apologize to our Hispanic audience members in advance, and also to anybody who might have been Jewish when they were mortal—?" He looked inquiringly at Imarte.

"I was *Chaldean*," she corrected him.

I put up my hand. "I was arrested by the Inquisition. Does that count?"

"I think that makes you an honorary Jew," Porfirio said.

"Okay," continued Einar, "just don't get sore. Now, before we begin, I'd like to serve refreshments." He went to the corner table and took down two big bowls of popcorn and handed them out. "Eat hearty. There will be brief intermissions when I change reels, because, no, ladies and gentlemen, this is not a holo! Tonight's entertainment comes to you in the authentic and time-honored medium of reel cinema." He gestured dramatically to the corner, where he'd opened out the primitive-looking projector and connected it with alligator clamps to a solar battery unit. "So without further ado, distinguished audience . . ."

Einar blew out the lamps one after another, killed the music, and stepped over Oscar to reach the projector. A click and a buzz, a white light on the screen briefly occluded by his head and shoulders as he groped his way back to his seat; then the flickering images held our attention, and the only sound was the faint whirring of the projector and the crunching of popcorn.

It was a great film. Horrible unrelenting tragedy, but you couldn't be depressed watching it, because you were constantly exhilarated at what a work of bloody genius it was. Have you ever seen it, señors? From the opening scenes in the mining town, where you meet this appalling, tender-hearted ogre who protects little birds but is willing to kill his fellow men with a backhand blow, to his astonishing transformation into a *dentist*, for Christ's sake, to the banal and doomed love story with the girl who won the lottery—their degeneration, she into a grasping harpy, he into a bestial drunk—and the murder, the chase across the desert, the final scenes where the poor monster finds himself handcuffed to a dead man on the floor of Death Valley, the last frames where he watches the expiring flutters of the damn canary he's brought along with him, cage and all, on his flight from justice—I tell you, it beats Hamlet for craziness and black humor in tragedy. Not a ray of hope in a frame of it.

So why did we sit there enthralled for nine hours, never saying a word? The last frames unrolled, the progressively longer shots of the wretched mortal's end winked out, and the screen went white. It was 0500 hours. There was silence but for Juan Bautista's stifled sob.

"That poor canary," he gasped.

Imarte began to applaud, and we all joined in, even Juan Bautista. And I think our applause counted for something. We're immortals, after all. We've watched history itself unspool before our eyes. It takes a lot to impress us. So even though the real Erich von Stroheim had yet to be born on the night we watched *Greed*, I hope his shade heard our ovation for his butchered masterpiece. I hope he was appeased, somewhere, somehow.

6

I WAS SO impressed with the film, I accessed the text of *McTeague* and read it through in the following days, as the inn drowsed between stagecoach visits.

On a good day we got two passing through, pausing long enough to let off or pick up mail or passengers. If one of the horses was in need of attention, Porfirio got out his farrier's tools while the passengers wandered up and down our little canyon or availed themselves of our remarkably clean and tidy outhouse. Imarte would hurry to entertain them; if it was a group of mixed couples, she'd leave off the feather boa and play gracious hostess rather than daughter of joy. She'd do whatever it took to get them talking to her about themselves. There were in-depth interviews with an Italian opera singer headed for San Francisco, a Scot in a genuine kilt (sporran and all), two Basque wool magnates who might have been identical twins though they weren't, and a Mormon patriarch from San Bernardino, who proposed marriage to Imarte on half an hour's acquaintance. She was genuinely regretful at having to turn him down. ("What an incredible opportunity to study a fascinating mutation of American folk morality!") I mostly slunk away into the oaks when passengers were around. Mortals got on my nerves, these days.

They never spent the night, unless they were Company operatives passing through. Porfirio would explain politely that all our rooms were presently occupied, and the *señores y señoras* would most certainly find lodging at the Garnier brothers' inn farther up the highway. If the *señores y señoras* got ugly about it, a bottle of aguardiente was offered for the road; if that failed to mollify them, Einar would swagger into sight with his bandoliers and look menacing.

But once in a while one of our own would climb out and have his or her trunk handed down, and there'd be anecdote swapping and aguardiente far into the night. Usually the trunks were full of high-tech stuff we'd ordered, processing credenza replacement parts or re-fills for Einar's tranquilizer gun. When they left on the next stage, they took with them DNA material, coded transcripts, and anything too solid to transmit or too small to bother shipping from the Lost City of the Lizard People.

I was out behind the stable one afternoon helping Einar crate up an antelope (obtained in Antelope Valley, where else?), when Juan Bautista came running to find us, hugging Erich awkwardly. The damn bird was growing.

"You guys! Come see, the stage just pulled in, and it's a Concord!"

"No kidding?" Einar dropped his pressure sealer, and we both ran to look, eager to admire the lines of the Rolls-Royce of stagecoaches. Butterfield had used *only* Concords, of course, which was maybe why it didn't want to risk them cross-country with a war on. So how had Banning managed to get his hands on the gorgeously engineered thing we saw sitting at our humble embarkation point? I never found out; and I never had much leisure to wonder about it, either, because while Einar and Juan Bautista were checking it out ("Body by Fisher, man!"), I realized with a start that I actually recognized a friend among the passengers.

Have you gentlemen ever noticed how rare that is with us im-mortals? Of course we run into acquaintances now and again—I had known Imarte before, unfortunately—but why is it that we almost never get stationed anywhere near old *friends*? Does this have some-thing to do with one of the Company's famous secret agendas? Not that I'd ask if I wasn't higher than a kite. It's the Theobromos talking.

The mortal passengers saw a rather bulky and foreign-looking gen-tleman help his drab wife out of the passenger compartment, and then raise his hand to assist their colored servant down from her seat by the driver. If they noticed his gallant gesture toward the black lady, they probably raised an eyebrow. But California was a Free State, and people didn't care as much about race relations out here, between blacks and whites anyway.

She was a beautiful woman. Tiny and elegant, with ebony skin that glowed as though polished and fine West African features. Her hair was braided up, but I knew that if she let it down and shook it out, it would wave around her shoulders like a storm cloud.

Nancy? I transmitted in astonishment.

She lifted her head, saw me, and smiled, and she still had the tiniest gap between her front teeth when she smiled. There had been a boy in our graduating class who wrote an impassioned poem to that little gap.

Mendoza? Can that be you?

I nodded dumbly, feeling every one of the years since the last time I saw her, at our commencement party in 1553. I was on a transport to Spain shortly after, and she went to do research work at a base under the Sahara. I heard later on that she'd had a very successful career in Italy and Algiers, but we never kept track of each other; you don't keep track when you're busy in the field. I never have, at least.

She lowered her eyes and played the docile maid for the mortal passengers, fetching the drab wife's reticule and parasol from where they'd been forgotten, while the big fellow saw to their trunks. Porfirio led up the change of horses, and I could see him double-taking on the wife, though she looked like Miss Kansas Corn to me. She turned to him, too, and there was evidently an exchange of some kind; for as soon as the stage rattled away, leaving the three immortals there, she screamed like a steam whistle and fell on him in an embrace.

"Porfirio! You goddam son of a whore, you look *great!*" she said.

"Eucharia!" he said, and they staggered around and around in a prolonged hug. The big man, meanwhile, took Nancy's hands in his and was leaning over her, evidently murmuring anxious queries as to her well-being during the ride. She smiled and said something reassuring. He bent and kissed her face.

I gawked. You see, *he was an immortal too.* In all the years I'd worked for Dr. Zeus, I never, ever saw a pair of immortals in love with each other. I thought it just didn't happen. Our teenaged neophytes have crushes on anything that moves, of course, but full-grown immortals put all that behind them. Don't they? Plenty of affectionate friendships, even noisily affectionate ones like what Porfirio and the bleached-out lady from the Midwest apparently shared, but romance? No.

She was leading him by his big bear paw up the slope to me, her eyes sparkling. "Dearest," she said to him, "allow me to present my oldest friend. Mendoza and I have known each other since we were neophytes together. How many years has it been?" She put out her arms, and we hugged. I hadn't hugged anybody since 1700. It felt strange.

"Three hundred and nine," I said. "But who's this?"

The big man bowed. "Vasilii Vasilievitch Kalugin, mademoiselle, at your service. I am indebted to you for an excellent botanical survey of the Novy Albion region, though you may not recall the occasion—?"

I accessed hurriedly and suddenly placed the name. "In 1831. *You* were that operative up at Fort Ross?"

"The very same. My eternal thanks." He took my hand and kissed it. The clothing was aristocratic Russian; but the accent was exquisitely Continental, as was hers now. She wore her servant's calico with her customary grace and style, and believe me, they didn't in the least look mismatched as a couple. Some of Kalugin's bulk was his Russian coat, but he was genuinely a big guy, with sort of harsh sneering features in a round pink face framed by amazing muttonchop whiskers. His eyes were timid and kindly, though, and he couldn't keep them turned from her for long.

"I'll just go bring up the trunks, shall I, my love?" He squeezed her hand. "Your pardon, mademoiselle. I return directly. I daresay you ladies have much to discuss, no?" He turned and bustled after the trunks like an anxious husband. Gosh, he was cute.

"Well!" I burst out laughing, and she just stood there looking happy. "When did *he* happen to you?"

"We've known each other since 1699," she said. "It's a long story."

Sixteen ninety-nine? That was just before I'd been posted to California. "I'll bet. And you're really—? He's really—? It's love?"

"Yes," she said, turning to watch him. "Oh, Mendy, it is."

Mendy. God, the years were rolling back. "So, like, are you married?"

"In a manner of speaking. Not as mortals marry, of course. We've exchanged certain vows of our own. Our work has parted us frequently, years at a time, on occasion. Fortunately the Company is understanding and arranges our work near each other whenever possible."

"What's he do?"

"He's a marine salvage technician," she said, and I nodded, because she was an art conservation specialist. I couldn't think their jobs would overlap much.

"So he's away at sea a lot? But what are you two doing here in California?"

"All those San Francisco millionaires are returning from Europe with art treasures for their mansions," she said. "Half of them will be beggars within the next five years, and their collections will be blown to the four winds. I'm doing a preliminary survey before Beckman's sent in. It should be easy to get domestic positions. I have several letters of recommendation from persons of the highest quality, all giving me an excellent character." She smiled, narrowing her eyes. "As you are doubtless aware, although California is technically a Free State, it is inadvisable for a Negress to travel alone. Kalugin has been assigned duties in San Francisco, and dear Eucharia agreed to travel with us to lend *respectability* to our journey."

Eucharia was stepping back from Porfirio and regarding him, hands on hips. "We'll have a high old time tonight," she said. "Got any tequila?"

"No, and no Southern Comfort, either," replied Porfirio, and that set both of them roaring with laughter. I guess there was some history there. I hadn't seen Porfirio smile like that in the whole time I'd been there, not a real smile like he was enjoying himself.

"But what of you?" Nancy took my hand. "Have you been happy?"

"Happy? I—well, of course. I've mostly worked alone, you know, back in the mountains. Remember how I wanted to come here after I graduated, how I made New World grains my specialty? Well, the Company finally noticed. Here I've been, years and years now."

"I heard about what happened in England," she said quietly, looking at my hand. "I was so sorry. I wrote to you."

I shivered. "I was in therapy for a while. I probably never got your letter. Well, it was a long time ago, and I'm over it now. But thank you for writing."

"Here we are!" Kalugin came puffing up the trail, a trunk under either arm. "Everything seems to have survived the journey, Nan. Will you do me the kindness of showing me where I can stow these, mademoiselle?"

"This way." I gestured, and took one of the trunks from him and swung it up to my shoulder. He made a little dismayed sound but followed me to the adobe, where I led them down the long corridor to the guest room that was kept for visiting operatives. "Here you are. Don't be scared of the cowhide bed, they're actually very comfortable," I said. "Dinner at 2000 hours, alfresco. The menu includes such authentic regional delicacies as grilled beef, frijoles, and tortillas, but I should warn you that a tortilla here bears no resemblance to the Spanish item of the same name."

"Yes, I've discovered that." Kalugin hastened to relieve me of the trunk. "Allow me, that really is too heavy for a lady."

I could lift a horse, let alone a trunk, if I had to, like any cyborg; but how sweet of the man.

I left them alone to get the dust of the journey out of their teeth, and went to pace around in the oak trees for a while. Was I happy for

my old friend? Yes, unquestionably; but I didn't want to be reminded
of being young, or of England, or of the mortal man who had died
there so long ago. He was after me again, following me relentlessly
from shadow to shadow through the trees.

Eucharia helped Porfirio prepare supper for the rest of us, but then
the two of them disappeared into the night with pistols, a small box
of ammunition, and a lot of aguardiente. Imarte was away on one of
her sleepovers at the Bella Union, thankfully, and Oscar had trekked
far afield on his quest for a buyer for the Criterion Patented Brassbound
Pie Safe; so the company around the cookfire was fairly intimate that
evening. Juan Bautista even brought out his guitar.

"But how charming," Nancy said. "That was made in Old Spain,
was it not? And by a master, to judge from the inlay work."

"Yes, ma'am," said Juan Bautista in a tiny voice. He'd fallen in
love with her, desperately, of course. "One of the mortal travelers left
it. Lucky chance, huh?"

"Can you play it?" I peered at him across the firelight. "I've never
seen you actually play it, Juan."

"Sure he can," said Einar, putting another log on the fire. "I hear
him practicing sometimes."

"I play for Erich von Stroheim," Juan Bautista said. When Nancy
and Kalugin stared at him, he hastened to add: "My condor. Baby
condor. I rescued him. It helps him get to sleep sometimes when he's
nervous."

"Ah, of course," Kalugin said with a nod of understanding.
"Would you perhaps do us the honor of playing for us now?"

Juan Bautista hung his head and fiddled with the tuning pegs.
"Sure," he muttered. I braced myself, expecting him to clutch painfully
at the frets in a beginner's "(I Can't Get No) Satisfaction," but to my
astonishment he went into a classic Segovia piece, and it flowed out
on the night air smooth as coffee with cream. He kept on with beautiful
classical stuff all evening, Rodrigo and de Falla and Five Jaguar, quiet
and unobtrusive, the background to our talk.

"I have to know," I said, leaning forward, "how the two of you
met. It's so rare, you know, for any of us to find . . . what you've
found."

"It was terribly romantic," Kalugin said, smiling where he lay with
his head in Nan's lap. "I'd been in a shipwreck, and washed up on the
coast of Morocco. She was all in silks and bangles, third wife to one
of the sultan's corsairs."

Einar leaned his chin on his fist and grunted. "Our anthropologist
will be disappointed she didn't get a chance to talk with you."

Nancy opened her reticule. "I'll leave her one of my calling cards. It is, after all, the correct thing to do in these circumstances in polite society."

"Calling cards," I said. She nodded serenely and handed me a tiny square of pasteboard, embossed, beautifully engraved. I read:

Mme. Nan D'Araignée

Salon Algeria

"D'Araignée?" I asked.

"An artistic decision," she said. "French for *spider*, you see. I have always retained the clearest memories of the folktales of my mortal parents. Indeed, I can scarcely recall anything else from my mortal life."

I remembered the angry four-year-old girl that she'd been, telling me how the spider god of her tribe had deserted them, saving only her.

"Anansi," she said. "The friend and helper of men, as I understand from my researches into the work of M. Griaule and Mr. Parrinder."

I stared into the fire. The immortal operative who'd rescued the child must have named her for the word she repeated most often, thinking it sounded like Nancy. Had the little girl been calling on her god? Had she finally made her peace with him now, since she'd taken his name for her own? I'd never made peace with mine.

But how wonderful, what style she had, to what good use she'd put her anger.

"What's Salon Algeria?" I asked.

"One of the Company safe houses in Paris," she said. "I reside there when Dr. Zeus has no pressing errand on which to send me. And it's useful, too; a certain segment of the artistic denizens on the Left Bank know that I am always interested in seeing canvases, and perhaps paying cash for them. Regretfully, members of the criminal class are also aware of this, and I'm afraid I have purchased stolen paintings on more than one occasion." She shrugged. "One has the consolation of knowing that everything one purchases in this way will survive for the ages rather than burn in the political upheavals with which France is so frequently visited these days."

I nodded. God, she even had a home.

"What were you doing in a shipwreck?" Juan Bautista raised his head and looked at Kalugin. "I thought we always know when a ship's going to sink."

"We do," Kalugin told him ruefully. "But when history records that a ship's going to disappear with all hands, young man, she becomes fair game for the Company. And when history records that she carries valuable cargo, the Company acts. Most people suppose a marine salvage technician is some sort of diver, and it's true; but, you see, I don't go down after the wreck. I go down *with* it."

This extraordinary statement was followed by a distant salvo of gunfire, followed by wild laughter from somewhere up the canyon. Porfirio and Eucharia were apparently target shooting by infrared.

"Anyone can dive down to retrieve gold or jewels," Kalugin explained. "They aren't spoiled by a little seawater. But what about manuscripts, paintings, Stradivarius violins? You need someone there, on the scene, someone with the knowledge of what's to come, who can secure all those perishable treasures in sealed containers before the ship sinks. You need someone to ride the poor wreck to her final resting place, and transmit exact coordinates on her location to a Company salvage team. You need someone to stay with her on the bottom, lest she drift, lest she break up and any of those carefully sealed boxes float away. And you need someone there to guard her, in her grave, lest the chance fisherman or swimmer should find her before the Company team arrives."

"You mean you stay in the wreck with all the dead guys?" Juan Bautista asked, horrified. His music faltered for a moment.

Kalugin nodded sadly.

"How can you stand that, man?" said Einar.

"I go into fugue," said Kalugin. "I shut down. I respond only when there's a threat to the ship. When the Company divers come, they pull me out, and I go bobbing up to the surface to breathe again. Wretched business, isn't it? To do one's work by impersonating a bloated corpse." He gave a little embarrassed laugh. Nancy took his hand and kissed it.

"But living on board with those guys, knowing all the time that they're doomed . . ." Einar shook his head.

Kalugin seemed to be choosing his words carefully. "Well, it's rather like what we all face every day, isn't it? Every mortal who stops here is doomed, eventually. All our fellow passengers in the stagecoach, every one of them bound for the unknown. I just . . . try not to think about it." He turned his face up to Nancy and smiled. "Fortunately, when not thinking becomes impossible—as it does—I have an angel to pray to."

A silence fell. Juan Bautista had stopped playing. I suppose we were all sitting there with identical expressions of appalled sympathy on our faces.

A voice began to sing, somewhere up on the hill, a woman's voice powerful and harsh, raw with emotion and alcohol, echoing in the night.

> *You hear no sound but my silenced voice.*
> *You feel no heat but the fire that burns me.*
> *You draw no breath but I come into you.*
> *Before you, behind you, I am the sea and the rock.*
> *I AM THE SEA AND THE ROCK!*

Juan Bautista lifted his head, recognizing the song, and so did I. It was by the twenty-first-century composer Whelan, from *The Unquiet Dead*, his Celtic reinterpretation of de Falla's *El amor brujo*. Juan Bautista flexed his clenched hands and improvised on the melody, and as the flow of guitar music began again, we all drew breath.

That night in bed, I tried to occupy my mind with how much better off I was than poor Kalugin, but all I could do was envy him and Nancy their good fortune. Whereas I was alone on the shore, like the girl in the song waiting for my lover to return from the other side . . . And now here he came, from the east, out of the sea. From the east? What coast was I on?

There was the track of foam breaking the water as he emerged. The white horse bore him up, he was coming on the wave, armored like a knight but all in seashells, and his charger in seashells likewise. Oh, the beautiful arrogance of his big body in armor, and how well he sat a horse! His lance was a narwhal's horn, a twisted ivory spear, and he wore no helmet but a tall hat banded with a trailing ribbon of seaweed. His eyes were the color of Spanish glass in his stern face, yes, and fixed on me as he came on, and he came faster now and was lowering his lance at me. Yes! I knew what he meant to do and tore at my clothing, baring my heart to his assault.

"Strike!" I screamed. "Strike, in God's name!"

He struck true, and what a great relief it was.

I awoke in darkness.

7

Early the next morning, I staggered out to make coffee, under the assumption that Porfirio wouldn't be in any condition to do so; but I was mistaken.

He was sitting beside the fire with Eucharia, and they were both watching the blue graniteware pot like pilgrims waiting for a miracle to happen. She looked pretty bad; she was clutching her whalebone corset, which I guess had been removed at some point during the target party for convenience, and her mauve taffeta ruffles were torn. As for him, I didn't think our eyes could sink that far back into our heads.

I noticed them only for a split second, because my attention was immediately drawn to the dead bear.

"That's a dead bear!" I yelled. They both winced.

"I'm sorry, okay?" Porfirio put his hands to his head. "I'm really sorry. Just keep your voice down."

"But we're trying to keep the damn things from going *extinct*," I hissed.

"It was my fault," Eucharia said shakily. "Wasn't it, babe? We were shooting at targets, and he just popped up against the skyline. Thought for a minute I was in a shooting gallery."

I paced around the bear. He had a neat bullet hole between his eyes. "That was some nice shooting, anyway."

"I thought Einar could salvage it for DNA," Porfirio said, reaching for the coffeepot with a trembling hand. "Oh, man. I need to metabolize some glucose. Mendoza, is there any of that pan dulce left?"

"I'll go see," I told him, and as I was entering the adobe, I passed Einar coming from his room. A moment later I heard his howl of dismay at the sight of the bear.

Nancy and Kalugin emerged slightly later, managing to look like an Arabian Nights illustration despite their primly Victorian morning wear. Nancy took one look at poor Eucharia and led her away, shaking her head. By the time they came out again, Eucharia had been dusted off and freshened up, and you wouldn't have known her for the gum-popping honey of the previous evening. She looked a lot like the farm wife in *American Gothic*. By the time the morning stage rolled in, the three of them were back in their roles completely: vaguely foreign gentleman, dull-eyed wife, and meek servant girl.

As Kalugin was seeing to their trunks, Nancy turned to me and reached out her hand. "Mendoza, will you be all right?"

Who, me, ashen-faced after a night of erotic death dreams? But I wasn't the one facing a stagecoach ride with a hungover fellow passenger. "Sure I will. I mean, here I am in the New World. I got what I wanted. Granted, this is a lousy place, but I've already put in my request to go back to the Ventana when this tour of duty's over. It'll be great. Green wilderness, Nancy, oak trees older than we are and not a mortal soul for miles. You should go up there sometime."

"I should love to," she said. "But, you know, my dear, it's going to become more difficult to find places in California where there aren't mortals. Nearly impossible, in another few decades. Where will you go then?"

And I realized, only then, that I had no clue, none at all. I guess it showed in my eyes, because she gave me a hug. "Oh, Mendoza, find something to make you happy! It's easier than it seems. You'd be surprised."

"Okay," I said, for lack of anything better to say, and the driver shouted, and we hugged again, quickly, and she was away and running to clamber up on her seat. I wondered how many centuries it would be before I saw her again. With the crack of a whip the stagecoach was off, up Cahuenga Pass, on its long journey to San Francisco.

Imarte had disembarked and brought a customer with her, her arm wound firmly through his, leading him up the trail to her lair.

"You're going to love it here, Mr. Kimberley, the climate's real nice," she was telling him. "I bet it's real cold in England, huh?"

"Wretched, dear lady," the john assured her, and he was definitely English. I shuddered at the sound of his voice. "Though England does have the advantage of a certain amount of stability. I trust there are no civil disturbances hereabouts? Relating to the present war, I mean?"

"No, honey, none at all," Imarte said, lying through her teeth, because there was a regular secessionist crowd that hung out at the Bella Union, and they not infrequently took potshots at fellow Americans whose accent sounded a bit Down East. Not that I understand how Maine can be *down* anything when it's as far north as you can go in the States.

She led the Englishman away with her, assuring him they had plenty of time before the next stage came through. I thought sourly that if the man had any inkling of how much talking he was expected to do in bed, he'd be running after the departing stage. I wandered away up the canyon to the little brook where you could occasionally find trout and sat there awhile, looking into the brown water, wondering where I *would* go when California filled up with mortals. Canada, I decided at last, and made a mental note to do some studies on the botany peculiar to our neighbor to the north. Yet I loved California; I was even beginning to like this ghastly corner of it, with its killers lurking in the sagebrush and its yet unborn movie industry.

And I thought to myself that things weren't that bad. I had my work, didn't I? There was my problem! I wasn't working enough, what with needing an escort for every field trip. That was why Nicholas was haunting me. Well, if I practiced harder with the Navy pistol, maybe Porfirio would decide it was safe to let me go out on my own. In the meanwhile, another good collecting trip was just the thing to chase away the blues.

By the time I mulled all this over and wandered back to the inn, the afternoon sun had fallen behind the ridge and the dust of the last stage had long settled. Nobody was in sight. I scanned and detected Porfirio and Imarte in the inn, and followed their signals to the pantry room, where Porfirio was kneading dough for a fresh batch of pan dulce. His eyes had come out of their caves a little. Imarte sat with her elbows on the table, watching him. She had a bitchy line between her eyebrows.

"Where is everybody?" I asked, pulling out a chair and sitting down.

"The kid's around here somewhere. Oscar, I don't know. Einar went off to Antelope Valley again."

"Nuts." I sighed. He probably wouldn't be home until the next afternoon. "I wanted to go out collecting tomorrow."

Porfirio shrugged. "You could go with Oscar," he suggested hopefully. Now there were two women with bitchy expressions in the room with him. "So, Imarte, what was the deal with the Englishman? Get any good material from him?"

"Virtually none," she said. "He never stopped asking *me* questions all afternoon! In fact he shut up for exactly five minutes, and I leave it to you to guess why. The rest of the time, I might as well have been a tour guide."

"Maybe you met up with a kindred soul," I said. "Dueling anthropologists."

"Very funny. I learned nothing of his home region or native customs. The best I could get out of him was that he's a mining engineer with the Albion Mining Syndicate. Apparently some confidence man persuaded a group of foreigners that there's been a gold strike on Santa Catalina Island, of all places."

I remembered the blue island I'd seen, way out there in the sea. "And it's a con, you think?"

"Certainly. Who ever heard of gold out there?" Imarte leaned back in her chair and stretched.

I actually asked Oscar about his rounds the next day, I was that desperate for work. He was only too happy to oblige; he hadn't made the West Hollywood sweep in a while, it seemed, and so next morning I crowded onto the seat of the peddler's cart with him, and we rolled off down the canyon.

"So, is it hard to get your foot in the door when you're making your pitch?" I asked as we turned right and headed west.

"Goodness no, not at all," Oscar said. "Not like in the States. I mean, the original thirteen. The local inhabitants are charming people, with a keen appreciation of the solid worth and delightful abundance of general merchandise offered by your humble servant. They'll welcome a salesman into their homes, indeed invite him to dine with them, which is certainly more than I can say for the inhabitants of Rhode Island. The folks here will sit patiently through a complete demonstration of every ingenious and laborsaving device I have to offer. Only problem is, they have no money."

"Really?"

"Nobody here has," he said. "All these Californio gentlemen, and the Yankee fellows too, have pitifully little cash. All they've got is the land and cows. The land's dirt cheap, but most of it's mortgaged to the last square inch, with the highest interest rates you've ever seen. Why, it's plain crazy." He shook his head in commiseration.

"Boom and bust, huh?" I said. Finance had never interested me, but I craved trivia just now, anything to tie me to the present place and time.

"And take this new silkworm business." He gestured angrily with the whip. "Fools planting mulberry trees, thousands of the darned things, everywhere, and importing cocoons from the Orient at great expense. Will it ever produce so much as a handkerchief's span of silk? No, sir! The whole enterprise is a sham, a bubble, a speculator's airy impertinence, and the end result will be *ruin*, you mark my words. And a lot of mulberry firewood."

Was that why my orders had included collecting samples from mulberry trees? I'd wondered about that; they weren't an indigenous plant. Sounded like another tulip fiasco: when speculation on bulbs wrecked Holland's economy and prices plummeted, nursery stock was destroyed en masse, and lots of genetic diversity disappeared.

"Will we be passing any mulberry plantations today?" I asked.

"More than likely," Oscar said.

"Good. I can take some cell samples. Got a customer lined up for your Criterion Patented Brassbound Pie Safe yet?"

"Just about," he said, brightening a little. "If my careful analysis of my customers is correct."

We followed the rocky track, which paralleled the foothills and continued west in a fairly straight line toward a tiny cluster of adobes, all facing one another on opposite sides of what would undoubtedly one day be an avenue, boulevard, or drive. Tilled fields and orchards took up a few acres around the hamlet; straggling fences of nopal cactus raised formidable paddles against bears, wandering longhorns, and chicken thieves. The place appeared deserted save for a dog lying in the dust in the middle of the avenue, boulevard, or drive, and I'm not sure he was alive.

"Now this," Oscar said, "is the ill-fated village of Sherman. I don't believe it's named after the redoubtable general of the same name. No, indeed, and it certainly won't live to be as famous. West Hollywood will obliterate it completely, as a matter of fact. Nevertheless, these people are as receptive to the improvement of their lives by beautiful and useful merchandise as any you'll find in more progressive communities."

"Really. Look, there's a grove of mulberry trees." I pointed at a double row of miserable little whippy seedlings, each with its green flame of young leaves waving at the top. "Do you know these people? Think you could get me permission to take samples?"

"Undoubtedly," he said, and clucked to Amelia to stop just in front of the first house. Describing it now will save my having to describe nearly any other structure in southern California from here on: a long adobe, its former whitewash peeling and cracked away in places, all of it badly eroded by the winter rains. Flat roofs of pink tile, cracked or missing here and there, held on by thick tar from the nearby La Brea pits. Wooden doors and window frames, closed shutters painted faded blue if they were painted at all. Most were of bare wood silvered and cracked with the weather.

"I don't think anybody's home," I said, as a chilly breeze whirled through the cactus.

"Nonsense. Always looks like this. Decent people stay indoors and mind their own business around here, that's all." Oscar hopped down and ran around to offer me his arm in descending. I looked up at several pockmarks in the nearest wall; if they weren't bullet holes, the place had damned big hailstones. Oscar didn't notice, seemingly; he strode right up to the door and knocked briskly. "Hello there! Buenos días, Señora Berreyesa, might I have a moment of your time?" I followed him slowly, ready to throw myself flat if a hail of shot came from anywhere. After a moment we heard a bolt drawn, and the door opened a trifle. A woman peered out at us.

"What do you require, señor?" she said in Mexican Spanish.

"Ah, Señora Berreyesa, what I require is not the issue at all," said Oscar, matching her Spanish pretty well. "It is what *you* require. Perhaps you recall me? I was here last autumn, before the rains. You purchased a splendid shaving razor for the señor of the house, which perhaps you will also recall. Doubtless you will be pleased to discover that I have returned, bringing even more splendid wares for your inspection."

"In that case, consider my house your own," she said, with great courtesy but less enthusiasm, standing aside to open the door. Oscar threw me a triumphant little smile and stepped inside, and I followed, murmuring my thanks to Señora Berreyesa.

The interior was typical of a reasonably well-to-do working-class family. A dirt floor, packed hard and pounded smooth, and smoothly plastered walls shading to an olive brown near the ceiling, from smoke, and almost black over the household shrine, where a couple of candles winked in jars of ruby glass before a little wooden figure of the Virgin of Guadalupe. This was a house of two rooms, and the fine oven and cooking hearth were built into the wall between the rooms, so as to warm both. There were stoneware jars with heavy lids ranged along the wall, and shelves above them displaying graniteware dishes. Several wooden chests; a solid table; and on it a chunk of fresh pork loin and a carving knife, which the señora had apparently been using when we arrived. She eyed the knife now, and looked at us in the hope that we'd be polite enough to leave soon and let her get back to her housework.

"And may I introduce Señora Mendoza, who was kind enough to accept my offer of transportation when her horse went lame? Very

good. I know your time is valuable, señora, so I won't waste it," Oscar
said, interpreting her expression correctly. "You should know I have
cakes of shaving soap available that fit precisely into the mug your
husband uses. And, if I recall correctly, you must be nearly out of
Morning Glory Laundry Bluing, and that was a particular favorite of
yours, was it not?"

"It is, señor," she said.

All this while, subtle unseen miniaturized cameras and recording
devices on and in Oscar's person were noting every detail of the house
and of its inhabitant. "Very good." He rubbed his hands together cheerfully. "I have all you could require. Now, let's see, your husband, do
I err in remembering that he's a vaquero?"

"No, señor, you do not," she said. "At the Rodeo de Las Aguas."

"Yes, so he is. And he's, ah, twenty-eight years old?"

"Twenty-six, señor."

"A good age for a man to begin looking after his teeth, wouldn't
you say? I don't believe I've ever shown you the fine assortment of
American brushes I carry for that very purpose. Regard this!" From
seemingly thin air he produced a bone-handled toothbrush. The señora
did not seem impressed at the sleight of hand, but the tiny brown boy
who had been watching from her skirts yelled with delight and pointed
at us.

"Well." Oscar hitched up the front of his trousers and crouched
down, smiling, turning his head for a good camera angle. "And who's
this little fellow? I don't believe I met *you* on my last visit, no, sir."

The child retreated a bit, staring in fascination. "He was asleep
then, señor," the mother explained. Oscar produced (again, from apparent thin air) a little wooden jointed doll and offered it to the boy.

"Well, here you go, sonny. Here's a dancing Uncle Sam to keep
you busy while your mama does the household chores, eh? No, no,
señora, it's a free gift, a trifle. And I'd like you to consider this brush
I was about to show you." He stood again, proffering the brush in one
fluid movement. She must have wondered how she found it in her
hand without consciously accepting it, but there it was; and he pulled
out a can of tooth powder and held it up before her puzzled eyes.

"Now, señora, I can see you've been favored by Nature with exceptionally beautiful and durable teeth. How fortunate you are. But as
a dutiful wife and mother, it falls to you to see to the well-being of
your spouse and little ones; and they may not be as dentally gifted as
yourself, if I may say so. Were you aware that it is the opinion of
most modern physicians that an astonishing number of diseases, dis-

temperatures, and infections find their root and origin in *poor dental hygiene?*"

"I know," she said. "Gingivitis."

"Er—well, yes, exactly so, señora. And yet, by following the simplest of daily regimens, one can preserve glowing dental health and, incidentally, the beauty of a radiant smile."

"It's true," she agreed. "You chew on sage leaves. Keeps away the gum sores, and your breath doesn't stink either. And they're free. They grow all over the hills here."

"To be sure," said Oscar, not missing a beat, "and I can see you're *exactly* the caring and concerned parent and mate who does her best to see to it that her family follows that oh-so-careful daily routine for their own good. For that very reason, I know you'll be interested in this splendid dentifrice applicator, manufactured out of the very finest materials by the Superior Brush Company of Ogdensburg, New York, USA, and guaranteed to withstand the most rigorous use. Only regard it, señora! Observe the bristles, designed to delve into the crevices between difficult-to-reach back teeth, where home remedies can so seldom penetrate. Now these bristles are derived from the splendid native American wild boar, and they have a particular flexibility unknown to the inferior European variety, which makes them the material of choice for delivering a sufficient dose of this excellent nostrum to the teeth and gums of the gratified user. Now this, señora, is Cleopatra's Smile Tooth Powder, not merely a solution to ensure dental health but a restorative of the natural whiteness of the tooth enamel itself. Tell me, señora, your husband's a vaquero: does he ever chew tobacco?"

"Never!" Señora Berreyesa said with a scowl. "I'd throw him out of the house if he took up a dirty habit like that."

"You would, of course, like any right-minded wife, I don't doubt it, but do you know that Cleopatra's Smile has removed stubborn tobacco stains even on those depraved unfortunates who practice the tobacco vice? Now let's address the question of tea and coffee, which we all enjoy from time to time. Cleopatra's Smile has been proven to remove tea or coffee stains from the teeth and restore snowy whiteness *after only one application.*" I think he was sweating just a little, but Fate smiled. Señora Berreyesa put her head to one side and considered the bright logo on the can.

"Will it do that for tablecloths too?" she asked.

"Well, why wouldn't it?" Oscar said. "If it was brushed in sufficiently, I bet it would! Now I'll tell you what I'll do, señora. I'll make you a complimentary gift of that very brush you hold in your hand.

Society matrons in the eastern States can't get Cleopatra's Smile for less than ten cents a can, but I'm able to offer it out here for a mere three red cents."

She thought about it. "Three cents? You will excuse me one moment, señor?" And she went into the adjoining room, with the little boy following her like a shadow.

"A can of tooth powder isn't a pie safe," I said to Oscar. "And you had to give away a doll and a toothbrush, plus a seven-cent markdown on the tooth powder."

"That's not the point," he murmured. "I'm building a clientele, don't you see? The point of the game is getting them to *want* this stuff. After want comes need, and once they need what you have, all you have to do is supply the demand."

"Will you remember to ask about the mulberry trees?"

"The what? Yes, yes, of course. And we'll just see about that pie safe, shall we?" He stuck his thumbs in his waistcoat pockets, looking mighty pleased with himself.

Señora Berreyesa returned and held out her hand. "Three American cents, señor. I will try a can of that powder."

"You won't regret it, señora," he assured her, pocketing the money and presenting her with the can. "And may I add that this is also a superlative remover of the stubborn and unsightly stains caused by the consumption of mulberries? Of which I notice you shall soon have abundance, by the way."

"Those?" She rolled her eyes. "If we ever see a berry from them, I'll fall over dead. My husband let Señor Workman plant them, after some crazy talk about silkworms. Chinese shawls growing on trees, he told him."

"Well, isn't that just like a man? But I wonder, señora, if you would allow my friend here to collect a couple of leaves from the young trees? She studies such things."

"You can take the whole damned orchard, as far as I'm concerned," she said to me. "Please, señora, help yourself. This way." She scooped up the little boy in her arms and led us out the back door to the garden beyond.

As I walked among the little trees, clipping off a likely-looking shoot here and there, Oscar cleared his throat. "I couldn't help noticing that our arrival interrupted preparations for a meal," he said.

"That's true, señor, but I can spare the time to speak with you," Señora Berreyesa lied graciously.

"Ah, but, busy woman as you are, you must frequently suffer interruptions in the course of your culinary duties, and food intended for human consumption may then be unintentionally exposed to the assault of common household pests. I'd like to suggest a means of ensuring that your foodstuffs stay safe and unmolested. Now I happen to have in my wagon a miracle of modern design: the Criterion Patented Brassbound Pie Safe! I believe it may be the answer to all your problems, and if you'll just step out to the cart and let me demonstrate its assorted features, I'm sure you'll—"

But Señora Berreyesa had stopped in her tracks, her face registering outrage as the import of his words sank in. "Are you suggesting that I have rats in my kitchen?" she said.

"Uh—why, no, certainly, but—"

She seized his sleeve. "You think I keep a dirty house? You think I leave food lying around to draw rats? You come in here and see." She dragged him back into the house, and I ran after them hastily, tucking trailing mulberry cuttings into my collecting basket. She gestured dramatically at the row of stone jars, each with its heavy stone lid.

"*There.* That keeps the food safe and cool. There is never any food left lying unprotected in my house, except when annoying little white men come to sell me things."

Oscar gulped and scuttled for the door. "Point taken, señora, point taken. I'll just be on my way, I guess. Buenos días."

"Buenos días, señora, and please excuse the discourtesy," I said as I followed him. She inclined her head stiffly in acknowledgement. The little boy stared at us with solemn eyes.

"Well, at least she bought the tooth powder," I said when we were out in the street.

"Tactical error," he admitted, taking out an immense spotted handkerchief and mopping his face with it. "Ought to have seen she was house proud. Well, well, I'll do better next time. Got your sample cuttings, did you? First-rate. Let's be off to the next customer."

Down the street we went, the mule sighing audibly.

Nobody answered our knock at the next few houses. Near one there came a little whine and a *ping*, and a puff of adobe and plaster flakes jumped off a nearby wall; so we kept on going, until we got to a board-and-batten shanty sitting by itself in a field. Smoke whirled from its tin chimney.

"Can this be a new customer?" Oscar stared at it keenly. "That place was abandoned, and somebody's been and fixed it up. Well, well. Cameras and audio at the ready! Care to come in with me?"

"Why not?" I said, scanning the house. I could pick up only one occupant, a female. No, there was a cat, too.

So we got out, and Oscar rapped smartly at the door. There was a silence and a scurrying, then someone tugged the door open from the inside, scraping it across the warped sill.

"You will excuse please," said the lady who had answered. "My door, it is wretchedly made. There are no good carpenters here, like in my country."

We beheld a mortal woman in her mid-thirties, with a plain freckled face and intense blue eyes. She had a vaquero's red bandanna bound tight on her head, like a Gypsy scarf, and the rest of her appearance produced that effect also: calico blouse and skirt of violently clashing colors, red morocco slippers with pointed-up toes, and brass hoop earrings so big, a mouse could have jumped through one. Around her neck were numerous strings of beads, some of crystal, some of cheap trade glass, some of bones and shells and little unidentifiable oddments. She wore a lot of rings, too, gimcrack stuff, the costume and curtain variety.

For once, Oscar was speechless; but not for long.

"And what country would that be, ma'am?" he asked, removing his derby.

"Grumania-Starstein," she said. "I am princess there. You are addressing Her Highness Sophia Sylvia Rodiamantikoff. Filthy conspirators brought about the downfall of the royal house. But I fled to safety through snows aided by loyal servants, chased by wolves all the way. I have come to this country to await restoration of monarchy by my secret friends in the palace."

Right. My guess, analyzing her accent, was that she'd been born in Pennsylvania (possibly Shamokin) and probably known some immigrant families. Oscar blinked, turned his derby around in his fingertips, and smiled.

"Why, isn't that interesting. It didn't leave you much time to pack a bag, did it? Is Your Highness provided with all the minor necessaries a lady requires for good health and hygiene?"

"I *had* such," she said with a melancholy sigh, lifting the back of her hand to her forehead. "Had beautiful set of tortoiseshell combs, given to my great-great-grandmother as a present from Ivan the Terrible, who was her godfather, you know. Alas! They are lost, along with solid gold comb-and-brush set I was given by my uncle the archduke. Gone, gone with my jewels and my crown!"

"Golly, that's really too bad," Oscar said sympathetically. "Fortunately, I happen to have a complete assortment of the finest toiletries and toilette accessories a lady could require, ready for your inspection. I'd be honored if you'd care to purchase any, ma'am—Your Highness, I mean."

She bunched the fingers of one hand together and set them in the middle of her forehead, frowning thoughtfully. "One second, if you please," she said. "I must consult spirit guides. Chief Running Deer! King Elisheazar! What you say, boys?"

In the silence that followed, I transmitted to Oscar: *So, is she nuts or a con artist?*

Your guess is as good as mine, he replied.

"We will consider your wares," she said at length, and stepped forth into the light of day. Behind her an evil-faced cat came to the doorway, peered out at us, and fled back inside. Oscar hastened to open up the side of his wagon, displaying a gaudy splendor of ribbons, brass thimbles and scissors, pack thread, playing cards, cheaply bound books, and various items for personal grooming.

"There, now, Your Highness, what d'you think of this?" he said, as though he expected her breath to be taken away by the glory of it all. I decided they were both nuts and turned my attention to a nice little specimen of *Lupinus* lifting spires of blue and purple from the edge of an irrigation ditch. Her Royal Highness Rodiamantikoff fussed and sniffed at the items on display, remarking plaintively that these things were very shoddily made, not like wares in dear old Grumania-Starstein, and occasionally her two spirit guides threw in their two cents about the quality of this bottle of toilet water or that pair of silver-plated sugar nippers. Oscar just poured on the ingratiating charm, bowing and scraping as though she were standing there in her royal finery.

She'd decided on three yards of scarlet ribbon and a deck of playing cards, explaining that her mother had been a Gypsy and taught her to read the future with them—this, by the way, was why the evil conspirators had not wanted her to inherit the throne and stole the crown for the prime minister's baseborn son Otto, who was the offspring of a chambermaid—when Chief Running Deer and King Elisheazar got into a fight over whether or not she should buy herself a peppermint stick. Chief Running Deer (she informed us) said she oughtn't to deny herself such a small pleasure, poor exiled creature that she was, but King Elisheazar told him he was a savage without any breeding and it showed, because *everybody* knew that royalty didn't buy themselves candy; such luxuries were given to them by loving subjects and by foreigners out of respect for the aura of rulership that hung about their persons despite unfortunate circumstances.

Oscar took the hint and presented her the peppermint stick with his compliments, which restored the good humor of the spirit guides, much to Her Highness's relief, for it *so* embarrassed her when they went at it like that. She paid a whole thirty-five cents for the cards and the ribbon, delving into her skinny bosom for it, and I guess it was more money than Oscar had made in days, because, encouraged by his success, he made so bold as to say:

"Now I wonder, Your Highness, if you'd be interested in purchasing a certain item I have here—and I've only the one, you see, you won't find its like this side of the Rockies, but you being royalty and all, I'd like to offer you first crack at it. Step this way if you please, Your Highness, and I'll give you a private viewing."

She followed his outstretched hand around to the other side of the wagon, where he opened up the panel and revealed the Criterion Patented Brassbound Pie Safe.

"You see here?" His face was shining with desperate hope. "*Your* eye, trained as it is in discernment and accustomed as it is to superior craftsmanship, *your* eye will surely appreciate the magnificence of this prime household appurtenance. Note the panels of polished rosewood. Note the decorative brass figuring: pineapples, the ancient symbol of abundance and hospitality. Now, I don't pretend that this is any match for the fine kitchen furniture they've got in your country, but I'll tell you plainly, Your Highness, that this is positively the finest the U.S. of A. has to offer, and no other lady in all of southern California has the like. Now, down east where I come from, the wives of millionaires would pay as much as twenty-five dollars for the likes of this—*if* they could get it! And of course out here, where everything has to be brought by ship, it's worth a lot more. Yet to you, Highness, to you I'll offer exclusive ownership for a mere token sum of eleven dollars— why, that won't even cover the shipping and handling—and the priceless privilege of numbering royalty among my customers." My God, he was actually getting down on one knee. "What do you say, eh? Shall I take it down for you?"

Ooo, he'd come so close. She'd been transfixed, listening with mouth half open, fascinated. But she didn't have that kind of money. She wrinkled her freckled nose in slightly disdainful regret.

"I think not, at the present time," she said. "Spirit guides advise that stars are not presently auspicious for buying furniture. Perhaps later, when vibrations are better."

He looked so crestfallen that she hastened to add, "Yet you may use my name. Yes, you may say truthfully that you are purveyor to Royal House of Rodiamantikoff." She swept past him to return to her shack. "In exile," she said, just before crossing the threshold. "Good day, mister. You are excused from the royal presence."

"Well, you've made thirty-eight cents so far," I said to Oscar as I helped him close up the panels on the wagon.

"Be-elzebub!" he said, grabbing his buggy whip. "I nearly had her, do you realize that? She saw it, she wanted it, she could envision its rich cabinetry making that dreary hovel a refined and gracious retreat. Nothing was lacking but *money!*"

"Well, that's always the way it is with mortals, isn't it?" I climbed up to my seat. "And think of the footage you got of her. Genuine California eccentric, wherever she's supposed to have been born. She's one for the archives, all right. But you know what? She's a gringa. If you sold it to her, you'd still lose the bet."

"I think not," he retorted grimly. "She says she's a refugee from a foreign land, and would any true gentleman impute falsehood to a lady? No sir, if Her Highness says she's not an American, I'll take her at her word."

A bullet came whining out of nowhere, drifting in to clip the top off a young oak tree nearby. Oscar whipped out a pistol and fired off three furious shots at the unseen gunman.

"I'll prevail, I say!" he shouted. "Do you hear me? I'll *sell* the darned thing! I say I will, by thunder!"

But he didn't, at least not on that day's rounds, and he was dull and taciturn—taciturn for him—by the time we returned to the inn that evening. He accepted his plate of grilled beef, tortillas, and frijoles from Porfirio and retired early.

Even though I was eager to get the mulberry samples to my processing credenza, I lingered over the food, because it was particularly good that evening, the beef fiery from a red chile marinade, the frijoles especially creamy, the tortillas unusually redolent of earth and corn and rain. I was still sitting in the clearing when Porfirio rose to his feet, stared off into the canyon and the night, turning his head for a better signal scan, and announced:

"Stranger approaching on horseback. Mortal male. Emotionally excited." He had a gun in either hand before he finished speaking, and Juan Bautista rose in haste to carry Erich von Stroheim indoors out of harm's way. The bird had got too big to button out of sight inside his shirt, though it kept trying to climb into its old refuge in times of stress. It croaked in protest as Juan Bautista passed Einar, who was emerging from the house with a loaded shotgun.

"Company, chief?" said Einar, cocking his weapon.

"Maybe," said Porfirio, though as the mortal drew nearer, we could tell that the excitement registering on the night air was the harmless, pleasurable kind: anticipatory, nonviolent. When he finally rode into the light of our fire, the mortal saw no weapons of any kind in evidence. Porfirio took a few steps toward him, hands outstretched in a peaceable gesture.

"You come for a room, señor? But we have no empty beds tonight. Bad luck, eh? Perhaps you'll ride on to Garnier's? Plenty of room there."

"Thanks, but that ain't why I'm here," the mortal said politely. "I come to see a lady, mister. Met her at the Bella Union. Said her name was Marthy, and she lived hereabouts. You wouldn't know where a man could find her, would you?"

"Ah. Marthy," said Porfirio, just as Imarte herself came sweeping to the door of the adobe, magnificent in her Love's Purple Passion negligee. She paused there in the doorway, holding up an oil lamp like one of those fancy figures that lift a lighting fixture on a newel post.

"Why, who is it at this time of night?" she said throatily.

"It's only me, Miss Marthy," said the stranger, dismounting and tying his reins to our hitching post. He stepped forward out of the shadows, hat in hand. "Only me, and perhaps you remember my name? Cyrus Jackson, ma'am. We met at the Bella Union, and you was so kind as to listen to my troubles."

"Why, to be sure," she cooed, "the *very* interesting man who hunted Apache scalps for bounty." She threw us all an arch glance as if to say, See what a trophy I bagged? "How well I remember your thrilling tales of adventure in old San Antonio! But what brings you here, sir, at this unaccustomed hour?"

He blushed. "Why, ma'am, I hope not to give offense—I sort of thought that you might receive callers after sundown, your trade being what it is. And, you know, I wasn't at my best when last we met— but I'm sober now, and I did remember that you was so taken with my recollections, that I wondered if you mightn't like to hear about when I was down in Nicaragua in '56."

"You rode with Walker in Nicaragua?" Her eyes lit up. She surged forward, bosom first, and placed a coy hand on his arm. "Why, sir, how fascinating! I wonder if you'd be so kind as to share the treasure of your eyewitness memories with an interested listener? In my private chamber, of course."

"Aw, ma'am, I'd be . . ." Words failed him, or perhaps they just couldn't make it through the barrier of his enormous foolish grin. He let himself be led by the arm into the house. Staring after Imarte, Porfirio shook his head.

"*Anthropologists,*" Einar muttered in agreement.

8

MORE BOXES ARRIVED on the next stage, and Einar ran off gleefully to his room with them. The next edition of the film festival featured hours of Charlie Chaplin, of Fatty Arbuckle and Mabel Normand. We sat in our finery in the dressed-up room and played Hollywood premiere again, sipping gin martinis and crunching on popcorn as the silver light flickered and Einar read the titles aloud in his master of ceremonies voice.

Now and then there were a few frames of a landscape we recognized: a smooth-backed elevation with a single line of trees, or a dirt road ascending a steep canyon, or tiny toylike frame houses perched high on the sides of hills and wide empty country all around them. Such a raw new place Hollywood would be, and how unlike the chaparral wilderness we inhabited. For, just as Einar had told me, it would be an eastern Yankee settlement in that time: there were the clapboard houses and the shop fronts and the front porches. It looked like any little town in Connecticut or Maryland, save that it sprawled over endless rolling hills. Edendale, Sunset Park, Lankershim, Burbank, the names to assure new arrivals they were back home and not in some barren wild place where coyotes trotted down the streets at night.

I didn't enjoy the comedies, as a whole, because so much heartache went with them. That world didn't even exist yet, that innocent place, and it was already lost. Those comedians weren't yet in their mothers' wombs, but their fates were known. It was hard to watch pretty Mabel and not look for the icy vivacity of cocaine, hard to watch Fatty hide his face in comic shame, knowing the doom one rowdy party would bring on him. Chaplin wasn't so bad; you knew he'd get off relatively easy for a mortal: long life, fame, lots of family—also scandal, disgrace, exile, quarrels. But the comedians were nearly as immortal as we were, and we gave them our applause.

9

THE DAYS GOT longer, and the green hills silvered and then went to gold. The wildflowers vanished as though somebody had rolled up the magic carpet and whisked it away, except for a few bright orange poppies that decorated the edges of roads. The heat of summer browned everything else. Even the eight-foot-tall thickets of wild mustard, which had bloomed in an electric Day-Glo yellow you could see for miles, went to brown; and the country took on a dry, businesslike look. The arriving and departing stages traveled in a permanent cloud of white dust.

The dust got everywhere. It covered every surface in the inn, and you shook it out of your blankets at night, and it greeted you in a fine sediment at the bottom of your morning coffee. The low-hanging branches of the oak trees, heavy with leaves, were thick with it, and dewy morning cobwebs in the grass looked like little brown rags by nightfall, they'd collected so much dust. And what had happened to all those burbling rills and freshets that had been so picturesque a couple of months earlier? Dry and dead; and in their places bone-dry trackways of sand and gravel, or deep piles of dead sycamore leaves. The cicadas started up a drone about 0700 hours in the morning, when the day would begin to heat up, and they rang in your ears like fever until sundown, when the crickets started up *their* song in the cool of the shadows.

No way you could have mistaken the place for England now, not a sight or sound or smell that was anything but Californian. You might think my specter would leave me alone now, and in truth I had no more gasping visitations that made Porfirio stare at me suspiciously the next morning; but the darkness was still there, beating like a sullen heart when I was alone in my room. I woke up one morning and realized I'd give anything for a breath of sea air.

"So, what's it like at San Pedro?" I said to Porfirio at breakfast.

"San Pedro?" He frowned. "Muddy. Used to be dangerous in the old days. It's not so bad now that Banning's running the place."

"It's the local seaport, right? Any chance Einar could take me down there for a visit, if he's going that way? I haven't seen a good-sized body of water in months."

Porfirio shrugged. "We've got some cargo due to come in. I've been meaning to send him down to the warehouses to see if it's arrived yet. You want to go with him? Nothing growing down there that I know of, though."

Einar, when approached on the subject, thought a day at the beach sounded like a great idea, so he busied himself hitching up the horses while I packed my collecting gear. In the midst of our preparations, Juan Bautista came out of the lean-to he shared with Erich von Stroheim, rubbing his eyes.

"What's going on?" he asked.

"Field trip to San Pedro," Einar said, giving me a hand up to the seat.

"The *beach*?" His eyes widened. "Can I come too? I haven't been swimming anywhere since I've been here!"

"San Pedro isn't exactly surf city, man," Einar said. "But if you want to come, sure. What will you do with Erich, though?"

"Oh," Juan Bautista said, turning guilty eyes to the condor, who had come staggering out after him. He wasn't a mature bird yet, according to Juan, but he was enormous. "I don't guess he should come. The seagulls might scare him. But I've never left him alone before. . . . Would you mind watching him for me?" He looked hopefully at Porfirio, who was just sitting down with his six-shooter, preparing to clean it.

Porfirio looked about as enthusiastic as one might expect. "Look, I've got work to do," he told the kid. "Put him in a cage for the day. I'll see to it he gets food and water."

Juan Bautista ran off to shoo the bird back to his room. Einar and I waited, listening to the croaks of protest as Erich von Stroheim was coerced into the aviary Juan had built for him. A moment later, Juan came running out with his towel and a short broad plank, planed smooth and rounded off at the corners. Behind him we heard a plaintive scream.

"Okay!" he said breathlessly, vaulting up into the back of the wagon. There was another scream, louder than the first.

"Is he gonna be all right?" asked Einar, releasing the brake and starting us down the canyon.

"Yes. He's just never been alone for very long," Juan said, turning around to get comfortable. Another scream rang out on the still morning air, echoing off the canyon walls. We could still hear the condor when we turned onto the road, and in fact the sound of his outrage carried for a good mile out into the plain.

"I hope he doesn't do that the whole time we're gone," I said, looking over my shoulder as the foothills receded into the distance behind us.

"Nah. He'll settle down and sleep. He likes to take a nap every morning," said Juan Bautista with confidence. I looked at Einar, who shrugged. We rolled on.

The sea was a lot farther than it had looked from the ridge above the Hollywood Bowl site. It took us five hours, rumbling along in the wagon, though Einar informed me that Banning could do it in two and a half in one of his Concords.

"Bully for him," I snarled, retreating even farther into the shade of my hat. Juan Bautista had set his piece of plank on his head and made a little tent for himself by draping his towel over it. He sat in the relative cool, humming a little tune.

"Yeah, that's the way to go, if you don't have freight to pick up. Banning's got regular stagecoach service from L.A. to the coast. Another few years, and there'll even be a railroad," Einar said. "Not that that does us much good now, of course."

Ahead of us, the sun on the summer sea lit up the sky, and Catalina Island hovered out there like a lovely cool mirage, blue and eternally remote. Just when I thought I couldn't take another mile of this wasteland (I'd thought Porfirio was kidding when he said nothing grew down here), we rolled up a little hill and over the top, and there it was: San Pedro Harbor.

Except it wasn't a harbor, yet, of course. It was a vast expanse of tidal mudflat, stretching away to shallow water and a distant line of white breakers. Hell, there wasn't even any sand.

But there was sea air, at least, if a bit swampy, and there was a little stream flowing through willows, blessedly green after all those parched miles.

"Surf's up, dudes!" crooned Einar. "Check it out!"

Juan Bautista obediently scrambled about and sat up to stare. He gave a cry of disappointment. "Where's the *water*?"

"Hey, this is Los Angeles! No water in the rivers, no water in the sea. No, seriously, access your Richard Henry Dana. This is the worst harbor on the coast right now. Tide flats are so shallow, cargo ships have to anchor way the hell out there and send in longboats to unload. Amazingly inconvenient. But see that big house being built over there?" Einar pointed to a vast edifice being framed about a mile inland. "That's the place Phineas Banning's building for himself. See those wharves? They're the latest step in his big plan to make this the next world port for shipping. Way off there"—he swung his arm around—"is the old San Pedro landing. Nobody lives there now but some fishermen. And see that island? That's Dead Man's Island. First recorded murder mystery of L.A., or so I'm told. Dead guy buried there is supposed to have been a British ship's captain, poisoned by somebody when he put in here to pick up a cargo of hides. Who slipped him the fatal glass of sherry? Nobody knows."

"Where's Malibu?" asked Juan Bautista, craning his neck, as if that would make yellow sands and clean surf appear.

"North of here. Nothing much there now either, kid. Nobody even goes there, except when a cow slips down a ledge and has to be retrieved from the rocks. Honest, it's just a little trail between the cliffs and the sand, and when we get earthquakes, it isn't even that."

"Sight-seeing is the art of disappointment," I quoted.

"I want to go surfing," said Juan Bautista sadly.

So we drove down the hill and took him as far out across the mud flats as we could without getting the wagon bogged down, and left him to walk out to the waves while we went over to the shipping warehouses.

I got down and walked to stretch my legs while Einar negotiated with the warehouse foreman, one of our paid mortals, a fisherman named Souza. It turned out that we did actually have goods to pick up: a box of printed materials for Porfirio and two crates for Oscar from the Acme Manufacturing Company of Boston, Massachusetts.

When everything had been signed for and Señor Souza had helped us load it all into the wagon, we drove out again, edging along the tidal flats as far as we dared before proceeding the rest of the way on foot. The mud was heavy clay, hard to walk through.

"That *is* the sea out there, yes?" I said, shading my eyes with my hand, peering ahead. "Not a special effect?"

"Just a little farther now," said Einar, swatting at midges. And sure enough, after we'd clambered over some slimy rocks and past a wrecked whaleboat, there were bright combers and surf breaking on rocks and even clean brown sand. Juan Bautista seemed to have got some surfing in, to judge by his piled clothing and his wet hair. But he was sitting in his drawers on the sand as we approached, cradling something in his bare arms. A big unsightly something. As we neared, it struggled and flapped.

"Easy, come on, take it easy," said Juan; and at his voice the bird calmed and turned its big rocket-shaped head to watch us.

"What do you have there?" Einar asked, crouching down to stare at it.

"Pelecanus occidentalis," Juan said. "Brown pelican. Old female. She's hurt. Look, I think that's fishing net cutting into her leg—I think her leg's broken—can you see? Can you get her leg free?"

"Sssh, ssh, let's see." Einar stretched out a careful hand. "You won't stab me, old lady, will you? No, you won't. Okay, that's fishing net, all right. I can try and cut it loose, but you'll have to hold her bill so she doesn't take a whack at me with it, okay, J. B.?"

"Okay," said Juan, his voice trembling.

I turned and walked away. I couldn't watch. It seemed to me the poor bird would have to be killed. I was profoundly grateful I was a botanist and free from the attachments people in other disciplines formed with the creatures they studied. Not that I didn't love plants. I walked up and down, looking out at the horizon where a couple of ships lay at anchor. I looked east, where Dead Man's Island raised its cone of mud. I looked at the ramshackle adobes and fishing boats beached at the old landing. I looked at the squared spaces where the new Union Army headquarters was being built, to save us all from joining a Confederacy in a distant and unreal world.

When I dared to look back, Einar was putting his knife away and talking in a soothing tone. "See how easy that was? Didn't hardly hurt the old lady at all. It's not a bad break, but it is broken, J. B. You need to make a decision now."

"We can't kill her!" the boy said in panic. "She's a brown pelican. They'll become endangered."

"I know. Okay, look. I can splint her leg now, and you can put it in a cast when you get her home, but what will happen then? How are you going to feed her? She eats fish, you know."

"There's trout in the stream," said Juan. "And I can give her food supplements, like I do with Erich. Please, Einar."

Einar was shaking his head, but he got a piece of driftwood and fashioned a splint for the bird's leg, cutting strands from the net to bind the leg securely.

I ventured close. "You have to remember, Juanito, she's an old bird," I felt obliged to say. "Even if this doesn't work, you've made what little time she has left more comfortable. So you mustn't feel bad if she doesn't make it. This happens to mortal things. Nature will make more of them."

"Not that many of *these*," he said, and I couldn't argue with that, so I kept my other helpful remarks to myself.

We took her with us, across the sloughs to the wagon, and Juan Bautista climbed into the back with her and wrapped her in his towel so she'd feel more secure during the long rattling drive home. By the time we reached La Nopalera that evening, she was still alive, and he'd named her Marie Dressler.

At about the point where we passed the future Hollywood Bowl, we began to hear something, and it wasn't Symphonies under the Stars. "What is that?" I asked.

Juan Bautista, dozing in the back with his arms around Marie, sat up guiltily.

"That's Erich," he said.

"Uh-oh," said Einar, and uh-oh was right. When we finally came creaking up our canyon trail to the inn, the screams were sounding out once every two seconds and Porfirio was sitting out by the cookfire, his hands over his ears.

Einar set the hand brake and jumped down. "Bird's upset, I guess."

"When did he start?" asked Juan Bautista, clambering out awkwardly, his arms full of Marie.

"Start? He never stopped," replied Porfirio through his teeth. "Not for ten seconds since you've been gone, muchacho. Please go in there *right now* and shut him up, okay?"

"Okay," said Juan Bautista, and ran for his room. As soon as he had gone inside and lit his lamp, the screams were replaced by happy little croodling sounds and a couple of dinosaur noises.

Porfirio's head sank to his knees. "Finally," he groaned. "Finally." Then he sat bolt upright. "Did he have *another* damn bird with him?"

"Another endangered rarity, chief," Einar said, getting the horses out of harness. "Just doing his job. California brown pelican with a busted leg. No big deal."

"We picked up some freight, too." I hastened to bring the box of periodicals. "Looks like you got your latest issue of *Punch*."

"How nice for me." Porfirio took the box with trembling hands. "Well, I think I'll go to bed now. I think I'll lie in bed and just read for a while. There's plenty to eat—Imarte and Oscar decided to dine out this evening. Help yourselves. Bye."

He got up and walked away, stiff-legged with controlled violence. I stared after him in frank admiration. I'd have wrung the bird's neck after the first hour.

10

Porfirio emerged from his room looking rested next morning, as I was trying to figure out how much coffee to make.

"Eight scoops or six?" I asked, fumbling with the coffeepot.

He rolled his eyes and took the pot from me. "Here, let me. Will you do me a favor?"

"Sure."

"Go wake up Juan Bautista and tell him I want to talk to him."

I went to knock on Juan Bautista's door. Nobody answered, so after a moment I entered.

It smelled like birds in there, and no wonder; one whole wall was cages, in which several dozen little nondescript-looking birds hopped and twittered. There were a couple of big cages, and in one of them Marie Dressler was enthroned, staring at me dolefully. Her broken leg, fixed in a cast, stuck out at an awkward angle. There was also a large perch next to the bed, clearly Erich von Stroheim's night roost. All the cages were spotlessly clean, the perch too, and all the water cups were full of fresh water and all the food cups full of fresh food. But the bed was an unmade wreck, and anything that was Juan's was either lying in a heap on the floor or piled on his one chair. He might have been an immortal cyborg like the rest of us, but he was also a seventeen-year-old boy.

As I was reflecting on this, the door opened behind me and he came in. Erich von Stroheim was perched on both his shoulders, straddling his head like a bizarre hat. Juan Bautista was carrying a little trout in either hand.

"Oh. Hello," he said, and stepped past me to open Marie Dressler's cage. "Here's your fish, lady. Just caught, see? Look, breakfast!" She looked at him as though he were crazy, then tilted up her head to receive his offering. After a few tries she got them down.

"I didn't know you kept birds in here," I said by way of polite conversation.

"This way I know coyotes won't get them. That's a chaparral bunting, and those are white flickers, and this is a pink-faced parrotlet, and that's an oak flycatcher, and that's a rufous-chinned sparrow. There's a little Neele's owl in here too, but he's hiding. All these guys will go extinct in the next fifty years. Except not really, because I've saved them." There was quiet pride in his voice. I remembered the first time I found and saved a rarity, how excited I'd been. *Ilex tormentosum*, the last known specimen, growing in a garden in England.

I put England out of my mind. "So, you're shipping them off to the Company aviaries?"

"When I've finished studying them." He nodded at his processing credenza, which I hadn't noticed because his guitar was leaning against it. "Except for Erich, I guess. He's kind of bonded to me."

"Uh . . . that reminds me. Porfirio would like to speak with you."

"Oh," he said, and slunk out of the room. I followed, not that I wanted a seat at his dressing-down, but I really needed some coffee.

The coffee wasn't ready yet when I came to the cookfire where Juan was facing Porfirio, head lowered meekly. I kept walking past them, deciding to disappear into the oak trees for a while, but I could still hear their conversation.

"Okay, before you say anything, I just want you to know that I understand it was really irresponsible of me to go off and leave Erich like that, and I'm really sorry he screamed all the time I was gone, and I hope it didn't bother the other operatives too much, and I promise it'll never happen again," recited Juan Bautista. He drew a deep breath.

Porfirio rubbed his unshaven chin. "You're never going swimming again, huh?"

"Well . . ."

"Never going to leave the bird alone for the night while you go out anywhere? Never going to go on field trips without him? How many endangered songbirds are you likely to catch with a condor perching on your head, kid?"

"Well . . ."

"Sit down, Juanito. We need to discuss your problem. It's not really that big a problem, as they go, but you need to understand a few things about life in the field."

"I thought I was doing a good job," said Juan, sounding stricken.

"You are. But you're going to be real unhappy, soon, and that's bad. It's especially bad for an immortal. We immortals need to avoid unhappiness at all costs, and do you know why? Because it's the only thing that can hurt us. Nothing else can get inside us and screw us up, not germs, not bullets, not poison—only unhappiness. And you can't do a good job when you're unhappy."

"Why am I going to be unhappy?"

Shit, the kid was so young.

"Because you have a pet. We don't have pets, Juan. Pets require time we haven't got, because we're operatives and all our time belongs to the Company. Pets require special housing and stuff we can't give them, because we never know when the Company is going to transfer us somewhere at a moment's notice. Pets require constant attention and love, and we can't afford to love them, because they're mortal and they'll die, which will make us unhappy, which will interfere with our doing a good job for the Company.

"See? Now, once in a while you people whose specialty is living things—ornithologists like you, or zoologists like Einar—will feel friendly toward something you've rescued. That's okay. Having friends is okay. Friends come and go, and it doesn't hurt much. But there's a different relationship involved here."

"Your problem is that this bird isn't a canary in a cage. It's a big, intelligent animal, and unfortunately its instinct is for complex social relations. It has bonded with you. That's bad, Juan, because when the time comes for you to go your way on your next mission, what do you do with Erich? You can't turn him loose. He doesn't know how to hunt. He doesn't know to be afraid of people. Access the whole history of the attempts to save his kind from extinction. Look at the problems condors have."

"I know."

"The only thing you're going to be able to do is ship him off with the rest of your collected specimens, because that's all he is: a specimen. That's all he can be to you. But it's going to hurt both of you, because he hasn't been a specimen, he's been your pet, your baby. You see what I'm saying here?"

"You're saying we shouldn't love the things we save from destruction." Juan's voice was muffled. He was crying. There was a long silence before Porfirio answered.

"Yeah," he said. "That's it, pretty much."

"I think it's crappy!"

"Yeah." Another long pause. "But it's the way things are."

A moment later, Porfirio continued: "This is not to say you can't love anything. Stuff that lasts forever, like your work or literature or cinema, that's safe. Look how happy Einar is. And look at those friends of Mendoza's who stayed here, they were actually in love with each other! Mortals, though . . . you want to avoid that. That can seriously screw you up. That'll make your present heartache look like a picnic. You just ask—" His voice broke off abruptly. I clenched my fists.

"So what do you want me to do?" Juan Bautista sniffed.

"No more pets. And start weaning yourself emotionally from the one you've got, all right? Better for you, better for him. Think how happy he'll be in the Company aviary. Once he has a mate, he'll forget all about you, and that's the way it should be."

"What about Marie?"

"She's a specimen. Once her leg has healed, she's off to the Company."

I put my face in my hands. Poor boy. I'd heard all this before, of course. Señors, when those clever twenty-fourth-century mortals devised us, they devised badly. Our fragile mortal bones are replaced with unbreakable ferroceramic; our weak mortal sinews are laced through with indestructible fiber, proof against any wrenching blow. Why not excise the wretched mortal heart too, give us a clean pump of steel, nothing that can weep at the appalling passage of the years? As I was weeping now, for the man I'd been unable to save.

I felt a hand touch my shoulder. But when I turned, there was nothing there but California, all sagebrush and red sand. What, was he going to start tormenting me in broad daylight? What had set him off now, the fact that it was an Englishman buried on Dead Man's Island? Was I never going to be free of England and dead Englishmen?

I ran down to the mouth of the canyon and out onto El Camino Real. I looked northward in longing for the forests of the coastal range. The road was free: it ran past me and kept going, skirting the dry hills, veering over to the coast, going on and on until it ended at what would one day be the Hyde Street Pier in San Francisco. If I stood there now, what cooler air I'd be breathing, what greener hills I'd see, and what a sound of the sea would be roaring in my ears!

As I stood there wishing myself anywhere but this flat-topped, sun-baked, bullet-ridden place, I picked up the approach of a mortal man, riding in from the city to the south. I scanned and dismissed him. It was the Yankee fellow who had come out to see Imarte, presumably back for another romantic interlude. To my dismay, he turned his horse's head in my direction and looked at me hopefully.

"Good morning, ma'am," he called out to me.

"Buenos días, señor," I said. Maybe if he thought I didn't speak English, he'd ride on.

"Ain't you the gal that works at the stagecoach stop, up there?" He pointed. "You know if Miss Marthy's at home to callers today?"

"No, señor, she is away," I said. "She is expected to arrive on the next stage, however."

"I reckon I'll wait for her, then," he said, but to my annoyance he continued to sit there on his horse and stare at me. "Uh . . . señorita? You know Miss Marthy very well?"

"Reasonably well, señor." What was this about? Had he caught something? It couldn't be from Imarte, not with the arsenal of amplified antibodies and God knew what else we Immortals carried in our systems.

"Well, would you know . . . ? I'd like to get her something, something grand like what she ain't never had, but I don't know the lady's taste. She's got all them books in her room, and it's clear to me she ain't the common trashy kind of girl, you see what I'm saying? I never seen a lady so cultivated and refined that was so beautiful too, all on top of earning her living as she does. You reckon she'd like a Shakespeare book?" His eyes were big and pleading.

Oh, dear, the mortal fool was falling in love with Imarte. Twice as stupid as falling in love with an ordinary whore.

"I think, señor, that her tastes do not run to literature," I said, choosing my words carefully. "I think she likes history better. I know she enjoys the company of men who have lived interesting lives."

"Oh, I seen that right away," he said, leaning forward in the saddle. "She thought no end of the stories I had to tell her about me tellin' off General Vallejo. Real interested in what I did in Nicaragua. Seems to me she don't come by her profession from natural inclination, wouldn't you think, señorita?"

"Probably not," I agreed, and even if I disagreed, he'd hear what he wanted to hear. "But you know how difficult it is for a lady to make a living in these parts, señor."

"Why, sure," he said. "Poor beautiful thing, to be down on her luck the way she is. You can tell she weren't born to it. Why, by rights she ought to have servants waiting on her. . . . You know what she reminds me of? There was this storybook my Uncle Jack had when I was a kid. He used to read from it, all about this beautiful queen whose husband thought women were no good and he'd marry a new one every night and have her killed with a sword every morning. Only *this* queen kept her wits about her and told him a great big old story every night, and he let her live till next evening so's he could hear how it come out, only she kept the story going so he never did hear the end, and after three years he decided the hell with it and kept her. That's kind of what it's like seeing Miss Marthy." He sighed. "Except I'm the one doing all the talking."

"She enjoys tales of adventure, señor, especially if they're true," I said, in no mood to have a mortal pour out his heart to me.

"I been thinking I could tell her about when I was up in Frisco last year," he said. "Hell of a joke. Bunch of fellows up there had a plan going to sell out California to the secessionists. Young fellow went by the name of Asbury Harpending (and ain't that the worst silly-ass name you ever hear?) was trying to raise him an army. I nearly joined, too. Reckon Miss Marthy would like that?"

"It sounds fascinating, señor," I said. "But, is that not the stage-coach? Perhaps even now your beloved is speeding like the wind to your embrace."

He gulped and turned in the saddle, and thank God it was true: here came the northbound stage, throwing out a wake of dust cloud like a malevolent djinn. The Scheherazade of Cahuenga Pass had returned.

"Thanks for the talk, señorita," called the Yankee over his shoulder, and galloped away to be there when she dismounted. I hope she hadn't brought a customer home or there was likely to be lead flying under the oak trees.

No shots rang out, however, and after a while I sneaked back and managed to get my field kit and vanish into the bushes for a while, all by myself for a change.

I had a productive day, without the distraction of conversation. I got a good sample of genetic material from a specimen of *Quercus morehus* and, wandering into a neighboring canyon, I found a lone *Symphoricarpus mollis*, which was on my priority (pharmaceuticals) list, as was *Ribes speciosum*, which I also bagged—several good specimens of that one. You never know when they're going to discover some miracle cure for something, up there in the twenty-fourth century. Three times now in my field career I've managed to win Favorable Mutation credits, earning me time out for private research. It occurred to me, that afternoon, that this might be a way to shake the dust of Los Diablos off my boots: find something so incredibly rare and useful that I'd win another holiday. I was in a great mood when I finally marched back to the inn that evening. Work always makes me happy. And I'd seen not one dour Protestant shade, not one reproachful phantom.

Porfirio, though, was glowering by the cookfire as I approached.

"No escort all day," he said sternly.

"Well, who was here to go with me?" I said. "The others have their jobs too. I need to be out every day, Porfirio, I have work to do. I'll take a Navy revolver, I promise."

"You didn't today," he said. "I'll issue you a holster. If you're going out alone, I want you to wear it at all times, understand?"

"When in Rome, et cetera," I grumbled. "Is this really necessary, though? Any trouble I ran into would be relayed simultaneously to the Company through the datafeed transmission. If I needed rescue—which I wouldn't anyway—Dr. Zeus would know immediately."

"Just because everything we see gets transmitted doesn't mean somebody's watching," Porfirio replied. "You think the Company's got enough personnel to watch every one of us around the clock? It may be months before somebody starts interpreting your signal, if ever."

"Why aren't you this restrictive on Imarte?" I complained, having no better argument.

"You think she doesn't carry a gun?" he said. "Beautiful little pearl-handled .22 in her reticule. Anyway her job is different, she's out in town most of the time, where she has some kind of law enforcement on her side if anything happens. If somebody tries to rape her or she goes to jail, no problem. She has a great time interviewing all the parties involved. You, you're out in the sagebrush, miles from where anybody can see. If you have a problem, you need to be able to solve it fast."

"Like Einar does." I shivered, remembering.

"Like Einar," Porfirio agreed. He looked as though he was about to say something else; but after an awkward moment he shrugged. "So, go put your stuff away. Dinner'll be ready in about fifteen minutes."

I went slowly, marveling at the gap between official policy and actual field procedure. We were always told that mortal life is incredibly precious and must never, ever be taken: they do enough of that themselves. We were warned that we would have to stand by and watch as mortals executed one another, or destroyed thousands of themselves in wars and riots. But *we* never take part in their primitive justice, never help them along their Malthusian path. Of course, there have always been rumors that the Company allows the occasional removal of a vile and evil mortal for the greater good. Sometimes, it's whispered, even an innocent mortal may die, if it's necessary for the success of a mission. I've even heard that tacitly admitted. Security techs like Porfirio would be the ones to take care of any unofficial assassinations; they're programmed for strong-arm work, the way facilitators are programmed to be devious and amoral.

But I didn't know what to make of how things were done in Los Angeles. Granted, most of the people sniping at travelers from the chaparral were murderers, either crazy or cold-blooded, whom any jury would hang in a second, so it made sense to kill them quickly and efficiently. But it was the speed and efficiency that had me unsettled. Got a problem? Bang, it's solved. No argument, no strategy, no getting to know your enemy.

I was still pondering this at dinner, over grilled beef and frijoles, and even Imarte's peculiar story didn't take my mind off it much.

"That man had the most *fascinating* account of rebel organizers in San Francisco," she said when she emerged for supper after a lengthy afternoon siesta.

"No kidding," said Porfirio, stirring the frijoles.

"You wouldn't believe the absurd and quixotic plans Southern sympathizers are forming up in the city. Even in places like Visalia. There is far more anti-Union sentiment in this region than I ever supposed." She sat, drawing a shawl about her. "This man was actually contacted by a cell trying to raise men for an army. Can you imagine what they could accomplish if they were able to recruit enough fighters? One of their plans was to intercept the gold shipments that provide Union funds for continuing the war, which I need hardly explain would cripple Lincoln's efforts."

I was surprised. I hadn't paid enough attention to the war to be concerned with such goings-on, but it seemed like a respectable plan. "Why didn't they go through with it?"

"I think it's because the majority of the organizers are young and hotheaded. My informant intimated that there was some sort of dissension among the members of the organizing cabal." Imarte accepted a plate of supper and frowned judiciously at it. "But the main reason, probably, was that the Comstock lode was discovered. Given the choice between resisting the tyrant's yoke and making a bundle, most of the nascent California Confederacy departed for Nevada."

"That figures," Porfirio said, and laughed. "I remember when all the Anglos deserted Los Angeles back in 1849, when the Gold Rush happened. Suddenly you couldn't get china, you couldn't get shoes— all the little stores were closed."

"Same thing in Monterey," I said, remembering the ghost town it had become. "Everybody went for the gold. That's so stupid, though, for the rebels! Just like the Japanese never getting around to bombing San Diego or Mare Island next century, which would win the Pacific war for them, but they never do it. Because, think about it. What would happen if the Confederates decided to play Sir Francis Drake and go privateering along the coast?"

"El Draque," said Porfirio, reminiscing as he rolled frijoles in a tortilla. "I saw him, once, for about ten minutes. Short little bastard."

"As it happens, that was part of the plan," Imarte told me. "The gold for the Union troops is shipped from San Francisco to Panama on the Pacific mail steamers. Seize those gold shipments, and you deal a serious blow to the Union. But apparently the logistical problems in obtaining a ship and ordnance for the enterprise were only just beginning to be dealt with when most of the conspirators left for Virginia City."

"This guy told all this top-secret stuff to a whore?" Porfirio shook his head. "No wonder the plot fell apart. Look at the blabber mouths they recruited."

"That must have been part of the problem," Imarte agreed. "Though I gather Mr. Jackson felt it safe to discuss the matter with me because the rebellion is pretty much a dead issue. Apparently the young man who was in charge of his cell departed for Veracruz."

"What's he gonna do down there? Fight with the ladrones to keep Maximilian out?" said Porfirio with disgust. "Shit, that's all they need, another Nicaragua."

Imarte shrugged. I washed down a tortilla with some lukewarm coffee. Who cared what the mortal monkeys did, anyway? We knew how it would turn out in the end. The Union would be saved, and poor old Abraham Lincoln would pick a bad night to go to the theater. France would get Mexico but wouldn't be able to keep it. I had work to do at my credenza.

"When did you see Sir Francis Drake?" Imarte asked Porfirio.

"Ha, gonna pick *my* brains, now? You anthropologist. It was in 1579. I was out with my brother's son. The kid was supposed to be delivering some silver on pack llamas from Tarapaca to Morro Morena, and I went with him to be sure he made it. Well, he didn't. About halfway there, who do we run into but this little stubby Englishman with a red beard, and—"

"Wait a minute!" I sat forward, staring. "Your brother's son? What are you talking about?"

"My brother's son," said Porfirio, looking down into his coffee as he stirred it. "I have family."

"But *none* of us have family," said Imarte. Even she was astonished. "It's Company policy to recruit orphaned children."

"Yes, it is," he said. "And I was orphaned. So was my brother . . .

My mortal father was a soldier under Bernal Diaz. From Hispaniola. All those gentlemen adventurers decided they could make a fortune by going over to Mexico with Cortés to get gold and estates for themselves. They did it, too, though most of them didn't live long enough to enjoy them. My father was awarded some relative of Moctezuma's as a bride. People gave the Spanish lots of girls, every one of them princesses, supposedly, hoping the tie of blood would make the new conquerors part of the family. I guess they kept some self-respect that way. You know: He's not a white god, he's just my son-in-law. Well, some minor king gave his daughter to Cortez, and Cortez already had all the wives he wanted, so he passed her on to one of his officers, who wasn't interested in women so *he* passed her on to one of his subordinates, and to make a long story short, she wound up with my father, who kept her.

"I guess they loved each other. I remember her crying and crying over him when he died. . . . But before that happened they had children. Two, me and my little brother, Agustin. I was four. Agustin was only a baby. I don't know what happened and don't want to know. All I remember is fire and blood and my father dying and my mother weeping over him. She told me to wait, to take care of Agustin, and she dragged my father's body outside. She never came back.

"Then the lady came. She told me she was going to take me away somewhere safe, where I'd never die, that a kind doctor was going to take care of me from now on. You know, the story we all hear, when they find us. She tried to make me go with her and leave Agustin, but I wouldn't. I yelled and picked him up and wouldn't let go of him. In the end she had to take us both.

"Well, when we got to the nearest Company base, they had a problem on their hands, because here they were with two little mortal kids saved from certain death, but only one of them—me—fit the physical profile for the immortality process. What to do with baby Agustin?

"They were kind enough about it. They inoculated him against diseases, and they found foster parents for him, a good, loving couple who wanted a child, and one day, while I was undergoing the first cranial surgery for augmentation, they gave him away. I was so mad when I woke up and found out. What was Agustin going to do without me? I was supposed to look after him.

"But the nurse explained how they'd given him to these really nice people, and how he'd live a wonderful long life and never die of smallpox, and my poor mother and father would have wanted that, and didn't I want them to be happy up there in heaven? Anyway, what could I do about it?

"Well, I did something." He gazed into the fire. "When I was grown, after I graduated, I accessed Company records and got the name of the couple who adopted Agustin, and I went and looked him up. He didn't remember me, of course, and I couldn't tell him who I was; but I struck up an acquaintance with him all the same. His adoptive father had land and money, and spoiled the kid. Agustin had everything, but he was beginning to get into trouble when I found him. You know the kind of trouble rich kids get into. They're bored. Life has no point. They don't love anybody, and they don't think anybody loves them. So it's cards, whores, drink, and raising hell. I beat some sense into him, and we became sworn friends after that.

"His foster father approved of me as a good influence. My brother and I went places, did things together, just as though I were a mortal. He fell in love with a girl and married her; I was best man. They had kids, and I was godfather to half of them. He worked hard, he made good investments. I had to leave now and then when the Company sent me places, but I always came back to check on Agustin.

"The business with Drake happened when Agustin had to pay some rents to the bishop at Morro Morena. He sent Dieguito—his oldest boy—with the rent in silver on a pack train of llamas. Thank God I went along. We were halfway there when out of nowhere we were surrounded by these lousy Englishmen, and I'm not using the term metaphorically. They were also armed to the teeth. They looked like they were starving. The leader was Francis Drake, a little short fat guy with a red beard. I wish I could tell you something memorable about him that would give you an invaluable insight into his character, but all he did was call us dogs and demand the llamas. He thought they were some kind of sheep. He was pretty happy when he found the silver.

"When his attention was distracted, I grabbed Dieguito, and we ran and got away. The English shot at us and called us filthy cowards—why they were sore about us running, I can't guess. Dieguito was humiliated and angry. He wanted to go back there and throw rocks at them or something. I grabbed him and asked him what he thought his father would rather have, a living son or a son killed by a bunch of pirates? Any father would like to know his son died bravely; but he'd much rather hear that there were going to be lots of grandchildren.

"When we got back, Dieguito saw that I was right, because Agustin wept and embraced his son, and embraced me, and said he would have given the boy's weight in silver to get him safe home again.

Agustin said it was a lucky day for him when I insulted him in that tavern. Drake sailed on up the coast and out of our lives, and the Company sent me away on a mission, and I was plenty busy for a while.

"But then, one time I came back after being away a couple of years . . ."

"And Agustin had died?" I guessed.

"No, though it felt like it. He'd aged. Begun to age, anyway. The first gray in his beard, his face sagging a little. And his kids were growing up. While I still looked twenty." Porfirio reached around for a branch and thrust it into the fire, opening up a red cavern of coals that breathed heat at us.

"So what did you do?" Imarte said.

"Learned appliance makeup real fast. Pretended to get sick and hang by a thread for months. Agustin came to see me every day . . . and when I made my recovery, everyone said the illness had aged me, which was what they were supposed to say, so things were okay for a while. It was a pain getting made up every morning, but it was worth it to be able to keep an eye on Agustin.

"But time kept passing. You know what happened, eventually. Little Agustin the fat baby, with his dimple and his shock of hair, became Agustin the tremulous old skeleton, toothless, blind, unable to remember things. He'd had his years and years of long life, just as the nurse promised me; and this was what it had done to him. I sat by his bed, every day; I held his hand and listened to him mutter and twitch, or breathe with a sound like clothes being dragged over a washboard. I myself was so weighed down with the crap I wore to make me look old, I could barely move.

"I went weeping to his funeral—so many great-grandchildren there!—and Dieguito, old Diego now, comforted me by telling me his father would see me in paradise. I couldn't tell him there was just one little problem with that: you have to die to go to heaven, and I couldn't.

"I pretended to, of course. I made up a wax dummy with my horrible old features, then had a hot shower and stripped away all the appliances, all the latex and paint and white hair, and paid a servant to see to my funeral. I walked out of my own house young and free, and I got on a horse and rode north."

Out in the night a coyote howled, mocking.

"But I wasn't free," Porfirio said with a sigh. "Who was going to look after the great-grandchildren? I stayed away ten years. The Company sent me to Nicaragua, to Chile, to Mexico, to Texas. I did a lot of good work and had some free time, so I went back to visit Agustin's grave. They'd buried my wax dummy beside him, wasn't that nice of them? And Dieguito, who would have remembered me best, was blind now. Cataracts. His kids had no sense, they'd led soft lives and were letting the estates go to hell. *Their* kids were wild and living like Indians. Somebody had to take a hand. So I followed the oldest of the young boys around, watching him, and one night he left a cantina drunk and was set upon by thieves. I killed them and brought him home."

Just like that, he killed them. Well, he was a security tech.

"The family—none of them knew who I was, I looked twenty-five at most—welcomed me, thanked me, gave me a job as majordomo. I held it for a while, long enough to set things to rights again. Dieguito died, and the baby I'd held in a baptismal robe I saw as an ancient creature lying gaunt in his coffin. It didn't matter. The son had a son, and I was such a member of the family by that time that I was the godfather, and I held the little fat brown boy while the old priest anointed him and named him Agustin.

"It's gone on like that, you see? For centuries now, and the Company has been very understanding. I have a big family, and they need me. Their fortunes have changed—our estates were lost after the Grito—but the family has survived. There was nothing I could do about Agustin's dying, but his blood still runs in his descendants. I stay with them awhile, I watch them get old and pretend to get old for a while myself; then I ride away and stay away until they need me again. One night a stranger will come; and if any of the old people think he looks like Uncle Porfirio, who used to teach them how to ride, well, it can't be more than coincidence, can it? Because Uncle Porfirio would of course be a very, very old man now, if anybody knew where he was."

After a long silence he shrugged. "I'll have to be more careful, now that photography has been invented," he concluded.

Imarte was sitting with stars in her eyes. "That is so *beautiful!* What a unique chance you've been given! Think what a cultural thesis you could make of it, three centuries of history as experienced by one family!"

"You think so?" He looked sidelong at her. "How'd you like to have that responsibility? I'm never free. Three hundred years, and I'm still obeying my mortal mother's last request."

I thought privately that he'd been too hard on poor Juan Bautista about the birds. It's all very well to break the news to a young operative that love is a mistake, that attachments can't be formed because of what we are. But Porfirio had found a way around that, hadn't he?

For him there was always a home fire burning somewhere, no matter how far he wandered on the dark plain, while the rest of us made do with ashes and ghosts.

Someone was standing on the other side of the fire, looking at me. The others didn't see him. I refused to lift my eyes.

"So, where are they now?" I asked. "Your family."

Porfirio shifted, uncomfortable. "Most of the direct line are working on a ranch in Durango. One of the girls married a man with some property, and all the brothers have moved in to work for them. They're doing all right, I guess. I haven't been down that way in ten years. I'll need to wait a few more years before I can go back there again."

I put his story out of my mind as I went to my room and set up my credenza for work, and I kept it out of my mind while I processed my specimens. In the end I had to shut it off and go to bed, though, and the second my head hit the pillow, the question leaped out at me like a thief from ambush: What had become of *my* family?

Long dead, their remains probably stacked in a charnel house beside some village church in Galicia. Had there been descendants? I'd had lots of brothers and sisters, so perhaps there were some distant relatives running around somewhere. There might be some woman even at this moment with my face, my hair, buying onions in the marketplace in Orense or Santiago de Compostela.

When I finally fell asleep, I had the nightmare again, the old nightmare that I always forget until I'm actually inside it once more, where I'm in my parents' house in the middle of the night. It's dead-black night, but the moon shines like an arc lamp, and I can see them all lying together in the one big bed. There is my skinny father and my ever-pregnant mother, and there are all the little children I used to fight with so bitterly for our shared toys, or a scrap of food, or our mother's attention. I know all their names, but I always forget them when I wake up.

My family is asleep, as silent as though they were underwater, and nothing will wake them. I'm the only one awake. I try my best, but I can't get anyone to wake up and be company for me. The moonlight is so white, the night is so still. I wander around the room disconsolately, but they never wake up to notice I'm there. They will sleep forever. Only I am awake; only I can never sleep.

This time, I couldn't bear it and ran outside into the moonlight. It was a mistake. Apple trees stretched in every direction, white with blossom, and the air was full of perfume. He was standing there under the trees, tall in his black robe, waiting for me. As I halted and stared, he extended his arm in its long sleeve, that graceful gesture that was one of the first things I'd ever noticed and loved in him. Inviting me, beckoning me, summoning me.

I struggled upright on my narrow cot, gasping like a fish out of water, soaked with chill sweat, and for one terrifying moment I thought the spectral moon was shining in here too, because it seemed to me there was a flash of eerie blue that faded and flickered away. I sagged against the wall and wept, not bothering to wipe away my tears. Here came the footsteps again, Porfirio running out to see what the disturbance was; but he stopped, and after a long while turned and went away without speaking.

I lay down again, shaking, pulled up the blanket, and curled on my side. I was so cold.

11

I wish we had some toast," Oscar was complaining at breakfast. "Oatmeal. Soft-boiled eggs. Real food."

"This isn't a civilized country yet, remember?" Porfirio said to him with a grin. "You'll get your oatmeal eventually."

"Anything would be preferable to this monotony of leftovers." Oscar rested his chin on his fist, staring glumly at the beef in the skillet.

"You want to talk to Dr. Zeus about allocating me a bigger budget to run this place?" Porfirio flipped the steaks adroitly. "So, hombre, how's that pie safe? Got a buyer for it yet? Should I start peeling those parsnips?"

Oscar pursed his lips. "I feel lucky today," he said. "Mendoza, will you come with me and bear witness?"

"To what?" I looked up groggily from my coffee. I hadn't been sleeping well lately, to put it mildly.

"I want someone present who can testify to my triumph."

"Oh. Actually I was going out into the temperate belt today, Oscar."

"We can go that way. There are houses out there. Why, I haven't even visited that area yet. Those people are probably desperate for good-quality merchandise at affordable prices." His eyes grew wide and reverent.

"Okay," I said, getting up to fetch my field gear. It'd save me a long walk; why not? When I came out, he'd already hitched up Amelia and was pacing back and forth, energized.

"Your chariot awaits, ma'am." He bowed me to my seat. "Where shall we go?"

"Take Franklin to Hollywood to Sunset," I said. We had all

adopted Einar's use of future street names, and that was the route that followed the foothills through the temperate belt. He gee-hawed to Amelia, and away we rolled.

This was a much prettier drive than the road that cut across the plain, with inviting green canyons that opened up to the north; unfortunately it was also a lot more dangerous, as bullets sang out of the thickets at regular intervals. We dodged them and shot back if they seemed too persistent; I scarcely wasted a thought on it now. I was able to get good specimens of *Vitis girdiana* near the future intersection of Laurel Canyon and Sunset Boulevard; I found an interesting mutation of *Chrysothamnus*, with possible commercially valuable properties, at Sunset and Queens Road. Oscar bore with my frequent stops patiently, but kept his eyes trained on a thin column of smoke that rose ahead.

When we finally came around a foothill and saw its source, he sighed in disappointment. The house was old, built of tules in the local Indian style, and in fact there was an Indian lady in the yard, standing on a rock to load acorns into a kind of basketwork silo. If not for the fact that she was wearing European clothing, we might be back in pre-Columbian days. She turned to stare at us as we pulled up before her yard.

"Good morning, señora," I called to her in Spanish.

"And to you," she said, getting down and wiping her hands on her apron.

"Look at that!" gasped Oscar. I thought he was enchanted by the primitiveness of it all, but it was the silo that had his attention. He was out of the wagon and into the yard much too fast for the dogs who lived there, for they surrounded him in a snarling mob before he could reach the lady.

"Please excuse him, señora, he means no harm," I said from my seat in the cart. She nodded and called the dogs off. Oscar had his hat in his hands at once.

"My apologies, a thousand pardons, señora, but I couldn't help seeing that you are in dire need of superior food-storage facilities!"

She just nodded and looked at him. Probably she was deciding that the white man was up to no good if he apologized to her this abjectly, but her face was blank, her expression mild.

Oscar gestured with his hat at the acorn silo. "This structure, señora, it's very ingenious and well made, but it's nothing more than *natural materials*. Are you not at the mercy of the ground squirrel, the raccoon, the scrub jay, and a host of other pests? Do they not voraciously deplete your larder?"

"Sometimes," she said.

"Well, allow me, señora, to offer you a solution to these depredations, a way of ensuring that your hours of backbreaking labor gathering the fruits of Jove's tree are not for naught!" He bowed her toward
the cart. She went with him, placidly folding her hands, no doubt
wondering who Jove was. The dogs snarled and followed, but kept
their menace low-key.

"What you need," Oscar said, unfastening the side of the cart, "is
a modern, sanitary method of preserving food. Now I think, señora, I
think you'll agree that what I have here just fits the bill. Behold!" He
flung back the side, displaying the pie safe gleaming among his wares
like the central diamond in a crown. "The Criterion Patented Brassbound Pie Safe!"

Her face remained perfectly still, but a light flickered in her eyes.
Then they grew a little bleak.

"It's very beautiful, señor," she said.

"Oscar—" I said. He ignored me.

"Regard the metal fittings. This is a first-rate device guaranteed to
be impervious to pests, whether of the gnawing, crawling, or pecking
variety. No less than eight separate compartments for the storage of
your acorns and, er, whatever other fine foods you wish to keep pure,
fresh, and unsullied. Now, I've a talent, if I may say so, señora, for
supplying needs, and I can see plainly that *you need this*. It may have
been designed for other forms of edible goods, but such is the versa-
tility of its design that it will admirably preserve foodstuffs from any
ethnic cuisine whatsoever."

"I'm sure it would, señor."

"Oscar—"

"Now, it may be," he said, raising a hand, "that you've put aside
hard-won savings, in the anticipation that Necessity may call at your,
uh, door. I might suggest that you could make no better investment
against Want than this splendid item, which will safely reserve your
stores against all possible losses. Ordinarily the Criterion Patented
Brassbound Pie Safe is sold for no less than thirty dollars; but for you,
señora, in your most obvious need, I will offer it for the special low
price of *ten* dollars. Only say the word, señora, and you need never
fear the loss of your acorns again."

I buried my face in my hands. She was taking them all in in a
long bitter stare, all those pretty and improbable things she'd never
thought of having and shouldn't have thought of having, because she'd
never have them.

"It is certainly a beautiful thing, señor," she said meekly. "I am afraid, though, that I have no money."

Oscar gaped. "Well—why, I'll tell you what, then. You can pay for it on the hire-purchase plan! Twenty easy installments of fifty cents each, how about that? With the first payment deferred six months. You can't afford not to take advantage of this once-only offer."

"Yes, I can," she said. "I have no money at all, señor. My husband works on the big rancho, and the man who owns it lets us stay here in return. We never have any money."

"But—but my good woman, how do you live?" he said.

She waved a hand at the acorns, at the venison jerky drying on the fence, at the neatly woven baskets of pinole meal.

"Come on, Oscar," I said.

"Uh, well. If you ever *should* obtain hard currency, I'm sure a thrifty housewife such as yourself will invest it in the wisest possible way," Oscar gabbled. "And may I present you with a complimentary volume of the poetry of Percy Bysshe Shelley? I trust you'll remember me, señora, when you require the finest in home furnishings. Good day."

"Thank you. Good day," she said, staring at the little book in its bright pasteboard binding. Oscar leaped into the seat, and we rocketed off.

"Shelley?" I asked.

"That was my low point, my absolute nadir," Oscar groaned. "Dear Lord, what possessed me? It was her need, you know, her utter need. It seduced me. I must supply where I see demand. It's a compulsion. Other operatives would be content with simply gathering valuable anthropological data or ferreting out hitherto unrecorded ethnographical statistics. I must be *more*. I must be the genuine article. That's my problem: my standards are too high."

"Well, it's not like you're a failure," I said helpfully. "You're doing great work for the Company."

"For Dr. Zeus, I'll grant you. But what about the worthy gentlemen at the Acme and Criterion Companies? Mere mortal merchants, say you; yet I believe in complete commitment, absolute fulfillment of all responsibilities, be they ever so trivial." He shook the reins with noble determination. "Giddap, Amelia! To the next customer."

But worse was yet to come.

Farther down the road, in a green clearing beside a still-bubbling spring, we saw a fine adobe and garden. The walls were freshly plastered, the window frames painted, and a tall paling fence warned trespassers away from the yard, where cabbages were growing in precise lines and peach and plum trees stood to attention.

"Now, look at that," said Oscar, laying down the reins in admiration. "Look at the industry and thrift evident in that pleasant scene. Surely this is the residence of a wage-earning individual. And his spouse. Prudent housewifery is in every line of that garden plot. I can taste that New England boiled dinner now."

"Those are awfully big dogs," I observed. They sat alert, one on either side of the door, watching us silently. I hadn't the slightest doubt that if Oscar so much as put his foot inside the gate, they'd tear it off.

"Hem, you're right. Well, let's not repeat my previous error." Oscar got down and went around to the back, where he drew out a pan and a long wooden spoon. He commenced to beat out a brisk tattoo on the pan, looking hopefully at the house. The dogs pricked up their ears but made no move.

"Good day! Hello there! Is there anyone at home?" he called. The door opened, and a woman looked out.

Whoops. I transmitted to Oscar. *She's an Anglo. Off-limits for your pie safe.*

He faltered only a moment in his disappointment. "Well, good morning, there, ma'am!" he said in English. "I wonder if you'd be interested in any of the superior merchandise I have to offer?"

"Nein," she said, and he shot me a look of triumph.

"You are German, madam?" he said in a close approximation of her regional accent. "From Bavaria, yes?"

"You, too?" Wonderingly she emerged from the house and came a little way toward him. "In this foreign land?"

"Many years now, but I assure you it is so. How pleasant it is to hear a cultivated voice again! Come now, my dear, I have many things here that you may need, though you may never have considered that in such a lawless and unimproved country they could be obtained. Come, see what I have to offer to you." Oscar put his hand on the latch, and the two dogs instantly sprang to their feet, growling. She shushed them and came a little closer, peering at us. He might have been a countryman, but he was still a peddler.

"Have you the polish with which to clean silver?" she said.

"Yes, *natürlich*! And I have additionally stove blacking, laundry bluing, wash powders, and these very fine clothespins that have a patent pending for the superior spring mechanism that they employ. Consider, here, the little figures of china bisque, very sweet, the little doves billing and cooing and the little shepherd boy playing love songs with his flute. And this pan for the baking of cakes, with the hearts printed in the bottom so as to make the design upon the finished cake, wouldn't you like to have this?"

"No," she said. "Just the polish for silver, thank you."

"Ah, but, my dear! Here is your silver polish, to be sure, but behold! Printed music for performance on the piano, the spinet, or the organ. And confections also, barley-sugar sticks in the flavors of apple, blackcurrant, or strawberry. And see what fine things I have for sewing."

"Thank you, no. How much for the silver polish?"

"Five cents American."

She raised her eyebrows slightly but fished in her apron pocket and paid him. He handed her the silver polish, and she turned to go. He nearly made a desperate lunge over the fence, which the dogs were only too happy to have him do.

"But, dear lady!" he screamed at her back. "See, here, this thing which you will find is an absolute necessity in this wild and dirty country. It is the Pie Safe Patented Criterion Brassbound." He flung wide the panel, revealing it in all its glory. "It keeps the bread loaves and the rolls from going stale. It keeps the mice, the rats, the insects from invading the pastries. You of all people would want such furniture for the kitchen that you bake in."

The woman turned and followed his gesture with her eyes. For a moment they were warm and approving. "Ah, yes," she agreed, nodding her head. "I do not know what I would do without the one I have."

"You have such a one?" Oscar asked, going pale.

"*Natürlich*, there in my kitchen inside the house. But mine is bigger than that, and bound not in brass but in nickel that is plated with silver. And it has not pineapples upon it but the design of pheasants." She looked closer, critically. "Also, yours does not have the egg timer or the barometer built into the cabinet, as mine has."

Immortal or not, I thought he'd keel over dead right there on the spot. She realized she'd dealt him some sort of near-fatal blow, though, because she hastened with a kindly word: "All the same, it is a very good pie safe, and you will certainly sell it to somebody. I have no need of it, however. Good day, my dear sir."

Well, I couldn't laugh, he looked so stricken when he crawled up on the seat beside me. We drove away in silence. About halfway back to La Nopalera, he drew a deep breath and said, "I'd be obliged to you, Mendoza, if you wouldn't mention this mortifying occasion to the others."

"Don't worry," I said. I had no wish to gloat. The day's outing had been successful for me; I had got a couple of good specimens not only on the drive out but also on the way back, I scored a previously unclassified member of the *Celastraceae*, some exotic low-elevation form of *Euonymus* by the look of it. Happy me.

12

I COULDN'T GET those green canyons out of my mind. Accessing topographical data, I decided that Laurel Canyon, with its drastic range in elevations, had the best chance of mutation-yielding micro-climates and diversified habitats. I was intrigued, also, by the blue-hazard notations on every reference to the area I encountered.

"I thought I'd stroll over to Laurel Canyon today," I said, one morning at breakfast, casually.

Porfirio choked on his coffee and glared at me.

"Are you nuts?" he said. "That's a blue-hazard precinct, dummy."

"So my files tell me, but I've never encountered one before. It's just a kind of energy sink, right? A locus of natural unnaturalness in the landscape?" I was a little taken aback by his reaction.

"You could say that," he growled, mopping spilled coffee from his chin with one hand. "It's just the biggest damn one on the continent, that's all."

"Oh," I said. "Does that mean I can't go there?"

"Not alone, you can't, you of all people, and not without the right field gear. What the hell do you want there, anyway?"

"Well . . . it has all those steep isolated canyons and drastic heights and depths. There are probably a lot of rare endemic species of plants growing there. I'd be stupid not to look for them. And what do you mean, me of all people?"

He looked over uneasily at Einar, who was grooming Marcus, and at Juan Bautista, who was watching him. "Okay," he said in a lower voice, not answering my question. "I guess there's stuff back up in there worth collecting at that. But you're going to take the following precautions, understand? Now listen carefully . . ."

Two hours later:

"God, I feel stupid," I moaned to Einar as we approached the canyon on horseback. "What if mortals see us?"

"We shoot 'em," he said glumly. I hoped he was joking. We were wearing absurd-looking helmets with Crome filter lenses and a lot of other cunning little mechanisms built into them with no consideration for style or convenience. We wore gauntlets full of wiring and large, ugly, and ill-fitting boots with circuitry patterns on the outside. Things like Batman's utility belt were cinched about our waists. To make matters worse, we were tethered each to the other by a long silver line. If one of our horses startled and bolted, somebody would be dragged.

"We look like extras in a cheap science-fiction film," I complained.

"In a damned expensive science-fiction film," Einar retorted. "You know how much it cost to make this stuff, here in 1862? And these are the only sets of this gear in the continental U.S. at this time. They were made just so we could go into Laurel Canyon, if we had to. So enjoy the fantasy. Tell yourself we're explorers on a forbidden planet or something."

"It can't be *that* weird, no matter what Porfirio says," I muttered. But as we came to the entrance of the canyon, I fell silent.

I saw a narrow passage between soaring walls of granite, thinly grown with whatever little plants could cling to their vertical surfaces. The way in followed a creek bed through which water was still cascading down. From the wreckage of broken trees and from the high-water mark on the cliff faces, you knew that this was no place to stand during the winter floods. Water must come thundering down that channel like cannon fire. A dramatic scene, with the leaning dead cottonwoods and the majestic atmosphere, the mountains impossibly high on either side. A little trail led into the canyon, a sandy embankment on the left-hand side above the water, and disappeared into dark trees.

Einar unslung his shotgun and cocked it. Cautiously we rode in.

"Now, remember," said Einar, "don't scan. Every conditioned reflex and instinct you've got is telling you to, but don't. Let the helmet do it for you. If you try, yourself, you're going to pick up data you won't believe."

"This is nuts," I said, as my horse picked its way timidly. "How are mortals going to live here? But they are, aren't they? And this is right in the heart of Hollywood."

"I know," he said. "They just . . . become part of the strangeness. Raymond Chandler wrote about it in his Philip Marlowe stories, but he didn't tell half of what he knew. There'll be a murder that happens right up *there*"—he pointed up a nearly vertical slope—"that he writes about in *The Big Sleep*. But it doesn't happen the way he says, it never makes the papers, and it's never solved, either. The guy isn't a pornography dealer, he's a high-ranking member of a hermetic brotherhood. There's a brilliant flash and a scream, all right, and a naked girl and some ancient earrings with a curse on them. The curse doesn't make it into the book, but a lot of the other details do."

"How lurid," I said, and then started, because I heard a sound I shouldn't have heard in that place, not for another half century at least. I turned my head to stare down the trail behind us. I knew that sound from cinema: the rattle of an internal combustion engine, the rush of displaced air as something sped toward us, but I had no visual input at all. Forgetting myself, I scanned, and *knew* there was something approaching. In my desperation I yanked up the Crome screen visor so I could see with my eyes.

"Mistake," Einar gasped. He was right. Without my visor the place lit up, every tree, rock, shrub, and blade of grass outlined in blue neon. The automobile was lit up like that too, a 1923 Avions Voisin, a lovely, elegant thing except for being glowing blue, slightly transparent, and a little out of place in 1862. Einar leaned over and got a firm grip on my horse's reins, or I'd have been away from there in an instant. The car zoomed up, till I was right between its bug-eyed headlights, and I got a clear glimpse of the hood ornament in the shape of a rearing cobra.

With a crackle of static the car whooshed through me and on, up the canyon. My mouth was open. Einar managed to reach out and click my visor down. Visual references were once again normal.

"Told you not to scan," he said reprovingly.

"Was that a ghost?" I asked at last. At least it hadn't been a sixteenth-century Protestant martyr.

"Or a temporal anomaly, or a hallucination, or—anything. Keep the visor down, don't scan, and start looking for rare plants *now*. The sooner you get what you're after, the sooner we get out of here."

"Okay," I said, and we rode on.

The road continued up, clinging to the hillside above the creek bed, and I saw condors wheeling in the sky and deer leaping away from us, and they were really there. I saw a coyote loping along in broad daylight across the canyon, and he was really there too. It was the sounds that dismayed. There were gunshots (which may or may not have been real), and there were more whizzing automobiles, and there was singing and chanting. How was I supposed to look for rare endemic plants with all that going on?

"All right," I said at last. "I give up. What's the deal here? And does it get any better, do we ride out of it?"

"No, it gets worse," Einar said. "We're still on the edge. We haven't come to Lookout Mountain Drive yet."

I frowned. "Lookout Mountain Drive? That sounds familiar."

"Here's the explanation as I understand it: weird geology around here. Look at all this decomposing granite. It's quartz-bearing, crystals all through the rock if you know where to look. There's another outcropping of high quartz concentration over in what'll be Griffith Park, and that place has some bizarre happenings of its own, but this place is the mother lode." Einar turned uneasily in his saddle, starting to scan, and stopped himself with visible effort. Something enormous went snorting and blowing past us, and we heard small trees snapping and big trees being pushed aside.

"I knew it would be bad, but not like this. The local Indians say the canyon was cut through by the God Himself, that He was chasing Coyote who'd stolen the moon, and Coyote had burrowed down under these mountains with it, and God grabbed the mountaintops and ripped them apart, made this long fissure, to get to where the moon was hidden. It was down so deep, though, that God gave up and threw a buffalo gourd up in the sky to be the moon instead, and the old moon's still buried here somewhere.

"An interesting story, in light of the fact that the biggest damn quartz deposit in the known universe lies about a thousand feet below the intersection of Laurel Canyon Drive and Lookout Mountain Drive. We know it's there; the Company did radar imaging of the whole area, once they noticed this place is so full of Crome's radiation, it can wipe out our sensory displays. Apparently there's a single crystal down there the size of—of that thing that just went stomping by us. And that's just some of what they found. Nothing supernatural or extraterrestrial, you understand, just the biggest naturally occurring Crome spectral sponge in the world. As near as Dr. Zeus can figure out, it stores Crome's radiation generated by anything passing over it that has a nervous system. Animals, Indians, and bandits is about all there is now; but as people begin moving in here, there will be a lot more energy absorbed.

"And every so often it discharges, and then all hell breaks loose, and that's what we're seeing now," Einar concluded.

"It figures, that this is supposed to be Coyote's fault," I said disgustedly. I saw a bush I didn't recognize and stopped. Handing the reins to Einar, I slid down and bent to examine it. Yes, it was really there. "But why are we seeing it now? There's nobody living up here yet to generate all this stuff," I argued, groping for my collecting gear. Damn this visor anyway. How was I supposed to take readings? "What's causing the blue lights and the auditory illusions?"

"It could be picking up Crome from us. One theory is that every time it discharges, it sets up a shock wave that puts stress on the temporal field, and the whole fabric of time ripples. My guess is, they're afraid we might slip through a hole or something, and that's why the connecting cable. If one of us goes through, the other can pull him out." Einar lifted his gun to his shoulder involuntarily, then lowered it. "We're also recording and broadcasting data to Central HQ, I'm sure. So, is that a rare plant?"

"Looks like a mutation of *Myrica californica*," I said in satisfaction. "Jackpot, on the first try. Not that I can tell much about it in all this armor."

"Cut a couple of branches and let's go, okay?"

"Are you scared?" I looked up at him. My own fear had evaporated the second the bush read positive for mutation. What else might I find up here?

"Me? Hell no, I'd love nothing better than to get myself sucked through a temporal rift into Jurassic times or something." Einar turned his head, sweeping the area visually. "Let's move on. Want to see where the Haunted Tavern will be? It's just up ahead."

"Neat," I replied, tucking the specimens into my collecting bag and climbing into the saddle again. We rode on, though unseen sirens screamed past us.

A few hundred feet ahead, the gorge widened to a sort of clearing, with another steep canyon opening to the left. Immense sycamores darkened the way ahead of us. We rode to the center of the clearing. For the moment, all we heard were natural sounds, the creek bubbling to our right, the wind in the leaves.

"Nice spot, isn't it?" said Einar, actually relaxing a little. "Someone will build a brick commercial building here. The top part will be the Canyon Store, eventually, and a lot of famous rock stars will buy their groceries here. Around the corner and downstairs, though"—he pointed over his horse's tail—"is where the Haunted Tavern will be. The earliest record of it is as a speakeasy, then later it's a cozy bar. Nice little watering hole for thirsty movie people going home to Encino after a day at RKO, or going home to Beverly Hills after a day at Universal or Republic. They'll shortcut through Laurel Canyon with a stop right here. It's private, it's unfashionable, it's hard for wives or reporters or detectives to find them in the little dark basement bar."

He leaned forward in the saddle, and his crazy smile looked crazier than usual under the visor of the absurd helmet.

"Now, you've heard the story about John Barrymore's wake? How, after he dies, a bunch of his drinking buddies steal his body from the funeral parlor and take it with them for one last night on the town? He's supposed to be carried all over Hollywood during this one long wild night before his funeral. That much is legendary.

"What didn't make it into the legend was how the party finished up. This part of the story is supposed to have been told to a male nurse at the hospital where W. C. Fields died. According to the nurse, the last stop on the route was this basement bar. The place was locked for the night, but Gene Fowler picked the lock, and they got in. Laid out cash on the bar and mixed themselves drinks. At this point, Barrymore is supposed to have sat up in his coffin and demanded to know where *his* drink was. They were in a pretty philosophical mood by that time, so they just poured him a martini. I don't know what's supposed to have happened after that, but people say . . ."

"What?" I shivered, hearing an invisible glass break.

"Well, the place operates on and off after that. Sometimes it's a bar, sometimes it's a restaurant, sometimes it closes down for years at a time. But whenever it's a bar, sooner or later, *John Barrymore comes in for a drink.* And once he's seen, the new owners know they might just as well give notice to the Realtor and move on; because before long the place is packed after hours with the thirsty dead, W. C. Fields and Victor McLaglen and Erroll Flynn, to name but a few. They drink the booze, they break the glasses, they have loud conversations in the parking lot at four A.M. Local residents get mad as hell and call the cops. What can the cops do? No use for the bar's owners to swear that they close at midnight, either. The place gets shut down again, until the next hapless guy comes along and decides it's a great place to open a cozy little bar."

Smash! This time it was a bottle breaking, and my horse shied and started forward.

"Let's go on," I said.

We rode up the canyon, with me stopping at frequent intervals to investigate the truly amazing number of unusual endemics that began to occur as we drew closer to Lookout Mountain Drive. I found a purple form of *Marah macrocarpus*, a variant of *Lonicera subspicata* with scarlet flowers, and the strangest-looking *Baccharis glutinosa* I'd ever encountered. I was so absorbed in my discoveries that I paid little attention to the trumpeting mammoths, trolley cars, and bagpipers that passed me on the way. Einar had to reach into his saddlebags, though, where he'd stashed a whole box of Theobromos, the Mexican kind that comes in six round cakes in an octagonal box. He just kept unwrapping them and wolfing them down, working his way through them as though they were rice cakes. As a result, he was mellower than usual by the time we got to Lookout Mountain Drive, and swaying gently in the saddle.

"An' here it is," he said, swinging an arm in a half circle. "The strange heart of all strangeness anyplace. Look normal to you? Ah, but we know better."

Actually it didn't look normal to me, even through the visor, though it was just a sunny clearing opening up to the sky. There was something a little skewed in the perspective. I couldn't quite tell how wide the clearing was.

"So this is the mystery spot?" I tried to sound nonchalant.

"Yes, but not some lousy little carney mystery spot with trick angles and optical illusions," said Einar. "If you took that visor off, this place would light up like Times Square. All kinds of unusual mortals will be drawn here. One guy, he'll be a naval officer and engineer with a wife who's a practicing witch. They'll settle here for a while, and he'll actually write an exposé of the place. Then he'll think things over and rewrite it as a piece of science fiction. Did you ever hear of Dr. Montgomery Sherrinford?"

I did a fast access on the name. All that turned up was a footnote in a biography of Aleister Crowley and a half paragraph in a work on theosophy.

"Some kind of Freemason?" I asked.

"Starts out as one. They eject him. He becomes a Rosicrucian, and they throw him out too. Same thing with the Order of the Golden Dawn. Madame Blavatsky gives him the heave-ho, and so do those people up at Summerland. He travels all over the place before he finds Lookout Mountain Drive, but *then*, man, his luck changes. He builds a kind of temple right there"—Einar pointed to our left—"and he builds a mansion up there on the hill. In later years people will call it Houdini's mansion, but no—it was built by Dr. Sherrinford. He *knows* the vibrations on this spot are like nothing else anywhere. Gets himself a cult going, becomes its high priest, lots of spooky goings-on all around this very intersection. A lot of famous players and their bosses too, from the early days of movies, come to 'services' here. Not because of the guy's charisma, but because he has real powers—also he knows where a lot of bodies are buried, metaphorically and otherwise."

"I never heard about any of this," I said doubtfully.

"You have to know where to look, but the references are there. In this correspondence, in that library collection. Anyway, Dr. Sherrinford has this big thing going. Silent-film stars at his beck and call. Blackmail money. Devoted followers who set about the task he sets them, which seems to be tunneling into Laurel Canyon. He gets them looking for the source of the power. He's never too clear on what it is, but he's got a good idea *where* it is. He'll completely undermine his temple with tunnels. And it seems he gets all the way down to the big crystal, too, because all these rumors start flying around of an incredible discovery and miracles and contact with the other world.

"Now, *we* know you can't do anything with Crome's radiation, not anything useful anyway. Dr. Sherrinford won't know that. He'll think it'll give him power. He builds an underground chapel a thousand feet below, reached by a little elevator going down a shaft, and he takes his disciples down there, and they hold chanting services.

"You know what happens when you have a lot of people generating a Crome-effect field around a spectral sponge. Just like electricity, it absorbs the charge, absorbs the charge, until finally it discharges, boom! And all hell breaks loose, ripples in the temporal field, ghosts, visions, apports, you name it. It happens, or seems to.

"That's what Dr. Sherrinford's disciples keep praying for. It's like a bunch of monkeys in a cage, hitting the same lever over and over again until the bell rings and a bucket of monkey treats are dumped on them. Or it's like somebody with a cup of nickels playing a slot machine. Mostly Dr. Sherrinford's crystal spirit ignores its worshipers, but every so often it blasts them with a miracle and a lot of stimulation of the hippocampal region of their brains.

"Harry Houdini is in California making a movie for Lasky, it's called *Terror Island*, and he's doing location shooting over on Catalina. And this guy comes up to him in the restaurant at the Hotel Metropole and tells him about the goings-on at Dr. Sherrinford's temple and asks if he wants to come attend a service there. It's implied that the dead speak at these parties.

"Well, that's just the right thing to say to Houdini—or the wrong thing, depending on your point of view. His mother died a few years previous, and he has this strong attachment to her, kind of a Freudian thing, you know? He's been positive she'll send him a message from the beyond, only years have gone by now and she hasn't, though he's paid plenty of bucks to spiritualists and mediums. Not that they don't claim she's trying to talk to him, but the messages are all obvious fakes.

"Finally he decides it's all a lot of bull and becomes an obsessive debunker. Inside, though, *he wants to believe*. So he flies back from

Catalina with this guy, and they go to Laurel Canyon. They meet Dr. Sherrinford. What happens next?

"Nobody ever gives complete testimony; but again, if you know where to look, you can piece it together, what happens down in the crystal chamber. Houdini goes there, all right, with Dr. Sherrinford and his disciples, and they hold a big ceremony with chanting and pull out all the stops, they're levitating and speaking in tongues. It sets off the crystal. And when it discharges, apparently a *lot* of dead guys want to speak with Houdini. Only problem is, some of them are ordinary dead and some of them claim to be dead guys from the future, from a time when there isn't time. And they aren't all agreed on the usual spirit patter about being happy on the other side and telling everyone that it's all niceness and harmony over there. In fact, they start to fight.

"They fight so violently, they cause something like a small earthquake. The tunnel collapses, or becomes blocked. What happens to Dr. Sherrinford and his gang is never known, but Houdini manages to escape by getting to the jammed elevator and worming his way through an air vent, after which he climbs the cable. He takes off down the canyon into the night.

"Why doesn't he call the cops? Why doesn't he make any attempt to rescue Dr. Sherrinford's people? We'll never know. Whatever took place, it scares Houdini half to death. He opens negotiations to buy that property, though, which shows that something about it has a hold on him. History's a little vague about whether he ever closes the deal, but there's an account that he's visited in his hotel room by one of the disciples, who may or may not be a survivor of the crystal chamber. Houdini leaves on the train for New York the same day, and never stays in Los Angeles again. In fact he leaves America a month later and goes on an extended tour abroad. Spends the rest of his life trying to prove that there *is* no other side and that the dead can't talk."

"So there'll be an earthquake," I said, shrugging. "It buries the cultists, and Houdini gets out because of his special abilities. Afterward somebody blackmails him about running off and leaving the others to die. Creepy, but not inexplicable."

"I'd agree," Einar said, grinning at me, "except for the fact that in 2072 a bunch of people in white robes come wading out of the surf off Bermuda claiming to be Montgomery Sherrinford and his disciples. They disappear into an asylum and out of the historical record pretty fast, though."

"Hoaxers," I said firmly, shaking my head. I caught sight of a weird-looking thing poking through the dead leaves at the base of a *Rhus laurina*. A kind of fungus? Root parasite? Urn-shaped flowers bright green—some member of the heath family? At *this* elevation? And what were those curling scales? I accessed at top speed and found not a single identification. If it were possible for my immortal heart to skip a beat, it would have done so then. Visions of Favorable Mutation bonuses for *Sarcodes mendozai* danced before my eyes.

"I'm going to dismount now," I informed Einar. "I think there's something really remarkable here."

"You can say that again," said Einar, taking firm hold of the cord that connected us. He watched as I slid down—and I could feel something through the soles of my boots, a pulsing. There was a cracking sound and a flash of bluest light. I grabbed at my saddle in panic, but that was no good either, the horse just swayed away from me. Einar seemed a long distance off. And where was the damned plant?

I looked around, expecting to see a landscape festooned with melting clocks. What I saw was no less strange. Immediately beside me, and stretching up and down the canyon, was a long river of gleaming rounded things, inching slowly forward in a stinking miasma of chemical smoke like so many mechanical turtles. They weren't blue. They weren't transparent. Behind smoked glass, open-mouthed faces stared at me.

"Einar." I felt blindly for the cord. "There are unborn here."

"I know." His voice was faint. I looked over at him, and he was staring at me in horror, just as solidly there as I was, as the vehicles were. "So much for the cord, huh? I guess it just pulled me after you."

"These are late-twentieth-century automobiles."

"Yes."

I found myself hyperventilating. It was a mistake among the gasoline fumes. I looked around wildly. Everywhere were strange Japanese names in chrome. To hell with *Sarcodes mendozai*. I scrambled back up on my horse. The cars didn't go away. People were pointing at us.

"They're pointing at us," I said. "What do we do, for God's sake? Will they shoot at us, will they start rioting?"

"Let's stay calm," Einar said, though his knuckles were white where he gripped the reins. "Let's ride straight up that ridge and out of here. Maybe we'll, like, snap back to 1862 painlessly. Okay?"

We didn't. From the ridge above, we looked out on a clutter of houses. And what was the matter with the distant plain? Had the sea level risen? No; that roaring, gleaming gridwork was a city, stretching away to the horizon. We stared at it in shock. It was a city in the future, which I had always thought would be beautiful, but it wasn't beautiful at all. The air was brown. The sunlight looked red through it, sunset color at midday.

"Now . . . this *isn't* possible," I said to Einar. "Right? You can't go forward past your own time. Everybody knows that."

He nodded mutely.

"So it's just an illusion. No transcendence field, no stasis gas, so we can't even have gone back in time, let alone forward."

He nodded again. "Except," he said reluctantly, "that there are some recorded instances of people doing it. People in old-fashioned clothes suddenly turning up in future traffic and getting hit by cars, for instance."

"And of course those have to be unsubstantiated fictions, because it can't really happen. Dr. Zeus says so." I drew in a lungful of the acrid air and coughed. "Is this *smog*? How can people live like this?"

"Come on." Einar turned his horse's head. "There's supposed to be a relay station in Hollywood in this time period. Jumping ahead through time may be impossible for Dr. Zeus, but it obviously ain't impossible for Lookout Mountain Drive."

We rode down the ridge, accessing coordinates as we went. Immediately to the south of us rose a gated wall topped by what would have been Ionic columns if they were ten times bigger. As it was, they looked cheesy. Beyond them was a sprawling community of flat-topped mansions in ghastly mid-twentieth-century style, roofs covered with white gravel, walls faced with Hawaiian lava, everything deliberately off-center and out of balance, from the winding front walks to the kidney-shaped pools in each backyard. Black letters on the wall told us this was MOUNT OLYMPUS.

We found our way in, past the corner of Vulcan Drive, and proceeded down Olympus Drive. "Oh, they *didn't*." I said. "Did they?"

Einar smiled wryly and pointed at a little cul-de-sac with the grand name of Zeus Drive. The architecture there was just as crappy, even on the house that was obviously our relay station, the one with the Dr. Zeus logo picked out in green pebbles on the red-pebble tessellation of the front walk. There wasn't a living soul in sight, which was a good thing, under the circumstances.

We rode up the concrete driveway and sat there looking uncertainly at the very ugly house. There were no stables anywhere that I could see, though there was a sensor array on the roof, disguised to look like satellite television equipment.

Uh . . . Operatives Einar and Mendoza reporting. Please provide codes, transmitted Einar. As we watched, the broad garage door swung open of its own accord to reveal a couple of frightened-looking techs in coveralls.

"Come inside. Hurry!" hissed one of them. We urged our horses forward, and as soon as we were inside, the garage door clanked down after us. Our horses, who had been patient and unflappable until then, spooked; I just scrambled off mine and dodged its panicky dance, but Einar controlled his with an iron hand and caught my mount's reins. The techs cowered in a corner.

"Whoa, whoa," said Einar. He dismounted and caught his horse's head, stroking its muzzle and looking into its eyes. "You don't want to step on anybody, do you? Of course you don't. That's a good boy. And how about you, sweetie, you want to calm down too? Pretty girl. Good girl."

"You're talking to the *horses*," said one of the techs in disbelief.

"Yeah," he said, and I don't think he noticed that they found it distasteful. I noticed, though. I knew who they were at once: operatives from the future, doing time on a mission in what was *their* past, though their past was more than a hundred years ahead of us. I've worked with that kind before. They're stuck-up.

"I guess you're wondering what we're doing here," Einar said, but the tech who had more buttons on his coveralls than the other snapped:

"No, we're not. There was a distortion in the temporal field. We monitored it. You're an anomaly. You'll have to report immediately to the temporal transference chamber for return to your point of origin. This way!" He pointed, and the other one opened a door in the wall beside what appeared to be late-twentieth-century laundry appliances.

"What about the horses?" I said.

The tech got a look of horror on his face. He wrung his hands. At last he replied, "They'll have to come too. Just hurry!"

They scuttled ahead of us through the door. Einar and I exchanged bemused glances, but led our respective mounts through the doorway.

Horses look *big* in houses. Ours clopped after us through what was apparently a kitchen, across a smooth substance that must have been linoleum tile—I didn't think it looked all that bad—but the sound of their hooves was muffled when we emerged into a much larger room, because it was carpeted in synthetic fiber of a sickly beige color.

I was disoriented at once. The floor was on a couple of different levels, for no reason I could understand, and one whole wall slanted inward. Across the room was another rise to the floor, and there was a fireplace with no mantelpiece, only flagstones set *around* it, flush into the wall instead of on the floor, where flagstones belonged. In front of the hearth, where the flagstones should have been, the beige

carpet went right up to the andirons. Stranger still, the entire west wall
of the room was made of glass: four enormous panes gave a breathtaking view of the roofs of other houses across the canyon but robbed
the room of any warmth or privacy.

The horses were disoriented too. Einar's gave its opinion of the
decor with one good lift of its tail.

The tech leader jumped three feet, clapping his hands over his
nose and mouth. "Aaagh! You *filthy*—oh, you *filthy*—"

Someone in the room burst out laughing. An immortal rose from
a shapeless piece of furniture and surveyed the mess. She wore the
unisex clothing of that era, ordinary jeans like Einar's and a plain white
cotton shirt. She turned to us.

"You must be the two unfortunates who surfed the temporal wave.
How do you feel?" she said pleasantly, as though what had happened
was no big deal.

"There is excrement on the floor. The carpet will have to be dis-
infected," said the tech.

"Oh, shut up and go get a shovel. If we've got one around here.
You'd have to be Zoologist Einar and, let's see, Botanist Mendoza,
wasn't it? Maire, regional facilitator." The immortal shook our hands,
for some reason pausing with me, but only a fraction of a second.
"Don't worry. We can deal with the Lookout Mountain anomaly a lot
better in this era; we've been studying it from this station for years
now. You'll be all right. I'd love to let you stay a couple of days and
show you around, but—"

"Those *things* have got to get out of here," said the tech. "What
if one of them does number one?"

"—as you see, we have a crisis on our hands," Maire said, indicating the tech with a grimace. "So if you don't mind, we'll just whisk
you back to 1862. Sorry we couldn't be more hospitable." With a wave
she directed us into a space beyond the room—there wasn't exactly a
doorway, and I couldn't quite figure the geometry of the house, but it
seemed to be an entry hall. One wall was covered with beige drapery.
She pulled a cord, and the draperies drew to one side, revealing not a
window but a glass chamber, smooth and featureless inside. It looked
like one of those streamlined aluminum travel trailers mortals will tow
around behind their automobiles in that century, but it seemed to have
been built into the house.

Maire pressed a series of buttons, and a door slid open. She gestured for us to enter. The horses didn't want to go, but Einar managed
to sweet-talk them over the silver threshold. As he was doing so, I
heard the roar of an automobile outside approaching the house, stop-

ping abruptly as it pulled into the driveway. Once the horses were in with us, the door slid shut, and we felt the cabin pressurizing.

"Nobody seems very surprised to see us," I murmured to Einar.

"Well, but they had to have known we were coming. The Temporal Concordance would have told them." Einar soothed and stroked my mount, which was more panicked than his.

"But if what we just did is impossible, you'd think they'd want to study us—" I broke off as Maire stepped forward to the control console.

She tapped in a combination on the buttons and stood back, looking at us through the window. She took a small cylinder from her pocket and spoke into it. Her voice came hollowly from the air above our heads. "It's warming up. Transcendence in approximately thirty seconds. Brace yourselves."

Yellow vapor began to curl into the air from no source I could see. I inhaled deeply; stasis gas is a lot easier on the lungs than smog. Beyond our window, the door opened, and a man entered the house, setting down a leather case and tossing his keys on the hall table. He was an immortal, in an expensive-looking twentieth-century suit that must have been tailored but somehow seemed too big on him. He looked familiar. As he turned his head to stare at us, I recognized him: Lewis, with whom I'd been stationed at New World One for years and years. Strange, I thought, two old friends in a matter of months. Lewis had been the last person I hugged back in 1700, when I said good-bye at the transport lounge before I came to California. Hadn't he been going to England? But that was three hundred years ago by this time. I smiled and waved. I could see Maire smiling too, pointing at us and explaining something to him, but of course I couldn't hear behind the glass.

He didn't hear her either, I don't think. He was staring at me with the most incredulous expression on his face, which had gone perfectly white. Suddenly he flung himself at the window, pounding on it, shouting silently at me. What on earth? And why the urgency? The air in the room grew suddenly icy, the yellow gas boiled around me and obscured his desperate face. I was growing numb with the transcendence, but I managed to read his lips.

Mendoza, for God's sake! Don't go with him!

I turned my head slowly to Einar. He was looking confused. He met my eyes and shrugged. I looked back at Lewis, shaking my head and holding out my hands. Were those tears in his eyes? He was mouthing *no* over and over, both palms pressed flat against the glass as if trying to push it in. The yellow gas was almost opaque now. I reached out my hand in slow motion and set it on the window, palm to palm with him through the glass, though I could no longer see his face. Then the transcendence came, and it was a lovely thing, pleasurable even with the feeling of infinite violence being done to one, as if you were picked up and thrown into the void forever, or flying ...

Then there was a strong wind blowing the fog away, and I stumbled and fell to my knees, choking. I was groping in red sand, trying to rise in a thicket of sagebrush and spurge laurel. There were the horses, flailing and struggling, and there was Einar, doubled up on hands and knees, gasping out yellow smoke.

I scanned blearily. No houses, no deadly city on the plain. We were on the ridge above Laurel Canyon, in the same space we'd occupied 134 years earlier. Later? Whatever. I sank down as Einar was doing and panted, clearing my lungs. Neither one of us said anything for a few minutes. Even the horses gave up and lay still while their mortal nervous systems recovered.

Finally Einar turned over and sat up, resting his head in his hands.

"What was up with that guy?" he asked. "Why didn't he want you to go with me?"

"No idea." I shook my head. "We used to be good friends, back before I came to California. I haven't seen him in ages."

I couldn't remember ever having seen Lewis that upset, even when his lady friends dumped him, as sometimes happened. He was one of those genuinely nice guys who somehow always wind up alone. I was always alone, myself. It had been what made us friends.

Einar and I both shrugged.

Once the horses were able to get up, we left that place, walking and leading them, because the trail down from the ridge was steep and tricky. Halfway back, my horse began to cough and shudder, then abruptly fell. Blood gushed from its wide nostrils as it gave one last convulsive twitch. The stress of the time journey, I guess. Einar sank down on his knees and cried.

It was hours before we stumbled into our own canyon, to the welcome smell of beef being grilled over a mesquite fire. There was blessed silence: no cars, no phantoms, only the oak trees and chaparral and one or two stars winking in the twilight sky. Porfirio was crouched over the fire, turning the steaks. He looked up as we approached.

"There you are. What happened to the mare?"

"She had an accident," said Einar sullenly, and led his mount away to the stable.

Porfirio winced, and I thought he was recalculating his operating budget. He looked at me. "And you? Any problems?"

"Not really," I said. Well, we'd come home in one piece, hadn't we? I sank down beside the fire.

Porfirio still stood, considering me for a long moment. "Mendoza," he said, "I'm a security tech. I can tell when people are lying."

I glared at him, señors, feeling very Spanish. How dare he say I was lying? Even if I was. "All right, something happened," I admitted, pulling off the stupid high-tech armor that hadn't worked. He swore. I snapped at him, "I don't know why you bothered to make us carry all this garbage. I suppose you had some communiqué from the Company about what was going to happen today? Did everybody but *me* know? One of those rules you're not supposed to break, about telling people what's in their future?"

"Something like that," Porfirio said.

"Why did you ask me, then, if you knew?"

"Because they didn't tell me much," he said bitterly. "They never do. Never enough to be of any use."

"That figures." I sighed and slumped forward. I was so tired. I was about to tell him about the accident when he took my breath away by asking:

"How long have you been a Crome generator?"

I began to shake. "I'm not! There was just one time, when I was young—only that once. My case officer thought—he said it was probably nothing. Never since then, I swear!"

"Mendoza," he said, "since you've been here, not one week has gone by that there hasn't been an incident. I've looked out and seen the blue light pouring through the cracks in the boards, as if you had lightning in there with you. You didn't know? You slept through it every time? What's been happening to you?"

I shook my head. How could I tell him, when I didn't know myself? Bad dreams? I debated telling him about my dead lover who had risen from his grave to follow me across three centuries, an ocean, and a continent to make my life intolerable in this already intolerable place. What I said instead was, "I appear to be malfunctioning."

We regarded each other in silence.

"Are you going to ship me out and send for a replacement botanist?" I asked. That was according to regulations. Ironic, isn't it, señors? I was holding my breath, petrified at the thought that my field career was over. If only he *had* shipped me out.

Porfirio shook his head grimly. "I don't do that to my people. You've done a lot of good work, Mendoza. If you throw enough Crome to read by, so what? It doesn't seem to be hurting anybody but you. I know you have some bad memories, but you never let them interfere with your work. Look . . . the rules are different down here. Don't give me a reason to have you replaced, and I won't. Okay? But don't ever lie to me, because I'll know. So what happened today?"

I told him, as he took the steaks off the fire with greatest care and arranged them on an iron platter. He listened without a word, going about the business of setting out the evening meal as though I were telling him the plot of a film I'd seen. At last I finished, and he handed me a plate of supper and sat down across from me as I ate.

"Mendoza," he said finally, "watch your back."

That was all he'd say on the subject.

Obviously he had an idea of what was coming. And on that day in 1996, Lewis *knew*, señors, what would happen, knew that I'd sit before you in this place now, telling you this story. He was trying to warn me. It was kind of him, though it did no good in the end, and I hope it didn't get him into trouble. This just proves once again the only unbreakable law I know: that history cannot be changed.

13

THE SUMMER WORE on; it grew hotter and browner and dustier, and then in the evenings the wind began to change. Big purple rifts of fog would come blowing in from the coast. In the brown canyons the big leaves of sycamores began to drift down, smelling spicy and sweet when one crunched through them. Deer began to descend from the brown hills, looking around hopefully for garden produce, which they didn't find; but we did get venison for a change. The moon got very big, very silver, and the coyotes rejoiced.

Porfirio began to stock up our supplies for the winter. Not that there was ever any snow, and we knew, as the mortals didn't, that this year there wouldn't even be winter rains to flood out the roads. But it was a safe bet that some disaster or other was going to strike, this being southern California, so it was just as well to be prepared.

So Einar was sent out time and again, to Los Angeles with lowing longhorns for Dr. Zeus, and he came back with wagonload after wagonload of crates, barrels, and sacks. Porfirio and Einar would haul them into the storeroom, where Juan Bautista and I (and Erich and Marie) would uncrate stuff and check it against the order list. Dozens of sacks of pink beans, dozens more of masa, enough coffee beans to wake the dead, jars of pickles and preserves, cones of brown sugar, boxes of salt . . . and seven cases of canned sardines.

"Jesus, why'd he order all the sardines?" I said, staring astonished into an opened crate. "They're not even on his list. Hey, Porfirio?" Juan Bautista got a funny look on his face and put up his hands to shush me, but Porfirio had already backed in, carrying one end of a barrel.

"What?" he grunted, backing in the rest of the way so Einar could ease his end down.

"Never mind, I figured it out," I said, but he turned frowning and noticed the funny-looking cans in the opened crate.

"What the hell are those?" He picked up one of the cans. "These are sardines! I didn't order these. None of you guys even like them."

"I like them," said Juan Bautista in a doomed voice.

There was a frozen moment, which unfortunately was broken by Marie Dressler limping across the room and looking up at Juan Bautista expectantly.

Porfirio blew his top, and then blew it louder when he found out that that opened case was one of seven, but I really thought the roof was going to come off the adobe when he discovered that Juan Bautista had added them to the station's order list, which meant that they'd been paid for out of the station's operating budget.

"Didn't I order the damn bird a sack of pelican chow?" shouted Porfirio.

Juan Bautista hung his head. "She's too old for it. It makes her droppings runny."

I left then and at some speed, not wishing to be there when Porfirio came down off the ceiling. Einar was already gone.

I was up in my favorite retreat by the creek, gloomily contemplating my future, when Juan Bautista came wandering along the creek bed half an hour later. Erich was perching on him and Marie was cradled in his arms. He was sniffling a little.

I cleared my throat, so he wouldn't think he was alone and go into some soliloquy of teenage despair.

"Oh," he said. "Hi." He came over and sat down beside me. I edged away slightly, not caring to be that close to Marie's beak. She had a wicked kind of hook on the end of it, like a mandarin's thumbnail.

"Is Porfirio through screaming?"

"I guess so," he said. "I guess I shouldn't have ordered seven cases. And it was wrong not to tell him about adding to his order. But what am I supposed to do? She's old. She's an endangered species. Fish is what she's supposed to eat. We can't take any more out of the creek, or the breeding population will go below sustainable levels. *He* ought to try that lousy pelican chow, see how *he* likes it."

This implied that Juan Bautista had sampled it himself, which I didn't want to think about. "Well, don't worry," I said. "If Imarte peddles her papayas vigorously enough, she'll earn back the budget deficit." But he wasn't amused, he was sunk in the self-righteous bitterness that only the very young can feel.

"Darned grandfather," he muttered.

We sat there a moment in silence. "What," I asked cautiously, "was that supposed to mean?"

"It was my grandfather got me into this."

"You mean, a real grandfather? Your mortal father's father?"

He nodded. After a moment, he drew a deep breath and began.

"We lived on one of the islands. I don't even know which one, San Miguel or Santa Rosa. All our people had left to go live at the mission, but Grandfather took us back—my father and mother, I mean. He wouldn't leave his holy place. He was the . . . I guess he was the priest. The word for it sounded like *sishwin*. Anyhow, his god told him he wasn't supposed to leave the island, so he had to go back. That meant my father had to go back, too, because he was supposed to be the sishwin after Grandfather died, and my mother went too, because she was going to have me. They went by canoe. My mother was sick the whole way. I remember she used to talk about it.

"She and my father had a lot of fights. I was born over there, and there weren't any medicine women to help when I was born, just my father, and she was always talking about that. She wanted to go back to the mission, she didn't mind being a Christian, and she talked about that a lot too. And she was always afraid I would fall off a cliff into the sea.

"My father didn't want to be there either. When they were speaking to each other, he'd tell her how mad he was at my grandfather, how our old god was fake nowadays and Grandfather was just being stubborn about staying on the island. I remember he said he could never be a sishwin, because even if the old god cared, Grandfather would never think my father was good enough.

"But they never said anything when Grandfather came into the house. They were scared of him. He was scary-looking. He looked at Daddy like he was dirt, and at Mommy the same way.

"He liked me. He used to take me out to his holy place. There was a big wooden statue of the god there with the sun and the moon on his head. There were big black ravens, and I guess they were bigger than the ones here on the mainland, because I've never seen them that big since I came back. Grandfather used to show me how to feed them. Some were tame and would hop on my hand and let me scratch their necks. Some could talk. I used to think that was magic, because back then I didn't know how smart the *corvidae* are.

"Grandfather told me a lot of stuff about how I belonged to his god, and how if Mommy and Daddy were bad weak people, *I* wasn't, and I was going to be a powerful sishwin just like him, and someday our god was going to send the bears to get all the bad weak people who stopped paying attention to him.

"I just kept quiet and played with the ravens. I liked to stroke their feathers. They were so shiny black, they were blue and reflected the sky. I thought they were the prettiest things.

"Then something bad happened. I don't know what it was. Daddy and Mommy were yelling at each other, and I sneaked away to play with the ravens. There was one that liked to have his neck scratched, behind the feathers, and he just wanted you to go on and on and he'd close his eyes like saying, I can't stand this, it's so good.

"Grandfather came and got me and put me in the canoe. He said a lot of scary things. We went across the sea, and sometimes he'd stand up in the canoe and shout at the sky. I curled up in the bottom of the canoe and closed my eyes.

"We came to the mainland, and Grandfather hid the canoe in a cave. We sneaked across the hills, so the soldiers wouldn't see us, and we came to the big mission. It was the biggest place I'd ever seen. There was a Christian priest sitting on the steps. I don't know why he was sitting out there in the middle of the night."

"I do," I said tensely. "Short man, was he, in a brown robe? Stocky? Little black eyes?"

"Uh-huh. Grandfather carried me up to him and said, Here, you take children, take this one. And he turned and walked away. He left me there. I never saw him again." Juan Bautista's eyes were red, but he didn't start blubbering, thank God.

"Well, the Christian was really surprised. He sat up and asked me what had happened. I told him everything I knew, which wasn't much. He was nice. He asked me a lot of questions and told me everything would be all right now. We went into the big kitchen in the dark, but the Christian could see in the dark, and he got me some food. Then he took me to his room and put me in his bed and told me to sleep. I asked him where he was going to sleep, and he said he didn't sleep."

"He doesn't," I said. "Not much, anyway."

"He hid me in his room a couple of days. He shaved my head, because of bugs, he said. He measured me and looked in my eyes. He let me play with a glass. I'd never seen glass before. It broke, and I cut my finger, and he took some of the blood and put it in something that was probably a machine, but it didn't look like one."

"And let me guess," I said, clenching my fists. "He sat you down and gave you a talk about how sad it was to get old and crazy like your grandfather, but *you* didn't ever have to get old or die."

"That's right."

"And I'll bet he told you that it was sad you'd lost your family, but you could have a wonderful new family who would help you become smart and live forever."

Juan Bautista looked at me. "I guess that's what we say to all the kids we rescue, huh? The next day, he brought me out and told the other Christians that I was a little orphan who'd been left at the mission, but that he'd discovered I had family at a rancheria up the coast, so he was going to take me there, because the mission couldn't provide for orphans anymore.

"We walked and walked, and after a couple of days we came to a big hill above the sea. You could see the islands from there. We stopped and built a fire and waited until dark. In the middle of the night the ship came, a big silver ship. It scared me half to death, but the Christian explained what it was.

"It landed, and the door opened, and nice people came out and took me inside. I was happy, for the first time I could remember except when I was with the ravens. Nobody ever fought or yelled. There was lots of food. And when they found out I liked birds, they made me an ornithologist." Juan Bautista sighed. "So I guess I'm better off now. I really shouldn't blame my grandfather. Because if he hadn't taken me to the Christian, I'd probably be dead or a slave. And it isn't Porfirio's fault that Marie is old and can't eat the pelican chow."

"No, it isn't." I gazed into the brown water of the creek.

"You want to go eat some sardines, old lady?" said Juan Bautista, burying his face in the spiky feathers on Marie's neck. "They're good for you. We'll go get some treats, and I'll play for you, how about that? I'm learning Nunuz's *Sinfonia Asturias*. She really likes the slow movement."

Erich von Stroheim reached down and groomed behind Juan's ears, tugging a long tail of silver hair and pulling it slowly through his beak until it stood out at an angle. He cocked his head, studying the results.

PART TWO

Babylon Is Fallen

14

THIS IS THE big one!" Einar said, leaping down from the wagon.

"What big one?" Porfirio asked uneasily, looking around at the hills as though he expected them to rock and roll.

"The epic. David Wark Griffith's *Intolerance*." Einar flourished a big silver film can at us. "It just came in. Polish up your rhinestones and press those tuxedos, ladies and gentlemen, 'cause we're going to Babylon tonight!"

There's nothing like a sense of occasion to lift your spirits. Imarte was delighted when she heard what was on the evening's bill, and prepared a special treat; in addition to our popcorn and non-bathtub gin we had little rose-flavored chunks of gummy candy, prepared (she assured us) exactly as it was served at Belshazzar's feast. She would know, I guess. Nor was that all; she and Einar made a last-minute trip over to Sherman and managed to get roses from somebody's garden, big trailing fronds of yellow rambler, and spent most of the afternoon picking off thorns and weaving them into serviceable crowns. We settled down amid the cushions wearing chaplets of roses, and a big yellow rose waved above Einar's right ear as he stood up and pretended to talk into a microphone.

"And welcome once again, my fellow immortals, to this evening's edition of the Cahuenga Pass Film Festival. Tonight's offering is maybe the quintessential Hollywood film, the first cinema epic, and has been hailed as one of the greatest films ever made *and* one of the worst. How did the inimitable D. W. manage to grab the brass ring while simultaneously falling off the painted pony and landing on his head?

"Budget and bad timing, folks, combined with the same wholesome naïveté that left him astonished when black audiences failed to enjoy his film glorifying the Ku Klux Klan. Nobody could ever say Griffith was a slow learner, though, and so for his next film he singled out a slightly safer group to pick on: prissy old ladies of both genders. You may not agree with his unique insights on psychology or his scholarly footnotes as the evening progresses, but I can promise you this much: the visuals are killer.

"Now, this print will not be accompanied by the original score, but we are fortunate enough to have in our audience an expert who will provide us with fascinating commentary and insights of her own." He bowed at Imarte, and we all applauded politely. She waved a gracious hand. "On matters Babylonian, Persian, and prostitutional we defer to thee, O scarlet one. So, everybody, breathe a silent prayer to Ishtar, the goddess at Heaven's Gate, and hold on to your cushions, because it's gonna be a truly bumpy ride!"

He clambered over Juan Bautista and Erich (Marie was more obliging about being left in her cage) and started the projector. We were briefly treated to his black shadow on the screen while he blew out the lamps; then we were silently told that we were watching IN-TOLERANCE, a Sun-Play of the Ages.

"What's a sun-play?" Juan Bautista asked.

"Photoplay, get it?" Porfirio explained.

"Oh."

The screen advised us that we were going to watch a story of the battle of the forces of Hatred and Intolerance versus Love and Charity. Great, I thought, as though a roomful of immortals hadn't seen *that* plotline a few hundred times already. But this was supposed to be a great classic, so I opened my mouth only to stuff in some popcorn.

"Okay, here's the great leitmotif," said Einar. OUT OF THE CRADLE ENDLESSLY ROCKING, the screen told us, and there was Lillian Gish rocking the biggest cradle I'd ever seen, while the Three Fates looked on from upstage. There followed something incoherent and vaguely poetical about eternal hopes and fears, eternal joys and sorrows, and then we were watching a grand ball for a wealthy modern (early-twentieth-century) industrialist and his spinster sister.

"What is that woman wearing on her head?" Oscar inquired, frowning at the screen. "She looks like a circus horse."

She did, too; she was aging and plain, which made her easy prey for the Uplifters, a villainous society of ladies who wanted her money so they could ruin everybody else's fun. Now that she was no longer attracting the boys, she just naturally fell into their clutches, and was persuaded to hand over her brother's millions to the cause of Reform.

"Notice the subtle misogyny in Griffith's depiction of older women," said Imarte with a sniff.

"Subtle!" I scoffed through my popcorn.

Now we got to meet the Little Dear One, portrayed by Mae Marsh, a teen miss given to hysterical displays of affection, living happily with her aged father (a mill worker for the wealthy industrialist) and a host of small barnyard animals. Next we met our hero, Bobby Herron, as the Boy, who sported a black mustache in defiance of all heroic convention.

"He looks like Gomez Addams," said Juan Bautista. Our giggles died as the scene advanced and Griffith showed us the gray laboring masses shuffling in lockstep through the gates of the mill. This was the Future, this was the Metropolis, this was the century that would bring us to 1984. Where would I be in 1984? Or 1996? I reached for my martini and had a bracing gulp.

The scene changed. There was Lillian Gish with the cradle again and then the two tablets of Mosaic law, and we were at the Jaffa Gate watching camels and old bearded men in striped headdresses. Griffith explained what a Pharisee was, making sure we didn't miss the parallel with the Uplifters, and then showed us some of the Judean variety praying ostentatiously.

Wham! Scene change to France, A.D. 1572, where problems between the Catholics and the Huguenots were about to come to the boil.

"Hey! Really good clothes," I said in surprise. Everyone nodded except Juan Bautista and Oscar, who hadn't lived through that century. Then we were shown Catherine de Medici, the villainous queen mother ("*That* meddling old hag!" snarled Imarte, with such venom, we all turned to look at her) and her two sons: the king, a slender fellow with a tendency to curl up sideways on his throne, and his brother the prince, an effeminate who kept puppies in his codpiece. We were shown the French court milling around in a large room; then we met our Huguenot heroine Brown Eyes (with a tight close-up on her face, so we got the idea) and her nonentity boyfriend, Prosper Latour. We also met an obviously villainous soldier who was smitten with lust for Brown Eyes.

"I bet I know what's going to happen," said Juan Bautista, sitting forward.

But before we could guess, we were whisked back to the twentieth century, where the poor mill workers were innocently dancing at an ice-cream social. The Little Dear One was there, gleeful as usual, and so was the industrialist oppressor, snooping on his workers and scavenging dropped change from the sidewalk. This was straight out of Dickens, only grayer and more banal.

"When do we get to Babylon?" I complained.

"Right about now," Einar said, and lo, we beheld the Imgur Bel Gate of Babylon! Intricate, massive, worked by twin capstans carven with lions rampant, manned by dozens of slaves. Elephants plodding through the streets, looking small as cows before the vast walls. Enormous winged bulls with the heads of bearded kings. Now *this* was imagery. We cheered and applauded.

"Shot right here, folks, on Griffith's lot off Hollywood Boulevard," said Einar.

"Actually it didn't look at all like that," Imarte said.

"Well, it ought to have," Porfirio said.

In the midst of the gorgeously costumed bustle there were a few people just sort of sitting around in the street as though they were waiting for the next bus, and Griffith made sure we noticed one of them, she whom the title card declared to be the Mountain Girl.

"So, is there some reason he never gives these people names?" Porfirio asked.

Einar shrugged. "It's poetical or something. The actress is Constance Talmadge."

"Good Lord, what does she have on her head?" Oscar exclaimed. We all looked intently. No gorgeous robes for this chick; she appeared to have a couple of fur rugs tied around her boyish figure, and on her head were eucalyptus nuts sewn to a felt beanie.

"Needless to say, this is *not* an accurate historical costume," Imarte remarked.

The Mountain Girl was no drooping harem lily; she was a tomboy, as cute and spunky as Mary Pickford. And here was somebody else waiting for the same bus: Griffith explained that this handsome barearmed guy with flowers in his hair was the Rhapsode, a warrior-singer-poet. He made eyes at the Mountain Girl, who of course—the little spitfire—rejected him indignantly.

"Now, get a load of his seduction line," said Einar.

"Dearest one—in the ash heaps of my backyard there will be small flowers; seven lilies—if thou wilt love me—but a little," read Juan Bautista uncomprehendingly, and we fell about laughing. The Mountain Girl wasn't impressed either. The scene changed, and we met the High Priest of Bel-Marduk and his god, both of them pretty sore that all the people were worshiping Ishtar these days. Another scene shift, and Griffith advised us that we were about to meet the ruling Prince of Babylon, Belshazzar, riding in his chariot along the top of his city walls, which were careful historical reconstructions of the real ones.

"Really?" we all wanted to know.

"They weren't quite that high," admitted Imarte. "But when you were arriving from a three-hut village and seeing them for the first time, the effect was very nearly the same."

Belshazzar, a slender creature in a tall hat, was the Apostle of Tolerance and Religious Freedom; and here was his bodyguard, the burly Two-Sword Man; and here were the Handmaidens from Ishtar's Temple of Love and Laughter. They came dancing crazily out through the gate before the big parade float that bore the statue of Ishtar. Next we met the Princess Beloved, much more the conventional harem-lily type, and she and Belshazzar made a lot of pseudo-Biblical protestations of love for each other. Yes, all was happiness in old Babylon. But now, Griffith told us, the Mountain Girl's Brother (he had no name either) was having trouble keeping her in line, so he was going to drag her off to "the First Known Court of Justice in the World" to make her behave. A scholarly title card explained how Babylon's ancient laws were the first to protect the weak from the strong.

"Occasionally," Imarte said. "And of course you're all aware that the Babylonians were not the inventors of law." We all nodded, watching the antics of the Mountain Girl before the judges. We knew about the Neanderthal Code of Punishable Acts. Of course, there'd always been the rumor that the Company had been involved in that, somehow . . . Whoops! The judges sentenced the Mountain Girl to be dragged off to the marriage market. We all leaned forward in anticipation.

"Damn," said Porfirio, as we jumped forward through time over the Cradle Endlessly Rocking and found ourselves back in the twentieth century, where the nasty old Uplifters had spent so much of the wealthy industrialist's money that he was obliged to cut wages at the mill by ten percent. So we got to see one of the dreary labor strikes of the twentieth century, complete with soldiers—or were they Pinkerton men?—firing on the protesters. THE SAME TODAY AS YESTERDAY read a sign painted on a fence; and we immortals silently acknowledged that bitter truth. The Loom of Fate wove death for the Boy's Father when he took a bullet, and in the aftermath everybody went off to the big city to look for other work: the Boy, the Little Dear One and *her* father, and another girl, the Friendless One.

"I want to see Babylon again," Oscar complained.

Instead, we got to watch as our nameless ones suffered the inevitable consequences of urban relocation: the Boy rolled a drunk and turned to a life of crime, the Friendless One met a pimp called, for no reason any of us could figure out, the Musketeer of the Slums, and the Little Dear One's hysteria grew more pronounced.

"This is depressing," said Juan Bautista, and then: "All right!" because there was Ms. Gish and her Cradle again, and we were back in Babylon at the marriage mart.

Griffith explained that in the ancient Babylonian marriage market, the money spent to purchase pretty girls was given to plain girls for dowries, so that all might be happily married, and that "Women Corresponding to Our Outcasts of the Street" became wards of church and state for life. Imarte shook her head sadly when I looked to her for commentary. The men in the room were keeping their eyes on the screen, however, as Griffith's camera moved slowly past pretty girls in various states of undress. And here was the Mountain Girl, swaggering little hoyden, chewing on a couple of scallions as she awaited her turn and sticking them sullenly in her bodice when told to stop.

"This episode is pure fabrication," Imarte said. "I find the scene noteworthy for what it reveals to us about the sexual repression of the early twentieth century, however. Of course, you're all aware that white slavery will be a popular motif of escapist cinema during that period, and it's interesting to regard the paradox of sexual bondage viewed as a liberating experience. In *The Sheik*, for example . . ."

I tuned her out. Of course the Mountain Girl was a failure in the marriage market, winsomely scowling and threatening her prospective husbands, and then raging when they laughed and refused to buy her. But, out of nowhere, Belshazzar appeared with his attendants and wanted to know what all the fuss was about. When her plight was explained to him, Belshazzar granted her the right to marry or not as she wished, with a nifty bit of stage business involving a cylinder seal rolled over a clay tablet, shown in tight close-up (Imarte interrupted her lecture long enough to remark approvingly on its verisimilitude). Exit Belshazzar, followed by moony stares from the Mountain Girl, clearly smitten with him.

But what was this? Now we had the Rhapsode, working in the tenements to convert backsliders to the true worship of Bel.

"So he's a missionary?" Oscar said with a frown. "I thought he was a poet-warrior-singer or something."

"He's an utterly imaginary creature," said Imarte dismissively, but I was intrigued. He was a potentially interesting character, this Rhapsode. Was Griffith going to develop his warrior and zealot sides? Was he a hero as well as pleasure-loving esthete? Was he going to have some kind of relationship with the spirited if somewhat gauche Mountain Girl? Maybe so, because here she came, and again he was making protestations of love to her. But the Mountain Girl drew back from him, declaring:

"Put away thy perfumes, thy garments of Assinu, the Female Man," read Oscar. "I shall love none but a soldier."

"I guess she told *him*," Porfirio said. But then the scene changed to the interior of the Temple of Ishtar, and the attention of all gentlemen present was riveted on the screen, as Griffith treated them to a nicely detailed study of the Virgins of Ishtar frolicking in various pools and fountains, or lounging around in—well, in no clothing at all, one or two of them.

"Wow," gasped Juan Bautista.

"Pre-Hays Code, guys," said Einar. "Cool, huh?"

"Now, this, actually, is fairly accurate," Imarte said. "Though there would have been rather more nudity. The ancients were considerably more realistic about sexual needs, to say nothing of the issues of climate and comfort. Notice the continual depiction of Babylon by Griffith as a model of humane and sensible government, which will be really rather daring of him, considering that American audiences of that era are inclined to take the Old Testament view of Babylon as depraved and vice-ridden."

Here was Belshazzar again, with the Princess Beloved, billing and cooing in the Temple, and he was promising to build her a city of her very own, because:

"The fragrant mystery of your body is greater than the mystery of life," read Juan Bautista.

"Roughly translated as, Gee, did you step in something one of the elephants left?" I jeered. But Griffith just kept piling on the splendors, the Virgins of the Sacred Fire of Life dancing in the Love Temple, the harpists and yawning harem guards, Belshazzar and the Princess Beloved standing at a high window viewing the magnificence of Babylon spread out below them. When he stuck to the images, the phenomenal images, you were caught up in this silly thing in spite of yourself.

"The Cradle again," said Juan Bautista, and here was the Little Dear One in her tenement, trying to get a Hopeful Geranium (actually a pelargonium) to thrive. When she wasn't doing that, the innocent creature was watching whores from her tenement window, practicing their walk so she'd be popular too. Griffith was inviting us to smile in fond amusement here, but you could see where it was leading, and, sure enough, the next scene took us to the Friendless One in her new job: sitting in a bar in her negligee, drinking gin. She got up to go solace herself with the Musketeer of the Slums, but their passionate moment was interrupted by the Boy, who was now a Barbarian of the Streets. You could tell, because he'd taken to wearing a derby and smoking.

Next scene, the Little Dear One and the Boy encountered each other at his newsstand (a blind for his more criminal activities, we were told) and she did her prostitute walk for him. It worked! The next thing we saw was the two of them in her hallway with him vowing eternal love, a little less poetically than Belshazzar. ("Say, kid, you're going to be my chicken," read out Juan Bautista.) But the Little Dear One's old father broke it up, dragging her upstairs to pray for forgiveness before a little plaster statue of the Holy Mother and Child. ("Notice the recurring goddess images here," instructed Imarte.) After a brief Cradle shot, we saw the old man lying stiff in his winding-sheet and the Little Dear One weeping by his corpse.

"We want Babylon, we want Babylon," chanted Einar. Instead we got the Wedding at Cana, with a very bouncy and giggly young couple being fed the first mouthful of chickpeas at their reception. Whether or not the bride was expected to smear the next handful on the groom's face we never got to see, because the scene shifted to a shot of some white doves and then the entry of Jesus. He looked just like Belshazzar, except he didn't have a hat. But here were those mean old Pharisees again, snooping around and remarking that there was Too Much Revelry and Pleasure-Seeking among the People. Not for long, though—the wedding party ran out of wine!

I set aside my popcorn and leaned forward, wondering what special effect Griffith had to wow us with the water-into-wine miracle. But all we saw was a long shot of Jesus praying over some jars, only you couldn't quite make him out. At first I thought it was some defect in the print, but then I got the trick: Jesus was nearly obscured by a cross-shaped shadow. "Notice the metaphor," Imarte said, "Divine Love being blotted out by the instrument of torture and execution."

"We noticed, thank you," I said. A thought occurred to me. "Hey, did *you* ever meet Jesus of Nazareth?"

"No." She took a sip of her martini. "I was stationed in Turkey at the time."

"But somebody must have. Surely the Company was in on that moment in history too, right?" I wondered aloud. "Is there footage in a Company archive somewhere of Jesus trashing the temple vendors, Jesus on his bloody cross, Jesus giving the Sermon on the Mount?"

"Yes," Einar said, as we watched the wedding guests celebrate the miracle. "A fundamentalist group paid the Company big bucks to catch the man's act on film. They didn't like what they saw, so they paid more big bucks to have it suppressed."

"You're kidding!" I leaned forward. "So he was real? So he worked miracles?"

"Oh, yeah," said Einar, nodding. "That wasn't the problem."

"What *was* the problem?" Had he been a Crome generator too?

"Sorry, guys, that's classified information," he said, and we booed him and threw popcorn until Juan Bautista cried:

"Whoa, how did we get to France again?" Because we were back in France, no question, and Brown Eyes and her family were having a cozy evening at home with visiting swain Prosper Latour. ("How come he gets a name when nobody else does?" asked Porfirio.) Prosper left to go home, and Brown Eyes saw him to the door, where the same mercenary soldier spotted her again. He made his moves, but she was a nice Protestant girl and declined his advances.

I took my eyes off the screen long enough to quaff some martini. When I looked up again, we were back in the twentieth century, and the Boy and Little Dear One were having an outing in the Good Old Summertime.

"Notice San Pedro standing in for Coney Island," Einar said.

They went back to the tenement, and the Boy tried to muscle his way into the Little Dear One's room, but she shut him out and prayed tearfully to the Holy Mother to help her be a Strong-Jawed Jane. I accessed my historical idiom file for a definition of this colorful phrase, without results.

Fate was smiling on the Little Dear One, because the Boy proposed marriage. We were shown briefly how the insidious Uplifters were gaining more and more power, and then—

"This is almost as disorienting as real time travel," I said, as we found ourselves watching the Pharisees spying on Jesus.

"Behold a man gluttonous and a winebibber, a friend of publicans and sinners," read Juan Bautista. There was Jesus sitting in what appeared to be a cafe, chatting pleasantly with a fellow customer. But wait! Here was the Woman Taken in Adultery, and the Pharisees all ready to stone her, rocks in hand like extras from a Monty Python sketch. Unbelievable overacting from the Pharisees when Jesus zinged them with his ruling, and unbelievably strange dancing when the Adulteress made her grateful exit. Jesus just sat there and looked benign, apparently the only good actor in Galilee.

We all groaned to find ourselves back in the twentieth century again, viewing more of the Uplifters' nasty handiwork. Griffith came right out and said it this time, that When Women Cease to Attract

Men, They Often Turn to Reform as a Second Choice. We booed and
threw popcorn as he showed how these villainous spinsters were responsible for bootlegging, secret poker games, and flirting in alleyways. Meanwhile, the Little Dear One was working her own
reformation on the Boy, extracting his promise to quit his criminal
gang, and her victory dance was truly savage and bizarre. And premature: for no sooner had the Boy quit his gang than the Musketeer
of the Slums got him framed for theft, and the Boy was whisked off
to prison.

Babylon again! We cheered, but there was trouble brewing; the
wicked High Priest was still interminably plotting, prophesying doom
if people didn't leave off this Ishtar nonsense and return to Bel-
Marduk. Enter Nabonidus, Belshazzar's crazy old father, excitedly
showing off his latest archaeological discovery and remembering to
mention that Oh by the way, Cyrus the Persian is massing with his
armies to destroy us.

"Notice the subtext of implicit condemnation of intellectual pur-
suits," observed Imarte.

"Whatever," I said. "Wow, these must be the Persians!" It was the
war camp of Cyrus. Griffith showed us milling soldiers, engines of
war, and chariots of fire. The exotic hordes of Cyrus, the Medes, the
Persians, the Ethiopians. ("Look, *real* black guys this time!" Einar said.
"Most of the Negroes in *Birth of a Nation* were white guys in black-
face.") There were some bone-gnawing white European males designated merely as Barbarians, then Cyrus himself, shouting orders from
his war chariot, turning sharply right, left, right, a big martial profile
from a wall painting. He looked like a Klingon member of Sergeant
Pepper's Lonely Hearts Club Band.

"Damn," yelled Porfirio, because in mid-spectacle we were hauled
back to the twentieth century, where the Little Dear One was now the
Little Mother. There was some touching footage of her playing with
her baby, but we knew tragedy was in the offing, and, sure enough,
the evil Uplifters were at it again: Griffith showed them descending
on slum neighborhoods like stiff harpies, and nailing the Little Mother
when they caught her with some whiskey she was taking as a cold
remedy. When they came for her baby, the Little Mother fought back
with such frenzy that they smashed her to the ground senseless, hefty
muscular broads as they were. We saw her clutching feebly at one
baby sock, dropped in the struggle, all she had left of her child.

"Emotionally involving," admitted Imarte, "though overall I *think*
Chaplin handled the same theme more effectively." I resisted an urge
to shush her, because it was an upsetting scene after all, but then

Griffith went and threw in the kitchen sink by showing us a Suffer Little Children to Come unto Me tableau, with Jesus and what must have been half the child population of Hollywood, happy little extras earning a day's wage.

Then, thankfully, we were back in France, watching the Catholics cower as the Huguenots ran around wild in the streets and smashed a perfectly good plaster statue. We can't have this kind of thing going on! announced Catherine de' Medici. Time to do something about those pesky Protestants.

But we escaped to Babylon again, and Cyrus jumped athletically into his chariot and ordered his armies to march on Belshazzar's city. And here was Belshazzar, mustering up the city guard, pausing only to bid a fond adieu to his Princess Beloved. She bid him one heck of a fond adieu herself:

"My Lord, like white pearls I shall keep my tears in an ark of silver for your return. I bite my thumb! I strike my girdle!" Juan Bautista read, and began to giggle helplessly. "If you return not, I go to the death halls of Aflat!"

"That's Allat," Imarte corrected him primly, which only made the rest of us snicker more. We watched as the Mountain Girl decked herself out in her brother's second-best armor and rushed out to help defend her city, just like Xena.

"Get ready, guys," said Einar, "this is one of *the* great cinema battles of all time."

He wasn't kidding. Thousands of costumed extras stormed those magnificent walls, battered those glorious gates, and, by God, life-sized siege towers were actually pushed into place by real elephants, because Griffith hadn't had any other way to move them. The Priests of Ishtar assumed odd positions and prayed to their goddess for deliverance. They made burnt offerings, the flame and smoke of their sacrifices flowing up with the flame and smoke of the battle. The Mountain Girl sent a rain of arrows down on the attacking hordes. The burly Two-Sword Man, fighting with (surprise) two swords, swopped off a Persian head as neatly as I've ever seen it done on film. More shots of the Mountain Girl fighting valiantly for her Prince, intercut with the Princess Beloved peering fearfully out the window at the battle, posturing dismay and terror with palms angled stiffly, and you knew she didn't deserve Belshazzar the way our plucky heroine did. The catapults of the attacking host launched rocks on the defenders, and the defenders pushed one of the siege towers outward, outward, until it tilted and fell, all eight stories, with a crash they must have heard in San Pedro.

And now the battle was going on into the night, with flames along the battlements to rival the burning of Atlanta in *Gone with the Wind*.

"Look at that!" said Oscar. We stared at the secret weapon of Babylon, an armored tank that Jules Verne might have designed if he'd been around in Belshazzar's day. It was huge, with spiked wheels that rolled it implacably forward and long nozzles that shot out jets of flame. How absurd, how improbable, how *marvelous!* We all applauded.

"A blatant anachronism," Imarte said, but we ignored her. Who were we, cyborgs in the Old West, to talk about anachronisms? We cheered as the engine of destruction laid waste to the Persians, burning and bringing down more siege towers in flaming ruin. The forces of Cyrus were routed! Wild celebration in Babylon! Dances of joy and bliss! What a spectacle!

Intermission.

"Rats," I said, as Einar crawled over to the projector to change reels.

"Stay cool," he said, groping for the film can. "The best is yet to be."

But when the silver world returned, we were in the twentieth century again, with more tragedy building: the Musketeer of the Slums now had his lustful eye on the forlorn Little Mother, intimating he might be able to rescue her baby from the clutches of the Uplifters. He was jealously shadowed by the Friendless One, however. The Boy got out of prison, but this did not discourage the Musketeer from his dastardly plan—

"Thank God," said Porfirio, because the Cradle appeared again, and Griffith told us we were about to behold the Feast of Belshazzar, "Imaged after the Splendor of an Olden Day."

Einar gave a whoop of excitement. "This is it, Babylon the Great! For those of you who were wondering what could possibly top the magnificence of that battle scene . . ."

But he didn't need to say anything more, because there before us was the first long shot of Hollywood Babylon in all her glory, and it took my immortal breath away. A central court so huge, it beggared all comprehension of scale, with gods and goddesses stories high, rearing elephants in stone, and thousands of tiny figures there below us on the wide stairs as the camera moved slowly in on the scene. How had he done it? And still the camera moved in, and yes, there were real people on those painted stairs, and your eye had to believe that this was no matte shot, no miniature, this truly was the ancient and massive splendor that had died away from the world, caught on silver nitrate by giants who were in the earth in those days.

The camera took us up the great stairs through the mad bacchanal, with all the little incidents to catch attention: the grim Two-Sword Man fondly stroking a white dove, the temple priestesses dancing stiff like wall paintings come to life, the Priests of Ishtar chanting praise to Her. I heard Imarte sniffling: was she crying? And here were Belshazzar and the Princess Beloved in all their glory, scarlet and purple, emerald and gold, glowing through the austere silver print.

Now we saw the Mountain Girl confidently expecting to walk into the banquet hall, but of course she was turned away, the little ragamuffin. Next we saw the High Priest of Bel, scheming to make his defeat a temporary one, summoning the Rhapsode and ordering him to ready the chariots for a secret visit to the camp of Cyrus. But what was this? Did the warrior-poet-singer-missionary balk at this base treachery? No! He looked confused, he abased himself, he ran off to do the High Priest's bidding. He wasn't really going to be a dupe and betray Babylon, was he? Surely he would form some clever plan to thwart Cyrus, the High Priest, and the rest of them. It wouldn't work out, of course, unless Griffith had decided to change history . . . but, having created such a potentially interesting hero, was Griffith really going to waste him? I drained my martini and fumbled around in the dark for the cocktail shaker. I had to pry it loose from Imarte's grip: she was staring at the screen as if mortally hurt, and she *was* crying. Son of a gun.

The Mountain Girl was thirsty, too; she was purchasing a drink of goat milk to celebrate, squatting down and milking the goat herself. Something about the motion must have reminded her of Belshazzar, for she promptly got that moony unrequited-love look on her face, with intercut shots of Belshazzar at his feast, and back to her tugging on the pendulous squirting udders. Einar and Porfirio were rolling on the floor, choking with laughter, and Oscar had his handkerchief up in front of his face.

More revelry, more splendor. We reclined at the table of a Babylonian noble crowned with flowers; we were invited to partake of spiced wine cooled with snow brought down from the mountains. We watched a Babylonian gallant idly stroking the head of a leopard, which lay bound and snarling through the roses in its jaws. We watched a tame bear being fed party delicacies. We watched a swaying-drunk soldier telling the cameraman about the little monkey that clung to his helmet. And here was the Mountain Girl again, and the Rhapsode coming around a corner to catch sight of her. Still smitten with her boyish charms, he made another pitch for her and was indignantly spurned. But he kept following her around and then—

I groaned and downed my martini in a gulp. So much for the potentially interesting hero. In his efforts to impress the Mountain Girl, the Rhapsode did it, he blabbed about the secret mission to Cyrus's camp.

What was Catherine de' Medici doing here? Oh, we were back in France. Pressure was being put on the King to sign the order allowing the Catholics to massacre the Huguenots. Would he do it? No, no, a thousand times no! He ran around the room screaming, he tore his hair, he stamped his feet, he curled up in his throne and kicked his legs. He signed it, though, as his nasty and effeminate brother played with a ball-and-paddle game. Next we saw sedate Protestant joy at the Brown Eyes residence as she and Prosper Latour were betrothed. Ominous foreshadowings as the happy family snuffed their candles before retiring for the night, and Prosper walking back to his lodgings and noticing those groups of soldiers going around chalking X's on the doors of the Protestants. Did he have a clue? Nope.

"In the Temple of Loooooove!" yodeled Einar, and we were back in Babylon again. Apparently an orgy was in progress. More harem hijinks, more voluptuaries rolling around in perfectly astonishing attitudes of invitation, more dancers on the grand stairway performing some kind of goose-stepping polka, another seminaked girl—

"Watch," Einar announced. "Long-distance gynecology. You won't see a shot like this one until *Basic Instinct* with Sharon Stone, 1992."

"Dear Lord!" Oscar went into a coughing fit, his eyes bugging out of his head.

Juan Bautista blushed furiously. "Could they *do* that back then?" he asked.

Einar grinned. "No Hays Code yet, like I said." Now we saw the Princess Beloved coyly sending a white rose in a little chariot drawn by two white doves across the banquet table to Belshazzar. But not everyone was celebrating: the evil High Priest and other objectionable members of the clergy climbed into their chariots and sneaked away to Cyrus's camp. Not unobserved. The clever Mountain Girl stole a chariot to follow them, riding like the wind past the Three Fates and Lillian Gish, to—

New York? What were we doing in this cramped tenement, with the Musketeer of the Slums attempting to rape the Little Mother? The Boy burst in and struggled with the Musketeer, while the Friendless One clung precariously to the window ledge outside, trying to get a clear shot. Bang! Huge clouds of smoke, the Musketeer staggered into the corridor to die, the Friendless One dropped the gun into the room and took to her heels, and in no time at all the Boy was on trial for his life in a huge courtroom. The Prosecution was clever—you could tell, because he wore pince-nez—while the Defense Attorney was a stammering novice, so we weren't left in much suspense about the outcome. Not so the Little Mother, who giggled encouragement across the courtroom at the Boy, at least until the brutal sentence was read, when she screamed and fainted. Somewhere in this scene we went to Jerusalem, briefly, where poor Jesus was struggling with his cross through the howling mob, and then we were back in the twentieth century again, where the Friendless One was trying to get up nerve to confess to her crime.

I had another martini, and it seemed to help. We went back to where Cyrus was greeting the High Priest and his cronies while the Mountain Girl listened in on the conspirators, but then we were interrupted by scenes of various efforts to save the Boy, and there were Model Ts racing back and forth, which inexplicably became chariots racing along the Euphrates, only Einar was explaining that it was really a slough down near Long Beach with some palm trees planted to make it look like the Euphrates, and there was Catherine de' Medici again!

"What the hell is she doing here?" I heard Porfirio inquire, but it soon became obvious, because Brown Eyes and her family were having a Terrible Awakening as the Catholic forces battered down their door.

Were those automobiles coming to the Huguenots' rescue? No, we were back in New York, and then we were racing along beside the Euphrates, and—hey! the Friendless One finally confessed! The Mountain Girl was racing ahead of the army advancing on poor Babylon, and the damn Cradle was rocking faster and faster. Two Model Ts chased each other, then it was a race car chasing a train, then the Boy was receiving last rites from a priest, then a priest was hiding a terrified Huguenot child under his cloak, then Belshazzar and the Princess Beloved were pitching woo all unmindful of the train bearing down on them or the Huguenots being slaughtered in the next room. Here came Jesus wearing a signboard, narrowly missed by the race car bearing the last-minute testimony that would reprieve the Boy, who was fainting in the priest's arms, no doubt at the graphic rape and murder of Brown Eyes by that darned mercenary ("*I knew* he was gonna do that!" said Juan Bautista). Prosper could have saved her, but he couldn't get through the crowds of soldiers massacring Protestants, and the same crowd was slowing down the Mountain Girl too, because it took her

forever to make her way to Belshazzar's party to let him know what
was going on, by which time it was too late to save Brown Eyes, but
at least the governor was willing to reprieve the Boy! And now it was
the train racing to get to the prison before the execution, but Belshazzar
could get only twelve men to help him defend Babylon, and the Princess Beloved couldn't get *anybody* to go with her to the Death Halls
of Allat. Oh hell, oh spite!

Prosper was killed, the Mountain Girl was killed, Belshazzar and
the Princess Beloved killed themselves, and there was a close-up of
the Mountain Girl lying killed, which irised out to show that the forlorn
little doves had pulled the rose-chariot up to her lifeless body. Juan
Bautista burst into tears, but Catherine de' Medici was pleased with
herself and so was Cyrus, who guffawed crudely right in the camera's
face, as meanwhile everybody piled out of the train and into another
car, which raced on to save—gee, who else was left alive?

Not Jesus. A confusing mass with a lot of smoke resolved itself
into Golgotha, with the three crosses dimly visible on a dark skyline.
So the car raced on, but the Boy was already mounting the scaffold,
they were binding his hands, they were binding his legs, they were
putting the black hood on him, and men with razors were standing by
to cut the cord that would drop the trap. *Would rescuers get there in
time?*

Surprise! They did. Dazed Boy being embraced by passionately
twitching Little Mother. General expressions of joy and satisfaction.
"Here comes the summation," Einar told us.

WHEN CANNON AND PRISON BARS WROUGHT IN THE FIRES OF IN-
TOLERANCE, read the titles, over scenes of battlefield and prison. A lot
of angels appeared, dangling in a rather crowded sky, and all the fighting stopped.

AND PERFECT LOVE SHALL BRING PEACE FOREVERMORE. More people staring up in confusion at the angels.

INSTEAD OF PRISON WALLS, BLOOM FLOWERY FIELDS. A scene
showing convicts in their striped uniforms walking through the walls
like ghosts and disappearing. Then an exterior shot of a prison doing
a vanishing act too, leaving the Hollywood Hills in the distance. Now
we saw little children disporting themselves at a church picnic. One
bold toddler grabbed a tiny playmate and gave her a big kiss.

"If he tried that in the twenty-first century, he'd be arrested and
put in therapy the rest of his life," said Porfirio gloomily. I was waiting
for a final title card that would finish Griffith's sentence, but instead
we saw a lot of people yelling glory hallelujah at the angels and then

one last shot of Lillian Gish and her Cradle, endlessly, endlessly rocking.

White light, flickering on a blank screen.

Einar moaned, stretching sensually.

"So, what happened to the Baby?" Porfirio asked.

"What happened to the goddamn Rhapsode?" I asked.

Before either of our questions could be answered, Imarte leaped to her feet, scattering popcorn in all directions.

"I must go there," she announced. "Now."

"Where?" Oscar stared at her in bewilderment. We were bewildered too; there hadn't been a peep out of her in the last few minutes, but now she turned on him with a snarl.

"I must go to Babylon!"

"Imarte, what'd you put in that rahat locum?" said Porfirio, but she pushed her chaplet of roses back from where it had slipped over one eye and fixed him with one of the scariest expressions I'd ever seen.

"I *will* go to Babylon, fairest of cities, beloved of Ishtar," she said. "I will not lose it again!"

"Cool," said Einar, scrambling unsteadily to his feet. "Let's go now. Come on, you guys, it's just over on Sunset. God knows there's no traffic. We can get there in no time."

I remember that Porfirio did some protesting, and so did Oscar, but one way or another we found ourselves galloping through the night. That is, Einar and Imarte galloped; the rest of us rode in the wagon, driven by Porfirio at a rattling clip as he tried to catch up with those two. I clutched at my chaplet of roses and wondered what I was doing as we thundered along through the damp night air under a very amused moon.

It was a wide sloping piece of ground where we stopped, an old floodplain with a view of the distant lights of Los Angeles and the more distant sea, pale and obscure under the moon. Was that Catalina Island out there?

Einar and Imarte had dismounted. She was standing motionless; he was striding with arms outstretched through the sagebrush and chamise.

"Right here," he was saying. "This will be the lot adjacent to the Fine Arts studio complex. Can you see it? And where I'm standing, babe, we're on that Grand Staircase! Look up there behind us in the moonlight, there are the elephants! There are the winged bulls bright as day. They're here, and more real than this empty place or the asphalt that covers it later. Silver nitrate's made Babylon eternal for all time, and the prophets can't do a thing about it. This is Ishtar's city of love and tolerance. Can you smell the incense? Can you hear the music?"

I very nearly could. I found I was still clutching the cocktail shaker and took a fortifying gulp. Imarte stretched out her arms to the moon and gave a plaintive cry. She began to dance, there in the moonlight, over the stones and red sand, through the yucca and the cactus and other herbs that never lifted bud or branch in Belshazzar's city so long fallen. It was no stiff absurd dance either, no attempt to choreograph a flat wall painting; it was lithe and savage, a little unsteady, something you'd really dance at a bacchanal.

"Is she nuts?" asked Juan Bautista, who cowered shivering beside me. "What's she doing?"

"She's just had enough gin, that's all," Porfirio told him.

"You think that's all it is?" I had another belt from the cocktail shaker. "She's crazy with pain. She's so much older than the rest of us, and she was really there, wasn't she, when Cyrus came crashing down on Babylon. What if you'd loved a place like that, and seen it go down in flames? What if you'd buried it in your heart for centuries, all that lost glory safely forgotten, and then one night, when you least expected it, something brought it to life for you again? How do you think you'd feel? How *will* you feel, kid, a hundred centuries from now, when you're as old as she is?"

"I won't be like that," said Juan Bautista. "That's not supposed to happen to us. We don't go crazy, we can't, we're perfect! Aren't we?"

"Shut up, Mendoza," said Porfirio quietly, and Oscar fumbled the cocktail shaker from my icy grasp.

"Of course we are, son, we're positively the last word in cyber-technology," he assured Juan Bautista.

I staggered to my feet and flung my chaplet of roses out into the middle of what would be Sunset Boulevard one day, when all this sweet wild land would be buried under an urban nightmare. And what would *I* be feeling, when I was as old as Imarte? What would have become of the places *I'd* loved? What if there were no more oak trees or redwoods, what if California itself slipped under the Pacific, drowned and broken up, as lost as Atlantis?

And I was going to lose it all, when that steel cancer of a future city was built. It wouldn't even take a global calamity: just millions of mortals moving west. I would lose my wilderness just as I'd lost Nicholas, and how would I live then?

I drew in my breath to howl at the moon, but Einar came bounding up to the wagon. He held up his pistol by its barrel, pretending it was a microphone again. "Let's hear what our studio audience has to say!

Sir, can you tell the wonderful people out there in the dark what personal revelations *you* had tonight?" He thrust it under Oscar's nose.

"Oh, this is silly," Oscar said. "But—very well." He took the gun and held it up. "If you really want to know, why, I think there's a brilliant message in that film, and Griffith really was a genius born too soon. He's telling us loud and clear just what's going to bring on that earthly paradise he envisions at the end, and you know what it is?

"Technology. Yes, sir, ladies and gentlemen, consider for a moment. What turns the tide of battle (albeit temporarily) against the Persians? None other than the superior technology of the Babylonians, as exemplified by their marvelous machine of war. And consider! Don't the other tragedies occur because prospective rescuers are delayed in their efforts by inferior means of transportation? Reflect upon the fact that, of all the stories presented, the one story that ends happily does so solely because of modern and efficient means of locomotion. Yes! The automobile brings the Boy's pardon! Now, just what would have happened if that Mountain Girl or the French fellow had had Fords with which to speed to the rescue of *their* loved ones?"

"What would have happened if Christ's apostles had had grenades and rocket launchers?" I said, dropping into the bed of the wagon.

"Precisely! That is, er, anyhow, it seems mighty clear to me that what the great David Wark Griffith was foreseeing was nothing less than us. For are we not the veritable saviors of Earth, the ultimate marriage of man's mechanical genius with his biological possibilities? Why should any cyborg feel shame? Is it not an honor to be descended from the noble Model T no less than from Adam? I don't know about you folks, but I'm proud, *proud* of my mingled heritage." Oscar flung his chaplet out into what would one day be the roof of the Kinemacolor lab. He handed the gun back to Einar, who was applauding.

"Bravo, Mr. O! And what about you, sir, do you have an epiphany you'd like to share with the folks listening at home?" He thrust the gun at Porfirio.

"What home?" I said. "We have no homes, none of us."

"Shut up." Porfirio put his hand on my shoulder. "You want to know what I think, pal? I think it's time to rein in this party. Maybe you should go catch Salome of the Seven Veils and get her back on her horse."

"No, man, she's okay," Einar's eyes were glowing. "Don't you see? She knows how to deal with this time thing. She understands. That's why she's dancing. She can *see* Babylon. It exists for her outside of time, it's neither past nor future but right now. Always.

"Haven't you guys figured it out yet? Don't you know what it really means to be immortals? We transcend time, it has no meaning for us, it ceases to exist, because it's all simultaneous. We're here *now*, and we're on Griffith's set *now*, and we're in 2355 *now! We're the ones controlling reality, from in here.*" He struck his fist against his indestructible skull.

"We are time machines! The truth's been right in front of our noses since cinema was invented. Hell, since photography was invented. Hell, since *writing* was invented. Make an image of something, and it escapes the flow of time. That's why it's forbidden! Dickens had a grasp on it with his ghosts, Mary Wollstonecraft Shelley almost got it, and Einstein came so close to the truth. The dead heroes are brought in to Odin, and they rise again, they feast all night and fight all day again, and their deaths mean nothing, because they've escaped time. That's the whole point of the metaphor with Dr. Zeus, you guys! He's the liberator. *Zeus defeats Chronos.* Everything's happening at once! We can perceive time in a way mortals can't, we can make it irrelevant. Don't you see?

"All you have to do is understand, and you're free! You're out of here!" With an ear-piercing whoop he snatched off his chaplet of roses and whirled it up, up, black against the moon for a second before it bounced down and rolled away in the direction of L. Frank Baum's house.

I did understand: Einar was mad as a hatter. There were rumors that some of the really Old Ones weren't too stable. I knew Imarte was several millennia old, and she'd lost a screw tonight. How old was Einar? That mention of Odin was probably a clue. He wasn't so crazy, he couldn't do his job; just crazy enough to be happy on this black plain, under this cold moon. Wasn't he the lucky guy?

Shuddering, I pulled my shawl around myself. I needed Theobromos. I'd have some as soon as I got back to the inn. No, I couldn't; I'd been drinking gin. Where had I heard that Theobromos and gin didn't combine well?

It's hell to be a cyborg and have immediate access to any stray memory that one rashly summons up. There I was at a New Year's ball, at a table with three other immortals. There was the little neophyte Latif, there was my damned demon godfather Joseph, and there was poor Lewis, who was feeling ill after overindulging. Precocious Latif had explained about the toxic effect of Theobromos combined with martinis.

Lewis. Somewhere my friend Lewis was weeping for me.

Juan Bautista's teeth were chattering in his head, and Imarte's dance had become so frenzied, she was a blur in the moonlight. Einar was dancing too, kicking up his boots and waving his long arms as he chanted a song, something in third-century Norwegian about hauling on the oars and steering for the land where palm trees grow.

Porfirio pitched his chaplet over the side of the wagon and drew his six-shooter.

"Our revels now are ended," he announced, and fired three shots into the air. Instantly we were all sober, converting the alcohol in our bloodstreams into water and sugar, as we were programmed to do when confronted by hazard.

"What on Earth—?" said Imarte. "How embarrassing." She got up from where she'd been rolling in the dust, near what would one day be the statue of Ishtar, and hastily brushed herself off. "Was I indulging in grief accommodation again?"

Einar was crawling out from under the wagon, where he'd vanished when the shots went off. He got to his feet and looked around sheepishly.

"Cold out here, isn't it?" was all he said.

"Well—we were only having a bit of fun, weren't we?" said Oscar.

"Speak for yourself," I said. Juan Bautista had his eyes closed; he was huddled up with his cheek pressed into Erich von Stroheim's feathers.

"Let's go, guys," Porfirio ordered. He took the reins and swung us back around for La Nopalera. Einar and Imarte climbed into their saddles and followed, all along the empty road, and the lights of Los Angeles grew fainter behind us, until they vanished like a dream.

15

IT HAD BEEN a great movie, all the same.

Thinking about it all, about Babylon and France and Jerusalem and that cold urban future, one tended to forget one was living in the midst of a historical upheaval just as impressive. France was finding that it was a great deal harder for the Second Empire to crush a bunch of ignorant mestizos than had ever been expected, while England and Spain sat back and watched in disgust. The North Americans were busy filling up the history books too: the Emancipation Proclamation was issued, for example. In future cinema it would be depicted by black hands stretching up toward beams of sunlight, broken manacles dangling from the wrists, to the accompaniment of a swelling chorus of this or that hymn, usually fading into a long shot of the Lincoln Memorial.

So sentimentally is the birth of a baby presented. The reality is far more an occasion of blood, of fear and uncertainty, of shock that displaces the joy that should be felt on such an occasion. While not one of those people to whom that piece of paper meant so much would ever have gone back to being slaves again, they must have known that the chains would be ten times as hard to break now that they were invisible and intangible.

But how could any of it matter to us? We went on about our daily life in a world where Watts and South Central were still Spanish land grants where vaqueros roped steers, and the longhorns herded down from the Tejon Ranch bore a brand of Cross above Crescent, commemorating the ancient victories of the Spanish Crusaders over the

Moors, and I still thought of black men as turbaned kings with scimitars. What did this Civil War have to do with me?

You see? I had no sense of Realpolitik at all. Not that I wasn't warned.

16

I WAS RETURNING from a profitable day in the less surreal regions of the temperate belt when I picked up the warning signal being broadcast by Porfirio. It told me to approach with caution, so I left the road and came overland through the sagebrush, straining to pick up more of the transmission. All I could hear was Porfirio's end of it, at first.

But why would I lie to you, señor? Señora Marta comes and goes as she pleases. You must know this. She pays rent on her room, and I don't ask her what she does in there and she doesn't tell me. Come and have some coffee.

Of course I would tell you if I knew, señor.

No, señor, I'm not in love with her. No.

She didn't tell me, señor. What about some coffee?

I don't love her, señor.

Yes, I would tell you. Would you like a cup of coffee, señor?

No, señor, I never said that. Señor, please, put the gun away. There's no need for that. Listen to me, señor, you know what? If he's with her when she comes home, I'll help you shoot him. Please stop waving the gun in the air and sit down and have some coffee—

There followed a salvo of shots.

Now, you see, señor? You're not at your best, or you'd have hit something for sure. And you don't want to hang, señor. Señora Marta would cry if you were to hang, eh? No, señor, she didn't tell me.

No, señor, I'm not in love with her.

Señor, you really would feel better with some coffee in you.

Mental note: no torturer in a dungeon cell ever devised anything as frustrating, as inescapable, as terrifyingly pointless as a conversation with a drunk.

Yes, señor, that's a good idea. Yes, by all means.

All right, señor, that's a very, very good idea. There is your horse.

No, she didn't tell me, señor. Maybe if you get on your horse and ride out now, you'll catch them.

Very good! Buenos noches, señor. That way. The road is that way. What would you want to shoot the horse for, señor?

Yes, you're right, that would show her. Yes, I'm sure she'd weep over your grave. I think you want to put it in your mouth, though, señor, not against the temple like that. There! You see how easy it is to miss?

Very well, señor, if you say so. Yes, that way. That way, señor. Buenos noches, señor. Vaya con sathanas.

When the all clear was finally broadcast, I came slinking down out of the hills to find Porfirio sitting beside the fire, mixing himself a double mocha by dissolving most of a cake of Theobromos in a pot of black coffee.

"Who was that?" I asked, shrugging off my pack.

"Mr. Cyrus Jackson," Porfirio said, baring his teeth. "Some knight chivalrous, huh? Good thing the 1600-hours stage is late, or there'd have been a nasty scene."

"Where is Imarte, anyway? I haven't seen her for a few days," I said, reaching for a tin plate and digging a spoon into the frijole pot.

"She went up north for something," Porfirio said. "Christ knows what. She didn't tell me." I joined with him on the last sentence.

Juan Bautista emerged from his lean-to, looking perturbed. "Is that drunk guy gone? I was scared he'd shoot at my birds."

"Gone but not forgotten, unfortunately," said Porfirio. He raised his head, listening. "And there's the stage. I think I'll just go dump this whole mess in Ms. Imarte's ever-ready lap." He took a terrific slug of Theobromos-adulterated java straight from the coffeepot and stalked off down the canyon, carrying the pot with him.

After a few minutes we heard the driver's whip crack as the stage continued its journey to Los Angeles, and Porfirio and Imarte came slowly up the canyon.

"I told you I was sorry. What on earth can I do?" Imarte was saying.

"You can deal with the guy, that's what you can do. You led him on, and now he's got a fit of killer jealousy. Why did you give him the idea he was anything but a customer to you, anyway?"

"He was a good source of data," Imarte said, drawing her feathered shawl around her against the twilight chill. "He provided me with no end of fascinating material that has, in fact, led me to an astonishing discovery. You wouldn't believe it, but the evidence is overwhelming, that not only is there an active Confederate plot—"

"He wants to kill you for being unfaithful to him," Porfirio said.

"Oh." She knitted her brows. "I'll have to do something, I suppose. Don't worry. We'll deal with the inconvenience somehow. Believe me, it's worth it. Have you any idea what his simple anecdotes have revealed?"

"Why don't you tell us?" I said, soaking a tortilla in steak juice.

She was so enthralled with her big news, she actually sat down beside me. "There is a conspiracy," she uttered in thrilled tones, "that may involve the highest-ranking members of Parliament, to take California for the *British*."

"The British? Why would they want California?"

Imarte gave me an arch look and paused dramatically, during which time the answer became obvious. Gold, vast natural resources, most of the Pacific coastline . . . Okay, any government in its right collective mind would covet California. But the British?

"I thought it was an odd series of coincidences at first," Imarte said, gazing pensively into the fire. "All those British nationals passing through, filing claims to search for gold on Catalina. Why Catalina, where no appreciable gold has ever been found? Why are they shipping engineering equipment over there? Why are they taking such pains to determine who actually owns title to the island? Because they are, you know. I slept with a man who informed me that a fortified base is being constructed by the Albion Mining Syndicate, to be called Queen City. Of course he didn't call it a fortified base, but by asking certain questions about this so-called mining town, I was able to determine that the site it occupies has considerable strategic importance and is, in fact, being prepared for ordnance emplacements. Moreover, no attempts whatsoever are being made to prospect for gold."

"Wow," said Juan Bautista. "What would happen if the English took over California?"

I rolled up frijoles in a tortilla and bit into it. "They won't, we know that, so what's the point of wondering? They gave up Oregon without a fight, didn't they? Why should they try to take the West Coast now, even if they want it?"

"Ah, but you see," Imarte said, holding up a forefinger, "the political situation has changed. The Americans, who might once have prevented them, are locked in a devastating civil war whose outcome is still unknown. Europe is making a play to regain lost empires in South America. If the continental royalty manages to conquer Mexico, if the American nation falls apart—and these mortals haven't our advantage of knowing how it all turns out in the end—why, then, Manifest Destiny comes undone and the whole of the New World is up for grabs again. There have even been rumors that the Russians are beginning to regret pulling out of California. Can anyone wonder if Queen Victoria's ministers"—she searched for a metaphor—"want to be first in line, shopping bags in hand, when the doors are flung open on the Great American Fire Sale?"

"What does it matter, anyway?" I said crossly.

"Don't you think it's fascinating? This is secret history. It lends so much more understanding, so much fire and color to the dramatic pageant unfolding before our eyes. Imagine all those British diplomats playing the Union and Confederate governments off against each other, deploring slavery while covertly aiding the rebels, yet planning still another layer of double cross by preparing to step in and seize territories from the survivors should the Confederacy win!" Her eyes were gleaming. "Given the size of the empire they control already, why should the British think it unreasonable to go on playing the Great Game here?"

"You're sure about this?" Porfirio asked, taking another swig from the coffeepot. "God knows they were eager enough to stick their fingers in the pie of Texas."

"I've been collecting information. Even now there's a plot brewing in San Francisco. The nephew of a British statesman has persuaded a stupid young American to join him in a privateering expedition—supposedly to aid the Confederacy by raiding the Pacific Mail and diverting the gold shipments from the San Francisco Mint to the Confederate cause. I don't yet know how they plan to do it, but I'm fairly sure the Albion Mining Syndicate is involved, from their base on Catalina Island. Are you aware that any maritime power positioned there with even minimal ordnance could effectively control the entire coastline of California at this point in time?"

"Pirates!" Porfirio slapped his knee. "Goddamn Francis Drake is at it again!"

"But that's awful!" said Juan Bautista. His eyes were big and worried.

"It's not going to happen, dummy," I said. "Access your files. If there actually ever is such a plot, somebody screws it up, because it never makes the history books."

"It might not be so bad if the British took over," said Porfirio with a grin. "Have we fared all that well under the Yankees? I'll bet General Vallejo kicks himself every day for not shooting John C. Fremont when he had the chance. And think about a colonial governor and the

Union Jack flying over the Plaza. All those damn cowboys and their guns expelled. Think how the future of California would change. No Prohibition, so no bootleggers, so no Mob. No cops with guns. No movie people either. Just lots of plantations run by old aristocratic families. It'd be Lower Canada, man! Nothing would *ever* happen here."

No freeways, no smog, low population density. That horrifying city on the plain I'd glimpsed would never exist. Would that be such a bad thing? But of course it was never going to happen. Catalina Island had a strange enough future ahead of it, but being the Californian Hong Kong wasn't part of the package.

I shrugged. "So what are you planning to do with all this fascinating secret knowledge?" I asked Imarte.

"Take notes. And so should all of you," she admonished us. "This is the life, the hidden motivation of mortal history. It concerns every one of us."

"It concerns *you*," I said. "I have more important things to occupy my time."

"Oh, yes, finding seventeen different mutations of mugwort *would* take precedence over the destinies of nations any day." She tossed her head.

"Can it, ladies," Porfirio said.

We heard the rattle and creak of Oscar's wagon approaching. He was leaning backward in the seat, peering down the canyon behind him. He was concerned. "Er, there appears to be a mortal fellow lying dead drunk in a ditch back there by the grade," he said. "His horse is unharmed, however."

Porfirio sighed.

I was afraid all this talk of the damned Brits would set the dreams off again, and I was right. It was a surprisingly quiet dream, though; at least it wasn't more endless replay of the past.

I was on a ship, not a miserable little dark galleon like the one I'd left La Coruña in so long ago, but a modern ship, one of those beautiful three-masted clippers the English were making nowadays, with iron-framed hulls, so much safer than the Yankee variety. Every detail exact. Salt spray, brisk chilly breeze, white clouds of canvas taking up miles of sky, nimble sailors mounting through the shrouds and rat-lines. This ship was taking somebody somewhere fast. I seemed to be having a *nice* dream for a change. I'd never been on a modern ship before. I wandered around, looking at things with great interest, observing Jack-Tars holystoning the deck and doing other terribly nautical things.

"Here now, girlie," croaked a voice in my ear, and I turned in astonishment to behold a black-bearded sailor grinning evilly at me. "Ain't you been in to see him yet?"

"Excuse me?" I said.

"He's aft there," said the seaman, "in the deckhouse. He's comin' through, ye know."

"Oh," I said.

Then the dream faded away into something else, something less vivid, and I thought that he wasn't coming after all, because I'd turned out to be a Crome generator. I woke crying, pitying myself.

17

Our immortal lives went on. The hills went from brown to a more weathered shade of brown. The leaves of the black walnut trees turned bright yellow, and so did the few cottonwoods; they were the only ones to make any ostentatious display of color. There were also bright scarlet berries on the toyon holly bushes, and they were pretty hanging in clumps among the dark serrate leaves; but the rest of southern California was unrelievedly drab.

The days dawned gray, which burned off to a glaring white sky around noon, hazy and painful to the eyes. Smoke from the cookfire hung in the cold, still air and did not dissipate. Small wonder smog would become a local institution. There was no rain to wash it away, either, though the dewfall was heavy and our adobe rooms became chill and dank unless lit braziers were kept in them half the day, which increased the smokiness. Oscar made a few wistful remarks about how good New England food would be now that the weather was getting nippy, but there were still no takers for his Criterion Patented Brass-bound Pie Safe.

If I were home in the Santa Lucia Range, what a dark green the mountains would be, what a dark blue the sky, with cold winds that drove out the summer fog. And the redwoods and the cypresses would stand like dark gods, offering up their own aromatic blood. The broad-leaf maples would blaze like flame, the stars glitter like broken glass. I could travel my secret ridge routes all day with no company but the sea hundreds of meters below me, and the occasional white sail on the far horizon to prove I wasn't the only living soul in the world.

And if I wanted company, or at least civilized food, I could always hike north to Monterey, or stop in at the Post's little rancho at

Soberanes Creek; though I didn't do that often, because I unnerved the settlers, and in any case I seldom wanted company. The trees and the sea were enough. Not even *he* could find me there, my wraith, unable to summon me from my restless bed when I didn't have one, unable to break my human heart when I'd transmuted it into green leaves and stars.

But here I was in this glaring purgatory of a cow town. Winter was decidedly not its best season. The weather wasn't our only problem; Imarte had given Cyrus Jackson the brush-off somehow, more or less tactfully, but he hadn't accepted it. Several times we spotted him by infrared, sitting off on the hills at night, watching our little canyon. As long as he did nothing but lurk, he was welcome to his miserable vigil; but you never know when mortals are going to decide to go out in a blaze of glory and try to take you with them, so we monitored him closely.

Imarte didn't care. She had her fascinating theories, her invaluable first-person narratives, and her wealth of irreplaceable historical detail. When she wrang a source dry, she dropped the source. I am afraid that, although an anthropologist, she lacked a certain love for her subject, or perhaps its immediate and particular personification: the human heart.

I should talk, eh, señors?

Anyway, we were all a little nervous, as the cold weather set in, scanning the dull hills for desperate mortals with guns. They were everywhere down here anyway, but now we had our own special desperate mortal with a gun.

One day, when the northbound stage stopped by, I went down to watch Porfirio change a shoe on the lead horse. I had seen him shoe horses before; but Einar was the only other person around, and he and I had taken to avoiding conversation with each other since our visit to 1996.

It wasn't a long stop; no passengers had to get on or off; they wouldn't have stopped except for the loose shoe. During the whole time, though, one of the passengers had his attention riveted on Porfirio. He was a young kid, maybe Juan Bautista's age, Mexican from the look of him and very well dressed, with a high shirt collar and the old-fashioned silk tie that stuck out like paddles from either side of the central knot. Leading the horse back to its place, Porfirio noticed the boy's intense regard and glanced up at him once, curious. The boy looked away immediately.

"What was with the kid who kept staring at you?" I asked as the stage went bounding and creaking away and we closed up the smithy shed.

"Beats me," Porfirio said. "I think I'll make some tamales dulces tomorrow, what do you say? It's early for Christmas, but I've really got a craving for something sweet."

He made hot chocolate that night instead of coffee, and we got into quite an elevated mood, sipping it around the fire and laughing. We all sobered up, though, the instant we picked up the mortal coming over the ridge to our immediate north.

"Chief?" Einar was on his feet at once, shotgun unslung and cocked.

"I read him." Porfirio was in the shadow of an oak tree faster than mortal eye could have followed, his Navy revolver out. Einar faded into the gloom behind the house.

" 'Scuse me," murmured Juan Bautista, grabbing up Marie Dressler, who clacked her beak at him in protest. He sprinted for his room clutching her in his arms, while Erich rode his head, balancing expertly.

I remained where I was, warming my hands on my mug and peering doubtfully up at the ridge. Yes, there he was on infrared, making his stealthy way down the hill in our direction. Carrying a gun, too. But it wasn't our lovelorn filibuster . . . Who the hell was this, creeping along like a thief, his heart thudding painfully? He raised the gun to sight on our circle of firelight, and I winked out on him, to continue my scan from the shadows under a spurge laurel. He lowered the gun, staring in disbelief at the deserted fire. This was a young male mortal, no intoxicants in his bloodstream but with a number of the toxins produced by fear and exhaustion. No disease signatures . . . some healed fractures, very old. Unhappiness. He didn't want to be here, he didn't want to be doing this. He was tired and cold. Where had the person gone, who'd been there a minute ago? he was thinking in Mexican Spanish.

I saw Porfirio and Einar working their way uphill toward him. Porfirio stopped about twenty feet below, and Einar circled around until he was just above him, only about ten feet away in the sagebrush, moving without a sound until he suddenly stood up black against the stars and said loudly:

"¿Qué pasa, amigo?"

The kid whirled, swinging his gun around, but Porfirio nailed him from behind before he could get off a single shot. That was that. He pitched forward, and I saw Porfirio and Einar closing in on him cautiously. I remembered my hot chocolate and took a sip. No reason to come out until they'd brought the body down. He wasn't dead yet, anyway, just unconscious and bleeding a lot.

Then what a howl of agony. Not out loud, I don't think it would have shaken the Earth that way if he'd been using only his voice: it was Porfirio's heart that was screaming, cutting through the subvocal ether like the sound of all possible things malfunctioning at once. My hair stood on end. I came blundering out through the bushes to see him crashing down the hillside, bearing the young mortal in his arms, and you couldn't have told who looked more deathlike, gray-faced Porfirio or the mortal. Einar was bounding along after him.

"Chief! Chief, what is it? What's wrong?"

"Code blue!" snarled Porfirio. "Equipment! Three pints Hemo-synth!"

Nobody can say we don't move fast in an emergency. The boy was restarted and stable in no time, bleeding stopped and wounds bound, all kinds of stuff pumping through him that wouldn't be discovered by mortals for decades. His nice clothes were ruined, of course, including the silk tie, which had come undone and was covered with blood. He was one lucky kid for all that. Porfirio's shot had missed his heart. We stretchered him into Porfirio's room, and Porfirio sat down beside him and told us all to get the hell out of there, which we did.

What to do after that but go to bed? Nobody was going to answer our questions; nobody was going to explain why the little creep had come sneaking back to gun for us, or why Porfirio had been so suddenly horrified, after plugging him with as neat a piece of cold-blooded shooting as I've ever seen, or why such pains had been taken to save his young life.

I was awakened at dawn by Porfirio coming into my room. He still hadn't washed the blood from his hands. "He's starting to come around," he said hoarsely. "He can't see me. Go to him, please."

"You want to tell me what's going on?" I said, swinging my legs over the side of the cot and groping for my boots.

Porfirio leaned against the doorway. "He's one of my family. I didn't recognize him. Haven't seen him since he was seven years old."

"So why was he shooting at you?" I stood up and pulled my shawl around my shoulders.

"I shot his father."

"You shot his father," I said, looking at him.

He was looking down at the dirt floor. "Yeah. You know how I recognized him? His father broke all the fingers on his hand that day.

Just held his little hand down on the table and pounded it with a bottle. The fingers healed crooked. That was how I recognized him."

"Oh," I said.

The boy didn't wake much. I gave him water and spoke to him soothingly in Spanish, telling him he was all right. Most of the time he was passed out, sedated while the miracle cures Porfirio had filled him with did their work. I examined his hand and found the evidence of old multiple injuries. It must have been a very little hand when it was hurt so badly. Whether or not Paradise exists, señors, there must be a hell. People who do such things to their children belong there, and for all eternity too.

Einar came in to take my place at noon, and I went out into the ghastly white day. Porfirio was nowhere in evidence, but Imarte was standing by the cookfire with an apron tied on over her whore's finery. Of all things, she appeared to be making lunch; she was tossing handfuls of barley into what smelled like goat stew.

"What's that supposed to be?" I asked, squinting at it through the glare.

"It's the only thing I know how to make," she said defensively. "It's a *very* old recipe."

"Where's Porfirio?"

"Asleep in my room, poor dear. Goddess, what a tragedy." She sighed. The subtext here was that she knew more about it than I did, so I just sat down and refrained from asking anything else until she couldn't stand not telling me a second longer.

"You know what happened, of course."

I shook my head. "Only that the kid is one of that family of his. There seems to be revenge mixed up in it somehow. And child abuse."

"If that were all! Remember when we asked Porfirio where his family is now? Remember he told us that a great-niece had married a ranchero, and her brothers had come to work on the rancho for him? Well, it seems this young man is her son, hers and the ranchero. The boy's father appears to have been one of those unfortunates with two personalities, a fairly decent one when he was sober and entirely another kind when he drank. A lot of unresolved rage there, apparently." She tossed in the last of the barley and looked around. She found the raisins she wanted and sprinkled them in too.

"In any case, after the child was born, the father's dark side came more into control. He was sober less of the time. Fortunately Porfirio (who was there) and the girl's brothers looked after the man's business affairs, but, as so often happens with this type of personality disorder, he was anything but grateful. More and more, his rage manifested itself in violence against his wife and, in time, no doubt as he perceived himself being displaced in her affections, against the child."

"So he showed them all by crippling the baby's hand." I rubbed my eyes wearily. I hated mortals.

"Ah, but that's not the whole story. The wife, for her part, had a classically codependent personality. She manifested her own feelings of low self-esteem by remaining with her husband in spite of their abusive relationship and, from what I understand, transferring *her* anger to her brothers and to her 'Uncle' Porfirio."

"It figures."

"Quite a standard pathology, actually," said Imarte, stirring the pot busily and frowning as she considered the seasoning. "And of course it broke Porfirio's heart. He seems to have loved the child and assumed the role of father in his life. He taught the boy to ride, he remembered his birthday with presents, he read to him from Cervantes. This, however, only brought about greater feelings of resentment and alienation from the actual father, and in time precipitated the final crisis. The tragedy occurred on one of their colorful fiesta days, the one with all the skeletons."

"The Day of the Dead."

"The family had made some attempt to celebrate, with decorations and candy for the little boy. The father, driven by his usual compulsion on festive occasions, began to drink early in the afternoon. Once again he was unable to deal with his rage, and by twilight he was fairly violent. The incident with the child's hand was apparently provoked when the child hid from his father behind a chair."

"I'm glad Porfirio shot the son of a bitch."

"Oh, he didn't shoot him in retaliation for the boy," Imarte said, sorting through the little cans of spices she'd set out. She found one she liked and dealt out a few dashes into the stew. "The wife was able to emerge from her passive role long enough to take the liquor bottle from her husband. He turned on her, accusing her of betrayal. He said he'd kill all three of them, then thrust the muzzle of his pistol in her mouth. At this point Porfirio and the brothers, who had just ridden up, intervened. As they burst through the door, the husband turned and shot at them. He wounded one of the brothers mortally. That was when Porfirio drew his own gun and shot the husband dead."

I drew my shawl over my head.

"As is usual in these cases, the woman blamed everyone but her abuser. She threw herself on her husband's body, shrieking incoherent lamentations and protestations of eternal love. The surviving brothers found Porfirio a horse and helped him to escape. The Company was obliging about stationing him as far away as possible. That was ten years ago. Last night, the young man made his attempt on Porfirio's life."

"He can't blame Porfirio for what happened!"

"You think not?" She gave me a sadly tolerant smile. "But you yourself are a product of Hispanic culture, you ought to understand. These male-dominated societies all follow the same code of honor. Porfirio killed the father, therefore the son must kill Porfirio. It's depressingly simple."

The immortal uncle was accustomed to solving the problems of this classic dysfunctional family, but he hadn't quite brought it off this time, had he? Poor man. Briefly I thanked God that my blood were strangers to me, if indeed the line hadn't died out.

"How do we explain to this kid that he can't finish his vendetta, because his target's an immortal?" I asked. Imarte shrugged gracefully.

Just then Porfirio emerged from the inn, carrying a blanket and a bag, and went straight to the stable without a word. A few minutes later, he came out, leading a saddled horse, and approached us. His face was blank, curtains drawn and shutters closed.

"I'm taking off," he said. "I'll be camping up the pass, if you need me. What you're going to tell Tomas is, I was just the blacksmith here, and you didn't know I was wanted for murder in Durango or anything else about my past. Tell him Einar runs the place, and when Einar found out what happened, he went for the sheriff in Los Angeles, but I ran away before I could be arrested. You have no idea where I've gone. Help him get well again and then put him on a stagecoach and send him back to Durango. Okay? I'll send you my location coordinates so you can let me know how he's doing."

"You want us to bring you supplies?" I asked. "Food, aguardiente, anything?"

He just shook his head and swung up into the saddle. We watched him urge his horse to a swift canter, and away he went down the canyon.

Imarte sighed deeply. "The grim history unfolds," she intoned. "How thoroughly characteristic of the American West, yet analogous to clan feuds in Corsica or Scotland. How unfortunate, but how fascinating, don't you think?"

"Unfortunate," I replied.

Tomas was out of danger pretty quickly, with no infections to complicate things; no fever, no ravings, only a pale polite boy with enormous dark eyes asking us if we knew where the blacksmith went. We told him what Porfirio told us to tell him, and he accepted that quietly enough, and was unconscious again. His body needed the sleep. Young mortals heal almost as fast as we do.

After a few days he was able to ask Einar to go recover his trunk, which he'd hidden in a bush in Encino after leaving the stagecoach at Garnier's. It contained two other suits of clothes, a shaving kit, and several small personal items, including a daguerreotype of a woman and child. His mother, no doubt, because the child standing stiffly beside her chair was certainly Tomas. He had a wistful little smile for the camera. She was dressed in black, and her eyes were black too, cold and angry. Was there maybe a resemblance to Porfirio in the shape of her face, the chill in her eyes?

Tomas asked for his gun back. We checked with Porfirio, who was hiding out in a high narrow canyon on Mount Hollywood; he sighed and then transmitted his okay to give it back to the boy, cleaned and loaded. This was Los Angeles, after all. We hung his gun belt over the bedpost. He woke up long enough to see it there and gave us his little grateful smile, just like the child in the picture. Then he slept again.

So there was this kid, in Porfirio's room, with his luggage and his weapon and his mystery. Imarte hovered over Tomas, attending to the tiniest details of nursing with perfection, hoping he'd murmur some part of his story in a delirium or gasp confidences into her motherly bosom. He didn't. He barely spoke at all, to any of us, and when he did finally speak, it was to Juan Bautista.

I was sitting by the bed, reading a back issue of *La Estrella* and waiting for Imarte to take her turn at vigil, when Juan Bautista entered the room. Tomas opened his eyes at the noise, and then opened them wider. It's not every day you see silver-haired Indian kids with condors perched on their heads.

"That guy came and wanted to talk to Imarte again, so I said I'd take over for you," Juan Bautista told me in Cinema Standard.

"Fine," I said, and rose from the chair. I was starving. As Juan Bautista sat down and I left the room, I heard Tomas asking shakily, in Spanish:

"Why do you have a bird standing on your head?"

I fixed myself a plate of Imarte's goat stew, that's how hungry I was, and sat down with my back against the wall to eat it. As I ate, I became aware that there was a conversation in Spanish going on in the room on the other side of the wall. Sharpening my reception, I was able to pick it up.

". . . and I feed her fish when I can get them," Juan Bautista was saying. "Mostly sardines, you know, in those little square cans with the funny openers?"

"That's really neat," I heard Tomas reply.

"Yeah. I thought about getting her some canned oysters, but they're *way* expensive."

"I had some oysters in Santa Fe one time. I didn't think much of them. What do you feed the other ones?"

"Just seeds and stuff. You know. Except for the little owls—I catch crickets for them. Watch out. He's telling you he needs to go to the bathroom. Here, give him back a minute. Good boy! See, I've trained him to let me know. Now you can hold him again."

"He's, like, the biggest parrot in the world or something," Tomas said, giggling weakly. "Boy, I'd love to have one of these guys to wear on my shoulder when I walk around the ranch. Condors don't talk, huh?"

"No. Only the *Psittacidae, Corvidae*, and *Sturnidae* talk. The *Sturnidae* are just mimics, though, they don't understand speech like parrots."

"We used to have a parrot when I was a kid." Tomas's voice was a little sad. "My father bought him for my mother. He was . . . a real man, my father."

"And he was killed by that blacksmith who worked here?" Juan Bautista said, cautiously. I frowned at my empty plate and wondered if he was going to let slip any details he shouldn't know.

"The same man who shot me."

"You came looking for him?" Juan Bautista asked.

"I didn't think I'd find him, I didn't think he would still be alive, not the kind of guy he was. I thought . . . if I could just find his grave or something, I could spit on it and go home and tell my mother I'd done that, at least. I was going up to San Francisco to look for the grave, because I'd heard they had a lot of criminals up there. But then the stagecoach stopped here, and there he was, and I knew I had to kill him. For my father."

"You loved your father?"

"I was only a kid when that son of a bitch killed him, but I remember we used to do stuff. He taught me how to ride. His favorite book was *Don Quixote*, and he used to read to me from it, and one year for my birthday, you know what he did? He made me a whole set of wooden figures from the book, he carved them himself. There was a Don Quixote with these long jointed legs, you could sit him on Rocinante or you could make him dance or turn somersaults. He had a lance and shield and helmet. There was a windmill with vanes that really turned, and there was a giant's face carved on it. There was a Sancho too, but he didn't do anything, he just sat on his mule. They were the best toys. . . . My father loved me better than anybody else ever did." Tomas's voice grew a little muffled.

"But . . . what happened to your fingers?" asked Juan Bautista, bewildered. He didn't get it.

"That was the other guy, the one who murdered my father. I don't remember what happened, I was too little, but my mother said he'd been drinking. He was this lowlife friend of my uncles'. They used to work on our ranch, and they brought this friend of theirs. He was our majordomo for a while. But he was a drunk, always getting into trouble. I remember he'd yell and break things, and I'd be scared. I don't know why my mother let him yell at her that way, she was so stupid. Wouldn't you think she'd just have told my father? *He* wouldn't have let anybody talk to his woman that way, if he'd known. But I guess he never found out about it, until that night."

Had the mother twisted the story for her son? Or had she simply never answered his questions? What was wrong with the mortal woman, anyway?

"You want some of this tea?" Juan Bautista's voice was a little shaky. "It's good for you."

"Thanks." There was a pause as Tomas drank, and then he continued:

"Sometimes I can remember a little. We were having a party. I was scared. I remember the yelling. There was a fight. That guy was drunk, and he hurt my hand and killed my father and one of my uncles when they came in. He ran away, and nobody ever caught him.

"After the funeral, my mother sent the rest of her brothers away, because it was their fault that guy came to the ranch. She said she'd rather have me be the man of the family than any of them. Sometimes, I wish she hadn't done that, because it's hard running the ranch without help. She's still angry after all these years."

Poor boy. What a weight on his shoulders.

"Still angry?" asked Juan Bautista.

"Oh, yeah. She told me I had to find that guy as soon as I was old enough and avenge my father's murder."

"Well . . ." I could hear Juan Bautista shifting around uncomfortably. "You know what? You could go back and tell her you got him. He shot you, but you shot him first, see? And I'd be a witness for you. We could write a letter. You know, like a deposition? Everybody here would sign it, telling her how you killed him. Then you could go home with proof, and it would be all over."

"I can't lie to her," Tomas said. "She always knows. . . . Anyhow, I don't want to go home until I've killed him. It wasn't until I saw his face that afternoon that I remembered how scary it used to be, how my mother cried. I have to kill him for her, but I also have to kill him for me, for taking away my father. I hadn't even remembered how much my father loved me until I saw that man."

"But he almost got you," Juan Bautista said. "He's a real good shot, and now he knows you're after him. You'll get killed next time."

"Maybe I'll kill him instead." Tomas didn't sound certain. "Or he'll kill me, and then I'll be in Paradise with my father. I don't care which. What would you do, if you were me?"

"I don't know," Juan Bautista said. "I'm an orphan." He sounded as though he was grateful for that. "But I wouldn't want to die for no reason. I mean . . . what if your mother got some of the details wrong?"

"She never gets details wrong."

"Have you asked your uncles about what happened?"

"How could I?" Tomas sounded tired. "She sent them away, and they never came back. I don't know where they went or if they're even still alive."

"You need to sleep some more," Juan Bautista said. "Your blood pressure's too low." I winced; this was the kind of cover-blowing remark young operatives make. He might as well tell the mortal boy he could scan him. "You can't do anything anyway until you get well. So you should rest and drink a lot of tea, okay?"

"Okay," said Tomas in a fading voice.

He rested and drank a lot of tea, and the color began to come back into his face as the days passed. Soon he was able to get out of bed and totter around the room, and then to put on his clothes and sit outside in the chilly November sunlight.

Tomas was a nice boy. He was quiet and courteous, for a seventeen-year-old; he didn't brag or try to impress us with how tough he was. He spoke respectfully to ladies and deferred to Einar and Oscar. He was really taken with Juan Bautista's aviary, and the two of them spent hours in there cleaning the cages and talking about birds. And wasn't he a good son? Ready to roam the face of the earth to deliver blazing death to a stranger, or suffer blazing death himself, for his mother's sake.

"What are we going to do?" said Juan Bautista, late one evening when Tomas was safely asleep in Porfirio's bed. "I never knew mortals were crazy like this. They look so normal. How are we going to stop him from going off to hunt for Porfirio, when he's better?"

You can't, transmitted Porfirio from the mountain. He sounded glum. *He won't go home looking like a fool or a coward. If I could take my head off and send it home with him as a trophy, I'd do it.*

"Why not simply let the lad continue with his search indefinitely?" said Oscar. "It doesn't sound to me as though his home is a terribly pleasant place. Perhaps he's better off wandering the world and having adventures. Certainly he won't expect you to come back here. We might see him on his way, and then you could come out of hiding."

What kind of adventures is he likely to have, poking his nose into every den of thieves he comes across, looking for me? Because that's what he'll do, you know that, and the next time he gets shot, I won't be there to hook him up to a life-support system.

"He's stubborn," Imarte said. "I've done my best to explain to him how this kind of primitive revenge ritual invariably results in the destruction of all parties. Regrettably, he comes from a society where a greater value is placed on abstract cultural values than individual human life. One is reminded of the Japanese custom of—"

"I don't suppose there's any way you could tell him the truth?" I asked Porfirio. "That his memories are all screwed up, that his father was the real bastard and you were the good guy?"

Can you think of any way I could get him to listen to me? transmitted Porfirio bitterly. *And even if I could, what then? He thinks he had a father who loved him and died in his mother's defense. Her version of the story's a lot more palatable, isn't it? What happens when the pretty paper is stripped off my ugly present of truth? His mother becomes a liar, at the very least.*

"She sounds like a crazy bitch anyway. Why should she hate *you*?" I said.

I killed the man she loved. She would have forgiven him anything, but she'll never forgive me. And I shouldn't be forgiven! I could have prevented this. If I'd been quicker, I might have stopped the bullet that killed Bartolo. I might have disabled Jaime without killing him. I might have been there for the boy all these years. God in heaven, see what she's done. The family is broken, scattered, when I'd fought so hard to keep them together where I could look out for them. How will I ever find Juan and Agustin again? Are they even alive? And she, look at what she's become, look at what she's done to that boy. If I had only stayed . . .

"You couldn't have, man," Einar said. "You know that. You belong to the Company. First time Dr. Zeus had a job for you somewhere else, you'd have had to go. And even if you'd stuck around, do you think you could have kept on micromanaging their lives forever? We may be immortals, but we can't control mortal destinies. We can help them when they want help, but that's it. When they want to destroy themselves, not even God can stop them."

"That is so true," I said, with all my weary heart. "It's that lousy rotten free will of theirs. All we do is run around cleaning up after it."

"We're the everlasting janitors in the Big Bathroom," Einar agreed. "Our only consolation is knowing how much worse things would be if we weren't part of the equation. Anyway, kids: here's an idea, culled from my centuries of wisdom and cinema expertise: We've all seen films where a guy fakes his own murder."

"I can think of several," Imarte said. And then, "Oh."

Let him shoot me?

"We'll load his gun with blanks and fix you up ahead of time with a full suit of charges and stage-blood bags. He'll think he's blown you away and go home with the revenge thing all finished." Einar jumped up in his excitement and began to pace. "Six Cawelti squibs, a sheet of body armor, some red dye and corn syrup—man, we can make you look like you had breakfast at the OK Corral!"

18

It took no more than a week to prepare, during which time Tomas was getting stronger. Against Imarte's entreaties, he set up a target on a tree and practiced shooting at it. Juan Bautista tried to talk him into going home, but there was no arguing with the boy: as soon as he was well enough, he planned to take the stagecoach out to Calabasas, famed locally for its bandit population, to see if Porfirio had gone there to hide from justice. On the day he was finally strong enough to ride, however, Einar came riding up from the bottom of the canyon at a dusty gallop.

"Hey! Amigo!" he called out in crude Texan Spanish. Tomas turned. He'd been target shooting. "Yeah, you. I think I finally got a line on that no-good murdering hombre that killed your pa. Looks like he's holed up not five miles from here. You want to go see if you can get him?"

I looked up from the cookfire to watch the boy's reaction. He stood frozen, staring with those enormous dark eyes. Slowly and deliberately he holstered the pistol. "Will you have the kindness to loan me a horse, señor?"

"Get him a horse, Juanito," Einar said.

Juan Bautista gulped. "You don't want to do this," he told Tomas. "Think how bad you'll feel afterward."

"No. If I get it over with, I can be my own man," said Tomas.

So Juan Bautista brought out a horse, saddled and bridled, and Tomas climbed awkwardly into the saddle. He looked sick and dizzy up there.

Einar reached over and took his pistol out of its holster. He spun the empty chambers. "Won't do you any good unless you reload, son.

Here, take mine." He handed off the gun full of blanks, and I looked meaningfully at Juan Bautista. First bit of stage business in our play accomplished.

Tomas stuck the gun in his belt and drew a deep breath. "Let's go, señor. Take me to that murdering son of a whore."

They rode away down the canyon, dust clouds spiraling up. Juan Bautista stood looking after them, wringing his hands. "I have to see," he said, and ran for the stable, from which he emerged a moment later leading another horse.

I ran to him as he got into the saddle. "Take me along. This ought to be some show."

He put out a hand, and I leaped up behind him, just as Imarte came running out of the inn. "What is it? Is it time? Don't tell me they've left—"

"We'll let you know how it went," I said, and we galloped away.

We followed the dust clouds north through the pass, up the grade to Dark Canyon, and over the flank of Cahuenga Peak. We were coming to the high ground behind Mount Hollywood, which sloped gently down toward the river, and I wondered if Einar had chosen the spot deliberately. You could call it an appropriate location for a shoot-out; this was the site of an immense graveyard in the distant future. Nearer our time, Griffith would shoot the battle sequence from *Birth of a Nation* here, and for all I knew the battle scene that ended *Intolerance* too. Einar had told us about it enough times, in his babbling enthusiasm. Now, before it became that famous place, it would serve as a small and private theater for a grim farce.

But where were the actors?

We saw the two horses tethered in a stand of oak trees. And, just creeping over a ridge and peering into the hollow beyond, there were Einar and Tomas. Juan Bautista urged our mount forward.

Porfirio was advertising his presence. A plume of smoke rose thinly. He'd made a cookfire.

"Up there," I said, pointing to our right. We could climb a winding trail for a better view. Juan Bautista hesitated, then swung the horse's head uphill, and we ascended hurriedly, peering through the oak trees.

Porfirio was sitting by his fire, warming his hands. He looked tired. He glanced up as Einar broadcast, *We're here, man. Is it a good day to die?*

Always. Porfirio looked down at the embers again, deliberately ignoring the mortal boy's clumsy approach through the weeds. Oh, God, the kid slipped, was tumbling down to land in a crouch not ten yards from where Porfirio sat. Did he really want to do this? Up on the ridge, Einar pulled out the little electronic control and waited.

Porfirio raised his face. Tomas made a stifled sound and staggered backward. We couldn't see his face, but we had a fine view of Porfirio as he got to his feet and held out his hands, his empty hands.

"Very good, *mi hijo*. It's my turn. Blood for blood, so you can be a man."

Then the boy was firing wildly, *bang bang bang*, and the charges detonated in perfect time with his shots. The blood bags exploded outward, and Porfirio spun and fell. The noise of the shots echoed; it hit the face of the ridge like a wave breaking and rolled back down the slope, prolonging the moment, washing us in the sound. Out on the valley floor beyond the river, a dog began to bark.

It's a wrap. Beautiful, Einar transmitted. *You all right?* He came jumping down the slope, stuffing the detonator remote into the pocket of his jeans.

Damn things hurt came the answering transmission. I confess I was relieved to hear Porfirio reply; that had been a truly convincing death scene. Look at him now, the way he lay there ashen and motionless, his lean villainous face frozen in a snarl like a dead animal's. But then, who could counterfeit death better than an Immortal? We see so much of the real thing.

Tomas had dropped the gun and was doubled up, retching. Einar caught him and steadied him. "Come on, boy. We have to get out of here. No sense getting yourself hanged. Let's go, let's go." He practically carried him up the slope and down the other side, to the place where their mounts were waiting. Juan Bautista spurred our horse through the sagebrush toward them.

"Did you get him?" I asked, playing my part.

"Got him, all right," Einar said, boosting Tomas into the saddle. "Now this boy's satisfied his debt of honor and he can go home to his ma with a clear conscience. Isn't that right, son?"

Juan Bautista rode up to Tomas and peered into his face worriedly. Tomas looked deathly ill again, as bad as on the night he'd been shot.

Then we all thundered away through the November evening, and the sun was setting red as blood, and the shadows were long. Tomas wept the whole way, and when we walked our horses into the innyard, he tumbled off his horse and into Imarte's waiting arms.

She folded him into her bosom.

"You poor brave boy. You come with me, tell Marta all about it," she cooed. *I trust everything went off as planned?*

You shoulda seen, Einar transmitted.

If anyone had bothered to tell me in time, I might have, she replied, giving me a nasty look. She turned and pulled Tomas away with her into the inn, doubtless to obtain a first-person narrative from him and gain valuable insights into the culture of machismo. The damned harpy.

She nursed him through the hysterics, and I think she rewarded him the way a man wants to be rewarded, and as the evening wore on it, she gave him aguardiente too to bolster his sense of worth. He cheered up tremendously and began to swagger and sing, as I'd never heard him do before. We all assumed it was the relief of being out from under this burden he'd carried his whole young life. But Juan Bautista listened for a while and then vanished silently up the canyon, taking Marie and Erich with him. I busied myself with making some plain beef stew—I'd had all the Chaldean Surprise I could stand—and Einar bounced around taking care of his innkeeper duties, still pleased with himself at the way his special effects had turned out. Even he began to look a little concerned, though, as the noise level in Imarte's room rose.

I was trying not to listen to what seemed to be an argument developing, when I picked up Porfirio on the ridge behind us, just arriving.

Mendoza?

Yes.

I could use some hot food.

Hang on.

I ran and got a blanket from my room, and half a case bottle of aguardiente, wrapping them together. I got a bowl of stew and a spoon and hurried up the canyon. As I ran, I could hear Tomas emerging from the inn, shouting to Imarte to leave him the hell alone.

"Whoa, son, where are you going?" Einar said, getting up.

"Set up the bottles!" the boy shouted. "Set up the bottles and give me that gun!"

Target shooting again? I shrugged and kept climbing.

Porfirio was sitting quietly in the darkness, gray as a ghost, which he looked like in his serape with the holes and bloodstains all over it. I put the bowl of stew into his hands and threw the blanket around his shoulders.

"Thanks." He turned the bowl in his hands, savoring the warmth. I sat down beside him and uncorked the aguardiente bottle.

"How is he?"

"I think he's having some kind of hysterical reaction," I answered delicately. "But I guess that's normal if you think you've just killed somebody. It looked great, by the way."

"The kid's drunk," Porfirio said with a scowl, gazing at the circle of light around our cookfire. "Listen to him."

Gunfire, followed by Tomas's shrill laughter. He was telling Einar to bring more bottles to shoot at. I had a gulp of aguardiente myself. Porfirio spooned stew into his mouth, but he never took his eyes from the fire. They were dark and cold.

"Listen to him, down there," he said. "He thinks he's some killer, he thinks he's one hell of a man."

"You did your best," I said. "What else could you do, Porfirio? At least this way he can go home and make his mother happy."

"She'll never be happy," he said, emptying the bottle and throwing it away. "My fault, I guess."

More shots. We could hear Einar making a very tactful suggestion and being refused indignantly. Porfirio exhaled hard.

"I was so relieved when she married Jaime. At last, I thought, somebody who'll take care of her, and he's even got money. But see how that turned out. I could go looking for Juan and Agustin, I guess, when this job is over; I could try to track them down and see if they've married, if they've kept the family going. But what am I going to do about her? And what am I going to do about that kid?

"Look at him down there, strutting around with his gun. He's bought into the whole damned lie about blood and honor and revenge. He was made to feel like a little nobody all his life, but now it's payback time. Nobody's ever going to tell *him* what to do again, not now that he's killed somebody. Ay, ay, ay."

Porfirio buried his head in his arms. "Who will take this curse off my family?" he asked the night.

The party didn't last much longer. Tomas got cold and ran out of things to shoot at, and Einar got tired of dodging bullets and vanished into the bushes, so Imarte came out and tried to get the boy to come to bed before he caught pneumonia or fell into the fire. He tried to hit her. You don't do that to an Immortal. She swiftly knocked him out and carried him indoors like a sack of flour.

Some time in the afternoon next day, Einar roused him and got him into a change of clothes. When the 1600-hours stage came rolling up, Tomas was bundled into a seat, still groggy, and Einar loaded on his trunk and paid for his passage southbound.

Porfirio came out of the hills, and our lives resumed their courses. I don't suppose I'll ever see that young man again; but I can imagine how he'll turn out.

Can't you, señors?

19

WELL, IT JUST got darker and crazier in bad old Los Diablos. Bad things come in by the armful and leave by inches, it's said. Winter came, but no rain; smallpox instead. It began in the old shacks on the hill where the poorer citizens lived, Sonoratown, the locals called it. The few remaining Indians were dying like flies, and then the Mexicans were being wiped out, and pretty soon there were even rows of coffins being carried to the Protestant cemetery. Stagecoach service became irregular, to say the least, in the dry and bitter cold.

Dry. There wasn't a creek or a freshet running. Our little stream became pools of standing water, shrinking perceptibly day by day. I don't know where the trout went. Our well hadn't given out, but we were taking serious measures to conserve water. Whatever water we used to wash I took to carrying out to the oak trees, to pour over their roots. Within hours after emptying a pail, you could see tiny blades of grass emerging where the water had been splashed. The land was desperate to cover itself with green; but the rain never fell, and next morning there would be deer slot everywhere, and the grass would all be gone.

There was water in the sky, all right; there was water vapor holding the haze together, which stung the eyes at midday and kept the adobe rooms cold as death. There was water in the slate clouds that rolled over us and kept going without releasing so much as a drop. The longhorns began to rove into people's vegetable patches, and the last of the old rancheros looked at the brown hills and wondered if they oughtn't borrow some more from the Yankee moneylenders to tide them over what might be an unprofitable year.

We froze, but we got no rain. San Francisco got rain; but, then,

San Francisco never doesn't get rain. It rained back east in Vicksburg, where another battle was fought, and we read rumors of soldiers drowning in their tents. It rained in Mexico, where Juárez sat in his room and calmly considered what he ought to do about Europe. Everybody else got rain, but we were dying of thirst.

And smallpox.

Oscar stayed home a lot, driving the rest of us crazy; but how was he going to sell anything with people hiding behind their doors, more afraid of the disease than they'd ever been of stray bullets? We saw almost nothing of Imarte, though, so it was a fair trade. She was having a field day, moving among the dying like a scarlet angel, easing their journey out of the world in exchange for life stories gasped out to the sympathetic stranger. To be fair, I believe she nursed a few back to health. When she wasn't busy compiling statistics on mortality, she found time to get some suspiciously British mining engineer to buy her a Peach and Honey at the bar of the Bella Union, and one or two spilled a few more details to support her pet conspiracy theory. The whole thing was so ludicrous, we actually encouraged her to talk about it, on the few occasions she came home; we needed the laughs.

And who wanted to celebrate Christmas, on the underside of hell? Time was when I enjoyed walking to a town and slipping into a pew to watch a *pastorela*, with the earnest mission Indians trying so hard to get to Bethlehem and all the teenaged boys in the parish portraying the devils who tried so hard to prevent them (a role so natural for any teenaged boy). I loved the way the spoken verses would echo in the old church, and the way the flames of the candles winked in their glass cups, and the way the sleepy mortals observed a reverent hush all around me. It was all so charming. And when the Indian pastores finally made it to the stable, after vanquishing Señor Satan (who always bore a close resemblance to a gentleman of Old Spain), and the central Mystery unfolded, how lovely to see the black-eyed Mother with her Indian cheekbones and serene smile as she displayed the tiny red Child with his shock of black hair. One could almost come to love mortals again.

Or not. Other years, I'd been alone in the night, where the great trees towered black against the stars, so many white stars, and the air was cold and full of the smell of evergreens. I'd been in the heart of the Mystery then, too. The stars rang like little bells at midnight, and one moment the air would be dead calm on the forest floor, and then a wind would spring up, just on that stroke of midnight, a wind magically warm and full of perfume, and you knew that the Light had begun to fight his way out of his grave, and winter would not last forever.

But this winter of 1862, that promise seemed to have failed. So many coffins, and not a drop of rain.

20

I DON'T SUPPOSE I need to tell you that the hauntings became worse, señors. Became strange. He still pursued me in the night, my dead love, but he seemed to have changed; we seemed to have lost England and gone to places I'd never been. I'll tell you the dream that's clearest in my mind.

I was in a jungle like a Rousseau painting, you know, all those botanical specimens so carefully delineated and dead-eyed jaguars staring forth here and there like so many stuffed toys. Something was coming after me, crashing through the fever-green forest, and where he passed, the palms and ferns and bromeliads all shook to life, lost their neat arrangements, and became real, pulsing and shooting toward the sun.

I'm not sure I was making any effort to run from him.

Then he was coming across a clearing at me, and I could see him at last, the savage, was that a Mayan with his high cheekbones and long curved nose? No, how could I have thought so? This was another kind of naked savage. He was tattooed fearsomely, swirling blue spirals all over his white body, his pale-blue eyes glittering with deadly laughter, and he was on me with the grace and weight of a lion. I went over like a rag doll. What was my stern Protestant metamorphosing into? What atavistic madness was this? He had a flint knife, and it was a beautiful thing, beautifully worked, and as he searched for my heart, I saw the fan palms waving above our twined bodies. I tried to tell him that the fan palm is the only member of the *Arecaceae* actually native to California, but I was distracted by the discovery that he had the front page of the London *Times* for January 6, 1863, tattooed on his chest.

I tried to read it as he was busily taking out my heart. Then we heard shots behind him, and he turned with a snarl. Looming above us was a vast blue pyramid, and from its base hunters were coming, sending lead singing through the air. He turned and looked back down at me, and I saw that his face was painted too, a pattern of red and white diagonals crossing on a blue field. No time, no time to do this properly! said somebody, and he rose above me and lifted the blade in both hands for the stroke of mercy.

But I was awake and moaning on my cot before he was able to give it, and blue light was crawling away, diminishing into darkness, leaving me miserably, eternally alive.

21

THE DAY THE actors came, we were taken by surprise. We'd been alone in our canyon for so many days, it was hard to imagine a stagecoach ever stopping here again. But—

"Incoming," announced Einar, and with sour laughter we hurried down the canyon to see who was arriving, departing, or just passing through. We heard the shouting as the stage pulled up.

"Are you mad, man? Are you demented, have you quite taken leave of your senses?" said a stentorian baritone. "Press on! Press on, though wolves howl and birds of prey darken the air. D'you want to die of the peste, for God's sake?"

"Mister, if that wheel comes off when we're coming down the grade, it ain't gonna be the smallpox kills you," said the driver. "Now you just hush up and set tight. We'll be on our way again soon's we get the spare on."

"Ay, what a wreck," said Porfirio, crouching down to look at the wheel. "You want this thing repaired, señor?"

"It'll have to be." The driver handed off the reins to his partner and jumped down. "We can't get new ones from the Concord folks nohow, what with the war. You got any spares here?"

"Sí." Porfirio jerked his thumb at the shed. "You leave the bad one, and I'll see if I can have it ready when you come back down, huh?"

"Fair enough," the driver said, going to unhitch the team. "Though I'm half minded to stay up in Frisco, the way things is going. This ain't no business to be in right now. You heard about the Indian attack this summer?"

"Indians?" queried a soprano voice, and the baritone thundered out:

"Driver, you categorically assured me there were no savages to be encountered on this route!"

"Aw, shut your damn pie hole," the driver said.

"What Indian attack?" Einar asked, bracing the corner of the wagon as Porfirio settled the jack under it preparatory to taking off the broken wheel.

"Happened in Minnesota," said the driver, leading the first of the team to our watering trough. "Seems the Secessionists are paying 'em to make trouble. They been cutting down telegraph poles, too. You ask me, I think they're smart enough to figure out they can raise all the hell they like with the Army busy fighting itself. Whoever's behind it, I sure don't fancy being stuck out here with a mess of Indians and Mormons and who knows what all between me and Teaneck, New Jersey."

There was a noise like an asthmatic goose honking; it came from the passenger compartment. Juan Bautista and I looked at each other in puzzlement. He walked around to the other side of the stage to see if in fact it was a bird, but just as he disappeared, the last honk ended on a shrill indrawn breath and became evident as a fit of hysterics on the part of the soprano.

"Oh, we shall not survive! Ingraham, one cannot venture—into such *places*—without appalling consequence. Such venues. Such wretched venues, and such (for want of a better word) men!" she shrieked.

"Have courage, Caroline. It may be that we have escaped the Pale Rider in one form only to encounter him in another; but I say we *shall* reach the Golden Gate, though calamity leap headlong into our path," said the baritone. I walked around the wagon to see why Juan Bautista hadn't reappeared.

He was staring as though transfixed at a wicker birdcage, which was tied on the back under the trunk enclosure. The leather cover hadn't been fastened down properly, and a flap had blown back, exposing a gnarled and clutching claw the size of a fist. What was in there, a dragon?

Juan Bautista's face was stony with anger. He began to work on the knots that held the cage in place.

"Hey," I said uncertainly. "Should you be doing that?"

He didn't answer me. The knots were proving intractable, so he took out a knife and cut them. He hauled the cage out and down, exposing its occupant. The ranting from the passenger compartment stopped abruptly.

"Caroline, I believe our trunks are under attack," said the baritone, and the gilded head of a cane thrust the window flap aside. A face glared out at us. "I thought so! Boy, I shall prosecute you with the utmost force of the law. How dare you?" the baritone snarled. He was a thinly bearded gent in a very loud checked coat. His gray gloves matched his beaver hat, though.

"How dare *you*?" Juan Bautista shouted, trembling with anger. I took a step backward. I guess he was mad about the treatment of the occupant of the cage, who was a very, very large something with talons. The cage was way too small for it; it must have been stuffed in there with tremendous trouble, and had scarcely any room to move. Its head was sealed in a leather hood like falconers use, and its legs were bound; all it could move were its talons, which were constantly clenching and unclenching on the floor of the cage, nasty with its droppings. Not even a perch, and no water or food. Erich von Stroheim gronked and snaked his head sideways to peer down at it.

"Put that back at once," said the baritone.

"No," said Juan Bautista. "Do you know what this is? It's a *Haliaeetus leucocephalus*. Where did you get it?"

"You are mistaken, sir, that is a bald eagle, and it might interest you to know that it was a present to me from Chief Two Ducks of the Wyandotte Tribe on the occasion of my successful charity gala in Sudbury, Ontario," said the baritone with a sneer. "Its name is Mister Liberty, and if you don't immediately replace it, I shall be obliged to descend from this conveyance and beat you like the little thief you are."

Juan Bautista proceeded to wrench the cage apart with his bare hands. It was only a wicker cage, of course, but the baritone was so shocked, it took him a full ten seconds to roar: "Damn your impudence. Driver! Are there no laws to protect passengers on this line? Driver!" He leaned across and shouted out the other window.

The driver and Einar came around the side of the stage just in time to see Juan Bautista grab up the poor bird and run with him. Erich was jolted from his customary perch and flapped along above them, and the three disappeared in the general direction of Hollywood Boulevard.

"Oh," said Einar.

"Well, God damn," the driver said, grinning. "I guess you'll just have to file a Damages and Loss Report, mister. It will be reviewed by our claims representative, and when and if an award is made, you'll be compensated by the company in the amount of the registered value of the goods as reported in the parcel manifest or in an amount up to but not exceeding the approximate value of said goods as defined in paragraph 3, article 2A in said document."

"Blow it out your arse," the baritone said.

"Ingraham!" gasped the soprano.

"My apologies, madam." Ingraham gave me a peremptory tip of his hat. "Has the word *lawsuit* any meaning to you rustics? I see it has. You will make every effort to recover Mr. Liberty now, this moment, or I shall own you."

"Aw, that bird was about dead anyhow," said the driver.

"That is immaterial, sir. Are we to be deprived even of the services of a taxidermist? And are you aware with whom you speak? I, sir, am Ingraham Drew Culliman, of the Marlborough Theatre. Perhaps *now* you'll wish to avail yourself of a post horse in the pursuit of my personal property?" Ingraham's voice had risen to a frightening pitch.

"Never heard of you," the driver said.

"A liar as well as insolent. And if I were to mention that the rara avis in dispute was to be the centerpiece in my latest variety spectacle, the Salute to Liberty? That the magnificent emblem of our presently divided nation was to be held aloft by Mrs. Culliman (herself gowned as Martha Washington) at the climax of a musical tribute certain to raise the spirits and cheer the hearts of our boys in blue? There are those, sir, who might construe your detestable negligence as the next thing to treason, which, let me remind you, is a hanging offense." Ingraham brandished his cane.

The driver explained where he was minded to put that cane if Mr. Culliman shook it at him one more time, and added that Mr. Culliman was going to find it uncomfortable to sing or, for that matter, dance in any shows with the cane in that particular location.

"Hey, hey," objected Einar, as Ingraham took off his gloves to engage in fisticuffs with the driver. "Take it easy. I don't reckon we can get the bird back for you, but we'll be glad to pay you for him. How'd that suit?"

Immediately Ingraham put on his gloves again. "Well, of course the bird was a gift, but, taking into consideration the difficulty of obtaining another when we reach our destination, which is San Francisco, where rates are astronomical . . ."

"Remuneration in gold, Ingraham," Mrs. Culliman advised him.

"I'd say I couldn't accept less than a twenty-dollar gold piece," said Mr. Culliman, and leaned back on his cane and frowned magisterially at us.

Einar blanched, thinking of our budget. "It's a deal," he said in a hollow voice. We waited while he ran up to the inn and raided the emergency fund.

Mr. Culliman inspected the gold piece critically, nipping it with a careful incisor before tucking it in the watch pocket of his flowered waistcoat. "I daresay that'll suffice. One really ought to inform the police in a matter of such flagrant disregard for laws concerning personal property, but as it's the season of charity and goodwill toward men, I will let the matter rest without further prosecution." He touched his hat brim with the ferrule of his cane. "Driver! Pray see to it that our trunks are better secured before we proceed."

He vaulted back into the compartment and let the window flap fall. We could hear Caroline demanding to see the gold piece. The driver gave him a particular salute and lounged back against a boulder, rolling himself a cigarette.

"Is there trouble?" Porfirio asked, returning from the shed with a spare wheel. Einar and I shook our heads mutely.

Juan Bautista didn't return until three hours later. Erich was back on his customary shoulder perch, and the eagle was still clutched in Juan Bautista's arms. It had had the blinding hood removed, and it was a bald eagle all right, though a pretty sorry specimen to have cost so much. A lot of its feathers had been pulled out; and though I'm no judge of avian expressions, its eyes had a kind of fixed and glassy stare of rage that I'm sure live birds don't usually display. It made Porfirio's expression look mild by comparison.

One look at him, though, was enough to reduce Juan Bautista to tears.

"I tried to set him free," he said. "I wasn't going to bring him home. But he can't fly. Somebody broke his wings, and they healed wrong. Please! Let me try to fix him. I can do surgery that'll fix it so he doesn't hurt anymore. I won't keep him, I promise."

"The bald eagle will be on the endangered-species list by the middle of the next century, you know," Einar said helpfully.

Porfirio gritted his teeth and swallowed the fire and brimstone he'd been preparing to spill. "Why should I care?" he said, throwing up his arms. "Go ahead. The stink from sardines in your room is already enough to knock over a Turk, but you're the one who has to live in there. Maybe *this* one'll eat all the goddamn pelican chow I ordered."

In fact, the eagle seemed to like it. John Barrymore (so named after lengthy debate between Juan Bautista and Einar) was definitely not a normal bird. Not cute or whimsical, either, after the months of abuse and neglect he'd suffered. Psychotic.

At least he didn't bite, and Juan Bautista managed to get him to stop pulling his own feathers out; but he destroyed every cage Juan Bautista made for him, no matter how roomy. Yet he never flew; he never even tried. He would stalk around like King Lear on the blasted heath, glaring at the whole world. Usually he followed Juan Bautista around, but occasionally he decided to travel his own path. It was unnerving, while reading the paper on one's cot, to look up into his accusatory stare not three feet away. The only thing that sent him into a homicidal frenzy was anyone attempting to pick him up, so rather than risk his talons, one had to lie there and yell for Juan Bautista to come coax him away. I got pretty tired of this after the third or fourth time. I don't know what the damn bird thought I'd ever done to him.

He was a symbol of many things, señors, not least of all this nation, crazed and self-destructive as it was. None of us could fly from that desolate place. Though the New Year arrived, there was a general feeling of the light going, waning, chilling, the feeling that we were journeying downward into darkness. The land sick, the people sick and crazy, certain ruin trundling toward us like a siege tower.

22

"WHAT A TEDIOUS time this is," said Oscar, hitching up his trousers to protect the crease as he sat down. "I haven't sold anything but black dye in weeks. All my Christmas business vanished in quarantine; with so many funerals going on, nobody wanted to buy presents."

"At least your business will pick up eventually," I said, pouring myself a cup of black coffee. "Mine's going to hell without a return ticket. You should see it out in the temperate belt these days. I have to fight off the longhorns to get to my specimens. Everything's being grazed right down to the ground. Extinctions, honest-to-God extinctions happening right before my eyes. Or would be, if I wasn't collecting."

"Oh, surely not," he said. "Isn't this region prone to droughts? Wouldn't the local flora be resistant?"

"It's resistant to drought, all right, but not to being eaten by starving cattle." I sipped my coffee. It was bitter, but I drank it anyway. "Think of the way things looked this time last year. Remember how green everything was? The cattle herds do. They wander out every day, looking for the green. All their instincts are telling them to head for the salad bar after a long winter. Salad bar's closed, unfortunately."

Oscar sat straighter, struck with inspiration. "Ah, if only there were a rainmaking apparatus. Talk about supplying demand! Imagine how that would win the trust and affection of one's consumers."

I tilted the last bitter drops out on the dry earth. "If it didn't work, you'd need a fast horse or a good tar remover."

"Never happened to me," he said, waving a hand airily. "I am no charlatan. I carry nothing but merchandise of the highest quality."

"You *are* a good little machine," I said.

"The best," he replied with conviction. "How can you persuade mortals to trust you if you lie to yourself? And where's the passion, the suspense, the triumph of the whole business, if it's all a sham? Really, the field material is almost of secondary importance, because you can't obtain worthwhile data in an artificial situation. I've worked with partners whose heart just wasn't in the Deal, if you know what I'm saying. No focus on the act of enticement at all, merely on obtaining data. They might as well have *been* clockwork automatons, and don't you think the mortal customers didn't sense it. No, sirree. They froze up and hadn't two words to say about themselves."

"Basic characterization," I said in agreement, remembering what we were taught in school. "Believe in your character, and the mortals will, too."

Oscar held up an admonitory finger. "More than that. Believe what your character believes, and the illusion is unbreakable. A method guaranteed never to fail, under the most adverse circumstances. When the most important thing in the world to me is getting that gentleman or lady to make a purchase—when I have them craving it, whatever it is—their souls open, and they reveal all manner of secrets about themselves. They would never suspect I wasn't human, even if they saw gears and cogwheels flying out of my mouth."

"Well, but—really, we *are* human," I said uncomfortably.

"Just so!" He nodded his approval. "That's the attitude to take if you want a successful career, you may depend upon it."

I stared at him, and at last I asked, "So . . . have you always been stationed in the New World?"

"Native of this country, I'm proud to say!" He smiled in fond remembrance. "Born if not bred here. That Croatoan affair. No memories of a mortal life at all, of course—recruited as an infant. Orphaned, I gather. Some nasty business with the local redskins. No hard feelings, naturally. Quite an irony, wouldn't you say, that savages with stone tomahawks were the shapers of my destiny, with all its splendid artifice? I went straight back into the field after my graduation, too, never been back to a base since. Never wanted to! Why in blazes would I want to loll around idling, watching holos, when all the glamor and excitement's out here?"

"You find this glamorous?" I jerked a thumb at the bleak hills.

"Heavens, yes." He was incredulous I should even ask. "This is the very edge of the world! You can't go any farther out in America, not until we acquire Alaska and Hawaii. And what's my function here? To document the forces of civilization at work, as they transform this murderous wilderness into a place where decent folks would want to live. The more savage it is, the greater the challenge. It would be exciting enough if one were only a spectator; but look at me. I'm not only bearing witness to Manifest Destiny, I'm an apostle of it, by gum!"

I decided he was crazy too. "How do you mean?" I asked.

"By advancing the standard of living through the availability of fine merchandise, of course. With every labor-saving device or can of stove polish I sell, chaos is dealt another blow in this wilderness. Even when I don't actually conclude a transaction, even when those penniless folk stare openmouthed at the splendor of my wares but come not forth to buy, they go home with visions of a better world dancing in their heads." Oscar rose to his feet and swept off his hat.

"And they'll *desire* those visions, and there will be those among them who dare to improve their mortal lot, that they might purchase some measure of that splendor, some glittering prize, though it be but a fragment of the glorious whole. The idle will seek employment, the chronically hapless will become sober and industrious, and noble ambition will animate the frames of those who now lie torpid and indifferent to what they *might* have, if only they would rise to embrace it."

There was a breathless pause.

"Oscar," I said at last, "you will go far."

"Excelsior!" he said, and thrust his hat skyward as far as he could reach.

At this moment, we both noticed the approach of a vehicle. It was the wrong time of day for a stagecoach. Whatever it was, it had turned off the Camino Real and was rolling up our own little canyon, going right to the door of the inn. We turned to stare.

It was a fine two-horse open carriage, slightly antique, oxblood in color, with the arms of some grand old Spanish family blazoned on the body. It had been blazoned there an awfully long time ago, though, to judge from the way it had faded. A black man in a red coat drove it, and seated within was a mortal lady of our mutual acquaintance.

Oscar gasped. He had been in the act of returning his hat to his head, but now he swept it off and bowed double.

"Princess Rodiamantikoff," he said.

It was even she; but how changed. Gone were the Gypsy silks and cheap baubles. She wasn't more tastefully dressed, you understand, but certainly more expensively, and there was now a coherence and even a dignity to her ensemble. She'd found some good luck somewhere. Her plain face was fuller by a few square meals, but the blue eyes were still knife-sharp, unwavering, superfocused. She extended a regal arm, pointing at Oscar with her parasol as the carriage braked to a stop.

"It is he," she said. "At last we find you. Chief Running Deer and King Elisheazar have not searched cosmic ether in vain. You may approach us, sir, for we would discuss with you matter of trade."

The effect on Oscar was—well, it was indecent. He was beside the wagon at once, planting a fervent kiss on her outstretched hand. The black coachman looked at him askance.

"Your Highness!" Oscar said. "How pleased I am to see that your fortunes have improved. Doubtless loyal friends at the distant court have contrived to send you support of a material nature?"

"Naturally," she said grandly, lying through her teeth, if her pulse and respiration rate were any indication. "Not to mention certain assistance rendered by dear Spirit Guides and others in realms above who are anxious to see that great work goes forward."

"And what great work would that be, ma'am?" Oscar asked, terribly interested.

"Ushering in of new era," she said. "Epoch when unhappy multitudes gain peace and enlightenment through communication with world beyond. Secrets known only to arcane secret societies will at last be revealed to all! Futures foretold through modern methods of cartomancy passed on from ancient Egypt through Gypsy race. Loved ones who have passed over will send advice and encouragement through gifted individuals. We are pleased to be humble instrument of Spirits' will. Spirits have told us you were also instrument, bringing cards for entertainment purposes only."

"So Your Highness has improved her situation by telling fortunes?" Oscar's eyes were wide with fascination, his cameras rolling.

"Please." She raised a hand. "Grateful clients have presented tokens of esteem for messages received from beyond. We are now enabled to live in gracious home in better area of City of Angels. But now, Spirit Guides have advised we must prepare doorway to Spirit realm through construction of beautiful altar. Offerings will open pathway for clients to speak with loved ones through intercession of Spirits. Common household object of beautiful design must be used for this. Spirits have directed us to purchase from you beautiful cabinet whose gross material purpose is keeping pies. It will be consecrated to higher use through addition of sacred plates of metal from ancient Egypt, location of which revealed to us in trance."

"The pie safe!" I think Oscar leaped a foot in the air. "You wish to buy the Criterion Patented Brassbound Pie Safe."

She nodded demurely. "Do you deliver?"

He certainly did.

23

YOU NEVER SAW a man, mortal or immortal, strut around so. It took us a few days to get all the ingredients for a New England boiled dinner together, during which time we were treated to multiple retellings of the story of the sale, with the hunt, the chase, and the astonishing moment of the kill. What a triumph for the good gentlemen of the Criterion company! What invaluable documentation of the development of spiritualism as a movement in America, throwing new light on its evolution on the West Coast!

The dinner itself consisted of a big chunk of beef brisket, boiled, with side bowls of boiled potatoes, boiled onions, boiled cabbage, and boiled parsnips. There was brown bread with raisins, but even that was water-cooked, steamed in a can over the coals, like a plum pudding. Everything was liberally buttered and mashed, with lots of salt and pepper, which it very much needed, especially the beef.

In honor of the occasion the meal was served indoors, on our rickety kitchen table made bright with a sheet of checked oilcloth. We crowded around, Oscar and Porfirio in our two chairs and Einar and I seated on kegs from the storeroom, basking in the steamy warmth. Juan Bautista was obliged to take his meals in his room nowadays, lest John Barrymore attempt to commit suicide in his absence, and Imarte was out on the prowl. It was pretty cheery in there, even with the Boiled Everything, especially after Porfirio brought out an earthenware jug he'd been keeping warm in a covered basket.

"Okay, Yankee man," he said, "it's time for a toast. Hot rum punch, courtesy of the house."

"Oh, my," said Oscar, rising unsteadily to his feet, doubtless feeling the powerful gravitational force exerted by his ingested supper.

"And isn't this just the weather for it, too. I haven't had rum punch in decades. You're a prince, sir."

"Hell, we always knew you'd sell that thing," Porfirio lied, carefully tilting the jug to fill our graniteware mugs. Out jetted a stream of something as red as a streetwalker's dress, dotted by bits of orange peel and clove and fragrant with fiery rum. We howled in anticipation and raised our drinks high.

"To a radiantly successful mission, Oscar," Porfirio said. "Not only for unloading the pie safe, but for the commendation the Company has decided to grant you for the sheer volume of sociological material you compiled while you were trying."

"Surprise!" Einar and I yelled, and Oscar turned pink.

Porfirio held out a hand for dignity and order. "And what could be more appropriate in your honor," he said, "than a polycultural cocktail? The cranberry of New England, the orange of Old Spain, the peach of Georgia, spices from the Far East, and rum from Jamaica, all boiled and served as hot as your pursuit of the Willing Customer. We wish you many more, man." He threw back his head and gulped the drink down, and we followed his example.

Oscar actually got misty-eyed. "I'd no idea," he said. "A commendation? Imagine. All I've ever wished was to do my job, you know, to the best of my limited abilities. Setting aside false modesty, though"—and he stuck out his chest with pride—"I must say, when once I set my mind to accomplish a thing, I can't be beat."

"And what do we have for the winner?" Einar said, jumping to his feet. He gestured gracefully at an invisible prize. "Two months' all-expenses-paid vacation at that fabulous Company resort, Pacifica Three, on the beautiful island of Molokai! You'll enjoy unlimited use of Company research facilities while dining on exotic tropical cuisine! When you're not lounging by the library pool, you can saddle up a pony and explore the island's natural wonders, or barter for anecdotal material at the friendly local leper colony. Other activities include windsurfing, spearfishing, and hot-air ballooning.

"But that's not all!" He turned and gestured in the other direction. "Tanned, relaxed, and refreshed, you'll return to an assignment personally selected by *you*. That's right. You may choose to go through either:

"Door number one, to the lush plains of the Oklahoma Territory, where you'll document consumerism in the developing settlement culture. Or,

"Door number two, just a canoe ride across to the beautiful Big

Island of Hawaii, to report on the growing dependency of the native population on manufactured trade goods. Or,

"Door number three, to that all-male Queen of the Pacific Northwest, Seattle! You'll cheer (and record) as the arrival of female citizens and quality merchandise changes this lumber boomtown into an American metropolis."

Well, that was too much. Oscar's legs gave way under him, and he sat, put his head in his hands, and cried for sheer happiness. I could have cried too, from envy. How often do immortals get choices of anything? And here was Oscar, who'd cheerfully trundle his peddler's wagon into hell if the Company told him to, given the opportunity I'd been pining for. It just goes to show why one should do one's best to be a good little machine.

I was preparing to drink to his health as Porfirio poured us another libation from the jug, when we were all alerted to the approaching presence of a mortal on the immortal arm of Imarte.

Porfirio halted in mid pour, scanning, and we tuned in as well. No trouble; the mortal was in a happy, lustful mood, slightly drunk, and Imarte wasn't concerned.

"Why, sir, I declare I am simply in love with England," she was gushing. "I do feel that what we colonists gained in liberty was *quite* outweighed by our loss in culture. This must all seem so terribly rude to a gentleman like you-all."

"My dear lady, who can feel the want of social graces in your fair presence?" was the gallant if somewhat adenoidal reply. We heard an indrawn breath, and then: "By Jove! Is that rum punch perfuming the night air?"

"I believe it's some of the other lodgers here . . ." We heard her voice sharpen a little as she bustled after him, for he was coming down the passage to our kitchen like a devil after a soul. A moment later, he had stepped into the circle of lamplight, and we beheld a slightly weedy mortal youth clutching a leather valise to himself. He resembled Charles III of England, with the same sad, remote eyes; and their expression chilled further as he found himself in a room full of strangers. You could see him brightening, however, when he noticed our weapons and decided we were colorful and exotic.

"Oh, I say, though. Are you banditti?"

"No, señor, we are merely the staff here," Porfirio said. "You must be aware that it is advisable to carry firearms in Los Angeles."

"Quite!" Our visitor gave a horsey little giggle. "The code duello seems to rule in your streets; and may I say that, while I find the brevity of life here appalling, it certainly is lived with a manly lack of hypocrisy and cowardice."

We blinked at him. "Thank you," said Porfirio at last. "May we offer you a glass of punch, señor?"

"Yes, please. I shan't be sorry for the warmth." He set down his valise and rubbed his hands together. "For a tropical country it's devilish cold here o'nights, you know."

"Subtropical," I corrected him absently.

"What?" He turned to stare at me, but then his attention focused on the glass Porfirio was holding out to him. "Oh, now *that's* something like. To your good health, all." He raised his glass to us and drank deeply. Imarte scowled at us from the doorway behind him.

"Mr. Rubery, dear, recollect what happens when a man mixes his liquors. We don't want Bacchus's vine to make it difficult for us to offer myrtle to Venus, do we?" she told him rather acidly. He smiled into his empty glass, licked his chops, and turned to her with an awful leer.

"I've a constitution of iron, my dear. But let it never be said of me that I kept a lady waiting. Gentlemen, madam, I'm obliged to you for the potation." He gave us a nod and set down the glass. Sliding an arm around Imarte's waist, he let himself be pulled off in the direction of her bedroom.

"She's going to be mad as hell with us if he passes out before she can get him talking about secret plans," Einar said, grinning as he raised another toast to Oscar.

"He left his valise," I said, nudging it with my boot.

"Don't open it. It probably has one of those trick locks that spray tear gas, as in *From Russia, with Love*," he warned me.

"More likely a spare pair of socks and a set of embroidered hankies," said Oscar disdainfully. "What a prime example of a weak and decadent aristocracy. Did you see the way his teeth—"

What problem he had with Mr. Rubery's teeth I was never to learn, for at that moment we all picked up the signal we had come to dread: a mortal out there in the night, drunk and wrathful, putting the spurs to his poor horse. Cyrus Jackson.

"Two kilometers out and coming in fast," Einar announced, getting to his feet.

"Riding," said Porfirio, pulling out his gun and checking the chambers.

"You can't kill him," Oscar said, blowing out the lamp. The room glowed as we switched to infrared. "There's a mortal witness. That Britisher."

"Damn. You can't even shoot him with a trank," I said, following them out the back door. The valise was right where I could trip over it; impatiently I grabbed it up and shoved it into a cupboard. "The witness would still think we'd killed the guy."

"But I'm getting tired of Señor Cyrus Jackson," Porfirio growled. "Tired of his staking us out all the damn time. I think the moment has come to nail his nasty ass to a wall."

"Uh-oh," said Einar, as we emerged into the clearing around the cookfire. Mr. Jackson's signal was growing louder and clearer as he galloped toward us, and it wasn't giving us the usual spectrum of his jealous misery and self-pity; it was off the scale. The man was in a homicidal rage. Einar leaned forward slightly, staring intently down the canyon. We heard the thunder of hoofbeats stop abruptly, and there was a thudding crash and a curse.

"I got his horse to throw him," Einar said. "And . . . shit, he's still coming."

There he was on visual now, a grotesque figure by infrared, crawling out of the bushes where he'd landed with the boneless impunity of a drunk and staggering to his feet. On he came, up our canyon trail, pulling his gun from its holster.

"It's your party, boys," I said, and winked out to the hillside, where I crouched down and did my best to resemble an ordinary rock formation. I still had a good view of the clearing, with the three of them standing undecided as the monster lurched toward them.

What's happening? Imarte broadcast in panic, having just noticed the approaching hazard.

Keep your Englishman quiet, Porfirio told her. *Maybe he should get his pants on, though.*

I'm staying inside with my birds, Juan Bautista transmitted from his room.

"We'd best get these poor creatures out of sight," Oscar said, nodding at the tethered mounts on which Imarte and Mr. Rubery had ridden in from Los Angeles. He took their bridles and led them off to the stable. "Might I suggest a timely visit from Michael Finn? I've a bottle of chloral hydrate I'd be most happy to contribute to the occasion."

"I don't think this guy's in any mood to sit down and have a drink with us," Porfirio said. "Thanks all the same."

"Smoke and mirrors, I guess, huh, chief?" Einar asked, rubbing his chin pensively. Porfirio nodded, and they winked out simultaneously, to reappear in the shadows on opposite sides of the clearing just as the mortal man came raving into sight.

He stopped when he saw the house. He stood swaying for a moment. His rage was building to a peak again. He groped around for the bottle he'd lost in his fall; when it failed to present itself, he let out an inarticulate roar.

A gasp from within the house, and some kind of half-smothered inquiry from Mr. Rubery, which fortunately Mr. Jackson was unable to hear. But he had recovered his bearings enough now to remember why he was there. Shambling forward, he addressed the house and drew a deep breath.

"Marthy!" he called. "You come on out of there, you faithless bitch!"

There was silence, at least as far as his mortal ears were concerned. I could hear the pounding of Mr. Rubery's terrified heart as he struggled to get back into his clothes.

"You come on out here where I've waited for you," roared Mr. Jackson. "You, no-good . . . you're a pitiless wanton. You're the goddamn woman in purple and scarlet, that's what you are. Marthy!"

I could hear Mr. Rubery whimpering, partly in terror and partly in pain as Imarte had hold of his arm in a viselike grip. In a low and exceedingly calm whisper she was explaining to him the dangers of heedless flight. Mr. Jackson, meanwhile, had leaned over backward until he looked likely to topple, staring in an accusatory way at the stars.

"I *defy* you stars!" he said, and hiccupped. "The way you looked down on me an' laughed. Marthy, ever' night I sat up there an' watched for you, an' waited for you, and it was so cold. You din't care none! Oh, Marthy, I'd 'a given you ever'thing that was mine, my good name and all, if you'd 'a loved me." At this point his gun went off accidentally, kicking up a spurt of dust in the starlight. He was thrown backward and fell on his ass.

At the sound of the gunshot, Mr. Rubery intensified his efforts to escape to such a degree that Imarte had to let go of his arm or break it. He blundered frantically down the passage into the kitchen, where he tripped over a chair with a crash. Even Mr. Jackson heard it, and he scrambled to his feet with an agility I would not have thought him capable of in his condition.

"All right, I know you're in there with her. Come out here, you no-good English nancy boy," he said. "You prancin' Ephebe! Bring him out, Marthy! Jesus God, woman, ain't it enough you've run my heart through with needles? Ain't I sat up there bleeding for you, crying in the dark with nobody to care?"

Mr. Rubery was going round and round in the kitchen like a

trapped rat. Oh, he must have been hunting for his valise. Mr. Jackson thrust his head forward, peering at the house through narrowed eyes. He had to have been one hell of a hunter when he was sober, because even liquored up he was pinpointing Mr. Rubery's location as accurately as I was.

"I got you, limey coward," he snarled. "We go down to hell together, but you go first." And he started for the house with an unnervingly steady stride; at least, until Einar popped up beside him.

"Sorry, pal, you just crossed the line," he said, and winked out again. Mr. Jackson jumped and stared; he looked all around and then turned to look behind him.

Einar popped into view again, not an inch from his face. "You could drop the gun," he suggested. Instead Mr. Jackson swung it up and fired wildly at him—or at the place he'd been, for of course Einar winked away once more. Even with the echoing gunfire, though, we all heard the crash as Mr. Rubery got the kitchen door open.

"Enough is enough," said Porfirio, appearing behind Mr. Jackson with the empty frijole pot in his hands. When Mr. Jackson whirled about to see who was speaking, Einar popped up again and gave him a good push. As Mr. Jackson toppled backward, Porfirio shoved the pot down over his head. Mr. Jackson dropped his gun to clutch at the pot with both hands as he fell, and Einar kicked the weapon out of reach. Then Mr. Jackson was on his hands and knees in the dust, struggling blindly to rise and shaking his head, but the pot wouldn't come off.

The poker materialized in Einar's hand, and Porfirio had one of his iron ladles, and the two of them began to rain blows on the pot, alternating like clockwork figures striking the hours. As they did so, Mr. Rubery went running for his life through the sagebrush, bounding up the hill behind the inn at really amazing speed, and vanished over the ridge. Mr. Jackson kept trying to get up, but the deafening noise was too much for him. He collapsed at last, stunned and nerveless. When he'd stopped twitching, Porfirio and Einar stopped hitting the pot. Porfirio took out a little medikit book and peeled off a trank patch, which he stuck on Mr. Jackson's back, right where the shirttail had come out of the pants.

"That'll keep him out for twenty-four hours," said Porfirio, shoving the book back in his coat pocket. I climbed down from my place on the hillside as Imarte came raging out of the inn, stark naked.

"Is that miserable sot of a mortal finally finished with?" she said. "Mr. Rubery! Alfred, dear! Please don't be alarmed. 'Tis safe to return, dear, the wretch has expired."

"I don't think he can hear you," I said. "He's probably halfway to San Francisco by now."

She glared at me and swore an oath that would have made Cyrus the Persian blanch and cover his ears. "I CANNOT TOLERATE THESE WORKING CONDITIONS," she screamed, then said, when the air had cleared and the little green bats had stopped flying out of her mouth, "Do you know the chance I've just lost? Do you know who that boy was?"

"No, but I think he left his valise behind," I said. "It's in the kitchen cupboard behind the table."

"His valise!" She got an intense look in her eyes. "You're sure?" She turned and went bouncing off to the kitchen, with never a backward glance at Mr. Jackson.

We stood there in bemusement, until a snore from inside the frijole pot recalled us to our immediate problem.

"So, uh, chief," said Einar. "What do we do with this guy? The witness is gone. I guess he could just turn up dead in a ditch."

Porfirio made a sour face. "It's not like he killed anybody. Not here, tonight, anyway. On the other hand, he really needs to go far, far away and never bother us again."

"Don't kill him," I found myself saying, to my surprise, because I've always thought mortals with the If I Can't Have You Nobody Can Have You kind of obsession to be one of the lowest forms of life. "There must be a way to get him out of the picture without violence. We could shanghai him."

"An excellent suggestion," Oscar said, popping up beside us. "An involuntary sea cruise is just the thing for him."

"It's a long drive to San Pedro at this time of night," Porfirio said, sighing as he took off his hat and ran his hand through his hair.

"I'll take him," I offered, astonishing myself again. Why on earth was I sorry for this mortal?

"And I'll drive," Oscar said. "I've done this before, you know. Plenty of nasty fellows shipped out of New Bedford feet first when they made a nuisance of themselves around the Company safe house there, let me tell you. It's generally a humane and reliable way to dispose of unwanted mortals."

So Mr. Cyrus Jackson made his final exit from Hollywood at last, trussed and snoring in the back of Oscar's cart, and I heard a numbing five hours of speculation on which assignment Oscar ought to choose as we rattled across the night plain toward the sea.

*   *   *

In San Pedro, we circled warily around Banning's turf and made for the fishermen's huts on Rattlesnake Island, across from the old landing. Dark shacks on pilings, with a single lantern burning low and red—not a good place to find yourself at three in the morning. But Oscar drove straight up and hopped out unconcernedly.

"I'll fetch the blackguard. You go waken Señor Souza and make the arrangements."

I hated talking to mortals; but I crept up to the shack with the lantern and knocked timidly. After a long moment, the door was opened. I recognized the sleepy and unshaven face that peered out at me.

"Souza? The doctor has work for you," I said, using the standard phrase.

His eyes widened, and he nodded. "One moment please, señora," he replied, and ducked back inside. He emerged a moment later, trousered and shod, just as Oscar came bustling up with Mr. Jackson draped across his shoulders.

"Hello there," Oscar said brightly, in Portuguese so perfect, you'd have sworn he was born in Lisbon. "Has my friend explained about the evil and desperate man I'm wearing?"

Souza blinked and rubbed the bridge of his nose, just below his Company control implant. "No, señor. You'd like him drowned?"

"Not at all. No, sir, we simply think he needs a change of air. Now, unless I'm much mistaken, that ship over yonder's full of lumber. Is she going on a long voyage, by any chance?"

Souza raised his eyes to the open sea, where a schooner rode at anchor. He grinned, white teeth distinct in the gloom. "Yes, señor, the *Elg*. She is bound for Norway with the tide. Two of her able-bodied seamen killed in a fight in Los Angeles, too, I hear. Very sad."

"And this is your boat moored over here, is it not?" Oscar strolled out along the rickety pier.

"I am proud to say so, señor," replied Souza, strolling beside him.

"Capital." Oscar shrugged off Mr. Jackson and dumped him into the bottom of the boat, where he lay moaning. Souza leaped in and untied the mooring rope. A moment later he was rowing steadily out through the darkness in the direction of the *Elg*.

"Good riddance to bad rubbish," Oscar said, adjusting his lapels and shooting his cuffs. "Faugh, what a smell of rye whiskey. This coat wants laundering, wouldn't you say?"

"Very much," I agreed, and we climbed back into the cart and wheeled around to return to Hollywood.

Oscar took up the conversation again as though it hadn't been interrupted, and for the next five hours I gave my morose opinion in negatives or affirmatives on the merits of Hawaii over the Oklahoma Territories. Altogether it was an excellent thing for Cyrus Jackson that he wake up alive in a bunk on board the *Elg*, with no more Imarte to break his mortal heart for him.

The red sun was well above the horizon by the time we got back, and still Oscar hadn't made up his mind about where he wanted to be posted next. Nor had he decided by the time we saw him off, a week later. But Immortals don't get choices very often in their eternal lives, and who could blame him for lingering over his decision?

We did receive a holocard from him, later, though, all the way from sunny Molokai, and it may well be the last I ever see of that absurd little machine: pinkly sunburned, smiling and waving from the gondola of a hot-air balloon, the untamed world his oyster.

24

UNFORTUNATELY, IN THE same Company communiqué that had contained Oscar's commendation there was a memo of a less positive nature. It seemed that Juan Bautista's quota of rescued birds hadn't been met for several months in a row, though his budget allocation for maintenance had been exceeded to a remarkable degree.

"I know, I know!" he groaned, sinking into a chair, which brought Erich von Stroheim down to eye level with us. "It's not my fault, though. How am I supposed to go out and look for anything? I can't leave John Barrymore alone for two minutes, and I have to take Erich every place I go. Marie's the only one who'll stay where I tell her to."

"I warned you about this, Juanito," said Porfirio, shaking his head. "Didn't I warn you about this? Now you don't have a choice. You crate up the big birds and ship them off to HQ. They'll be all right. What's more important, you'll be able to get back to your work."

Juan Bautista's face went pale. "Please, just give me a little more time. I think I'm finally beginning to make some progress with John Barrymore. The microsurgery's all healed up, and lately he's even started to act like a normal bird sometimes. Please? One more month. As soon as the weather's better, I swear I'll send them away."

Porfirio leaned forward. "You don't seem to get it. This is not me telling you. This is Dr. Zeus *officially* telling you that you have screwed up. You're not doing your job. That's not acceptable, kid. You do understand that, don't you? And it doesn't take a lot of brains to figure out what your next move has to be, and you have brains to spare, thanks to Dr. Zeus. This is tough enough; don't make it tougher."

"What if I was able to catch up on my quota?" said Juan Bautista.

"I know I've fallen behind, but it's not the birds' fault. I'll learn to manage my time better. I'll bring my work up to speed, you'll see. Couldn't I keep them just another month, if I was able to do that? Would one more month make any difference, if I was able to make the Company happy?"

This was too much for me. I had to slink out, so I didn't catch the rest of the conversation; but I gathered that Porfirio gave in again, because no big birds were crated up or shipped off in the next few days. All the stock of songbirds and little owls went, though, tagged in their wicker cages; and Juan Bautista was admirably industrious for a whole day in front of his room, weaving new cages for the new stock he had sworn to bring in.

Imarte was industrious, too. We never saw Alfred Rubery again, but he *had* left his valise behind. She spent days locked in her room with it, going over the contents in minute detail and making copies of what she found. We only saw her at mealtimes, and the transformation from whore to scribe was unsettling: inky fingers, disheveled hair, stained dressing gown. She looked radiantly happy, though, with whatever lode of cryptohistory she'd struck. I confess I was curious, but not curious enough to bring myself to ask her about it.

And Einar was certainly industrious. Longhorns were going for ridiculously low prices now, and he was acquiring them every day and conducting cattle minidrives into Los Angeles. Porfirio was always busy, of course. The one advantage to the drought was that no roads washed out that winter, and now that the smallpox epidemic was tapering off, the stagecoaches were running regularly again. Banning seemed to be deferring maintenance on the coaches, though, or maybe his regular crew had died of the pox, because there were repairs to be made at our smithy nearly every day.

I was the only one with nothing to do. Why was that, señors? There was nothing left for me to save. Everything that grew in the temperate belt had either been collected by me or grazed down to bare earth by starving cattle. There were no rarities left to find, unless I cared to venture into the Canyon of Lunacy again. But no prize on earth could have tempted me back into that place where I might glimpse the deadly city again, the future desolation.

Now, you would think, wouldn't you, that Dr. Zeus might give me a pat on the head and tell me to run along now, back to my beautiful green Ventana? I certainly thought so. I wasn't expecting commendations or prizes, or even thanks for a job well done; but I did expect a new posting, and none came, though I checked the Company directives pouch every time Einar returned from Los Diablos.

Bureaucratic willfulness, or some subtle punishment to make me work harder, to improve my attitude? Why was I being ignored, señors? Was it simply that nobody noticed that I was stranded there, unable to do the work I'd been programmed for, the work I needed? The work that kept my demon at bay?

Or did the Company know? Did you know what would happen next? Did you know and sit there like God, silent, remorseless, useless? What happens if I sit here in silence, too? What if I never give you my all-important testimony, eh?

But of course you couldn't have known. You're stuck here in 1863, just like me. I don't imagine our masters up there in the future would tell you if they knew, either. No operative is ever told any personal detail of the Temporal Concordance. It's forbidden to tell. Though Lewis tried . . . Will you punish him, too?

More Theobromos? Well, thank you so very much. You damned well better anesthetize me now, if you want me to go on with this.

25

So there we were, all happily going about our work except for me. I sat huddled in my room most days, wrapped in a blanket and viewing holos hour after hour. Not as much fun as old-style cinema, overall. There is a pleasant sense of camaraderie with the rest of the audience, watching cinema. You know: throwing popcorn at the flat screen and cheering and sharing moments of excitement, like when Luke Skywalker is shooting down the bad guys pursuing the *Millennium Falcon*, or any part of *The Rocky Horror Picture Show*.

It's true that a holo takes you right into the center of the action; but that illusion is not always a good thing. The leeches scene from *The African Queen* comes shudderingly to mind. *Sunset Boulevard*, too. Who the hell wants to get unbearably close to Norma Desmond's scary eyes in that last scene? And let's not even talk about Hitchcock's films. Though it's no better, really, in the films you *want* to be a part of, because you're still isolated, you're like a ghost. No amount of technological cleverness can make Sean Connery take you in his arms, and no Good Witch will ever take you by the hand and welcome you to Oz. They won't see you, they won't hear you, because their reality is complete and you are not a part of it.

At last I gave it up and started following the war news again. Depressing, inconclusive, inaccurate, but at least it was really happening. I feel badly that it absorbed my attention so much. If it hadn't, I might have noticed the noises in Juan Bautista's room that awful day.

Not that I could have done anything if I had, of course.

You see, encouraged by the progress that John Barrymore seemed to be making, Juan had taken to leaving him shut in his room when he went out on his collecting trips. Erich von Stroheim he kept in

Einar's room, liberally dosed with bird dope of some kind, so the damn creature was quiet all day. He didn't like to do it, of course, but the idea was that it was only temporary, until he caught up on his quota and reassured Dr. Zeus that he too was a good little machine.

In my opinion he should have been doing this all along. It was no effort for Juan Bautista to catch birds: all he had to do was stand still, and the bloody things would light all over him. But he was seventeen! Sloppy and disorganized and stupid as youth will always be, no matter how cyberaugmented it's made. Perhaps that was why he filled his room to the ceiling with flimsy woven cages full of the miserable cheeping little things, and left a psychotic predator in there with them while he went out each day to hunt for more.

Do I have to tell you what happened, señors?

It was as bad as you could imagine. I heard his wail of horror when he opened his door. I came stumbling from my room in time to see John Barrymore bouncing clumsily out into the clearing. Porfirio and Einar emerged from the house too, and stopped dead at the sight of the eagle.

Not that he was covered with gore, or anything like that. Well, a little blood, and some few bright feathers from some little victim. He regained his composure and took a few paces sideways, cocking his head to stare at us in a puzzled way. But there was the most heartbroken sobbing from Juan Bautista's room.

The irony was that John Barrymore had been making progress. While he was sick and mad, he tried only to kill himself. It was when he began to heal that he felt the normal urge to do what predators do. But Juan Bautista was in no condition to appreciate this, as he emerged from his room with a little torn body in either hand.

"You *bastard*," he screamed. "How could you do this?"

He ran at John Barrymore, who started and crouched in alarm. Then, with a wild flapping of wings, the big bird rose into the air and floated onto the roof of the inn. He looked down at us all, and we stood looking up at him with open mouths. Experimentally he beat his wings again, twice, three times, and we felt the rush of air in our faces as he nearly lifted off. Had the madness left any room for joy, when it vacated that narrow killer's skull of his? What was in his flat blank eyes, when he beat his wings again with a noise like a stiff breeze filling canvas? I don't know. In the next moment he leaned into the evening air and sailed away on spread wings, effortlessly, a long curve ascending. Up and up he went, high enough at last to catch the last light of the sun, and then he flew northward and was gone.

Marie Dressler had survived; she had managed to get into the clutter under Juan Bautista's bed and defend herself from there with her formidable old bill. And of course Erich von Stroheim was fine; he'd slept through it all in Einar's room. But the boy who loved them had changed.

Do you remember that terrible moment, señors, when the self-righteousness of your youth died? When all the stern warnings of your elders, ignored until the consequences abruptly came crashing down on your head, made you see in a flash that the warnings hadn't been unfair or mean-spirited or blind, they'd been *right*? All along your elders had been trying to tell you about the black joke that is life, trying to help you and save you from pain. But you insisted on running straight into the trap, mocking them as you ran, to the agony that was irreversible and permanent, with no one to blame, finally, but yourself.

It's not good to see yourself in the mirror then. Juan Bautista was reflected in the eyes of every one of the little dead birds he had to clean out of his room.

Next time Einar loaded up the wagon for the trip into Los Diablos, there were two big cages among his cargo. Marie sat patiently in hers, considering her new fate with a calculating eye; but Erich von Stroheim croaked and hissed with anxiety, trying to muscle through the wire mesh that kept him from Juan Bautista. When the wagon started up and he found himself rolling away from the boy, he started up the piercing scream we knew all too well. Juan Bautista just stood there, watching, his face like stone. It took a long time and a lot of distance for the screams to fade to silence.

"It's better this way, muchacho," Porfirio said at last. "They'll be safe, they'll be happy, they'll have great lives in the Company aviary."

Juan Bautista nodded, but I knew what he was thinking: no way now he could kill them, either, with his well-meaning mistakes or unintentional neglect or selfish love. I wondered if he'd ever dare love anything mortal again. Some of us don't.

26

IT WAS MARCH 13, 1863. I was struggling back and forth between
our galvanized bathtub and the nearest oak tree, carrying buckets of
cold and slightly soapy water in my unending irrigation efforts, when
I looked up to see Einar returning from Los Diablos in the wagon,
trailing a cloud of dust several stories high. I squinted in the glare and
frowned; he'd brought back a load of crates, something so heavy the
wagon was low on its springs. Porfirio picked up the question I was
broadcasting and came out to see.

"What the hell are those?" he said, wiping his floury hands on a
dish towel. "He's brought back eight pianos? Where's the olive oil I
ordered?"

"Wasn't room, chief," Einar called. "When I got to HQ, these guys
were waiting for me. Ladies, I mean; they're eight tule elk does in
stasis, and they've all been bred. I've got some marching orders.
They're supposed to go over Tejon Pass out to Buttonwillow, to be
released into the wild. You're tagged to assist me."

"Great," said Porfirio, throwing down the dish towel. "Just what I
needed. A trip to beautiful Buttonwillow at this time of year."

I didn't envy them. If there was a place more desolate than Los
Angeles, Buttonwillow was it; the only possible advantage being that
there were almost no mortals there in this era.

Einar shrugged apologetically. "It shouldn't take us more than a
week," he said. "We have to leave ASAP, though. 0500 hours tomorrow okay with you?"

Porfirio sighed. "That's life in the service. All right, tomorrow it
is; I guess the pass is clear by now. No killer camels this time, huh?"
Referring to the legend of deadly dromedaries haunting the mountains.

"That was just a joke, chief. Honest. But look at what else was waiting for me at HQ." Einar held up a big silver film can. "*Grand Hotel*, 1932! Greta Garbo, two Barrymores, Joan Crawford, Wallace Beery. We can have another night of the film festival when we get back, what do you say?"

I filled my bucket again and went trudging off to water the oak trees. How about Walt Disney's *Fantasia*, I wondered nastily. Weren't we all sorcerer's apprentices? Bucket-carrying brooms impossible to kill.

They left next morning in the bleak dark, bundled in their coats on the springboard of the wagon.

"You have plenty of supplies," Porfirio told Imarte and me. She had got up to see them off. "And there's most of a pot of fresh coffee on the fire over there. You ladies look after the kid, okay? And no cat fights in my absence, please."

Imarte and I looked at each other in disdain. "Wouldn't bother," I said.

"Don't give it a moment's thought," Imarte agreed.

He looked at us searchingly, his black eyes troubled. "No going out without wearing a loaded sidearm at all times, remember?"

"Hey, man, these are immortal girls," Einar said. "They can take care of themselves. Ciao, ladies; get your hankies laundered and ready, 'cause *Grand Hotel* has one of the really great tearjerker endings of all time!"

He gave a crack of his whip, and the wagon rolled away into the gloom, creaking under the weight of its improbable cargo. I hoped they wouldn't break an axle going over the Grapevine Grade. As though he had heard my thought—I wasn't broadcasting—Porfirio turned around in his seat and looked at me. What an uncertain look on his scarred devil's face. He was wearing it still when they turned onto El Camino Real and vanished from sight.

I stood there a moment longer, shivering in the mists. Then I remembered there was coffee. Imarte was already helping herself to the pot. I hurried to find my mug.

We managed to restrain ourselves from hair pulling and all that fun stuff, mostly because after she filled her mug she disappeared back into her room to continue her studies of the amazing secret-agent valise. Juan Bautista came moping out a while later, and I grilled him some beef for breakfast. He didn't stick around to talk; very shortly he disappeared up the canyon with half a dozen empty wicker cages, which had to be filled with endangered species. I knew a little of what he was feeling; he'd come to the place we all come to, sooner or later, when the work is all you have, all you can depend on.

So I was alone all day. There weren't even any passengers dismounting from the stages. It was a lovely, surreal feeling, all that peace and quiet. My ghost, too, left me quite alone. I made a stew of leftover grilled beef for supper, and built up the cookfire to a nice blaze afterward. In the interests of peace and harmony I broadcast a meal call to Imarte, and a moment later she actually emerged from the house.

"You prepared a meal?" she said in surprise.

"I know several recipes," I said. "Not that one can do a lot without olive oil."

"Goddess, that's true," she said, sounding astonished that we had found a common opinion. She made up for it by picking most of the chilies out of her dish, however, and flicking them into the dark. We sat there awhile in unpleasant silence, before she finally cleared her throat and spoke. "I believe I'll take the stage north tomorrow," she said.

"Really?" I asked. Where did she get off, leaving me with the responsibility of running the place? "You cleared it with Porfirio before he left, I suppose?"

"Oh, he knew I had a research trip to make," she said evasively. I just shrugged and kept eating. After a moment she gave up trying to keep her news to herself. "The contents of that valise contained the most incredible—"

"Is there any supper left?" asked Juan Bautista, appearing from the shadows. He was holding something bundled in his coat. I pretended not to notice as I ladled him a bowl of stew, but Imarte leaned forward and peered, frowning.

"Are you hiding something, child?"

"I'm—it's just a raven, that's all," he said. "She has a broken wing. I thought I could fix it with microsurgery. I seem to be pretty good at that."

She missed the bitterness of his last remark and sailed right on. "That's nice. Well, as I was saying, when I examined the contents of the valise—"

Juan Bautista's eyes widened with excitement. "Are you finally going to tell us what was in it? I've been wondering about that. Were there really, like, secret documents?"

"Incredibly secret," she said, her voice dropping to a dramatic whisper. "Lists of persons to be contacted, with their addresses. Communications from Judah Benjamin and John Bright. Letters of introduction. Documents pertaining to the Order of the Golden Circle.

Drafts on the Bank of England, without countersignature, amounts to be filled in at the discretion of the bearer. Two pasteboard tubes filled with golden sovereigns, sealed with stamped wax. Timetables, instructions, and letters in coded phrases.

"Several letters of a most incriminating nature between a person named Greathouse and several Canadian nationals, to say nothing of some *very* interesting overtures from the Prime Minister to Benito Juárez." She leaned forward after an impressive pause. "Last but certainly not least, letters referring to some technological discovery, made in a place designated only by code. All written in a lovely violet ink, chosen undoubtedly not for its color but for the remarkable chemical properties that enable it to vanish without a trace when exposed to water."

"Wow," said Juan Bautista. "All you'd have to do is dip a page in water to get rid of the evidence? I guess he really *was* an English spy."

"A conspirator, I think," Imarte said judiciously. "Not spy material, or he'd have been back for the valise by now. But thanks to some cross-referencing of available data, I now have important information about just who these conspirators are. I found an invaluable text entitled 'The Great Diamond Hoax.' It purports to be a firsthand narrative, by one Asbury Harpending, of the true circumstances of what will be known as the Chapman Piracy Case, which I gather is the name the San Francisco papers will give my pet conspiracy when it resoundingly fails."

"You mean, they'll be caught?" I asked, glancing over at the little black thing in Juan Bautista's coat, which had stirred feebly.

"In a matter of hours," Imarte said. "If only I'd found Harpending's narrative sooner. It would appear that quite shortly our dear Mr. Rubery and his Secessionist friends will be cooling their heels in prison, thanks to some astonishing errors of judgment. My theory is that their bungling will be due to the loss of the vital information in the valise. Of course the plot fails, but somehow the British will manage to cover their involvement completely. I must know how! You can see this is important, I trust? It's absolutely necessary that the Company have a qualified observer on the scene. One of the most concerted covert efforts by a foreign power to overthrow an American government in this century, and somehow it will be made to seem nothing more than a boyish prank, a footnote in a minor chapter in history."

"I certainly won't stop you," I said. "Go, by all means. Have a grand time. And bring us back a loaf of sourdough bread." A little more flip than the occasion called for, particularly as I thought her obsession sounded kind of interesting for once; but she always brought out my worst side.

She narrowed her eyes at me. A chilly silence fell. It was finally broken by Juan Bautista, who said, "I was wondering . . ."

"What?" I turned my attention back to him.

"Did the Company ever try the immortality process on animals?"

"There are stories," I said. "It almost works, but not quite. Animals can be made smarter, or nearly immortal, but not all the way and not as smart as us. I know for a fact it was done with one of the higher primates, but the program never went further than the prototype."

"So you could make an animal as smart as a mortal human?"

"Sure you could," I said. "But why would anyone want to? Mortals are unhappy enough with the brains they have. Why inflict self-awareness on an animal?"

He didn't answer. Shortly after that, he went to bed, carefully cradling the little black thing in his bundled coat. Imarte flounced off too, doubtless to pack her bag for her trip to San Francisco. I stayed up a while, looking at the stars. I could hear Juan Bautista playing his guitar in his room. It was the first time he'd touched it in days.

PART THREE

The Island Out There

27

MARCH 15, 1863. A day to remember, señors.

I woke early and was quite happy grinding coffee beans, grilling beef. I thought to myself that perhaps there was a future for me in the food service industry, if the Company had no further use for me as a botanist. Juan Bautista ate hurriedly and vanished into the brown wilderness, so I was the only one there to see Imarte off when she came out to meet the stagecoach, bag in hand. She was all tarted up again, hair curled and ink stains scrubbed away, corseted for action.

"I'm on my way," she said. "It's unlikely I'll return before the end of the month. Convey my apologies to Porfirio, but I'm certain he'll understand why this was necessary when I have a chance to explain it to him."

"Fine with me," I said. "Aren't you taking the secret valise, though?"

"No, of course not!" She shifted her bag to her other hand and leaned close to lower her voice, though we were the only living souls for a good six kilometers around. "That material is far too incriminating to carry abroad. I rather imagine some sort of effort will be made to recover it, so I've left it in plain sight in my room. Should any suspicious-looking persons call, let them take it. I've made a detailed copy of everything."

"We're not going to be visited by angry Union Army troops or police, are we?" I asked.

"A ridiculous idea. At this particular point in time my conspirators are blissfully unaware of any trouble brewing for them, and my research indicates that the attention of the law will be focused entirely on their activities in San Francisco. The fact that the conspirators also had a cabal in Los Angeles seems to have disappeared in the Historical Event Shadow," she said, glancing at her chronophase. "We're perfectly safe. Now, if you'll excuse me, I have a stagecoach to catch."

I watched her go sashaying down the trail, scarlet ribbons and curls bouncing, Immortal Babylon insatiably after a good time. The fact that her pleasure derived from history rather than from pretty boys made it no less delicious. A deeper and more subtle pleasure, no doubt. If there really are gods and goddesses, this must be how they amuse themselves, not with the pettiness of individual men but with the sins of nations, the follies of kings.

So I had the inn to myself. I wandered into the storeroom and poked through Porfirio's groceries. I found a cake of Theobromos and made off with the whole thing, luxuriating in a sense of selfishness. But wait, there was more: six months of back issues of *Punch* I'd never got around to reading, and nobody to complain about the way I folded them. I dug them out from under Porfirio's bed and settled in the kitchen, putting my feet up on a chair. Should I make myself another pot of coffee? Should I eat all the Theobromos now or save half for later? Maybe I'd eat a whole cone of piloncillo sugar too. Oh, the sins I could indulge in with nobody to see.

But even as I turned my attention to the latest nasty caricature of Abraham Lincoln, I picked up the signal of a mortal approaching. So much for blessed solitude.

I ignored it as long as I could, which wasn't very long. What the hell was this mortal doing? I set down the papers, got up, and went outside.

It was a male, very much in control of his thoughts and emotions, wary but not particularly afraid or even disturbed. No, he was concentrating intently on his activity of the moment, which seemed to be the covert surveillance of our humble establishment. I faded back into the doorway and scanned.

Yes, there he was on the ridgeline, a barely visible figure having a nice leisurely look at us through a pair of field glasses. They were all I could distinguish on visual alone. Infrared in broad daylight gave me a sketchy little scarlet ghost, but judging from the proportions, he was large. There were large animal readings, too; the man must have had a horse tethered just out of sight.

Over the next hour he worked his way around our canyon, studying us from all sides. I gave up and went indoors, deciding he was after the valise. He was welcome to it, as far as I was concerned. He didn't read like a mortal intent on violence, so I settled back in the kitchen, put my feet up again, and resumed my perusal of the British funny papers. I did make sure that my gun belt was fastened properly and my Navy revolver was loose in its holster, though.

Was he going to have his look and go sneakily away, leaving me in peace? No, damn it, here he was again, riding up the trail on horseback like a proper visitor. He was going to come to the door. I had him on audio now; there were the plodding hoofbeats of his horse; I could hear his breathing and his heartbeat. There was something unsettling about them. I eased my gun from its holster and held it concealed behind the copy of *Punch* I had been reading. I hoped I wouldn't have to blow a hole through that comic poem about highwaymen. He was a *very* large man, too. Would one bullet stop him?

"Hello? Is anyone here?" he called out.

And his words might have been a bullet through me, such an impact they had on this immortal body I wear, señors. I jerked as though I'd taken a hit, cursing silently and wondering whether I was having some sort of malfunction, some electronic seizure. My chair squeaked a good two inches backward. I did a self-diagnostic in the fraction of a second it took for the echo of his words to die away, but found nothing wrong.

The man heard the noise my chair made and was coming to the door. Angrily I got to my feet, holstering my weapon—why, I don't know—and tossing away the papers. Every defensive sense I had was activated. There, he had stepped through the doorway and halted, looking into the kitchen at me.

A big mortal indeed, absurdly so, even without the tall hat he was in the act of removing. He wore the tailored clothing of a Continental gentleman, in subtle tones of gray and brown that had just incidentally made him nearly impossible to see in the underbrush. You couldn't have told he'd been out there crawling around in the purple sage, though; not a wrinkle nor a stain on the man, not a single twig in his lank fair hair.

He was even wearing gloves; at least the hand that held the Spanish-English phrasebook was gloved. He was wearing a gun, too, though that was discreetly holstered under his left arm and would have been invisible to another mortal. He smiled at me with a great deal of charm and no little confidence. When he smiled, his pale-blue eyes narrowed and his high wide cheekbones seemed to slant upward, which made his long broken nose look longer.

He was, señors, the living image of the man I had last seen bound to a stake, screaming in flames, three centuries ago and half the world away. How could I not know him, my one and only lover? He had died in those flames, and my human heart had gone into the fire with

him and become the charred thing it was. But here he was now, he'd
smashed through the barrier of dreams and come to claim me in no
more hauntings but in living flesh. My doom had come upon me, as
the lady in the poem said.

"Please excuse me, señorita," he said in perfect Castilian Spanish.
He pretended to read from the phrasebook. "Is this the inn where one
may meet the coach to San Francisco?"

It was the same voice, too, that dark tenor of such power, such
beauty. When he'd preached to the avid spectators from the flames,
even they had been moved to tears.

I found myself perfectly calm. Well, I wasn't a mortal woman
who might have fainted or wept, was I? I was the same cyborg creature
who'd watched Nicholas Harpole die, and I knew he was dead, and
this man could not be my lover miraculously returned to me. "I speak
English, señor," I said.

"*Do* you?" he replied. "How very convenient for us both." His
smile widened, and the phrasebook disappeared into his pocket with a
single graceful movement. Dear God help me, he was an Englishman.
Not *my* Englishman, of course. I was going to be rational about this
if it killed me.

Who did I think he was, you ask? Give me more Theobromos,
and I'll tell you my friend Joseph's theory of genetic stability.

Thanks so much. Joseph calls it the English Character Actor Phenomenon. Have you ever had occasion to watch a lot of British cinema,
or look at British portraits or photographs? You may have noticed that
many of the faces are identical, though separated by decades or even
centuries. Compare a cast photo of the D'Oyly Carte company from
1885 with one from 1973, for example. Some of them could be the
same people, as immortal as we are. Of course they're not; and there's
no need to grope for a mystical reason to explain the resemblance,
either. It's a simple matter of genetics on a rather small island. There
are only so many faces, only so many physical types in that gene pool.
You can find the same sort of recurring appearances in other communities that tend to disapprove of marriage outside one's race.

Older operatives with countless lifetimes behind them—like Joseph, for example, whose theory this is—are always running into people who could be identical twins to mortals they knew centuries earlier.
I'm told one gets over the surprise fairly soon. Perhaps I would, too.

"By your leave, señorita," said the mortal man, holding my gaze
steadily as he stepped forward with a caution that indicated he'd noticed my weapon and taken my measure. "I believe we have acquaintances in common. I was informed at the Bella Union Hotel that there

was a well-spoken daughter of joy who kept a private house at this location. Have I the pleasure of her company?"

"No, señor," I said. "She is away. I do not expect her return for some days."

"Ah." He tilted his head a little to one side, considering me. "You are perhaps in her employ?"

I blinked at him. It actually took me a moment to realize that this magnificent stranger was asking me to have sex with him. He thought I was a whore, my long-lost beloved.

On the other hand, I had been celibate for just over three centuries now, and the nearness of his mortal flesh and the sound of his voice were more than I could bear.

Why not? Why deny myself this thing?

"Yes," I said.

"Very well," he said, drawing off his remaining glove and tucking it in his hat with the other one. "I trust you have the afternoon free? Where may we be undisturbed?"

I led him into Imarte's room without a word.

The light flickered over his eyes as he took in the dimensions of the room, rapidly noting placement of doors and windows, locking mechanisms, possible traps. He was *scanning*, señors, as ably as one of us, if without electronic assistance. He spotted the valise under Imarte's table—no change in his expression at all—and turned his attention to me with nothing but expectant and straightforward lust. Had I always been able to read him like this? But I was so young when I met my man, and so many years of hard living since then had sharpened my perceptions.

"What is your pleasure, señor?" I asked after an awkward pause. Wasn't that what whores said?

He drew his eyebrows together slightly. "Well, under the circumstances, I believe it's customary for one to undress," he said, just a hint of irony in that well-bred voice. Undress, right. I unbuckled my gun belt, and he held out his hand to take it. "Allow me."

He hung it over a chair, well out of my reach. I watched as he turned back to me, and our eyes met, acknowledging that he'd scored the first touch. He stepped back a pace to indicate that I should proceed.

So I took them off, the drab and convenient garments of my life, the long walking skirt with its slightly muddy hem, the plain dark blouse and bodice, the battered high-topped boots and threadbare black stockings. My lingerie was a disgrace, shabby gray cotton I'd mended with pack thread; but I had never expected to sleep with anyone again.

It just goes to show that you ought to invest in good underwear, because you never know, do you, when a long-dead lover will pop up and whisk you into bed. At least my flesh was presentable: to all appearances that of the same eighteen-year-old girl who'd loved the man in England. Immortality has that much consolation.

He watched me intently, and only when he'd seen that I had no other weapons concealed in any other possible place did the good red blood rise into his face, and a certain ready warmth into his eyes.

"Charming" was all he said; and setting down his hat and gloves, he shrugged out of his coat. There was his holster, for anyone to see, with a revolver snugly tucked away in it. He acknowledged my stare with a frank smile. "Lest one fall amongst thieves whilst traveling," he explained. He took it off and hung it on the chair next to mine, but rather closer to the bed. While removing his boots, he was able to get a good look under the bed and satisfy himself that nobody was lurking there. Off came his waistcoat with its watch in the little pocket, off came his flowing tie; and that was as undressed as he was going to get, except for letting his suspenders down and unbuttoning where necessary. What a pity; I wondered if the rest of him was eerily identical to Nicholas Harpole. What I could see as he unbuttoned was gorgeously the same.

We sank down on the counterpane together and, yes, if this wasn't the same man, there was something wildly wrong with the universe. He kissed like Nicholas, used his hands with the same masterful expertise, played my body like a rare instrument just as Nicholas had done, as though I were something beautiful.

There was only one moment of trouble, when an expression of amazement crossed his face, and he rose on his elbows and gave me a sharp wondering look; but the music was playing too sweetly to stop the dance now, and we went leaping on. I didn't try to guess what he was thinking. Would *you* have?

I won't describe the physical pleasure. You wouldn't believe it, señors. I don't know that I believed it myself. One moment the world had been the sad ordinary place I'd lived in for the better part of three centuries, and the next it had shattered and fallen away like an image painted on glass, a dreary illusion gone forever. If this day was possible, then angels might exist, fairies too, miracles and wonders, even a loving God.

I think we made love for hours. He was a determined sensualist, as perfect and as tireless as one of us, and seemed intent on exhausting me, which of course he couldn't do, except emotionally. A long while later, I lay weeping silently, curled against him. He leaned up on one elbow to regard me.

My God, the same dear face, flushed in the same way after his pleasure. His eyes were sharp and considering; and yet I could sense no desire to harm me, though I'd detected at least three more weapons concealed on his person during our lovemaking. What on earth was he, a professional assassin?

Well, why else would he be carrying all those weapons? He'd been sent for the valise, and I was the only witness.

This realization hit me like a thunderbolt, in the precise moment that he casually draped an arm over me and pulled me close again. Without apparent effort on his part I found myself caught against him, my arms securely pinioned and the weight of his big body holding me down. If I'd been a mortal woman, I couldn't have escaped. My heart raced all the same.

He looked into my eyes, probing for something. "That was delightful, my dear," he told me suavely. "But you're not a whore, are you?"

"No, señor," I said. "My apologies for the deception."

"You were in fact a virgin, were you not?" He sounded regretful, not for my lost innocence but because he was afraid there might have to be a death in this room, and he was sincerely hoping it wouldn't be necessary.

I stared. I couldn't tell him that if I seemed a virgin, it might be because I hadn't slept with anybody since March 1555. Did you know our bodily regeneration was that thorough? I hadn't known. "Yes, señor, I was," I answered.

He smiled slightly. "I don't flatter myself that my personal attractions led you to sacrifice something of such value to a young lady. Why, then, did you lie to me concerning your . . . vocation?"

What he intended to do next depended on my answer to that question. What was the right answer? No way to tell him the truth. At least I was in fair control of myself. Time was when even a mortal in a temper would have had me winking out in nervous terror. Killer apes, I'd called them; but this was a killer angel. You may think he was a monster, señors, prepared as he was to quietly kill a woman he'd just pleasured; but I tell you it maddened me with new desire, and isn't *that* monstrous? But who in the hell knows what's clean or unclean in love?

"I needed the money, señor," I lied, as frankly as I knew how. "Bereavement has left me a pauper, without refuge. In the past few days my situation has become desperate. The whore of this place is absent, I told you the truth of that; and when you came inquiring for her, it appeared that fate had placed a terrible opportunity before me. You seemed like a decent man, señor."

"Or at least a wealthy one?" He raised one eyebrow and studied me. His body was relaxing. "And this, then, was the occasion of your fall from grace? I trust you won't take offense if I observe that you don't seem suited for this occupation. Are you aware you never even set me a price, my dear? Pleasant as our dalliance was—and believe me, señorita, it was a pleasure indeed—I think this is not the life for you."

He was amused. He was deciding there was no need for unpleasantness. He wasn't through with me yet, though. Was I disappointed?

"What price ought I to have charged, señor?" I asked.

He smiled wryly. "The price of a good dowry in this backward country, or whatever donation the nearest convent requires to take in a novice. I believe I have a fair idea of the exchange rate at the present time. I'll leave that sum in gold; but you must promise me you'll use it for the one purpose or the other, as your inclination directs. Harlotry's a dangerous business."

He was a professional killer, and so far as he knew, I was a wretched nonentity he might just as easily have discarded, by one means or another. Instead he had opted to *do the decent thing*. Who was this man? Who sent him here, to this miserable place? Queen Victoria's Foreign Office?

"Thank you, señor" was all I could think to say.

He smiled again and kissed me, releasing my arms. "There's a good girl. Now, shall we seal the bargain with a toast? What wine or spirits does the resident strumpet keep here?" He rolled off me and sat up.

"There's aguardiente," I said.

"Your local brandy, yes. That'll do. Fetch us a bottle of the best and two glasses, and we'll drink to your future as an honest woman."

I hastened to obey, so readily that I was on my way back from the pantry with the bottle and glasses before I remembered that I was stark naked. He smiled engagingly at me as I scurried back to him where he lounged against the headboard of the bed. He was concealing something in one hand, however.

"Many thanks," he said, taking the bottle and one of the glasses. He poured a drink for me, dispensing a white powder into my glass as he did so with beautifully neat sleight of hand. It dissolved without a trace in the aguardiente. He handed me my glass and poured one for himself. "Back into bed, now. Climb under the blankets. There's rather a chill in the air."

There certainly was. I analyzed the contents of my glass, smiling ingenuously at him. Not poison, at least; something to make me sleep. Sleep while he did what? Made off with the valise, of course. What was I going to do now?

"To your good health and moral reclamation," he said, lifting his glass. I lifted mine too. He drank, but as soon as he saw that I wasn't drinking with him, his attention was fixed on me again.

"Perhaps you don't indulge in spirits, my dear?" he inquired, in a way as delicate as the perfect spring mechanism of a steel trap.

"Not often," I said, lowering my glass. I leaned affectionately on his right arm. "Never mind, señor. You know, it's only just occurred to me how you must have come to hear of this place. You must be a friend of Mr. Alfred Rubery."

Ha, that startled him. Nobody but a cyborg who was reading his pulse and skin conductivity could have told, however. His eyes narrowed in that dangerous smile.

"The young ass," he said. "Yes, he was quite taken with Madam Martha."

"I hope he was able to get back to his hotel safely? Really, señor, you'd have laughed if you were here to see it. A perfect farce! Except that he really was in danger of being shot by the jealous lover. He barely escaped with his clothing as it was. In fact . . ." I looked around the room as though searching, then pointed a finger at the valise as though I'd only just discovered it. "There it is, señor, that's Mr. Rubery's valise. He left it here in his haste. We expected he'd send for it, but ever so many days have passed. I assume he's afraid to come back here. Would you perhaps be so kind as to take it with you when you return to the Bella Union?"

"Anything to oblige a lady," he said, kissing my hand, all cozy gallantry, but there was a coldly inquiring look in his eyes. Had I overplayed the scene? Had I swung too quickly from vulnerable waif to cheerful servant girl? I rather think I had. He looked again at the glass I wasn't touching and sighed. I had given him a way to exit gracefully with the valise, but something about me rang false, and he couldn't afford to leave a loose end.

Damn. I do *not* interact gracefully with mortals. They can always tell.

"This is all quite pleasant," he said, getting his right arm free and sliding it around me snugly. "And may I say, my dear, that you speak

English beautifully? I am really quite astonished at your command of the language."

Oh dear.

"My mother was English," I temporized. It was happening again; three hundred years, and another tissue of lies to conceal what I truly was. Talk about déjà vu.

"Was she?" He had another sip of his aguardiente. "How did she come to be here, might one ask?"

How indeed. Pirates? Kidnapping? Shipwreck?

"She came in search of her brother," I said carefully. "He emigrated, you see, señor, first to America and then to Texas, when the Mexican government was inviting settlers to farm the land. He sent word that he had a fine farm and was prospering. Her parents died, and there had been some thievery by solicitors—what, I never knew precisely, but she was left nearly penniless. She wrote to her brother to expect her and spent the little she had inherited to buy passage to Texas."

He was nodding thoughtfully. Nothing improbably romantic, nothing that clashed with geographical or historical facts.

"Unfortunately," I continued, "it appeared that her brother had exaggerated his success. He had become, in fact, little more than a beggar. The New World had failed to reform the prodigal vices of his youth. His parents were well-born, you understand, small gentry of an old family, but not rich. Yet he lived as though he had a fortune to inherit, drinking and gambling. That was why he'd been obliged to emigrate in the first place." I monitored his reactions to my story. Was that all right, that little intimation of good bloodlines to appeal to his English snobbery? Yes, he was accepting it.

"So, she arrived in Texas and found that her brother was not only not prosperous but sitting in the village prison for vagrancy, and all her prospects were dashed forever. I am afraid she quite collapsed. Luckily, as she sat weeping in the street, she drew the attention of a gentleman who had come to Texas to see to some business affairs he had there. He was a kind and gallant man, and he rescued her from her plight.

"That man was my father, Don Rodrigo Mendoza. He was not a Mexican, you understand, señor, he was born in Old Spain, the youngest son of a house of ancient valor but no fortune. All his parents could procure for him was an officer's commission, and he made the best of it. He came with the army to New Spain and won a grant of land in Alta California from his king. After the Revolution he remained here; there was nothing in Europe to draw him back, and he had come to love this New World." There, a little more aristocratic ancestry, a father who was an officer and a gentleman. How was he taking that? He was still listening.

"My father was no longer a young man when he befriended my mother, but such was their love that he married her and brought her back to Alta California with him. They lived happily at his rancho near"—what was the most remote and unlikely spot I could think of?—"San Luis Obispo. I was born there, and they had no other children. I was educated in all that a lady of property need learn, and more, for my father had a great admiration for classical studies. I also had to learn what it is to manage an estate. We thought we would always be happy, but the coming of the Americans ruined my father's fortunes, and we lost our home." My Englishman was quite interested by that, to judge from his heart rate and respiration; but he merely made a sympathetic noise. I drew breath and went on.

"The shame killed him, señor. To be cheated out of what he had won with his sword, by shrewd Yankee traders. And my mother did not long survive him, such was her grief. I was left with the clothes on my back and a determination to live. For five years I have won my bread by honest means, cooking and cleaning for strangers; and if it was menial work that my own maids would have scorned to do, when I was a cosseted child, at least I had the satisfaction of knowing that I had never descended into another kind of shame." How was that playing? Pretty well. His pupils were dilated; always a sure sign he was moved about something.

At least, that had been true for Nicholas Harpole, who was not this man.

"Two years I have been the cook at this station, señor, and it has been enough to keep me. But times are hard, señor, surely you know that. The American war, the floods, and then the smallpox, and now the drought. Men run mad, and this land is dying. I have not been paid in weeks. Can you blame me for the despair that led me to this bed? The inn is nearly deserted now, and I fear it will be abandoned soon. Where shall I go then? How am I to live?"

There, I'd written myself a role to play. This was Hollywood, after all. Though the slight tremor in my voice was genuine. My fear and misery were real enough; if they could be made to convince this glorious stranger of my sincerity, so much the better. But had I convinced him?

Maybe.

He was excited about something I'd said, intrigued, not suspicious. His blood was racing. And now he turned to look down into my eyes, and there was a genuine emotion visible for a second behind the smooth opportunistic facade. Was it sympathy? Not love by a long shot, but a good start; and a damned sight better than the reluctant intent to kill me. Yes, we were coming along splendidly.

"Where will you go?" he said, taking my face in his fine strong hands and kissing me. "Why, wherever in this wide world you please, with such a brave heart. You've no need to sell yourself to strangers, my dear; you can make your own terms for a husband. If you once catch the eye of a man of property, your fortune's made, and he's a damned lucky fellow!"

Well, *that* rang false, though I doubt a mortal girl could have told. He wanted something from me. Some detail of my pathetic story had suggested an opportunity to him. What did I care? I loved the taste of his mouth.

"You are married, I suppose," I sighed.

"I? No. My line of work prevents that indulgence; travel, you know. And I'm no man of property, unfortunately. No, my dear, you can do better for yourself than me; but if you'll allow me to come to your assistance, I think there are certain measures that can be taken to ease your entry into better society." He looked deep into my eyes, and the fact that he had thought of a use for me didn't make his smile any less sincere. "Upon my word I do."

"I am in no position to refuse assistance, señor," I told him guardedly.

"No, poor child, and God knows that's none of your doing," he said, settling me gently into the pillows. How persuasive and silken his voice, and how nicely he smiled with that wide humorous mouth of his. "See here: I represent the interests of Imperial Export of London. My firm would pay handsomely for the exclusive rights to supply British manufactured goods to the inhabitants of this coast. That's not our main object, however. You may be aware that British textile industries have suffered from the American conflict. Cotton production in the Southern states (on which our mills depend) has come to a virtual halt, and the little that is being produced is blockaded. Meanwhile our researches indicate that the prevailing weather in this part of California would be ideal for cotton.

"At the present time, the vast pastoral ranchos of your childhood lie fallow and desolate, mortgaged to unscrupulous Yankee moneylenders, and the hereditary gentry of your people are impoverished—not merely by debt but also by the present drought, which has driven the price of cattle down so far as to ruin them. Your countrymen have exchanged independence for a dubious citizenship in a nation that despises them. How they must regret signing the treaty of Guadalupe Hidalgo," he said, not too theatrically, and had another sip of brandy.

"Assuredly they do," I said. "But what is to be done? Were we able to defend ourselves? Our cavalry was magnificent, señor, but we were something short on weapons. Perhaps before gold was discovered here we might have driven them out; after that, never in the world. The United States of America won't relinquish California willingly. We must resign ourselves to being a conquered people."

How intently he was listening to me. His face didn't show it, though, as he moved his hand idly along my thigh.

"And if this Civil War of theirs should alter the situation in your favor . . . ?"

"I try not to hope for anything these days, señor," I said, watching his hand. "Life is so uncertain."

"How very true. But consider what might happen if a benevolent interest were to buy up the debts of your countrymen. What if they found themselves once again in free and clear possession of their lands, with that same benevolent interest offering to lease their abundant acreage at handsome terms for a new industry?"

"The British want to grow cotton here, señor?" I asked, drawing my brows together. I was beginning to understand Imarte's blather about the fascination of secret history. "But . . . where would you get the workers, señor? Most of the Indian population has been wiped out. Who would pick this cotton?"

"Not Negro slaves, certainly," he said, smiling as his hand traveled. "But former slaves have a great deal of agricultural expertise, and if they were offered good wages for honest employment, I daresay many of them would find their way here. Irrigation would present a difficulty, but one easily surmounted by the best engineers an empire could provide. All this remains to be worked out. At the present time, my principal interest is in arranging to meet with the prominent rancheros of your father's race and determining whether they might be interested in Imperial Export's offer. I truly feel that such an arrangement would be in California's best interests.

"And," he continued, tracing the curve of my shoulder with a finger, "if I were to engage in negotiations with a representative of the displaced ruling class at my side, one who could advise me as to local customs and relationships . . . my chances of success would be greatly improved." Had his teeth always been that long? Yes, in that saturnine smile. I realized that it looked strange to me because I'd so seldom seen my poor godly Nicholas laugh. We'd been happy, though, at least at first . . .

"I don't know if I could be as much use to you as all that, señor," I felt obliged to say. "It's hardly as though I have the ear of Pio Pico. I'm a cook in a stagecoach inn, nothing more."

"But you know the land, you know the people," he said. "And you yourself are one of the deposed *gentes de razón*. Your experience with the Yankees is common to them all. Should they not be more readily disposed to listen to my offer of better treatment at British hands if you added your charming voice to mine?"

I smiled at him and stretched. "Am I to be your Malinche, señor? You know the story? She was born near Campeche, where your English pirates used to make so merry. Long before that time, however, the Aztecs enslaved her people and were exacting cruel tribute from them. One day Cortés came from the sea and offered to free her people. She became his interpreter, and led him into Aztec lands to overthrow her tribe's oppressors. Are you planning a revolution, señor?"

"Nothing so uncivilized." He took my hand and kissed the fingertips. "Surely there's been enough blood shed in this poor country. Wouldn't you like to live in a city where you could walk down the streets without fear of being shot? I can assure you, in her native land your mother had no need to wear a pistol. Order and safety and the rule of law, that's the blessing of a modern empire."

"That was what the Yankees promised us, too," I said lazily, tickling him. He arched his back and reached for my hair.

"Well, can one really expect better from Brother Jonathan?" He loosed the end of my long braid. "His nation of liberty was founded on the backs of Negro slaves and at the cost of exterminating the aborigines. As far as I can tell, the Yankee's idea of freedom is his right to carry a pistol with which he may shoot strangers in the street. No wonder his Union has crumbled. My expectation is that it will shortly expire of its own viciousness; and when that happens, California will have the chance to begin anew."

"Under Britain's guidance."

"Of course," he said, unraveling the serpentine twists of my braid.

It all seemed like a great idea to me, except for the fact that I knew it would never happen, thanks to whatever critical mistakes Mr. Rubery was even now in the act of making. All because he had set his valise down in the wrong spot. But why shouldn't I go along with it? What a splendid ride it would be, with this polished and dangerous mortal man, and who cared when it came to a stop? I had no idea what bizarre decision of God's had placed my lover in my arms again, in defiance of reason and death; but now that I had him back, damned if I would ever let him go again.

"Exigua pars est vitae quam nos vivimus," I said.

To my astonishment, he looked blank and then furrowed his brow. "Brief is that part of life ..." he translated haltingly.

"The part of life we actually live is too short," I said in English. I switched to the Latin in which I'd flirted with Nicholas Harpole centuries past. "What is this, young man, have you forgotten your grammar?"

In schoolboy Latin, with several pauses, he said, "The sword, when it is not drawn daily, rusts." He leaned back and looked at me, and there was that flicker of real feeling again for a second. Was it grudging respect I saw there? Maybe even the beginning of admiration? "You *have* had a classical education. And your memory is better than mine, I fear. Tell me, can you actually shoot with that pistol of yours?"

"To kill," I said.

What a gleam came into his eyes. I had him now, and he was determined to have me. My hair coiled in his fingers like snakes as he pulled my face close for a kiss.

"Madness, to leave you scrubbing pots for vaqueros," he murmured. "You'll have a house in London, if that's your pleasure, or rule a plantation here that would be the envy of some queens. I've the wherewithal to free you from this miserable life, my girl, if you'll accept my offer on Imperial Export's behalf. And consider the benefit to your countrymen, Señorita Mendoza. What, pray, is your Christian name?"

"Dolores," I said, because that was what I'd been using for the last few decades or so. Then I remembered that my mother was supposed to have been English. "Dolores Alice Elizabeth Mendoza."

"Delighted to make your acquaintance," he said. "Allow me to introduce myself. Edward Alton Bell-Fairfax."

"Charmed, Señor Bell-Fairfax." Dear God, what a Victorian name. It suited him, though. "I'd be lying if I told you your offer of financial assistance didn't attract me, and I seldom lie, señor," I said, and bit his lower lip gently. "But I rather imagine the Americans will have something to say about the Verdugos and the Picos signing lucrative contracts with a foreign power."

He took my untasted glass and set it atop the headboard. Rising to lean over me, he took my two hands in his own. "Let me make an analogy, if I may," he said. "I think of California as a beautiful girl, lost beyond the mountains. In her veins runs the mingled blood of the Latins, passionate and heroic, and the cooler blood of the pragmatic races. Now, she is nominally under the protection of her two step-brothers, the lantern-jawed gentlemen Jonathan"—he took my left hand and stretched it out above my head—"and Sam"—he took my right hand and stretched it out too, and lowered his face inches from mine. He went on. "But they have not dealt with her in a brotherly fashion, have in fact spent her inheritance recklessly. This would be bad enough; but Jonathan and Sam are now locked in a fratricidal struggle, tumbling perhaps to their destruction. And what of the lovely California?"

What indeed, I wondered, as our lips met in a fierce kiss. He rose on his elbows again. "Who will defend her? For she must be defended. Cruel eyes watch from the howling wasteland and plot her ravishment. To the south is the French beast, and his contemptible lackey the Austrian." He raised one hand and brought it down, down, threatening my left breast. "What they have planned for the fair maiden is too terrible to be imagined, except in the mind of a lascivious Frenchman. And what is this to the north?" He lifted his other hand and poised it over my right breast. "Dimly seen on the horizon, shambling down from the region of ice and snow where he is monarch, the Russian bear. What is his intention? What has it ever been, my dear, but rape and pillage?

"Who will defend her from them?" he said, leaning down to me, laughter glinting in his wicked eyes. "She cannot flee to the east— savages bar the way, and Mormons, only too eager to seize her. She cannot flee to the west, either. But she has one friend, I assure you, one stout friend who will rise to help her, who will bring her peace and contentment, who will look after her best interests, and invest her dowry wisely. And that stalwart stands ready to crown her with the wealth of a prosperous empire, if only she will raise her eyes to him."

We embraced. In the subsequent tumult the brandy glass was knocked from its place on the headboard, and it fell behind the bed and shattered, so the sweet narcotic spilled out. And the whole time, I swear to you, a little brass band was playing "Rule Britannia" in the air just above our frantic bodies.

And that was how I became a double agent, señors, a spy in the pay of Her Britannic Majesty. And, you know something? I'm not sorry. I wish it *had* worked out. Would Lower Canada have been so bad, really? But the laws of nations count for nothing, in the end. The only law that matters is the one that states that history cannot be changed.

28

W<small>E DECIDED</small> I should accompany him back into Los Angeles, where Mr. Edward Alton Bell-Fairfax had some correspondence to look to, since he had only just arrived yesterday from Veracruz. Then the first order of business would be to find me some clothing suitable to my role as Imperial Export's cultural liaison. Following that, we would make a brief sea voyage across the channel to Catalina Island. It seemed that there were some other representatives of Imperial Export on the island, doing scientific research for possible investment proposals. They had made quite a comfortable camp there, away from the gunfire and generally insalubrious air of Los Diablos. Perhaps we might stay over there a few days, while we planned a strategy for gaining the support of the rancheros.

Once we had managed to pry ourselves apart, I got dressed first and went out to leave a note on the credenza in my room. This also gave Edward a discreet opportunity to go through the valise and make sure that all its contents were as they ought to be. I realized with a start that we'd been in bed a lot longer than I'd imagined; the sun had already dipped down behind the ridge. That surprise was minor compared to my shock at encountering Juan Bautista, coming down the canyon with a couple of wicker cages. He seemed like a ghost, so unreal had my former life become in the last few hours.

He stopped and stared at me, openmouthed. "Is something wrong? You look different."

"Nothing's wrong," I said. "But I'm going into the field for a while myself. I may not be back any time soon. Let the others know everything's okay." After all, if Imarte could do it, why couldn't I? But

Juan Bautista had noticed Edward's horse, and was lifting his head and scanning.

"Who's the mortal?" he said. "And—hey! Who's going to fix dinner tonight?"

"Fix your own damned dinner," I snapped. "Look, you know that special research Imarte's doing? About the English? Well, tell her I'm following up a lead for her. Tell her I'll bring her back some invaluable first-person narratives."

"But you're a botanist," he said.

"Have you noticed there are no plants left to study around here? I'm making myself useful, that's all. And if you want to do the same, why don't you go saddle me a horse?" I said, putting every ounce of authority I had into the request. He nodded meekly and set down his cages, hurrying off to obey. And it seemed to me, señors, that my reason was a perfectly valid one. I was indeed contributing to another operative's research. Perhaps even you would have accepted that as an excuse. If only the rest hadn't happened.

Edward emerged from the inn, fully dressed, hat in one hand and valise in the other. He had to duck to avoid the top of the doorway. "With whom were you speaking, Señorita Mendoza?" he asked politely.

"The stable boy. Only an Indian, señor, and he knows nothing," I said. "He's fetching me a horse."

"Good," he said, and set his hat on his head, which made him nearly seven feet tall. Just like Nicholas. The extraordinary height must have been something of a disadvantage for a spy. He went to fasten the valise securely into a saddlebag. When he had made fast the buckles and straps, he vaulted easily into the saddle and sat, reins in one gloved hand, waiting as Juan Bautista led out my horse. It took me a moment to notice Juan Bautista standing there helpfully, ready to give me a foot up onto my own mount.

Edward Alton Bell-Fairfax looked like a god in the saddle. I had a moment of lurching terror as I realized how much I loved this man, whoever he was. His long-ago death had blasted my immortal life. What would it do to me, if it should happen again?

But this wasn't the same man, was it? He was certainly no saint and martyr, as my Nicholas had been. Subtle, politic, quite capable of a double cross, I should think, and certainly of cold-blooded murder if duty required it. He hadn't expressed any religious opinions, and I'd be willing to bet he had none, to be in his line of work. Could I be happy with this man?

I was insanely happy.

And that is, finally, the only reason I can give you for why I swung into the saddle, snarled, "There's cold beef in the pantry" to Juan Bautista in Spanish, and rode away with Edward Alton Bell-Fairfax.

We went at a swift canter through the slanting red sunlight, toward the place that would one day be black towers blighting the sky but for now was only the adobe sprawl I'd come to loathe so much. We were shot at only twice, and both times Edward sent off a lead riposte with a speed that was breathtaking, for a mortal. We made such good time that the sun was setting as we rode down Calle Principal.

Edward made for the telegraph office while I waited in the saddle. He emerged with a communication he'd received on flimsy paper. I read it upside down without his noticing.

E. A. BELL-FAIRFAX, REP. IMPERIAL EXPORT CO.
YOURS OF 14TH REC'D 11:P.M. BEST REGARDS FROM
GOLDEN GATE. SUCCESSFULLY RECOVERED FROM LA
GRIPPE AND LOOK FORWARD TO PROFITABLE
VENTURE WITH CHAPMAN. A. RUBERY, SALES MGR.

Edward exhaled angrily, but there was a certain satisfaction in his eyes as he mounted again, and we ventured once more into the mean streets.

"Good news, señor?" I asked.

"Tolerably good," he said. "It seems my young idiot of a friend has managed to succeed in his affairs, against my expectations. Alfred never had much head for business. Privilege tends to soften the brain, or so I've observed."

I reflected on that opinion. "I should have thought *you* were a member of the privileged classes, señor."

"Hardly, my dear. My ancestry's good enough; but will you understand if I explain that my birth represented a certain inconvenience for my parents? I trust that won't dismay you. My upbringing was discreetly anonymous, and my inheritance is nil. So I've had to shift for myself rather. Another reason I'm not a suitable husband, by the way," he added slyly. My God, that was Nicholas to the life, that trick of talking out of the side of his mouth when he was being ironical.

"Señor, your excellent qualities outweigh any consideration of clerical sanction," I said with an airy wave of my hand. He was grinning, about to answer, when his expression suddenly changed, became ice-cold. I followed his gaze but could see nothing except a pair of men hurrying into the Bella Union Hotel down the street. That was our destination too. Yet now Edward pulled abruptly on his horse's reins and spurred down a side street. I followed silently. A few more streets over, and he turned in his saddle to address me.

All the easy warmth of the day's pleasure had gone, with all the high color from his face. There was a look of strain in his eyes, though his voice was composed when he spoke.

"My dear, I'm afraid there's been a change of plan. Regrettable, but it can't be helped. There were two gentlemen entering the Bella Union just now—perhaps you saw them? I know them, unfortunately, and their presence indicates that they know I'm here. It would appear our friend Mr. Rubery made a few more blunders than I thought. Please accept this as a token of my esteem." He reached into his saddlebag and drew out a small leather pouch. He passed it to me over my horse's neck; it was heavy for its size. "That should enable you to find a more hospitable corner of the world in which to live. I believe you're clever enough to see that my presence shall shortly be a very dangerous place indeed, so I'd advise you to ride, and quickly."

"Not in this life, señor," I said in a low voice, leaning forward in the saddle. "I know the country, as you said, and I think you need a swift way out of here. You can't go back to the Bella Union. Will those men think to look for you at the stagecoach inn when you fail to return to your room?"

"Possibly," he said. "I must assume they've already discovered certain things. You're owed an explanation. You'll have it if you can get us both out of here alive."

"Follow," I said, and urged my horse forward. He followed, to my relief, and I immediately accessed a detailed street map. There was a narrow alley that ran along the base of the long low hill, and we made for that and galloped its length, behind its houses out of town. We encountered nobody but a dead man; our mounts slowed to pick their delicate way over him where he lay staring placidly at the new stars, and we sped on as the twilight deepened.

So back toward Hollywood, but not the way we'd come. I found us a route over torn earth, where cattle and vaqueros had passed in the dozens, and widened my scanning range to eight kilometers. Nobody was following us; nobody was lying in wait for us. The people whose delight it was to lie in the underbrush and take potshots at passersby were evidently on their dinner breaks. So far, so good. We made a wide turn, avoiding Cahuenga Pass, and rode for a winding canyon about a mile west of it.

About a kilometer in, there was a great branching sycamore tree near a spring that bubbled out of the sand, and we reined in under the shadows there. The tree was occasionally used to hang thieves, and so local residents tended to avoid the area after dark. "Well, Señor Bell-Fairfax?" I said.

"Well, Señorita Mendoza," he said. "You were indeed correct in your assumption that what's left of the Yankee government wouldn't approve of our plans for profitable trade with the locals. Apparently certain agents in the employ of Mr. Allan Pinkerton have got wind of something, doubtless thanks to Mr. Rubery's lack of discretion."

So this was how it had failed? "The game is over, then, señor?" I asked, hoping we'd make the best of a bad business and get out of the heat.

"By no means," he said, "since we were able to escape with our lives. Our proposal for your countrymen will simply be delayed, and they may be even more willing to listen by that time. If you're still game, of course?"

"I am." Though I didn't like his persistence in the face of danger. Better to give it up, go home, live to spy another day. "What about getting over to Catalina Island?"

"Hm. That's compromised now. I had engaged a reliable fellow to take me across tomorrow evening, but if my room has been searched, I daresay he'll be watched." He looked thoughtful in the darkness, but the color had returned to his face. After a moment he turned, surveying the night. He couldn't have been able to see anything; to a mortal the black shadow would have been complete and impenetrable. "I'm afraid I must impose on your bravery and your hospitality a while longer, my dear. I'd like to move on. We need a secure retreat with a decent view of the surrounding countryside. Do you know of any such?"

"I think I know a place," I said, and we rode on up the canyon.

It twisted steeply for a few miles, and we followed a sandy creek bed under black avenues of trees. There was no water there now, but cool air currents flowed past our faces in the darkness until we emerged, riding straight uphill toward rimrock. To one side below us a splendid view of the plain opened out, and there was a tiny cluster of yellow lights to show us where the village of Sherman slept. I wondered if Señora Berreyesa had survived the smallpox. What a lifetime ago that had been.

We stopped climbing and made our way north through the hilltops, keeping well below the rimrock, and our horses picked their way carefully through black sliding piles of scree. I found a trail to take us around and down, until we emerged on another view: the San Fernando Valley lying vast and silent in the darkness. There below us was the northern end of Cahuenga Pass, beyond was the gigantic wall of Mount Hollywood, and far, far out on the valley floor was the tumbled ruin of what had been Mission San Fernando, its graceful arcade broken open to the stars. Not that a mortal could have made it out at that distance. I remembered chatting with a friar in its tidy mission garden, once, and felt a pang of loneliness.

"My compliments," whispered Edward beside me. "A fine panoramic view. All we need is a defensible spot." How could he tell there was a fine panoramic view? I was seeing it by infrared, but he was a mortal man.

"Up here," I murmured, gesturing to a small steep hill like a turret that was crowned with a stand of trees. We rode up into the cover they provided. On the other side of the hill was a little terrace, wooded and dropping to a rocky saddleback ridge. To either edge the land fell sharply away in deep canyons. Below us, nearly invisible in the night and the trees, was a rough square of leaning wooden huts.

"You want a defensible spot?" I said to Edward. "This was one of Fremont's outposts. It's been abandoned for years. Nobody for miles but Cielo the farmer, and he won't be able to see us from his house."

Edward nodded.

I let him reconnoiter while I gathered wood for a fire. I'd told him the literal truth, we really were the only people for kilometers except for Mr. Cielo; so he returned satisfied as to our security. The largest of the buildings had a crude stone hearth, and I cleared it enough to start a small fire. No furniture left, but at least the creaking plank floor was dry. Edward saw to our horses and then came in and sat down beside me, carrying the saddlebag. He pulled out his watch and looked at it.

"Twenty-four hours," he said, with some satisfaction.

"Is that significant, señor?" I asked.

"Yes, I think so," he said, closing the watch and slipping it back into his waistcoat pocket. Without explaining further, he took out the valise and opened it. "I daresay you examined the contents of this whilst it was left at your inn?"

"No, señor," I said truthfully. "But I'm fairly sure Martha went through it."

"Yes, I'd gathered someone had. Damn." He looked up as an idea struck him. "Where has that intriguing lady got to, by the way? You said she was gone; where did she go?"

"San Francisco," I answered.

He stopped in the act of taking out the neat little stoppered bottle of violet ink. "When?" he said in a voice too calm.

"Just this morning, señor," I said. "If you'd arrived two hours earlier, you'd have met her."

He relaxed visibly, but his expression was still grim.

"Now, I wonder," he said, pulling a pen from an inner pocket and removing the cap that protected the nib. "I wonder how well you're acquainted with the lady."

"Quite well, señor."

"She had rather a reputation at the Bella Union as a sympathizer with the Secessionist cause, and was reputed to have had a particular fondness for Britons. I assume this was how Mr. Rubery chanced to be enjoying her favors at the moment her jealous friend stepped on-stage." He pulled out a sheaf of papers, half sheets that appeared to be printed in the same violet ink, and thumbed through them carefully. "Was the lady what she seemed to be, in your opinion?"

"I don't think she's a Federal spy, señor. I think she serves her own interests, like most whores."

"Yet she made no attempt to pilfer the contents of this valise." He held up the sheaf. "These are drafts on the Bank of England; useless without a countersignature, but a dedicated thief would attempt to forge one. And there's a considerable sum in coin as well, but apart from prising up the seal to look at it, she left that quite untouched. She may also have read through certain other papers here, the idea of which is rather unsettling." He rested the valise on his knee to use as a writing surface. Dipping his pen in the violet ink, he selected a draft and filled out an amount. He signed it with a flourish and carefully put his pen back in his inner breast pocket. "I put the question to you: having examined these things, what was the lady's object in departing for San Francisco this morning?"

"She didn't say," I lied, looking thoughtful. "If she was intending to betray your cause, I should imagine she'd have taken the valise straight to Fort Drum down here. Would she have learned from the papers that your friend was now in San Francisco?"

"Yes," he said, waving the check in the air to dry it.

"Well, then, perhaps she's gone up there to blackmail him. That might explain why she left the valise."

"It might well." He stared into the fire. "In which case, we have nothing to fear from that quarter, at least at present."

"We haven't?"

"No," he said. Groping with his free hand, he pulled a kind of envelope of oilcloth out of the valise. It was exactly big enough for a half sheet. He tucked the check inside and handed it to me. "There, my dear. Less immediately negotiable than the gold, but if we should be separated, this will get you to London, where you'll find you have friends. Take care not to get it wet; even perspiration is enough to make that ink vanish like a dream."

"You're too generous, señor," I said, opening it to peer at the amount. My jaw dropped. I had to read twice before I was sure. I looked at him in confusion. "Señor! That's—it is too much."

He gave a brief shake of his head, putting away the contents of the valise. "You may well earn it before this business is done. Let me tell you honestly that your life may stand at hazard, Señorita Mendoza. I shall certainly think no less of you if you wish to withdraw at this point and travel elsewhere. Indeed, I'm obliged to tell you it's in your best interests to do so at once. The money's yours, regardless." He reached back into the saddlebag and brought out a small box.

"This is more than a matter of trade, isn't it?" I said.

Edward looked at me for a long moment before he answered. "It is a game of nations," he said. He drew his gun from its holster and opened the box, which contained small tools, ammunition, and a chamois cloth. Methodically he removed the remaining bullets from his gun and began to clean it.

I watched him awhile before I spoke again. "I suspected as much. Well. Señor, I will not leave you. This involves my honor, after all."

He was shaking his head. "That won't do, my dear. Marriage is really not—"

"You mistake my meaning," I said. "You are a stranger in my country, and you have shown me kindness, and now our common enemies hunt for you. I will not leave your side, señor, while I can be of use to you. That's my honor, and I won't surrender it." Only lines spoken by the character I was playing; but I meant them all the same.

Real emotion in his eyes again, before the cold businesslike look returned. What kind of man lay behind the role *he* was playing? "Señorita, you do credit to your father's sword," he said. "By God, I hope we can win through to London."

"What are our chances?" I settled back, hoping he couldn't hear the way my heart was pounding.

He took up his gun again and spun the empty cylinders. "Not poor, I think," he said, reloading. Oh, his heart was pounding too. "If we can avoid capture for another day or so, and if we can get across to Santa Catalina Island, we'll do very well indeed. The difficulty will be finding a vessel to take us."

I remembered Señor Souza and his dark house on its pilings.

"I can manage that, señor," I said. "I know a fisherman with a house on the slough, below the old landing place."

"His name?" Edward gave the weapon a final inspection and returned it to its holster.

"Souza. A Portuguese gentleman. There was a doctor who resided at the inn for a while, to whom he's indebted. I'll call in a favor on his behalf."

"Can you?" Edward said, putting away the box. He leaned back and stretched out his long legs. "Then we'll hope for the best and prepare for the worst, and God defend the right."

Flames were dancing in his eyes. Flames running up his shirt, sputtering in his fair hair, Nicholas had stared at me until the agony broke his concentration . . .

I had to close my eyes and draw a deep breath. When I opened them, Edward was sitting forward and frowning at me. "Are you well, señorita?" he asked.

I stared at him. "Do you believe in God, señor?"

He looked disconcerted. "I suppose so," he said at length. "Certainly religion is a civilizing influence, if it's not taken too far. I imagine you're a Roman Catholic?"

"I was born one," I said, which was the truth.

"I won't offend you, then. But I think we can agree that zealots of any persuasion do a great deal of harm. All the same, men need commandments of some kind."

"Do you think there's a true religion?"

"Do I? Yes, the C. of E., I suppose. But if I were a Hottentot, I'd tell you that my great wooden idol was better than anyone else's. I doubt that distinct creeds matter much, so long as civilized behavior is observed." He looked at me askance. "Is the matter of doctrine very important to you, my dear?"

No, this man wasn't one to die for his God, and I'd have to remember to thank God for it, next time I believed in Him. I wasn't sure I didn't believe in Him right now. Could my lover have been reconstituted *without* the faith that had killed him?

In my relief I stammered, "Not to me, señor, but I feared it might matter to you." I drew breath and temporized. "My mother owned an English book about Protestant martyrs, *Foxe's Acts and Monuments*. You understand, she became a Catholic when she married my father, but since this book had been given to her as a girl, she kept it for sentiment's sake. Well, I read it when I was learning to read English, and what a terrible business. Such hatred the Catholics and Protestants felt for each other! So I drew the conclusion that Englishmen might feel strongly on the matter even now."

"And many do," he admitted. "But that was three centuries ago.

If all nations brooded interminably on old scores, there'd never be an end to the vengeance. Most of the Catholics I've known have been reasonably decent chaps. A certain amount of tolerance is essential to civilized behavior. Barbarity is the force to be fought, not differences of dogma. Wouldn't you agree?"

"Yes!" How direct, how enlightened. Nicholas's intellect and humanity, everything I'd adored in him, without his late medieval prejudices.

Possibly encouraged by my enthralled look, Edward continued: "Religion has its place, certainly, in reinforcing ethical behavior amongst the masses, but any sufficiently enlightened secular laws will have the same effect. After all, most of the creeds of the world have essentially the same purpose, have they not? To enjoin men to be what we call moral, which is to say *civilized*. A civilized man obeys the rule of law, he acknowledges that he must not injure his neighbors, and if injured by them, he must appeal to law for satisfaction rather than indulge in burning their houses over their heads as they sleep. Civilization is the ideal for which we strive, with so little perceptible success; yet we do succeed, in inches and over years.

"Consider." He sat forward, resting his elbows on his knees, and the intensity of his eyes made my heart flame. "What was Britain when the Romans found her? A wilderness of howling savages. And Rome, a thousand times more civilized, yet was so barbaric, she held spectacles of slaughter for her citizens, and her rulers were guilty of the most hideous crimes.

"Still, the Pax Romana tamed the wilderness, taught the savages, and, as imperfect as she was, Rome sent the idea of civilization working throughout the world. Even her fall into decadence could not stay the forces she had set in motion."

"Other people were what we'd call civilized, before Rome," I said with effort. His voice was so magnificent, I hated to interrupt him.

"Certainly. The Greeks, in fact, were more so. They lacked, however, Rome's peculiar genius at organization and her insistence that civilization be spread. That, in my opinion, was Rome's great contribution to the world, and that is the inheritance she passed on to Britain: the moral imperative to bring the rule of law to barbarians, through the operative mechanisms of empire." He moved closer to me. There was a purpose to all this, of course: he wanted to win me to his government's side. But look how his eyes glowed. All the easy, deceitful charm had fallen away, and passionate conviction was shining out of them like light.

"That is the cause in which I labor. What force can bring the greatest good to the greatest number of men? Only the modern empire, with its constitution to guarantee their individual rights, and its power to bring them prosperity. A missionary may persuade a painted savage to worship a cross rather than an idol; but he will not make laws that send that savage's children to school, where they might learn to make the desert they inhabit another Eden by means of the advanced sciences. He may persuade his flock to love one another for his God's sake, but he'll invariably urge them to slaughter any neighboring tribe that still worships stone idols. This is the failure of religion as a force for the common welfare," he said.

"Señor, you have the truth of it," I said from my heart. How had Victorian England brought forth a man like this? "And surely this is the way to a better world, is it not, this secular enlightenment? Even the Americans have deduced this, with their separation of church and state."

"Ah, the Yankees." He sneered elegantly. "What have they achieved but violent chaos? And I'll tell you why, my dear. Liberty (as they conceive of it) and loyalty are opposing concepts. Having rebelled against the hereditary ruler who was the embodiment of their nation, to what will they be loyal? Their flag? But see what has happened now: half the nation, asserting its liberty to keep slaves, has rebelled and taken up arms to defend that liberty. It won't end there, either, you know. Any brute will demand his right to be a law unto himself, beating his wife and his children as he pleases, and defend that right with his father's rifle and think himself a patriot." He used his big hands so well when he spoke, with graceful economical gestures to make his point.

"The difficulty, I think, is that liberty is too abstract an idea for human nature to grasp. It is too easily twisted into lawlessness, as has happened in America. Most men are incapable of reverencing a mere principle; that principle must be embodied in a living person to effectively hold their allegiance. This is where empire inspires, and democracy fails in inspiration: love of one's monarch."

What a spell he was weaving, jarred only by my mental image of dumpy little Victoria and her priggish prince. No, I certainly couldn't agree with him on that one. But he swept on and took my breath away by saying:

"Mind you, royals and their attendant baggage of toadies, cretins, and thieves are seldom an inspiring lot in and of themselves, but in a constitutional commonwealth they need not be. I believe that my sovereign has deplorable taste in art, is devoid of much talent to rule, and certainly couldn't compete with Venus for beauty. But she in her person is the empire personified, the driving force of civilization, and as such I serve her, reverence her, and will, when necessity commands, die for her."

The wickedly confidential way in which he said this was so delightful that it took a moment for the last part to sink in on me.

"I trust, señor, you've no intention of dying soon," I said.

His eyes narrowed, and he shrugged. "No intention at all. But my occupation carries that risk, always. I imagine I came rather close to the awful specter this evening. Certainly I'd hate to lose my life as the result of some fool's incompetence. Should there come a time, however, when my death would serve the purpose of empire, then I hope I will die without hesitation. As the bard of Avon says, 'Live we how we can, yet die we must.' And that being the inevitable case, one can at least have the satisfaction of accomplishing something with one's death."

It has probably already occurred to you, señors, but it was only at that moment that I realized that this *was* the same man I had loved. He had exactly the same inner drive that had got him burned at the stake; only the focus of his devotion had shifted. As I stared at him in horror, he leaned back and went on:

"I don't imagine I'd much care to live to decrepit old age, to tell you the truth. End one's days being pushed about in a bath chair? Not for me. Better a brief life lived intensely, with a keen appreciation of its pleasures." He gave me a meaningful smile. "It's no more than the bargain soldiers make, after all, self-sacrifice for the greater good."

He was the perfect operative. Brilliant intellect, no life of his own, utterly focused on his duty to make the world a better place, thoroughly convinced that his masters were wise and good. He was just what I was supposed to be.

"But—isn't human sacrifice one of the barbarisms you're working to put an end to?" I protested, rising up on my knees. "Whether willing or unwilling? And how can you *know*, señor, that your death will really have accomplished anything? Secrets of espionage are the most transitory. And who can ever say how history will play out? Consider, consider those same English martyrs!"

I felt my voice shaking and tried desperately to control it, but everything I'd wanted to say to him for three hundred years came howling up from my heart. "They let themselves be burned in droves, señor, and for what? They died for *nothing*. If they'd only kept their mouths shut and lain low, they'd have lived to see a better day, because in short order Bloody Mary died and Elizabeth succeeded her, and restored their stupid Protestant faith to power. So how can you know, señor, that you wouldn't be throwing your life away, that you wouldn't serve your cause better as a living man?"

Was I convincing him, señors? No, I was only arousing him. He found the throb of my voice, the firelight on my hair, and the angry blood in my cheeks exciting. But he did make an effort to reply seriously rather than simply grab me and pull me down.

"I am astonished at how well you know English history, my dear," he said. "Granting your point—without foreknowledge of history, what else could those Protestant heroes have done? Nor can you say with real certainty that their deaths accomplished nothing. If they hadn't died as bravely as they did, if they had not so publicly denounced Mary's tyranny, might not her husband Philip of Spain have been emboldened to seize the crown after her death? Setting aside the immediate salvation that martyrdom is reputed to confer on the martyr." His eyes glinted, reflecting fire.

How could I tell him that *I* had known how history was going to play out, and I'd failed to save him, even so? He continued:

"The instinct to preserve life is natural for your sex, my dear; it's a fine and appropriate womanly inclination. And when the ideal is reached at last and the world is civilized, I trust there shall be no more need of martyrs to die in any cause. At present, however, we live in a world that requires certain regrettable actions in order to bring about the better world we desire. I myself have been required to commit crimes, to do things I would certainly rather have avoided. And when my blood must be shed to atone for those acts, then at least I'll face oblivion with a clean score. It works out, you see."

"In the minds of wicked old men who make governments, it works out," I said in despair. "They know they can always count on a ready supply of brave men who'll die for a cause, like you, and so they continue to wage wars and spend lives to keep themselves in power. But if all the heroes refused to play that great game, what then, señor? If the nations had no means of waging war on one another, wouldn't they be obliged to find some more civilized means of settling their differences?"

I thought he wasn't listening to me, so hungry were his eyes. Even now he was moving forward with one hand out to wind it in my hair and pull my face close to his. He kissed greedily, but when we came up for air he growled:

"No, my dear, they wouldn't. Come, come, do you suppose the politicians are the only ones responsible for wars? When one shepherd will steal his neighbor's flock, when one child will pick up a stone to fling at a child from the next village over? Things are by no means so simply drawn as you imagine, and the causes of war are far too complicated to gloss over with a pacifist cliché."

He bore me backward, and we wrestled as he very adroitly unbuttoned and unhooked. "If all the statesmen in the world signed a universal peace tomorrow, some spiteful fool would find a way to bare his bum at his former enemies, and the whole misery would begin all over again. It will take a great deal more subtle work, over a much longer period of time, to bring peace to the world."

And of course he was right about that, and I *had* used a pacifist cliché. Really, what other man could argue like that while in the throes of carnal passion? Only one I'd ever known, a long time ago in a land far away.

Edward put his face close to mine and looked into my eyes, and I was so spellbound by his gaze and the music of his voice, I very nearly missed the meaning of his words, which would have been a pity, because it was extraordinary.

"And *when* there is peace at last, and *when* men are no longer distracted by the ravages of war and crime, then the real work begins. Mankind has grasped at science and invention to improve his lot; when he truly understands that he can wield those tools to improve *himself*, he will lay the cornerstone of the earthly paradise," Edward said. "What might not science achieve, in a world where a nation's resources weren't continually drained by strife? What if that nation made a remarkable discovery, one that gave new meaning to old legends of a golden age? What if it were possible to utterly change the human condition? What if it were possible to put an end forever to disease? To age? To death itself? And where will men ever make those discoveries but in a stable and peaceful empire?"

How did he know? Was the man a bloody prophet? How could he foresee so clearly what the future would hold once the Company was founded? And how the hell could he prophesy so, with our hearts thundering against each other and our bodies locked in the most intimate embrace? I didn't know, I had never known, but just so had my lover spoken three centuries before. And now as then, I fled from the meaning of his words and lost myself in the worship of his magnificent mortal flesh.

So we burned together beside that little fire, in the leaning ruin of Fremont's outpost, and the shades of Manifest Destiny and Imperialism looked on with sardonic smiles. If the flames had risen and consumed us in each other's arms, señors, we'd have felt no pain. If only we were lying there now, our quiet ashes mingled together!

*   *   *

I opened my eyes and saw him, in the chilly morning light. For a moment I thought I was lying in a garret room in England, awake at last after a nightmare of terrible sorrow and interminable length. But no, this was my new lover, who by an amazing coincidence was identical in every respect to Nicholas. Limited gene pool indeed! I had never once in all the intervening centuries met another mortal with his face. He wasn't conventionally handsome, with that broken nose and that wide mouth; but the combination of features that would have made another man a leering gargoyle were elegant in Edward-who-had-been-Nicholas. Part of the trick was the way he used his face, the responsive liveliness of expression, the movement of his eyes. He fascinated, he charmed, he *moved* well, and one never realized that the big man didn't quite look human—something odd in the angle of the cheekbones, in the way the head sat on the powerful neck. But he hid his strangeness far better than I, who looked human.

It was going to be tricky keeping him alive and safe, in his line of work, but I could do it, if I stayed by him the rest of his life. How to manage that? I'd find some way. Porfirio had his pet mortals, didn't he? The Company let him go to them, stay with them, help them when they needed his help. All I'd need do is learn clever makeup skills, appear to age with Edward as he aged.

Full body appliance makeup to make me look like an old woman with my clothes off obviously wouldn't work. What then, live with him as is and hope for the best? The best would be some mortal disease felling him comparatively early, before he could notice that his hair was graying while I still looked eighteen.

If I took the chance and lived an idyll with him, and if he loved me enough, might I gradually let him in on my little secret? But look what had happened the last time he discovered I wasn't human.

But we were in the modern era now, and this was a man with a strong belief in the virtues of science, unlikely to attribute my inexplicable abilities to Satan. Maybe I could explain, maybe he could be brought to understand, maybe he could become one of Dr. Zeus's paid mortals with a control implant . . .

No. But something would suggest itself, something could be worked out. Who knows, perhaps we'd live blissfully awhile and then lose interest in each other, as so many mortals did, as *we* might have if he'd lived, and go our separate ways without pain. Perhaps fate had brought him back for just that closure on the events of 1555, to heal my life at last.

When he opened his eyes, though, I stopped thinking.

"Good morning, my dear," he said, alert at once. The charm went

on as though a switch had been flipped, and his courtly smirk acknowledged that he'd very much enjoyed my company last night, wink wink,
squeeze squeeze, yet his eyes also tracked around the room. Saddlebags still there, weapons still there, no intruders. Having ticked these
off his mental list, he smiled down at me. "I trust you slept well?"

"Very well indeed, señor," I said, smiling back at him, but I had
logistical problems of my own: here was a mortal man who'd been
without food or water for at least twenty hours. "Though the land of
dreams is a poor place to visit after one has been to heaven."

"Ah, but *I* was in paradise all night," he said gallantly, getting to
his feet and offering me his hand to rise. "Now, my dear, our first
business is to feed and water the horses. Where did the redoubtable
John Charles Fremont attend to such things?"

I accessed a topographical survey. The nearest water should be a
little creek flowing down a ravine just over our turreted hill. What was
this footnote? Future site of Harrison Ford residence? I made a mental
note not to download map information from Einar again. Movie star
homes, my foot. Was the damn creek there in time of drought, that
was the information I needed. I smiled prettily at Edward and pointed
vaguely north. "Woman's intuition tells me, señor, that there is a spring
in yonder canyon."

We led the horses to where there was a little green forage. But
the spring had dwindled to a seep, an uninviting trickle in a black
muddy bog at the canyon bottom, full of amoebic guests that wouldn't
bother a horse but would be only too happy to give a mortal dysentery.
We had to prise up a couple of big rocks and grub out a hole for the
water to collect in so the horses could drink. No bullwhip-wielding
hero showed up to offer us assistance, but it was 1863, after all. My
own hero produced a canteen from his saddlebag and offered it to me.

"You'll find it brackish, I'm afraid, but safe," he said. How did
he know about the shigella I had detected here? And see how expertly
he was avoiding the poison oak as he looked for a clean place to sit
down. He settled on a boulder at the approximate location of what
would one day be Mr. Ford's front step, and nonchalantly proceeded
to shave himself with a clasp knife that appeared in his hand out of
nowhere.

I was distracted from my awestruck contemplation of this feat (no
soap, no water, and he didn't nick himself once) by an annoying little
signal pulsing through the ether.

Mendoza?

What is it, Juan Bautista? I'm busy.

Are you coming back today?

No. Fix your own breakfast. Wait, this is important. I need you to put some food together and bring it up to me. Make it look as though you'd fixed yourself a very large picnic lunch. I'm going to lead my mortal friend back in your direction, and we're going to just accidentally on purpose run into you as you're out hunting, okay?

What's going on?

I'm doing fieldwork for Imarte.

Hey, is that guy a real British secret agent? Like in the James Bond movies?

Uh, yes, I guess he is.

Edward was standing up, neatly folding away the clasp knife. A day and a night of living rough in the field, and he hadn't so much as a smudge on those fawn wool trousers of his. Whatever secret device kept James Bond's tuxedo impeccably pressed, it seemed to have been already in use by the British secret service in 1863.

Neat! Can I help with whatever it is you're doing?

No, just bring us food. And this is secret, okay, J. B.? I'm trying to keep this man out of danger while I find out more about his plot.

Right.

I'll broadcast a directional signal as we come. Do your best to look surprised when you meet us. Spanish only, and remember, he probably understands it as well as you do, so watch what you say.

Gotcha.

Edward was coming toward me. "Well, my dear," he said. "I find nothing especially edible hereabouts, with the possible exception of rattlesnakes. What are the chances we might purchase food from that farmer you mentioned?"

"He is an inhospitable man," I said. It might have been true, too, for all I knew. "I recollect a farm near the Rodeo de Las Aguas where they are friendlier. It would be our wisest course to keep to the heights and work our way over there. We will pass near the stagecoach inn, but not near enough to be seen. Does that suit you, señor?"

"Very well indeed," he said.

We saddled our horses and rode out, working our way back in the direction of the inn, with me broadcasting a steady signal to Juan Bautista. As we were edging our way down onto what would one day be Mulholland Drive, I spotted him lounging ever-so-casually against a rock.

"Ay," he said in Mexican Spanish. "Señora Mendoza, I was afraid when you did not return last night. I am out hunting, as you see." He waved one of our rifles unconvincingly. Edward raised an eyebrow at him.

"And I am safe, as *you* see. Is that food you have in your basket, boy?" I said.

"Oh, yes—I packed myself a lunch." Juan Bautista was trying not to stare at Edward. "It's a very good lunch."

"Well, listen to me, I'm going to ask you for it. My friend here is a kind gentleman who is being pursued by thieves. We had to flee Los Diablos last night, and he has had nothing to eat. We would go back to the inn for a meal, but I am afraid they may come looking for him there."

"Oh, they have already," Juan Bautista said.

"What?" *What? Why the hell didn't you tell me?*

I thought you knew. "Yes, señora, two Yankee men. They said they were the friends of the Englishman who had been there. They came to collect the valise he left behind. I pretended not to understand them because, as you know, I do not trust the Yankee oppressors of our people." Juan Bautista gave the rifle a dramatic flourish.

I turned to look at Edward. His face was a perfect mask of polite incomprehension, but he had turned pale. "Señor," I told him, "the boy says that two Yankee men came to the inn asking for the valise an Englishman left there. He doesn't like Yankees, so he wouldn't speak with them."

"Really," Edward drawled. He made an odd little gesture that I would have taken for a shrug, if I hadn't known where all his concealed weapons were. He was quietly assuring himself each was in place. "Ask him when they were at the inn."

"When was this, Juanito?"

You're scared, aren't you? What's wrong? "It was this morning, señora, just after first light."

They'll kill him if they find him. "And are they still there now, boy?"

"No, señora, but I think they did not go far away. I think they are hiding to watch the stagecoach come and go, but, as you know, I am an Indian and white men cannot conceal themselves from me." *Can I help? Can I be your Indian guide? Please? I could throw the bad guys off the scent if they followed us.*

God damn it, this isn't a movie. "He says they were here at dawn," I told Edward. "He says they left, but he thinks they're still hiding in the pass, waiting for you to come."

Edward just nodded. I was feeling a slow anger building in him, sullen and exasperated. Not much fear, though for all he knew the Yankees might have had him in their sights at that very moment. But *I* was terrified for him, señors.

"I think you ought to ambush and kill those Yankees, Juanito," I said. "I assure you they are very bad men."

Juan Bautista did a good job of looking crafty. "Perhaps that can be arranged, señora." *So what do you want me to do about them, really?*

Like I said.

That shook Juan Bautista's little world. Even though Einar had been nailing mortal hides to the wall for months. After all, wasn't this Los Angeles, where such things were done every day? The boy shuffled his feet and looked at the ground. *Mendoza, I can't kill mortals.*

Why not? James Bond does.

Edward apparently came to some kind of decision, because he looked up at this point and said, "Thank the boy and tell him to go on with his business. If he meets the Yankees again, on no account is he to mention that he's seen me. But he should avoid them if he can, because they are very dangerous men."

"Give me that food now," I told Juan Bautista. "My friend offers his thanks and says to stay away from those Yankees, but don't tell them about him if you do encounter them. I assume this means he does not wish them to die. What a pity. However, your soul is free of two mortal sins. How fortunate for you."

Juan Bautista was too unnerved to play back. He just handed me the lunch basket and muttered, "Good day, good fortune on your journey," before vanishing into the sagebrush.

I hefted the basket and flashed Edward a brittle smile. "The boy has kindly surrendered his luncheon repast to our greater need. Poor fare, señor, but sustaining. I suggest we find a secure place to eat and revise our plans."

He shook his head grimly. "If I were a free man, we'd be riding for San Francisco this moment. Unfortunately I have a duty to salvage what I can from Rubery's incompetence."

This gave me an idea, but all I said was "One cannot make decisions on an empty stomach. Let us ride back to the high ground, señor."

We returned to the vicinity of Fremont's outpost and stopped in a grove of oak trees on the saddleback ridge just below. We still had a good view of the north end of the pass, but from a more sheltered spot. If anyone tracking us should find our previous night's camp, we'd have warning of their presence and a reasonably clear shot at them.

I unpacked the basket. Left to himself, Juan Bautista had grilled beef and made severely deformed tortillas for supper last night, and we had lots of the leftovers. He had also included a jug of water, a jar of olives, some cheese, a can of sardines, and a couple of cakes of Theobromos.

I should mention that I didn't have to explain any of the food to Edward, or show him how to roll up a filling in a tortilla. He'd learned how, somewhere. Perhaps in secret agent school; more likely in Veracruz, whatever he'd been doing there. From his saddlebag, he drew out an immense white handkerchief and spread it across his lap. I watched in amazement as he made himself sardine tacos and ate them without getting one spot of oil on those immaculate clothes.

"As regards this plan, señor," I said at length, when we'd consumed half the contents of the basket and neatly packed the rest for later. "As I said: my honor will not permit me to leave you. But clearly we are dealing in matters of life and death now. For your sake, I will be my father's sword at the throat of your enemies. Yet I begin to question whether your government is wise enough to rule the world. What fool ever trusted your Mr. Rubery with important papers?"

Yes, that touched a nerve. What a cold, bleak look in his eyes as he stared out at Cahuenga Pass, and how well I remembered the bitter anger that pulled the corners of his mouth down. He mastered his temper, though, and turned to face me with a rueful smile and a shrug.

"I can't deny the truth, my dear, particularly in this instance, since we're facing considerable danger as a result of it. I have at least the satisfaction of pointing out that well-born imbeciles tend to get themselves killed before they manage to breed, leaving room for men of ability to replace them. And not all well-born men are idiots! I can assure you that there is an office in Whitehall where a very wise and noble man makes national policy, one whose judgment I'd utterly trust, for all that he's seldom quoted in the *Times*. That same man who made the decision to give Alfred a task he was barely fit for had the foresight to send me after him, guessing no doubt that Alfred would make the wretched mess he has."

I shook my head. "Why send the boy in the first place? If your people think you're expendable, their aristocratic brains are no better than Mr. Rubery's. I'll grant you, the idea of this land in peace and prosperity under British rule is a splendid one. I'd die myself if that would bring it into being. But I don't see how it can be accomplished now, do you? Martha must have gone straight to the Yankees and told them about the valise; or if she did not, some other indiscretion of Mr. Rubery's put them on the scent. They surely know everything now. I don't see how your masters can blame you for pulling out and saving what you can of the affair."

"Ah, but the Yankees *don't* know everything now," he said. He pushed his lank hair back from his forehead with the flat of his hand and set his hat straight on his head. "If they did, they wouldn't be after the valise. Whatever else we do, it mustn't fall into their hands."

"Shouldn't we destroy the papers, then?" I asked.

"No. If we can salvage any part of this, we'll need them. And, my dear, the game's not over yet. Alfred's an idiot, but at least he's a British idiot, and despite the business with the valise he's managed to accomplish successfully another part of his task." He glanced down involuntarily at his watch pocket. "So. All we need do is evade our Yankee opposite numbers until we can get across to Santa Catalina Island. My compliments to Abraham Lincoln, I must say. Certainly no one thought he had the resources to spend anything on counterespionage in this corner of the nation. But he can't keep it up for long, I think. And if the Union loses to the Confederacy, it won't matter whether he knows about us or not." He rose to his feet briskly and extended his hand to me. "We'll triumph yet. Are you still game, my love?"

My love. The earth wobbled in its orbit, just for a second, there. Against all my better judgment I let him pull me to my feet, and tried to look every inch the fearless secret agent's girlfriend. "I'll go with you, señor!"

So much for my attempt to seduce him away from his duty. He was unstoppable, señors, and he always had been. What an operative he'd have made for Dr. Zeus, eh? Our agents are always so adroit at stepping in and whisking away unwanted children. Where were they when Nicholas Harpole made his unwelcome entrance into this world, or Edward Alton Bell-Fairfax? Sublime bastards both of them, with a courage and determination and nobility of character I'd never possessed. What imbecile chance selected me for immortality, when *he* could have made so much better use of an eternal life? He didn't fit the optimum physical parameters, I'll admit; and that was absolutely the only bar I could see.

Consider his ability to inspire. I had been lost in the dark wood, on this wretched posting, and despair owned me. I'd seen at last the future we'd all been promised, and I knew it for the hard and ugly thing it was. I'd seen the madness that descends on older immortals, and it wasn't an enjoyable prospect to contemplate for myself. Nevertheless, others of my kind have in their differing ways found a certain happiness, a sense of purpose, even love. I had my work; but the work dried up, like the seasonal streams of this accursed place, and in its absence I had glimpsed the hideous dry void it covered. What if the

Company gave me new work? The void was still there. Besides, I had now the growing suspicion that the work was meaningless, a pointless series of tasks devised to keep busy a thing that couldn't die, since its creators could find no way to unsay the spell that had set it in motion.

But this man walked back into my life and changed everything.

Surely, I thought, his mere existence argued that there was a greater power than the Company, that there was more going on here than our pitiful creators imagined! You see? There might be a point to this eternal life business after all, a purpose and a meaning I couldn't see. Had he not come back to me, like a good angel in my darkest hour, and started my dead heart beating again?

Theobromos, please. Thank you. You want to know what we did next, not listen to my opinions. I see, though, that some of you recognize the feeling. Yes, and some of you are as frightened of the future as I am. Your eyes give it away. So much the worse for you. What's the old saying, don't rejoice at my troubles, because when they're old news, yours will have just started? You have no refuge, any more than I; unbearable Time is master of us all, who thought we had defeated him. Will he treat you with more charity than he's treated me?

We rode, señors, by devious and careful paths, down from that ridge and quickly across the grade to Dark Canyon Road. The plan was to work our way around behind Mount Hollywood, then cut across the lands of the old haunted rancho on the other side, crossing the river at some point. Los Angeles being what it was, this could be done with dry shoes most years; especially so in this year of drought. Edward looked around him in wonder as our horses picked their way through the sand and river cobbles.

"But—this is the principal river in southern California," he murmured.

"So it is," I said. "Not at its best just now, unfortunately. In a normal year, however, it is at least two feet across. Sometimes even three."

He frowned and fell silent. I imagine he was wondering how even the most brilliant British engineers could irrigate this desolation to the point where cotton could be grown.

"Wheat might grow here, señor," I said helpfully. "Cotton, never, unless you bring water down from the north. Plenty of water up there. It's a green paradise; parts of it even look like your England. You would like it there."

He wasn't comforted. Perhaps he was beginning to doubt the feasibility of the grand design after all. In a pigeonhole in some fine antique oaken desk in Whitehall, there was a map of southern California;

and some Briton had looked at this wavy line that described itself as a river and made plans accordingly, without understanding that Los Angeles never plays by the rules, whether of geography, law, or anything else.

And of course I knew, I who rode faithful at his side, that the whole business would fall to pieces anyway. Even now Alfred Rubery was probably sitting in a San Francisco jail, having been unable to get any part of his mission right. The British would never own California. Edward and I would at least enjoy a holiday on Catalina Island first. But when the piracy case hit the world newspapers, surely Britain would throw in the towel and call its operatives home.

And what would we do then? What would I do in England, on which I'd turned my back with the earnest hope that the island sink entirely into the sea? I hadn't seen the place since before the Industrial Revolution. It had been crude, cold, and violent, still largely medieval then, with all the attendant lustful bawdiness that implied. What would I make of the new Victorian propriety? What would I make of the mill towns and mine towns that had turned the green fields black? There were railways there now, and canals, and no one was burned at the stake anymore; all peace and prosperity. Except for the workhouses, of course, and the children freezing in alleyways and drinking gin to warm themselves, and the typhus and tuberculosis . . . But what other nation in the world hadn't the same problems, or worse? No gunfights in the public streets, at least.

It occurred to me that I'd like to go to Rochester, to the open place near the cathedral where Nicholas was burned. To walk there in my Victorian clothes, on the arm of my Victorian Nicholas, and laugh in the face of Death.

I'd have to make some accommodation to the Company, explain my actions and propose a plan that would serve its interests as well as mine. Hadn't they been understanding of Porfirio's needs? After all the years I'd served them, surely they could afford to make some allowances for me. Yes, and it should even be possible to break the truth to Edward. What was the Company, after all, but the ultimate expression of the civilizing force to which he'd dedicated his life? And if he too should become a double agent? Oh, but of a much higher order than a flunky like Souza. It would have worked, señors. We could have made it work.

So I rode over that barren ground, with my head in the rainy clouds of England.

We went up into the foothills to avoid Sonoratown as we approached Los Angeles, though scanning from a distance, I could tell that it was virtually deserted. Best to be safe. We climbed, screened by laurel and oak scrub, until we were peering down on the city we'd left in such haste only the night before. It looked flat and desolate, the whole scene filtered through a yellow haze of dust raised by cattle and horses. Terrible dust, for of course there'd been no rain. And the smell of manure rose up, and of roofing tar, and mesquite smoke, and, faintly under all these, the smell of death.

But out on the horizon, what was that poking up blue into the high clean air?

"Catalina Island, señor," I said, stretching out an arm. "If only we could fly there."

His face was somber as he surveyed the distance, and his gaze dropped back down to the uninviting prospect below us. "I must warn you, my dear, that our road to the sea will be watched. It would be pleasant to think that they've simply posted a man to observe the stage line to San Pedro; but I rather think they know I've got wind of them by now. Is there a fairly straight route to the sea that avoids the pueblo?"

There would be, when the 710 freeway was built. I accessed information hurriedly and superimposed a twentieth-century grid over the present-day map. No reason why we couldn't follow the freeway route through the sagebrush and sand. It would take us right down to the future site of Long Beach, just south of Souza's landing. I plotted a course and nodded. "This way, señor," I said, urging my horse forward, and Edward followed.

So we went down across the wide plain, keeping the smoke of Los Angeles on our right, through a wilderness that would one day be East Los Angeles and various urban housing tracts called Maywood, Bell Gardens, South Gate, Downey, Compton. Such orderly Yankee names for a place that was now only a desert of trampled earth and bleaching cattle bones. Would there be an interval of little Yankee towns with gardens and cottages here too? And would they too vanish in their time, asphalted over, shadowed by the steel towers that would themselves vanish in the urban wars? And what pair of lovers would one day pick their way across a desolation not of sagebrush but of rust and broken paving, under a poisoned sky, past the bleaching bones of men? Full circle for this place, but not for me. With any luck I'd never see Los Angeles again. I'd be off to Great Britain. I'd have to find some way of persuading Edward to give up this nonsense about dying for Queen and country, though . . .

We had gone on our way about an hour when I edged my horse close enough to speak to Edward in a low voice.

"A question, señor. You understand that I have every confidence in your ability, and absolute faith in your word. To look at the matter coldly, however—what shall I do if we do not succeed? What will the Yankees do if they apprehend us?"

He gave a brief, humorless laugh. "My government is in no position to come to my assistance. The Yankees, for their part, cannot fight a war with Britain just at the present moment, being preoccupied with rather more pressing matters. They'd dearly love to obtain all the particulars of our business here, make no mistake about that. But I doubt very much they'll go to the trouble of declaring me persona non grata and paying my passage home. Much more likely, I'll quietly vanish into a shallow grave, and the contents of the valise will be forwarded to Washington. This is, you understand, the worst possible chance; but it is a possibility. All the more reason to avoid capture, my dear." He looked up and gave me a brisk smile, cold and bright as the winter sun. "Are you reconsidering your offer? I should, if I were you. You see what it is to be a pawn on this particular chessboard."

I might demoralize him, but I couldn't dissuade him.

With his gloved hand he reached over and took mine, and held it tight. "Dolores," he said. He stopped and drew breath. "I don't know what impression of me you've formed in the last twenty-four hours, but I think you see clearly enough that I'm unlikely to end my days quietly. Men in my profession do not. Women in my profession (and there are a few) are as much at risk, indeed at risk of worse. I will never marry you, I will never settle in a pleasant cottage by the sea with you, and we will never raise children together. You are clearly intelligent enough to have perceived this."

"I know, señor. Your life is not your own."

He gripped my hand more tightly and went on. "And it's not that it isn't a glorious life. Giving yourself to a noble cause. True, sometimes one must disregard certain moral considerations to achieve a desired end. One might go to a great deal of trouble to obtain a useful tool, sharp and bright and perfect for the job, a really remarkable tool to find in so unlikely a place. One might have no intention of discarding that tool, either, when its use had been served—though the use might well destroy the tool. A man who seduces a girl into prostitution is vile enough; what would you call a man who persuades a girl to risk her life?"

"Not a liar, at all events," I said with a shrug. "Your conscience should give you a rest, señor. I understand the danger here."

"But I did not, twenty-four hours ago. The ground has shifted since then. Don't share a shallow grave with me, my dear."

"I have no intention of dying," I replied. "And you're not a dead man yet. Catalina, señor, look at it out there, isn't it beautiful? Only a few more miles of this hideous desert, and then it's all blue water. We'll make it, and then we'll have all the time in the world to discuss what further use I can be to Imperial Export."

"By God," he said, looking away from me. "If only we'd met some other place or time."

We had. It hadn't worked out; would it work out now?

We rode on in silence.

29

I WANTED TO ask him about himself, to find out where he'd been born, who those highborn relations were who had hushed up his birth but evidently found him some back entrance into the corridors of power. The secret child grew up into a secret man, terrifically useful but never to be publicly acknowledged. And when his usefulness ended? When he finally failed to accomplish a task that had been set for him, or began to question the wisdom of the masters who paid him, as I think he must already have begun to do? How did any secret service reward an agent who couldn't do the job, whether through his fault or through the folly of his superiors? Silence and abandonment, disappearance without a trace. I knew that much. Within our own Company there were always rumors that certain operatives had been retired, though nobody knew what that involved exactly. . . . It's unsafe to inquire after fellow immortals one hasn't seen in a while. I guess I'm going to find out where bad cyborgs go, eh, señors?

But I couldn't ask Edward anything, about his personal life or our plans once we got to Catalina, for a number of reasons. The most immediate reason being that we were trying to cross a dangerous place quickly and in silence.

I could access the historical record, though.

It was so easy, it never occurred to me. All I had to do was access the files I was given codes for when I came to California. I was given whole libraries full of stuff on its history, its future, much more detailed information than I ever bothered to use. When you spend most of your time in a coastal mountain range miles from the nearest mortal soul, you don't need to know who will run for third mayor of Pasadena. But was Edward Alton Bell-Fairfax mentioned in the history of

California? Perhaps in some connection with Catalina Island? There would be no mention of me, of course. No Dr. Zeus operative is ever given information about his or her own future, so if I appeared in any footnote in the historical record, it would have been carefully excised from my files.

But I might find references to Edward. I set my primary consciousness to automatic scan and focused on the material behind my eyes.

California, Channel Islands, Santa Catalina Island. One of eight channel islands. Geology: crystalline metamorphic rock, principally quartzite, also steatite, lead, silver—only traces of gold. Botany: several rare endemics (how fascinating, why hadn't I ever been sent there?). Zoology: biggest predator a small fox; goats introduced by the Spanish doing very well. Ornithology, archaeology . . . nothing I wanted here.

Any record of British involvement? I scanned the records of ownership.

The Indians first, obviously, for about 30,000 years. Thirty *thousand?* Wasn't that a little early? And what was this nonsense about sunken continents, reports of white Indians, and seven-foot-tall skeletons found in the oldest burial mounds? Then assorted Spanish galleons stopping by for souvenirs over the next couple of centuries, doing no harm for once. Russian fur hunters, Yankee sea captains, meddling Franciscans finally causing the place to be abandoned by its native population, who went over to the mission communities on the mainland, where they all died of smallpox.

First owner to hold any kind of title, thanks to Juan Rodríguez Cabrillo: King Charles of Aragon and Castile, later the Emperor Charles, father of my old acquaintance Philip II of Spain, husband of that very same Mary Tudor who had my Nicholas burned at the stake. Small world. And then subsequent kings of Spain, until the Revolution in 1822, when Mexico claimed it. Modern times, now: when Pio Pico was dodging the invading Yankees, he granted title to the island to his friend Thomas M. Robbins. That was in 1846.

Robbins sold the island to José Maria Covarrubias in 1850, and in 1853 it passed out of his hands, sold to one Albert Packard of San Francisco, who had it now and would keep it until at least 1864.

But here the records grew confusing, incomplete. Somebody named Eugene L. Sullivan was claiming part title as early as 1858. And who was this James H. Ray claiming to be Packard's agent, traveling back east *now*, 1863, and bragging to potential investors that he "about had a deal with John Bull"? British parties were interested in buying the property, if clear title could be established. And here was Ray buying out Packard's interest in the island and immediately selling shares in the title to a consortium of men with fairly British-sounding names. Were they the Britons Ray had boasted about? Good Lord, by next year they would own Catalina Island.

I scanned further, fascinated. No—they wouldn't hold the place long. Here was the American government stepping in and seizing the island, ordering everybody off. They'd build a Union Army barracks over there. When would this happen?

January 1, 1864. Nine months from now. A General West would arrive with Union troops, forcibly remove all settlers—including the Albion Mining Syndicate, who had developed an area on a defensible bay and named it Queen City—and build a Union Army barracks at the narrow isthmus that connected the two halves of the island. Under government orders, West would name the two opposing bays Catalina Harbor and Union Harbor. The schooner *Jessup* would be outfitted with a pivot gun and put into service as an armed supply vessel for the Union troops there. In short, Civil War or no Civil War, Abraham Lincoln would find the time and resources to come down on any funny business on Catalina Island like a ton of bricks. Why?

I sped through document titles and froze on one: "Winfield Scott Hancock's Threat Evaluation. Survey Performed on Orders of Edwin M. Stanton, Secretary of War, November 26, 1863." Eight months from now.

So something that happened within the next eight months would cause the secretary of war in far-off Washington to order a survey of Catalina Island with national defense in mind. I scanned the report. What had Hancock found?

That the population of the island consisted of a few squatter families who had been there since the 1850s, sheepherders and fishermen only—and approximately one hundred miners (most of whom were British nationals), who arrived abruptly, proceeded to fortify a little crescent-shaped harbor, and engaged in no observable mining activity.

That the island's coast was rife with small, accessible harbors, many of which had adequate capacity for vessels of war. Hancock felt the island had dangerous potential for a military base: "any major maritime power" could, with minimal ordnance, control the entire coastline of California from a base on that island, preferably one located in the two-square-mile area around the isthmus. What major maritime power? The Confederacy, desperately dodging blockades or busy hunting Union ships in the Atlantic? It hadn't the wherewithal to send a fleet around Cape Horn. Britain, though, had ships all over the

Pacific, and as recently as 1842 the U.S. was so afraid that Britain was going to make a play for California that they'd rushed ashore and prematurely raised the Stars and Stripes at Monterey, which, by an inconvenient little quirk of international law, still happened to belong to Mexico.

What a sharp-eyed fellow he'd been, this Winfield Scott Hancock, and how quickly the secretary of war had acted on his request. Whatever tipped off the secretary of war to order the survey in the first place (doubtless something relating to Mr. Rubery's big mouth, or possibly even Mr. James H. Ray's), in less than a year the whole British plot would come unraveled, and Catalina Island would be firmly under the control of the U.S. government. What a shame, though at least it seemed to have happened without any bloodshed. No mention of any Edward Alton Bell-Fairfax.

Quite an interesting little episode in local history. Imarte had been right: it was all utterly fascinating. So that was the end of British attempts on Catalina . . .

Wait a minute: what was this? The U.S. government would pull out its forces in September 1864. None of the miners would ever return to the island to press their claims (not surprising, since no substantial amount of gold had ever been located), and a man named James Lick would seek out the consortium members and purchase their titles to the island. There was a lot of correspondence from certain parties in the Department of Indian Affairs, who thought the island would be a great place to dump the unwanted Indian population of Humboldt County, but this would never come to anything, because of the fact (or perhaps in spite of the fact) that Catalina Island had almost no fresh water or arable land, and also because James Lick would be by this time the sole and legal owner, with a clear title.

And here was Lick, in 1872, the Army long out of the picture, offering an option on the island to a Major Max von Stroble. The major would go to London to form an English syndicate to take up the option. Curiously, on the morning he was to sign the papers and collect the money, he would be found dead in his hotel room.

What the hell? And next? Here was George Shatto, the developer, buying the island from Lick in 1887 and selling an option to an *English mining syndicate*. With the money he would receive, Shatto would busy himself laying out the little resort town of Avalon. But there would be problems: the English were supposedly mining silver this time, but then they would leave suddenly, and Shatto would default on payments and lose the island. Shortly afterward, he would reportedly fall from the back of a moving train.

The island would revert to the Lick trustees, who would sell it in 1892 to the Banning brothers. And who were they? The sons of our present staunch pro-Union stagecoach tycoon Phineas Banning, the little boys who'd grow to manhood in that nice mansion being built above San Pedro even now. William, Joseph, and Hancock Banning, the youngest having been named for his father's good friend Winfield Scott Hancock, who'd written the threat estimate fingering the British. Very small world.

So the island would remain firmly in American hands from then on, though the Bannings would experience some trouble: fighting on the waterfront, mysterious sabotage attempts, and arson in 1915 that would destroy the Hotel Metropole (where Harry Houdini stayed) and most of the resort buildings. In the end, the brothers would be bought out by the millionaire Wrigley, of chewing gum fame, who would rebuild Avalon along grander lines. Oh, look: here was a reference to a visit by the Chronos Photo-Play Company, for the purposes of shooting a movie. Chronos Photo-Play was an early alias for Dr. Zeus's entertainment division. I wondered if Einar would be involved in that.

Decades of peace and prosperity for Avalon, then, a pretty little resort town dreaming in the island sun, all its bizarre history long forgotten. No more mysterious deaths, no more British strangers lurking around. The only bit of trivia to stand out of the record was that Wrigley would pay to have an extensive geologic survey done and then suppress the results . . .

What was going on here?

For half a century, in absolute silence and in deadly earnest, two world powers would wrestle for control of this tiny island. At the beginning, its strategic importance was undeniable. But why would the British keep coming back, long after they'd lost any chance of adding it to their empire? What would they be looking for that required engineering and mining teams? What would Wrigley's geologic survey reveal? Not gold, which had never been found in enough quantity to merit attention of this kind. Not the various buried treasures reported to be there: every island had its tales of buried treasure. What were the British after? What had Imarte told me, something about letters referring to an astonishing technological discovery, made at a place designated only by code. Was the place Catalina? Had they unearthed something there they wanted to study?

Did Edward know?

I remembered his face above me by firelight, shining with the sweat of passion, while he said something about a remarkable discovery, one that might enable men to defeat death. What did Edward know?

I scanned forward through the records. With the Second World War, the strangeness would begin again. The island would be closed to the public once more, and the OSS, forerunner of the CIA, would be quartered there. Oh my. There would be rumors of visits by Allied scientists, particularly the British, and of classified projects at science bases in the island's interior. From that time onward, access to the island's interior would be strictly controlled, even after the war, when the resort areas reopened. A conservancy would be formed in 1972, closing off most of the island to anyone but authorized residents. Access to certain areas was completely restricted, the reason given being that these were rare ecosystems where endemic plants thrived.

I noticed something interesting in the successive editions of the island's history. The earlier works said the Union Army barracks were built to discourage Confederate sympathizers who might try to turn privateer, which doubtless related to whatever Mr. Rubery had been involved in. But later editions began to change the story: the barracks were built to patrol the Indian reservation that had been planned for the island. Still later, the story was that the barracks were built to guard against opium smugglers, and later still (by which point mortals were clearly losing their grasp of history) that they were built to prevent bootleggers from bringing in cases of whiskey.

The same thing happened with the successive maps. Here was one from 1912, nicely detailed, showing a lot of the interior features: the old mine adits and in particular Silver Canyon, where the English would work until their swift departure in 1887. Perhaps they got what they were after. But here was a map from 1938—where were the mines? And here was one from 1976, with interior roads and hiking trails but few other features. Silver Canyon was not marked. Over this I superimposed a map published by the conservancy in 1982. There was *nothing* on the map in that section of the island, not even topographical lines to show ridges or streams, though they appeared everywhere else. The Silver Canyon region was white, blank, featureless. Who was taking such pains to obliterate its memory?

Ah, but a cross-reference in the text indicated the conservancy's involvement with a twentieth-century holding company for Dr. Zeus.

Here were the records for the twenty-first century, and the UFO sightings that would begin on Catalina Island—over the Silver Canyon area, by the way. We all know, of course, that UFO sightings will be a gigantic hoax, costumed nonsense to conceal Company experiments in some cases and mass hysteria in all others. We know that, because the Company told us so. Although nobody ever bothered to explain to me about those little pale men I ran into back in 1860, or why all the material I collected on that job was confiscated. But doubt the Company's word? Inconceivable.

In any case, the Company was surely responsible for those sightings on the island, because here was name after corporate name becoming entangled in the conservancy's affairs, and nearly every one of them was some pseudonym of Dr. Zeus. And it was undoubtedly Dr. Zeus who would provide the islanders with the armament enabling them to close their harbor to mainland vessels after the Second Civil War broke out in mid century, Dr. Zeus who would patrol their waters for them, Dr. Zeus who would develop the advanced agrarian technology that would make them self-sufficient when foodstuffs could no longer be imported from the poisoned mainland.

And it would be Dr. Zeus who established the secret libraries and archives there. When Los Angeles is the toxic, riot-ridden hell it will become, Catalina Island, like sixth-century Ireland, will be a peaceful and remote sanctuary beyond the sea, where knowledge is preserved and research conducted.

Look at the names: Olympian Technologies, Kronos Diversified, Jupiter Cyberceuticals, Lightning-A Company, Jovian Integrated Systems. Every one of them the Company. Will the Company be behind the bizarre incidents that occur on Catalina Island in the twenty-second century? The rash of Kaspar Hausers who come wandering down onto the golf course in Avalon over a three-month period in 2136, babbling in no known language? The weeping man, found floating off Long Point in a fishing boat of antique design, who says his name is Emilio Machado and swears it is the year 1901? The persistent rumors that a Scots actor, famous for his adventure films of the twentieth century, is somehow still alive and well and can be glimpsed occasionally dining at the Avalon Country Club? What is Dr. Zeus up to?

Señors, if I wasn't meant to know these things, I should never have been given the access codes. Or was it simply that nobody ever thought that one of us would reference this particular subject matter, connect this particular chain of events? I'm fairly sure I wasn't supposed to find out that the CEOs of Olympian Technologies, Jupiter Cyberceuticals, and the rest are, to a man and woman, loyal subjects of Henry X of England. But that must be a coincidence. We were always taught that Dr. Zeus was a multinational entity, drawing the best brains in science and finance from every nation on Earth. There are undoubtedly plenty of Czechs and Kenyans, too, on the board of directors. Anyway . . .

I raised my eyes to the distant island; it loomed out there like a dream, as I had seen it every day and night of my sojourn here. I turned to Edward Alton Bell-Fairfax, who was now ten times the enigma he had been before. I opened my mouth to ask him a question.

But I never did ask him, because at that moment I picked up the signal of the mortal man approaching through the brush ahead of us. My head snapped around, and I focused on him. Mortal male, two meters tall, thirty to thirty-five years of age, sober, approximately 270 pounds, blood pressure slightly elevated, brainwave pattern suggesting he was hunting. Mounted, and urging his horse forward at a brisk trot. Armed. Rifle and two Navy revolvers.

"Edward," I said in a low voice, "we'd better get off the trail." He looked at me sharply but turned his horse's head at once, and we found our way down a gully and into the partial shade of a scrub oak.

If only he hadn't been so tall.

The mortal must have caught a glimpse of that tall hat, because he sent a bullet whistling through the sagebrush at us. That was no more than conversation in Los Angeles, and it missed by a good ten feet. But here he came, galloping after it, emitting the signal I'd come to know too well: a mortal after blood.

We slid from our saddles, and I found myself flattened between Edward and an undercut clay bank, where the storms of 1862 had hollowed out a space. The clay was just about the same color as those miraculous trousers of his, which were still spotless, by the way. Edward's gun was already in his hand. Damn, here still came the mortal, and even if he didn't spot me and Chameleon Man, he'd see the horses.

He did, too; he saw them first. A long searching stare along the gully, and he saw Edward as well. He grinned in delight, taking in the details of Edward's appearance, his tailored clothing.

"Now I just bet you're that limey bastard," he said. "Let me hear you say something, friend. Talk for me." And he raised the barrel of his rifle.

Bang. Just like in the movies, a red dot appeared in the center of his forehead and a dark red drop ran down. Just like that. He sat there a moment in the saddle, his grin frozen, then fell slowly to one side. His horse didn't appreciate that at all; it stepped clear of him and kicked impatiently to clear his dead foot from the stirrup.

Edward rolled away and looked at me in astonishment. "Good shot, my dear," he said.

That was when I realized I had just killed a mortal. The gun was there in my hand, a bullet gone from the cylinder.

We don't do such things. Einar's mad, he doesn't count; Porfirio had immediately saved the life of the only person I ever saw him shoot. We don't kill. We reason, we run away, we lie to our attackers or confuse them or project illusions to hide ourselves, but we never, ever rob them of their miserable brief lives, because we have so much and they have so little. Unlike us, they have mothers who mourn for them. They have families who starve.

I was crushed with such a sense of sin as I had never felt in my wretched long life. I was a true Angeleno now, wasn't I? At last I'd fired a gun at a total stranger, and blown him away too. But no audience cheered for me, as would have happened in the movies.

Edward took the gun from my nerveless hand, stroked back my hair, looked straight into my eyes. "Dolores, my dear. This was your first time, I think?"

Nice of him, to help a lady so gently on the occasion of retching after her first kill.

"My apologies, señor," I murmured at last.

He waved a dismissive hand. "It quite shocks the system," he said, "the first time. But I think you ought not to take this up as steady work, however good your aim. One can accustom oneself to the act of necessary murder, but does one wish to?"

Yes indeed, something to be seriously considered by the young woman contemplating her entrance into Victorian society.

We mounted and rode on.

The sun was dropping into the west now, and we were nearing San Pedro and the probable cordon, so the danger was greater than ever. We arrived at Long Beach before it was quite dark, splashing across the slough. I wondered if D. W. Griffith's men would plant palm trees here one day, preparing the scene for the desperate chariot race to warn Babylon.

It seemed preferable to wait until full cover of night before making our way to Souza's. Accordingly we found a dry stream bed under an oak tree along the outskirts of Señor Tempe's rancho and reined in there, to dismount for a while.

Edward jumped down first and put up his hands to catch me as I slid from my saddle. I fell into his arms. The brief hold became an embrace, and without quite meaning to we were kissing hungrily. It was going to happen again; nothing we could do about it, other than unlock for a moment as Edward staggered over to loop the horses' reins around an oak branch. He came back, breathing hard. I knelt in the sand; he swept off his hat and knelt beside me.

And really it was like prayer, señors, desperate prayer for forgiveness, an appeal for mercy, an act of life in that deadly place. I gave him pleasure to atone for the death I'd given the stranger. He gave me absolution for what I'd done, and found his own blessing of acquittal in my arms. Violent prayer, struggle and assault, shuddering ecstatic confirmation that we were still alive, though without our bower walls were dogs and enchanters, whoremongers and murderers.

We lay there afterward, looking up awhile at the red evening sky through the black leaves.

"What are you?" Edward whispered.

"Your mate," I said. "As meaningless as that is, for us both. We'll never marry. We'll never settle in a cottage by the sea. We'll never raise children. Death and time stalk us like a pair of hounds. But we were formed in the mind of God from the same piece of steel, for what purpose I cannot imagine."

He was silent for a while. His hand traveled up and closed on my breast. "Death and time," he said at last. "What would our life be like, if we could live?"

"Oh, we'd make the world the place it should have been," I answered with a grand wave. "We'd blaze across the sky like meteors, and our masters would look upon us and tremble. We'd bring down the palace of Death as though it were so many cards. You'd take the flaming sword and smash the lock on the gates to Eden, and let our children into the garden. I'd teach them how to grow corn, and you'd give them laws. Everything would begin again, except sorrow."

He laughed, softly. "So it would," he said. "And then, perhaps, the world could look after its own affairs for a while. Imagine not having to justify one's existence, ever, to anybody."

"Imagine having the freedom to travel where one wished."

"Imagine having the time," he sighed, and I sighed with him. Somewhere out in the evening a sea bird cried, a high thin far-off piping, a lonely sound.

Perhaps it made the moment too surreal, brought home to him just how strange our conversation was. I felt his mood changing, his wariness returning.

"Dolores Alice Elizabeth Mendoza," he said musingly. "You're far too young to understand this business as well as you do, and to kill with such precision. But for your age, I could imagine you were one of Juárez's agents, or even that buffoon Napoleon's, though I can't see how or why. You were certainly a virgin, and yet I've known Eastern whores with less expertise in the arts of love. Less enthusiasm, too. What am I to make of you, my dear?"

I lay very still. "You might accept the truth as I told it to you," I said. Of all the mortals in that English hall, long ago, Nicholas had been the only one to suspect what I was. It had been a game between us, a delightful game of question and evasion, until he discovered the truth. Then he tried to kill me.

"Well, my love, but it doesn't quite convince," said Edward. "I add together all the figures you've given me, and they simply don't produce the sum of you." He stretched luxuriously, in that motion bringing at least two of his concealed weapons into place for immediate deployment. "A sensible man in my line of work would have disposed of you—by some means or other—hours ago. I am, however, reluctant to lose such a charming companion. And it is a fact that your objective and mine would seem to coincide." He smiled, narrow-eyed, waiting to see what I would say.

I gave the faintest of shrugs, a tilt of the head, and spoke in the most reasonable of voices. "Señor. If my intent were to betray you, I might easily have led you to the Yankees by now. If my intent were to secure the contents of the valise—I had all the time in the world to do that when it sat at the inn, before ever you came looking for it. If you find my knowledge or my skill with a pistol remarkable, all I can tell you is that there's not much for a well-born girl to do in San Luis Obispo, save read and practice shooting at targets or the occasional bandit. I believe it's customary for a gentleman to accept a lady's word without question, is it not?"

"It is," he said. "Though I expect you'll appreciate the difficulty I'm in just now, my love, as regards the luxury of trusting anyone."

"I do." I looked up into his eyes. The pupils were dilated, enormous. He really did not want to kill me. "I point out that you have little choice in the matter, señor."

His dark smile deepened, melting me, even with the point of his hidden knife inches from my heart. "So the question remains: What are you? I find myself with a price on my head in a foreign land. My associates have bungled and miscalculated to such a degree that I may well be unlikely to escape with my life. I'm in a very narrow little corner indeed, and my only ally is a remarkable young lady who seems, by some unlikely trick of metempsychosis, to be a fused reincarnation of Boadicea and Cleopatra. A very bad business. And I can't for the life of me think why you're not having a fit of hysterics now, or angry tears."

"Metempsychosis," I said thoughtfully. "Now, that was Pythagoras's theory of the transmigration of souls, was it not? Rebirth, after death, in a new body. Possibly I trust you because we were lovers once, in some previous life. Possibly you trust me for the same reason. It makes as much sense as anything else, señor."

He drew a deep breath and struck the earth beside my head with the flat of his hand. "Now, how in hell do you know what metempsychosis means? Whoever you are," he said, "whoever you've been, if we get out of this with our lives, I *will* marry you. See if you can keep the truth from me then!"

The stars came out, and the chill of evening set in, but we didn't notice. What stamina he had. And what good fortune for us that no bounty hunters chanced to come near that particular oak tree, on that night of the sixteenth of March, 1863.

Much later we arose and rode out again, and I led us through the marshy tidelands and the shallow sea of reeds by scanning for solid ground along Rattlesnake Island. If we made noise, the frogs and the night creatures made more; and so we came in safety to the huts of the fishermen, and I was so grateful to ride up onto the causeway and behold Souza's night lamp burning.

"I will talk for us," I told Edward as I rapped softly on the door. He nodded, and when Souza opened and peered out, I said in Portuguese, "The doctor has a request to make of you, Souza. This gentleman and I need to go across to the big island out there, in silence and secret. When can you take us?"

He yawned and rubbed his eyes. "With the tide, lady. Six hours more."

"Have you a secure place we can rest until then?" I asked.

Of course he had; it was a Company safe house, after all. He bowed us through his low door and showed us to the little closet of a room kept for Dr. Zeus agents who were passing through. Not spacious, but the low, wide bed was clean and dry. There was a chair, on which Edward deposited his saddlebag; there were a washstand and a table with a candlestick on it. Souza lit the candle for us and went to see to our horses. We undressed by candlelight—it flickered, from a little draft coming through the plank walls off the sea—and we sat up by its light long enough to make a late supper out of the last of Juan Bautista's picnic lunch. We barely spoke for exhaustion.

Edward got up once, to make certain the door was secured to his standards, and I lay in bed and watched him. Not one mark, not one scar on his body, same as Nicholas. Really rather remarkable for a man in his profession. But, then, he seemed to be as perceptive of danger as an immortal. Anybody who ever contemplated sending a bullet or knife his way must have been fatally beaten to the draw.

And what was he? I was a woman of mystery to him, but his existence posed a far greater question. Setting aside for a moment that we were somehow in bed together again after three centuries had passed—how was he connected to the technocrats who would one day found my own Company?

I opened my mouth to ask him, but somehow the only question that popped out was "How did you break your nose?"

He turned, peering at me curiously. Naked there by candlelight, no Victorian trappings, and he was Nicholas in every line.

"I've never broken my nose," he replied, coming back to get into bed beside me. He believed what he was saying, too. I lifted my hand to his face and ran my thumb along the irregularity in the bridge that had always so fascinated me.

"But it *has* been broken, just here," I insisted. I could feel the scar in the cartilage, an old injury, healed long ago. "You must have noticed."

"I've noticed the ugly fellow in my shaving mirror, yes, but he's looked that way as long as I remember," Edward said wryly. "It's a family feature, I assume. I'm not sufficiently acquainted with my relations to know. But I assure you, my dear, I've never taken a blow to the face. One of the few advantages of being exceptionally tall; it's difficult for one's assailants to reach so far."

"Ah," I said. I'd never asked how Nicholas broke his nose. He'd had quite a reputation as a university brawler, and I assumed he did it in a fight. "Perhaps you broke it in infancy, then, and don't remember?"

"Perhaps," he said, yawning. He leaned up on his elbow and blew out the candle, and drew me into his arms. We snuggled into safety, there in that room where the wind sighed in the corners, bearing on it the smell and the sound of the sea. Sleep came at once.

We were almost there, señors.

30

MARCH 17, 1863. I had no nightmares, I seemed to have had no sleep at all before there came the discreet knock and Souza's apologetic murmur advising us that the tide had turned. There was a lingering impression that I'd been having an earnest conversation with someone about Catalina Island and its absurd history, going over and over the cryptic records. The person, who must have been Edward, was patiently explaining that everything was all right because we were really on the same side after all, that the office that employed him would hand on its discovery to the first cabal that would become Dr. Zeus, and that the contents of document D . . . the *what?*

I opened my eyes groggily, shivering, reaching for the shreds of memories, and of course they disintegrated into meaninglessness. I saw no blue light in the room, though. Edward's arm came out of the darkness, bracing around my shoulders. How hot his skin was.

"Wake up, my love," he said. "We've a crossing to make."

We washed and dressed, and he didn't take the trouble to shave, this time. Every concealed weapon had miraculously found its way into place again, though, and his gloves and hat were firmly on as we stepped out into the morning darkness.

Wide black sky, wide black horizon, and the glint of water between the waving reeds. Freshening wind and the promise of morning, much more of a smack of the sea and less of tidal mud. Souza was crouched in his boat, clearing away nets for seating space. He rose up and offered me his hand into the boat.

"We need to leave now," he said. I nodded and made room for Edward, who stepped in easily and silently and placed his saddlebag among the nets. Souza cast off and bent to his oars. We moved out, bearing well to the east of Dead Man's Island. Slowly we worked our way out of the shallows, past that island of bad reputation, and at length we felt the pull of the tide taking us into deep water. The wind rose. Edward helped Souza run up our little sail, Point Fermin began to recede behind us, and the black threat of the mainland dwindled away.

We had done it, we had got clear. The sky began to pale with morning, and we could see the island now, fair across open water, twenty miles out. I was making for a destiny of which I'd never dreamed, with the missing half of my soul beside me, and it didn't matter what we came to in the end. The morning shone with more promise than any I'd known in my long life.

Edward was leaning back on his saddlebag, watching the mainland shrink. He turned a speculative eye on Souza; then sat up and addressed me in his awkward Latin.

"The fisherman," he asked. "Does he speak my tongue?"

"No, he does not," I replied.

"Good." He continued in English, but kept his voice low all the same. "I estimate we'll make landfall shortly before noon, if this breeze continues steady. Friends will be waiting for us there."

"Englishmen conducting their scientific studies, yes, you told me," I said, smiling at him. And they must have made one hell of a scientific discovery, to judge from the tug-of-war that the British and Americans would be playing soon. Whatever it was, Edward and I would have flown to some further safety by then.

"Ye-es," Edward said. "And some others. Assuming he managed to find a competent pilot on his own, Mr. Rubery and a party of friends should also be arriving, at very nearly the same moment we do. You may be rather surprised at the company he keeps."

"Why, señor?" I asked, folding my hands in my lap and looking expectantly at him. Now would come his explanation of the piracy business.

"There will be certain American gentlemen with Alfred," Edward said, sitting up to face me, "who are under the impression that Her Majesty's government will assist them in a privateering venture in aid of the Confederacy, and that my colleagues on the island have been preparing a base for them from which they may prey on the Pacific Mail steamers. This is, of course, not precisely the case; but we aren't anxious that they should learn the truth immediately."

Asbury Harpending, that was the fool's name.

"It will be useful, in the event that they are caught," Edward continued, "to have the venture assumed to be a purely Confederate conspiracy. We will endeavor to supply them with all they need to make a fearful reputation for themselves, and with any luck their depredations will help push the War of Secession to a speedy conclusion. With funds from the San Francisco Mint cut off, Lincoln will surely sue for peace."

And California would be up for grabs, isolated on a distant coast.

"At this point," Edward said, smiling a cold smile, "there will be certain changes of plan suggested for the privateers. It is to be hoped, by that time, that Southern gentlemen will form only a minority of the crew—having been replaced gradually by gentlemen adventurers of Californian birth, whom I shall have recruited with your able assistance, my dear. We can also expect fresh numbers of my countrymen, once the American hostilities have ended and they can move with greater openness."

He leaned forward and spoke more quietly, and so smoothly. "But there will be an interval during which great tact and persuasion are called for, to convince the enthusiasts of the erstwhile Confederacy that a change of loyalties is in their best interests. It will fall to me to attempt this conversion, on a case-by-case basis. Those Southern gentlemen who cannot be induced to exchange the Stars and Bars for the Union Jack will meet with unfortunate accidents, and I regret to say that the arrangements for those accidents will also fall to me." He looked into my eyes, reading my reaction.

Yes, I know, it was murder he was talking about, but of tobacco-chewing bastards who trafficked in black slaves and had the temerity to dress up their shame in plumes and epaulets. I'd seen those belligerent Southern boys in the bar of the Bella Union. Someone might urge mercy for their kind, but it wouldn't be me. I nodded for him to continue.

"Shortly thereafter, my dear, you and I will have a number of journeys to make," he said. "If we can persuade certain persons of certain things—for example, that a league of amity between Great Britain and Mexico would benefit both parties—then various and assorted efforts by several persons in several countries should bear fruit. That being the case, happy days will ensue. And I will at last be more than Alfred Rubery's long shadow, and you will be whatever you choose to be, in whatever country you choose to reside."

"I may choose to travel, señor," I said, giving him my most meaningful look. He smiled and settled his tall hat more securely on his head, for the wind was blowing strongly now. Souza politely ignored us, leaning on the tiller.

I had no doubt Edward could talk Confederate privateers into supporting the cause of Britain, or persuade Benito Juárez that Her Majesty desired to assist him. The mystery, to me, was why a man with his abilities hadn't gone further. But being illegitimate put the wrong sort of stripe on his old school tie, and that carried so much negative weight with the English. It meant that superb men like Edward lived and died in obscurity, while their nation was run by second-rate boobs who'd lose that empire he was working so hard for. Eventually. Years from now.

Or would they?

This particular plan was already defeated—there would be no British-backed privateers stalking the Pacific Mail—but what about the other part of the plot, involving some discovery the British had made on the island? How would Dr. Zeus become involved? There was every indication that England—in that far-off future when it was no longer even the United Kingdom—would somehow slip into the director's chair at Dr. Zeus. And Dr. Zeus *did* rule the world. Secretly, of course. Would they be able to do this because of what they'd found on Catalina Island in 1862? And what could they possibly have found?

"I've never been to this island," I said. "Though of course I have heard the stories." This was a prompt, but it didn't work.

"What stories would those be, my dear?" Edward asked, extending his hand and clasping mine.

Damn. I sped through reference files. Any old farrago of nonsense would do to get the conversational ball rolling.

"The Indians used to believe that there was once a great continent here in the West, which drowned in much the same way as we believe Plato's Atlantis did," I said. "The Indians claimed there were white men who lived there, extraordinarily tall. They called the place Lemuria."

Edward looked puzzled. "Unusual name. Were there lemurs there as well?"

"I've no idea. In any case, these islands in the channel are thought to be the highest mountaintops of the submerged continent, the only part to survive the deluge. The white men who lived there were unable to prevent the sinking of their world, but they were mechanically brilliant—so the stories say—and produced engines of genius that far surpassed the modern railway or ironclad warship."

Ha, Edward reacted to that, if only in the pulse of his blood. His face showed nothing, however. "What an extraordinary story," he said. "I suppose it's all nonsense, though."

They *had* found something, and he knew about it. Was it some kind of technology? But whose? There had never been any real Lemurians.

I shrugged. "The Indians used to tell fantastic tales. The priests discouraged it, of course, as a lot of superstitious nonsense."

"As well they might," Edward said. "Though there is a growing opinion that the mythologies of primitive peoples ought to be collected and studied. Conquering races tend to destroy such things, to their own loss. Science now indicates that what were once thought to be fantastical myths may well have some basis in historical fact."

"For example?" I asked, sitting forward in anticipation.

He removed his tall hat and pushed his hair back from his forehead before setting the hat on his head again. "In Dover, I was recently shown the complete skeleton of an antediluvian monster, fossilized in solid rock. Educated persons had dismissed accounts of dragons as no more than fairy stories. And yet here was the leviathan himself, and any reasonably observant peasant must conclude it was a real creature that had lived once. And so it had: not galloping after knights and virgins, but sporting in vanished seas."

"An ichthyosaur," I said in disappointment. He wasn't going to tell me what they'd found on the island.

"That was its name, to be sure," he said, squinting at me in the sunlight. "Don't tell me you were trained in palaeozoology as well!"

"No, of course not," I said. "I saw an article in a San Francisco newspaper."

He nodded slowly, a speculative look on his face. "I do look forward," he said, "to the leisure for more of these conversations with you, my dear."

So much for artlessly digging information out of him. How much did he know about what had been found? I was never to find out. But I daresay you know, señors.

The sun was well up now, the little boat sped on and on, and with each hour the island became more than a blue outline. We could see the steep canyons and vast mountains in the interior. We were going directly across, in the shortest line, to the west end of the island: not near the future site of Avalon, but to the double harbor where the Union Army would build its barracks soon. From the sea, you might think Catalina was two islands here, a little range just west of the main mass; but they were connected by a half mile of level isthmus just above sea level, making a neck you could cross in five minutes' lazy walk.

It looked brown and dry, terribly overgrazed by sheep—not like a place you'd find fascinating endemic species of plants. But, then, there was more to this island than met the eye, wasn't there?

Edward took out his field glasses and scanned, and I scanned right with him. A few miles west of the isthmus was where the construction was going on. It was no simple field camp. I could see where they were preparing gun emplacements, and really the little bay they'd chosen was superbly suited for a defensive position. Neat field shelters and some kind of equipment, too, though it didn't look like anything connected with mining. A couple of plumes of smoke: small tidy breakfast fires, I'd bet, preparing kippers and whatever else Englishmen were eating for breakfast these days. I shuddered at the memory of the sardine tacos. Could I see the mysterious Silver Canyon from here?

No, it was back on the windward side of the island. Well, perhaps I'd have a chance to explore the area on foot.

I became aware that Edward had turned beside me and was peering at the far western end of the island, up the coast from the fortifications. I turned too.

There was a ship out there, rolling at anchor, her sails furled.

"Ah," said Edward with satisfaction. "Now, what should this be but the good ship *Chapman*, bearing her crew of traitors and pirates? And the slightly competent Alfred Rubery. Have the boatsman change course. Let's go cheer on the gallant Confederate cause, shall we?"

I gave the order to Souza, but my heart was in my mouth. That couldn't be the *Chapman*, because history had recorded that Rubery and the other conspirators were caught before they could leave San Francisco Bay. They should be in jail cells by now. So there was no way the *Chapman* could be arriving here at its appointed rendezvous, right on schedule. But if that ship wasn't the *Chapman*, what was it?

"Why is she just sitting out there, señor?" I asked. "Oughtn't she have moored in the bay before the camp?"

He shrugged. "Alfred may be following orders at last. He was to wait until I came aboard before taking her into the bay. I'd have been here by now, if all had fallen out as planned. So there he waits, like an obedient boy, for me to bring the valise and further orders. I daresay he'll be glad to see the money. It's rather difficult to recruit a crew on promises."

I scanned the ship. There was a crew on board, but at this range I couldn't tell much more. Nothing to do but sit and wait as we sped across the blue water; nothing but access the historical record.

I hurried through data files. What was the source Imarte found? *The Great Diamond Hoax*, here it was. And other stirring incidents, supposedly, in the life of Asbury Harpending. Just who was Harpending?

Liar, traitor, and swindler, according to historians; scion of a fine old Kentucky family of wealthy landowners, according to himself, as well as a philanthropic speculator, developer, and crusader for truth. In this year of 1863 he was only about twenty-one, though, with a long career of shady dealing before him.

I sped through the chapters. Here were the abortive attempts to stage a Confederate uprising, failed because of hysteria, lack of nerve, and the discovery of the Comstock lode. Just as Imarte had said. Here were the gallant Confederate sympathizers attempting to regroup with an eye to privateering, under the leadership of Harpending. Here Mr. Rubery entered the picture—callow British youth (I'll say) with a sympathy for Southern aristocracy and a love of adventure. Even Harpending made him out to be something of an idiot; though I wondered how much of the privateering scheme had come into shape *after* they met and not before, and whether Harpending was really their leader.

They spent money feverishly, buying the *Chapman*, buying cutlasses, cannons, firearms, and ammunition, and probably a Jolly Roger and cocked hats too. There was no mention of Rubery's making a trip to Veracruz to obtain more funds, but he must have done so, with a stopover in Los Angeles on his way back. Thanks to Cyrus Jackson's jealous passion, Rubery fled back to San Francisco empty-handed; and not only had he left the money behind, he'd come away without the list of contacts who would have helped the next part of the plan along.

For here it was in print: the conspirators were unable to find a navigator anywhere in San Francisco. They'd made inquiries, they'd had friends and acquaintances make inquiries for them; and word had evidently gotten around to the authorities that a band of young men with known Confederate sympathies was looking for an able-bodied navigator likewise eager to overthrow the Union government.

So one came forward, courtesy of the San Francisco Police Department, a man named William Law (surely a broad hint if ever there was one). The conspirators took Law into their confidence. He signed on readily and just as readily took all details of the plot to Captain of Police I. W. Lees.

Lees, being a wise man, opted to wait until all the birds were in the net. If Edward could read this, his hair would go gray. Law went along with all the preparations and agreed to be on board the *Chapman* well before her scheduled sailing time of eleven o'clock in the evening of March 14, 1863. That had been the meaning of the coded telegram Edward picked up the following day.

At ten o'clock on the 14th, I had been sitting in front of the cook-fire, listening to Juan Bautista play his guitar. Edward had just arrived from Veracruz and was settling into his room at the Bella Union. And Alfred Rubery and Asbury Harpending were just going on board the *Chapman* and discovering that Law was nowhere to be found.

Was this enough to warn them off? No, they left a sentry to watch for Law and went to bed in their bunks on the *Chapman*. The trusty sentinel dozed off too, it seemed, because the next thing they knew, it was broad daylight on March 15 and the U.S. warship *Cyane* had her guns trained on them. Boatloads of marines were bearing down on them from all sides, to say nothing of a tugboat full of San Francisco police.

And then? Off to Alcatraz with them for interrogation, at just about the time Edward was watching me undress.

News of the foiled plot went out over the telegraph that same day, to the whole world, as Edward and I lay in bed together. If we'd been in any other city, we'd have heard the newsboys crying the story under our windows; but we were in a coaching inn on the edge of nowhere, and we never knew a thing.

What did Rubery tell the police, under interrogation? Something to occasion those two Pinkerton men to go hurrying into the Bella Union as Edward and I approached it that evening? Were they tipped off by an alert telegraph operator, who compared the names on Edward's yet unclaimed message with the names in the breaking story? I cringed inside. No wonder there were bounty hunters after us the following day. Everyone must know now, Queen Victoria on her distant throne must know by now. Everyone knew but Edward.

I fast-forwarded through the details, desperate to see what would happen. The conspirators would be convicted of treason. Possibly because it would seem so obviously a stupidly boyish game, they would be sentenced to fines and imprisonment instead of death. Alfred Rubery's Parliamentary uncle would step in and wheedle a free pardon for him from Abraham Lincoln. Rubery would be thrown out of the country all the same, though, shipped out on one of the Pacific Mail steamers and transferred to a British vessel at Panama.

And that would be the end of the matter.

No villainous British plot to invade the state would ever be publicly uncovered, no scandal of foreign nationals preparing fortifications on Catalina Island. No mention at all of an Edward Alton Bell-Fairfax.

And yet the secretary of war would know enough to send the Army to Catalina. How would he make the connection between a bunch of silly young men wanting to play pirates for the Confederacy, all the way up there in San Francisco, and the activities of certain Britons on an obscure island off the coast of Los Angeles? All Harpending ever said in his memoirs was that they had a general plan to base themselves in some islands *off the coast of Mexico*. But then, he hadn't known about the whole plot, had he? And had he protested when he discovered the use to which his pirate ship was to be put, my smiling Edward would have been there to slip an inconspicuous knife between his ribs.

Did the authorities tell Alfred Rubery that he faced the prospect of being shot as a spy? He must have sung like a damned canary.

We were near the ship now, and there wasn't a soul on deck. She looked as deserted as the *Mary Celeste*. I realized, as we drew near, that whoever had anchored her in that particular little cove chose the spot with coy discretion: we were able to spot her from the open sea, but the men at the British camp on the other side of Arrow Point could have no idea she was there.

There were men on board, alive, alert, and waiting for us.

"Edward," I said, "this isn't right."

He didn't lower his field glasses, for he was studying the ship intently. "Not right? Moral qualms, my dear?"

How could I tell him what I knew? "Not that—there's something the matter here. Why isn't your friend on deck, watching for you?"

"That's a good question," he said, slowly adjusting the long focus. "How can you tell there's no one on deck at this distance, my dear?"

It was like a faceful of ice water, señors. He hadn't mentioned what he was seeing, and he knew I had no field glasses of my own. There was a sadness in his face when he lowered the glasses to look at me, but a certain shivery distance, too.

Nothing to do but brazen it out.

"I have trained eyesight," I explained, as though impatiently. "I was raised to count cattle on hills five miles away, señor. Can't your English shepherds do the same? Look." I pointed to the ship. "See the stain on her jib sail? See the red rag tied to her wheel? The three belaying pins on that rail there at the left, and the five at the right? Look there, that's a brown pelican lighting on her aft deck now. Stupid creature expects someone to toss it a fish. Do you see it, señor?"

"Yes," he said, looking through the glasses again.

"And do you see a living soul on deck?"

"No, my dear, I don't."

"And does that seem reasonable to you?"

"No, it doesn't." He lowered the glasses and looked at me again, not quite sure what to think. "You never cease to amaze me, Dolores. It should make our continued acquaintance interesting indeed. However—Alfred hasn't much experience with maritime customs such as leaving a watch on duty. Neither, I suspect, have his fellow privateers. They may all be belowdecks playing whist." He looked through the glasses again. "Or there may be something wrong. I doubt it, though. Sails reefed, anchor down, everything in order, both boats there."

"How do you even know that's Mr. Rubery's ship?" I was in agony. Nearer we flew and nearer, across the lovely clear water, closer to the ones who were waiting for us.

"That is another good question," he said coolly. He didn't know what to make of my terror, but he wasn't about to panic himself. "Let's just see, shall we? You!" he addressed Souza in Spanish. "Take us in, under her stern."

Souza looked inquiringly at me—though he understood Spanish perfectly well—and I nodded weakly. We made straight for her now, then angled around so that we were coming in with a good view of the aft cabin. There was her name, in big blocky letters: J. M. CHAPMAN. Her boarding ladder was down, in open invitation.

Behind my eyes, a line of text jumped out at me, Harpending peevishly complaining that the name of the vessel was the plain *Chapman*, though for some reason journalists had seen fit to refer to it in all the papers as the *J. M. Chapman*.

"It's she," said Edward briskly. He said to Souza, "Bring her alongside."

I stared up at the painted name. Freshly painted name. Wait, no. The J. and the M. and the CH were duller; only the APMAN gleamed with new enamel. I subjected it to infrared scanning and saw, underneath, the letters ISHOLM. This ship had been the *J. M. Chisholm* not long ago. Who had altered her name, and why?

"Señor," I said, keeping my voice as reasonable as I could. "Call it woman's intuition. I fear treachery here. What if Mr. Rubery has met with some misfortune?"

Edward gave me a long speculative look. "Then he'll need my assistance," he said. "In any case, it's my duty to find him. Are you frightened, Dolores? You needn't go on board if you are. This shouldn't take long."

He took up his saddlebag and caught hold of the ladder, climbing nimbly despite his awkward grip. I sat there and watched him a dull moment, before rising and scrambling after with a sob of desperation. If I couldn't prevent him from walking into the trap, perhaps I could get him out of it. Perhaps nothing very bad would happen after all. Mr. Rubery, twit that he was, would come out of this with no more than a slap on the wrist and deportation, so perhaps Edward and I would escape once more, sailing free into the sunset after amazing adventures.

We boarded the *J. M. Chapman* and stood on her empty deck. All sunlight and silence, but for the creaking of the rigging and the sough of breakers on the shore nearby.

"Edward," I whispered. "There are mortal men below decks."

He raised an eyebrow. "*Mortal* men?" he said, smiling a little. He set off down the deck and then halted, turning to me with the strangest look in his eyes. "What did you—?"

Yes, señors, I'd given myself away. Not that it mattered, however.

With only the slightest sound, the door of the aft cabin opened, and a man emerged. He was a clean-shaven nondescript in a neat gray suit, smiling as he leveled a pistol at Edward. "Commander Bell-Fairfax?" He had a pleasant flat American voice. "You're under arrest, sir. Could you set down that bag, please?"

Edward went white as a sheet, but he smiled that cold and narrow-eyed smile.

"Ah," he said. "This bag?" He set it down very carefully. He opened it. The Pinkerton agent made a sharp little noise, stepped toward him, thrusting out his pistol—but Edward held up both hands in a pacifying motion and slowly drew out the valise.

"This is what you want, I expect," he said, and held it up. The agent smiled and stepped forward, holding out his hand.

Edward shot him.

I had the American's pistol out of his hand before he fell. "Jump!" I screamed to Edward, for I could hear the men below hatches boiling from beneath us, coming up on deck as the wounded agent rolled and cried for help. I turned to see Edward composedly opening the valise and scattering its contents over the side, papers fluttering and falling, and the lovely violet ink blurring and melting away to nothing as soon as the pages settled on the water. The Americans would never learn the whole truth now. They'd get the island, but they wouldn't know what its secret was or where, and the British would find a way to creep back and take it from under their noses.

"Jump, for God's sake!" I ran to him, but the bullets got there first.

It didn't happen in picturesque slow motion. He neither jerked nor spun about. He coughed once, with the first hit; then he squared his big back and took the shots, doing his best to ignore them as he sent the last of the papers into the sea and dropped the valise after them. He pushed himself around to face me and the crew of Pinkerton agents who had surrounded us.

He met my gaze with an ironical smile. Oh, he was falling; his legs weren't working anymore. He toppled forward, and I caught him, and we sank to the deck in a welter of bright blood. His hat came off and rolled away.

I was sobbing, catching my breath in ugly little cries as I rocked him in my arms, trying to get enough air for a scream. Blood was coming up out of his mouth. He gave one grimace of pain and he stiffened; but then something seemed to get easier, and he opened his eyes and peered up at me with an inquiring expression, as though I had just made a remark he didn't quite hear and was hoping I'd repeat it.

The world had shrunk to that little space on the deck. Our enemies might have been a circle of statues, for all we noticed them. His world was shrinking even faster; he was fighting to keep his eyes focused on mine.

"Wh—what *are* you?" he asked, quietly, as though we were lying in a green garden somewhere and no blood was running down his chin.

The only gift I could give him now was the truth. My throat was like stone, but I got the words out, whispering to him.

"I'm not a mortal woman, *mi amor*. But it was science and medicine that made me so, not magic. I exist because your masters discovered something that enabled them to make immortal creatures like me, to do their work for them here in the past. They *will* create a race that can never age nor die, just as you said. This is what you have bought with your life."

He was knitting his brows, his breath was rasping and wet as he strained to hear me. Suddenly there was comprehension in his eyes, and they brightened. He gave a gurgling chuckle. He knew.

I fought to suck in a breath. His death was coming for him. I leaned closer and said, "Listen to me, my love. I'm trapped by centuries, I can't follow you. Come back for me and break my chains. Set me free. Will you set me free?"

He nodded. He looked into my eyes, trying to say something. He had neither the strength nor the time. A wind gusted across the deck toward us. His soul slipped away with it.

I bent over him, hiding his dead face with my hair.

"I hear no sound but your silenced voice," I murmured. "I feel no heat but the fire that burns you, I draw no breath but you come into me, before me, behind me, you are the sea and the rock!"

"Johnston's dead," someone announced. "Who's this woman?"

"The whore from the Bella Union, ain't she?" someone else said.

"God damn," said a voice directly above me. "I guess you could say this didn't turn out so well. What'll we do with this one?" A booted foot tapped Edward's leg.

"Weight the body," someone said. "We'll put out to sea and drop him in the channel. No evidence, gentlemen."

"Come on, girlie, get up." A hand closed on my wrist. "You're under arrest."

I don't really have a clear memory of what happened next, señors, only a few impressions. I remember seeing Souza in the distance, rowing away for his life. I remember the Americans screaming and trying to hide. If you want the details, you can check my video transmission. I know what I must have done; because when that longboat full of British voices came around the point to see what was going on, I remember throwing human heads at them. And an arm. I didn't kill the Englishmen, though, I'm fairly certain. I think they retreated in some haste. And then of course your security operatives came and found me, doubtless because poor Souza's control implant was broadcasting his horror.

And that's it, señors, that's the end of the story. I had a second chance to save my love, and I failed. I took unauthorized leave and I committed murder. I did find out a great many interesting things about the genesis of our Company, but I have a feeling that the information was classified, not for my eyes at all.

I was a bad machine.

But I've told you the truth, señors, every word. Now, you wouldn't have one more piece of Theobromos to spare, would you, for a poor old thing like me?

31

HOW VERY EMBARRASSING to read one's own testimony. If the hearing panel hadn't given me so much Theobromos, I'd have told them the story in half the time.

As it was, I lay in the worst case of theobromine poisoning I'd ever had, for three days and three nights, before they came for me and gave me to understand there would be no trial, no further action. I was only to be sent off to my new posting immediately. I was still groggy when they helped me into the silver box, and I heard the hiss, breathed in the yellow gas, and was abruptly *here*.

And where exactly is here? Ah, that's the cream of the jest. I crawled out of the box and wandered around in bewilderment for several minutes before I found the crates and dispatch case that had been sent with me. I fumbled open the seal and read my orders.

I am now the managing operative of a Dr. Zeus agricultural station, located—where else?—on Catalina Island, and the present year is 153,020 B.C.E. I am in fact the sole personnel assigned to this station, but after all I'm an immortal with unlimited strength, so I find myself adequate for the job. Plenty of heavy equipment I can drive, plenty of supplies sent as I request them. No company at all.

Is it my job to collect the rare endemic species that grow here and nurture them along? Not exactly. My assignment is to grow produce for the Company's Day Six resort on Santa Cruz Island, some miles north of here. I supply the salad bars of wealthy twenty-fourth-century vacationers, who pay out a considerable chunk of their income to be herded into cramped shuttles and thrown back through time to an unspoiled and unpolluted paradise where they can sport-fish, have their holos taken with dwarf woolly mammoths, or just relax by the pool. I read that in a brochure somebody dropped on the loading dock where I deliver the crates of radicchio, squash blossoms, and endive that I raise. I never stay to watch the ship arrive. I don't like talking to people.

My heart aches when I think of the Ventana and Big Sur. I can never go back there again. I'm forbidden to leave this garden I've made. And some violence has been done to my electronic memory, I fear. Something's been deleted. I can't access all those fascinating historical records of this island now, nor the successive altered maps. They don't seem to have realized that the information still exists in my human memory. But since I can't download the information to another operative, maybe they don't care, especially as I'm unlikely to see anyone I know back here. Even Joseph won't be born for a hundred thousand years. Longer for Lewis and the others. No way at all to talk about my discoveries, which is undoubtedly why I've been put so far in the past.

All things considered, though, the Company has treated me very well. One door closes, another one opens. This is a beautiful island right now, not at all the dry and rocky place it will become. There are immense forests here, ironwoods the equal of any sequoias you might find on the mainland, deep groves of mahogany trees, great spreading oaks and pines. Very little flat land, but what there is I have covered with neat green rows of vegetables, tidy orchards, and a small area for my own botanical experiments. No animals bigger than the little fox. Plenty of birds. No mortals at all . . . yet.

I'm to watch for them, though. This is very, very secret. Really I shouldn't be writing it down here, but who the hell will ever see? I'm to watch for certain people, odd-looking people with pale skins, who will arrive one day. They will not be Ancient Lemurians. It is expected they will arrive in well-designed oared galleys or perhaps even in gliders of some kind. It is expected they will settle in the Silver Canyon region. It is expected they will dig themselves in under a mountain and hide there, safe from marauding Neanderthal or Cro-Magnon primitives. I'm to report their arrival to the Company at once, and then I'm to monitor them unobtrusively for the next few centuries. When they've reached a certain level of technological development, when a certain energy signature begins to appear, I'm to alert Dr. Zeus. I suspect the Company will come in and slaughter them, then, and make off with their peculiar inventions.

Talk about piracy. But the Company won't take everything. Something will be deliberately left for the British to find in 1862 or whenever, some bit of machinery that will be hidden away in a military laboratory for decades, until some Briton finally discovers how to make it work, and gains thereby insight into certain dimensional principles that enable him to solve the problem of time travel. Dr. Zeus will have guaranteed its own birth, built the foundation of its empire. And Edward will have been the sacrificed hero whose blood mortared its cornerstone.

Pretty sneaky, eh?

It was a few centuries before I could bring myself to climb over to the west end of this island and look down into the anchorage where Edward died. I half-expected to see the ship lying there, and his poor mortal body sprawled on the deck. But none of that's happened yet. Thousands of years yet before the acorns fall that will grow into the trees that make up the timbers of the *J. M. Chapman* of fatal memory. Edward's distant ancestors are at this time knapping flints for hand axes. I would bet, though, that in some tribe on some cold green island there is one very tall savage who has learned how to put a wooden handle on his ax, or perhaps to draw reindeer on his cave wall. It will so unnerve his fellow cavemen that they'll grab him at the next spring equinox and sacrifice him to their gods. Perhaps some wretched little proto-Celtic girl will weep for him and wring her hands, too.

Who knows? We may have been in this dance since time began, and could never see the pattern until Dr. Zeus made me an immortal, unable to die or to forget. When Nicholas died, I was still too young to see what was going on. This last time with Edward gave them away, however. I don't believe in reincarnation, but surely even the Hindus don't imagine it works like this. What's the point? The same man circling through lives like a blazing comet, always returning on the same course, meeting the same inevitable doom before he vanishes into darkness, serving somebody's purpose with his death but never his own. The game is fixed. Whoever is running it—and I can guess at the identity, though not the reason—it's fixed.

But now at least I know.

I don't expect I'll see him again for a while. But I will see him again. He will come back and set me free, because he said he would. And it may not be on our next encounter, or the next, but one day the pattern of his sacrifice and death will be broken. We will make something better than this, he and I, and God help our masters if they try to prevent us.

In the meanwhile I tend my rows of corn and tomatoes, or wander on this narrow cobblestone crescent and admire the blue sea, or sit outside my shelter at night and watch the sky. I'm patient; I can wait.

He will come again.

The Graveyard Game

This one's for absent friends.

Miss you, Dave.

What Has Gone Before

T HIS IS THE *fourth book in the unofficial history of Dr. Zeus Incorporated.*

In the twenty-fourth century, a research and development firm invented a means of time travel. It also discovered the secret of immortality. There were, however, certain limitations that prevented the Company from bestowing these gifts left and right. But since the past could now be looted to increase corporate earnings, the stockholders were happy.

In the Garden Of Iden *introduced Botanist Mendoza, rescued as a child from the dungeons of the Inquisition in sixteenth-century Spain by a Company operative, Facilitator Joseph. In exchange for being given immortality and a fantastically augmented body and mind, she would work in the past for the future, saving certain plants from extinction.*

On her first mission as an adult, Mendoza was sent with Joseph to England, where she fell in love with a mortal, with bitter consequences.

Sky Coyote *opened over a century later, as Joseph arrived at the research base at New World One to look up his protégée and inform her they had both been drafted for a Company mission in Alta California. Mendoza said goodbye to the one friend she had made at New World One—Lewis—and went with Joseph.*

Near a Chumash Indian village she met a number of the mortal masters from the future, and was appalled to find them bigoted and fearful of their cyborg servants. Joseph learned unsettling facts about the Company that brought to mind a warning he'd been given long ago by Budu, the Enforcer who recruited him.

Why was it that, though the immortal operatives were provided with information and other entertainment from the future, nothing they received was ever dated later than the year 2355?

At the conclusion of the mission, Mendoza remained in the wilderness of the coastal forests, working alone as a botanist.

Mendoza in Hollywood *opened in 1862, as Mendoza journeyed reluctantly to her new posting: a stagecoach inn at a remote spot that one day would be known as Hollywood. There, near the violent little pueblo of Los Angeles (one murder a night, not counting Indians), she was to collect rare plants scheduled to go extinct in the coming drought.*

Mendoza found herself now haunted by visions of her mortal lover, and she was giving off Crome's radiation again, the spectral blue fire of paranormal abilities that no cyborg was supposed to possess.

In a local spot known for strangeness, she encountered an anomaly that threw her temporarily into the future. There she glimpsed her friend Lewis, who tried frantically to tell her of an impending disaster.

Into her life came another mortal—Edward Alton Bell-Fairfax, an English spy involved in a plot to grab California for the British Empire. Edward looked enough like Mendoza's first love to have been cloned from him. Mendoza abandoned her post and ran away with Edward.

As they raced for sanctuary on Catalina Island, pursued by American agents and bounty hunters, Edward began to suspect that Mendoza was far more than a coaching-inn servant. Mendoza discovered that Edward too was more than he seemed, in fact was connected to the Company in some way.

But before the lovers could solve their mutual riddle, their luck ran out. Edward was shot to death, and Mendoza went berserk with grief. The Company sent her to a penal station hundreds of millennia in the past—the preferred method of disposing of troublesome immortals . . .

Joseph in the Darkness

You KNOW SOMETHING, father? Sin exists. It really does.

I'm not talking about guilt, I'm talking about cause and effect. Every single thing we do wrong comes back to get us, sooner or later. You knew that, didn't you? And you told me, and I . . . well, I was so much more flexible than you, wasn't I? I could see all sides of every question. You saw black and white, and I saw all those gray tones.

For the longest time, I thought I was the one who had it right. I mean, you wound up here at last, didn't you? And I'm still free, as free goes. But whatever you're feeling, in there, I'll bet your conscience isn't bothering you.

You'd have let the little girl die, I know. Sized Mendoza up with that calm ruthless look, seen what she was and given your judgment: unsuitable for augmentation. Sent her back to die of starvation in the dungeons. She'd only have lasted another couple of days, she was so weak. Maybe I'd have let her die too, if I hadn't thought there was a chance they might interrogate her again before she died, and use the hot coals on her this time.

That was why I lied, father. It seemed doable at the time. Rescue the kid, make her one of us, give her a wonderful new life working for the Company. Nobody would ever find out about that freaky little something extra she had. Hell, every living thing generates the Crome's stuff from time to time. Only one person in a million ever manages to produce enough to do things like walk through walls or be in two places at once. How was I to know . . . ?

You're right, it was still wrong. And did anybody ever thank me for my random act of kindness? Not little Mendoza, that's for damned sure. Not on that day in England in 1555 when I stood beside her watching her mortal lover burn. How could she thank me? Her heart was in shreds and she could never die, no matter how much she wanted to, and it was my fault.

And I wouldn't be here now, either, would I, father? Going from vault to vault, looking up at the blind silent faces, to see if one of them is hers. Hoping to find her here in one of these houses of the near dead, even if I can't set her free this time, praying she's here: because there are worse places she might be.

I guess I was a lousy father to her. I hope I've been a better son to you. Yes, father, there's sin, and there's eternal punishment for sin. It's like a rat gnawing at your guts.

Sorry about the metaphor. Don't take it personally.

Look, we've got all night: and you're not going anywhere. I'll tell you about it.

Hollywood, 1996

SOMETHING ODD HAD happened.

Unless you possessed the temporally keen senses of an immortal cyborg, though, you wouldn't have noticed, over all the racket floating up from the roaring, grinding city. Lewis, being an immortal cyborg, frowned slightly as he accelerated up Mount Olympus Drive and scanned the thick air. He was a dapper man, with the appearance of someone who has wandered out of a Noel Coward play and got lost in a less gracious place.

Earthquake? No, or there would have been car alarms shrieking and people standing out on the sidewalk, a place the inhabitants of Los Angeles County seldom ventured nowadays without body armor.

Still, there was a sense of insult on the fabric of space and time, a residual shuddering Lewis couldn't identify at all.

He turned left into Zeus Drive and nosed his jade-green BMW into the driveway of the house. Nothing out of the ordinary here that he could see. He shut off the engine, removed his polarized sunglasses and put them in their case, removed his studio parking tag, and carefully put glasses and tag in the glove compartment. Only then did he emerge from the car and look about, sniffing the air.

Other than a higher than normal amount of ozone and an inexplicable whiff of horse, the air wasn't any worse than usual. Lewis shrugged, took up his briefcase, locked the car, and entered Company HQ.

What was that high-pitched whine? Lewis set down his briefcase, tossed his keys on the hall table, and looked into what would have been an ordinary suburban living room if it hadn't had a time tran-

scendence chamber in one wall. Maire, the station's Facilitator, was
activating it. She turned to him.

"You should have been here, Lewis. We've had quite an afternoon," she said.

He barely heard her, his gaze drawn to the window of the chamber.
He gaped, astonished to see a pair of very uneasy horses and two oddly
dressed people in there, just beginning to be obscured by the rising
stasis gas.

One of the people raised her hand and waved. She was a sharp-
featured woman, with cold black eyes and hair bound back in a long
braid. She smiled at him. He knew the smile. It made her eyes less
cold. The woman was the Botanist Mendoza.

Lewis had loved her, quietly, for several centuries, and she had
never once noticed. They were stationed at the same research base for
many years before she was transferred. He thought of writing to her
after that, but then lost his chance, because she made a terrible mistake.

So terrible, in fact, that it was impossible that she could be standing there now smiling at him.

Then he connected the horses with the nineteenth-century clothing
she was wearing. Was he seeing her, somehow, before the commission
of her mistake? Was there any chance he might warn her, prevent the
catastrophe?

No, because you couldn't violate the laws of temporal physics.
You couldn't change history. He knew that perfectly well and yet
found himself running to the chamber as the gas boiled up around her,
beating on the window with his fists.

"Mendoza!" he shouted. "Mendoza, for God's sake! Don't go with
him!"

She stared, taken aback, and then turned her wondering face to
her companion. Lewis realized in despair she thought he meant the
other immortal, and cried, "No!"

She looked back at him and shook her head, shrugging.

"No, no!" Lewis shouted, and he could feel tears welling in his
eyes as he pressed his hands against the glass, to push across time by
main force. Futile. She was vanishing from his sight even now, as the
yellow gas obscured everything.

Out of the clouds, her hand emerged for a moment. She set it
against the window, palm to palm with his flattened hand, a gesture
he would have died for once, rendered less personal by the thickness
of the glass.

Then she was gone, he had lost her again, and he staggered back
from the chamber and became aware that Maire was standing beside

him. He turned and looked into her amazed eyes, struggled to compose himself.

"Er—what's going on?" he inquired, in the coolest voice he could summon.

"You tell me!" was Maire's reply.

In the end, though, she had to explain first. What he had seen was a temporal anomaly—nothing the Company couldn't handle. In fact Maire had received advance warning this morning from Future HQ. It was all listed in the Temporal Concordance. Everyone knew that weird things happened at the Mount Olympus HQ anyway, overlooking as it did Laurel Canyon's notorious Lookout Mountain Drive. It had been built to monitor that very location, actually.

This didn't do a lot to clear up Lewis's confusion. Temporal Concordance or not, it was still supposed to be impossible for anybody in the past to jump *forward* through time. When he mentioned this, Maire glanced at the techs and drew him aside.

"She was your friend, wasn't she?"

"Yes," said Lewis. "A—a coworker. We were close."

Maire said in a low voice:

"Then you knew she was a Crome generator."

Lewis hadn't known. He was unable to hide his shock. Watching his face go pale, Maire lowered her voice even more.

"Lewis, I'm sorry. I'm afraid it's true. Something latent that wasn't caught when she was recruited, apparently. You know what those people are; she might have warped the field any one of a dozen ways. What can I tell you? The impossible happens, sometimes."

He nodded, silent, afraid the tears might come again. Maire looked him up and down and pursed her lips.

"Under the circumstances, you see why there wasn't anything you could have done to help her," she said, in a tone that was gentle but suggested he'd better get a grip on himself now.

Lewis gulped and nodded.

Nothing more was said that night, and he thought the matter would slip by without further discussion. But next morning at breakfast, Maire said, "You're still upset. I can tell."

"I guess I made a fool of myself," Lewis replied, sipping his coffee. "She was a good friend."

"I wouldn't worry about it, Lewis," she told him, stirring sugar into her cup. The tech who was on his hands and knees scrubbing a large stain off the carpet looked up to glare at her. She glared back and slowly lifted her coffee, drinking it in elaborate enjoyment. "I might have done the same thing in your shoes. Besides, you're a valued Company operative."

"That's nice to know," said Lewis mildly, but he felt the hair stand on the back of his neck. He modified the slight tremor into a sad shake of his head. "Poor Mendoza. But, after all, a Crome generator! At least the rumors make sense now."

"Yes," Maire agreed. "Cream?"

"Thank you." Lewis held out his cup. The tech made a disgusted noise. He was a relatively young immortal, having traveled to 1996 from the year 2332 and not liking the past at all. He didn't care for decadent old immortals who indulged in disgusting controlled-substance abuse either. Coffee, cream, and chocolate were all illegal in his era. More: they were immoral.

"Unfortunate, but the sooner we put it behind us the better," Maire continued. She rose and wandered over to the picture window, which looked out across Laurel Canyon. It was a hazy morning in midsummer, with the sky a delicate yellow shading to blue at the zenith. The yellow was from internal combustion engines. The air burned, acrid on one's palate, and was full of the wailing of sirens and the thudding beat of helicopter blades. Maire was fifteen thousand years old, but the late twentieth century didn't bother her much; she'd seen worse. Besides, this was Hollywood.

Behind her, Lewis drained his coffee and set down his saucer and cup. "Sound advice," he said. "Well, I'd better hit the road. I'm going up to San Francisco today. That fellow with the Marion Davies correspondence has settled on a price at last."

"No, really?" Maire grinned. "I suppose you'll pay a little visit to . . ." She dropped her eyes to the tech, who was still scrubbing away, and looked back up at Lewis. *Ghirardelli's?* she transmitted on a private channel.

Lewis stood and took her hand. *Shall I bring you back a box of little Theobromos cable car?* he transmitted back.

Her smile widened, showing a lot of beautiful and very white teeth. She squeezed his hand. She was a strong woman. *You're a dear.*

"To Fisherman's Wharf? Certainly. Shall I bring you back a loaf of sourdough bread?" Lewis asked.

"You're a dear! Boudin's, please." She glanced down at the tech mischievously. "I wonder if they'll still pack up those boiled crabs in ice chests for you."

The tech looked horrified.

"I'll find out." Lewis slipped his hand free and took his briefcase and keys. "Ta-ta, then. If I have to stay over, I'll give you a call."

"Oh, stay over," Maire ordered, waving him to the door. "Too long a drive to make twice in one day. Besides, you could use a little vacation. Get this unfortunate incident out of your mind."

"Oh, that," said Lewis, as though he'd forgotten already. "Yes, well, I imagine a ride on a cable car will lighten my spirits."

He wasn't referring to the popular tourist transit. *Theobroma cacao* has a unique effect on the nervous systems of immortals. Maire chuckled at his joke. The tech looked over his shoulder in a surly kind of way as Lewis stepped out into the heat and light of a Southern California morning.

He walked once around his car to inspect it for vandalism. When this Company HQ had been built, thirty years earlier, the gated community in which it was situated was regularly patrolled, to say nothing of being perched so far up on such a steep hill as to deter most criminals. Times had changed.

Sooner or later, they always did.

Satisfied that his leased transport was safe for operation, Lewis got in. Carefully he fastened his seatbelt and put on his sunglasses; carefully he backed out onto Zeus Drive and headed over the top of the hill to the less crowded exit from Mount Olympus. As he descended, he had a brief view of the city that stretched to the sea. Beyond that it had once been possible to see Catalina Island. The island was still there, but the smog hid it. Only once in a great while, when atmospheric conditions were just right, could it be glimpsed.

He proceeded down to Hollywood Boulevard and headed north through Cahuenga Pass, where he got on the Hollywood Freeway. He bore east to Interstate 5. After Mission San Fernando he followed the old stagecoach road, now a multilane highway into the mountains. It took him north, under arches restored since the last earthquake.

Long high miles brought him to Tejon Ranch, where the road dropped like a narrow sawmill flume between towering mountains preposterously out of scale. At the top, the San Joaquin Valley hung before his eyes like a curtain, and far down and away there the tiny road raced across it, straight as an arrow.

He shivered, remembering how bad the grim old Ridge Route had been, especially in the season of flash floods, or forest fires, or blizzards, or summer heat so extreme, it made automobile tires explode. The modern road had only the drawback of the San Andreas Fault, which lay directly beneath it.

But there was no earthquake scheduled today, so as he shot down onto the plain through a miasma of burning brakes he muttered a little prayer of thanks to Apollo, in whom he did not particularly believe, but one really ought to thank *somebody* for getting safely down that pass.

For the next four hours the view was the same: the lion-yellow Diablo Range on his left, flat field on his right, stretching across the floor of the valley to the Sierra Nevadas, the eastern wall of the world. Straight ahead lay the highway, shimmering in the heat. Memory rose like a ghost from the bright silent monotony.

He did not want to remember himself striding along the front walk of Botany Residential with a bouquet of red roses, and he was even whistling, for God's sake, he was that happy. Could anything have been more of a cliché? Right in through the lobby, past all the mortal servants and the Botany staff leaving for early dinners, and he didn't care who saw him. He waited at the elevator, still whistling. He might as well have had a neon sign on his forehead: I AM A HAPPY MAN.

The elevator doors opened, and there stood Botanist Mendoza, ice bucket in hand. She smiled at him, briefly. She didn't smile at many people, but once at a party he'd been casually kind to her. It hadn't amounted to much; he'd seen her alone at a table, miserably unhappy, and brought her a handful of cocktail napkins to dry her eyes. Could he help? No, she explained with brittle dignity: it was only that she'd once loved a mortal man, and he'd been dead now for forty years, and she hadn't realized it had been that long until something at the party reminded her. She didn't really want company, but Lewis stayed long enough to be sure she was all right.

He smiled and nodded at her now, and she nodded back. They stepped past each other, she to the ice machine and he to ascend into realms of delight. He thought.

As it turned out, he got ice too.

Ten minutes later he was standing outside the elevator on the fifth floor of Botany Residential, in the act of tossing the roses into the trash chute, when the door opened and Mendoza was standing there again, witness to his bitter gesture. Her eyes widened. He drew himself up, summoning what shreds of self-respect he had left, and adjusted his lace cuffs.

"Hello, Mendoza," he said.

"Oh, Lewis. I'm sorry," she said.

She took him down the hall to her apartment, and he didn't mean to pour out his woes, but he did, and she listened.

They stayed there for hours, until he talked it all out, and then it seemed like a good idea for them to sneak down to the bar in the lobby and go on talking over drinks. For some reason she decided to let him past the wall of sarcasm with which she kept the rest of the world at bay. It couldn't have been his little moment of chivalry with the cocktail napkins. Lewis had been kind to a lot of women. But, laughing with her in that cramped little bar, he spent the best evening he'd had in a long time. And they were seen.

"You went out with the Ice Witch?" hooted Eliakim from Archives. "*Mendoza?* Botanist Mendoza? You took a flamethrower instead of a bottle or something?"

"None of your business," Lewis said. "But it might interest you to know that she's a perfectly delightful woman."

"This is the redhead we're talking about, right?" Junius from Catering leaned over the back of his chair, eyes wide with disbelief. "The workaholic? The one who isn't interested in *anybody?* I tried to kiss her once at a Solstice party, and I thought I'd have to get a skin graft for the frostbite!" He looked at Lewis with a certain awe that Lewis found flattering.

He merely shrugged. "It doesn't bear discussion."

Of course they promptly went out and told most of New World One, and for about two weeks rumors flew. He went to Mendoza to apologize.

"To hell with them," she said philosophically. "Us a couple? Are they nuts? What a bunch of nasty little academic gossips, and what overblown imaginations."

"I just wanted you to understand that none of it came from me," he said, not that pleased.

"I know," she replied, looking at him with a fondness that made his heart skip a beat. "You're a good man, Lewis. You're the nicest immortal I've ever known."

She kissed him, then, on the cheek, and tousled his hair.

They never became lovers, but she was affectionate with him in a way she never was with anyone else. He accepted that. They became great friends. When he was transferred to England, he found he missed her terribly. When he learned what had happened to her, years later in Los Angeles, he was sick at heart.

San Francisco

He gave a sigh of relief when at last he turned west through the Altamont Pass, fighting the wind until he got through to the East Bay cities, leaving the golden desolation well behind him.

Chrome and glass, sea air, the Oakland Bay Bridge with its section that had fallen out during the last big earthquake—all nicely replaced now, millions of busy commuters never gave it so much as a thought anymore, but Lewis's knuckles were white on the steering wheel until he had crossed into the city.

He made his way along the diagonal of Columbus, where he turned up a steep and narrow street and called upon a man in a dark rear apartment. A price was named and met; several bundles of cash were removed from Lewis's leather briefcase, to be replaced by a certain packet of letters. Lewis got back into his car and checked his internal chronometer.

Three hours ahead of schedule.

He started the car and took it up the long spiral to Coit Tower, apologizing to the transmission. There he parked and walked to the edge of the terrace, to all appearances a young executive taking an afternoon off to admire the spectacular view.

He removed his sunglasses and folded them away in his breast pocket. He looked out across the bay at Marin County. Somewhere over there . . . ? He transmitted a tentative inquiry. It was returned immediately, from the depths of the city at his feet:

Receiving your signal. Who's that?

Literature Specialist Lewis. Joseph?

Lewis! What are you doing up here?

We have something to discuss in private. Coordinates, please?

Directions were transmitted. Lewis got back into his car and drove down from Coit Tower, apologizing this time to the brakes and promising to go nowhere near Lombard Street's notorious block.

He drove to another tourist attraction instead: the great outdoor shopping mall on Pier 39. Parking, he wandered through the mortal throng, the Europeans with cameras, performance artists, recovering addicts hawking cheap jewelry from card tables. Near the entrance Lewis spotted the location he sought. It was an amusement arcade of the modern variety, promising the thrills, so popular in this late twentieth century, of vicarious mass destruction and simulated murder. Cautiously he went in, politely declining a handbill that would have got him twenty cents off a frozen yogurt cone.

He stood peering down a long dark corridor filled with electronic games, tuning his hearing to sort through the wall of noise. Beeps, crashes, screams, roaring, and a familiar voice:

". . . so your place would be the first, Jeff. We're willing to throw in the service plan for free, too. But, you know, I really think this model sells itself. I mean, I couldn't believe it when I saw the resolution, personally."

"Yeah, I like the graphics," somebody said, almost won over but wanting a bit more assurance. Lewis walked around a console where an adolescent boy was piloting a flying motorcycle through flames and winged demons. He beheld two bearded men, spotlighted in reflection from the sunlit world outside.

One was a young mortal, in nondescript casual clothes. The other was an immortal, a short and rather stockily built male in an Armani suit. His ancestry might have been Spanish, or Jewish, or Italian, or Greek; in fact he had been born centuries before any of those nations existed, though he appeared to be in his early thirties. He wore a neatly trimmed black mustache and beard, which gave him a cheerfully villainous look.

Open on the floor at his feet was a bulky white case bearing the logo of a well-known special effects house based in Marin County. He was holding a curious visored helmet in his hands, extending it to the mortal.

Both men turned to look at Lewis as he approached.

"Do you have a soda machine in here?" Lewis inquired.

"Sorry, no," the mortal told him, but the man in the Armani suit reached out a beckoning hand.

"Hey, friend, have you got a minute? Would you mind being part of an impromptu demonstration here?"

"Not at all," Lewis said. The immortal reached out to shake his hand.

What are you doing?

Bear with me.

"Name is Joseph X. Capra, how're you doing today? Great. Listen, I'm just offering my friend here some of the latest virtual reality technology for his business, and I'd like to get an unbiased opinion of this new helmet. Would you mind trying it on?"

"Not at all," said Lewis graciously, setting his briefcase between his feet. "Of course, I don't play VR games much—"

"That's okay, friend. That's even better, you know? You won't know what to expect." Joseph stepped around the case and set the helmet on Lewis's head. He fastened down the visor, and Lewis found himself in total darkness, listening to the voices outside.

"Now, just hang in there a minute, friend. You'll experience maybe a second of disorientation, but I promise you, the room won't be moving. Let's see, would you like to try the walk through Stonehenge? That's a neat one, let's get you set up for that."

"Sure," Lewis said.

Jeff said doubtfully: "I understand the Japanese have stuff now that's five years ahead of anything we have, so this is probably already obsolete—"

"This they don't have," said Joseph firmly. "Trust me on this one, pal. Here we go, the walk through Stonehenge!"

Lewis heard a click, and ethereal New Age music began to play in his headphones as Salisbury Plain opened out before him. He seemed to be drifting across it like a cloud, advancing on the Neolithic monument as it might have looked shortly after its completion. White-robed druids were moving in procession around it, chanting.

Really, Joseph, there weren't any druids yet when Stonehenge was finished. I was one, I should know. "Gosh, this is—quite amazing," said Lewis.

"You like those visuals, huh? Aren't they killer?" *Yeah, I know. What do you want? The artist is a neopagan reincarnated shaman in his spare time.* "But the best part's coming up in just a couple of seconds. Hang in there—"

Lewis felt a hand grip his shoulder, and it was just as well, because there was a sudden flash within the helmet that left him with a pattern of stars dancing before his eyes. The virtual world around him skewed and broke up. He could tell he was supposed to be watching the arrival of the sun god Belenos, but the image was fragmented. He felt sick and dizzy.

"Oh—ah—wow! What an experience!" he chirped desperately. *What in God's name did you just do to me?*

"You like that?" The grip did not leave his shoulder. "Think you'd come back to my friend's operation, here, to play this one?" *I'll explain when we're out of here.*

"Yes, certainly. Can't wait!" *I'd sooner have my liver torn out by harpies!*

"Unfortunately, this is only a sampler program, so you only get an excerpt," Joseph said, as the music stopped and the picture went to black. There was another click, and the Great Pyramid began to loom into view as Joseph lifted the helmet away. Lewis stood blinking, running a self-diagnostic.

Something's wrong! There's an error in my data transmission.

Yeah, it's fried for the next twenty-four hours. Mine too.

He was referring to the constant flow of data that went back to a Company terminal somewhere, the visual and auditory impressions from every immortal operative. It guaranteed that an operative in the field was always being watched over, could be rescued in time of trouble; but it also made private conversation impossible, except through subvocal transmission, which required a lot of concentration.

Are you out of your mind? Lewis transmitted.

No, but the Company's out of yours. Joseph was grinning, shaking his hand again. "I'd like to thank you for your valuable time and opinion. Great meeting you." *Go outside and wait. I'll be finished here in just a minute.* He turned to Jeff and said, "So okay, that's a guy who doesn't regularly use your product, and see the effect it had on him? Now. Because this is practically the prototype, Mr. Lucas feels . . ."

Lewis tottered outside and groped hurriedly for his sunglasses. He bought a Calistoga water at a snack stand and sat down on a bench with it. His hands shook as he poured the drink into a paper cup and sipped carefully.

He watched Joseph emerge from the arcade with Jeff, deep in conversation. They went across the street to what was obviously Joseph's car—a black Lexus sports coupe, gold package—and loaded the case into the trunk. Finally Joseph shook Jeff's hand and walked back with him as far as the arcade entrance, talking earnestly and persuasively the whole while. They shook hands again, and the mortal went back inside. Joseph stood there a moment, going through a routine of finding and putting on his Ray-Bans, shooting his cuffs, patting his pockets for his keys, as Lewis got up and strolled toward him.

So, want to take my car?

I'd really rather not drive in this condition, thank you. Lewis frowned slightly as he finished his mineral water and put the cup in a trash receptacle.

Trust me, the dizziness won't last, Joseph told him as they walked across the street, pretending not to notice each other. *But you sounded like you had something private to discuss, and now we can discuss it out loud. Neat trick, huh?*

Remarkable, but couldn't you have invented something a little less painful?

Joseph pulled out his keys, making his car beep twice as it unlocked for him. *I didn't invent it. Total fluke discovery. The particular hardware in that particular helmet plus the glitch in that particular sample program. Nothing the Company could ever have anticipated when they designed us. I'm working on reproducing the effect in something smaller and more portable, though.* He got into the car, and Lewis got in on the other side.

Dear Lord! You'd better be careful, Joseph. Is it safe to talk in here?

"Oh, yeah," said Joseph, looking over his shoulder as he backed out of his parking space. "But I'd wait till we get where we're going."

"Where are we going?"

"Chinatown!" Joseph grinned and peeled away from the curb.

They parked in Portsmouth Square near the Stevenson Monument. Lewis looked around nervously at the towering buildings. "A lot of these are unreinforced brick, you know," he remarked.

"Uh-huh," said Joseph, striding away up the street. "But we both know there's no earthquake today, so what's the problem?"

"It's the principle of the thing," Lewis objected, hurrying after him. "I don't see how you can overcome the basic hazard-avoidance programming."

"You live long enough, you can figure out ways around almost anything," said Joseph, stopping to look up at a rusting pink neon sign. "Come on, this is it. Good old Sam Pan's."

He stepped through a narrow doorway into what was apparently a restaurant, and spoke in fluid Cantonese to an elderly man in a stained apron. Lewis waited in the doorway, peering doubtfully into the tiny dim kitchen. Before him a steep flight of wooden stairs ascended next to the yawning mouth of a dumbwaiter. It opened on a black shaft whose impenetrable darkness stank like a crypt.

The elderly man nodded and sent a slightly less elderly man to lead them up the stairs. On the third floor landing they emerged into a lofty dining room with card tables lined up along the street windows, through which the afternoon sun poured like gold. Flies whirled merrily in the sunbeams. The waiter settled them at a table and shuffled away to the dumbwaiter, where two bottles of beer rose smoothly into sight. He brought them to Joseph and went off to sit at the table by the staircase, where he proceeded to remove his right shoe and sock and examine his corns.

"We're not going to eat here, are we?" murmured Lewis.

"What are you, nuts?" Joseph's eyes widened as he opened their beers. "But isn't this a great place to talk in private? Can you imagine any Company operative coming in here for any reason at all? Get a load of *this*." He jabbed with a chopstick between two of the bricks in the bare wall; ancient mortar trickled down like fine sand. "Any quake over 6.2 and, boy—"

"Don't." Lewis closed his eyes.

"Hey, it's okay. Next big one isn't scheduled for—" Joseph looked at his chronometer. "Well, a while, anyway. So, what did you want to talk about?" He lifted his bottle and drank.

Lewis drew a deep breath. "You know I was posted to the Laurel Canyon HQ back in '65."

"The Mount Olympus place?" Joseph frowned. "That's the one that monitors the Lookout Mountain Drive anomaly, huh? It's a full-service HQ now?"

"Budget reasons," Lewis said.

Joseph sighed and shook his head. "Jesus. One of these days that whole place will get sucked into some black hole, you know? So, what happened? Was there a disturbance?"

"Yes, apparently, though it was over by the time I got there," said Lewis. He wondered how to tell Joseph what he had to say next. Finally he just said it. "Joseph, I saw Mendoza."

He wasn't prepared for the reaction. Something flared for a moment in Joseph's eyes, then burned out as fast as it had appeared. He lifted his beer and took another swallow. "Really?" he said casually. "No kidding? How's she doing these days?"

"What do you mean, how's she doing these days?" gasped Lewis, staring at him.

Joseph looked for a long moment into Lewis's white face. "Oh," he said. He set the beer down carefully. He put his head in his hands.

"You mean you didn't know?" Lewis was horrified. "I'd have thought you of all people would have been notified!"

"Yes and no," said Joseph in a muffled voice.

"All these years I thought you *knew*." Lewis sagged back in his chair. "My God. I was never officially notified myself, I came across the partial transcript in my case officer's files."

"What happened to her?" Joseph lifted his face. His eyes were cold now. "You tell me. I'd rather hear it from you."

"She was arrested," Lewis said. "And . . . retired from active duty. Joseph, I'm sorry, I never thought—"

"Arrested? What the hell did she do? When was this?"

"1863. She was stationed in Los Angeles, and—"

"LA?" Joseph said. "They sent her down there? What did they do that for? She was in the Ventana, she was okay. Nothing grows in Los Angeles! Nothing natural, anyhow."

"Well, things used to, before the 1863 drought. There's that temperate belt, remember? She was stationed in the old Cahuenga Pass HQ."

"Bleeding Jesus!"

"Well, she was doing all right. Apparently. She'd completed her mission and everything, but . . . From what I can tell, the job ended, and she wasn't reassigned anywhere else." Lewis swallowed hard. "You know how layovers can be."

Joseph nodded. "If trouble's going to happen, it happens on a layover. Every time. Some goddam idiot of a posting officer . . . Tell me the rest."

Lewis wrung his hands. "I'm not clear on the details. As far as I could make out, somehow everybody was away from the HQ one day except for Mendoza and a junior operative. And . . . a mortal came to the station while the boy was in the field. She, er, ran off with the mortal. Deserted."

"With a mortal?" Joseph stared. "But she couldn't stand being around mortals! Not since—" He halted. "Who was this guy? Did anybody find out?"

"Oh, yes, the boy testified. It was his testimony transcript I saw, actually. Rather weird; the mortal seems to have been one of those Englishmen their foreign office sent out back then to court the Confederacy." Lewis stopped. Joseph had gone a nasty putty color under his tan.

"You did say Englishman, right?"

"I know. Bad luck, wasn't it? After what happened to her in England all that time before." Lewis shook his head. "Maybe the coincidence—I don't know. But it ended rather quickly. And unpleasantly. The Englishman died, I know that much."

"You're sure about that," said Joseph.

"Well—yes."

"What did they do with her? Where did they send her?" Joseph asked.

Lewis made a sad gesture, turning his empty palms up on the table.

"But you said you saw her!"

Lewis nodded. "I told you there was a disturbance. It was in 1862, before the incident happened. She and a fellow operative went into Laurel Canyon hunting for specimens. I don't know what could have possessed them to do it, but they rode up to Lookout Mountain Drive. And somehow or other the temporal wave sucked them *forward*, into 1996."

"Forward." Joseph gaped at him. "No, that's nuts, you must have misunderstood. We can't go forward. They must have been pulled from 2062. You heard wrong."

"Joseph, I saw them," said Lewis quietly. "They were wearing nineteenth-century clothes. They'd been riding horses, even the horses had been pulled along with them!"

"But—" Joseph was too stunned to continue.

"I got there just as they were being sent back," Lewis explained. "They were already in the transcendence chamber. And I saw her there, and I just—" He paused. "I tried to warn her about what she was going to do. I had to! And she couldn't understand me through the glass, she just stood there looking bewildered." He had to stop.

Joseph reached out and patted his arm. "It was a good try. There'll be trouble over that, though, you know."

"Oh, it's not that bad," Lewis said. "My case officer and I get along. I think I smoothed it over. It's not as though it did any good." He laughed bitterly. "History cannot be changed."

"Watch out, all the same." Joseph was still puzzled. He looked sharply at Lewis. "When did all this happen?"

"Yesterday afternoon."

"The place must be swarming with techs trying to find out how it happened. How'd you get away?"

"Well, I had business up here anyway and I thought—I thought you knew about her, you see, so you might have an idea where she's being kept. It was one thing to learn about her arrest and feel awful for years, but then to see her! Suddenly I just couldn't stand it anymore. As for how it happened, well, isn't it obvious?"

"No. Would you mind letting me in on the little secret?" said Joseph harshly. "Because in—what, twenty-odd thousand years of going around the block?—this is the first time I've ever heard of anybody defying the laws of temporal physics!"

Lewis looked at him miserably. "It was Mendoza, Joseph. She'd become a Crome generator. *She* set off the temporal wave. You didn't know that either?"

Joseph was silent for about thirty seconds. Then, moving too quickly for mortal sight, he leaped to his feet and hurled his beer bottle across the room. It smashed against the brick wall. The waiter looked at him reproachfully.

"Let's get out of here," croaked Joseph. "I need to do myself some damage." He pulled out his wallet and withdrew a fifty-dollar bill, which he thrust at the waiter as he shouldered past him. He ran clattering down the stairs, Lewis following him closely.

The waiter thrust the money into his pocket and, sighing, got a couple of paper napkins from the cutlery stand. Careful not to step in the broken glass with his bare foot, he crouched to shove it all together in a small pile between the two napkins. He scraped up as much as he could into the napkins. Looking around, he finally dropped them down the dumbwaiter shaft. The rest he pushed up against the baseboard, into a spacious crack there. Wiping his hands on his apron, he put on his sock and shoe again and limped downstairs. His corns hurt.

There are a lot of strange people in San Francisco, and if you work there, you soon grow used to occasional peculiarities in your customers; but the girl behind the cash register at Ghirardelli's decided that this took weirdness to new heights. Two executives in tailored business suits were sitting at one of the little white tables in the soda fountain area, glaring hungrily at the fountain worker who was preparing their eighth round of hot chocolate. They had marched in, put down a hundred-dollar bill, and told her to keep the drinks coming. On the floor between their respective briefcases was a souvenir bag stuffed with boxes of chocolate cable cars, and the table was littered with foil wrappers from the chocolate they had already consumed.

To make matters stranger, they had the appearance of junior delegates from opposing sides of a celestial peace conference: the dark one with his little diabolic beard and the fair-haired one with his fragile good looks. As she watched, the devil jumped up the second his order number was called and went swiftly, if unsteadily, to take his tray. He grabbed the cocoa-powder canister on his return. Sitting down across from the angel, he added a generous helping of cocoa to his hot chocolate. Then, apparently seized by an afterthought, he opened the canister and shook out a couple of spoonfuls onto the marble tabletop. Giggling guiltily, he pulled out an American Express card and began scraping the cocoa powder into neat lines.

"Danny!" She stopped the busboy as he came through the turnstile. "Look at him! Is he really going to—?"

He was. He did. The angel went into gales of high-pitched laughter and fell off his chair. The devil sighed in bliss and leaned down for a pass with the other nostril.

"I don't know what's wrong with them," said the girl in bewilderment. "I swear to God they were both sober when they came in here, and all they've ordered is hot chocolate."

"Maybe they just really like hot chocolate?" said the busboy.

"So, anyway," Joseph said, brushing cocoa powder off his lapels. "Where was I?"

"That thing you were going to tell me about," Lewis replied from the floor, where he was on his hands and knees searching for his chair.

"Yeah. Well, see, I don't think Mendoza's been deactivated. And I'll tell you why."

"I'm glad we're doing Theobromos," said Lewis as his head reappeared above the level of the table. "I don't think I could bear to discuss this if we weren't, you know? I just think I'd cry and cry." He drank most of his hot chocolate in a gulp.

"Me too." Joseph lifted his mug and quaffed mightily as well. "But this is okay. So. You ever go over to Catalina Island?"

Lewis blinked, remembering.

"Once or twice. Second-unit work. Who was I stunt-doubling for? Was it Fredric March or Richard Barthelmess? I know I've been over there. Go on."

"You remember the big white hotel? It's not there anymore, they tore it down in the sixties, but back then it was brand-new." Joseph sighed, remembering. He reached into the souvenir bag and pulled out another bar, unwrapping it absentmindedly.

"Big white hotel. Right." Lewis frowned solemnly. "Oh! The Hotel Saint Catherine. I remember now, because one used to be able to get, uh . . ."

"Yeah, liquor in the bar, because there were bootleggers all over the place." Joseph looked around on the tabletop, trying to see where his chocolate had gone. "Did I eat that already? Christ."

"I hope you're leaving me some of the ones without almonds."

"Uh-huh. So I was over there in 1923. I was trying to corner somebody, Chaplin or Stan Laurel or I forget who, to get him interested in a deal with Paramount."

"Was he?" Lewis drank the rest of his hot chocolate and signaled to the counter man for more.

"Interested? Hell no, complete waste of time. But it was a job. So I'm at the bar, see? And I'm talking up a great line, hoping to make the guy sorry he's not a player, you know, and I glance over into the dining room and—there she is." Joseph gulped. Tears started in his eyes. He reached blindly for his hot chocolate and drank the rest of it.

"Who?"

"Mendoza. I'm telling you, Lewis. Sitting at a table in the restaurant. Sleeveless dress, peach silk with a bead fringe on the skirt, white sun hat, string of pearls. She had a glass of white wine in front of her. So did he."

"Who?"

"The guy," said Joseph, and put his head down on the table and began to weep. It's disconcerting when a baritone weeps. Lewis was at a loss. He looked up as the fountain attendant, who had given up trying to get their attention, approached with their next hot chocolates.

"Um, I think my friend has had enough," he enunciated with care. "You can leave both of those, though, I'll drink them."

"Can you drive?" said Joseph foggily.

"Uh . . . no."

"Well, I can't."

"That's okay," said Lewis. "We'll just take a cable car."

"I live in Sausalito."

"Oh." Lewis drank half of one of the hot chocolates. "Cable cars don't go across the Golden Gate, do they?"

Joseph shook his head, reached for the cocoa powder again.

"Oh, busboy!" Lewis stood up and nearly fell over. "Would you call us a taxi, please? Thank you. There we go! All settled. So, anyway. The girl in the peach silk dress. She turned out not to be Mendoza, obviously."

"Yeah. No, it was her. I'm telling you, Lewis, I saw her!"

"Who was the fellow she was with?"

"That was what I couldn't dope out." Joseph rose up on one elbow, staring at him. He mopped tears and cocoa powder from his face with a paper napkin. "He shouldn't have been there. Couldn't have been, the big arrogant bastard! But they both looked up and saw me. Recognized me, I'd swear. I pushed away from the bar and went through the crowd to get to them, but that was a hell of a crowded watering hole, and by the time I got into the restaurant, they were gone."

"You're sure they were really there in the first place?"

"No," Joseph admitted. "Except . . . their wine was still there, on the table. And the terrace door was open."

"Where are you going?" shouted the busboy from the phone, putting his hand over the mouthpiece.

Where indeed? wondered Lewis.

"Sausalito," shouted Joseph.

They sat looking at each other.

"We must find her," Joseph said.

"I was hoping you'd say that." Lewis began to smile.

"It's impossible she managed to escape from wherever they stashed her, but what if she did? She might need help. And I have to know whether or not she was really there."

"We couldn't get into trouble, could we, just making a few discreet inquiries?"

"It might take us years to find out anything."

"So much the better." Lewis held out his hands. "We'll be less obvious that way."

"What was it the man said about the free French garrison, Louie?" Joseph began to giggle, reaching for Lewis's half-finished drink.

At that moment another immortal entered the room. He was a security tech. He was dressed as a sport cyclist, in the bright tight-fitting cycling ensemble of that era, and carried his helmet and sunglasses under his arm. He swept the room once with a cold gray stare and acquired the two businessmen sitting at the little table under the time clock. He closed on them at once.

"Operatives? You stopped transmitting three hours ago. Are you in need of assistance?" he inquired in a low voice. They stared up at him, momentarily sobered. Someone must have been monitoring their data transmissions.

"Oh, gee, I'm sorry!" Joseph said. "You know what it was? We were in this arcade, and one of the damn electronic games fritzed. We were standing too close to it. Happens every now and then. We're okay, really."

"Honest," Lewis said.

The security tech scanned them and recoiled slightly at the level of Theobromos in their systems. He surveyed the litter of foil wrappers and empty cups, regarded the cocoa powder in Joseph's beard, and sighed. Two old professionals on a sloppy bender. And it was true that there were occasional inexplicable flares and shortings-out in San Francisco, which was as weird in its way as Laurel Canyon, not because of any geologic anomaly but because the place seemed to attract Crome-generating mortals in droves. It made his job more complicated than that of most security personnel.

"All right," he said. "I don't really need to report this, if you two senile delinquents will promise me you won't try to drive in your condition."

"We've already sent for a taxi," Lewis assured him.

"Gonna go home and order a pizza and sleep it off. Trust me, kid." Joseph reached up and patted the security tech's white helmet. He left cocoa-powdered fingerprints.

Lewis sat up abruptly and stared around, wishing he hadn't. He had a terrible headache, and his skin was crawling. He was ravenously hungry, too. At least he remembered where he was: a houseboat in Sausalito. Rank wind off the tidal flats and the cry of sea birds confirmed his memory.

He remained on the couch for a moment, surveying the litter of the dimly recalled previous evening. Five pizza boxes and two empty five-liter bottles of Coca-Cola. Lewis lifted the lid on the nearest box, hoping there was some crust left. There wasn't. How sad. He needed carbohydrates terribly just now.

Resting his head in his hands, he tried to remember his dream, but it was fading so quickly: Mendoza laughing with him at one of the base administrator's parties, over some ridiculous costume Houbert had worn. They hadn't been able to stop giggling. He'd master himself, fix all his features in a look of prim attention, and she'd take one look at him and go into fresh gales of laughter, which would set him off again. They'd had to stagger outside at last, leaning on each other.

Mendoza looked so young when she laughed. Apparent age, in immortals, is largely a matter of facial expression. Most of the time she seemed older, austere and withdrawn. Lewis thought he must be the only person who'd ever seen her eyes sparkle, her cheeks flush. That is, outside the mortal men who'd loved her.

Resolutely, he got to his feet and peered into the empty bedroom. The bed was neatly made, though Joseph must have been in bad shape when he woke. Funny how army training never wore off, especially when one had been a centurion. He sent a vague questing signal, and there came a response, faint through hills and traffic: *Getting the car. You can borrow one of my shirts.*

Thanks.

Lewis stepped into the kitchen and opened Joseph's refrigerator. There was more Theobromos, which he couldn't bear to look at. There were several six-packs of Anchor Steam beer. There was a loaf of Roman Meal bread and a package of unidentifiable sliced delicatessen product. Lewis groaned and opened the freezer. Ah! Ten boxes of frozen fettuccine Alfredo. He slid out the whole stack, opened them all, and put them in the microwave. Then he went to take a shower, uttering another silent prayer of thanks to Apollo, lord of civilized amenities.

Only after he'd eaten all the fettuccine did he gather up the pizza boxes and liter bottles and little black plastic dishes and fill a trash bag, which he set carefully beside Joseph's front door. He found an ironing board and was pressing his suit when he heard the Lexus pull into the carport.

A moment later Joseph came across the gangplank and let himself in, rather awkwardly because he was carrying a large cardboard box.

"I got two dozen doughnuts," he said, offering it. "I think there's a couple left. I meant to leave more. Sorry."

"Oh, no, thank you, you needn't have. I ate all your fettuccine Alfredo."

"Okay then," said Joseph, and sat down to eat the remaining doughnuts. No Armani suit today; he was wearing a brilliant Hawaiian shirt over black Levis, and black high-top sneakers. "I phoned in sick," he explained through a mouthful of doughnut, taking in Lewis's stare. "We need to talk to somebody today. Do you have to get back anytime soon?"

"Not immediately, no." Lewis unplugged the iron and pulled on his pants. "With whom do we need to talk?"

"I did some checking," Joseph said, licking glazed sugar from his fingers. "On the operatives who were posted at Cahuenga Pass with Mendoza. One of them is still in California. Right here in Marin County, in fact."

"That's convenient." Lewis tied his tie carefully.

"It gets better. It's the ornithologist. The kid who was there with her when she went AWOL. The one who testified. Who actually saw the Englishman." Joseph's eyes were black and shiny as coal this morning, his gaze hard and direct. "So. We have another six hours before the effect of the helmet wears off and we start transmitting data to the Company again. Here's what we do. We go see this guy right now, somehow or other we get him to put on the helmet and walk through Stonehenge, and then we ask him a few questions. Okay?"

"*Nunc aut nunquam,*" said Lewis grimly, slipping on his coat.

"You said it, kiddo." Joseph picked up his car keys and rose to his feet.

They took Highway I north, winding along coastline and cutting over to Tomales Bay. In the late twentieth century this was all pastoral land, dairy pastures on sea-facing hills, with redwoods along the creeks and wild rose and blackberry bramble thick beside the road. Here and there an isolated farmhouse sat back in the shadows under its grove of laurel trees, unchanged in a hundred years except for a satellite dish for television reception.

At last there was a steel-framed gate across a dirt road on their left, with a posted sign. Joseph slowed and stopped as they came abreast of it. It read:

AUDUBON SANCTUARY, TOMALES BAY
RESTRICTED ENTRY

"Good place for an ornithologist," said Lewis.

"Nice and isolated, too." Joseph backed up and made a sharp turn across the highway, pulling up to the gate. There was a little communications box with a push button at one side. He got out and pressed the button. A moment later a voice responded, tinny and distorted by the weathered speaker.

"Are you here to see the smews?"

"Uh—" Joseph and Lewis exchanged a look.

"Or are you here to see the Hitchcock set?" the voice went on, in a slightly annoyed tone.

"Yeah, actually," Joseph said.

"I have to tell you, you're really missing an opportunity if you don't see the smews while they're here."

"Ornithologist Grade Two Juan Bautista?"

"Oh." The voice altered completely. "I'm sorry. Who's that?"

"Facilitator Joseph and Literature Specialist Lewis."

"Okay." There was a loud buzz and click as the gate unlocked. "Please close up again after you come through."

Once through the gate, they followed the road across a meadow and down the hill toward the bay. It led to a promontory where a frame house sat, shaded by three enormous cypress trees, looking out on a little boat dock. The location seemed eerily familiar.

"*Alfred* Hitchcock," said Joseph abruptly, slapping his forehead. "It's the house from *The Birds!*"

"Well, no wonder we drove up here to see it," said Lewis in delight.

"Perfect," Joseph growled, pulling up to the garage from which Rod, Tippi, Jessica, and Veronica made their final desperate escape.

As they approached the house, they heard what appeared to be a violent argument going on between a child and an adult, though it ceased abruptly when Lewis knocked. The door opened, and an immortal stood there staring at them. He wore a khaki uniform with a plastic tag over the pocket that read JOHN GREY EAGLE, SITE DOCENT. His long hair, which had once been silver, was now dyed jet black and braided behind him.

"Hi," he said. There was a violent flapping of wings from the room beyond, and a raven suddenly landed on his shoulder. He reached up swiftly and closed its beak between his thumb and forefinger.

"Whoa." Joseph stepped back, laughing. "Is that one of the cast members still hanging around?"

"No," said the man with a trace of sullenness. "This is just Raven. You guys understand that birds never, ever really behave that way, right? It was just a horror movie. Ravens never hurt mortals, and neither do seagulls, for that matter."

"Well, sure, but it's still a great movie." Joseph thrust out his hand. "Hi. I'm Joseph and this is Lewis. We came to see the set, but—say, what *is* a smew, anyway?"

"I'm Juan Bautista. *Mergellus albellus*, it's a Eurasian merganser, and they're only accidental here, but we have a mated pair! Do you have any idea how rare that is?" said Juan Bautista, shaking hands.

"Amazing," said Joseph. "So. Can we see the house?"

"All right," sighed Juan Bautista, stepping back from the door. Then he stopped, staring at Joseph. "Do I know you from somewhere?"

"Gee, I suppose it's possible. I get around a lot," said Joseph. "Come on, I want to see the fireplace where the sparrows attacked."

There wasn't really much to see, since no attempt had been made to reproduce any of the film's furnishings. Juan showed them through the rooms anyway and recited a few film facts for their edification: that Hitchcock had thrown a lot of innocent helpless birds at Tippi Hedrin, and that the schoolhouse where the ravens massed for their completely out-of-character attack was now a private residence and thought to be haunted, though not by Suzanne Pleshette. The raven clacked its beak derisively.

"Well, isn't that just fascinating," said Lewis appreciatively.

"Want to go see the smews now?"

"Great," said Joseph.

A smew looked like a fat little black-and-white duck with a crest, though Juan Bautista insisted a merganser wasn't a duck. They admired one paddling about on a reedy backwater for a few minutes, then started back to the house.

"I guess you don't get into the city much," said Joseph as they crossed the lawn.

"Me? No. What do you guys do?"

"Lewis here works for the studios in Hollywood—" Juan Bautista turned to stare at him, impressed. "Dealing in rare research stuff and old scripts."

"I was stationed in Hollywood once," said Juan Bautista. "It wasn't there yet, though, so I never got to see any movie stars."

"Yeah, that's life in the service, isn't it?" Joseph shook his head ruefully. "I don't see many in my line of work, either. I work for— Say, I've just remembered, I have that helmet in the car!"

"That's right, you do," said Lewis. "Let's show him."

Juan Bautista looked from one to the other. "What?"

"You'll love this. It's *so* cool." Joseph ran to the Lexus and popped the trunk.

"He was showing me only yesterday," Lewis told Juan Bautista. "No end of fun, virtual reality stuff."

Juan Bautista's eyes lit up. "The graphics are still pretty crappy, but I understand they're getting better."

"Wait'll you see this." Joseph chortled, digging the white crate out of the trunk. "Come on, let's take it in the house. It's a prototype. You can try it out."

"You work for *those* guys?" Juan Bautista recognized the logo on the box. "Wow."

"Yeah, but I'm never involved in the movies themselves." Joseph pushed the door open and set the box down. "Right now I'm a salesman for their cybernetic entertainment division. There are certain developments Dr. Zeus wants monitored. You know." He lifted out the helmet. "Just sit down and get comfortable."

"Okay." Juan Bautista handed the raven off to a perch—it gronked and protested—and took a seat on his couch. Joseph stepped close and placed the helmet carefully on Juan Bautista's head. Lewis winced and retreated a few paces. The raven cocked its head to look at him and looked back at Juan Bautista uneasily.

"Here we go!" Joseph took a small control out of his pocket and inserted a minidisc. "This is the sampler. My favorite's the walk through Stonehenge, it's the first one on the program. Check it out." He thumbed the control and stepped well away from the couch. The raven ducked its head and began to flutter its wings, crying.

"Oh, shut up, bird. Hey, this is really something," said Juan Bautista muffledly. "It's a *lot* better than the other stuff I—ow!"

He began to fumble with the helmet. The raven flew off its perch and went straight for Joseph's eyes, screaming, "Get it off him! Get it off him right now!"

Joseph dropped the control to defend himself and got a grip around the raven's wings, trapping them. He held it out at arm's length. Juan Bautista pushed off the helmet, panting. There was a moment of silence.

"Did that bird just talk?" asked Lewis at last.

"Uh—sure. Ravens can be taught to talk, you know," said Juan Bautista, in a frantically reasonable voice. "Just like parrots. All the *Corvidae* are really intelligent."

"Get it off him, get it off him right now," said the raven rather lamely. "Polly wants a cracker, awk, awk, awk."

"Nice try," said Joseph, glaring at it. "Why don't you do the nevermore bit next?"

"I hate that stupid poem," said the raven. Juan Bautista groaned and slid down on the couch. "I'm sorry, Dad," it added contritely.

Joseph grinned unpleasantly. Lewis was reminded that Joseph had worked for the Spanish Inquisition.

"Well, well," he chuckled. "You're not just any birdbrain, are you? Somebody's done an augmentation job on you. Boy, that's really illegal. The Company wouldn't be at all happy if they found out. I wonder who could have done such a thing?"

"Dad didn't do it!" shrieked the raven. "It was somebody else. Not Dad."

"Shut *up*," said Juan Bautista desperately.

"Oh, pal, have we ever got your ass in a sling," Joseph said. "To say nothing of your bird in my hand. But, you know what? This is your lucky day. The Company won't ever find out, because that helmet just shorted out your automatic datalink."

"For a period of twenty-four hours," Lewis added.

Juan Bautista looked from one to the other, then ran his self-diagnostic. "My God, it has," he said after a moment. He scowled at Joseph. "Okay, what's going on? Who are you guys? I'm sure I know you from somewhere."

"Don't worry. We just needed to ask you some questions in private, and the helmet was the only way to do it," Lewis assured him.

"Let Raven go, and maybe I'll talk to you," Juan Bautista said.

"Okay, Raven, are you augmented enough to know what'll happen to you if you go after me again?" Joseph asked her.

"I'll be good," the raven snarled. Juan Bautista put out his hand and she went to him, scurrying up his arm to busy herself with grooming his hair through the whole of the following conversation.

"Look, there's no need for unpleasantness. We just want some information you might have about something that happened to a friend of ours," said Lewis.

"You don't tell anybody about this conversation," said Joseph, pulling up a chair, "and we won't tell anybody about your little friend. A deal? And if there are any inquiries about why you weren't transmitting for twenty-four hours, no problem." Joseph held up his index finger. "We came here to see the Hitchcock set, got to talking, I persuaded you to try on the helmet, and it zapped you. You can tell it exactly as it happened. Then Lewis and I looked at each other and exclaimed, 'My gosh, it must have been the helmet all along. It's defective.' I apologized, and we promised to take it apart tomorrow to see what's wrong with it, which I'm going to anyway, so it's not even a lie. Okay? That's what you tell any security tech who comes to check on you. If they ask us, we'll corroborate, and everybody's happy."

"Do you mind if I ask you a question, though?" Lewis stepped closer. "How did you manage to do the augmentation without being found out?"

Juan Bautista nodded in the direction of Tomales Bay. "The San Andreas Fault runs right along under there. Every time there's any seismic activity at all, the electromagnetic disturbance shuts out transmissions for hours. I have a lot of time to myself, actually. The Company just ignores it, now, since there's nothing they can do."

"Neat," said Joseph in awe. "For Christ's sake don't ever tell anybody else, though."

"I'd heard rumors that storms will do it too," said Lewis.

Juan Bautista nodded. "Bad electrical ones," he said.

"It's true," Joseph admitted. "To let you in on a little Facilitator classified information. But you're not supposed to know. So you don't know, right, guys? And you'll never speak or think about it again, after today." He glanced at his chronometer. "After about fifteen hundred hours today. So let's talk fast."

"Indeed." Lewis came and sat down gingerly on the couch, as far away as he could get from the raven. "Do you remember working with the Botanist Mendoza?"

Juan Bautista's eyes widened. "Yes," he said unhappily.

"You testified against her," stated Joseph.

"Not *against* her," Juan Bautista said. "Just about her! I just—oh, man, can't I ever leave this behind me? I caught hell from my case officer, I had to testify."

"But you have a real nice posting now, and you wouldn't want to lose it, so let's move on," said Joseph flatly. "1863. What happened?"

"I don't know what happened," Juan Bautista said. "I swear to God I don't. All I remember is, Mendoza's job was finished, and her transfer never came through, and she was getting really mean. There was a drought that ruined the rancheros, and all the plants died, and there was smallpox. Were either of you guys there? It was bad. I was only seventeen, my first time out in the field."

Joseph's face twisted oddly. Lewis glanced at him and took the initiative.

"I've heard about it. I was in England at the time, and glad to be there. The man who came to see Mendoza, he was an Englishman, wasn't he?"

Juan Bautista nodded emphatically. "An espionage guy. Like an early-day James Bond. There were American secret service agents, or whatever they had back then, chasing him, and Mendoza was helping him hide."

"You have any idea why she was helping him?" said Joseph.

Juan Bautista looked very uncomfortable. His hand wandered up to stroke the raven's neck feathers, but she clacked her beak at him irritably. "Stop that!" she snapped. "I'm doing the grooming here."

Juan Bautista looked out the window at the bright waters of the bay. "Well—Mendoza and the Englishman, they went to bed together, apparently." He exhaled. "Do you guys really want to know all this?"

"No, no," Lewis said soothingly. "So there was some relationship between them, that's why Mendoza was helping the mortal. How did she explain what she was doing?"

"She said it was research," Juan Bautista said. "There was some kind of weird British conspiracy going on. Our anthropologist knew all about it. I think this guy was part of the plot. The one that Mendoza ran off with. He came after Imarte left, and suddenly Mendoza was all interested. She told me she was going off to check things for Imarte. I thought it was weird, because she and Imarte couldn't stand each other."

"That's true," said Joseph.

"When I came home that afternoon, Mendoza and the British guy were about to ride away. She told me I had to fix my own dinner." Juan Bautista sighed, remembering. "Didn't come home all night. Next morning two Yankees came looking for the Englishman, said they were his friends. I was pretty dumb back then, but I played dumber. Next thing I know, Mendoza transmitted, said she and the Englishman had to hide out, and could I bring them some food? So I did. I told them about the Yankees. You should have seen her, she was so scared. And mad . . ."

There was a moment of silence, broken only by the rustling of the raven's feathers.

"What happened then?" said Joseph.

"Nothing. I never saw her again. I was all alone the next two days. The Yankees never came back, either. But the night after that, security techs came and took all Mendoza's stuff, and started searching the place. And in the middle of it Porfirio—he was my case officer—came galloping up, and they started yelling at each other." Juan Bautista closed his eyes at the memory.

"They left with her stuff. Porfirio reamed me out, he really did. Like it was my fault! But then they came back and got both of us. They took us to some place in Los Angeles, and I didn't see Porfirio again after that. They questioned me over and over, but I didn't know anything. Then they transferred me. And that was all that happened.

"What did he look like?" Joseph asked.

"Porfirio?"

"No, the Englishman. Did he look like James Bond?"

"No," Juan Bautista said. "He just looked . . . like an Englishman. But he was really tall."

Joseph began to pace the room. He took a pencil and paper from Juan Bautista's desk and thrust them at him. "Draw the guy for me," he said. "Give me a photographic likeness."

It was a simple request to make of a Company operative, with total recall and photographic memory at his disposal. Juan Bautista shrugged. He worked for about five minutes, as Joseph and Lewis watched him. Long before he had finished and handed the portrait to Lewis, Joseph was across the room beating his head against the wall.

Lewis studied the portrait: a very tall figure looking down from horseback. He was dressed in the clothing a gentleman wore for travel in 1862, elegantly tailored, which somewhat obscured the fact that he was rather lankily built. He had a long broken nose and high broad cheekbones. Lewis found the picture disturbing, though he couldn't have said why, other than the obvious fact that something about it was making Joseph bang his head against the wall. Juan Bautista watched, horrified.

"You know," said Lewis carefully, pretending not to notice what Joseph was doing, "this fellow reminds me of . . . the way Mendoza used to describe the mortal she knew in England. The, ah, attitude."

"And how," groaned Joseph. He staggered to a chair and sat down. "Give me the picture."

Lewis handed it to him. Joseph stared at it for a long moment before crumpling it up and squeezing the wad of paper between both hands.

"Did I offend you somehow?" Juan Bautista asked cautiously.

"No. No, you didn't, pal, and I owe you one. We're going to go, now, and with any luck our paths won't ever cross again." Joseph got up. "Come on, Lewis."

"Thank you, Juan," said Lewis. "And rest assured we won't tell anyone about the raven."

Juan Bautista watched as Joseph scooped up the helmet and its case and stalked out, with Lewis following.

"*Did* he know you from somewhere?" Lewis asked quietly, as they paused at the car to put away the helmet.

"He was one of my recruits," Joseph said, slamming the trunk lid down. "Haven't seen him since he was four. Great father, ain't I?"

Juan Bautista went to the window to be certain they left.

"I'm glad they're going," said Raven, fussing with her master's hair. "I didn't like them at all. I wanted to peck out his eyes, that mean man. Just like in the scary movie."

"Hush," Juan Bautista said, watching the two immortals drive away. His hand rose in the habitual gesture to stroke her neck feathers, and this time she let him.

"You're driving rather fast," remarked Lewis. It was the first word either of them had spoken. They were halfway back to San Francisco, following the highway along the cliffs above the sea.

"Sorry," Joseph said. He pulled the car over on the narrow stony verge, stopped the engine, and got out. For a moment Lewis had the strangest conviction that Joseph was going to jump; instead he pulled back his arm and threw something, hurling it with a grunt of fury toward the steel-colored ocean. It seemed to hang in the air a moment before it dropped, a little white ball of wadded paper.

"Would you mind explaining?" asked Lewis, when Joseph got back in and slammed the door.

"We made a decision yesterday when we were both bombed out of our skulls. But the ante, Lewis, just got upped. If you knew just how high it is now," Joseph said, "I don't think you'd want to keep playing."

Lewis turned to stare at him. "I beg your pardon," he said coldly. "That's my decision to make, I believe. Mendoza was my friend. If there's anything I can do to help her, wherever she is now, I'm going to do it."

Joseph sighed. "We may not be able to do anything for her. Even finding out where she is will be dangerous. I may have some chance, on my own. What I do, what we do, depends on what I turn up. But I may not turn up anything for years. You see what I'm saying?"

"Yes, I do." Lewis set his chin. "But you have to understand my position. There she was, about to walk into tragedy, and I knew it but there was nothing on earth I could do."

"Oh, I think I know how you felt," said Joseph bleakly.

"You recognized the man in the picture. Who was he?"

Joseph disengaged the emergency brake and started the Lexus again. Watching carefully for oncoming traffic, he pulled back onto the highway. "Somebody who died and should have stayed dead," he said at last.

They were nearly back in Sausalito before Lewis spoke again. "You'll let me know when you discover where she is?"

"I promise. Now, I think we shouldn't contact each other again for a few years. You may not hear from me until after the war. You probably won't be stationed in LA much longer."

Lewis shrugged. "Not the way things are going, no." He looked at his chronometer. "Goodness, how time flies," he said lightly.

Joseph nodded. They were talking about the Oakland Raiders when data transmission resumed a few minutes later.

Lewis reclaimed his car and drove back to Hollywood that afternoon, arriving long after dark. He didn't see Joseph again for thirty years.

Joseph in the Darkness

So, FATHER, YOU'RE the expert on death. Why can't we die?

Right now you'd be giving me that flat patient stare that meant I'd asked a really dumb question. But, seriously, think about this for a minute: what step in the immortality process makes us permanent problems for our masters, instead of just terribly long-lived ones?

The conditioning to avoid danger at all costs can be worked around, if you psych yourself up to it. Takes a lot of practice, but it can be done.

The pineal tribrantine 3 gives us eternal youth, but it doesn't make us indestructible.

The ferroceramic skeletal structure can't be damaged, but the soft tissues around it are as vulnerable as a mortal's to injury—or would be, if we didn't have the speed and agility to avoid bullets, knives, shrapnel, et cetera.

The millions of biomechanicals circulating through us, each one custom-designed to the individual operative's DNA, are tougher to beat. If my heart was cut out of my body (assuming I held still long enough to let somebody do that, which I wouldn't, because I'm afraid of pain), I'd just go into fugue and my biomechanicals would grow a new heart. They repair, replace, revive, detoxify, and probably they could keep us immortal all on their own, if it wasn't for the fact that they're susceptible to damage too.

Each system backs up the other systems, functions overlap, and the whole design works so well that Preservers almost never incur damage bad enough to land them in a repair facility. Smash us to bits—sooner or later we'll rise up in one piece again, like the bucket-carrying brooms in the *Sorcerer's Apprentice*, and go on about our work. Not only that, we make more of ourselves, out of the unwanted orphans of history. And we're smarter than the masters who created us. God knows I'd be scared of me, if I was a mortal.

So I can just imagine our masters sitting around a table in an ivory tower up there in the twenty-fourth century, thumbing frantically through some big book of spells trying to find the one that will turn us off.

But better minds than theirs have tackled the problem, and nobody's ever managed. I'm talking about suicide attempts, of course. All of us immortals have felt like dying, at some time. Some of us have wanted it bad enough to try. There are a lot of stories, hilarious in a black kind of way, about what happened. The best of them is the one about the guy who overcame his hazard avoidance programming enough to position himself at ground zero in Hiroshima. Next thing he knew, he was wandering around in the mountains with big chunks of his memory gone, and the locals were reporting sightings of Charcoal Faceless Ghost-Man.

Why wasn't he vaporized, ferroceramic skeleton and all? I don't know. My guess is, no matter how badly he consciously wanted to die, something in his unconscious got him out of there at hyperspeed at the last possible second.

If we can survive something like that, what can't we survive?

And how would our masters even begin to find out? How could they experiment without tipping us off? What would we do to them if we caught them at it?

But if they did find some silver bullet, how would they manage to hunt down every single one of thousands of ancient, cunning, superintelligent, and extremely survival-oriented cyborgs so they could use it?

To say nothing of the fact that it would have to be one hell of a silver bullet, capable of destroying every single biomechanical in a cyborg's body. If it missed even one, the little thing would reproduce frantically, and soon there would be enough to begin repair. Months or years later, some body would claw its way out of an unmarked grave, and if it wasn't pissed off about the way it had been treated, I'd be real surprised. The masters would be surprised, too. Maybe in their beds, maybe in lonely places.

No wonder they monitor every word we say.

Austin, 2025

THE CEMETERY WAS a modern one, parklike and smooth, with neat
flat headstones set flush in the manicured lawn; so it had taken a lot
of work and enthusiasm to give it an appropriate holiday look. Garden
edging had been used here and there to enclose graves in little pavil-
ions festooned with black and orange crepe paper, or strung with electronic pumpkin and skeleton lights. Every grave had its jack-o'-lantern
or bouquet of marigolds and chrysanthemums. The infants' section was
particularly bright, with little plastic trick-or-treat buckets, tiny pumpkins, black and orange pinwheels, tissue-paper ghosts.

The living children in their costumes wandered between the graves
reading names and dates, or thronged at the edge of the cemetery,
where a produce stand had a pumpkin patch and hayride. Normally a
row of dilapidated tractors was ranged along the edge of the property
line; today there were dummies mounted in the rusting seats, old
clothes stuffed with newspaper and surmounted with rubber masks.
There was a vampire, a werewolf, Frankenstein's monster.

Señor and Señora Death were busy packing up the leftovers of a
tailgate picnic, nesting empty Tupperware containers and wadding up
plastic bags. Señor Death turned to look at the horizon, where slate-
blue clouds advanced. He frowned. He shouted, "Kids! Are you going
trick-or-treating or what? Come on."

They came running from the hayride, the ballerina and Snow
White and the baby tiger. Teenage Death strolled after them, being
irritating, too cool to hurry.

Señor Death exhaled sharply and shook his head. The ballerina
outpaced her little brother and sister and said breathlessly, "Uncle Frio!

The man at the pumpkin patch says it's going to rain. Will that short out Daddy's lights?"

"No." Señor Death crouched down by the grave and lifted the wire that connected the four little jack-o'-lanterns carved with the four names: GILBERT, TINA, BRANDY, AGUSTIN. "It's outdoor grade wire, the microchip's insulated. They'll shine all night, no matter what the weather does."

"Mommy, can I have an orange soda?" asked the baby tiger.

"Not in the car, mijo," Señora Death said firmly. "When you get home." The baby tiger started to pout.

"Tricker-treat, tricker-treat, tricker-treat," chanted Snow White, which distracted the baby tiger, and he took up the chant too. They bounced up and down in great excitement.

"You're practically jumping on Daddy's grave!" the ballerina fretted.

"I think he'd kind of like it," Señor Death told her. "They're little, Brandy. It's okay."

Teenage Death made his leisurely arrival and bent to lift the cooler over the tailgate for his mother. He fished inside and drew out a bottle of orange soda. Instantly the baby tiger stopped bouncing and pointed an accusatory finger. "How come *he* gets to have one?" he yelled.

"Because I won't barf all over the inside of the truck, baby," said his brother.

"Agustin, it won't kill you to wait ten minutes until we get home. Put the soda back," Señor Death ordered. Agustin gave him an insolent stare, so Señor Death added, "If you want to go to that party tonight—"

"Nazi," muttered the boy, but he put the soda back.

"Come on, kids." Señora Death was kneeling by the grave, making the sign of the cross. The younger children knelt beside her and crossed themselves too. Señor Death and Agustin stood to pray, reciting the Hail Mary and Our Father with them. When they finished, the children scrambled to their feet and climbed into the truck, crouching under the camper shell. Agustin closed the tailgate on them and stood beside Señor Death, waiting somberly as his mother bent to the gravestone and kissed it. Her white makeup left the print of her lips on the stone that read:

PHILIP BERNARD AGUILAR
LOVING HUSBAND AND FATHER
1990–2021

They got into the truck and drove away, following a road east through low rolling hills and scrub oaks, into a pleasant lakeside housing development shaded by sycamore trees. The storm clouds had advanced with breathtaking speed, bringing early darkness. Already people were putting out lighted pumpkins or turning on strings of Halloween lights. As they pulled into their driveway, a tiny devil and superheroine emerged from the house next door, clutching loot bags.

"Mommy, Robin and Maria are starting!" shrieked Snow White. "Uncle Frio, can't we go now?"

Señor Death shut off the motor and scowled up at the sky. "Yes, go early, that's a good idea. Agustin! Watch them like a hawk. If it starts to rain, go to the Circle K and call me. I'll come drive you home."

"Okay." Agustin slid from the cab seat. "Drive me to Sasha's later?"

Señor Death nodded. Brandy ran into the house and returned with their loot bags and a flashlight for each child. Waving them like light sabers, the children hastened down the street. Señor Death watched them go. He could smell autumn leaves, candle-charring pumpkins, dinners cooking in a dozen kitchens; over all that, the heavy smell of the storm, very strong, worrisome.

He hefted the cooler out of the back and tilted it in the driveway, letting the melted ice drain out. As he bent there, something came through the twilight to him, some signal through the ether he couldn't define. He stood up sharply and stared, turning his bone-white face this way and that, but he couldn't locate it.

Shrugging, he carried the cooler into the house.

Señora Death was just sliding a covered dish into the oven. "You can go first," she told him. "The cotton balls and the Noxema are all laid out." There was a certain courteous reserve in her tone, a formality, respect and affection without intimacy.

"Thanks," he said. He made his way through the darkening house, turning on lights as he went, not out of any need—he could see by infrared—but out of a mounting edginess. Near the door of the bathroom he nearly stepped on a UFO Abductee Barbie. Muttering to himself, he picked it up and went to the door of the girls' room, where he turned on the light before tossing it on Tina's bed. Nothing out of place, everything normal: Brandy's side fussily neat, Tina's a wreckage of toys and crayons. He heard a faint scrape and hiss, smelled something burning. Annette was lighting the jack-o'-lantern and setting it in the front window.

He went back to the bathroom and shrugged out of his black robe. Leaning forward over the sink, he began carefully removing the white from his face. It was an involved process, because he had to avoid removing the more subtle makeup that disguised him as a forty-five-year-old mortal man.

He was sponging the last of it out of his mustache when Annette was beside him suddenly, her alarm magnified by the black grease-paint around her eyes.

"Porfirio, I thought I saw a man in the backyard."

I knew it, he told himself. "Well, let's see," he said grimly. He stepped into his bedroom and emerged with a shotgun. Cocking it, he stepped out on the back porch and looked into the deepening shadow.

"Luisa said the marshal shot two Freemen in Spicewood," Annette hissed.

"Maybe," he replied. It had been three years since the war, but now and then somebody came lurching out of the back country, desperate for supplies.

But there was no crazed survivalist in this suburban backyard, and nothing out of place either: Gilbert's wading pool full of water-logged oak leaves, bicycles, the tree house made of pallets, the rope swing over the edge of the lake. For a split second he thought he saw something wrong. An outline, a ghost, in the tree house? As he stared, it melted into nothing. Or nearly nothing. He snarled silently.

Miles away, there was a flicker on the horizon. A long moment later the faint thunder came.

"It's okay," he called to Annette. "Nobody out here stupid enough to trespass."

He went back indoors.

They ate supper in the kitchen, interrupted occasionally by trick-or-treaters. The storm held off. The children came home, and Annette fed the younger ones while Agustin got a change of clothes and his sleeping bag. Porfirio drove him to his party. On the way back the lightning flashes were nearer, the thunder following more closely. As he let himself in, the first drops just began to fall, and as he crossed the threshold, a blue-white blaze lit the whole street.

Annette was sitting on the couch clutching his shotgun, her eyes enormous.

He locked the door behind him and shot the bolt. "Did you see somebody again?"

"No. I was getting Gilbert out of the tub, and Brandy came running in screaming she'd seen somebody in the kids' tree house. We looked with the flashlight. I couldn't see anybody, but—"

He came and put an arm around her. "Probably just a coyote. Too many spooks this Halloween, huh? Don't worry. It's raining pretty hard now, listen. At least they can't get into much trouble at that party.

You go on to bed. I'll sit up and watch the yard for a while. Nothing's going to prowl for long if I get a clear shot at it."

Boom! Blue light flared, and the windows rattled with the force of the thunder. She jumped and held him more tightly than she meant to.

"All right," she said, deciding not to argue. In the time since he'd shown up on her doorstep the day after Philip's funeral, she had learned not to ask him too many questions. It was a small price to pay for security, even if she had her suspicions that he was not really Philip's long-lost cousin.

He walked her to her bedroom, turned on the light, checked the closets. Nothing out of place. He kissed her on the forehead and went off to check the locks. Lightning flashed. Thunder split the sky, and rain fell in torrents.

Porfirio went into the dark kitchen and stood looking out into the yard. He could see the man clearly now, huddled in the tree house, flinching at every blast of livid fire. Porfirio grinned. He went into the living room and tapped in a combination on the customized entertainment center. A soothing tone filled the air, inaudible to mortal ears. The children sank deeper into dreams, and Annette, who'd been staring tensely into darkness, suddenly relaxed and was blissfully unconscious.

Porfirio went back into the kitchen and opened the back door. Ozone was filling the air with an acrid electric smell. Between one flash and the next the man stood beside him on the porch, dripping and shivering.

"Goddam storm took forever to break," he gasped. "I've been waiting out there for hours."

"That's a shame," said Porfirio. "Not that you have any business in my yard. You want to tell me who you are and what you're doing here?"

"Joseph, Facilitator Grade One," the other said, jumping when lightning struck close by. "Can we continue this conversation indoors?"

Porfirio stepped inside, and the other followed him readily. He went on:

"I know this is sort of unorthodox, but I needed to ask you something in private, about somebody you worked with once. I'm trying to find out what happened to her. I thought you might know."

Porfirio looked at him in silence. His visitor was dressed, most improbably, in complete fly fisherman's gear, including waders, utility vest, flannel plaid shirt, and shapeless hat. "And you had to wait for an electrical storm, so the data transmission would be knocked out? Smart guy. I just might report you anyway, pal."

"Aw, don't do that," implored Joseph. He looked around the kitchen, hungrily inhaling the fragrances of Halloween night. "Nice place. How'd you get posted with a mortal family?"

"You don't need to know," Porfirio told him, opening the liquor cabinet and pouring a shot of bourbon. He offered it to Joseph, who was drifting wide-eyed toward the big bowl of candy on the kitchen counter.

"My God, those are Almond Joys! May I? Thanks." He tossed back the bourbon in a gulp. "You're right, I don't need to know. Look, I'll make this short: back in 1862 you worked with the Botanist Mendoza, yes?"

Porfirio started. Joseph, watching him, peeled the wrapper off a candy miniature and popped it in his mouth. "I thought so," he said, chewing. "I was her case officer once myself. I'm trying to find out where she went. I'm not asking for your help, just for some information."

Exhaling, Porfirio got down a couple of highball glasses and poured out more bourbon. He handed one to Joseph and took the other. "Let's go sit. And leave the candy alone. The kids will kill me if it's gone in the morning."

Boom! All over the neighborhood, in other houses people were sitting huddled up, unable to sleep for the thunder, but Annette and her children slept on. Porfirio lit the gas logs. Joseph relaxed on the couch, watching the firelight play on the ceiling, watching the jack-o'-lantern's flame.

"I guess this is part of the Gradual Retirement Plan, huh?" he said. "Mendoza didn't get gradually retired, though, did she? She was arrested. Something nasty happened."

"Very nasty," Porfirio agreed, sipping his bourbon.

"I think you tried to help her. I think you went on record as making some kind of formal protest about what they did to her." Joseph gulped his bourbon and set the glass aside. "So tell me, friend: do you have any idea where she is?"

"Out of commission, as far as I know," said Porfirio. "She got a raw deal. Still, she killed six mortals and went AWOL. You don't get off with a slap on the wrist for something like that. I believe she had a lot of drug therapy, and in the end they transferred her to—" He dipped his finger in the bourbon and drew on the table a line of three little arrows pointing left.

Joseph might have gone pale; it was hard to tell in the wavering light. After a moment he asked, "Did you see her after she was arrested?"

"I tried. They wouldn't let me."

"Thank you, anyway," Joseph said.

Porfirio looked at him thoughtfully and had another sip of bourbon. "What's it to you, anyway?" he asked.

Joseph avoided his gaze, staring into the fire. "I recruited her," he said.

"And? You must have recruited a lot of kids in your time. You're old. Why follow up on what happened to this one?"

"Most of the time I ship them out, and I never see them after they've been augmented, but I saw Mendoza a lot after she came back. I was with her on her first field mission. She's the closest thing I have to a daughter. I always felt kind of responsible for her."

"Okay, that I can understand," said Porfirio, nodding. His dark stare intensified. "You must have known she was a Crome generator, then."

Joseph winced. "Not really," he lied. "I have this habit of ignoring things that might bother me. So. Was that how she got into trouble? Something to do with the Crome's radiation?"

"No," Porfirio said. "Although now that I come to think of it . . . maybe it did after all. She'd been throwing Crome's like . . . that storm outside. Every damn night practically, mostly while she was asleep. It was never a problem, though, until one day when she went up into the Laurel Canyon anomaly."

"I heard about that," said Joseph uneasily.

"So you have a good idea why the Company doesn't want anybody to find out what happened there. I'd like to know how *you* found out about it, actually." Porfirio raised one eyebrow.

Joseph just shook his head grimly. Porfirio shrugged and continued:

"She got back okay, but in my opinion it was just a matter of time after that before Dr. Zeus found a reason to put her away. Pretty soon she gave them a reason, too, one in technicolor." He lifted his glass again and stopped, struck by a thought. "I wonder if that's why they kept delaying her new posting."

"I heard that they left her on layover indefinitely," said Joseph, rubbing his temples. "You're saying the Company *wanted* her to get into trouble so they could take her out?"

Porfirio nodded almost imperceptibly.

"And then the Englishman came," said Joseph in a tight voice.

"I don't know anything about that part. That had all happened by the time I came back."

"Did you see the guy?"

"No. He was already dead by then."

"Do you have any idea who he was?"

"Nope." Porfirio set his glass down.

"You said she killed six mortals. Did she kill him?"

"No. She killed the guys who shot him, and I sure as hell know who *they* were, because it cost the Company a lot to cover up their disappearances. Pinkerton agents employed by the Union government. This was during the Civil War. They were after him for some reason, and for some reason she was helping him. I've always thought she was susceptible to him because of that incident in her file, the thing that happened back in England on her first mission." Porfirio looked sharply across at Joseph. "You were on that posting. You must know all about it."

"Yeah," said Joseph. "She never got over it, really."

"Plus the fact that Crome generators have been known to go nuts," said Porfirio, watching the effect of his words as Joseph flinched again.

"You think she did?"

"Who knows? Something weird happened, that's for sure." Porfirio leaned forward and spoke in a cold voice. "And she's not the only one who suffered for it, my friend. All of us who were there got a black mark in some way or other as a result of that incident. The Company dragged my ass over the coals, let me tell you. They scared the hell out of the only other witness, nice little kid on his first mission. There was an anthropologist who wasn't even there when it happened, and I know for a fact they pulled her in and did a data erasure on her.

"And there was an operative who went with Mendoza on that trip into Laurel Canyon and got pulled into the anomaly too. I sent him along to cover her. Nice guy, had a good attitude, never a moment of trouble for the Company. He wasn't there when she went AWOL either, he was on a job. I was with him, for crying out loud. But you know what? Within twenty-four hours of Mendoza's little mistake, a security team showed up at our camp at Tejon and took him away with them. He just grinned and went. Never seen him since. I can't even find out where he was reassigned, and I've tried."

"Jesus." Joseph put his head in his hands.

"Some body count, huh?" Porfirio's voice was harsh. "And maybe it's all because an operative got careless one time, when he was scanning a potential recruit, and didn't bother to check for Crome's. You think that's maybe the case?"

"Could be," said Joseph in a muffled voice.

"I've carried the same guilt," said Porfirio reflectively. "How did I miss what was coming? Was there any way I could have stopped it? Could I have helped her? And poor old Einar, I was the one who gave him the order to go with Mendoza into Laurel Canyon, and now he's out of the picture. I thought I was responsible. Maybe I'm not, though." He turned to Joseph. "Maybe I'll just dump all this guilt on you now, pal."

"Thanks," said Joseph listlessly.

"You're welcome. Listen: I told you all this because I respect the fact that you're trying to help your daughter. And she was a good operative, before the incident. Mendoza did good work." Porfirio sighed. "But I have family of my own I'm looking out for, so I don't ever want to see your face or hear about this again."

"Family?" Joseph sat up, sudden comprehension in his face. "Is that what you're doing here?"

Porfirio nodded. "They're descendants of the brother I had when I was mortal. I've kept track of them all down the years."

"The Company lets you do that?"

"They want to keep me happy. I'm a problem solver."

"Oh," said Joseph in a small voice. "One of those guys who gets rid of—"

"Yeah. Anyway, this is all your responsibility now, right?" Porfirio stretched. "Find out what happened to her, if you can. Help her if you can. If you can find out what happened to a Zoologist and Cinema Preservationist named Einar, that would be nice too. But I never met you, I never talked to you, and you're going to stay the hell away from me and my family for the rest of your eternal life."

"You got it," Joseph agreed. He looked across at the window, where the rain beat steadily but with less and less punctuation of lightning. "I guess I'll be going now. Thanks for the help, all the same."

"You need a ride anywhere?" Porfirio relaxed somewhat.

"No, that's okay." Joseph gave a slightly embarrassed grin. "My canoe's tied up at your neighbor's dock. I'll just row back up the lake to the public campground. I'm supposed to be on a fishing vacation, it's part of my gradual retirement. Smooth, huh?"

Porfirio almost smiled. He stood, and Joseph stood, and they went out through the kitchen, where Joseph cast a longing eye at the Halloween candy.

"One for the road?" he suggested.

"What the hell." Porfirio tossed him an Almond Joy. He caught it neatly and slipped out though the back door into the steadily falling rain, silent as a coyote. Porfirio went to the window and watched. A moment later he saw the dark shape of a canoe moving out on the lake, and a dark oarsman rowing. It backed around and headed north, and a moment later was lost in the rain and the night.

Porfirio locked the door and slid its deadbolt home. He keyed in the security combination that protected the house. Returning to the living room, he turned the lever to extinguish the gas fire, went to the front window and drew the drapes against the night. He leaned over the pumpkin and blew out its little candle. Darkness, and a plume of white smoke.

Joseph in the Darkness

WELL, THAT WAS that. Now I knew where Mendoza was, if only in a general way. I knew I couldn't rescue her myself; and Lewis had no chance at all. There were only two immortals I could turn to.

One of them was Suleyman, the North African Section Head. He's built up a private power base in Morocco, a huge machine, employs mortals and immortals alike as his agents. They do a good job for him, too, because he's a good man. Believes in all that Honor, Integrity, and Service stuff that was so important to you, Father. I'd trust Suleyman with my life . . . but I didn't think he would trust me. We go back a ways, he and I, so it would be sort of hard for him to believe I was really only trying to find my daughter. See what happens when you get a reputation for being a slimy little guy?

The other one was you, Father, and I hadn't seen you in a thousand years. You'd turned rogue, gone underground, and I hadn't lifted a finger to help you. Never even looked for you, though you gave me a clue. It sat undecrypted in my tertiary consciousness for ten centuries, because I was scared to look at it. It might even be useless by now. I guess you'd tell me it serves me right. But Mendoza, and the operatives she took down in her fall, is paying for my cowardice.

The whole sin thing works just like the Almighty said it does: innocent people get punished for things they didn't do. Unto the fourth and fifth generation. You make your mistake, and not only do you get screwed forever, the screwing spreads out in circles like ripples from a body dropped into quiet water. A body with a millstone about its neck.

That's why slash and burn was your way of dealing with the bad guys, wasn't it? Make examples of them, terrify the others so they'll never dare to break the laws. Free will? Forget it. Obedience was what you demanded and got. Very Pentateuch.

I wonder . . . did you ever work around Ur of the Chaldees? Ever lay some law on a shepherd named Abram? With Company special effects, maybe?

But theater was never your way. You'd have marched up to the shepherd, grabbed him by the front of his robe, and told him you would be running his life from then on, for his own good. You didn't beat around the bush.

Times changed, though. The Company had to stop being that direct. I think you understood this, maybe you alone of all the old Enforcers; though it didn't help you in the end. You realized what was going on when your kind began disappearing, didn't you? You knew how the Company was solving the problem of operatives it no longer needed.

Did you do what I'm doing now, investigating, searching? But it's a little harder for me, Father, the Company's more devious these days, as 2355 draws closer. The Preservers are being given a nice package deal, it's called gradual retirement.

The argument is, as the future world comes nearer, there's less work for us, who were created to rescue endangered things from humanity's folly. Mortals, finally becoming wise and good, don't need our services as much to preserve their priceless works of art from the ravages of war, to prevent extinctions of rare plants and animals due to overcrowding, overdevelopment. There is very little and soon will be *no* more war, overcrowding, or development.

Personally I have my doubts about this. Maybe they've just run out of stuff for us to save.

But anyway. We've all been told the Company will start rewarding us now for our millennia of faithful service. Giving us little treats, vacations, personal lives. This is the way it'll be all the time after 2355, they say: we can go anywhere we want, do anything we want. Just as though we weren't slaves.

It's taken me so many years to be able to say that word.

Slaves? Us? Not when the Company is starting to let us choose our own postings. Not when the Company is permitting us lasting relationships with the mortals with whom we have to work. Not when the Company is relaxing the old rules about personal property, schedules, and Theobromos consumption. We have choices now, at least some of the time. We can live our own lives, except when the Company needs us to do something.

The reason gradual retirement is so gradual, of course, is that all our programming directly opposes the idea. We have to be eased into a life of leisure. Our work is all we want, all we need, all that has kept us going through centuries of immortal heartbreak. Time on our hands makes us seriously uncomfortable. Look what it did to a Conservationist like poor Mendoza. Drove her crazy . . .

I assume she went crazy when she killed those mortals. A Conservationist killing, that's almost unheard of. Guys like you made pyramids of trophy heads, I know, and problem solvers like Porfirio work their silent way through the sewers of the world taking out two-legged vermin. Even Facilitators have been known to do a little quiet unofficial termination now and then.

But Mendoza? I'd never have thought her anger could push her that far. It was a rotten trick the Company played on her, taking her work away, letting her sit there in the middle of desolation with nothing to keep the old memories at bay. No wonder she went with the damned Englishman . . .

But which Englishman?

Who the hell was he?

What was he?

London, 2026

TREVOR AND ANITA sat waiting in the front parlor of the shop in Euston Road. They were uncomfortable. It was a very well known antiquarian bookshop, the kind that did almost no business out of the shopfront but relied principally on private clientele and Web orders. Nevertheless there was not a speck of dust anywhere, and the furniture in the parlor was expensive.

Trevor and Anita were not well off. They were hoping to be; artistic, creative, and talented, they were busily working at several concurrent schemes to make a bundle. One of these schemes was buying and restoring old houses, doing the work themselves to cut overhead, and reselling at handsome profits. Although to date there had been no profits, due to the union fines they had to pay. Then they found the old box.

It was so old, its leather panels were peeling away, and now it was wrapped in a green polythene garbage sack. Trevor held it on his lap. A white cardboard carton would have been more elegant, or brown paper. Looking uneasily around at the fifteenth-century Italian manuscripts under glass, Trevor and Anita regretted that they had found nothing better to put the old box in.

After a half hour of raised eyebrows from immaculately groomed persons who came and went through the office, Trevor and Anita were ready to sink through the floor. They had just decided to sneak out with their nasty little bag when a young man descended the stairs from the private offices on the first floor. He looked inquiringly at them.

He too was immaculately groomed, and wore a very expensive suit, though it seemed a little too big for him. He was handsome in a well-bred sort of way, with chiseled features and a resolute chin, rather like a romantic lead from the cinema of a century before. His eyes were the color of twilight.

"Excuse me," he said. "You wouldn't happen to be my three o'clock provenance case, would you?"

They stared at him, nonplussed.

"Um—you described it on the phone? Old wood-and-leather box found in an attic?" He gestured helpfully. "About this big? Full of possibly Victorian papers?"

"Yes!" The couple rose as one.

"So sorry I kept you waiting," he said, advancing on them and shaking hands. "Owen Lewis. You must be Trevor and Anita? Is this the box?"

"It is—"

"There was an iron bed frame in the attic room, and I don't think anybody had moved it in just, well, ages—"

"And this was wedged in underneath, we would never have known it was there if we hadn't moved the bed, and it took both of us—"

"The lid just fell apart when we prized it off—"

"Gosh, how exciting," Lewis exclaimed, rubbing his hands together. "Let's take it up to my office and have a look, shall we?"

He led them up the stairs, and they followed happily, completely set at ease. This was a nice, unintimidating man.

"My, this really has come to pieces, hasn't it?" said Lewis, when they were all gathered around his desk and he'd gingerly cut away the green bag. "Good idea to have brought it in in plastic. This is what we in the trade call a basket case."

Trevor and Anita smiled at each other, validated.

"Pity the box fell apart," Trevor said.

"Don't feel too badly," Lewis told him, taking a pair of latex gloves from a drawer and pulling them on with fastidious care. "From the pieces I'd say it's early Victorian, but rather cheap for its time. Mass-produced. You say it was in the attic? Where's the house?"

"Number 10, Albany Crescent," Trevor and Anita chorused.

"Ah." Lewis lifted away the ruin of the lid, piece by piece. "I know the neighborhood. Upstairs-downstairs, once, with a full staff of servants. Parlormaids and footmen and undergardeners and, here we are! A packet of letters. Let's just set these aside for the moment, shall we? This looks like a certificate of discharge from the army; this is a clipping from the London *Times* for—" Lewis tilted his head to look at it. "13 April 1840. And here's an old-fashioned pen."

"I thought people wrote with feathers back then," said Trevor.

"Not by 1840, actually. See this? It's the sort of wooden pen you could buy cheaply in any stationer's shop. I think all this belonged to a servant. The stains here? These are your man's fingerprints, just imagine!" Lewis set it carefully aside. "More newspaper clippings. Something underneath, looks like a book, and . . . a picture . . ."

"Oh," said Anita, leaning forward to look. "An old photograph! Do you suppose this is him?"

There was a moment's silence. Trevor and Anita looked up to see Lewis staring fixedly at the old picture. But he lifted his eyes to them, smiled, and in a perfectly normal voice said, "Probably not. This man's in a naval officer's uniform. A daguerreotype, too, I should say from about the year 1850. Somebody the servant knew, perhaps."

"He's rather odd-looking," Anita said, frowning at the image. "So stern."

"Yes, well, naval officers had to be." Lewis gave a slightly breathless laugh. "But let's see the book, shall we?" He lifted it out and opened it gingerly. "This'll be your real treasure, or I miss my guess. Your man must have been the butler at number ten. This is his household accounts book. Not a record of the finances, you understand, sort of a handbook he'd have compiled on how to run that particular household. Everything from recipes for silver polish to how to cure hiccups in a lady's maid. Here we go—here's his name, Robert Richardson, 19 January 1822. Two hundred and four years ago."

"Is it worth money?" Trevor said.

"The book? Almost certainly. I can put you in touch with at least three or four research libraries who have standing offers out for this sort of thing." Lewis set the book down.

"How much money are we looking at?" Anita said.

Lewis spread out his hands as though inviting them to guess. "Four thousand pounds? Five? The material has to be verified first. I can get to work on it at once, but it may be a few days before I can give you a real estimate."

Trevor and Anita looked at each other. Four thousand pounds would enable them to finish installing a modern climate-control system and pay off the union bully for the next month.

"Please go ahead, then," Trevor said.

While they waited, Lewis opened each of the letters in turn and ran a scanner over them to make a quick electronic record of their number and contents. There were two letters of reference from former employers and one from a regimental colonel attesting to the worthiness and reliability of Robert Richardson as a servant and soldier. There were three letters from someone named Edward, of a personal nature. The newspaper clippings were scanned and recorded, the book recorded page by page, the daguerreotype image recorded. The ancient pen and a half stick of sealing wax found at the bottom of the box were also duly noted.

Lewis transferred the scan to a master and opened the keyboard of his desk console. He keyed in a command to copy. A moment later the console ejected a little golden disk.

"And there you are." Taking it carefully by the edges, Lewis slid it into a plastic case and presented it to Anita. "Your record. Sign here on the tablet and leave your contact site, please. I should have some preliminary results for you by tomorrow afternoon."

Trevor and Anita left the office walking on air, and drifted away through the London afternoon into the rest of their lives, which do not figure further in this story.

Lewis sat alone in his office, contemplating the heap of yellowed paper, the blackened fragments of the box, the daguerreotype in its felt-backed case. At last he took up the picture and looked at it directly.

There could be no doubt.

It was an authentic image. The mortal wore the uniform of a naval commander, and from the cut Lewis guessed the image dated from about the year 1845. The young commander's face was extraordinary. Lewis had seen that face only once before, in his long life, and it was distinctive enough to stand out from any other.

As the mortal woman had remarked, the commander looked very stern, stiffly upright with his cockaded hat under his arm, frowning at the camera. He had high cheekbones and a long nose. His eyes were deepset, colorless silver in the image, perhaps pale blue. His wide mouth looked mobile and businesslike, ready to rap out some sort of nautical order or other. Ordinary features, but in their composition there was some quality that defied description, that fascinated or repelled. His hands were big but beautifully shaped.

And if the plaster Roman column against the backdrop was any measure of scale, he had been an extremely tall young man.

Lewis sighed and closed his eyes.

He saw in the darkness, for a moment; the commander's face, then the sketch he had seen thirty years earlier, the arrogant stranger staring down from horseback. The two faces were identical. They faded, to be replaced by a woman's face.

Her face, pale with unhappiness, looking paler in the darkness at the back of the booth. Where had they been? The old El Galleon at New World One, to be sure, in a secluded booth suitable for lovers . . .

Mendoza had lifted her glass and gazed into it a moment without drinking.

"Nicholas was the tallest mortal I ever saw," she said. "I had no idea they came that tall. He couldn't walk through any doorway without having to duck.

And I had to tilt my head back to look into his face, and—and such a remarkable face he had." She closed her eyes, red from crying. "Even looking sullen like that. How he disapproved of me! Little Spanish Papist girl, he thought. Daughter of Eve, source of all sin. I'd say we're Lilith's children, though, wouldn't you . . . ?"

She opened her eyes long enough to take a sip of her drink, and closed them again, the better to focus on her memory. "Big Roman nose, broken once. High cheekbones, wide mouth, quite a sensual mouth too, as I found out . . ."

Mendoza opened her eyes again and stared at Lewis, with that black intensity that connected like a physical blow. "I'm not giving you any idea of what Nicholas looked like, am I? He must sound absurd to you, homely as a mule. I tell you, though, no god was ever more beautiful."

"I can't see the man," Lewis admitted, "but I can see the man's soul, I think. You're describing what your heart saw when you looked at him."

She nodded in emphatic agreement, her face flushed. "His soul, yes, it was the animating spirit in his eyes that was so . . . I couldn't stop looking at them. Winter-sky eyes paler for colorless lashes, kind of small, actually, way up there peering out from their caves . . . But when Nicholas regarded you with those eyes . . ."

Her breath caught, and she looked so young, with the scarlet color draining away and leaving her pale as ashes again. Lewis caught his breath too, but the moment had gone; the young girl had retreated, and there was the austere old woman, the widow pulling her shawl closer against the cold.

She shook her head and picked up her drink again. "You see? All these years later, and I still go to pieces. Is God a cruel bastard or what, to make love so painful?"

He reached out and took her hand. "And mortal love is the hardest," he said.

She laughed harshly, tilting her glass to peer at the last of her margarita. "Oh, look, we're out," she said. "Shall we order another round? 'Stay me with flagons, comfort me with apples; for I am sick of love. . . .'" And she crumpled into herself in such an agony of grief that Lewis hurried to her side and put an arm around her. She wept in desperate silence as he held her.

Lewis opened his eyes now and looked at the old picture.

It was the Englishman Mendoza had run away with in 1863. What had been the name Lewis glimpsed in the arrest report? Bell-Something? And yet Nicholas Harpole too must have looked very like this, Mendoza's Nicholas who had been burned for his faith in 1555. Lewis was seeing, suddenly, the extraordinary quality she'd tried so hard to describe. His heart lurched. He wasn't sure what to make of this.

He sat up in his chair and put the daguerreotype and the other contents of the old box in a neat white carton. Drawing off his gloves, he set the carton aside, went to his bookcase, and withdrew a slender volume. It was not what you'd expect to find in an antiquarian's case; had been printed only a half century before, and big bouncy letters on its cheaply lithographed cover announced that it was the *Chocoholic's Almanac*, containing all sorts or interesting lore and legends to delight lovers of *Theobroma cacao*.

He sat down at his desk with it and drew out a manila shipping envelope, addressing it in neat script. Then he keyed in an order to his printer, which hummed and promptly provided him with a copy of the image on the daguerreotype. He scribbled something across the bottom and slipped it into the *Chocoholic's Almanac*; wrote a brief note and enclosed that too, and sealed up the book in the envelope. That done, he arose, slipped on his coat, took his package across the landing to the office's postal franking machine, which scanned, weighed, and inked it with the necessary bar code.

Lewis ran lightly down the stairs and out through the lobby to the street, leaving his package in the office's outgoing parcels bin. The parcel courier's van was already pulling up as Lewis rounded the corner and walked away down Tottenham Court Road.

Houston, 2026

"**Y**OU GOT A package, boss," said Musicologist Donal, peering at it as he returned to the breakfast nook.

"Have you been sending off for more of those bondage fetish disks again?" asked Muriel innocently, looking up from her coffee. She was an Anthropologist.

"Ha ha," said Joseph, scowling at her. He accepted the package and peered at the label. "One of these days I'm going to find out which one of you did that, and then—"

He was interrupted by the Art Preservationist, who came thundering down the stairs, pulling on his coat. "My alarm didn't go off. Why didn't anybody wake me?"

They gaped at him in surprise as he buttoned his coat.

"We didn't know you were on that tight a schedule, Andrei," Muriel said.

"My car's in the shop, and I've got to be in Corpus Christi by noon," he said, grabbing a brioche from the basket on the table. "The hurricane's scheduled to hit on the twenty-seventh, you know. I don't have much time, and there's even less if I have to take goddam public transit on this job."

"Okay, okay," sighed Joseph, getting up and tucking the unopened package into his briefcase. "I'll drive you. It's not as though I had anything important to do today. Just kiss Governor Gleason's ass until he agrees to veto that land appropriation bill. But I can do that any time, right? I'm under no pressure, not old Joseph."

"I appreciate this," Andrei said, dancing in impatience by the door. "I'll even mail the governor's office for you in the car while you drive. Tell him you're calling in sick or something."

"Let's go," Joseph said, following him out the door and down the hall.

"Have a nice day," Donal called after them.

Outside the apartment building it was already uncomfortably warm, and Andrei had shed his coat by the time they got into Joseph's black Saturn Avocet. However, the temperature fell rapidly over the next two hours, and he was bundled up again by the time Joseph dropped him off on the outskirts of town.

"Will you need a ride back tonight?" Joseph leaned out the window.

"No. I'm probably staying a few days this time. I'll call HQ later and let you know, okay?" Andrei shouted, turning up his coat collar.

"Okay," said Joseph.

"Bye." Andrei waved, and sprinted off to get out of the wind.

Joseph circled back to the highway. Before he had gone very far, however, hail began dropping out of the sky. He cursed and pulled off to the side of the road to wait out the cloudburst. Other motorists were doing the same.

He sighed and switched off the engine. His gaze fell on his briefcase; carefully he took out the package and opened it.

There was a note and a book: *The Chocoholic's Almanac.* He nodded gamely, setting the book aside. He read the note.

Hello there, old man! Came across this in an estate sale and was reminded of the days when we used to paint the City cocoa-powder brown. You might find it instructive. Can you get Ghirardelli's in the Lone Star State?

I'm in the other City now. Come across for a weekend, and we can discuss old times over a cup of Cadbury's, ha ha. Ave, Lewis.

Grinning, Joseph picked up the little book and opened it. He came upon the printout of the naval officer tucked inside, and his grin froze on his face. The officer regarded him severely. Under the picture Lewis had written, in a waggish scrawl: NO THEOBROMOS PERMITTED IN THE DORMITORY.

Joseph drew a long breath through clenched teeth, eyes fixed on the picture. The hail was coming down harder now, big stones hitting the Avocet's shell and putting a thousand little spiderweb fractures in its just-waxed finish, but Joseph barely noticed. When the storm passed, his was the first car to leave the side of the road, peeling out with a lurch and fishtailing slightly as he sped away through the slush. He might have maintained better control of the car if he'd kept both hands on the wheel, but he was busily making a flight reservation on the dash console as he drove.

London

LEWIS SPOTTED HIM from the end of the street, a businessman in a rumpled if costly suit, waiting on the front step like a patient dog. Joseph rose to his feet, grinning as Lewis approached, but there was a certain flinty quality in his eyes.

That was quick, Lewis transmitted to him.

"Hey, Lewis, great to see you." *Where did you find that picture? Who is he?*

"Joseph, you old rake." Lewis bounced up the steps and shook hands vigorously. *His name was Edward Alton Bell-Fairfax. I have a lot to tell you. Did you ever perfect that signal disrupter?*

"Nice place the Company's set you up in." Joseph waved a hand at the building. "Restored Georgian, isn't it?" *Not quite yet. Anyway we shouldn't use it this time out. Somebody would be bound to wonder why we fry our circuits every time we get together.*

"Yes." Lewis keyed in the entry combination. "Lots of style, but the closets are impossible and the heating bills are worse. On the other hand, I needn't commute, and there's a really first-class vindaloo place around the corner."

The door swung open, and he gestured for Joseph to precede him. Joseph put his suitcase down in the hall and looked around brightly, scanning. "Quite the bachelor pad, huh?"

"It's all done in Mid-Twentieth Century Revival," Lewis said, keying in the security, lighting, and temperature control. The rooms had a certain spartan, masculine style, black vinyl and brass, framed abstract prints, a whole wall given over to books. Everything was spotlessly clean and in perfect order. It looked like a movie set for an espionage film.

"Boy, you must sit here in the evenings and pretend you're James Bond," said Joseph, hanging up his coat on the hall stand.

Funny you should say that. "It's quite comfortable, all things considered. How long can you stay?"

"Oh, just for the weekend. I'm taking a suborbital back Sunday night." *What did you find out?*

More than I can tell you subvocally. Are you sure it's dangerous to discuss out loud, even in here? "Well, let's make good use of our time. Come on, I'll give you the grand tour. That's the den, and the kitchen's in there. Lavatory and two bedrooms upstairs. You'll want to unpack, I imagine." Lewis led Joseph up the stairs.

Especially in here. I know what we can do, though. Got any DVDs?

"And maybe you'd like to watch a movie after dinner?" Lewis suggested. "I've got rather an extensive collection of classics."

"Great." Joseph edged into the tiny guest bedroom and looked around. It was all navy blue and brass, with yachting prints on the walls. *We just put on a movie and settle back to watch it. Then we can talk subvocally without having to improvise chatter for some security tech's benefit.*

Seems a bit paranoid, but you're the Facilitator.

After Joseph unpacked, they walked down to the corner for takeaway curry, chatting pleasantly and audibly on unobjectionable topics. The nearest wine shop had closed for the day, in accordance with the tighter new laws, but Lewis had a cabinet nicely stocked with Californian white varietals. He filled a couple of goblets, and they sat on his black couch in companionable silence, eating from the cartons as they watched Humphrey Bogart face down Conrad Veidt in the latest remastered rerelease of *Casablanca*.

So, you were saying? Edward Alton who?

Bell-Fairfax. *Nice young couple of mortals renovating an old house found an ancient box of papers in the attic and brought it to me, pound signs dancing before their eyes. Among the papers was that daguerreotype. He's the man the ornithologist sketched, isn't he? That day we went to the Hitchcock house?*

Maybe. What he definitely is is the exact double of a first-class son of a bitch named Nicholas Harpole, whom I had the pleasure of watching burn at the stake in 1555.

The man in the daguerreotype looks just like Nicholas?

The spit and image.

How remarkable, transmitted Lewis calmly, though his pulse was racing.

Remarkable ain't the word, Lewis. I wonder what we're dealing with here. Coincidence? Genetic hyperstability on this damn little island? You've lived here on and off for centuries, Lewis. Did you ever see another Englishman who even remotely resembled that big scarecrow?

Actually he seemed rather well-dressed to me. But—no, I can't say that I have. I've been trying to find out more about him.

You've tracked down his death certificate, I hope?

I haven't, though there's a registry of baptism in an obscure little country parish, and he's listed as illegitimate.

That figures.

There's more. He appears to have written three of the letters in this collection. The young master writing home to the old family retainer, as it were. I've been using the references in the letters to track him, to follow his career. He was in the royal navy for a while, but then he left under something of a cloud.

I'll bet.

I've only started seriously looking, but I have several leads to follow up. Did you find out where Mendoza was sent?

Yeah.

Where, for God's sake? When were you going to tell me?

Joseph shifted uncomfortably on the couch, as Paul Henreid ordered a champagne cocktail for himself and Ingrid Bergman.

I was getting around to it. Lewis, we can't help her. She . . . Did you ever hear rumors about a place called Back Way Back?

Lewis reached out in a leisurely way and picked up his wineglass. His hand shook only very slightly as he took a sip of chilled Chardonnay.

I see, he said at last.

She may be perfectly okay! But she's out of the picture, Lewis. Permanently. Even if there was something I could do for her—and I'm not ruling that out—there's sure as hell nothing you could do.

Lewis set his wine down carefully. For a moment his face was astonishingly transformed by rage. *Damn them. And damn you. Are you writing her off?*

Look, Joseph said, *all this is beside the point. Wherever Mendoza is, she'll be staying put. I'm following another lead right now, something completely unrelated, but it just might give me some leverage. I'll need all the advantages I can get if I'm going to even attempt to help her. See? So you must bear with me.*

What sort of lead?

Somebody gave me a set of coordinates once . . . I'll tell you the story sometime, but the bottom line is, I need to look them up. What I'm searching for may be long gone by now, but I have to see. One of the locations is in Yorkshire. You know that area?

Yes, actually. I had a job there a few years back.

Great. Do you have a car?

I can get the Austin from the garage. It might be an overnight trip, though.

It's only a couple of hundred miles. Just pretend you're back in California. And even if we do stay over, I have my own credit line these days, I can pay for a hotel. All we need is a plausible reason for visiting there, so we don't rouse suspicions.

Lewis frowned thoughtfully. *A literary pilgrimage? Lot of writers in that part of the world. The Brontës, Herriot, Knollys . . .*

Sounds unbelievably boring, but what the hell. You're a literature guy, right? Any Theobromos action up there?

I don't believe so.

Oh, well. We can always get some Aero bars at a newsagent's or somewhere for the trip.

Lewis sipped more of his wine. *You're on another jag? I'd better lay in a few dozen tins of spaghetti. So you think this search of yours might help Mendoza?*

Possibly. Though she's been out of the picture since 1863.

Aren't you forgetting something? You saw her in 1923. And she was with him, *wasn't she? That man in the daguerreotype, who looks just like her Nicholas?*

Lewis, that has to have been a hallucination. I couldn't have seen either one of them. I know that now. Even if she managed to escape Back Way Back somehow, what about him? That picture dates from, what, 1850? By 1923 he'd have been damn near a hundred. But he wasn't. He didn't look a day older than the last time I saw him, just before a powder key turned him into a human torch. Joseph crunched into a pappadum savagely and continued. *In any case, what does it matter? We know that the gene pool over here produced not one but two of the rotten stinking lousy guys. We know that somehow, by the worst coincidence in the world, guy number two managed to find my poor little recruit and screw up her life even worse than guy number one did. End of story, except that if this island somehow manages to produce another one, I swear I'll kill him myself, because God only knows what's left for him to do to her.*

Lewis looked at him sidelong. *Would you mind not gnashing your teeth? You're spitting pappadum flakes all over my couch. You really hated the man, didn't you? It's affecting your judgment, you know. You've completely overlooked one possibility.*

Which would be?

Mendoza was a Crome generator, Joseph. There have been no other immortals with that condition. It's impossible to say what she can do.

True. But all the same—

She loved Nicholas desperately. I know. She was never reconciled to his death. What if she somehow reincarnated him?

Lewis, that is nuts. Have you been reading romance novels?

Of course I have, but that's beside the point. In the nearly two thousand years I've been alive, I've seen my share of the inexplicable. And if you tell me you haven't seen more anomalies than I have in your twenty thousand, then all I have to say is you're either blind or a damned liar.

Joseph picked up his wine and drank it down like water. He sagged back in the vinyl upholstery, staring at the old film, watching the exquisite play of black shadow on white, on silvertone, on ash gray, silhouettes of palm fronds, window blinds, pale smoke curling in the midnight air. Bogart took another drag on the cigarette that would kill him and pondered the cruelty of chance meetings.

Yorkshire

"THIS USED TO be Ermine Street, didn't it?" Joseph asked, squinting into the wind.

Lewis drove an Austin Taranis electric convertible, gunmetal gray, and the sporty windscreen didn't deflect much. "Good old Roman roads," he said, slipping them through the last poky AI traffic emerging from London and cautiously increasing his speed. "I daresay you've marched along a few of these in your time."

"Yeah," Joseph replied, a little gloomily. "This very road, if you want the truth."

"Really? I wish I'd been stationed here then. Or in Rome. I never really got to know that side of my organic heritage, you know. The Company sent me straight into Ireland as soon as I graduated, and I was stuck there for the next few centuries," Lewis said. "By the time I was finally stationed in England, Roman Britain was long gone. I've always rather regretted that."

"You like army life?" Joseph unwrapped an Aero bar and took a bite.

"Well, no—at least, I don't suppose I would. Literary Preservationists don't see a lot of that sort of assignment," Lewis said. "But, you know, all those legions tramping through the mists, the sort of thing you imagine when you listen to Respighi's music. It has a certain romantic appeal."

"Respighi should have done some time carrying a hundred-pound pack through Cumbria, that's all I've got to say," said Joseph. "And your feet froze all the time in those damn caligae. What brain trust came up with an open-toed combat boot? Goddam slaves got better shoes. And of course the poor auxiliaries died like flies from the cold, because we had guys from Africa and Hispania sent up here, naturally, and ex-Visigoths sent down to patrol villages in Egypt. Military intelligence."

"Eat the other Aero bar, for God's sake." Lewis shifted gears and sped around a lorry trundling Japanese sewing machines to a minor industrial town.

"Okay, okay. Let's see, what can I say that's positive about the Roman army? Good engineers, but everybody knows that. Lots of incentives, and they really took care of their veterans. Had to; most stayed in the service until they were gray and toothless, which wasn't actually all that long, given the life expectancy in those days." Joseph balled up the wrapper and stuffed it in the Austin's map pocket after looking around vainly for an ashtray.

"I suppose I shouldn't ask further." Lewis sighed. "Not if I want to keep any illusions about the blessings of the Pax Romana with all those centrally heated public buildings and orderly little towns."

"A little Rome went a long way, believe me," Joseph said.

Lewis pulled over to let a speeding Jaguar pass him. "Now—it's funny, I've known for years you'd been a centurion, but it's only just occurred to me to wonder—what on earth would one of us be doing in *any* army? How could you possibly have dealt with being on a battlefield?"

"I ducked a lot," Joseph told him. "And as for what I was doing there, you don't need to know."

"Ah," said Lewis, nodding sagely, and appeared to concentrate very closely on the road for the next few miles.

No, seriously, can you tell me what you were doing?

The Company needed an observer to fill in an event shadow. I was with the Ninth Hispania, operating out of Eboracum. York, I mean.

The Ninth? The famous lost legion?

Yeah.

And the Company planted you among them so you could find out what happened to it?

That's right.

But I thought it turned out they were never lost after all. Didn't someone discover they were simply transferred to Cappadocia or somewhere?

Those were the replacement guys. Haven't you been in this business long enough to know that most questions have to be answered with yes and no? There was a good reason the legend of the lost legion got started.

Well?

We got sent on a stupid march through the Pennines, and about a million Brigantes came down on our heads. It wasn't as bad as when Quintilius Varus got massacred, but it was bad enough. They cut us into little pieces. All except me, of course. Joseph unwrapped the other Aero bar and ate it in three bites.

That's all?

It didn't take long, either, the Ninth was already in such bad shape.

But . . . why were no remains ever found? No rusting armor, no spears, no coins?

Why do you think? Joseph stared out at the green countryside, where a bulldozer was methodically destroying a hedgerow eleven centuries old.

Lewis's jaw dropped. He put the car on autopilot a moment while he went through the motions of opening out the audio case for a leisurely inspection of its contents. He selected one disc at last, a symphonic piece by Ian Anderson, and slipped it into the music system. Only then did he place both hands firmly back on the wheel and ask, *Are you saying the Company had you strip the bodies?*

Joseph gave a barely perceptible shrug. *Something like that. You know how much future collectors will pay for authentic relics of the lost legion? With the old IX Hispania insignia?*

I can imagine, Lewis said. He drove on, pale and shaken, as a flute melody of haunting sweetness wafted out of the Austin's speakers. At last he shook his head. *You know—I've been thinking, lately, that all this paranoia and strong-arm work was something new for the Company, some reaction perhaps to the fact that we're nearing the year of the Silence. I assumed that Dr. Zeus used to operate in a more civilized and humane manner.*

Nope.

North and north the car sped on, along the well-metaled road.

They went west on the A635 and meandered westward for a while to the A629, past Denby Dale, past Kirkburton, through Huddersfield and Halifax, and at last Lewis announced brightly, "Well, we're almost there. Stop one of our Yorkshire literary tour. We'll see the famous parsonage at Haworth, where the ill-fated but creative Brontë family lived, loved and died to the last member. You've read the novels, of course?"

"I've seen the movies," Joseph said. "I worked at MGM when they were making the *Wuthering Heights* with Larry Olivier."

"So you've never read the novels?" Lewis's lips thinned slightly.

"I might have scanned them in school." Joseph shrugged, refusing to admit to anything. "Real men don't read *Jane Eyre*. Unless you're a Literature Specialist, I guess," he added soothingly.

"Thank you." Lewis downshifted with a bit more force than was required. "Well, you're going to enjoy this anyway, damn it. Look at these heathery moors! Look at the wild and lonely prospects! Imagine those fantastically talented and sickly children in their claustrophobic little parsonage, growing up into doomed, brilliant youth. Not a one of them made it into their forties, did you know that? They burnt out like flares. Is it any wonder they were able to produce masterworks of savage passion and searing romance?"

"*Jane Eyre*, that was the one with the governess, right?" Joseph yawned.

"You know perfectly well it was. Look, there's the parsonage museum." Lewis turned off and steered for the car park.

"Do they have a souvenir stand?" asked Joseph.

They stopped and got out. There for their edification was the little church with its parsonage, islands in a sea of tombstones, and the moors rolling down on the back of the parsonage like a never-breaking wave. There were a few other cars in the park, but no tourists visible. The two immortals strolled toward the parsonage.

Is this going to help you at all in your investigation?

Not really. We need to go farther north. Still, it's a good blind. We'll see the sights, buy a couple of souvenirs, and move on, okay?

How very cloak-and-dagger.

As they came around the corner, they saw an impressive conveyance, a long wagon with a team of six coal-black draft horses in its traces. It was an omnibus of some kind, fitted with rows of seats and roofed over by an awning. A man in nineteenth-century coachman's dress waited, immobile as a waxwork figure by the horses. Joseph and Lewis halted, staring at the moment out of time.

Before either of them could comment, the door of the parsonage opened, and out filed a line of persons, also in nineteenth-century costume in varying funereal shades, all looking rather self-conscious except for the formidable lady at their head. She spotted Joseph and Lewis gaping at them. Directing her companions to the wagon, she turned and made straight for the immortals.

"If you are interested in the tour, gentlemen, you must purchase tickets in the gift shop," she said. She was a small stout lady of the iron-sinewed maiden-aunt variety. "However, I must advise you that appropriate dress is required, which fortunately you may rent for a reasonable sum from the wardrobe mistress."

"Okay," said Joseph.

"Oh! Oh! This is one of those total immersion reenactor events, isn't it?" said Lewis in excitement. "How utterly magical! And I imagine you're Charlotte Brontë?"

"I am, sir," said the actress.

"Delighted to make your acquaintance, Miss Brontë." Lewis swept her hand to his lips. "I have so enjoyed your novels. May I introduce myself? Mr. Owen Lewis, and this American gentleman is my friend, Mr. Capra."

"Hi," said Joseph.

Charlotte Brontë inclined graciously and peered down at the watch pinned to her bosom. "Thank you. Today's tour includes the authentic locations that inspired my late sister Emily in her depiction of the principal scenes from *Wuthering Heights*. We depart presently; shall we wait for you to join us?"

"How much are the tickets?" Joseph asked.

"Thirty pounds," said Miss Brontë coolly. "Per person."

"Jesus H. Christ," Joseph said.

"You may, of course, elect to wait in the parsonage until the costumed tour returns in three hours, when the bargain-rate tour will be given." Miss Brontë stared him down. "Though I must warn you that the parsonage has, of course, no central heating, a fact which led, indirectly or otherwise, to the early deaths of several of my dear sisters."

"Joseph, you'll regret it if we pass up an opportunity like this," Lewis cajoled. "I know I will."

"I said I had a credit line, not a money tree."

"We won't be a moment," promised Lewis, and grabbing Joseph by the elbow, he hurried away to the parsonage. Miss Brontë sauntered back to the omnibus, swinging her reticule with an air of triumph.

"That cost a goddam fortune," growled Joseph five minutes later, as they emerged from the parsonage decked in Inverness cloaks and rather poorly made felt top hats. "And this is *really* not a guy thing, Lewis."

"For heaven's sake, can't you at least enjoy the irony of it all?" said Lewis. *Besides, if you don't want the Company to think you're planning something, this is certainly a good cover. What possible reason could you have for doing something like this other than impulsive, spur-of-the-moment fun?*

Joseph just growled again. They hurried to the omnibus, presented their tickets to Miss Brontë, and took their seats.

Three hours later they returned to the car, pausing to open the boot of the Austin.

"I can't believe you didn't enjoy that," said Lewis, as Joseph carefully loaded in the six jugs of Brontë liqueur he had purchased at the gift shop.

"I guess I'm just not literary," Joseph said, changing his mind and removing one of the jugs. He carried it around to the front of the car and got in.

"You've no appreciation of high romance, that's your trouble," Lewis said, climbing in and starting the motor.

Joseph nodded somberly. "Boy meets girl, girl loses boy, everybody dies. I just don't get it. What those kids needed was some tuberculosis inoculations and a whole lot of Prozac." He broke the seal on the jug and sampled the liqueur. "Wow. Or this. Want some?"

"Not while I'm driving. Do you want to get us arrested?" Lewis headed them back in the direction of the A629.

"At least that would be a guy thing," Joseph retorted.

They zigzagged back and forth across the Yorkshire Dales, gradually working their way north. They stopped at a Herriot museum and had their photographs taken with a Clydesdale horse; bought *All Creatures Great and Small* tea towels and a Yorkshire Dale cake in a tin enameled with scenes from Herriot's books; passed through villages with names like Blubberhouses, Winksley, Snape, and Patrick Brompton.

"Where are we going now?" Joseph said, taking another gulp from the liqueur jug.

"Quite a historically significant spot, actually," Lewis said, brushing crumbs of Dale cake from his tie as he accelerated. "Swaledale Anti-Farm, home of the late Audrey Knollys and setting of her celebrated heroic epic trilogy, *Commonwealth of Innocents*. Don't tell me: you haven't read it."

"What, the Beast Liberation lady?" Joseph shrugged. "Wrote kind of a cross between *Animal Farm* and *Watership Down?* I've heard of it. Those are the books that will get the Mandated Vegan Laws passed over here, right?"

"And over there, too, in what will be left of the United States," Lewis said. "There's already a Beast Liberation Party flexing its muscles in London. Ironically enough, none of the locals want it here; the economy's still based in farming. Eventually, though, the BLP will get the Herriot places closed down as mere glorifications of beast exploitation. Hang on to those tea towels; they'll be worth a fortune some-day."

"I guess so," said Joseph in awe.

He was silent as they continued west, and silent when they turned north at Hardraw. A short distance on, he sat upright and peered around suspiciously.

What's wrong? Lewis transmitted, keeping his eyes on the road.

Nothing. Nothing now, anyway. But it was right around here that the Ninth got creamed.

Gosh, really? Lewis slowed the car, looking about as if he expected to see hapless auxiliaries being chased by howling blue savages.

I guess I sort of erased the memory. It wasn't fun. But, you know something else? This is also pretty damn close to the coordinates I was tracing.

Lewis gnawed his lower lip. *That's an awfully big coincidence. It's also rather close to the location of that job I had up here.*

No kidding? Weird.

They drove on in silence. A moment later they came upon a wayside inn and gift shop styled THE INNOCENTS, beyond which loomed the flank of a steep hill.

Suggest that this looks like a good place to stop, transmitted Joseph urgently. *Out loud, now!*

"I wonder if this shop sells Bournville bars?" mused Lewis obediently, pulling into the row of graveled parking spaces. "Would you mind if we looked? I must confess I'm finding the scenery a bit depressing."

"Sure," said Joseph in his most casual voice. "Say, look at those clouds. Might be a good idea to remember there's a hotel here, if we get caught in a storm. Should we put the top up?"

Lewis keyed in a command on the dash, and the convertible's top creaked out over them like an opening wing. "May as well do it now, in case it starts while we're inside." *What is it? Have we reached your coordinates?*

This is the spot.

They got out and crunched across the gravel to the shop, looking up doubtfully at the dark sky. A bitter cold wind was sweeping under it, piercing through their coats. They opened the door and stepped into the relative warmth of the shop and an atmosphere of tinkling chimes, fragrant incense, and a vast distant mooing that Lewis, after a milli-second's startled analysis, identified as recorded whale songs.

"It's California again," muttered Joseph.

As if on cue, an American voice spoke from behind a display of crystal pendants. "Can I help you find something?"

"Hello?" Lewis peered around the display and beheld a thin intense lady wearing purple and a lot of neolithic-styled jewelry. "Do you have any Bournville bars?"

By way of answer the lady pointed to a display stand gratifyingly loaded with sweets. "Right over there, next to the books."

"So they are." Lewis smiled his thanks. Joseph followed him around to inspect them.

"Get me some mints too, will you? Hey, look," he said loudly. "Here are those great books you were recommending. The, uh, *Commonwealth of Innocents.*"

Must you be devious about everything? Lewis said in exasperation.

"Oh, you have to read those!" the lady informed him, heat and light coming into her voice. She emerged from behind the counter possessively. "You know where you are, don't you? You're right smack in the middle of where all her stories are set."

"I thought Swaledale must be nearby," Lewis said. "I've read them, of course."

"Aren't they just—?" The lady put one hand on her bosom, expressing that words failed her. "We named this place for the trilogy, you know, Jeffrey and I. We just couldn't believe it when we got up here and found out that there's no museum or plaque or *anything* about Knollys up at the Anti-Farm. It's just sitting there vacant! We're starting a fund to establish a museum. Donations are always welcome."

"What a wonderful idea," said Lewis, gallantly pulling out his wallet.

The lady nodded in vigorous affirmation, ringing up his purchases.

"Right up the road a couple of miles is the meadow with the copse where Silverbell the Gentle is martyred," she went on, referring to the eponymous bovine saint of the trilogy's first volume. "And, you won't believe this, but right in back of us is the very hill where Jeremiah the Valiant leads the Innocents against the Vulpos!"

She was referring to the trilogy's controversial third volume, wherein the peace-loving barnyard folk band together to exterminate all foxes in one great crusade to rid their world of vicious predators. Lewis explained this in a brief transmission to Joseph, adding:

There have always been rumors of a new trilogy Audrey Knollys was working on at the time of her death, in which the Innocents go after cats and dogs too. No notes ever surfaced, but the mere idea has already caused a schism among her followers.

Joseph gave Lewis a bright inquisitive look. *I bet there really were notes, in fact I'd bet there was a completed first draft. Gee, I wonder what could have happened to it?* He opened the mints and popped one in his mouth.

I had nothing to do with her accident, if that's what you're implying, Lewis said sharply. *I simply got there before her executors did.* He pressed a ten-pound note into the lady's hand. "No, keep the change for the museum fund. Please. Is there any kind of tour one can take? Any guidebook to the real-life locations?"

The lady shook her head. "It's shameful, but there really isn't. Someday, I just know there will be, but right now—" She lowered her voice. "It's this country. Don't get me wrong, I love England and all, but there's just no initiative here. You know what I mean? I mean, haven't you noticed that?"

"Absolutely. Is there anybody local we could pay to show us around?" said Joseph.

At this moment a youngish man shouldered open the door, puffing with effort because he was quite stout. He set down the cardboard boxes he'd been carrying and straightened up to glower at the two immortals. He wore black and more neolithic-styled jewelry, and had cultivated a little sinister beard and mustache to rival Joseph's.

"Jeffrey, these men are interested in a tour of the trilogy sites," said his wife hopefully.

"And we'll pay," added Joseph.

"Well then," Jeffrey said, drawing himself up. "Five pounds apiece, just to cover the gas, okay? I'll take you in the Landrover."

"Deal," Joseph said. Lewis fished out another ten-pound note.

Ten minutes later they were rumbling along a cow path in an old Landrover, listening to Jeffrey talk. Jeffrey spoke sonorously, pontifically, and at great length, and if either Joseph or Lewis had been actually interested in the trilogy, Jeffrey would have been a great guide, because he clearly knew the books by heart. As it was, they were able to hold a fairly uninterrupted subvocal conversation during his narration, only pausing now and then to murmur appreciatively when he emphasized something with a dramatic silence or sweeping gesture.

They wobbled past the semiruined Swaledale Anti-Farm, acres of weedy earth and a few stone buildings, "the site of Audrey Knollys's magnificently daring Nonhuman experiment"; they visited various chattering becks or heathery hillsides that had inspired scenes where unforgettably heroic beasts had loved, suffered, and/or died; and at last they charged bumping up a great hill, following its ridge as along the spine of a beached whale. At the highest point Jeffrey turned off the motor, set the emergency brake firmly, and announced:

"We're getting out here, gentlemen." He swung open the driver's door and stepped into a roaring blast of wind.

"Er . . . I don't like to seem overcautious, but isn't this spot rather exposed to lightning?" Lewis said, clambering from the Landrover after him. Joseph followed even more reluctantly. They stood there with their coats whipping behind them as Jeffrey struck an attitude.

"Now, *this* is my favorite spot. From this point you can see just about every important place mentioned in the entire trilogy, except for the parts set in Leeds, of course. But, see? Back there is the Anti-Farm, and Silverbell's Copse is clearly visible just over there, and . . ."

Lewis was smiling and nodding, pretending to follow the lecture attentively even as his teeth chattered. Joseph wasn't watching. He was staring fixedly into a place just below where they were standing, a smooth depression in the flank of the hill, more than a ledge, less than a valley. It was the sort of place where exhausted hikers might sprawl before going on to the top, or perhaps where a handful of desperate men might make a last stand, unable to go any higher.

This is what he was remembering:

Brigantia, A.D. 120

"WELL, *THIS* ISN'T going to work," said Ron, staring down at the last of the Brigantes, who had noticed their retreat. He was very, very big—all six of the "Cimmerians" were very, very big men with dun-colored hair and light blue eyes. They also shared other distinct and unusual physical characteristics, which was why the Company had felt it advisable to slip them into the legion as auxiliaries from a nonexistent northern race. Joseph came to peer over the edge and backed away, pale.

"Do you think they'll try to come up here after us?" he asked, groping for his short sword.

"Oh, yeah," said Bayard, coming to stand beside Ron. "As soon as they're done mopping up down there. Poor old Ninth. Ouch! They just took out Gaius Favonius. That's it. The last of the Syrians are running like hell."

"Are they getting away?" Gozo and Albert came to watch. The four giants stood there a moment in silence, staring, before Ron said briefly:

"Nope."

Bogdan and Pancha, who had been scanning the hilltop above the ledge, gave up and joined them, and after a moment's hesitation Joseph edged close again. He looked out on the carnage below and shuddered. "I'm sorry," he said desperately.

To a man, the Enforcers shrugged.

"It was their fate," said Ron. "Soldiers kill, soldiers get killed. Don't feel bad. You can take some revenge on the Brigantes, if you want. They're going to be up here any minute."

Joseph's blade trembled in his hand, and Gozo burst out laughing.

"Don't sweat it." Leaning down, he knocked playfully on Joseph's helmet. "We'll do our job, centurion baby. We got what the Company wanted, didn't we? You were able to observe the whole thing. Now this event shadow's filled in, Dr. Zeus knows what happened to the original Ninth, and all we've got to do is clean up."

"There's still the goddam Brigantes," said Joseph through his teeth, pushing his helmet back on his head.

"You can say that again." Ron's voice sharpened as he stepped back. "Here they come. Joseph, stay down, and we'll keep them off. You're the observer; just keep those cameras rolling. Axes, guys!"

Joseph sheathed his sword and crouched down, fighting every programmed instinct to wink out in hyperfunction and not touch ground until he was a good five miles away. He obeyed his orders, which had not come from Rome; he held his tiny patch of ground and kept his eyes open, recording what he saw.

The Enforcers cast away the little round auxilio shields and drew from their cases the particular native weapons of their own unit. These were not ballistae, nor were they slings or curved bows. They were flint axes of enormous size, bound to oak hafts in leather thongs, beautifully worked, heavily weighted to crush with the blunt ends, slice like razors on the edge. Each Enforcer had two axes.

"Hhhhaaai-ai-ai!" Bogdan said reverently. "Death!"

"Ready them," said Ron. "Hand-to-hand in thirty seconds. Shit, look at that. Down axes, prepare for javelin cast! Take out that front line!"

Joseph dragged himself to the edge and looked down. The Brigantes were coming, not swiftly. Winded from the fight below, they advanced almost lazily, chatting among themselves as they came up the face of the hill. They were followed by the fresh reinforcements that had just arrived, walking easily through the mutilated bodies and the ruined baggage train. He estimated their number at a hundred and six.

The foremost looked up at the ledge, and Joseph saw their eyes widen slightly. Then he heard the noise behind him, the creak of leather armor on six bodies bending all together like the great machines they were, just before they fired in perfect unison and with inhuman force.

No mortal eye could have seen the flight of spears, so swift it was; but Joseph watched them hurtling down the hill and through the Brigantes. Literally through, men two and three deep were falling, shrieking, with gaping wounds front and back as the spears shot on downward, clattering to rest at last on the stones of the little stream below.

The advance halted. The barbari looked at one another big-eyed, drew into groups, muttered together, stared up at the ledge uncertainly now. Joseph turned to look too. The Enforcers had taken up their axes and come to the edge and were just standing there, six very big men, motionless as mountains.

Joseph could see the Brigantes looking, turning to each other and mouthing, *Is that all?* and shrugging at last and beginning the cautious advance again, flatfooted up the hill, keeping their eyes on the very big men.

Ron drew a deep breath.

"Father of battles," he moaned. "Lord of justice, drink the blood of the unjust!"

The whole line of the Enforcers began to sway together, in that eerie unison with which they had launched their javelin cast. Their pupils had dilated enormously. To a man, they were smiling now as they rocked in place and contemplated the advancing mortals. First one and then another began to chant, softly at first, apparently disconnected phrases in a language forty thousand years old, a chaos of harmonies that unified into descant on a single melody, beautiful and terrifying, sweet tenor voices from those monstrous chests, those thick necks.

Joseph remembered the language. It was a very simple song: its meaning was only that the wicked must be punished so the innocent might live in peace.

Albert and Bogdan stepped forward and began to walk down the hill, still singing, swinging their flint axes in either massive hand.

The Brigantes halted, gaping; then someone screamed, and they charged, swarming up the hill.

Almost at once Albert and Bogdan vanished in the press of mortal bodies. You could see the axes rising and falling, though, and occasionally catch a glimpse of a great red hand or arm. Pancha and Bayard were walking down now, reaching out almost casually to knock in the skulls of the first Brigantes to reach them, disappearing in their turn under the screaming mob. Ron and Gozo waded in after them.

It didn't last long. The fighting moved back down the hill, for the simple reason that none of them could keep their footing, everyone was sliding in the blood and mud. Not only mortal blood, now; Joseph saw a lucky blow take off Albert's head, the trunk fountaining scarlet as it fought on a full ten seconds before dropping in fugue. Bayard was down, he'd been damaged. Brigantii were all over him like flies on a corpse, desperately trying to knife him where he lay, but his arms still rose and fell, rose and fell like machines, beating and breaking any mortal thing in range. The terrified mortals were stabbing frantically at the other Enforcers, delivering wound after wound with dagger or sword or spear, and the big men slowed as their blood ran down, but they did not stop killing.

Then it was over, all at once. Ron was the last one standing. He staggered back and sat down heavily. Joseph heard him sigh. There was a silence, except for the wind coming up the valley. There wasn't a Brigante left alive.

Joseph was on his hands and knees then, scrambling and crawling down the hill to Ron's side.

Ron blinked sleepily, not even looking at the mess that had spilled into his lap, though he was making an effort to hold it in with one hand. He was bleeding from wounds on every exposed surface of his body, from little thin scratches to the worst one in his neck, which had a short sword rather comically still protruding from it. It looked like a party novelty.

"That was close," he told Joseph, and spat out blood. "Got 'em all, though."

"The other guys are all down," Joseph meant to say firmly, but it came out in a whimper. "Don't worry. The retrieval team will be along any minute. I'm so sorry."

"Aw, don't be," Ron said. He looked down at the hideous carnage with a fond expression. "Damn, that was fun. That was like old times. How long has it been since a bunch of the Old Guard have been able to get together for a party like this?" He coughed and spat out a piece of something; Joseph avoided looking to see what exactly. "And I'll bet that's about the last time we get to mix it up. We look too different now from the mortals. I ain't looking forward to being demobilized, I can tell you."

Joseph shook his head. "They won't stick you behind a desk. They'll have to find something better for you. Maybe you can fly transports or something fun like that."

Ron smiled at him. "Company'll manage. They made us like killing. Maybe they can make us like something else. Just reprogram us, I guess." He shrugged and winced; putting his hand up in bewilderment, he encountered the sword sticking out of his neck. His incredulous giggle turned into a roar of laughter.

"Look at this stupid thing! How long were you going to wait before telling me some mortal left his sword in my neck? I wonder when that happened?" He took a firm grip and pulled it out. A gout of bright blood followed.

"Uh-oh." Ron's face grew still suddenly. "Not good. Blood loss unacceptable. Going into fugue, I guess. Bye-bye, Joseph. See you sometime . . ."

He closed his eyes and sank backward, like a tree going down in a storm.

Joseph got unsteadily to his feet. Panting, he looked around at the desolation. After a long moment he sighed and went down the hill, slipping and falling a few times in unspeakable muck, to retrieve Albert's head where it had rolled into a gorse bush. He had even nastier work over the next few minutes, locating the other Enforcers under piles of chopped Brigantii and hauling five enormous bodies up the hill to lay them out beside Ron.

He was standing there, gasping, watching Albert hopefully to see if the head might reattach where he'd set it on the neck stump—he didn't think so, the process of fugue was too far advanced, already the wounds had exuded the antiseptic ichor and sealed themselves over—when he heard little bells ringing. He turned.

Winding its way along the crest of the hill above him was a pack train of mules, bells on their harnesses announcing their approach. They were led by an immortal he vaguely recognized, accompanied by two maintenance techs.

"Facilitator Grade One Joseph, I presume?" called the leader cheerily. "Nennius, Facilitator General for the Northern Sector. Another successful mission, eh?"

"I guess you could call it that," Joseph said. He watched as they negotiated their way down the steep slope. "I thought they'd send an air transport."

"Are you mad? It's broad daylight. Anyway the mules will do perfectly well, the repair facility is nearby." Nennius tsk-tsked as he saw the Enforcers. "Poor old fellows! Blood lust got the better of them again, did it?"

Joseph shook his head. "Actually it was a last-minute bunch of enemy reinforcements. You should have been here! The bastards just kept coming. Our guys followed orders, sir, you'd have been proud of them."

"I'm sure I would have." Nennius nodded, gesturing. The two maintenance techs lifted Albert's body between them and threw it over the back of a mule, where they bound it in place. A moment later they came back with a bucket for his head. Nennius watched briefly and then turned back to Joseph.

"So. The lamentable end of the original Ninth Hispania! All the details were recorded for data transmission?"

"Yes, sir." Suddenly the horror of the last three days caught up with Joseph, the long trailing march, the snipers and skirmishes, the inexorably rising body count, the last full assault on an exhausted and demoralized remnant legion. His knees wanted to buckle. He settled for sitting down in the presence of a superior and leaning his head on his arms. "These are the last. No survivors. You'll find the previous casualties in cairns along the route. I left a signaling device at each one."

"They've already been collected," Nennius assured him. "And if you'll just be kind enough to do the same for the bodies down there, a transport will be along to get them after dark."

"Okay," said Joseph wearily. "Do you want the Brigantes too?"

"Heavens no. Leave them where they fell. We only want the legionaries, and of course all the gear and material from the baggage train. Mustn't leave any evidence to conflict with recorded history, after all." Nennius smiled graciously. "Though of course you know that, experienced field operator that you are. Really, you handled this very well, Joseph. Full marks."

"Thank you," Joseph replied, looking up to watch as Ron's body was hauled away to the pack train. Nennius turned and pulled out a good-sized leather satchel and dropped it beside Joseph.

"Now, when you've finished sorting and stacking the corpses, you'll need to remove everything you're wearing and leave it with the rest. There's a change of clothing for you in here, as well as money and trade goods to get you to the west coast. There'll be a ship waiting in Morecambe Bay. We're sending you back to Spain for a while, but you need to stop at a particular village on the way . . ."

Joseph just recorded and nodded, letting his awareness slip away.

He was back down on the field, poking through the bodies of his mortal command, when he glanced up to see the pack train winding away along the skyline, making for an even bigger and more steep-sided hill in the near distance. The next time he looked up, laboring antlike under his burden of carrion, the pack train had vanished.

Yorkshire, 2026

. . . WHERE THE WAVES of Vulpos plunged screaming from their foul dens, racing in their sharp-toothed hatred toward the firm hooves of the Innocents!" shouted Jeffrey at the top of his lungs, flinging his arms wide as his black coat billowed theatrically behind him. As if on cue, there was a blue-white flash, and thunder boomed. For a second the mortal looked panicked, and then very pleased with himself indeed.

"Oh, dear, I think we'd better head back, don't you?" said Lewis from inside the Landrover, where he had more or less materialized a split second after the lightning struck. Joseph, however, remained where he stood, staring slack-jawed at the high steep hill, the setting of Jeffrey's narrative.

"If you like," Jeffrey said grandly, sauntering back to the car. "Sorry if I alarmed you. As you can see, this is a place of Powers."

Joseph came to himself and scurried for the car.

You seemed spellbound, said Lewis worriedly. *I didn't think he was all that good a storyteller, frankly.*

It had nothing to do with him, Joseph replied. *I just made a connection, that's all.*

You'll have to tell me about it later.

Sure. Later.

Jeffrey drove rather recklessly down through the rain that had begun to fall. By the time they reached the Innocents, it was a solid torrent, sheets of water drenching them as they ran into the shop.

Jeffrey was in an expansive mood, suddenly more talkative than Lotus (the lady in purple) and very much in charge. They must stay for dinner, he informed them: savory tofu lasagna with its perfect accompaniment, Australian merlot. And they really ought to stay the night. This storm was not about to let up before morning, if *he* knew anything. The charge for a night was normally ninety pounds, but if they were short of cash—

"No, no, that's all right." Lewis waved his fork dismissively. "We'd planned on staying somewhere in the vicinity, and why not here? What remarkable luck we stopped in, eh, Joseph?"

"Mm," said Joseph in a ghost of a voice.

"Your friend seems shaken by our little experience up there," Jeffrey told Lewis, filling their glasses. He settled back in his chair, basking. "Understandable. It's a powerful place . . ."

"Yes," Lewis agreed, tasting the wine, "it simply reeks of power."

"Normally I prefer not to let—well—outsiders in on our secrets, but you seem to be fairly discreet gentlemen," Jeffrey began.

"There are all kinds of local legends!" said Lotus, coming back from the kitchen with the Choc-Tofu-Treats that were their dessert. "The name of the hill behind us is Arthur's Seat, you know."

"Oh?" Joseph turned to look at her.

"Is it really?" Lewis said. "How fascinating. Any connection with King Arthur?"

"Well, they say that—"

"It's the sleeping knights legend," Jeffrey said, firmly retrieving the lead. "You can find it in a few other places in England, but this is our local version. Supposedly there's a cave somewhere under that hill where Arthur's knights lie sleeping in their armor, waiting until Arthur comes again. When England's in its greatest hour of need, they'll wake and join in the battle of good versus evil."

"Personally I think it's Guinevere who's coming back, not Arthur," asserted Lotus.

"No, really?" Lewis looked fascinated, managing at the same time to conceal most of a chunk of lasagna in his paper serviette. "What an original idea."

"I have reason to believe that the whole legend predates Arthur and Christianity and all the rest of them." Jeffrey raised his voice a little. "And I'll tell you something: Audrey Knollys knew that when she set the scene of the final battle out there. She knew it was a place of power. There are certain people who hold the opinion," he leaned forward and dropped his voice like a garment, "that her death was *no accident.*"

"She knew too much?" said Lewis, unobtrusively conveying the serviette into his coat pocket.

"No, that she didn't really die at all! That, in fact, she was able to arrange her own advancement to a higher plane of existence to continue her work more effectively," Jeffrey told him, perfectly serious.

"You don't say," said Lewis in a shocked tone.

Joseph had been looking steadily grayer as the conversation progressed, but here he asked, *Did this lady really die?*

She was attempting to get a muffin out of a toaster with her fork and got electrocuted, Lewis replied, sipping his merlot and listening to Jeffrey with a rapt expression. Gratified, Jeffrey expanded on his revelations of mystic power and theories of ancient gods.

Outside, the dining room window made a tiny square of light in the miles of darkness. The rain fell, the thunder rolled, and the high steep hill loomed behind the house as though it were watching.

After a while the yellow light winked out, to reappear shortly in another window higher up, and then there were three lights briefly; then darkness entire.

Joseph sat on his bed, eating Polo mints one after another and waiting until the mortals slept. He was still wearing the suit and overcoat in which he'd traveled all day.

Shortly after midnight he rose in silence and left his tiny cold room, going down through the house to the private entrance. As he slid the bolt, he heard light quick steps descending the stairs behind him, and turned to look into Lewis's narrowed eyes.

I knew you were going to do something like this, Lewis said angrily.

This is so classified, you can't even imagine. Please go back and forget you saw anything.

I haven't seen anything. What is it, for God's sake? Something to do with your mysterious coordinates? What did you discover while we were up there?

Yes, it has to do with the coordinates. I wasn't going to investigate further this time, because I have you with me and it's just too dangerous. But then the electrical storm started and our data feed to the Company went down again.

Yes, I noticed that.

I just can't pass up the chance. Do you know how long I had to wait to get the timing right before I could get a private interview with Mendoza's last case officer during a storm and still make it look like it happened totally by accident? Twenty-five years. And we come here, and another storm is just thrown in my lap! I have to go out there to see.

Well, whatever it is you're looking for, I'm going too.

Joseph shook his head sadly. He opened the door, and they went out into the rain.

The back garden rose in terraces up the hill a short way, ending in a line of leaning snow fence that was easily stepped over. They found a little track through the heather up there, someone's favorite ramble perhaps, and they followed it around the lower slopes and up the northern face a few hundred meters. The storm hadn't stopped. They tramped on through mud and bursts of painful illumination back-lighting the falling rain, bringing out garish and alien colors in the purple heather.

Suddenly Joseph stopped in his tracks and pointed. Lewis looked up uncertainly, wiping the rain from his eyes.

There, that rock face. Look close. What do you see?

A nasty place for climbing, a treacherous rotten stretch of over-hung rock that any hiker would avoid. It looked crumbly and difficult to get to. Even the little animal trails went above or below it, but nowhere near. This is what a mortal would have seen, would have been intended to see. Joseph and Lewis, staring intently and using a visual filter mortals didn't possess, saw more.

They beheld a smooth path leading up to a sealed door.

"God," said Lewis faintly.

Joseph strode up the path. He crouched in the overhang, examining the door. There was a via pad there, tuned to Facilitator-grade clearance. He flattened his palm against it. After a moment the door opened smoothly, revealing utter darkness that breathed out a current of warm air, a promise of dryness, cleanliness. Half frozen in his soaked clothing, he found it pleasant.

He became aware that Lewis was standing beside him, staring with horror into the dark.

"This is what you were after," Lewis said.

"I guess so," Joseph said.

Lewis swallowed hard. "Is Mendoza down there?"

"I have no idea." Joseph tilted his head and considered the black depth. "Probably not, though. How could she be? We both know where they sent her. No, I'm looking for somebody else."

"But—even if Mendoza was sent back a million years, she'd get to the present eventually, just by living through the past a day at a time," stammered Lewis. "Wouldn't she? I mean, I never believed those rumors of Back Way Back for just that reason. If the Company wanted to get rid of its immortals, sending them into the past wouldn't be a permanent solution."

"You have a point there," said Joseph, advancing cautiously through the doorway, scanning as he went.

"So—she might be here after all. Is that what you think is down there? Some kind of holding facility for immortals?" Lewis's teeth were chattering in his head. He attempted to follow Joseph across the threshold but drew back, gasping as though he'd been struck a physical blow.

Joseph turned swiftly. "You ought to be able to cross that threshold," he said, puzzled. "I deactivated the repulsion system. What's wrong with you?"

"Well, let's see: violent electrical storm making my hair stand on end, crumbling cliffs in danger of dropping on us at any minute, and the only safety a yawning mouth of darkness. I suppose I'm terrified."

"You ought to be able to come in even so, there's no physical barrier. But stay here. I'll try not to be long. Just stop talking."

Lewis fell silent, and Joseph paced away into the darkness.

As tunnels into the absolute black unknown went, it wasn't bad: smooth and gradual of descent, full of a faint fragrance that was unidentifiable but familiar. Joseph could, of course, see perfectly well in the dark, and every programmed instinct he had was telling him he was much safer here than out in the middle of an electrical storm.

He had descended perhaps a hundred meters, and the tunnel had begun to level out ahead of him and reveal a glow of blue light, when he heard a clatter of shoes behind him. Lewis was racing down the tunnel, eyes wide.

What? Is something after you?

No, I just—had a hallucination or something. I can't be alone up there!

Joseph bared his teeth in exasperation and stalked on ahead. *I warned you.*

I know. Gasping, unsteady, Lewis followed him.

A few meters farther on, though, he staggered and fell. Joseph swung about to find him huddled against the wall, pale and sweating.

What the hell is wrong now?

Lewis turned a sick face up to him. *I seem to be having some sort of suppressed memory retrieval.*

Of what?

I, uh, appear to be remembering my death.

Joseph crouched beside him. *We're immortal. We don't die.*

I'm perfectly aware of that, thank you.

You know we're not supposed to be here, right? So you're probably feeling whatever trauma you went through before the Company recruited you as a kid. Dr. Zeus uses them to keep us in line, like the conditioning nightmares. Break the rules, and you start reliving whatever jam you were in before some nice Company operative appeared out of nowhere and rescued you. Me, I remember the guys who exterminated my tribe.

But I never went through any trauma like that! Lewis said. *I was taken by the Company as a newborn. I have no memories of mortal life, you see?* He drew his knees up and stared at the blue light with haunted eyes. *That's not it. But something happened to me in Ireland once, and I think it gave me amnesia . . .*

We don't get that either, Lewis. Joseph rose to his feet impatiently. *But you stay put and remember whatever you're remembering. I have something to check out.*

He walked away down the tunnel and vanished into the blue light.

Lewis hugged his knees. There had been a child chained in a cell. Not a child. Something all malevolence, hideously wise. There had been a mortal man, a Christian monk. The images were crowding on Lewis thick and fast, incoherent, inexplicable, impossible, and he realized that he could not sit there alone with them. The blue unknown was less horrible. He clawed his way upright again and went tottering off down the passage after Joseph, fighting panic every step of the way.

When he finally emerged from the tunnel's mouth, though, he stopped in blank surprise. It wasn't what he had expected at all.

He stood in a great vaulted bunker opening out before him into gentle gloom. The blue light was coming from regeneration vats, which were arranged in neat rows under the vaults. There were hundreds of them, and every one he could see was occupied by a pale floating figure. Joseph was sitting on the floor with his back against the nearest one. He lifted a tear-streaked face as Lewis came forward into the bunker.

"Oh, man," he said hoarsely. "I wish you hadn't come in here."

"But—it's just some kind of infirmary. These are only regeneration vats," said Lewis wonderingly. He came closer, peering up at the floating body. After a moment his mouth fell open in astonishment.

"Good God," he cried. "What are they?"

The vault's occupant was an immortal male, but there any resemblance to Lewis or Joseph ended. He was enormously tall, even allowing for the magnifying qualities of the transparent tank, probably eight feet if he were standing; enormously broad and deep in the chest and shoulders, with a peculiar articulation of the powerful neck and arms.

His head was even more peculiar, not human at all, with a wide-domed helmet shape. The face was comparably strange: great protruding brows made caves of the blind eyes. An enormous nose, flat cheekbones, the suggestion of unusual dentition in the heavy jaws. The skin was fair. The hair and beard, long and drifting in the tank's slight current, were the dun color of an autumn field after rain.

He wore nothing but a circlet of copper-colored metal on his brow.

The vault next to him contained another such, not identical but clearly of the same strange race. So did the one beyond that vault, and the one beyond that, and so on as far as Lewis could see. They were all males.

"They're . . . Neanderthals?" Lewis guessed. "No, they can't be, they're so big. That's not quite the skull shape, either. All the same . . . what kind of monsters are these?"

"They're not monsters," Joseph said, wiping his eyes on his sleeve. "They're heroes."

Lewis stared at him in incomprehension.

Joseph got to his feet, slowly, moving like an old mortal. "There's more than one kind of operative," he said.

"I know," Lewis said. "Facilitators, Conservationists, Techs."

Joseph shook his head. "Those are all Preservers. You, me, Mendoza. All you've ever seen is Preservers. The Company doesn't make these big guys anymore. We used to call them Enforcers."

"What did they enforce?" Lewis looked up at the sleeping giant nervously.

"Peace," replied Joseph. "You've heard of the Great Goat Cult?"

"Certainly. They were a fanatic religious movement back in prehistory. Insisted on tattoos. Wiped out any tribe that rose above a certain technological level. They delayed the birth of civilization by ten thousand years, and the Company was powerless to stop them."

"It wasn't." Joseph shook his head sadly. "Dr. Zeus got tired of waiting. Wouldn't you have got tired of waiting? Watching *Homo sapiens* work its way up from the monkeys, and just as it starts to produce art and culture worth preserving, somebody starts a religion that demands mass slaughter of sinners. The Goats were pretty good at it, too, they killed half the population of Europe and Asia before the Company made the decision to interfere.

"But the Company couldn't send in Preservers to stop the cult. We were designed to run, not to fight. We're sneak thieves, smooth talkers, nice guys. We don't get involved in mortal quarrels. We let mortals go their own way to hell while we rescue what we can, and we never, ever risk our own skins. Pain scares us. We don't do danger."

"Rather unflatteringly put, but essentially true." Lewis couldn't take his eyes off the man in the vault.

"Yeah, well, the Company needed somebody who *could* do danger. They played around with the available gene pool and came up with these guys."

"You mean they made recombinants?" Lewis asked, horrified.

"No, just some controlled breeding experiments, which is nastier, if you ask me. Where they got the results they wanted, they made the kids into immortals, but not Preservers: killers. Warriors, though, not assassins. Braver than you or I could ever possibly be, guys who'd think nothing of charging into oncoming spears, guys who could be shot so full of arrows they would look like porcupines and still keep fighting." Joseph glanced up at the vault, remembering.

"I can't imagine that," Lewis murmured. He jumped as the big man moved galvanically, flexed, and then relaxed.

"You're programmed not to," Joseph told him. "So am I. Not these guys. Anyway, the Company turned them loose on the Great Goat Cult. Kill all killers. Simple instruction. And they weren't stupid, either; these guys were as smart as you or I, just motivated differently. They went after any mortals who practiced violence. You know why mortal civilization was finally able to get started? Because these guys did their job."

"Perhaps they shouldn't have stopped, given the way civilization progressed."

"They thought so, too," said Joseph quietly.

"Oh," Lewis said. After a poignant silence, he went on: "And so the Company locked them up here? No wonder you didn't want me to find out about this."

"I didn't know about it," said Joseph in a wretched voice. "I just guessed. The problems were supposed to have been worked out. The Enforcers were supposed to have been retrained, reprogrammed, reassigned. Mostly to Company bases, because as time went on, the mortal races started looking different, and these guys couldn't pass anymore. I used to see a few of them now and then, back in the early days. Less and less as time went on. I didn't think anything of it. I didn't want to."

"What changed your mind?" Lewis drew back as the giant clenched his enormous and well-made hands, then relaxed them.

"Looking for Mendoza," said Joseph. "I hadn't wanted to think about *her*, either. I just shoved my official notification of her arrest into a file in my tertiary consciousness and never accessed it until that day in Sam Pan's when you told you saw her."

"I remember. But—"

"I had other data in that file," Joseph went on steadily. "And when I accessed the notification about Mendoza, it popped up. It was information somebody passed me a long time ago, something I didn't want to know anything about because it was really dangerous."

"Those coordinates?"

Joseph nodded.

"And they led you here?"

"The first set did."

"You mean there are other places like this? Full of these . . . ?"

"Probably. This is the first one I've checked." Joseph sighed. "I didn't want you to know about them at all. You're now one of probably ten people in the world who have seen this place, and we are in sooo much trouble if the Company finds out, Lewis. Remember back in San Francisco, when I said the stakes had got way too high for you? You should see them now."

"I heard a rumor, once." Lewis began to pace along the rows of vaults, looking at their occupants. "Supposedly passed back from some operative in the future. It's that, when we finally do reach the twenty-fourth century, our mortal masters will make us all wear an emblem. A clock with its hands missing. They'll tell us it's a badge of honor for all our work in time, but really it'll be a way to mark us out for the day when they . . . dispose of us somehow."

"I heard that rumor too."

"But I never believed it. And I've seen . . ." Lewis was walking faster now. "What were you hoping to find?"

"Somebody I owe." Joseph followed him. "Somebody who might be able to help me free Mendoza, if she can be freed. If he's here. If I can get him out of here."

They moved along the aisles between the vaults, looking up fearfully at the occupants.

"At least it seems humane enough," Lewis whispered. "They're safe. They're alive. They're not in any pain. I spent ten years in one of these tanks, once."

"Jesus, what happened to you?"

"I'm not sure. It was after Ireland."

"Maybe you did nearly die, then. Ten years! They must have had to replace most of your organic parts." Joseph shuddered. "You never mentioned this before."

"Would *you* want to talk about it?"

"But what kind of danger could a Literature Preservation Specialist get himself into—" Joseph stopped at one vault, and Lewis came instantly to his side.

"No," said Joseph, both relieved and disappointed. This vault's occupant was a Preserver, a woman, but not one he knew. She looked tiny, elfin compared with the Enforcers; her black hair waved around her like long silk. After a moment Joseph and Lewis moved on.

There were five hundred vaults in the bunker, four hundred and eighty of which contained sleeping Enforcers. Of the remaining twenty, nine contained Preservers, six males and three females, none of whom was Mendoza. Eleven vaults were empty.

There were rooms opening off one side. One room contained drums of regenerant concentrate and cleaning supplies. Another seemed to be a repair area, with an operating table and cabinets that might have contained tools. The third room had a bank of terminals, blinking quietly, and a cot. On the wall was a chalkboard, on which someone had printed, in straggling Latin:

ABDIEL HAS DONE HIS APPOINTED WORK HERE
9 NOVEMBER 2025–30 NOVEMBER 2025

There was nothing else.

"How many other bunkers like this are there?" said Lewis, aghast.

"You don't want to know," Joseph said.

"And your friend might be in any one of them. We'll have to search them all, won't we?"

"No way." Joseph stopped and glared at him. "Not you. Lewis, what have I been telling you over and over again? I'm a Facilitator, there's less danger for me. Is this how you wound up in a tank for ten years, taking stupid risks?"

Lewis scowled back. "I took a vow to help Mendoza, and I'll keep it even if the Company locks me away for two thousand years." He considered the nearest one. "How long do you suppose these poor devils have been here?"

"About two thousand years," said Joseph in a lifeless voice. "That one, anyway. He was brought here in 120 A.D. So were those five over there. We were in the Ninth Legion together."

Lotus and Jeffrey were terribly disappointed next morning to discover their guests had departed early, though they were somewhat comforted by the considerable tip the gentlemen had left.

Shortly afterward, the clerk in the York Rowntree Factory shop was startled by the abrupt appearance of two men at her counter. Their eyes were red-rimmed with exhaustion, their expensive suits needed pressing, and they had in their combined shopping baskets at least a hundred pounds' worth of assorted chocolate bars. They seemed a bit on edge.

Lewis dropped Joseph off at London City Airport and watched him board his suborbital flight. Weaving a little as he climbed the boarding ramp, Joseph turned at the door and threw Lewis a shaky Roman salute.

"Ave," murmured Lewis, waving back. *"Magna est veritas, et prevalebit."*

A full century was to pass before they saw each other again.

Joseph in the Darkness

So now I had opened the great big Pandora's box from hell in my hunt for you, father. I was finding out a lot more about the Company's secrets than I'd ever wanted to know, and Lewis—what kind of box had he opened for himself? All kinds of things were swarming out of the darkness of his memory to say hello to him. Poor bastard.

At least he was too busy to think about them much. We were all overworked in the second half of the twenty-first century, gearing up for when things were going to get crazy. Way too much to do for a lot of followup on the other bunker locations. I did find a couple, one in New Mexico and one in Siberia, but I wasn't able to do more than locate the concealed doorways. The Company kept me running.

Here's what would have interested you about that century, father: Information was king, and technological advances went at breakneck speed, if unevenly. Electric cars everywhere except the United States. Bullet trains, boom and bust, new religions, new leases on life for old religions. Fossil fuels began to run out. Islam sheathed its sword and went sort of Amish, concentrating on farming, at least in the former OPEC nations. They hadn't much choice.

The neopagan religious movement, with all its Wiccan and quasi-Wiccan subsets, finally realized that what it lacked was a certain coherence of doctrine. In 2082 they all got together in Malta to hold the First Maternal Synod. They debated questions like divine polarity (Was the Great God equal with the Great Goddess? They decided he wasn't) and whether males had souls. They agreed on common goals: The ancient city of Ephesus and its temple to the Goddess, for example, had to be reclaimed and restored for the faithful.

There were a couple of schisms—both the Diannic Feminist extremists and the Sons of Cernunnos walked out of the synod, and terrorists from both factions bombed each others' shrines. At the end of a year, though, they'd managed to put together a book of holy scripture and forge a new maternalistic religion every bit as violent and repressive as the old paternalistic ones had been. With the shoe now firmly on the other foot, the nonsecular world limped on.

I don't think it was a judgment of Jehovah—or Diana either, for that matter—but about this time the Sattes virus swept through the prisons of the world, killing off most of the inmates as well as the guards and their families. In every nation on Earth. How much did you know about that one, father? Was it planned? Would you have forbidden it, if you'd been able? Well, the mortals lived up to your expectations, I'm afraid. The stupefying improbability of it all was mostly ignored, the official investigations perfunctory at best, because everyone was so secretly grateful.

Then the virus broke out in the world's armies, and they weren't so happy anymore.

When it ended, abruptly and mysteriously as it had begun, there were a lot fewer people; but the infrastructure for the new world was intact, so a boom period of prosperity followed. Wages were up, labor was satisfied. No wars for a while, except in places where it never stopped, with or without armies.

Like Northern Ireland. Somebody nuked Belfast, with a dirty little stolen bomb, probably one of the old ones misplaced by the former superpowers. Nobody's quite sure who was responsible. But, surprise: when the mushroom cloud dissipated, the place was neither green nor orange. It was dead. Did that teach them anything? You'd bet it wouldn't, father, and you'd be so right.

America had its troubles too, race wars and a growing antifederalist movement, until the epidemic hit. Things went steadily on to hell in California, with two big earthquakes and an urban war in the south before the epidemic. Most of the population fled to the northern end of the state. Fusion power finally made the scene, and New York sued New Jersey to get its garbage back, now that the stuff could be used to power generators. Taxes went up. The pieces began to fall into place for the Second Civil War. I saw it, working in Texas, which was a big economic giant flexing its muscles. None of the mortals saw it coming, though.

Things went on in China and Africa about like they always had, insane repressions and bloodbaths in some places that made the news, peace and relative prosperity in other places that didn't. Same with India. Quebec split from Canada and tried, without success, to join the European Union. The Inuits got a full-fledged nation to themselves up in the Arctic Circle. Parts of Japan sank following three major earthquakes in a row, and Mexico suddenly found its lap full of yen. Europe manufactured things and grew a lot of genetically improved vegetables.

The first Luna colonies were founded, and boomed, because the colonists got rich in short order. Even the janitors became millionaires up there. High wages, nothing to spend them on, good benefits. People fought to go.

And the Recombinant was born. And died.

In the Netherlands, as it happened. Some laboratory had been working away, unfettered by any laws against genetic engineering, and one day announced proudly to the world that they'd produced the first designer human being. Not only that: they'd done it six years ago, and the perfectly normal, healthy boy was now of an age to make statements to the press.

Though he didn't, much. I remember seeing the footage of a terrified little kid at a press conference, holding tight to the hands of the two scientists who'd raised him. He was slender and dark, and all he said for the cameras was that he was very happy to meet people and really looked forward going to school. That didn't disarm the people who screamed that his very existence was blasphemy. Maybe in time they would have been disarmed; but then the new plague began, all around the boy. Children he played with got it. People he shook hands with got it.

A mob broke into the house where the kid lived and shot him and the scientists who'd raised him.

They burned the house, with the bodies and the laboratory and all the records of the experiment. I personally doubt that the work was lost. Dr. Zeus must have had somebody on the scene to retrieve all that data. But every nation in the world signed an agreement: Never again would anyone attempt to create another Recombinant.

And if there were any of us immortals who still believed that the day would come when Dr. Zeus proudly introduced us to an astonished world—Look, these are the wonderful cyborgs we created to save the planet for you, and now that they're retiring, they'd like to move into your neighborhood—if there were any of us who still believed that, well, we must have been a little shaken.

The twenty-second century arrived, and the year 2355 was another century closer.

London, 2142

LEWIS WALKED QUICKLY along Euston Road, past the bomb crater where the antiquarian bookshop once stood. He'd cleared out its treasures in one exhausting night just before the bomb went off, and managed to invite all his mortal coworkers out to breakfast an hour before the explosion, so that when the blast came, they were all sitting in a cafe arguing the merits of Thai iced coffee over Thai iced tea.

That was the last time he was able to afford inviting anyone out to breakfast.

England was poor now, like Lewis. Cutting loose Northern Ireland had seemed a good idea, but nobody had foreseen Belfast, and now there were roving Ulster Revenge League bombers carrying out reprisals for the Great Betrayal, as they termed England's disengagement. A number of historic buildings were no more, including Lewis's former place of employment. So far King Richard IV (dubbed Lucky Dicky because of his uncanny ability to dodge snipers' bullets) and Parliament (who were less skilled in that regard than their sovereign, and died frequently) had been unable to come to terms with any of the several faction leaders demanding restitution.

It hadn't helped when Scotland broke away. Terrorism was too tame for the Scots: they used lawyers. Richard's predecessor, George VII (even less lucky than Parliament), signed away the Union of Crowns and was promptly assassinated by an enraged imperialist. Now Wales was threatening to exit what was left of the United Kingdom, though its separatists were presently quarreling too violently among themselves to be able to draft a resolution to that effect.

London was once again a chilly place where people stood in queues for food, where children played in bombed-out ruins, where amputees hauled themselves along begging for change, where shop-windows were boarded up. Things would improve, eventually. They generally did.

Lewis pulled his coat tight about himself and sprinted up the dark narrow stair to his garret bed-sitter. Safely locked in, he took off his coat long enough to unpack the groceries he'd been carrying strapped to his body, chlorilar pouches worn like a diver's weight belt: beans, consommé, mixed pickle, tomatoes, pilchards, raspberry jam, green peas. Not his favorites, but what he'd been able to get, and a nicely balanced haul. He lined them up on his shelf, rejoicing in a sense of abundance.

No evidence of mice this afternoon. Perhaps his latest strategy had worked. He made himself a jam sandwich, whistling, and wandered over to his communication terminal.

He had no fear the power wouldn't come on. In these days of cold fusion, even England had dependable electricity. Not only that, the streets were kept tidy as people scavenged for trash to sell to the reactor stations. Taking a bite from his bread and jam, Lewis sat down and logged on.

On the little table at his elbow, Edward Alton Bell-Fairfax stared out at the world. Lewis had himself purchased the daguerreotype, and now it was one of several framed images Lewis owned and represented to his occasional mortal guests as long-departed family members. Usually, after identifying various nonexistent grandfathers and great-aunts, he'd tap Edward's daguerreotype fondly and tell some story about a great-great-great-uncle who'd been a disgrace to the British Navy. His guests were invariably amused, and this kind of faked incidental detail never hurt when one was passing oneself off as a mortal.

Lewis had been working sporadically on what he had come to think of, ever since that long-ago weekend in Yorkshire, as the Edward Mystery. He hadn't heard from Joseph in decades. For all he knew, Joseph had been arrested, and in any case Lewis didn't want to think about underground bunkers and what was inside them. He had refused to admit that he was powerless to help Mendoza. He had stubbornly clung to the notion that following the long-cold trail of this mortal man might turn up some helpful detail, some useful clue.

Besides, Lewis found he had become unaccountably fascinated by Edward Alton Bell-Fairfax himself, who in some way was also the reincarnation of Nicholas Harpole. Lewis was beginning to understand how Mendoza could have loved these mortals to such a degree that she never stopped mourning one and threw away her career for the other.

Taking another bite from his bread and jam, Lewis clicked in. A particular combination of keystrokes encrypted all he saw and everything he was to upload that afternoon. Anyone monitoring his automatic transmission to the Company would read it as a long series of entries on the literature of the Socialist movement in Britain, guaranteed to send them channel-surfing on to monitor some other operative's more interesting datafeed.

He opened the file headed EASILY AND BEST FORGOTTEN. There before him were the three letters in facsimile. The originals had long since passed into the possession of a museum in Southhampton, where they no doubt lay forgotten in some cabinet. It didn't matter. Lewis knew them by heart now.

16th May 1843
My dear Richardson,

Here he is in all the full glory of his dress uniform—you'd scarcely know him, would you? Pray accept this remembrance from The Damned Boy as a token of his sincerest regard.

I fear all your assertions in respect to Navy life and morals prove more true than I can conveniently relate, and I would not grieve you in any case with a recitation of my adventures. Suffice it to say that I cannot thank you enough for that advice on the removal of certain stains from one's dress tunic, to say nothing of where to find the best purveyors of French letters.

You may hear something of the *Osiris* and her crew soon. I fervently hope so. Ten weeks of whist parties with the best small gentry of Southhampton—elderly daughters and solicitous mammas—I leave it to your imagination! I would welcome a howling Buonapartist, pistols in either paw. Especially at one of these whist parties.
I remain
Edward

10th February 1847
My dear Richardson,

You will undoubtedly have been informed by now. I maintain, and will maintain, that I did no wrong. I was derelict in no duty, disobeyed no order, indulged in no cowardice, conspired in no mutiny. I did strike a superior, if a vicious and stupid monkey in a uniform may be dignified with that title.

I am fully aware that my case is lost before it has even begun. Neither my conduct in the late engagements with the blackbirders nor the testimony of the common sailors whose capricious murder I prevented will weigh in my defence, given the birth and breeding of Captain Southbey.

Indeed, my only regret is that I did not kill the man outright, since his continued career ensures a drain on Her Majesty's purse and certain danger to any men so unfortunate as to come under his command. There are certain offences to which I intend to testify, knowing full well they will not serve to acquit me but which must be shouted aloud. 'Tell truth and shame the devil,' says the poet, and so I must. He, at least, will suffer the indignity of hearing his particular monstrousness named before his peers. I WILL NOT BE SILENCED.

You cannot receive this news with any light heart, I know. Moreover, it has been forcibly given to me to understand that He of Whom We Must Not Speak has been seriously displeased by the news of my impending trial. How little I esteem his opinion you may well imagine, but the prospect of grieving your good heart is intolerable to me. You MUST understand that I have done nothing of which you would be ashamed, nor ever shall.

I remain
Edward

23rd September 1852
My dear old Richardson,

It grieves me more than I can express that I am unable to visit you at this time. None but you taught me the meaning of Duty, and mine requires my continued efforts here for the present, as I am certain you will understand, old soldier that you are. There will not pass one hour of the day when you are not continually in my thoughts.

You must get well, old man, you must obey Dr. Malcolm in every particular and avoid all care! I cannot imagine how No. 10 could continue without your 'mailed and terrible fist' to keep them all in line, and moreover, to whom shall I write if you leave me quite alone in this world?

For though One had the natural title and refused it, and Another assumed the title but bore it *in absentia*, God knows only you have ever done the office of a true Father to
your Damned Boy
Edward

Lewis sighed, as he usually did on reading the last paragraph. There wasn't a lot of material to run with, but over the years, through patient hours of cross-referencing and through the meticulous search of ancient archives, he had been able to piece together the following story.

On approximately August I, 1825, a boy—almost certainly illegitimate—was born in a small country house near Shipbourne, owned by one Mrs. Moreston, who kept the establishment to accommodate well-born young ladies who needed a nine-month country retreat. One week later he was baptized Edward Alton Fairfax in St. Nicholas's Church in Sevenoaks.

At this point in time, the property at No. 10 Albany Crescent in London was owned by one Septimus Bell, who resided there, childless, with his wife Dorothea and servants, chief of whom was the butler, Robert Richardson, a former sergeant in the 32nd Regiment of Foot. Mr. Bell's occupation was listed as Gentleman.

Lewis had never been able to determine just how the infant wound up in the Bell household, but in 1834 young Edward Alton Bell-Fairfax was enrolled in Overton School, and his guardian's address was given as No. 10, et cetera. On discovering this, Lewis searched out Mr. Septimus Bell's bank records, and found evidence of quarterly deposits of large sums of money beginning in 1825, though so far he had been unable to trace the source. The deposits continued even after Mr. and Mrs. Bell were lost in a shipwreck off the coast of Italy during a grand tour, late in young Edward's first term at Overton.

Edward's progress in school was exceptional, particularly in maths, at which he excelled, though there were disciplinary actions on two occasions for fighting. Scholastic brilliance notwithstanding, at the age of fourteen he was pulled from school and entered the Royal Navy as a midshipman. Admiralty records revealed that young Edward progressed with remarkable speed to the rank of lieutenant, and within five years was given command of a schooner and sent to the coast of Africa to patrol against the slave trade.

This was not the reward it might appear. It was dirty work and dangerous, given to young officers in no position to protest being sent in humble little boats to chase after slave ships. It appeared, however, that Edward turned the slight to his advantage. Mangrove swamps, poisoned spears, fever, alcohol, shipwreck: none of them managed to take him out. He distinguished himself by conducting a ferocious campaign against the slave traders, proving so effective a fighter that he was promptly pulled from the job, made a commander, and reassigned to a man-of-war doing nothing in particular off the coast of France.

And this appeared to be his downfall; he "violently quarreled" with a Captain Southbey over the matter of a flogging ordered for an ordinary seaman "in excess of a hundred strokes." However violent the quarrel may have been, Edward must have received some help from the unknown benefactor he so disdained; for the threatened court-martial never materialized. He was instead allowed to retire, retaining his rank of commander and on half pay. Captain Southbey, on the other hand, was murdered by his own crew the following year.

That was all the Admiralty records had to say on the subject of Edward Alton Bell-Fairfax, and for many years Lewis was unable to trace him any further.

But Lewis was patient as only an immortal can be, and had decades of gray London evenings to spend combing through every records cache that had survived the intervening centuries.

No record of marriage for Edward, no record of children, no record of what duties kept him from going to see Robert Richardson in his last illness—the old soldier died on October 10, 1852, and was buried in a churchyard in London, one of the tiny crowded places Dickens described. Lewis went to the grave site, found the ancient stone with its nearly effaced inscription; but there was no corresponding stone for Edward in any cemetery that kept records.

Lewis checked the ones without records, too, spent interminable sunless weekends pacing between leaning headstones, broken angels, toppled urns, wildernesses of moss and ivy. Passersby sometimes glanced through rusted railings and were startled by the slight man in the long coat, like a ghost himself.

Year after year Lewis searched, not knowing what he wanted to find or what he sought to prove. He cautiously admitted to himself that the hunt for Edward Alton Bell-Fairfax had become more than a hobby for him. The mystery possessed all the elements of a novel: the highborn foundling infant, the brilliant boy cut off from human affection except for an old servant, the heroic career at sea and in the coastal swamps of Africa, the furious protest against injustice and evil—and then nothing but the hint of some secret duty that prevented him from coming home. How did the story end?

Or, rather, how did it end with Edward's dying in Mendoza's arms in far-off California? How had this man, who'd risked his life repeatedly to prevent slaves from being taken, wind up shot to death by agents of a nation fighting to end slavery?

Lewis invented half a hundred scenarios, none of them satisfactory. To be a Literature Specialist is not necessarily to be able to write, though Lewis longed to. The fantasy was like a fire that kept the chill out of his immortal bones: he'd gaze off between the crumbling tombs and the willows and see the couple embracing there for a moment, the bright wraiths of the stern young man and the black-eyed girl. Edward smart in the uniform he'd worn for his portrait and Mendoza happy as Lewis had never seen her, wearing a summer dress of peach silk . . .

The image sustained him somehow. And it kept away the quiet horrors of his own life.

The nightmares came on Lewis gradually, after the return from the Yorkshire trip, and had nothing to do with the downscaled standard of living or the bombs in the streets, or even with living alone in a garret. They had everything to do with what he had forgotten about Ireland.

Sometimes he would be fine for years on end, and then something would set the nightmares off. Once he was in the Tube when the lights failed, and that did it. Once he tuned into a BBC program on the pathetic survivors of the human cloning experiment (it had worked, but the resulting children all suffered from progeria). Once it was no more than a customer bringing in a book to sell, a late-twentieth-century facsimile of the *Book of Kells*.

The symptoms were always the same, just what mortals suffered: shortness of breath, pounding heart, cold sweats. He'd sit up reading until he was exhausted, fearful of turning out the light. The nightmares would come eventually anyway, sometimes when he thought he was still awake.

They tended to begin with sleep paralysis. He knew he was awake, sitting up in a well-lighted room, safe and in full possession of his immortal faculties. He was completely paralyzed, however, and as soon as he acknowledged this to himself, the real horror began, a sensation of slipping downward into shadows.

After that followed chaos, darkness, and a sense of imminent and personal danger. There was a voice that spoke in Latin. A cell with a trick door. Children crowding into a tunnel. A suffocating smell. Red lightning. Sometimes the specific sequence of these events was confused, but they built, always, to the same conclusion: he would begin to go gradually blind. He'd be lying somewhere, helpless, unable to see, and he could hear his own voice saying, *My God, is this what it's like?*

Lewis never woke screaming. He'd get his sensation and his sight back a little at a time, finding himself at last perched on a chair or sprawled on the day bed in his clothes. He would be cold as ice, shivering, nauseated. Running a self-diagnostic never revealed anything wrong with him.

And then six months ago, something different happened.

The nightmare began again—this time simply an oddly familiar face glimpsed in the street had done it. He fell into dreams and was shuddering in the dark, fighting back the panic, knowing he was too damaged to stop them, knowing he might die, really die, the way mortals died—

Someone took hold of his hand.

Complete sensory confusion, sight flowing up his arm from his hand, caught hard in the grip of the other hand. It was pulling him out of the darkness. The sight reached his eyes, and he found himself staring into Edward Alton Bell-Fairfax's stern young face.

Edward kept pulling, and the darkness snarled and flowed away from Lewis like a fast tide receding. He found himself standing on a London street in his modern clothes, as the shuttle traffic roared past, as cripples pulled themselves along and shopkeepers unlocked their iron gates for the morning's commerce. But Edward was still standing there before him, in his nineteenth-century naval officer's uniform, frowning down at Lewis from his great height.

Pale blue eyes, just as Lewis had always thought, and high color in his face, yes, just as Mendoza had described it. Mendoza! If he could only tell Edward, if he could warn him, as he hadn't been able to warn Mendoza—

"I will not be silenced," Edward said grimly, looking him in the eye. Having said that, he straightened, kept going up and up, lengthening, and he seemed to have stepped back into the facade of a building too. No, he had *become* part of the facade behind him. For a second Lewis could still make out his face, rigid in stone; then the features faded, and Lewis was staring up at a great Ionic column, one of three holding up the pediment of an enormous neoclassical public building.

He knew the building, it dated from the early twenty-first century and was a copy of the Temple of Zeus at Lemnos. Lewis looked around in confusion, uncertain whether he had just awakened after a spectacular episode of sleepwalking. Cripples, pigeons, shopkeepers, traffic, all very real, and here was the morning sunlight just creeping over to illuminate the inscription in sedate Roman capitals on the front of the building:

NEW SYON HOUSE
2355 BOND STREET

"Surely, that's wrong, though," he found himself saying to his reading lamp. He sat up. He was in his room in the gray morning light.

And in fact the address proved to be wrong, when he showered, shaved, and went running out into the real morning of London to see; though only in respect to being at No. 205 Bond Street. Every other detail was just as he had seen it in his nightmare. Was that even a suggestion of an aloof face, in the design of the capital on the middle column?

Lewis murmured a prayer of thanks to Carl Jung. He even did a little skipping dance in his honor as he hurried home, for this was the intuitive leap he had needed to make.

New Syon House was some sort of government office. You could go in and fill out forms on the ground floor, and the clerk would forward them somewhere for you. Lewis knew, as any other operative of Dr. Zeus knew, that the place was actually a dump for outworn state secrets. It was an archive of documents that had never been declassified but that were now so old, there was nobody left alive who even knew why they had been secrets in the first place or (in the case of some encoded material to which the keys had been lost) what they even were about.

When the time came to transform moldy sheepskin into magnetic ink, somebody dutifully encrypted everything and shredded the originals. There the secrets hid, to this day, in databanks never accessed from one year's end to the next, masses of arcane gibberish.

For an immortal with empty nights to fill after eight hours a day in a grubby little bookshop, and no transfer to a better posting in sight, New Syon House was like one of those old Christmas calendars with twenty-five little windows: a new one to be opened every day, with no idea of what treat might be behind it, while one grew closer and closer to the window with the ultimate treat.

It took Lewis three months to scan the inventory. It took another month to sort out encryptions dating from the nineteenth century. Two weeks sufficed to break the old-fashioned code; all he had to do then was search for any occurrences of the name Edward Alton Bell-Fairfax.

The first reference was a list of members of a Redking's Club for the years 1849 to 1869. The list was profoundly interesting. For a smallish club, Redking's appeared to have had a disproportionate number of members whose names had made it into history books. There were politicians, there were men of science, there was a writer or two—and a virtual nobody, a retired naval officer on half pay. Lewis marveled. What was Edward doing in company like this? And why was this information classified?

Lewis found another peculiarity on the members list: the name of one William Fitzwalter Nennys. Lewis remembered this man perfectly, for the simple reason that he was in reality Nennius, an immortal with whom Lewis had worked briefly in the 1830s. Nennius was a Facilitator, and nothing was more likely than that he'd be strategically positioned in an exclusive club whose fellow members were in politics.

The next reference to Edward turned up when Lewis found a list of members of a Gentlemen's Speculative Society. Edward Alton Bell-Fairfax was one of their number. So were most of the other members of Redking's Club, including William Fitzwalter Nennys.

Lewis frowned as he read. Wasn't there something disreputable about the Gentleman's Speculative Society? A moment's hasty access of *Smith's History of Esoteric Cults*, volumes 1 through 10, brought it back to him:

In the year 1885 a mortal named David Addison Ramsay held several public lectures, claiming to be a representative of a hitherto secret brotherhood that presently went by the name of the Gentlemen's Speculative Society. He was unwise enough to mention several prominent statesmen and academics whom he claimed were fellow members.

He said further that their purpose was to advance humanity to a state of perfection through scientific means. This, he claimed, was where similarly well-intentioned secret societies had missed the mark: by clinging to outworn magical and religious rituals.

Ramsay then displayed what he claimed were inventions that had been suppressed out of religious superstition and ignorance. He apparently got quite a reaction out of his audience with his "thermoluminous globe," "speaking automaton," "true philosopher's stone," and several other remarkable objects. These inventions, he claimed, were not new; the Gentlemen's Speculative Society had rescued and collected them from laboratories of persecuted martyrs to the cause of Science. Da Vinci had contributed several, as had Dr. John Dee, who had also been a member of the Society, though in a former time when it bore another name.

Ramsay concluded by saying that the purpose of this demonstration was not merely to enlighten or entertain, but to enlist uninitiated Britons in the great cause for which he and his fellow Gentlemen labored. He admitted that his brother members did not entirely agree with him that the need for secrecy was past, but he believed that in this age of steam propulsion and industrial capitalism, mankind was ready to understand what science might achieve, if unfettered. He intimated that all the fantastic possibilities of legend were not beyond man's grasp, even, indeed most particularly, immortality itself.

All that was wanting was *capital*. He stood ready to accept the donations that must flow in from the noble Britons in his audience, who surely understood that every rational man must labor in the cause of the perfection and advancement of humanity.

Ramsay wasn't quite hooted off the stage, but the papers very nearly murdered him. His inventions were denounced as nothing more than brilliant stage effects. Worse, the powerful individuals he named all stated flatly that they never heard of him, or of the Gentlemen's Speculative Society to which they supposedly belonged. He was a common charlatan, they said, a humbug, an utter sham.

Ramsay hotly denied these charges and promised to provide proof. He didn't; he simply disappeared, along with his inventions.

This was the sort of thing that professed skeptics liked to giggle over. Even Lewis, himself an immortal being created by the efforts of a cabal of scientists and investors, smiled as he read the account. His smile faded as he considered the fact that he'd just found evidence—in classified documents, no less—that there *had* been a Gentlemen's Speculative Society, at least as early as 1849, and that the august persons who denied knowing David Addison Ramsay *had* been members. And so had Edward Alton Bell-Fairfax.

And so had William Fitzwalter Nennys, who, like Lewis, was an immortal being created by the efforts of a cabal of scientists and investors . . .

What on earth had Nennius been doing? What had *Edward* been doing?

Lewis followed up his next hunch: searching for other references to the Gentlemen's Speculative Society in the classified records. He was mildly astonished at what he found.

It was the Gentlemen's Speculative Society since 1755; prior to that its members called themselves the Fellowship of the Green Lion, during which time Sir Isaac Newton was one of their number.

The Fellowship of the Green Lion was reliably recorded as having existed as far back as 1660. It seemed to have sprung from a group calling itself the House of Solomon, almost certainly led by Sir Francis Bacon.

That particular fraternity of scholars previously met under the name of the Servants of the Temple of Albion, an organization that could be traced back through the era of Elizabeth I—persons as disparate as Dr. Dee and Sir Francis Drake were members—to the year 1250, when Roger Bacon was apparently its guiding light. There were intimations that Bacon inherited a tradition that began at an even earlier date.

All of this in a file the British government had chosen to keep secret, had chosen to keep *so* secret, it went to the trouble of encrypting it and burying it far from the light of day in New Syon House.

It was at about this time that Lewis began to feel a creeping sensation of knowing too much for comfort.

So he turned his attention to the biographical data on William Fitzwalter Nennys.

Born 1803—ha ha. Lewis knew for a fact that Nennius had come over in a galley at the order of the emperor Claudius; this he learned in the course of a pleasant evening in a coffeehouse back in 1836, during a chat with Nennius about old times. Lewis's current identification disc gave his own date of birth as the year 2116, when 103 A.D. was nearer the mark. Well, and what had Nennius done with that lifetime?

Here were the names of parents he never had, followed by a list of schools he never attended; and here the statement that in 1832 he became headmaster of Overton School . . .

Edward's school. He'd been Edward's headmaster.

Lewis's gasp in his chilly room puffed out like smoke. Distractedly he got up and turned on the climate-control unit, standing in front of its heating vent while he collected his memories and spread them out to try to make sense of them.

Nennius *had* been a headmaster, yes, that was what the meeting at the coffeehouse was all about—Nennius brought a sheaf of inky student papers to deliver to Lewis for the Company archives. Lewis didn't ask why, Lewis didn't even read them, just passed them on to the Company courier who came for them the following week. Dr. Zeus was always making off with ephemera like that. Lewis was more interested in the prospect of pumping Nennius for details about the old empire. They sat up late, getting mildly buzzed on drinking chocolate and laughing about how it was impossible to find a decently heated room in Britain since the legions pulled out . . .

Closing his eyes, Lewis dove back through his visual record. There! There were the papers, he was laughing with Nennius as he opened the leather case, and Nennius was saying:

"—lad may be somebody someday, but you know how it is with the archivists, they ask for the damnedest trivia—"

Freeze frame. Part of the top page was visible. What did it say? Enlarge and enhance. There were the slightly uneven letters of a boy not yet perfect in his copperplate hand: *Dulce et decorus pro patria mori, which is very true I think if you have got no other way of helping anybody or, for example, stopping the Hindoos from doing things such as burning up their widows. I would like to—*

Reeling slightly, Lewis put a hand to the wall. Compare frame with EASILY AND BEST FORGOTTEN file documents A, B, and C. Points of similarity? Singularity? Statistical likelihood of the same hand?

Ninety-five per cent.

And though the feeling of impending danger was very, very strong just then, Lewis leaped out into the middle of his room and executed a few shuffling tap steps, finishing on one knee with both arms flung out in triumph.

Nennius was young Edward's headmaster. Nennius belonged to the Gentlemen's Speculative Society and Redking's Club at the same time his former pupil was a member of them. Coincidence? Or had he sponsored Edward's admission into those august bodies? Given Edward's obscure birth and blighted naval career, it seemed likely he had. Why? Unless of course Edward was admitted at the urging of the unknown benefactor who prevented his court-martial and paid for his upbringing. But, then, what did Nennius have to do—?

Lewis was barely able to sleep that night, but he had no nightmares. Not that night, not any night since the plot began to thicken. And this was why he whistled, today, tapping away at the keyboard in his room.

He couldn't remember when he'd been happier, even as his awareness of risk grew. He very nearly got in touch with Nennius (a scan of Company records showed him that Nennius was currently stationed in the Breton Republic), but common sense prevailed. He was contenting himself now with following up Nennius's subsequent career.

It appeared that his fellow immortal had worked a very long shift indeed as William Fitzwalter Nennys, finally pretending to die in 1886. All the appliance aging makeup must have been hideously uncomfortable.

Ah, but not so uncomfortable he hadn't been able to—what was this? To attend a last meeting of the Gentlemen's Speculative Society. Yes, and vote with the other members, old and new—and, my, what interesting new members had joined since 1849, George Bernard Shaw and young Herbert George Wells, for example—to *change the name of the Gentlemen due to the recent scandal.* What did they decide to call themselves this time?

Lewis read on eagerly and then stopped.

He got up, made himself a cup of tea, went to the window, and stared down into the street for a while. When he finished the tea, he went to his tiny sink and rinsed out the cup, setting it carefully in the drainer. At last he walked back to his workstation, pulled out his chair, sat down, and looked again at the screen.

Yes, it really did say that the new name they chose was the Kronos Diversified Stock Company.

The reason Lewis was having trouble believing what he saw, of course, was that Kronos Diversified was one of the names under which Dr. Zeus, Incorporated, did business throughout the centuries.

He got up once more and went to his cupboard. Taking out a bottle of gin, he poured himself a small silver cocktail and went to the window again. He half-expected to see Edward Alton Bell-Fairfax looking up at him from the pavement, as the late traffic went by.

You won't be silenced. You meant it, didn't you? thought Lewis. *Have you refused to let go, are you haunting me somehow? What does all this mean about the Company, and why have you shown me? Are you trying to tell Mendoza? Can't you find her, either?*

Fez

"**I**F THERE'S AN eternity, boy, I wouldn't mind spending it like this," said Joseph, drifting gently into the coping at the edge of the pool.

"Contemplating the eternal stars?" Suleyman leaned back to look up at them where they glittered in the wide square of night sky, framed by the high white walls of the old garden.

"Floating in your pool with a piña colada, actually."

"Asses' milk, you infidel moron," jeered Latif. "Do you want to scandalize the servants?"

"All right, so it's coconut pineapple asses' milk with extract of Jamaican sugar cane," Joseph said. "God forbid I should upset the help, you lousy little squirt."

Latif, who had known Joseph since childhood, just sneered at him. He had long since attained his considerable adult height and had the lean and dangerous profile of a North African corsair. Suleyman laughed quietly and thumbed the control that lowered his deck chair into a reclining position so he could view the stars in greater comfort. Suleyman was very dark, with the classical features of Mali, so he didn't look like a corsair—though he had been one in his time.

"Isn't that something, about poor old Polaris?" he mused. "All these tens of centuries it's been the one thing you could depend on, in this hemisphere, anyway. Byword for constancy, and what does it go and do but slip out of place at last? What will mortals use to navigate, with the North Star gone astray?"

"Things change," said Joseph.

"So they do, little man. So they do."

A silence fell, with a shade of meaning in it that the two younger immortals missed. Donal sighed in contentment and switched off his headset, flipping up the televisor.

"That was that," he informed the others. "The Pirates took the match, six to nothing. Not one goal for the Assassins."

"The office pool is mine," said Latif.

"Yaah," Joseph said.

"Yaah yourself, you loser," Latif told him, grinning white in the darkness. He sprawled backward like a man at his ease, but there was an alertness in the lines of his body. He went on: "So, this vacation thing you're doing. You actually want to go see a *necropolis* tomorrow?"

"That's what I said, kid."

"Well, that's certainly my idea of a good time. Ride out into the foothills, where it gets hot enough to boil rice on the rocks at noon, and crawl around a bunch of mortal graves all stuccoed over to look like the biggest seagull splash in the world. What's that phrase, *whited sepulchers?* What a party guy you turned out to be."

"It's psychological," Joseph said, pushing away from the coping and rotating slowly in his pool float. "People are designed by nature to need a last resting place. The idea of one, anyway. We immortal guys never get graves. The programming we're given in school keeps the urge off for the first few millennia, but after a while you find yourself wondering what it would be like to just—lie down in a tomb and stop moving forever. So it helps, see, to go and look at the reality. Bones and dust. Makes you glad to be alive."

"Really?" Donal sounded appalled.

"No, he's giving us a lot of bullshit as usual," Latif said.

"Sounds creepy to me," Donal went on, shuddering. "I was recruited out of some kind of tunnel or catacomb place. I'd never want to visit one."

"I'll show him the necropolis," Suleyman said. "I know what he's talking about, after all. You kids go hang out at the bazaar. Milo Rousseau's added a third show at Palais Aziz, did I tell you? If you hang around the window and whine, I'll bet you can get tickets."

"What's his backup band?" Latif sat bolt upright.

"The Dead Weights."

"We're there," Latif said. He regarded Donal with curiosity. "Now, what was that about catacombs? I thought you were recruited out of San Francisco."

"Plenty of catacombs in San Francisco," Joseph said, draining his glass and setting it on the coping. "Place has everything. Of course,

the catacombs are mostly in Chinatown," he added, tilting to peer at
Donal. "You were an Irish immigrant kid, right?"

"As far as I know," said Donal. "I was only about three when the
Company rescued me."

"So what were you doing in a catacomb?" Latif persisted.

"He may not feel like talking about it, you know," Suleyman said.

"No, it's okay. It's just—it seems so *silly*." Donal shook his head.
"I was supposed to have been rescued from the 1906 earthquake, but
I don't remember that at all. I remember something else entirely . . ."

"Which was?" Latif prompted.

"This sounds so stupid. As God is my witness, what I remember
is that the Bad Toymaker carried me off, down to this place with all
these dead Chinese guys. And then Uncle Jimmy—I mean Victor,
that's the operative who recruited me—came and rescued me."

"Dead Chinese guys," said Joseph thoughtfully. "That would fit
with your being in a catacomb. It wouldn't explain who took you there,
though, or why."

"Bad *Toymaker?*" Latif looked incredulous.

"See, it's all mixed up in my mind." Donal closed his eyes in an
attempt to think. "There was this show my mortal parents took me to,
on that last night. I found out since it was *Babes in Toyland*, by Victor
Herbert. So what I remember is mixed up with the Bad Toymaker and
some bears. I thought it was a big bear at first, but it was a man. I
thought he was going to break my neck. He'd hurt Uncle Jimmy already, there was blood on Uncle Jimmy's shirt." Donal's voice slowed
unconsciously, took on traces of an early accent. "I was scared, but
then Uncle Jimmy spit on him, and it, like, broke the spell or something. The Toymaker had to let me go. We climbed a ladder. Then I
got to ride in a motor car, the little Chinese doll gave me chocolate,
and we went on the ship."

"That's very interesting," said Suleyman at last.

"It sounds like some of it was just a nightmare," said Latif.

"Yeah, that's what I've always thought, too." Donal sighed. "I still
see that big bear sometimes in my sleep, and the bunks down there,
and the dead men. Uncle Jimmy, Victor I mean, arguing with him."

"Victor," said Suleyman. "The Facilitator Victor? Little white man
with a red beard, usually plays an Englishman? Did you ever ask him
about it?"

"I only met him once, since then," Donal said. "I couldn't ask,
somehow. He was, I don't know, sort of stiff and formal, not at all
like when he was being Uncle Jimmy. Do you know him?"

"He stops in to see Nan, when he's in this part of the world," Suleyman said. "And he is a little unapproachable, I must admit."

"The big-bear guy," asked Latif, "what did he look like?"

"*Big*. Twice as big as Uncle Jimmy. A giant, an ogre. And he smelled awful. It'd knock you down, that smell, not like dirt but like musk. He had huge teeth, a big nose."

Joseph splashed a little. "What color were his eyes?" he asked, perhaps a shade too casually.

"His eyes? I don't remember. Yes, I do. Really pale blue. Like, uh, Coke bottle glass used to be?"

"Weird," Joseph remarked.

"And you say he was arguing with Victor," said Suleyman. "Can you remember what they were arguing about?"

"It must have been a hell of a fight," said Latif. "What kind of mortal could draw blood on one of us, no matter how big he was? It's impossible."

Joseph said nothing.

Donal groped for his drink. "This is creeping me out. I don't want to think any more about this. Not to be rude—"

"No, it's all right," Suleyman assured him. "We all have our own nightmares. Let's change the subject."

"Thanks. I'm sorry, I just—"

"It's okay, kid, perfectly okay," said Joseph.

Latif looked narrow-eyed from Suleyman to Joseph. However, one of the qualities that made him an able second-in-command was his ability to sense, without being told, when to leave something alone. So he yawned, stretched, and said, "How about those Pirates? What were you thinking, Joseph? You *knew* Wilker's averages."

Joseph, about to reply colorfully, caught his breath as a woman emerged from the lamplit terrace and came down the steps into the garden.

She was tiny, like an ebony figurine, with exquisite aristocratic features. Over her nightdress she wore a blue silk robe, the same shade as the evening sky. Her bearing was upright, she walked unconcernedly with her hands in the robe pockets; but there was a certain darkness in her gaze that brought to mind storm clouds.

Instantly the mood in the garden changed. Suleyman rose to his feet.

"My apologies, Nan," he said gently. "Were we keeping you awake?"

She shook her head. "I hadn't retired, to tell you the truth. I thought I'd sit out here and watch the stars for a while." Latif was already up and opening a lawn chair for her, arranging the woven cover and pillows with the deference one shows a princess or a widow. She stood watching in silence, unnervingly motionless. When he stepped back with a gesture of presentation, she gave him a smile.

"Thank you, dear," she said, and sat down.

"How's the work going?" Donal asked.

"Quite nicely, thank you," Nan replied. She wasn't referring to the mosaic she was restoring, and neither was he; but no one there wanted to speak of what she had been doing, alone in her room at her workstation, making endless inquiry for information she could never seem to get, searching for a man who had disappeared.

Joseph watched with compassion as she stretched out and sighed, turning her face to the sky, making an effort to relax the stiffness of rage. He couldn't think of anything to say that wouldn't seem clumsy, but he remembered that she loved the music of the twenty-first-century composer Jacques Soulier. He began to sing, very softly, Soulier's wordless *Sea Lullabye*. His baritone resonated off the water, off the high walls that enclosed them. He hadn't a bad voice.

After a moment Suleyman took up the bass part, and the two voices wove together, becoming the slow currents in the night sea. Donal listened for the first tenor part, describing the reflection of the evening star, and joined in on cue. Latif took the second tenor part when its turn came, the music of the breakers on the reef, that was always played by trumpets when the piece was done symphonically.

It was late, they'd been drinking a little, felt no need to cramp themselves to sound like mortal men. Within the house an old servant awoke and lay silent, listening in joy and terror. He had lived long enough to know that Allah did things like this, sometimes, beautiful and inexplicable things like sending angels to sing in a garden at night. It wouldn't do to blaspheme, though, by running to the window to see if they were really there. The music was gift enough.

Nan looked up at the stars and wondered, for the thousandth time, what had happened to Kalugin.

I have a question for you, little man.

Joseph looked off blandly across the floor of the desert, where the tombs shone like impossible snow. *I'll bet it's the same question I was going to ask you.*

Suleyman shifted gears on the little electric Moke, and it charged the next hill with a whine before he replied, as they went bumping on, leaving the elegant city farther and farther behind them, *Quite probably. But I outrank you, and I brought the subject up first.*

Okay.

You listened pretty attentively when the boys were discussing Donal's memories. Why?

What, about the Toymaker? You were paying close attention yourself, I noticed. The guy just sounded like someone I used to know. Joseph looked out at the tombs again and wiped sweat from his brow. "It's hot," he said out loud. "I bet this used to take forever on a camel, huh?"

"Just about," Suleyman said. *Is Budu the name I'm groping after, by any chance?*

Joseph's eyes widened. "Say, is there any tea left in the thermos, or did you finish it off?" he said in a bright voice. *Budu, Budu. Old Hungarian name, isn't it?*

"Plenty of tea. Help yourself." *Stop this. I need to know.*

Why do you need to know? Joseph groped about and found the thermos. He gulped thirstily.

Because I've been on his trail for the last three centuries. Suleyman shifted gears again, and the Moke obeyed him, complaining.

So have I, give or take a century. I can't imagine what he'd be doing in an opium den in San Francisco right before the 1906 earthquake, but it sure sounds like him.

I see. Why are you looking for him, Joseph?

Isn't everybody?

Answer me, please.

I owe the guy. And I need help, and he's the only one I can think of to ask.

Tell me why you owe anything to a mass-murdering Neanderthal freak.

He's not a Neanderthal, you know, they were really short. All the Enforcers were hybrids.

Hybrids? What are you talking about?

There was a protracted silence, as the Moke bumped along in the ruts of the road.

Let's start over, said Suleyman. *I have been looking for an Immortal named Budu. Very large, resembling a Neanderthal in certain respects, evil incarnate and able to travel nearly anywhere in the world without the Company being able to find him. Officially AWOL since 1099 A.D.*

I see.

Now you talk.

I've been looking for a big ugly guy named Budu who has coincidentally been on the lam from the Company since 1099. The one I

knew wasn't evil incarnate, though. Or a freak. He was just an En-
forcer, the best and smartest of them. He never hurt anyone who was
innocent. He saved my life when I was a kid. Recruited me.

Suleyman nodded, narrow-eyed with anger but controlling it well.

All right, now I understand your point of view. You should know,
though, that he kills without discrimination these days, and so do his
people.

His people? But—all the old Enforcers have been retired.

I'm not talking about the old Enforcers, Joseph. I'm talking about
a cabal hidden within the Company, operatives he's managed to talk
around to his point of view. He wants the Earth's population forcibly
reduced. Kill them all, and God will know his own, wasn't that the old
motto for soldiers?

Joseph did not reply, staring forward through the dust of the windscreen, clutching the thermos bottle.

Suleyman exhaled and continued. *You remember when the epi-*
demics started up again, in the late twentieth century, even before
Sattes? AIDS, all those hemorrhagic fevers like Ebola and Marburg?
Do you remember how badly Africa was hit? All we were supposed to
do, my people and I, was watch. Salvage certain cultural treasures the
Company wanted and perhaps the occasional child for recruitment,
but nothing else. Let the mortals die, it's their fate after all, history
can't be changed. Do you think I could do nothing more than watch?
Do you know how many millions on this continent died, while the rest
of the world looked the other way? Well, I didn't look the other way,
Joseph. I worked with the epidemiologists. We tracked the outbreaks
to their sources. Do you know what we found?

Joseph shifted in his seat. *I always heard it was stuff that had been*
around for centuries, only it'd lain dormant in the rain forests until
people started cutting them down.

No, Joseph. We traced most of them to one point of origin, a cave
in Mount Elgon. One cave, Joseph. And there the epidemiologists hit
a dead end, literally, couldn't figure out how the diseases had all
originated in one simple little hole in the earth. They left, defeated.

But it wasn't a simple little hole in the earth, Joseph. It was the
entrance to a Company supply tunnel. That was when I knew.

Joseph squeezed his eyes shut. *Jesus.*

Someone within the Company was doing it. Using Africa as a
testing ground, I think.

Not Budu. He'd never have done a thing like that, never in a
million years. You didn't know him. Anyway he wasn't with the Com-
pany by that time. He's been on the run since 1099, you said so your-

self. Where did you get the idea it was him? How did you even find out about the old Enforcers? They were way before your time.

I was old before the first stone was set in Zimbabwe's wall, you know that. I knew there were warriors once among the immortals, used for a specific purpose and then reprogrammed. Set to constructive tasks. I'm told you'd never know, now, what they used to do, they're indistinguishable from the rest of us. Suleyman steered expertly around a dead dog.

Well, there you're wrong. Joseph ground his teeth. *They were a different model from us, Suleyman. They were braver than lions, and they loved justice. War was their element, like air for the birds. Dr. Zeus designed them that way. You think Budu was a freak because you never saw the others.*

They sound like monsters.

Maybe they were. But they did their job, and you know how the Company thanked them once they'd done their job? Tricked them into underground bunkers one by one and took their brains offline. Budu was the last. He went rogue so it wouldn't happen to him. I can see him going after Dr. Zeus, maybe, but not doing the kind of filthy work you're talking about.

Suleyman looked at him sidelong as he drove. *I'm sorry. But I went hunting, Joseph, I set Latif and the best of my people on this. I can show you the evidence they've gathered. There is a group operating within the Company, betraying its ideals. Such as they are. The Sattes virus was their work. The Church of God-A took the blame in the history books, but Budu's cabal was guilty. It took him centuries to build it up, but he got a circle of disciples among the Preservers. I've seen their master plan. By the year 2355 there'll be so few mortals left, they can be rounded up and kept in patrolled villages. Peace at last. And any of the immortals who dispute their agenda will be taken out. How, I haven't discovered yet.*

"Boy, it's hot," said Joseph, pulling out a tissue. "I'm sweating bullets." He mopped tears from his face. *I can see him targeting the armies and the criminal population,* he admitted. *But why would he go after Third World civilians? Or homosexuals?*

Who would stand up for them? Suleyman responded grimly. *They're the easiest target. And look how well the economies of the world are doing, now that there are fewer people. Just like it was after the Black Death. Little towns abandoned and going back to nature. The grass grows greener, the trees grow taller with nobody to cut them down. The air is cleaner. But millions have been sacrificed for this.*

You have proof. Joseph sighed. It wasn't a question. Suleyman just nodded.

They drove along in silence for a while. At last Joseph blew his nose and asked, *Is it at the highest levels?*

Not really. But it goes deep.

You know—all I started out to do was find a friend of mine. A kid I recruited, once, who got into trouble.

The Botanist Mendoza?

Yeah. Christ, you wouldn't know where she is?

No. Just that she was a friend of Nan's. I take it she's become one of the disappeared, like poor old Kalugin?

Yeah.

This is why you want to see the necropolis, isn't it? You think there's a bunker underneath. You think your child might be in there.

She might be.

You think Kalugin might be in there?

Who knows? But we can't check today. You can only get into these places under cover of an electrical storm, so your datafeed to the Company gets knocked out.

Is that what you've been doing? Suleyman glanced at him, grinning. *Waiting for storms? Aie! How long has it taken you to get even this far? Pay attention, now, little man, and learn something.*

He sent the Moke charging recklessly up the nearest slope, swerving over the most rutted part of the road deliberately, at a decidedly unsafe speed. Joseph yelped and held on; but all that happened was that at the crest of the hill the Moke suddenly froze in its tracks.

"Shit." Suleyman thumped the steering wheel. "The power cell's knocked loose again. Give me a hand, here." He swung open the driver's side door and hopped out, pulling a tool kit from under the seat. Joseph got out and came around the fender uncertainly, meeting him in front of the car.

"Here," Suleyman said, thrusting the tool kit at him. "Open that and get me out a C-rod spanner."

Joseph obeyed and looked on as Suleyman lifted the hood of the car and peered in, making a disgusted sound. "Look at that. I tell that kid and I tell him, bungee cord's no good. Replace the hold-down clamp, I tell him. Does he listen? Kids!"

The power cell had indeed jumped half out of its little shaped space, and one connection had jostled loose. Suleyman tugged at his gold earring in annoyance. Then he reached out and grasped the connection with one hand, while reaching for the spanner with the other.

In the second that his hand touched the spanner that Joseph still held out to him, there was a brief flash and click.

"And no more datafeed for the next six hours," Suleyman announced.

"Wow," Joseph said. "That's brilliant. I never thought a simple car power cell would have enough charge to blow out the link!"

"They don't." Suleyman tugged his earring again. "But this does."

Joseph stared openmouthed. "My God. Where did you get that?"

"Latif designed it. Clever child, wouldn't you say? We used to have a few virtual reality games, back when they first came out. Some of them had some interesting glitches."

Joseph said something profane in a long-dead language. "Do you know how many years it's taken me to make one of those? And it's twice that size!"

Suleyman just smiled and reconnected the power cell. They got back in the car and drove on.

"Now, you understand," Suleyman resumed, "that I can't trust you."

Joseph sighed.

"We've known each other a long time, and I mean it as a compliment when I say you're the most Company man I've ever seen. You're also a lying little bastard when you need to be. That's a good thing, given your line of work. Unfortunately, I think you lie to yourself too.

"If you're working for the Company and reporting on what I'm doing—well, it isn't as though I haven't tried to tell them. I think the Company knows about Budu's group, and they're tolerating him because the Company can benefit from his work without getting its own hands dirty." Suleyman pulled up before the necropolis and switched off the engine. "However, the devil will call for payment one of these days."

They got out and trudged toward the gleaming white terraces. The heat was astonishing, making the horizon dance and waver in currents of boiling air.

"The other possibility is that you're here from Budu himself," Suleyman went on composedly. "You've made it clear you still think of him as a hero. You wouldn't feel that way if you walked with me through a children's hospital in Uganda, though, unless you've changed a lot from the days when you and I worked together. And we immortals don't change. It's one of the things that makes us immortals."

"My point exactly," said Joseph. "Budu wouldn't change either, not to the point where he'd orchestrate something like this."

"Maybe. Anyway—if you *are* here from your old Enforcer, if you're leading me into a trap, disabling me won't help you. Quite apart from the fact that little Latif would be very, very annoyed with you, and he knows where you live, by the way, I've taken a lot of pains to see that my work will go on without me."

"I work alone, myself," Joseph said. "I wish I had the kind of resources you have."

"I made some good investments when Dr. Zeus started permitting us private incomes," Suleyman conceded. "Latif, too. And it helps, of course, to have advance knowledge of the market."

"How did you manage that?" Joseph asked, as they made their way up a long mud-brick stair between walls so white, their shadows were iridescent blue, under a sky blue as blue tile. "You'd have to get a look at the Temporal Concordance to get information like that, and everybody knows we're not allowed to see that stuff."

"Nor do we," Suleyman said imperturbably. "If we could get a look at the Temporal Concordance past the present calendar date, we'd be all omnipotent as gods. Latif just analyzes the Company invest-ments, and we go with his projections. I said he's a clever child. Strong, too. I recruited him out of a slave ship, you know. Watched him, down there in the hold, beside his dying mother. Frightened little baby, but he was angry. His anger made him strong. We're all of us angry when we come into this immortal life; keeps us motivated to fight for humanity against evil.

"The question is, how long can we fight without coming to see humanity itself as the source of evil?" Suleyman stopped on the stair, turning to Joseph. "Of course, we've been given immortal wisdom, with immortal strength, to avoid such a pitfall."

"Well, there's that old saw of Nietzsche's about becoming a dragon yourself if you fight dragons too long," Joseph said, drinking from the thermos again. "I still don't think Budu's guilty. And I haven't led you into an ambush. In fact, I'm going to show you some-thing really useful, to somebody with the ability to use it." He climbed again, scanning as he went, until he abruptly stepped off to the left into one of the white terraces.

He paced along a short distance, Suleyman following closely, and stopped at one particular tomb midway along the line.

"Ah." Suleyman looked close. "This door is in good repair. Very unusual."

"Isn't it?" Joseph ran his hand down the frame. He found what he was searching for, what any operative with Facilitator clearance could have found, if he knew it was there. The door clicked and swung inward.

There were several dead persons in the tomb, in varying degrees of becoming dust. The front and side walls of the tomb were of mud brick; the back wall was the hillside itself, an irregular rock outcropping. Joseph pointed at it silently, and Suleyman nodded.

"Clever," he remarked. Had any one of the mortal occupants of the tomb come to life again for a moment, he would have been astounded to watch as Joseph and Suleyman walked toward the rock wall and through it, vanishing into a gloom deeper than even a corpse would be comfortable with.

But Joseph and Suleyman, able to see by infrared, clearly saw the smooth and sloping walls of the tunnel they traveled.

It was just like the tunnel in Yorkshire had been, to look at; had the same faint pleasant scent, too. Presently they emerged into another vast and vaulted room, blue-lit from the rows of regeneration tanks, each with its floating occupant.

"This is some kind of repair facility," said Suleyman, frowning.

"You'd think so, but look at these guys." Joseph went close. "See! Here's your proof. *These* were the old Enforcers."

Suleyman followed him reluctantly, staring up at the vaults. His eyes widened.

"Name of the Merciful," he said quietly.

"What else do you do with an immortal you don't want anymore? You can't kill them," said Joseph. "I guess you could blast them into space, but they might find a way back, and then—"

Suleyman looked up at a chalkboard on the wall. There, in Latin, were the words:

ABDIEL HAS DONE HIS APPOINTED WORK HERE
MARCH 6, 2143–MARCH 23, 2143

He looked back at Joseph's anguished face. "All right," he said. "I bear witness."

Joseph began to hurry back and forth among the vaults, looking up at the occupant of each one, and Suleyman followed him.

"You're not looking for your child," Suleyman realized. "You're looking for Budu."

Joseph nodded. "I think they must have caught him at last. I'm betting he's in one of these vaults. If I can find him, and wake him up—I pity whoever spread all those viruses from that supply tunnel."

He skidded to a stop in front of a vault where a male Preserver floated. "Kalugin might be here, too. Would you recognize him if we found him?"

"I would," Suleyman replied grimly, standing beside Joseph. "I performed his marriage ceremony."

"They got *married?* He and Nan? Two immortals?"

"It happens," said Suleyman.

"Amazing." Joseph turned a corner and started working his way along a new row of vaults. "So I guess we're wondering just exactly what Donal saw in 1906? How did the Company catch up with Budu? Why did Budu grab Donal? It was right before the big earthquake. Was Budu maybe doing some recruiting?"

"Unlikely," Suleyman said. "Unless his people have a way of performing the immortality process themselves, and if they'd managed to infiltrate the Company far enough to get *that* secret, they wouldn't have needed to send their own leader into a salvage zone to steal one mortal child."

"I guess so," Joseph said. "Donal said Budu and Victor were fighting, didn't he? Victor had blood on his shirt. Can you imagine what it would be like fighting with an Enforcer? Why wasn't Victor smashed like a bug?"

Suleyman nodded in agreement, stopping in front of one vault to peer at someone he thought he recognized. After a moment he moved on. "Donal said that Victor spat on Budu. That suggests the use of some kind of toxin."

"Poison? But *no* poison works on us. And if the Company finally found one, why wouldn't they use it to kill off all these Enforcers instead of keeping them here?"

"I don't know." Suleyman looked up at an olive-skinned girl with a sweet-sad face. "Unless it only disabled the old monster."

"Here's another scenario. What if Budu did start some group to try to change. Company policy? And what if his people double-crossed him, and somebody else has been running the cabal since 1906? Have your people found any trace of Budu in the last two hundred years?"

After a long moment Suleyman said, "As a matter of fact, no. Not since the end of the nineteenth century. Plenty of evidence of his group, though."

"There," Joseph said. "There's your answer."

"It's not an answer, little man. It's many, many more questions."

"You know who we have to talk to now, of course."

"Victor." Suleyman came to the last row of vaults and turned, starting back.

"And Victor's either on the side of the Company or he's one of the bad guys." Joseph strode to keep up. "If he's still Company, he may be the problem solver who finally caught up with Budu."

"A dangerous man to talk to, in either case."

"I liked Victor," said Joseph plaintively. "The guy did me a favor once, when he was stationed at New World One."

"He's always been the most pleasant and courteous of guests, when he stops in to visit Nan," Suleyman said.

"They're old friends?"

"So it seems."

"Would she talk to him? Can she find anything out for us?"

Suleyman looked down at him as they walked. "What are the chances that any of this will help her learn what happened to Kalugin?"

"I can promise to look for him," said Joseph. "I already have a shopping list of missing operatives."

"Then she'll talk to Victor."

They emerged from the tomb unseen. A plume of dust rose up behind them as they headed back for the city. Joseph sagged in his seat, watching the distant minarets against the sky.

"This is really depressing. At least I'm starting to get an idea of what will happen in 2355. There's the Company, and then there's this antihumanity cabal within the Company, and then there are people like you and me who are just trying to do their jobs. I can think of a lot of ways the Silence might fall."

"I guess we'll find out," Suleyman said.

"And the Company has it coming. Will we all wind up in those bunkers, or wearing those clock emblems? It's just the kind of thing I can see the twenty-fourth-century investors ordering. We make them nervous."

"I don't blame them for being nervous. It's sad . . . Now and then, to obtain something the Company wanted, I've had to impersonate supernatural creatures."

"Me too."

"I've played a djinn, once or twice. There's some interesting folklore about djinns. The story goes that Allah made men from clay, but the djinns he made from subtle fire. In his wisdom Allah gave them tremendous power, but gave mankind chains to bind that power, lest the djinns prey on them. So djinns were slaves to wise men and served their purposes. King Solomon commanded whole armies of them."

"I've heard that, too."

"The story goes on to say that the djinns must continue as faithful slaves until Judgment Day. Then, when the first blast of the trumpet sounds, they all die, since they have no souls with which to enter Paradise."

"Talk about raw deals." Joseph grinned bitterly.

"Who argues with the Almighty?" Suleyman made a gesture with his hand as though flicking away a speck of dust. "No point. "Maybe the djinns don't mind. Maybe they're glad to rest at last. Don't forget that Allah is all-merciful and utterly just. Unlike the mortal masters who created us."

"Now I'm *really* depressed," muttered Joseph.

The city grew nearer. After a while Joseph asked, "So. If I wanted to get a message to you without going through Company channels, how would I do that?"

Suleyman chuckled. "You do count on trust. I'll tell you, though. Look up a religious order calling themselves the Compassionates of Allah. If you're in the right city, and you leave a message, it will filter back to me."

Fez

THEY STROLLED TOGETHER through the city, the immortal gentleman and lady.

He was a dapper white man with small precise features. His eyes were green as a cat's, his hair and pointed beard red as fire. He wore a white suit of perfectly pressed, tropical-weight linen, rather retro in its cut, and a wide-brimmed hat against the sun. Formal as his appearance was, there was a sense of deliberate parody, a hint of the bizarre. Something too much like an insect's pincers in the way his oiled mustache swept up; something suggestive of a mime's exaggeration in his walk. Despite the heat, he wore white gloves.

Nan wore a peacock-blue afternoon ensemble from the premier designer house in Senegal, with matching hat and veil, like a beautifully dressed doll. Her parasol threw a shadow of deeper blue.

Slowly they made their way along the old streets, in and out of the islands of shadow from the great palm trees, through arcaded quarters plastered and painted in all shades of white and blue. They spoke quietly together. That either of them could hear what the other said was remarkable, given the small mortal child who danced along behind them, following closely as though drawn on a string. He carried on his shoulder a SoundBox 3000 that screamed out the latest album by Little Fairuza: ten songs of love and longing in the teen world of Islam.

Every now and then a passerby frowned severely at the child. It wasn't so much that the music's content was objectionable—when has any culture approved of love and longing for the under-sixteen set?—but for such a big SoundBox the speakers were execrable, buzzing and roaring with distortion. The child danced along, oblivious.

The white man cast a dubious look over one shoulder as they

walked slowly down Rue Meridien. "You're quite sure this is necessary?"

"Yes. The generator renders our conversation unintelligible."

Victor nodded, stroking his beard. "Well. Lunch alfresco? I seem
to remember a place in the next street over that does a splendid b'stila."

"I'd like that." Nan took his arm, and they bore right through a
winding maze of connected courtyards, emerging at last in a dim garden where a central fountain played. There a waiter served them from
a cart, presenting them with two neat chlorilar plates of b'stila and
uttering brief harsh words to the child, who hopped over the garden
wall, turned up the volume, and busied himself with an exhibition of
ape dancing for the edification of onlookers.

Nan and Victor set their plates on the wall and nibbled away tidily
at their crispy pastries. Victor made sounds of dignified pleasure, lifting a forkful of savory filling to admire it.

"Of all the things one never thought one would miss," he said, "I
must say *chicken* is the most unlikely. Do you know it's impossible
to get over there at all, now?"

"Really?"

"Yes. Thanks to the Beast Liberation Party, chickens are no longer
being bred. They're very nearly extinct in England."

"Extinct?" Nan looked astonished.

"Poor creatures were apparently too stupid to make use of the gift
of civil liberty," Victor said, carefully brushing confectioner's sugar
from his beard. "Wandering onto motorways or into the path of packs
of feral dogs, who have made much better use of their civil liberty."

Nan shook her head. "Why do all these attempts to stop cruelty
result in greater cruelty?" she said.

"Cruelty is a natural element in the world, like sand," Victor said,
smiling thinly. "Mortals may shovel it out of one place, but it merely
accumulates in a pile somewhere else. Clear your house and bury your
neighbor's. Yet the futile efforts persist."

"As we do," she said.

His smile faded, and he looked down at his plate again. "Have
you had any success?"

"I haven't found him, no. Though I wouldn't say my efforts have
met with complete failure."

"May I hear what you've learned?" Victor asked, taking her empty
plate on his and dropping them, with the forks, down the nearest fusion
hopper. He then pulled off his soiled gloves and tucked them away in
one pocket. From another pocket he produced a fresh pair and pulled

them on. Nan waited patiently, setting her parasol on her shoulder again.

He offered her his arm, and they strolled from the garden. The mortal child took up his SoundBox and moved after them.

As they paced across the courtyard outside the university, Nan said: "I was able to break into his personnel file, but there isn't much after 2038. Kalugin was at Kamchatka, he finished whatever he was doing there, he returned to Polar Base Two. He requested recreational leave, and then he was transferred to a location designated only by a number. After that his record simply stops."

"Perhaps he's still on duty at that site?" Victor suggested. "Involved in something classified."

"He'd have sent me word, in all these years," said Nan quietly. "You know that."

Victor reflected that she was right, that violating a mandatory communications lockdown to talk to his wife was exactly the sort of thing Kalugin would have done. He didn't say this, however. He simply watched Nan from under the brim of his hat and wondered, for the thousandth time, what his life might have been like if Nan had not loved Vasilii Vasilievitch Kalugin.

"So he would have," he said. "You've found nothing further, then?"

"I didn't say that." Nan glanced over her shoulder, and the mortal child walked nearer. She spoke in a measured, dispassionate way, as though she were discussing a subject of only mildly mutual interest. "It occurred to me to study the phenomenon of disappearance itself. Does it happen often? To whom, and why?"

"Sensible way to approach the problem," Victor said.

"I accessed Company personnel files, traced them, cross-referenced them. Never mind how I obtained the codes. I learned that disappearance is not recent, not the result of our masters' paranoia as we approach their time period.

"It has always happened. There are any number of files that simply stop, Victor. After a certain date they contain no entries. Sometimes it happens following injury."

Victor nodded. "Pretty damned infrequently, I'd think."

"More often than you'd think. An operative will be sent to a base for repair—and never released. Sometimes, it follows an arrest. An operative is sent to the nearest base for disciplinary action and counseling. After that, the operative is reassigned, but to a numbered location that cannot be traced in the Company files, regardless of what search parameters are used."

"I see." Victor smoothed his mustache uneasily.

Nan's voice sharpened as she went on: "Then there are operatives who disappear simply because they were associated with operatives who also disappeared." She let go of his arm and turned to face him abruptly. "They go to numbered sites too, Victor. Why? What did they witness? Do you know?"

Victor caught his breath at her fury, at her perfect lips drawn back from her white teeth. He raised his hands in a palms-up shrug, aware that the gloves made the gesture outrageously theatrical.

"I'm only a Facilitator, Nan. But we're both old enough to know the Company has its ugly little secrets. Dr. Zeus may have found it convenient to lose some of us."

"How can it just *lose* us?" Nan demanded. "I remember being told that I might sink under the polar ice, or be buried in an ocean of sand, and the Company would still be able to rescue me."

Victor took her arm again. She let him. "If you never incur the wrath of all-seeing Zeus, you'll be rescued. But certain persons . . . certain persons, madame, may have been careless."

She looked at him without speaking, and for a moment he thought she was going to strike him. His pulse quickened, but she turned away. The little mortal behind them looked from one to the other and frowned.

"Forgive me," said Victor.

Nan shook her head. "You were only telling the truth."

"Not always a prudent thing to do."

"And we mustn't be imprudent, must we?" Her voice shook slightly. "It's a mortal weakness."

At the word *weakness* Victor thought of Kalugin. Nan, gazing out across Rue Atlas, was thinking of something else . . .

"No, that would be weak. I wouldn't ever fall in love with anybody," eight-year-old Mendoza had announced, chinning herself on the bar. She pulled herself along and dropped into the swing next to Nan's. "Look at the stupid things mortals do when they're in love." She rolled her eyes to heaven and clasped her hands. "Ooh, darling, I can't live without you! I burn for your kiss! I die!" She threw herself backward recklessly, almost falling out of the swing. Catching herself at the last moment, she added, "Would you ever want your life to depend on somebody else's?"

"If I was really in love with somebody, it would be worth it," Nan had insisted. "People need other people. I bet you start singing a different tune when we hit puberty."

"Yuck! I bet I won't," Mendoza said, swinging faster now, punctuating each rise with "Never, never, *never*. Love! Who needs that kind of grief? Why take the risk?"

So saying, she had launched herself from the swing at the top of the next arc, hurtling into open air with outstretched arms.

Why take the risk? thought Nan bitterly. She turned now to regard Victor, standing beside her with eyes downcast, lost in equally bitter memories.

"Will you do something for me, Victor dear?"

He looked up, startled, and his gloved hands flew to his heart. "Anything, madame! What may I do?"

"Do you know the Facilitator Joseph?"

She watched as his face changed, became cautious and closed. The mortal child watched too, and decided it was time to set down the SoundBox. He stepped between them, shaking a tiny fist, and angrily told the white man he'd better not insult the *reine noir*.

The SoundBox wailed on:

> How can I tell my mother of our love?
> How can we hide from my father and my brothers?
> The world has a thousand eyes to spy on us!
> Oh, why did the Almighty make me a teenager in love?

Mexico

ON HIS LUNCH hour, Joseph strolled between the street vendor's carts of Little Kobe, looking up between the carved and gilded beams where the fish banners flew. It was a tourist trap, but a great place to get a fast bowl of rice. There was the beef bowl home-style, gray ribbons of beef on brown rice with julienned carrots, or the beef bowl Mazatlan-style, brown shreds of beef on orange rice with cubed carrots. The taste depended on what sauce you poured over it.

His present posting was unobjectionable. He was a departmental supervisor in a civic office that granted permits to archaeologists, and all the Company needed him to do was ensure that certain permit requests were granted and others refused. He was allowed to keep the weekly salary he earned (another benefit of gradual retirement), which enabled him to live in a very nice little box in a high-rise not two blocks from his office. Sticking up twenty stories, the building looked like a soda straw by comparison with the surrounding adobes. The Japanese developers couldn't seem to break themselves of the habit of conserving space, even in a country of sprawling deserts. The view from his one tiny window was fabulous, though.

Joseph finished his rice and dropped the paper bowl into a conveniently placed fusion hopper, where it vanished with a whoosh. Consulting an internal chronometer, he decided he had time to check his mail before going back for the afternoon shift. He wandered up to the nearest public terminal and stood in line, waiting patiently for his turn. Then he stepped up to the keyboard and tapped in his communication code.

Yes, he had mail. Water bill, a public service announcement about Park Beautification Week, and a letter from Morocco. Well, well.

It was encrypted, like most personal correspondence. He shunted it into his tertiary consciousness undecrypted, paid his water bill, and stepped away, relinquishing the terminal to a harried-looking little abuela with a string bag full of groceries. Hands in his coat pockets, he wandered back to his office.

At his desk he was able to decrypt the message as he busied himself with inputting a monthly report. The letter was brief:

> *Victor would prefer to speak with you privately. He feels that Regent's Park in London is a suitable location. His communication code is VdV@24Q83/09.*
> *Very best wishes,*
> *Nan D'Arraignee*

Joseph finished his report and leaned back from his keyboard, rubbing his neck. He closed his eyes and concentrated on draining the blood from his face, giving himself an unsightly pallor. A little careful work turned the skin under his eyes dark. He checked his reflection in a pocket mirror and hastily revised a little; he wanted to look sick, not dead. Then he got up and tottered into the manager's department to explain that he'd apparently eaten a bad tuna roll and needed to go home early.

His color returned to normal as he hurried down the street to his building. In his room he paused only long enough to pack an overnight bag. Back out on Calle Nakamura, he found an unoccupied public terminal. There he purchased a ticket to London for a tenth of what he'd spent the last time he went there, and sent a message to a certain bookstore in Gower Street.

Stepping away from the terminal to let two small members of a soccer team log on, Joseph spotted an electric tram trundling toward its stop. He sprinted to catch the tram, and rode standing as it took him out to the airport. He made his suborbital with ten minutes to spare, settling back in his seat as the flight attendant offered him a chlorilar pouch of green tea.

London

Forty-five minutes later Joseph stepped through the exit at London City Airport, having satisfied the customs officials that he was not a URL terrorist with a concealed explosive device. He boarded the Tube and exited at Gower Street, having shaken off the attentions of three desperates who wanted his overnight bag.

"What the hell have things come to in this country when a man has to fight for three pair of cotton socks and a shaving kit?" he growled as he strode into the small dark shop, redolent of moldy paper, where Lewis sat behind a counter.

"Oh, I'll bet there are pajamas in there, too," Lewis said. "You have no idea what flannel pajamas go for over here."

"So, hi." Joseph set down his bag. "Long time no see. I'm in town on business, and I thought I'd bunk at your place, okay?" *And I can bring you up to speed on what I've found out lately.*

"I'd love the company, though I'm afraid this isn't nearly as nice as where I was last time," Lewis said brightly. *I have rather a lot to tell you, too.*

"Hey, how bad can it be?" Joseph said, waving his hand dismissively.

"A rathole," he remarked fifteen minutes later, in Lewis's garret. "But *spacious*."

"Artistic and airy, too," suggested Lewis. "All I need are a few half-finished canvases and a bong."

"This is the kind of place the Company puts you up in nowadays?" Joseph set down his bag, looking worried.

"I've lived in worse," Lewis said, wrestling a bulky object out of a cupboard. He set it on the floor, yanked a lever, and staggered back as an air mattress self-inflated with a roar. "There, you see? I can even accommodate a guest. And we've plenty of gin. Let the good times roll."

No security techs snooping around? No fallout from that trip to Yorkshire? Joseph asked, poking doubtfully at the air mattress with his foot. It gulped in air in a last hissing spasm, like a dragon with gas, and lay quiet.

Techs? No, nothing like that. A few bad dreams now and then. Lewis reached deeper into the cupboard and pulled out a sleeping bag, which he unrolled on the mattress with a flourish. It lay there sullenly exuding a smell of British army surplus shop.

This was how it began sometimes, Joseph thought uneasily, postings that got worse and worse, jobs that got more and more pointless. Never any official acknowledgment of Dr. Zeus's displeasure, but over the great span of years the Company had to play with you, an ever-increasing number of opportunities to hang yourself, and lots of rope.

"The worst time was during the Blitz," Lewis mused. He folded back the slatted screen that closed off his bathroom, displaying the dingy porcelain delights beyond. "Those poor mortals. At least the bombs don't generally fall from the sky anymore. And look, all the hot water your heart desires, and no shillings needed. It's a vast improvement on the old days, let me tell you."

"Gin, huh?" Joseph rubbed his hands together. "Are the bootleggers any good?"

"Oh, the best," Lewis assured him. "It's all brought across the border from Scotland. Though if you'd like a cider or beer, they're still legal. There's a sandwich shop on the corner with a nice selection. I can't afford to eat there myself, but—"

"My treat," said Joseph, suppressing an urge to wring his hands. "Come on, let's go down there."

The place was small, dark, and overheated, but Lewis seemed to revel in the atmosphere.

"Gosh, this is like the old days," he said happily. In the dim light his face looked gaunt. Joseph staved off feelings of guilt by remembering that Lewis looked like a tragic poet at the best of times. He ordered most of the menu.

"You gentlemen aren't driving or operating machinery after this, I hope," said the barmaid sternly, bringing their beers.

"No fear!" Lewis toasted her, grinning. She seemed about to respond with a reluctant pleasantry when she gasped and dove for the floor, just as the sound of some heavy vehicle roaring by outside filled the room.

"Down!" Lewis yelled, and Joseph needed no urging. He found himself crouching in the darkness under the table as shots chattered in the street. There were a few screams and a lot of curses. He heard the distinctive ping and rattle of a bullet coming through a windowpane.

"Don't worry," Lewis said, sipping his beer, which he had brought under the table with him. "It's all safety glass in these places."

"Great," Joseph muttered. Three more shots followed in quick succession and broke another window, the lamp over the bar, and the holo-pinball machine in the corner. The machine didn't die quietly; it began to short out in great gouts of sparks and flame, to say nothing of low-level microwaves. The barmaid shrieked and scrambled on her hands and knees for a fire extinguisher. Joseph, who knew an opportunity when he saw one, reached into his coat pocket and switched on a tidy little device Suleyman had given him. He felt a click and a slight chill. So did Lewis, who lowered his beer and looked questioningly at Joseph.

The vehicle roared on, and now one could hear sirens screaming in pursuit. The barmaid got up and doused the fire. Grumbling, she went behind the bar for a potholder, with which she unplugged the defunct machine.

"I *knew* this bloody thing wasn't safe," she said. "Edwin! Get the tape, please."

A slender youth emerged from the kitchen and proceeded to tape brown paper over the broken windows. This seemed to be the signal for the other diners to emerge from under their tables. Within five minutes the glass had been swept up, candles had been lit at the bar, and conversation resumed as though nothing out of the ordinary had happened. Actually, nothing out of the ordinary *had* happened, except to the two immortals at the table near the door.

"I gather you've finally perfected that little device you were working on?" Lewis said, taking another sip of beer.

"Sort of," Joseph replied. "We can talk for about six hours."

"Good," Lewis said. He set down his beer. "Any new clues in our mystery?"

"I'm still following up leads." Joseph lifted his beer and drank, after scanning it cautiously for broken glass.

"I've continued sleuthing too," said Lewis. "You remember our friend Edward Alton Bell-Fairfax?"

Joseph grimaced and set down his beer. "That guy. Lewis, he's even deader now than he was when you found his picture. What's the point of investigating *him?*"

"I've learned several positively fascinating things," said Lewis. At this point the barmaid brought their orders: chips and beans, vegemite sandwiches, and spaghetti carbonara made with SoyHam bits.

"I'm not really interested in him, Lewis," Joseph said, looking around vainly for salt for his chips. He settled for vinegar.

"He's part of a bigger picture. Tell me, wouldn't you be interested in finding out how Edward—after being as good as court-martialed—gained entrance to one of the more exclusive clubs in London? And to an even more exclusive secret society whose origins are lost in the mists of time?"

"You're going to tell me he was a Freemason, right?" Joseph said, splashing vinegar all over his plate.

"Ever hear of the Gentlemen's Speculative Society?"

Joseph shoveled in a mouthful of chips. "Sounds like something that meets at a grange hall."

Lewis pointed with his fork. "Nowadays they call themselves the Kronos Diversified Stock Company."

Joseph choked slightly. "That's a Company DBA," he said when he had his breath back.

"Precisely," Lewis said. "And it means that the Company doesn't begin in 2318, as we've always been told, but much earlier. When that bunch of twenty-fourth-century technocrats get together and incorporate under the Dr. Zeus logo, they'll just be taking a new name. I'm beginning to suspect they're not even responsible for the technology that created us."

"They will invent pineal tribrantine three, though," Joseph said. "I've talked to the guy who came up with that. An idiot savant mortal by the name of Bugleg."

"Really? Well, I'm positive they didn't invent the time transcendence field on their own. Almost the first thing the Company did was guarantee its own existence by setting up a temporal paradox and stationing operatives throughout time in this one secret society. It's been based in Britain, almost from the beginning; though there's some indication that it was relocated before recorded history began from what is now Egypt. Tell me, did you ever go by the name Imhotep?"

Joseph jumped as though he'd been shot.

"Ha! Well, somebody using that name passed a few Company secrets to a progressive-minded group of priests, and carefully guided what use they made of the material. You might have been part of it without even being aware. And Edward Alton Bell-Fairfax was closely connected with the Victorian group, the Gentlemen's Speculative Society." Lewis pushed aside the empty plate that had contained the spaghetti and started on the beans and chips.

Joseph gulped down half his beer. "I guess you have proof."

"This time a month ago I had nothing more than inferences and conjectures—a few suspicious coincidences, one or two blatant clues. Evidence that the Company had closely monitored the progress through life of our friend the young naval officer, but no reason why." Lewis speared three chips on his fork and nibbled them delicately. "Ah, but then!"

"What?"

"I was able to break into the files of a long-defunct department of the British Foreign Office." Lewis grinned at him. "Doing semi-public business as the Imperial Export Company of London."

"Oh, for Christ's sake. Like in the James Bond books? Lewis—"

"No, no, that was Universal Export. You really ought to read something besides Raymond Chandler, you know. Anyway, need I tell you that the gentlemen involved in Imperial Export were all members of the same London club *and* the same secret fraternity? And that one of them was a retired naval officer by the name of Edward Alton Bell-Fairfax?" Lewis leaned across the table and spoke in a lower voice. "I found his dossier, Joseph. You wouldn't believe the things he did for Queen and country."

"I'll bet I would."

"A lot of them weren't very nice," Lewis admitted. "But he was awfully good at his job. Something of a problem solver, you see? Until he disappeared on his last job, in California, in 1863."

Joseph put down his sandwich. "Does this place sell hot chocolate?"

"Yes, but you're going to want to hear this first."

"I don't want to hear what he did to Mendoza."

"Listen, Joseph. There was a full-scale expedition to California, supposedly under the auspices of the Foreign Office but spearheaded by the Gentlemen's Speculative Society. The object was to secure Santa Catalina Island for Great Britain."

Joseph stared. "The place the chewing-gum guy owned? With the Avalon Ballroom? And the hotel where—"

"Where you thought you saw Mendoza, yes." Lewis leaned back and steepled his fingers like Sherlock Holmes. "And oh, Joseph, the things I've found out about Santa Catalina Island! Were you aware the Company maintains a steady presence there, in fact has quite a few research facilities and other involvements? And do you know why the Company remains interested in the place?"

"Because it's a safe zone, like Switzerland and Canada, where nothing ever happens," Joseph said.

Lewis shook his head. "It's a safe zone because the Company has made it so, Joseph. The gentlemen desperately wanted something that was thought to be located on that island!"

"What?"

"I haven't found that out yet," said Lewis. "The records keep referring to something called Document D. It was discovered in the Royal Archives by a highly placed member of the Gentlemen's Speculative Society who had security clearance—and who was nudged in the direction of his 'discovery' by one of our operatives. And promptly thereafter they sent their covert invasion force."

"But the Brits never invaded Catalina," Joseph objected. "Hell, they never even tried."

"As a matter of fact, they did try." Lewis took up his fork again and began to finish off his chips and beans. "It's quite a story, once you track down all the details. They set up a base camp on the island, in 1862. Though the expedition found what they'd been searching for, apparently the Yanks twigged to something and prevented them from taking it away.

"But the Gentlemen persisted. After the war they came back, they bought mining rights, and they kept trying to purchase the island itself. They were never able to buy it; but they do seem to have finally made off with the mysterious object."

"This is Indiana Jones stuff, Lewis," said Joseph wearily.

"And just how much do you know about the Ark of the Covenant, may I ask?" Lewis retorted.

"I forget. Barmaid?" Joseph waved. "Could we get a couple of hot chocolates over here, please? Thanks, sweetheart."

"What got the Yanks suspicious by 1863 was a breach of security, some inexperienced political who was caught, and talked. He'd left a valise containing incriminating evidence in a stagecoach inn in Los Angeles," Lewis continued.

Joseph groaned. "The one where Mendoza was stuck between postings."

"And Edward was sent to retrieve the valise, and this is where he disappears from history," Lewis said. "I could probably find out more if I were able to get into the Yanks' classified archives, and perhaps after the war I shall. The British Foreign Office never knew what happened to Edward, although the Yanks evidently never got hold of the valise. There's a confused report of a mystery ship that moored off the island near the British base there, where some sort of massacre evidently took place. Then the ship disappeared before they could investigate further.

"They kept Edward's file open for years before they declared him missing, presumed deceased. He had a reputation for surviving sticky situations. Of course, they didn't know what we know."

"That he dragged Mendoza into whatever trouble he was in," said Joseph hoarsely. "That the Pinkerton agents blew him away right in front of her eyes, and she went nuts and killed them. And the Company stepped in and mopped up so the mortals would never find out about her."

"Or about *him!*" Lewis said. "Hasn't the import of all this sunk in on you? The Company wanted Edward mopped up after too. He was on Company business when he died. Mendoza was helping him. In fact—" He halted before he could blurt out what had just occurred to him.

The barmaid, coming to their table, looked in concern at the American gentleman who'd ordered the hot chocolate. "Here, is he all right? Shall I call a medic?" she asked his friend.

The American lifted his head and gave his friend a look that quite unnerved the barmaid, who (as should be evident by now) did not unnerve easily. Without waiting for a reply, she set down the chocolate, murmured something polite, and scuttled away to the safety of the kitchen.

"They set her up," said Joseph through his teeth.

"I—I suppose."

"They left her there deliberately so she'd meet him. They knew it would happen! She helped him get rid of the evidence. If she hadn't, the Yanks would have found out about what the British were looking for and grabbed it for themselves, and maybe then there would never have been any Dr. Zeus Incorporated."

"And then the Company arrested her and put her away," said Lewis in a ghost of a voice, "but not because she'd gone AWOL. Not even because she killed those mortals. A Crome generator who has the ability to go forward through time could find out what happens when the Silence falls in 2355 and—"

"Lewis, don't go there. Okay? Not another word about that, if you value my life, let alone your own," said Joseph quickly. He noticed the chocolate and grabbed for it. "But that wraps up a whole bunch of problems for them, like what do they do with an operative who's a Crome generator when the Company says there aren't any. Thanks,

Mendoza, for helping us get started, and here's your one-way ticket to two million years ago."

Lewis sat silent, horrified. He looked down at the last piece of his sandwich and set it carefully on his plate, as though it might explode.

"Great Caesar's Ghost. And Edward—"

"Edward was their goddam bait to snare her!"

"But, don't you see? He was set up too," Lewis said. "I've traced his whole life—the Company groomed him for the work they wanted him to do. From the time he was at school. Our people were there monitoring him, Joseph, I've seen the proof. The Company wanted a man who'd be willing to die for a cause, a man with no family, a man who could disappear. He was a member of the Gentlemen, he knew their secrets and must have believed in their work. He was their operative!"

"You don't have to tell me any more about the guy." Joseph drank down his hot chocolate and made a face. "What is this made with, soy milk?"

"How can you just sit there?" Lewis demanded, his voice shaking. "Knowing what the Company did to Mendoza!"

"Yeah, soy milk, all right," said Joseph woodenly. "Who am I going to jump up and kill, Lewis? I never got a shot at Edward Alton Bell-Fairfax."

Regent's Park

THE TREES WERE still there, and so was Queen Mary's Garden; but its lawns hadn't been mown in years, so most of the park was hip-high weedy wilderness and young woodland. There were stories that tigers had been released into it when the London Zoo was closed down, and lurked in the tall grass even now, leaping out to eat the occasional homeless person. It wasn't true, of course. The tigers had been dutifully flown to Asia and released into a preserve there, where they were promptly shot by poachers.

There had been a movement to box up the swans and ship them off to wherever it was swans hailed from originally, but no one was really sure that swans didn't belong in that part of the world, and anyway they were free to go if they wanted to. It was pointed out, moreover, that the act of catching them even for the purpose of repatriation would be a violation of their civil rights. There the matter rested.

So one could still stand in the middle of the footbridge and watch the swans gliding to and fro where there was open water, and this is what Joseph and Lewis were doing as they waited for Victor. That, and arguing.

No, I've known Victor for years, Lewis insisted. *He was at New World One for nearly a century when I was there, don't you remember? He did the most wickedly funny imitation of Director General Houbert. Before that I think he was based in Europe, at least I recall seeing him once at EuroBase One—*

He broke off with an odd expression on his face.

I did see him there, he went on. *But that was right after I—*

Lewis, this is not a social visit, said Joseph. *You may be old pals, but he won't be expecting to see both of us. He may not feel like talking to me at all, if he sees you here. Not to be rude or anything, but—*

All right, I'll go poke around in the ruins of the mosque. I know when I'm not wanted. Lewis pulled his coat about himself and stalked away into the jungle that grew along the Outer Circle.

Joseph watched him go and sighed. Almost at once he was aware of another immortal approaching from the opposite direction, and turned on his heel to see Victor staring after Lewis with an expression of dismay.

"It's Victor, isn't it?" Joseph bustled up to him and extended a hand.

After a moment's hesitation Victor shook his hand, without removing the gloves he wore. "Wasn't that Lewis? The literature fellow?" he asked.

"Uh—yeah." Joseph cursed silently. "That's right, you would have seen each other at New World One, wouldn't you? Small world. He'll be sorry he missed you."

Victor shrugged. "We were slightly acquainted." *I agreed to talk to you alone.*

We're alone now. Joseph surveyed Victor. He looked thin and pale, as everyone did in London; but he was considerably better dressed than most, in smartly tailored clothes that had come from somewhere expensive on the Continent. "Some coincidence, huh?" Joseph said.

"Quite," replied Victor coldly. *I understand you have questions about something that happened in San Francisco. Why do you need to know?*

I'm looking for somebody who disappeared. You recruited a Musicologist named Donal there, yes? From the 1906 earthquake?

Victor's eyes narrowed and became, if such a thing were possible, colder. He glanced elaborately at his chronometer. "Heavens, look at the time. I'd love to stay and chat, but—"

Wait. I need to know—because your kid barely remembers it. Who did you rescue him from? Was it Budu? "Can I ask you a favor, first? Do you know of any snack stands around here? I'd kill for a Mars Bar right about now."

Victor stood for a moment, apparently lost in thought. "You know, I believe there is one here? Or was. I think it's over this way. I wouldn't mind a Mars Bar myself, now that you mention it."

He turned and started off along the trail, and Joseph hurried after him, thinking that Victor had changed. He'd noticed a similar alteration in some operatives and had assumed it had something to do with being out in the field too long. Certain lines of strain around the eyes, a certain indefinable sense of shadow.

You were one of Budu's recruits, weren't you? Victor asked warily.

Yeah. Though I understand he went crazy or something. Look, let me set your mind at rest. All I want to know is if the old guy is all right. Did they finally bring him in? Did the Company repair him? This is kind of a filial duty thing for me. It just breaks my heart to think of him roaming around damaged on his own somewhere, lost—

Spare me, please.

Where is he?

I was his recruit, too, as it happens.

Joseph halted at that, and pretended to have trouble with a shoelace. "Hang on a second, something's caught my shoe. Say, there aren't any tigers roaming around here, are there? That's just one of those urban legends, right?" *Really?*

"Of course. There are no tigers." *Yes. And, since we both know the sort of creature he was, why don't you drop the pretense of filial love?*

But I did love him, protested Joseph. *He was a hero. I'll admit I've heard stories, and maybe they're true—but he must have gone nuts. Was that him in San Francisco, in 1906?* He straightened up. "Okay, lead on."

Victor turned and walked. *He was there, the night before the earthquake.*

You saw him? He talked to you? Donal seemed to think there was a fight of some kind. That's absurd, though, because nobody fights with Budu and wins. He was damaged, right?

He was damaged.

And so obviously you got Donal away from him, and Dr. Zeus was able to get Budu back, and he's okay now.

No, Joseph.

No, Dr. Zeus didn't get him back, or no, he's not okay?

Both. "Oh, dear," said Victor. "This doesn't look promising." The refreshment pavilion loomed ahead of them; boarded up and in an advanced state of disuse.

"Damn! Can we go up close and see? Maybe they're just closed for lunch," said Joseph. *Please tell me. Was he arrested?*

No, Joseph, he wasn't.

He got away?

No, he didn't.

For Christ's sake, what then?

They made a slow circle around the refreshment pavilion, trying all the doors, before Victor replied. *I can tell you where to look for him. You understand this is classified?*

Please.

"No, I'm afraid we're out of luck, old boy," said Victor. *He's in Chinatown. On Sacramento Street, about a block up from Waverly Place.* "You might try the newsagent's in Marylebone Road. *And if you should find him at home—pray tell him that Victor sends his sincerest regrets.*

Regrets? Is that sarcasm?

No. I never loved him, and he knows it, but I'm ashamed of what I did there. Tell him that. I had no idea what would happen. I've since taken steps to make sure that it won't happen again. Victor wrung his gloved hands briefly. "And now, if you'll excuse me? I really must run."

He strode off in the direction of Chester Road.

Joseph stood staring after him, openmouthed. Finally he shivered and looked around him at the abandoned pavilion and the high weeds, uncertain whether he heard a low staccato growl, caught a glimpse of striped flank. He set off for the Outer Circle, making his way along the overgrown path in some haste.

So, what did he have to say? transmitted Latif, emerging from the trees behind him and pacing after in silence. Joseph started violently but managed to avoid looking around.

Give a guy some warning! How long have you been there?

Before either of you.

What do you have, some kind of masking field?

Right, like you need to know. Want to tell me what Victor said so I can get the hell out of here and back to a civilized country? One that's not so cold, anyway.

Joseph turned along a loop of trail and wandered aimlessly, kicking at fragments of bombed wreckage. *It was pretty cryptic. He doesn't think much of Budu either. But it sounded like Budu's out of the picture, some way or other.*

Did Victor know where he is? Did he tell you?

Sort of.

Joseph heard the exhalation of impatience. *Are you going to tell me?*

I'd kind of like to see for myself first. Can you cut me that much slack? I'll let you know everything once I've got the truth. If it's something really bad—I'd rather it was me found him. He recruited me. How would you feel if it was Suleyman?

Suleyman wouldn't go that way.

I never thought Budu would, kid.

Okay. As soon as you know anything, though, you send us word. Suleyman says he told you how to get in touch with him.

He did, and I will. Trust me.

He also said you were right about something.

What?

We reviewed all the information we've collected on Budu. There isn't anything after 1906. No sightings, no intercepted messages, no evidence he was running the Plague Club after that time. All the evidence indicates Facilitator General Labienus stepped into his place immediately after Budu dropped out of sight.

That guy. Joseph shivered.

You know him?

Cold-hearted SOB. I've had to work with Labienus a couple of times. Never liked him.

He taught me. I can't say I'm surprised he'd be part of this cabal. The man's ruthless.

He is. So, why don't you set your machine on him?

We already have.

Well, that's nice to know. Joseph picked his way to the Outer Circle and stood looking across at the ruins of the London Mosque. Lewis, wandering in the rubble, had picked up a piece of old inscribed tile and was studying it, head cocked to one side.

That's Lewis, isn't it? The guy who used to run Guest Services at New World One? transmitted Latif.

That's him. Do you remember that New Years' ball, when you were tiny? You came and sat at the table with us, and he was there too.

Of course I remember. You and Lewis and that lady, the Botanist, Mendoza.

The Botanist Mendoza. Yeah.

Do you remember what she said that night? Something about how the four of us would probably never find ourselves together in the same place again? But here we are, you and Lewis and I. Almost all of us.

Almost.

Joseph in the Darkness

IT WAS LIKE—like I set out to find just the pieces of the puzzle with blue sky, but somehow I kept reaching into the box and coming up with bits with fishing boats, rooftops, and elephants. Details I didn't want or need, and the growing feeling that the picture I was going to see when they were all assembled wouldn't be the nice simple scene I'd expected.

What had I learned so far?

A lot, actually. I knew that my old heroes the Enforcers had been double-crossed, were stashed away indefinitely, along with some of the Preservers.

I knew that Mendoza's fall from grace had been engineered, that the Company had used her for its purposes and thrown her away.

I knew that the goddam tall Englishman was connected with the Company somehow, that he'd been used and thrown away too, and I didn't really want to think about the implications of that. I should have, though.

I knew that the Company was a lot older than it said it was, and it didn't want that fact known. I knew it had lied about other stuff, like our being unable to travel forward through time—though maybe that wasn't exactly a lie. Maybe only Mendoza had ever managed that.

I knew that the Company had found something it wanted really badly on Catalina Island, something for which it was willing to sac-rifice people.

I found out that there are at least three groups competing for power within the Company: the people officially in charge, who are probably Old Ones, like Nennius, who pull the strings of our mortal masters; the Plague Club, who favor biological warfare against humanity, and who may have been started by you, father; and Suleyman's people, who are working against the Plague Club. Hell, you could probably count a fourth faction if you throw in the mortal masters themselves. If they have any brains at all, they must have some plot in the works to take their immortals out.

So who gave the orders to put Mendoza in harm's way? Who put away the Enforcers? Who the hell thought it would be funny to resurrect Nicholas Harpole Edward Alton Whatever-His-Name-Was and use him as a mortal Company operative? And how did they do that?

Why should the Company hide the fact of its origins from its own operatives?

And who was Victor working for, and where the hell were *you*, father? Were you masterminding a really evil bunch of people from a subterranean lair in Chinatown? Or were you living there in quiet gradual retirement, a victim of slander? How did you manage to disable your datalink?

Every time I thought I'd found an answer to something, it turned out to be a fistful of questions instead, and they were multiplying geometrically. Lewis was no help, plunging ahead with more enthusiasm than good sense, like a man digging for treasure and tossing sand into the hole somebody else was digging, completely unaware that a tidal wave was coming in . . .

So I left his chilly little garret and flew back to my cozy little box in Mazatlan, and tried to push everything to the back of my mind in the hopes it would straighten itself out.

My plan was, I'd go looking for you next. Eventually. I wanted to hear the story from your mouth. I knew if push came to shove, I'd have to side with Suleyman's people. But maybe he was mistaken about you. I hoped like hell he was.

Though Suleyman is almost never mistaken, about anything.

But I had to wait and let a good amount of time go by before I took any spur-of-the moment vacation weekends to San Francisco. The Second American Civil War was just about to start, and Company personnel were quietly getting the hell out of the States. Even without benefit of the Temporal Concordance, we all knew the Yanks were headed for trouble.

I guess the main difficulty was that their founding fathers never did really solve the problem of E Pluribus Unum back when they put their constitution together, in that locked room with the press kept firmly away so the American people wouldn't know what they were doing. Small wonder the succeeding generations of government felt they weren't accountable to the public; things had been done that way from the beginning, hadn't they?

Eventually, though, the public had enough. Everybody knew the government lied to the people. It lied about assassination conspiracies, unidentified flying objects, unpopular wars. So the powder and fuse of resentment were ready and waiting for the spark.

It went off in 2150. The West had fallen on hard times. Industries shut down or moved east. There were plagues. There were earthquakes and floods. The government made things worse by closing down the military bases. Dumb move, as it turned out.

You know your history, you know what happens when people think they have nothing to lose but their chains. A handful of cranks with a lot of guns took the California state capitol building and read an antifederalist manifesto. They were in the right place at the right time and hit the right nerve. Suddenly California was seceding from the Union. Nobody was surprised when Montana and Utah seceded too, but then Nevada went, and Colorado. What really tore it was when Texas joined the secessionists, because Texas had money and an intact infrastructure.

Within hours, most of the other western states had declared, and the South woke up in astonishment and jumped on the wagon too. Everything was happening so fast, and everyone was so confused, there might have been a real shooting war, with bombers and disrupter rifles this time, if the earthquake hadn't hit.

It was estimated at a ten on the Richter scale, and it hit the Eastern seaboard. The last time that happened, in the middle of the nineteenth century, the Mississippi river ran backward for three days.

It did it this time, too. New York was destroyed, Washington DC was destroyed, any place with highrise buildings and a dense urban population was destroyed. Millions of people died. The remaining United States found themselves with no way to refuse the secessionists.

Funny thing happened, though. The Americans were aghast at what had happened, abruptly aware of how vulnerable they were. Hurried meetings were held among the survivors. A loose federation was patched together, all parties agreeing to disagree.

The result was a bloc composed of most of the northeastern states, a bloc of southern and central states, an independent Republic of Texas, and a handful of Native American nations. The Mormon Church got Utah. Canada debated whether to accept the few bordering strays who petitioned for admittance. California fragmented into about five little independent republics. Hawaii set up a constitutional monarchy, since it had thoughtfully kept its royals. All parties retired to lick their wounds and burn their dead.

And that was it. You couldn't really call it a war, because Mother Nature was the only one who did the fighting; but Second Civil War sounds good in the history books. A lot of wealthy Asian and European countries looked thoughtfully at the mess and wondered what might be grabbed. Things might have gone badly for the Yanks if some guy in the American Community hadn't discovered—or, rather, rediscovered—antigravity.

What a joke! Antigravity proved to operate on a principle so moronically simple, most scientists refused to acknowledge it at first out of sheer embarrassment, except for a few rogue Egyptologists who laughed and laughed. The American Community had the sense to see it had been dealt a trump card, though. Cash flowed into the renascent union, and the old experiment of government of the people, by the people, for the people was back up and running. With all their politicians buried under tons of rubble, they just maybe had a chance this time.

It's easy to rebuild after an earthquake when you have antigravity to help you, and Megalith Nouveau became the next hot architectural style. The Yanks became the world's first manufacturer of the antigravity car, after having been the only holdouts in the world who were still stubbornly making internal combustion engines.

You can zip all over the known landscape in an agcar, you can even take them across water on a still day, they use almost no power and are a whole lot cheaper to make than electric cars. Everyone in the world wanted antigravity technology. The Yanks made a fortune selling the secret, until other nations figured out how simple it was.

Just as people were congratulating themselves on things returning to normal, the plagues broke out again—in China and India this time. Millions more died. Labienus's work, I guess. And then a good-sized earthquake hit England, of all places, and took out a lot of highrise London. That was in 2198.

The Brits rebuilt with antigravity technology. By the year 2205 London was back in business, though there were a lot fewer people. At least the last of the terrorists seemed to have been killed in the earthquake. England had enough of chaos: it reinvented its peerage and gave ruling power to a house of lords, hereditary bureaucrats who promptly formed social committees and tidied up everything. Europe went pretty much the same way: the Hapsburgs (talk about comebacks) emerged from the woodwork and made the antigravity trams run on time, and people were only too glad to let them.

In a way it was the post-holocaust world people had been expecting since the atomic age: old familiar institutions gone, humanity scarce on the ground and returning to feudalism. Instead of grinning leather-clad bandit punks, though, corporate functionaries were the rulers. People clustered together in smaller communities, linked online, and held tight to their comforts. Technological innovation stopped dead after antigravity. We had the global village at last and, surprise, a village was exactly what it was. With a shared culture, mortals became more provincial, not less.

The world looked inward, not ahead, and history-reenactment clubs became more popular than they had ever been. Even the people going out to Luna carried historical clichés with them, proud to be pioneers seeking Lebensraum. The future was looking more and more like the past, especially to anybody who watched Rome's long slow slide into night.

Oh, and Japan kept sinking. They had one earthquake after another, though none of them did much damage anymore, because most of the Japanese had relocated to Mexico. By 2205 about all that was left above sea level was Mount Fuji, and downtown Mazatlan was really crowded at lunch hour. By that time I was glad to be working again in Spain, which had changed beyond recognition in some ways and not at all in others.

Just like everything else.

London, 2225

Lᴇᴡɪꜱ ᴄʜᴇᴄᴋᴇᴅ ʜɪꜱ internal chronometer and wondered whether he ought to finish up lunch. It didn't really matter whether he took one hour or three, because almost nobody ever came into the Historic Books Annex of the London Metropolitan Library. Some days he never saw a single patron. It wasn't surprising; anything that anyone in this day and age might conceivably wish to read was long since online. In fact, *historic* books were the only kind that existed anymore, as nobody had printed on paper in decades.

The fact that the entrance to the annex was on a dark little side street made traffic less likely still. Lewis reflected that he might have indulged in a seven-course meal with brandy and cigars, if he'd wanted to (and if such things still existed); the chances of seeing a mortal before closing time were one in a hundred.

On the Buke screen at his desk a little animated figure of Edward Alton Bell-Fairfax stalked up and down on the quarterdeck of a nineteenth-century warship. The sea pitched and rolled most realistically, and about every seventh wave a seagull would swoop across the upper right-hand corner of the scene. It had taken Lewis months to program, getting all the details right, and he was rather proud of it. He no longer kept the daguerreotype on display—it was fabulously antique now—but he liked being able to see Edward.

Lewis leaned back in his chair and picked again at the mixed green salad, wondering sadly how a country so thoroughly vegan as Britain had gone could somehow fail to produce decent lettuce. He peered at what might have been a wholemeal crouton or a piece of romaine and gave up in disgust, tossing the catering box into the dustbin. No matter. He'd skip over to Paris this weekend and treat himself. He could afford to do such things nowadays. The gold letters on the inner door read LEWIS MARCH, CHIEF CURATOR.

Yes, the wheel of Fortune had turned; now he had a nice modern house in one of the New Parks that had been created on the site of the former high-rise district. Plenty of central heating and plumbing, all the sunlight London ever offered, and something else that hadn't used to be available at all in an urban area: fresh air. His present assignment—buying old books for the library and smoothly making off with the rare ones Dr. Zeus wanted—was unbelievably dull, but it left him a lot of time for his private research. Lewis didn't mind gradual retirement much.

He had been quietly monitoring the present-day activities of the Kronos Diversified Stock Company, and had noted that two of his fellow immortals sat on its board of directors. He had also hacked into the American classified archives—as he had suspected, this became a great deal easier after the war—and was able to confirm a great many details of the 1863 incident, including the unsolved disappearance of six Pinkerton agents. There was no record of any capture of a British agent, however, or even of one being shot while trying to escape, and nothing about any woman that might have been Mendoza.

The nightmares marched on relentlessly. He dreamed, often, about a sixth-century monk with the sort of sideways tonsure the Irish had defiantly worn. A big man, bearded, with ink on his hands. Lewis almost knew the mortal's name. He didn't want to.

It wasn't that he was afraid of the mortal—the man seemed quite nice, in fact he was trying to remind Lewis of something—but Lewis invariably woke in a cold sweat just as the man was about to tell him what it was.

He brushed away the crumbs of his lunch, standing up to be certain he hadn't got salad oil on his beautifully pressed trousers. No, all tidy. Satisfied, he settled down and cleared the screen for the personal project he was working on, his secret indulgence. He opened it and reviewed what he'd written that morning, frowning thoughtfully.

> Lieutenant Dumfries saluted and said nervously, "But, Commander, how are we to penetrate the mangrove swamps against the tide? There's not a breath of wind to fill the longboat's sails!"
> By way of answer Edward drew his cutlass and vaulted ashore, where a few brief efficient chops at a stand of bamboo produced three serviceable poles, each some eight feet in length when trimmed.

"Were you never at Cambridge, man?" he snapped.
"Pretend the damned thing's a punt. Now, gentlemen, step
lively! We've got a good deal of this damned swamp to
cross if we're to rendezvous with Jenkins's men before
Señor Delarosa and King Dalba—

Before they what? Lewis ran a hand through his limp hair, sighing
in frustration. What exactly was the point of the rendezvous? And did
bamboo grow in Africa? And wouldn't it be faster for them to sail
across the lagoon rather than work their way through the swamp? And
how had King Dalba met up with Señor Delarosa again so quickly?

Lewis wrote a few more lines and then stopped, realizing he hadn't
mentioned Edward's vaulting back *into* the boat before it pushed off.
He was busy deleting when the outer door opened, and Edward had
just leaped athletically onto the gunwale (a move that would almost
certainly have landed the heroic young commander in four feet of
swamp) when the inner door opened. Someone came to the counter
and stood there.

Lewis turned in his chair. "May I help you—?" was as far as he
got before he choked and levitated out of the chair so quickly, he
knocked it over. He stood behind it, shaking. The nightmares were
coming again, he could hear them baying for his blood in the distance.
His visitor did not seem to have noticed the accident.

"I have to use a terminal," said the visitor.

Lewis scanned, controlling himself. Nothing to be afraid of after
all. His visitor was only a mortal, rather a small one with some kind
of developmental disability. Male, about thirty-five, badly dressed,
with big weak-looking dark eyes that reminded Lewis of a rabbit's.
Pasty complexion. Big-domed oddly shaped head with an extremely
receding hairline. He was carrying a string bag containing a sipper
bottle of water and an orange.

"Er, sorry about that," Lewis giggled in embarrassment. "I'm a
little jumpy today. What are you looking for, Mr.—?"

"I have to use a terminal," repeated his visitor in a drippy little
voice.

Lewis walked out into the main reading room and pointed to the
closest bank of terminals. "Here you are. Please let me know if you
need any—" But the visitor had already marched past him, sat down,
and begun to type away with blinding speed. Lewis retreated behind
the counter gladly enough.

"I'll just continue my research, then, shall I?" he said, for no reason he could think of. The visitor ignored him. The rattling of keys in the echoing room sounded like a hailstorm.

Lewis sat down again, attempting to return his attention to the adventures of Commander Bell-Fairfax. What part of a boat was a gunwale anyway? And should it be cane instead of bamboo Edward cut for the poles? Mendoza could have told him . . .

He was accessing internal datafiles for his answers when the pattering of keys stopped. Lewis felt the hair rise on the back of his neck and turned in his chair to see the visitor advancing on him. What was so familiar about the creature?

"That terminal doesn't work," said the man.

"Oh, dear," Lewis said. "What are you trying to locate? Perhaps I can—"

"I need to call home," said the man, staring at him.

"Oh, I see, you need a public terminal," Lewis said. "I'm so sorry for the misunderstanding. None of these are linked to a public line, I'm afraid. They're for accessing information in the archives."

"Oh," said the visitor.

"Yes," said Lewis.

"Got any Nasowipes?"

Lewis pulled out a handful of tissues and thrust them at the visitor, who accepted them without a word, turned, and went back into the reading room. Lewis leaned over the counter, staring after him.

"But don't you want to—?" The visitor gave no sign of hearing him. Lewis shrugged and went back to his Buke. After a moment of staring at the last line, wherein Commander Bell-Fairfax had just rescued a frantic British tar who'd fallen into leech-infested water, Lewis adjusted his chair and console pullout so he was no longer sitting with his back to the reading room.

"Please, Commander, get 'em off me!" begged Johnson desperately.

"Courage, man." Coolly, Edward lit up a long cheroot. "This is likely to be a bit unpleasant. Close your eyes." The other sailors looked on in horror as Edward, having produced a red and glowing ember on the end of his cigar, reached down with his fine hand and applied it carefully to the horrible

"Got any paper clips?" the visitor asked, appearing at Lewis's elbow like a ghost. Lewis restrained himself from levitating again and groped in a pigeonhole of the desk. He found a handful of paper clips and offered them to the man.

The man took them, turned, and headed back to the reading room. Lewis looked after him, wiping his hand on his coat lapel unconsciously. The man's hand had been long, thin, and clammy.

Lewis revised:

applied it carefully to the disgusting

"Any magnedots?" asked the visitor. Lewis yanked open the drawer where he kept file labels and fished out a strip of magnedots for him. The visitor took them without a word and trudged away. Lewis sat jittering a moment before he resumed:

applied it carefully to the loathsome, blood-engorged

The street door was opening. Two mortals came hurriedly toward him, a man and a woman, passing through the inner door. They wore uniforms and were radiating alarm.

"Excuse me, please," said the young woman. "We're looking for a little man."

"Ah," said Lewis.

"We're from the Neasden Adult Residential Facility," said her companion. "We were taking our guests on an outing to the library, and Mr. Fancod seems to have wandered off. He's about five feet tall—"

"Mr. Fancod!" exclaimed the young woman, catching sight of the visitor through the reading room arch. "How clever of you to find your way in here. Come along now, dear, your friends are very worried about you." She rushed into the reading room, closely followed by her associate.

"I have to call home," said Mr. Fancod.

"Oh, but we're going home, Mr. Fancod," the man assured him.

"I'm not finished yet."

"Well, I'm afraid we really must ask you to come along anyhow . . ."

"Ask the cyborg if he has any raisins."

Cyborg? Lewis sat perfectly still, heart pounding. He heard the male attendant stifling a chuckle. "Now then, Mr. Fancod, I think it's time you stopped having fun with us. If you'll come along now, we'll stop at Prashant's, and you can buy more raisins."

"Okay," said Mr. Fancod, and Lewis heard them coming out of the reading room. He glanced up cautiously. The two mortals were making apologetic faces at him. Mr. Fancod, following them obediently, had taken out his orange and was peeling it as they went along, staring at it in utter absorption. He dropped pieces of peel on the floor as he walked.

Gnawing on his lower lip, Lewis watched them go. He looked down at his Buke and typed in:

applied it carefully to one of the loathsome, blood-engorged??????

He saved the document and closed the Buke. Rising, he got a tissue and carefully collected all the discarded orange peel. He tossed it in the dustbin. Wiping his hands, he ventured into the reading room to see if all was well.

It wasn't.

All the consoles, except the nearest one, bore a cheery greeting above the logo and menu for the London Metropolitan Library. That was normal. What wasn't normal was the black screen on the nearest console, crossed from top to bottom in something that resembled binary code but wasn't quite. Lewis approached it reluctantly and stood looking down at the screen. He reached out at arm's length and gave the command key a tentative tap.

The inexplicable code went away and was replaced by a menu. It said:

DR. ZEUS COMMUNICATION REQUEST
INITIALIZE
INITIAL REPLY
MEMO
DEPARTMENT METHODICAL
LEFT MODE
ENTER PERSONAL NOW:

His eyes went very wide. He looked over his shoulder and looked back at the screen. He leaned forward and examined the console. It was a moment before he found the small panel that had been broken out at one side, and the little alteration sticking out of it, made of paper clips and magnedots.

He looked around the room once more before crawling quickly underneath the seat recess to unplug the console. He found an OUT OF ORDER sign and spread it across the screen before scurrying back to his desk.

Opening his Buke again, he linked up with the Greater London

Communication Listings and entered a search request for the name FANCOD.

There was only one. Thurwood Fancod, care of Neasden Adult Residential Facility. Registered challenged adult. Employed: Self-Reliance In-Home Data Entry Program. Sponsor: Jovian Integrated Systems.

Jovian Integrated Systems was one of the holding companies for Dr. Zeus Incorporated.

Lewis leaned back. "Oh dear," he murmured. He exited the listings and swiveled in his chair, this way and that like a compass needle seeking true north. He closed his eyes to concentrate more deeply and at last found the frequency he sought.

Xenophon? Literature Specialist Lewis requesting reception.

Xenophon receiving, came the reply.

There seems to have been a security breach of some kind. My cover's been compromised.

Specify.

A mortal named Thurwood Fancod has access to material quite a bit beyond my need to know.

Xenophon swore electronically. *Details?*

He identified me as a cyborg in front of two other mortals. They didn't take him seriously, but he knew. And . . . he modified one of the library terminals to hack into a Dr. Zeus database. Seems to have been going after something classified.

Damn!

Should I run?

Yes, you'd better. We'll send a team over right away to confiscate the modified unit and replace it. I suppose somebody had better deal with Fancod, too. Where can we reach you?

Lewis gave him a set of coordinates.

Very good. Your new assignment and paperwork will be forwarded to you at that address on 7 March. Ave, Lewis.

Ave.

Sighing, Lewis got up and slipped his Buke into its case. He made a quick search through his desk drawers for any personal items he might want. There were none. He pulled on his coat, stowed the Buke case in an inner pocket, and took one last wistful look at his name in its gold lettering before walking out.

In the morning someone with unquestionable credentials as his next of kin would tearfully notify the library of an accident, or sudden death, or some terrible emergency. Shortly thereafter a person with splendid references would be perfectly positioned for promotion to the position of chief curator, and the space Lewis March had left in the world would vanish like a footprint in sand. It was standard operating procedure for a security breach, and he'd been warned that this sort of thing might begin to occur more frequently as he got closer to the Company's end of time.

He caught an antigravity transport at the corner and rode the short distance to his house, where he packed a suitcase with his shaving bag and a change of clothes. Just before closing it, he went to a cabinet and took out a little bubblewrap package containing the old daguerreotype of Edward, nesting it between two shirts.

Lewis carried his suitcase down to the front hall and paused again, looking around at the comfortable rooms, the entertainment center, the furniture, the paintings. Within the next six hours there would be Company techs in here loading everything into a van. This time tomorrow the place would be spotless, silent, and empty, awaiting a rental agent's powers of description. It had been nice while it lasted.

He put that out of his mind as he stepped outside, locked the door behind him, and walked away. Immortals say a lot of goodbyes.

It wasn't until Lewis was on the LPA transport bucketing along to Newhaven that he groaned and smacked his forehead. "The cheroot!" he said out loud. "How would he light the damned thing?" A mortal woman looked across at him in affronted silence. She wasn't affronted enough to go inform a Public Health Monitor that there was a man talking to himself on the transport, however, so Lewis made it to the Dieppe ferry without incident.

Once on board, he went quickly up to the deserted upper deck and found himself a cozy seat near the tea station, a corner booth with a table. There he wedged his suitcase in securely, took out his Buke, and within minutes was lost in the problem of how to light a cigar in a longboat in a swamp on the Guinea Coast in 1845.

He had concluded that it really wouldn't be all that improbable for Edward to be carrying sulfur friction matches (might even have had one of the new boxes with a safety striking surface), when two men clambered unsteadily onto the upper deck and sat down opposite the tea station.

Lewis frowned down at his last paragraph. Leeches. *Loathsome and blood-engorged* were a little overripe. So was *slimy*. What about *. . . vile gray creatures?*

But leeches were black, not gray, weren't they? Lewis sat back to think. Slugs were gray, and so were—he raised his eyes to scan the mortals who sat across from him. His mouth fell open in surprise.

They got up abruptly and came and sat on either side of him.

"Don't shout," said one of them.

"No," said the other one.

Lewis stared from one to the other. "I beg your pardon?" he said at last.

"No use to beg," the first speaker told him.

They were very odd-looking mortals. White suits in England? In March? And very large black sunglasses, and fairly stupid hats: one wore a knitted ski hat, the other a shapeless canvas porkpie. They were small and spindly enough to make Lewis seem like a gorilla by comparison. Both had drippy little voices, just like Mr. Fancod's.

They were quite the most feeble and ridiculous things Lewis had seen in a long while, even including Mr. Fancod. Nevertheless, he felt a sudden urge to leap over the side and swim back to Newhaven.

Getting a grip on his nerves, Lewis affected a certain composure as he saved and closed his novel once again.

"Would you mind telling me who you fellows are?" he said.

"Yes," said the man in the ski hat.

Lewis returned his Buke to its case, scanning them more closely. "You're carrying weapons, aren't you?" he said. They started.

"Yes," agreed the one in the ski hat.

"No," said the one in the porkpie.

"No," the one in the ski hat corrected himself.

Lewis pursed his lips. "I see. But you were threatening me, weren't you? And if you're not carrying weapons, how do you propose to make your threats good?"

The two men looked at each other in silence for a moment. Then they nodded and each drew from within his coat a pistol and pointed it at Lewis.

"We have weapons," admitted the one in the porkpie.

Lewis looked at the pistols. They appeared to be modern disrupters but were not of any design he'd ever seen. All he could determine, on scanning them, was that they contained circuitry whose purpose seemed to be generating a wave field of some kind.

He folded his hands on the table and thought very carefully about the situation in which he found himself.

No danger at all, on the face of it. He might simply wink out from between the two little men, run down into the main lounge, and alert the Public Safety Monitor that there were lunatics with weapons on board. Of course, then there would be a scene, which was not something a running operative particularly wanted. No way to avoid being asked to make a statement to the authorities, and perhaps to the press, either of which would be in direct violation of Company policy as regarded quiet exits.

He could wrest the weapons away and throw them overboard, which seemed like a good idea actually, though Lewis disliked hurting mortals. These particular mortals looked as though they might snap like toothpicks if he tried anything the least bit forceful, and that would cause a scene as well.

If he were Edward Alton Bell-Fairfax, he'd have casually killed the two with a backhand chop five minutes ago and tossed them, guns and all, discreetly over the side into the Channel. He wasn't Edward Alton Bell-Fairfax.

"Well, then," Lewis said, as politely as he could. "What do you want?"

"To take you home," said the one in the porkpie.

Lewis suppressed a smile. "Um—and what happens if I don't want to go home with you?"

"We shoot you," the other one informed him. "Then we take you anyhow."

"Yes," the one in the porkpie agreed.

"I'd rather you didn't shoot me," Lewis said, drumming his fingertips on the table.

"Yes. We know," said the one in the ski hat.

Realizing in panic that he was looking at three and a half more hours of conversation like this, Lewis attempted to transmit to Xenophon. There was no response. He felt the proverbial sensation of ice water along his spine.

"Are you jamming my signal?" he asked.

"Yes."

"So you know what I am?"

"Yes." Both of them nodded their heads. "You're a cyborg."

"How do you know?"

"We have been looking for you," said the one in the porkpie.

Lewis closed his eyes. Ireland. In that moment, years of denial ended abruptly. The nightmares had him. Grinning, they pulled off their masks, and he remembered the cave under Dun Govaun, the creatures who hadn't been children after all but small men, weak and stupid yet masters of a weapon that could disable the cleverest cyborg, if he walked into their hiding place. And Lewis had. The erasure field had crippled him, but it hadn't quite killed him. His captors didn't mind, because they had him now, so they could take him apart and see how he was made and make the weapon stronger, better, more deadly . . .

"Well then," he said in a light voice, opening his eyes again. "If you've been hunting me this long, you must know I don't want to be caught."

"Yes," said the one in the ski hat, nodding again.

"I think it's only fair to warn you, I'll probably run as soon as we get off this boat," Lewis said.

"That would be dumb," said the one in the porkpie, disapproval in his voice. "Because we'd shoot you, and then you'd be broken."

"Well, probably; but that's all the more reason for me to do something desperate, you see?" Lewis spread out his hands as though presenting them with an irrefutable argument. "So, there it is. If you're smart, you'll keep those guns trained on me."

"Oh, we're smart," the one in the ski hat said.

"We're the smartest ones," said the one in the porkpie.

"Yes, I can see that," Lewis agreed. "Well. I can't run anywhere until we land at Dieppe, so I think I'll just go on with my writing."

"It won't help," said the one in the ski hat.

"Then there's no reason for you to stop me, is there?" said Lewis smoothly, drawing his Buke from its case again. His captors appeared to be thinking that over.

"No," they said at last.

Lewis called up a Company line, and found to his frustration that although he was able to access the channel, he was unable to send any messages. Apparently whatever was jamming his personal transmission was able to block the Buke's as well. After several efforts he entered in the last communication code he had on file for Joseph.

Joseph wasn't home. His automatic response picked up the call, and Lewis beheld a brilliant yellow screen with bouncy red letters, giving the following cheery message in Castilian Spanish:

> Hola! If you're calling about the sofa and loveseat, they're still for sale. I'm on vacation this week, but please leave your comm code and I'll return your call as soon as I get back. If this is really important, you can reach me care of the Hotel Elissamburu, Irun, Eskual Herriraino, at HtEli546/C/882. I'll be there until the 30th. Bye.

Lewis exhaled in annoyance. He attempted to leave a message, but was blocked once again. After staring at the screen in frustration, he logged off and reopened his story file again and typed:

> applied it carefully to one of the filthy little creatures, and had the satisfaction of watching it shrivel and drop away.

Over the next three hours Edward Alton Bell-Fairfax and company got rid of the leeches, found their way through the mangrove swamp by a secret shortcut that was actually faster than sailing across the lagoon, descended on one of Delarosa's notorious barracoons, and burned it to the ground after setting free all the slaves, one of whom was the captive daughter of King Bahou, and very grateful she was too. But just as she was about to express her thanks, who should emerge from the steaming, fever-ridden jungle but the treacherous Diego Luna, determined to make good his threat to kill the English commander . . .

Lewis, on the other hand, sat in an increasingly chilly upper deck lounge praying that somebody would come open the tea station and perhaps notice his unwelcome companions. Nobody did.

Dieppe, en Route
to Paris

IT WAS DARK by the time the ferry landed at Dieppe. Lewis put away his Buke and groped for his suitcase. "Well, gentlemen, it's time to disembark," he told his captors.

"Not yet," they said together, threatening with their pistols. "We're supposed to wait until everybody goes."

So they waited, as the passengers from the lower decks trailed up the gangway, departing in ones and twos for the customs building. When the last one had trundled his baggage ashore, the little men rose to their feet.

"We're supposed to go now," said the one in the porkpie. "You're supposed to walk in front of us."

"Okay," Lewis said, hauling out his suitcase. "But I'm warning you, I'll almost certainly try to run away."

"Stupid cyborg," said the one in the ski hat. Lewis shrugged and walked ahead of them, down to the main deck and up the gangway to the quay. They followed closely, keeping their pistols trained on him the whole time. As he approached the customs building, Lewis glanced over his shoulder at them.

"I'll probably make my attempt in here," he said, and walked quickly up the ramp into the lighted hall with the turnstile and customs officers at its far end. They followed him, keeping their guns well up and pointed at his head. It was a long, long walk across the floor.

"Bonsoir, Monsieur," yawned the guard at the nearest turnstile.

"Regardez-vous les disrupters, s'il vous plait," Lewis said through his teeth, smiling. The guard's gaze skimmed past Lewis at the two little men and their guns.

"Merde!" he cried. The two little men stopped in their tracks, startled.

"Merci. Bonsoir," Lewis said pleasantly, largely unheard in the commotion of five large customs officers tackling his would-be captors. He walked over to Luggage Analysis, set his suitcase on the conveyor belt, and followed it through on the designated footpath without incident.

Before boarding the express to Paris he stopped at the snack bar and bought three Toblerones, and had finished one by the time he was seated in the deserted passenger car. The train left the station and picked up speed. Lewis was unwrapping the second Toblerone with trembling hands when two more strangers in white suits emerged from the car behind him and sat down, one to his left and one immediately in front of him.

They were quite similar to the first pair, though not so perfectly matched in size; one wore a beret, and the other a baseball cap. The one with the beret also had a tiny chin-tuft of beard.

"Don't try that again," he told Lewis menacingly. "We have weapons too."

"How many of you people are there?" Lewis asked.

"All of us," the one with the cap said.

"I'd really rather not go with you," said Lewis. "Why do you think you can frighten me with your guns? I'm a cyborg, you know."

"Because these can hurt you," the one in the beret said, gesturing with the hand he was careful to keep firmly in his pocket. "We hurt you once before. We have these now. We can do it again."

"Please don't." Lewis swallowed hard and leaned back into his seat.

Eogan, that had been the mortal's name. Lewis was in Ireland securing illuminated manuscripts for the Company. He'd been working at the remote monastery with Eogan. A monk had been carried off in the night by persons unknown, presumably the fair folk. The abbess, aware that Lewis had some unusual abilities, sent him out with Eogan to search and rescue if possible. They ventured into a hollow hill where the fair folk were thought to live. Lewis didn't believe in fairies, of course, the whole thing seemed like a lark; but when he found the concealed entrance under Dun Govaun, he was so intrigued . . .

So he and Eogan went down the passage under the hill, Lewis confidently assuring his companion there was nothing to fear, until they stepped across the metal plate set in the floor, and Lewis knew rending agony for the first time in his immortal life, and then red darkness.

A confusion of impressions after that, blurred perhaps by the intensity of his fear and pain: a quiet, venomous little voice telling a story about three brothers. Two were strong and clever, but the third was weak and small, stupid except insofar as he was able to devise wonders to hide him from his brothers. The strong brothers tried to steal the devised wonders, but the weak one fled and hid himself in a cave. So did his children who came after him, and the hunt continued over the ages as the weaklings were driven to invent greater and greater wonders to keep themselves hidden, a branch of humanity lost in shadows, forgotten except in legend.

The storyteller went on to say that always the weaklings managed to keep ahead of their pursuers, until from the other end of time the strong ones came up with a device of their own: immortal servants, full of machinery, who were cleverer and stronger even than their masters. These cyborgs succeeded in finding the weaklings' caves and robbing them.

So then they had to work harder, poor little weaklings, they had to find a way to break the cyborgs. With all the moronic intensity of their peculiar genius, they devised a disrupter field to disable biomechanicals. And Lewis, their first experimental subject, lay paralyzed in their warren, seriously damaged by the field, self-repair offline and organic components dying inside him.

But he didn't die, not inside the hill. Eogan escaped with him, carried him out. He tried to make Eogan understand about the distress signal to Dr. Zeus, that the Company would come for him. The monk wept, tried to save Lewis by baptizing him so he'd have an immortal soul. A nice thought, but it didn't help. His organic heart stopped. His organic parts began to die.

He looked now at the two little men. "Tell me something," he said wearily. "Why me? It's been two thousand years. You're not immortals. You weren't even born when your people caught me before. How did you know to look for me?"

"We all remember," said the man in the cap.

"Everything," said the man in the beret.

Lewis nodded slowly. "Hive memory? I see. And what are you going to do with me, now that you have me?"

"Take you back," the man in the beret said. "You got away before we could learn about you."

"Ah." Lewis sighed. "That's right. You were going to take me

apart, weren't you?" He felt something beading on his brow and realized it was the sweat of mortal fear. Then something occurred to
him. "Wait a minute. You mean you've been hunting for me all these
years simply because I happened to be the one you caught before?"

"Yes," said the one in the cap.

"But you could have learned what you wanted to know from any
Company operative. You mean you never tried to capture any of the
others?" Lewis's voice rose with incredulity, and he began to grin in
spite of himself.

"Yes," said the one in the cap, looking confused.

"Don't laugh at us!" The one in the beret scowled. "You won't
laugh when we get you home, slave."

Lewis sobered. Sweat was running down his face. He calmed himself and concentrated, trying to bring a greenish cast to his features. It
wasn't particularly difficult.

"Oh, dear, no, I'm frightened," he assured his captors. "I'm so
frightened, I think I'm going to be sick. It was Mr. Fancod, wasn't it?
You found me through him."

"Yes," the one in the cap said.

"But he's stupid," said the one in the beret with just a trace of
pride. "He's not like us."

"No, he couldn't be, could he? He lives with humans. Though I
suppose you're some form of humanity too—" Lewis made a choking
sound and hastily pulled out a tissue. "I really am going to be sick."

His captors backed away in alarm, but not far enough.

"Please let me go to the lavatory," Lewis gasped, rising in his seat.
"You don't want vomit on your shoes, do you?"

"No," said the one in the cap. They let him get up but pushed
closely behind him as he stumbled in the direction of the door marked
HOMMES. He went in, and they crowded into the tiny space after him,
so tightly packed that they were unable to raise their arms from their
sides.

That was when he winked out and slammed the door from the
outside, twisting the handle until the metal bent, effectively jamming
the lock. He heard a splash and a faint cry from within; perhaps one
of the guns had fallen into the toilet. He tore apart the nearest seat and
pulled out a tubular piece of steel, which he punched through the
lavatory's door jamb as an impromptu bolt.

Even as he was doing this, however, he felt a tingling sensation
and numbness in the hand that had touched the door. He backed away,
terrified. Turning and grabbing his suitcase with his left hand, he ran

down the aisle between the seats to the opposite end of the car. There he crouched, staring back in dread as the train rattled on through the night, and the distant lights winked out across the black fields.

Lewis flexed his hand and felt sensation returning. A hasty self-diagnostic told him that there was some tissue damage, ruptured cells, biomechanicals compromised but resetting themselves. Drawing himself up, he shoved through the exit and stood for a moment on the tiny swaying platform between the cars, expecting to see Rod Serling standing there on the point of going into a speech.

Gasping for breath, he disabled the alarm and forced the boarding door. He focused on the passing terrain and, timing it to the split second, hurled first his suitcase and then himself out into the darkness.

Being an immortal, he landed lightly on his feet and pitched forward to lie flat on the embankment until the train had roared past. Then he got up, dusted himself off, found his suitcase, and walked back along the tracks to Neufchatel.

There, on a quiet residential street, he stole an agcar. He felt rather badly about it. He hadn't stolen anything from a mortal since that briefcase of Ernest Hemingway's, three centuries past. He drove all night, through Normandy, through Maine, through Anjou and Poitou, where once he had been a troubadour.

At daybreak he abandoned the car in a field and walked into Bordeaux, where he caught a train that took him across the border into Biarritz, and there he checked into a very nice hotel. Having showered, shaved and put on a fresh suit, he went down to the hotel's restaurant and ordered lunch. His hands were still shaking.

While waiting for the regional specialty to arrive, Lewis fortified himself with a glass of real wine (France and its neighbors to the south had refused to have anything to do with the ban on alcoholic drinks, thank God) and set up his Buke. He keyed in the communication code to the Hotel Elissamburu and confirmed that a Joseph Denham was registered there. He left a message indicating he would be interested in purchasing the sofa and love seat and would call at the hotel to discuss it that afternoon. He sent the message, holding his breath; to his relief it went through, and the hotel confirmed reception.

Leaning back in his seat, he took another swallow of wine and peered cautiously at his right hand. Full sensation now; in fact, it hurt. It looked badly bruised, purpling under the surface of the skin.

He set down the wine and leaned forward again over his keyboard, spinning the story like a cloak, wrapping the words around to comfort himself.

"I will regret having defeated you, Commander Bell-Fairfax," sneered Diego Luna. "For I assure you, only in you have I ever found an opponent worthy of my steel!"

Edward looked along his cutlass at the wily Portuguese.

"You may find," he drawled, "that I'm a rather difficult man to kill."

Irun del Mar, Basque Republic

JOSEPH SAT IN the hotel garden, all suited up as a tourist on vacation. He wore a brilliantly colored sweater emblazoned with the logo of the local pelote team, black beret, and terrorist pants. He wasn't wearing espadrilles only because it was March. He was in a strange mood.

There were several reasons why. He hadn't been back to what was now Irun Del Mar in twenty thousand years, give or take a few centuries, and the degree to which things had changed (and hadn't changed) was profoundly unsettling to him.

He'd also been speaking Euskaran for the last week, which was enough to bend reality on its own.

Then too, he'd just received a cryptic mailing from Lewis, which probably meant that Lewis had news of some kind. It might be good news, or it might be some further tidbit about the life and exploits of Edward Alton Bell-Fairfax, of whom Joseph was sick of hearing. Mostly, though, he was bemused by a local phenomenon he had observed, and didn't quite know how he felt about it.

He waved cheerily enough, though, as Lewis, looking even more gaunt than usual, came to the garden gate. "Hi," said Joseph.

"What have you been doing, blowing up Spanish peers?" Lewis asked, regarding Joseph's ensemble in horror. He sat down at the table.

"I've been trying to summon a sense of ethnic identity," Joseph said.

"Is it working?" Lewis signaled to a waiter.

"No," Joseph admitted. "But check this out." He pointed at the transport trundling slowly down the street. It was a double-decker, and the upper deck was filled with some kind of sporting team, cheering rowdily and waving little pennants.

Lewis looked at them, and his mouth fell open. "Great Caesar's ghost," he said. "You've been cloned!"

"Weird, isn't it?" said Joseph. And in fact, every person on the bus could have been Joseph or a near relation. Short and stocky to a man and woman, same black button eyes, same ironic mouth. Lewis stared at them until the waiter came, and as he looked at the mortal to order a gin martini, he nearly jumped out of his skin. Joseph appeared to be in two places at once, a very badly dressed Joseph seated at his left and a Joseph in a white apron standing deferentially to his right, waiting with a little order plaquette.

Lewis changed his mind. "Hot chocolate, please," he said. Joseph repeated the order in Euskaran, the waiter keyed in his order and went away, and Lewis sagged backward in his chair.

"You know what's *really* weird?" said Joseph. "Nobody notices."

"Just when I thought things couldn't get any stranger, I was proven wrong." Lewis began to giggle helplessly.

"You don't look good," Joseph observed, frowning at him.

"I don't suppose I do. I've had a difficult couple of days, and I'm a little short on sleep."

"What's wrong? Are you in trouble?"

Lewis went into gales of high-pitched laughter. Passersby on the sidewalk turned toward him and frowned just like Joseph, which didn't help. Joseph looked around uncertainly and finally reached for his water glass, preparing to dash the contents into Lewis's face, but Lewis sobered abruptly. "Don't. This suit is Bond Street linen," he snapped. "And it's my best silk tie. I'm sorry. I'm running, if you must know."

"Christ! Somebody blow your cover?" Joseph set down the water glass.

"Yes. It was very strange. A vile-looking little idiot savant named Fancod walked into my office, modified an archives terminal with paper clips, and proceeded to break into the Company's database," Lewis said. "When his keepers came to take him away, he publicly identified me as a cyborg. They didn't believe him, of course, but he'd done it all the same. Then he threw orange peel all over the floor on his way out."

"Fancod?" Joseph stared.

"I cleaned up what I could, including the orange peel, you know procedure, and I ran." The waiter brought Lewis's hot chocolate, and

Lewis reached for it desperately. "Oh, my, look at this, real whipped cream."

"Bad break, but it doesn't sound like it's your fault." Joseph waved his credit disk, indicating to the waiter that he was paying. "I don't see how that could get you in trouble."

"Mm." Lewis gulped hot chocolate. *Then on the boat two more vile-looking little idiot savants attempted to abduct me. They had some kind of disrupter pistols. I shook them off at customs and got on the train, and two more popped out of the woodwork. We had quite a little chat. I got away from them too, but not before they managed to do this.* He held up his right hand for Joseph to see the bruise there. *This happened seventeen hours ago.*

Joseph's eyes widened. He leaned forward and examined the bruise, which ought to have vanished within an hour of Lewis's injury.

There's worse, I'm afraid. I've found out more than I ever ought to have known—and I remembered exactly what happened to me in Ireland—and I'm sorry to go to pieces like this, but I think the Company is out to make me disappear. Lewis drained the last of the chocolate and slumped in exhaustion.

Joseph looked around. *Okay. I was confused before. Now I'm scared and confused. We need to talk somewhere.* "I wouldn't worry," he said out loud. "You've always done your job. Look, you need to relax. I was just about to go catch some People's Shakespeare. Why don't you come along? Ever seen Shakespeare in Euskaran?"

"I can't say that I have." Lewis opened his eyes, remembering in amazement that he had thought everything would return to normal if he could just contact Joseph.

"Neither have I, so this ought to be interesting." Joseph pushed back his chair and got up. "Come on."

They walked down a few streets to a park, where a big flatbed freight hauler had been parked to make an impromptu stage. Several dozen Joseph clones stood or sat around watching the performance, which was being given by a group of young people, also Joseph clones, in worker's clothes. The front of the truck was draped in red banners and Marxist slogans.

"They're Communists?" Lewis asked.

"It takes a while for ideas to reach this country," Joseph explained, embarrassed.

Lewis nodded in mute acceptance as a stalwart maiden in work boots strode to the front of the stage and held up the tree branch, decorated with a star and crescent moon cut of sheet metal, that signified this was the Wood near Athens.

Readers will have to use their imaginations to picture what Eus-karan (a language that renders "I take the glass from the waitress" as "Glass the waitress the from in the act of taking I have it from her") would do to *A Midsummer Night's Dream.* The performance took eight hours without counting intermissions. Plenty of time for Lewis to ex-plain what a long strange trip he'd had and why, as he and Joseph relaxed on a park bench and fairies fought over a mortal boy.

It was almost dark by the time Lewis finished. Peaseblossom, Cob-web, Moth, and Mustardseed were leading Bottom away in chains of flowers.

Joseph was silent a long moment, nodding thoughtfully. *These little morons, do you think they're human? Some branch of the mortal race who became troglodytes? And with inbreeding or whatever, au-tistic genius became a dominant genetic trait?*

And lack of fashion sense, added Lewis, shuddering.

But, you know something? I don't think this is the Company's doing. If the Company wanted to get you, they'd have done it by now.

You think so? But the alternative is even more frightening, Joseph. It means that the Company has an enemy out there with comparative technology, and they know about us. Me, anyway. What's more, they have a way to disable us.

Joseph moved to one side as a stage manager climbed on the bench to hang a probe light from a tree branch. *I'll bet the Company knows a lot more about what happened to you in Ireland than they've let you know. I'll bet that's why it took ten years to get you back online. They must have been studying what the little creeps did to you so they could work up a defense. Wouldn't you think? I'd be really surprised if every operative recruited after that time hasn't got some kind of protection built in. Hell, I remember being called in for an upgrade around 600 A.D. I bet we've all got it now, you included.*

What about this? Lewis flexed his right hand.

It's healing, isn't it? Whereas when they got you the first time, they fried your biomechanicals, from the sound of it. You weren't in as much danger this time as you thought.

I'd certainly prefer to believe that.

You know what you've got to do now, of course: make a full report to the Company. Joseph looked hard at him. *Tell them everything that happened, or it will look funny. Worse! If these people have come up with some new improved way of getting to us, or you at least, the Company needs to know so they can take countermeasures. They'll cream the little bastards. Hell, if a Literature Specialist could outguess them, think what a team of security techs could do.*

I resent that, Lewis said, glaring at the stage.

No offense, pal. But you weren't designed for cloak-and-dagger stuff, were you? You were made to traffic in manuscripts and first editions, not dirty tricks. It's time to step back and let the professionals take over. Joseph leaned across and patted him on the shoulder. "I don't know about you, but this is getting real old. What do you say we go get some dinner?"

As they walked back to the hotel, Joseph transmitted: *The only thing that doesn't fit is this Fancod guy. Who the hell is he? You said he's working for the Company? He's got access codes? And yet he's one of these little creepy people?*

Yes! As much like the others as—as you're like all these Basques. That was why I thought it was a Company double cross at first. What is the Company doing employing one of them?

Maybe he was a spy, Joseph speculated. *Posing in an adult care facility as an autistic genius so he could hack into Company files.*

You think so?

Maybe. I don't know. But it makes a good story, and if I were you, I'd tell the Company that's what you think he was. And I'll bet they give you a pat on the back for being so smart, and that's the last you'll hear of the business, except for maybe an update later on, telling you they've caught the guy and everything's been taken care of. They turned in at the garden entrance and crossed the courtyard to the indoor dining room. Joseph stopped in the lighted doorway to look seriously at Lewis.

Sounds peachy, Lewis replied bitterly. A waiter appeared—not quite so much of a clone this time, more like an elderly uncle of Joseph's—and led them to a cozy dark booth. *I don't suppose you've had any leads on your friend since last we met?*

Only negative ones. One of the bunkers is up here. I got inside it two days ago. Lots of missing people, lots of Enforcers, but not him. So we can rule this one out.

I'm glad you've been doing something, at least—

"Hi, guys, sorry I'm late," said an immortal, sliding into the booth beside Lewis. "Security Tech Chilon. Literature Specialist Lewis? You okay? What the hell's been going on?"

"About time one of you people showed up," said Joseph. "My friend here's had quite a run. Waiter?" He flagged down the elderly mortal, and they had a brief but infinitely convoluted conversation in Euskaran.

"A lot has happened," Lewis said.

"Your transmission's been broken or intermittent since you got on the boat at Newhaven," Chilon informed him.

"That's nothing." Lewis stuck out his right hand. "Look at this."

"What?" Chilon peered at it in the dim light.

"There's a bruise."

"Oh." Chilon looked more closely. "So there is. How—"

"It's a really bloodcurdling story," Joseph said, settling back. "I've just ordered us wine and a couple of roast ducks. My friend here needs to make a full report. Get your ears on; this'll take a while."

It lasted, in fact, through dinner, dessert, and after-dinner drinks. Chilon, who was rather pleasanter and a bit more intelligent than most security techs Joseph had met, listened with an increasingly grim expression, though he was unfailingly polite and sympathetic in his reactions to Lewis's story.

"It sounds as though we have a lot of work to do, here," he said when Lewis finished. He was pushing his glass of Pernod around on the table without drinking.

"Indeed." Lewis leaned forward and tried to look confidential. "Now, I realize I've inadvertently turned up some information the Company didn't want generally known, and I can't tell you how embarrassed I am. I'm only a Literature Specialist, after all. I'd really rather not get involved with any of this. But, you know, it seems to me that the mortal Fancod must be some kind of spy for these creatures. How else could he have known about me? And he's been getting into Company files! I realize my opinion doesn't count for much, but something ought to be done about him, don't you think?"

Joseph applauded silently.

Chilon said, "You're absolutely right about that. We've already handled Fancod, so don't worry. As for the other stuff—well, you aren't likely to go blurting the information out to anybody, are you? Other than to Joseph here."

Joseph held his breath, but Lewis nodded and caught the ball. "I reported to the first Facilitator I could find. Technically it should have been Xenophon, I know, but I wasn't sure I could reach him, and for all I know that channel's not secured."

Right answer. Both Chilon and Joseph relaxed.

Chilon had a sip of Pernod. "Good point," he said.

"So, what happens now?" Lewis looked from one to the other.

"We're going to monitor you pretty closely for a while, to be sure these people leave you alone," Chilon said. "We'll see if we can grab the ones being held by the French authorities. I imagine the guys you trapped in the toilet had some explaining to do." He grinned. "But we must do some event effacement too, so the mortals don't get a lot of messy information they don't need. Don't worry about any of that. In fact, we can do a memory wipe, if you want."

Lewis's knuckles whitened on his glass, but he just shook his head with a slight frown. "I'd rather not go that far, thank you. If I meet up with them again, I want to be able to defend myself."

"You're right there." Joseph nodded.

"Okay." Chilon finished his drink. "Then here's what I propose: you could use a vacation anyway, after all this, and I know you were going to Paris, but why don't you hang out down here for a couple of weeks? Joseph and I can keep an eye on you while the Company clears up the fallout. Paris is a little crowded right now."

"Sounds like a plan," said Lewis cautiously.

"They'll probably want you to report to Eurobase One for a debriefing and a diagnostic," Chilon went on smoothly. "To see why that bruise is still there."

"Absolutely, yes."

Joseph's eyes flickered from Chilon to Lewis and back. "So what do you want to do now, Lewis?" he said. "You want to get a room here? We can take in one of those Minoan-style bullfights they're reintroducing. Or, I was planning on going to the Painted Cave Museum tomorrow. You want to tag along?"

"Oh, my gosh, I forgot." Lewis's face lit up. "They're your mortal father's paintings, aren't they? What an experience for you. I'd love to come. I left my suitcase at the hotel in Biarritz, though."

"No problem," said Chilon. "I have a car. I'll take you there tonight and bring you back up tomorrow. I ought to stick close anyway, until the operation's in place. There may be more of the little morons running around."

Lewis shivered.

It was growing late, so Chilon and Lewis left to walk back to Chilon's car. Joseph stood in the doorway of the hotel, watching them go down the street in the lamplight as they chatted about the fabled luxury of Eurobase One. The larger man put his hand on Lewis's shoulder, in a friendly way.

Joseph sighed, wondering if he'd ever see Lewis again.

But next morning there came no call officially informing him that Lewis had been transferred to a distant location, and as Joseph was sitting over his breakfast, he heard the two coming through the hotel lobby, discussing the relative merits of Toblerone over Perugina.

"In here." He leaned out and waved from the restaurant. They saw him and smiled. He thought that Lewis looked more tired than the day before, if that was possible, with new lines of strain in his face. Lewis seemed cheerful enough as he sat down and ordered coffee, however.

"No weird visitors lying in wait at your hotel, I guess?" Joseph inquired.

"Nope." Lewis shook out his napkin. "Though I can't say I had the most pleasant dreams."

"How's the investigation going?" Joseph asked Chilon.

"Up and running," Chilon said, reaching into the roll basket and selecting a brioche. He broke it open and daubed it with fruit paste.

Joseph knew better than to ask for details. He turned to Lewis and said casually, "So, are you all ready to give me emotional support? This should be some experience. I haven't seen those paintings since I was twenty, when I sealed them up."

"Wow," said Chilon through a mouthful.

"Will we have to do any spelunking or anything like that to get to them?" Lewis asked, worried. "Because I'm not really dressed—"

"No, no, we won't be going into the real cave. That's been re-sealed. This is the exhibit they built outside. It's all holosimulation. They say you can't tell the difference, except that you can walk through without getting mud on your shoes, and there's a gift shop."

"So you won't really get to see your father's paintings, then," said Lewis.

Joseph shrugged. "What's real? I'm a simulation too, when you come down to it. Besides, a lot of people died in that cave. I've put off coming back here my whole life, to be honest. Now that there's this nice sanitary replica, I thought I'd see if I could take it."

"This was where your mortal parents were killed?" Chilon asked.

"That's right," said Joseph.

The site was in a pleasant wooded valley, only a kilometer inland from the sea. Along one side were cliffs bordering a river, with a rock overhang that had long been known as a Neolithic shelter. The cave itself opened out of an escarpment some thirty meters east, and the modern exhibit and carpark were located in a meadow just below.

They drove up in Chilon's car and paid their admission. They walked through the museum with its display of flint tools and skulls, through the hall of dioramas with its creepy models of fur-clad ancients poised around cook fires, and at last to the painted cave itself. Chilon paused at the gift shop to rent an audio unit before they went in.

"You want one?" He gestured at the display rack as he put on his earshells.

"Nah. What can they tell me I don't already know?" said Joseph. They walked into darkness and memory.

The first area, skillfully lit as if by rush lamp for maximum dramatic effect, was the Gallery of the Dancers. It reminded Lewis of the opening night of Stravinsky's *Rite of Spring*, with the bear-robed shuffling figures that dominated the last act. Not that the pictures showed anything that easily identifiable: hundreds of wavy black lines only gradually resolved themselves for the eye and became capering thighs, a pair of arms outflung, a profile bowing over a flute. No single form was complete and coherent.

Lewis and Chilon looked up respectfully. After a moment Chilon's audio docent directed him into the next chamber, and he moved along obediently.

Lewis sidled over to Joseph, who was stone-faced. "Why are the lines all drawn on top of each other?" he whispered.

"Because nobody'd invented erasers yet," Joseph replied. "And the man was a doodler. He couldn't finish anything."

"Oh."

"It drove my mother crazy." Joseph surveyed the illusion and found a particular fall of rock, reproduced in perfect holographic detail. "She died right over there," he added, pointing. "Great Goat cultist with an axe."

"I'm sorry," said Lewis, appalled.

"I don't feel anything. Funny, isn't it?"

There followed a silence, in which they listened to Chilon's footsteps getting fainter as he moved farther in.

I'm going to transmit a code to you. Lewis reached out and touched Joseph's forehead. Before Joseph could reply, the code came, a jumble of something that might have been binary but wasn't quite. Joseph blinked, received it, and shunted it into his tertiary consciousness.

What the hell was that?

It's what Fancod used to pull up a Company menu. I tried it last night, when I couldn't sleep. I got into the personnel files, not the general biographies but the classified material. I thought I'd see if I could find out what Mendoza was doing on Catalina with Edward in 1923. Joseph, the Company sent her Back Way Back, but they didn't keep her there. She was sent to Agricultural Station One on March 24, 1863, linear time. But later that day she was transferred from there to a place called Site 317. That's the last entry in her file.

Jesus, Lewis!

Listen to me. It's more involved than it sounds. Agricultural Sta-

tion One existed from 200,000 B.C. to 50,000 B.C., and it was on Catalina Island too. They kept her there from 153,000 to 150,000. She was in Back Way Back three thousand years, Joseph, before they let her out! I couldn't find any information on the other place, Site 317. But if you saw her on Catalina in 1923, and Site 317 is her last known location, maybe they're one and the same.

Lewis, are you crazy? Didn't I warn you about this? "Come on," Joseph said, striding after Chilon. "I'm getting depressed here."

They walked unseeing through the Grotto of the Lions, the Red Room, and the Room of Noah, and caught up with Chilon in front of a whole wall of silhouettes of human hands of every possible size.

When they emerged blinking into the morning light, Chilon said, not unkindly, "Did you make peace with your ghosts?"

"There weren't any," Joseph said. "Can you beat that?"

"Perhaps because it's only a replica," suggested Lewis.

"Could be. But none of the rest of the landscape does anything for me either. I thought I'd feel a connection or something, you know? A sense of belonging, coming up here? I don't. No kinship at all, even when every guy in the street looks like my twin brother."

They contemplated that while getting into the car. Chilon switched on the agdrive, and the car rose to its accustomed two feet above the surface of the ground. The propellant motor bore them away.

"I had the same experience," Chilon remarked. "When I went back to Sparta thinking it would feel like home. I don't know if it was that so much time had passed and everything about my memories was totally irrelevant, or what. But I wasn't one of those people. They weren't part of me."

"We're Company men," said Joseph gloomily.

"I guess so."

Lewis settled back and gave thanks yet again that he had been acquired by the Company before he could form any memory whatever of mortal life. He had enough problems as it was. "Have you ever thought," he said carefully, "of where you'll live after 2355? Assuming, you know—"

"Yeah," said Chilon.

"Beyond gradual retirement, we can live anywhere we like, right? Settle down?"

"I'd always kind of thought I'd come back here," said Joseph. "I don't guess I will, though."

"I'm not sure where I'd go," said Lewis. "Just what it would have to have. Fine libraries and shops. A certain degree of gracious civilization. Good restaurants. Decent weather."

"Santa Barbara," Joseph suggested.

"No wine or gin there anymore," Lewis reminded him. "Paris, maybe. Or Monte Carlo. And yet, you know, I've never felt culturally identified with the French? What a pity we can't go backward. I'd love to live in Old Rome at the height of her glory."

Joseph had, and very nearly said something pungent and to the point about Old Rome. He looked at Lewis's weary face and confined himself to remarking, "No gin."

"I suppose not." Lewis sighed.

"And no Theobromos either," Chilon said. "The future's all there is, guys. Pie in the sky as time goes by."

"Good one," Joseph chuckled, and Lewis smiled politely.

Chilon left them off in front of Joseph's hotel while he looked for a place to park, because the technological advances of the twenty-third century not yet solved that problem. They went back to the lobby to see about getting two more rooms.

Will you check into that code? Lewis asked.

When it's safe. When I'm alone. Lewis, do you have a death wish or something?

Absolutely not. Lewis looked grim. *I found that out on the train from Dieppe, believe me. But this information was dropped in our laps, and we'd be insane not to make use of it. A mere Literature Specialist can't find out where Site 317 is, but a Facilitator might. Don't you want to solve the mystery once and for all?*

Joseph did not reply immediately. They stepped up to the front desk, and he had a long conversation with the clerk in Euskaran that amounted to, "My friends are staying on. Do you have two more rooms?" and "Yes. Please sign here." As Lewis was signing in, Joseph transmitted, *Something to think about, Lewis. Suppose we find Mendoza, switched off in one of those vaults. What will we be able to do for her? Get her out? Revive her? Hide her? Where the hell can we hide from the Company? What would she do with herself? The next chapter in that story is that all three of us wind up in vaults in the same bunker, per omnia secula seculorum.*

Lewis blanched, but answered doggedly, *I don't believe she's in one of those vaults, Joseph. What if they let her go after she served her time Back Way Back? We have no idea what Site 317 is. If it's the Hotel St. Catherine on Catalina Island, if for example that's her gradual retirement, and she's still there with Edward—*

Will you let go of that? You know damn well the Edward guy died, and the odds against Nature's spitting out not two but three *guys who look just like him—it's absurd.*

Lewis gestured impatiently at the lobby full of Josephs playing backgammon. *Somehow it doesn't seem as unlikely as it used to.*

Joseph looked around and went pale. *Oh, no. You don't suppose there's some weird little genetic pocket in England like there is here, do you? I never thought about that.*

Well, think about it now.

All right. I'll see what I can find out. But you have to drop this, Lewis! Mendoza was my recruit, after all. If I'm not obsessed with this past the point of good sense, you shouldn't be. What was she to you?

My dearest friend, Lewis told him. *You should understand, after where we've been today. We don't have families, we don't have homes, we don't even have nationalities. Nothing remains except us, and all we have is each other.*

Joseph was silent a moment. *Sometimes,* he replied. *Mostly, all we really have is ourselves, Lewis. Do you want to lose yourself? You spent ten years switched off once. Do you want that permanently?*

There are worse things. Joseph, I'm tired of worrying about me! We live such miserable lives when we live for ourselves. When our work is over, what will I have? A nice little villa for one somewhere and an endless supply of reading matter?

Hey, you might meet somebody. It's been known to happen.

Never to me. And very seldom to any of the rest of us, as far as I can tell. Except Mendoza. She loved, and gave up everything she had for it. And then, three thousand years in prison, Joseph!

I know.

Don't you see? When all this is over, I don't really care if I'm relegated to a vault or rewarded with a villa in St. Tropez. What I want, with my whole heart, is to know that Mendoza's story had a happy ending. That love triumphed, and bravery, against impossible odds. That you really saw them together there on Catalina Island.

And if you get yourself arrested or worse, trying to make the story come out right? What does that leave for you, *Lewis?*

My honor.

You are the most dangerous incurable romantic I have ever known.

Joseph spotted Chilon and waved. "We got you a room. Come in and sign for it," he called.

"You would not believe how far I had to go before I found a parking space," groused Chilon.

Joseph in the Darkness

I WENT WITH LEWIS to Eurobase One. Father, you wouldn't recognize it now! When I was little, when you led the troops out to battle and we kids watched you in breathless admiration, it was such a raw place: partly a twenty-fourth-century field camp with a limited budget, partly a Neolithic stockade, but one hundred percent military base, up in those rough cold Cévennes.

You should see it today. It's a neoclassical Art Deco kind of fantasy, like a resort hotel might be if the Olympian gods built one. I always thought New World One was classy, but it had nothing on this place. Statues by Praxiteles and a lot of other classical masters, gorgeous landscaped gardens, Roman-style banquets with French culinary style, and a bathhouse like something dreamed up by William Randolph Hearst. Aegeus, the guy who'd been running it the last two millennia, had picked and chosen the best elements of the ages that rolled by the place.

There was a big staff of mortal servants to keep it all immaculate too, fairly surly French peasants. I heard rumors while I was there that this hadn't always been the case, that Aegeus had got away with some exploitative stuff that would have made our mortal masters' hair stand on end, if they'd known about it. But that, if it happened, was long in the past. I didn't see a single togaed girl or boy slave while I was there.

Lewis was too nervous to enjoy it much. This was the place he'd been brought after the little stupid guys fried his circuits the first time, after all, the place where he spent ten years in a regeneration vat. More unpleasant memories seemed to be bubbling up to the surface of his consciousness, but he didn't talk about them much. And though he tested out physically okay, with the damage to his hand all self-repaired, and though he got through his debriefing without arousing any suspicion (as far as I could tell), something was wrong.

He seemed to expect to see little freaks in white suits everywhere we went. In the sensational neoclassical gymnasium he thought he saw them lurking behind the homoerotic Greek bronzes. In the vast billiard parlor hung with lost Renoirs, jolly studies of boozing sports parties, he thought he spotted them under the tables. In the restaurant (Le Grenouille en Vin, a five-star place if ever there was one, the wine cellar alone went down five stories into the bedrock of the Cévennes), he jittered when a white-coated waiter stepped out a little too suddenly from behind a potted palm. Even the Robert Louis Stevenson shrine, with its holo statue of the writer, gave him pause. Maybe it was those huge starry eyes Stevenson had and the pipe-cleaner skinniness of his limbs. I knew the guy; even in the flesh, Louis looked too weird to be human.

But no phantoms seized the other Lewis. After about a week, his new posting orders and identification disk arrived, and the Company sent him on to a nice safe job in New Zealand, pilfering old documents from a university library. I saw him to his transport and then got the hell out of Euro One myself. I was tired of all the grandeur.

I sound pretty philistine, don't I? But this was my first home, other than that rock shelter. I had some good memories of the old base, when I was young and as idealistic as I was ever going to be. The world was a swell place, and we were all safe, father, because of you and the rest of the big guys. Nobody thought you were monsters then.

But what did the old stockade have to do with this pink carpeting, indirect lighting, gilt and crystal? And where in this world would you fit, now? I'm not so sure I fit myself anymore.

I went back to my job in Spain, assistant to an archaeology team sponsored by the local rabbinical school, making sure they uncovered the miraculously preserved relics of a twelfth-century synagogue, digging up what Nahum and I buried so carefully all those years ago. I made plans to go back to California the next time I could get a few weeks off, but somehow the time just sped by. Was I scared to come look for you, father? Probably. I sure as hell didn't feel like going to Catalina to see if Mendoza was shacked up there with another Englishman, no matter what I'd promised Lewis.

Things are safe enough in the American Community, at least, no worries about that. Everything is prim and proper and politically correct there now. They've outlawed alcohol again in most of the former states. Also meat, dairy products, tobacco, coffee, tea, chocolate, refined sugar, recreational drugs of any kind, competitive sports, and most great literature. So has England, and so have most of the rest of what used to be called First World countries.

This means boom economies for those little nations, like the Celtic Federation, who thumb their noses at the others and continue to produce whiskey and lamb chops. Still, most of the world's farmed acreage is given over to soybeans. Religion isn't illegal but is increasingly being regarded with genteel horror by most people, except the Ephesians. Faith is so . . . psychologically incorrect.

Sex isn't illegal, but there isn't a lot of it going on these days. There's talk about how it's a distasteful animal urge, how it victimizes women and robs men of their primal power. It creates codependency. It presents a terrible risk of catching a communicable disease. Relationships of any kind, in fact, are probably a bad idea.

I don't know exactly when this problem became widespread among the mortals, but I know that a lot of operatives of my acquaintance are climbing the walls or beginning to date other immortals, which is sort of unusual. We're not really comfortable in bed with each other as a rule, you know?

There is something beginning to be wrong with the mortals, a certain lack of interest and ability. The birth rate has plummeted all over the world. There are millions of inner children and fewer and fewer real ones. I remember seeing a holo feature on a certain famous amusement park: roller coasters and merry-go-rounds packed with forty-year-olds clutching the wonder of childhood to themselves like harpies, and not one little face in the crowd. Neverland has been invaded by the grownups, no children allowed. It's better than having lots of real kids starving in gutters, at least.

Mind you, it isn't like this everywhere. There are still plenty of places a retrograde old guy or gal can be an adult. You can get a beer, a steak, or a roll in the hay, and merry-go-rounds be damned; but you'll be branded a sociopath if anybody finds out.

Not surprisingly, a lot of people have taken to alternative lifestyles, like living outside national boundaries so they can indulge what appetites they still have without interference. How do they manage this?

It's being called the Second Golden Age of Sail.

Steam ended the days of the old sailing ships so long ago that most mortals can't imagine why such lovely, graceful craft were pushed out of existence by squat metal tubs. Being mortals, of course, they weren't around in the days when foot-long cockroaches swarmed in wooden forecastles or sailors clung to frozen ropes, attempting to take in sails with numb hands. Probably for that reason, a tall ship has come to symbolize the romance of the high seas in a way no chunky cruise boat can ever match, no matter how many Las Vegas revues it books.

Forget about space cruises. Think of an economy air transport, only more cramped, with worse food, and no chance in hell of surviving an accident. People don't go to Luna to have fun; they go there to work. And Mars will be even more work once mortals are able to go there.

No, consumers wanted something pretty, something comfortingly retro. Tall ships were the answer, updated with modern technology.

You don't need to climb to dizzying heights or learn a bunch of arcane phrases: the ship's computer will do it all for you now, with smoothly efficient servomotors and composite cables. It judges the wind and keeps to a course as ably as the crustiest old salt, with the added advantage of weather satellite links. Add a little fusion drive to get you places in a dead calm, and the system is nearly perfect. Employ a couple of able-bodied sailors in case of fouls or repairs, and you even keep the unions happy. Any dope can sail a three-masted clipper now, and lots do, and that means Freedom.

On a good-sized vessel you can store enough booze and contraband food to last a couple of years, and you can enjoy them without a Public Health Monitor breathing down your neck, as long as you stay outside the jurisdiction of the local coast guard. You can play music as loud as you want. You can be overweight, light up a pipe of tobacco, and indulge in other behavior that would get you shut away in a mental hospital if you tried it anyplace else nowadays.

Mortals have taken to the sea in droves, becoming semipermanent residents. Little piddly thirty-foot yachts have become the trailers of the new age. People with real money have custom sailing ships built, mansions under acres of sail.

For a while there was a lot of enthusiastic talk about how eco-friendly sail was, since it utilized wind power, and a lot of commercial freight vessels got built before people figured out it was cheaper just to send stuff by big fusion-driven cargo barges. But for the private sector sail is in, it's stylish, it's a political antistatement, and so waterfronts are once again forested with masts.

I have to admit they're easy on the eyes, those big graceful square-riggers flying along under clouds of canvas; and, unlike the old days, there are no rats, roaches, rotting timbers, or rotting food.

Freedom and adventure on the high seas. Cruise lines make a fortune on consumers who can't afford their own ships by offering six-month package tours during which they can partake of forbidden pleasures like pizza or hot fudge sundaes.

I guess that was why Lewis utilized some gradual retirement time and booked himself a cruise on the Olympian Clipper Line's Unrepentant Monarch.

The Company must have decided it was the perfect place to bait the trap.

Twelve Hundred Kilometers North-Northeast of Auckland, 2275

T AKE THAT FOR you?" asked the deck steward, gesturing at Lewis's empty martini glass.

"Thanks." Lewis looked up from his text of *The Moon and Six-pence.*

"Another?"

"Not now."

Lewis turned his attention to the bookscreen again, but at that moment a little party boat came into sight to starboard, tacking about to give its passengers a better view of the *Unrepentant Monarch*. They hooted and screamed and waved at the great ship, clinging to the rail of their schooner, and there seemed to be a costume party in progress, because most of them were dressed as pirates. As Lewis smiled and waved back, somebody on board fired their signal cannon. Ping, a broadside, if they had been using shot instead of a sound chip. But even if they used shot, the cruise vessel would have no more noticed a one-pound ball than an elephant would notice a mosquito.

The mortals on board the schooner nevertheless danced and whooped, and the mortals on the *Unrepentant* catcalled back to them as though there were a real assault going on.

Lewis, who remembered vividly what it was like to be on a ship under attack by French privateers, offered up a prayer of gratitude to Neptune. All things taken into consideration, he preferred reclining in a deck chair with a novel to running around on a blood-smeared deck dodging real cannon fire.

Though the experience had made for one of his better chapters, he felt. The scene where Edward and his command take on the slaver *Whydah Queen* was his favorite, full of authentic little touches, the one he'd rewritten least over the years. *The Tall Englishman* was unbelievably long now, seventeen volumes at last count.

Lewis had hit a dry spell lately, as he drew inevitably closer to the point where Edward (now a political, supposedly in the pay of Her Majesty's Foreign Office but in reality an agent of the Gentlemen's Speculative Society) was to be given his assignment to go to California. Quite apart from the fact that he wasn't looking forward to killing off his hero, Lewis had certain qualms about depicting Edward's relationship with Mendoza. It seemed an invasion of privacy, unforgivably frivolous to dramatize something that had resulted in heartbreak for her not to mention ruin.

He had made some attempts to block out a different scenario, one with a happy ending, but it had given off no more warmth than a painted fire. Nothing to do but set the whole project aside for a few decades and see if something suggested itself . . .

Lewis sighed and leaned back, looking up at the sky with its Mercator lines of cable crossing. Vast canvas walls straining in the brisk breeze, the *Unrepentant Monarch* skimmed along like a seabird. Perhaps Edward had come to America on a clipper. Ought Lewis take notes for a future scene?

He couldn't let the story alone, could he? He closed his eyes, sorted through his mental list of gods, and invoked Apollo and the Muses to grant him inspiration.

"I say, aren't you Literature Specialist Lewis?"

Lewis opened his eyes. There before him, leaning on the rail, was Facilitator Nennius, nattily dressed in white cruise attire. In some other dimension, Apollo smirked and threw Lewis a salute.

"Nennius, isn't it?" he said, after a moment's stupefaction. "Heavens, how long has it been? 1836, wasn't it?"

corner, and not a word of complaint or a cough or an impatient look from him."

"Johnson's," Lewis said, remembering.

"Abominable coffee, but a lovely place for privacy. Gone long since, I suppose."

"Utterly. That whole block went during the Blitz."

"That's right, you were stationed over there then, weren't you? You've had some lively postings over the years. I was there until the twentieth century. Then I was off to Greece, thank God." Nennius waved indulgently at the mortal pirate party, which was making another pass along the starboard bow. "Look at the silly little beggars. They do everything they can to make their world as dull and inhibited as it can possibly be, and run off at weekend to pretend they're having adventures. They do love their adventures."

"So few of them ever get to have real ones," Lewis said.

"True. Good thing too, on the whole. Though I remember one who did, by God!" Nennius reached for his glass. "Do you recall those papers I gave you for the archives, that night in 1836? Nasty inky schoolboy mess the Company wanted, for some unimaginable reason?"

Lewis felt the shiver of warning, sensed the pit thinly screened with branches. He stared out at the wide horizon, pretending to think. "Vaguely. I was more interested in your anecdotes about Londinium."

"So you were. The leather-knickers-down-the-well story." Nennius sniggered. "And to think they ended up in a museum exhibit! Anyway. I was a headmaster at a public school at the time, and the papers were nothing more than exercises I'd set one of my pupils. Remarkable boy, really, though I thought he'd no future at all. Illegitimate, you see, even if he was the bastard of somebody awfully important. They'd paid to send him to Overton, at least. But you know how it was back then: you simply had no place in the world with that kind of mark against you, unless you cut one out for yourself.

"I never thought the boy would manage it. Too fond of using his fists to answer an argument, though he was certainly a clever little fellow. He was shaping up into a scholar of some promise, actually, but then he was nearly sent down for fighting, so his people—whoever they were—took him out of school and sent him off to the Navy for a midshipman, and I thought, well, that's the last I'll hear of *him*. Our padre was desolated. He had some idea the little brute could have gone out for divinity!"

"Was he a religious boy?" Lewis asked.

"Oh, he was full of idealistic nonsense at first, but he woke up to the reality of the world pretty damn quickly. No fool he."

"To be sure. That evening at Johnson's." Nennius stepped forwar surefooted though the *Unrepentant* was rising on a particularly moun tainous swell just then, and settled himself into the deck chair next t Lewis. He was a tall immortal, dark and aristocratic-looking. "Well well, what are the odds of this? Are you taking the whole cruise?"

"As far as Panama. I'm on my way to my next posting," Lewis replied, fighting down panic. Was it so remarkable they should run into one another again, after four hundred years? He looked on as Nennius ordered a bottle of Chateau Rothschild from the deck steward and wondered how on earth he could refrain from leading the conversation around to Edward, whom this man had actually known, spoken with, perhaps even set on his course in life.

"I'm on holiday, personally," Nennius said, lounging back. "And a damned well-earned one, I might add. I've just come off forty years as a politician in Australia. I envy you Conservationist chaps, I really do. When you're done with a job, you've at least got something to show for it. How I'd love to have an old book or a painting or *anything* I could point to and say, 'There, that was my work, I rescued that for the ages.' But nothing we Facilitators do shows, you know, in the long run."

"Well, but surely that's the point," Lewis said. "If your work's done well, it doesn't show. It's a much more difficult job being a Facilitator. You're the men behind the scenes, the stage managers for history, the men in black?"

"A very flattering assessment."

"True, all the same."

"Well, thank you."

They fell silent as the steward brought the wine—service was superb on these cruises—and Nennius accepted his glass, inhaled, sipped, and approved. The steward, waiting until Nennius's nod, vanished unobtrusively. Nennius watched him go and shook his head.

"What that chap could teach his fellow mortals. Does it seem to you they've gotten ruder as the ages roll by? To think the day would come when you'd have to go on a cruise like this to experience courtesy!"

"It's one of the things promised in the brochure," Lewis said. "Every one of the staff has to take social interaction classes."

"Not like the old days, eh?" Nennius drank with relish. "The little monkeys might have been ignorant and bloodthirsty, but by God they knew how to be polite when they had to. Remember that night we sat up talking till all hours at Johnson's? That waiter *waited*, there in the

"Really," said Lewis, trying to sound bored but polite.

"Edward Bell-Fairfax, that was his name," Nennius said, and Lewis's heart contracted painfully. He raised a hand in a casual gesture, and the deck steward stepped within earshot, inquiringly.

"Another martini, please," Lewis said. The steward ducked his head and hastened away.

Nennius went on: "So anyway, a dozen years went by, and then a few more, and I'd long since forgotten about Bell-Fairfax. In those days I used to belong to Redking's Club. There was a cabinet minister I was dogging on the Company's behalf—you don't need to know whom, of course, but it was more of what you so kindly call stage-managing history. Well, we had our annual function welcoming new members, and to my utter astonishment I found myself seated opposite Bell-Fairfax."

"What a surprise," agreed Lewis. "I suppose that sort of man didn't get into that sort of club?"

"I should say not! But there was no mistaking Bell-Fairfax: remarkably ugly fellow, big horse-faced gawk with a broken nose, so tall he couldn't walk through a doorway with his hat on. Beautiful speaking voice, though," Nennius said, "and tremendously charming when he wanted to be. At any rate he'd charmed his way into the club. A retired naval commander on half pay, mind you! I thought it must be his people who'd arranged it, of course. Funnily enough, I was dead wrong." Nennius poured himself another glass of wine.

"Was he some sort of hero?" Lewis said carefully.

"Oh, I gather he'd served with some distinction off the Ivory Coast. Been sent out there to fight the slave trade, you know, probably some of that youthful idealism coming to the fore. But he got himself into trouble again. Nobody spoke of it to his face, but the rumor was he'd very nearly been court-martialed. Fighting again, just as he'd done in school. This time he'd laid his hands on a superior officer, and from what I heard, the only reason he was allowed to retire honorably was that he threatened to make the damnedest scandal." Nennius looked arch. "The captain in question was notorious for certain things, even by the standards of the British Navy."

"Rum, sodomy, and the lash," quoted Lewis.

"Oh, rather worse than that, I think. However it happened, Bell-Fairfax came out of it all right." Nennius watched as the deck steward set down Lewis's martini and slipped away. "After all, there he was, across the table from me. Properly respectful, of course, to his old headmaster, and I was obliged to converse with him. I was gratified to discover that he hadn't rotted away his brain on grog, or turned into one of those blustering seafaring gentlemen. Actually rather learned, for a Navy man. Superb command of rhetoric, though his Latin was abysmal."

"Not much call for it in the Navy, I suppose." Lewis took a bracing sip of his cocktail.

"No. No. But still a fine raconteur, quite dryly clever, and I found myself liking him. We became friends, as much as a former pupil and master can, saw one another at the club when he wasn't traveling abroad. He did a lot of traveling abroad," Nennius added in a meaningful tone.

Lewis merely raised his eyebrows in inquiry, not trusting himself to speak.

"You'll recollect I said I was wrong to assume his people had bribed the admittance council," Nennius continued. "Well. He had been sponsored by one of the Old Members!"

"You don't say," said Lewis faintly, marveling at the permanence of certain things Victorian.

"It seems he got in with a rather remarkable set." Nennius lifted his glass and studied it. "A clique of Foreign Office people with certain esoteric interests."

"Freemasons?" Lewis wondered to what god he ought to pray just now. Mercury, god of liars? Minerva, goddess of wisdom?

"No. You remember how it was back then, most of the ruling classes were Freemasons. That was old hat compared with what Bell-Fairfax and these other people—most distinguished some of them were, too—were doing." Nennius looked sternly across at Lewis. "Did you ever hear of the Gentlemen's Speculative Society?"

Mercury, Lewis decided, and as he wrinkled his brow in apparent perplexity, he uttered a silent but profound prayer of supplication. "Debating team at Oxford?" he said at last.

Nennius laughed. "Not likely," he said scornfully. "Imagine a secret fraternity that might admit Victor Frankenstein, Jules Verne, and Indiana Jones on equal terms. Sounds like a hoax, doesn't it? However, I happen to know it was very real indeed, and Bell-Fairfax was a member."

Nennius himself had been a member. Did he know Lewis knew? Was this a trap? Or was he simply leaving out his own involvement in order to be able to tell the tale? "Your mortal must have had no end of adventures," said Lewis.

"Perfectly astonishing ones, if rumor prove true," said Nennius. "Of course, at this late date very little evidence remains. I can assure you, though, that there were any number of quasi-scientific expeditions

authorized by my cabinet member, who was also one of the Gentle-
mens' number, as were some of the best scientific brains in England
at the time. Their goal seems to have been world domination, in a mild
sort of way.

"That was where Bell-Fairfax fit in, you see. He was no scientific
genius, but he was frightfully clever and a damned good man of his
hands, if you take my meaning: he'd grown accustomed to dirty work
in a just cause and could be relied on utterly. He was one of their best
agents, I believe."

Lewis giggled shakily. "What a novel this would make."

"If mortals read such things anymore," said Nennius, looking out
at the pirate ship in contempt.

"Well, but go on. This is fascinating," Lewis said, remembering
his martini and gulping half of it down. "I worked in Hollywood once,
you know. I can't help thinking what John Ford might have done with
such a story."

"Unfortunately, I don't know many details." Nennius shook his
head. "They sent him to Egypt, and Jerusalem, and once—I believe—
to a Jewish ghetto in Poland, of all places. Bell-Fairfax was a closed-
mouthed chap, though. Wouldn't have been much of a political if he
hadn't been. No, I got most of what I learned of his adventures from
my cabinet member, who was rather a fool."

"A ghetto," said Lewis. New chapters were dancing before his
eyes, in spite of his fear.

"The only mission I have any detailed knowledge of is his last
one: poor old Bell-Fairfax disappeared, presumed killed." Nennius
sighed. "We kept his room at the club for seven years. Still, the adventure must have been choice. Ever hear of Santa Catalina Island?
But you must have, you worked in Hollywood. I understand it became
a fashionable resort in the early twentieth century."

Lewis nodded, light-headed. "Twenty-six miles from the mainland.
One used to be able to see it, on clear days, when there still were any
in Los Angeles. I suppose one can again, now."

Nennius leaned forward and lowered his voice. "As near as I could
piece it together, the Gentlemen had got hold of a mysterious document
that dated back to God only knew when and lay forgotten in the royal
archives. An early explorer was out there, it seems, and discovered
something damned queer on Santa Catalina. There were supposed to
have been artifacts with the document, but I was never able to confirm
that. The rumors, though! Hints about Atlantis, the Fountain of Youth,
fabulous treasure. Whatever was actually there, the Gentlemen felt

strongly enough about it to send an expedition, and so of course they prodded the Foreign Office into mounting one."

"Now we're getting into George Lucas's territory," said Lewis, surprised at his own sangfroid.

"Yes, aren't we? The only difficulty with the plan was that the Yanks found out about it, and weren't about to let a foreign power grab a bit of their coastline, especially when they had a civil war going on. This was in 1862, you see.

"Something went wrong, just as the expedition was beginning to make real progress. Bell-Fairfax was sent in to salvage what he could from some fool's mistake. They never saw him again."

"And did they ever find the treasure?" asked Lewis.

Nennius shrugged. "My cabinet minister died not long after, so I lost my primary source of information. I have a general impression they kept sneaking back to search for it, and for Bell-Fairfax too. Do you know, you're the only person I've told about this, in the four centuries since it happened? It seems like the wildest cheap literature, I know. I wouldn't believe it myself if I hadn't known the parties involved."

"You say they kept searching for Edward?" Lewis asked distractedly.

Nennius was silent a moment, noting his familiar use of the name. He smiled at Lewis, thinking that it certainly wasn't difficult to snare a Preserver. All one needed for a literature drone was a good story.

He yawned and said, "Perhaps they hoped he wasn't really dead, after all the tight corners he'd got himself out of without a scratch. I'd like to believe that. I was rather fond of him, at least as fond as one can be of the monkeys."

"But he must have died," Lewis said.

"Well, of course. And yet, you know, rumors persisted that he'd been seen, much later than was possible for a mortal."

Lewis caught his breath. "Really?"

"Yes. Who knows? Perhaps all that nonsense about a Fountain of Youth was true. Certainly they did find something remarkable, in a cave on the windward side of the island." Nennius observed Lewis's reaction. "Or so I heard. I must admit I've felt the urge to go out there and see for myself if Bell-Fairfax is still strutting about. Wouldn't you? What if he somehow dragged himself into that cave and cheated death?"

Lewis smiled but was silent, thinking very hard. Not hard enough, however, as it turned out.

*   *   *

That night he dreamed of a cave in the hills behind Avalon. He was in the long passage that led into the cave, terrified, though it was a pleasant passage, full of sweet melancholy perfume. It glowed with a white light that deepened to blue as he went farther in and farther down. Joseph was with him.

They emerged into a great vaulted room that stretched away into unfathomable darkness, lit only by white screens where films were playing, old films from Hollywood's golden age, when he'd lived there. He saw Sean Connery and Michael Caine being British adventurers: *The Man Who Would Be King.* And there was Harrison Ford in Egypt in *Raiders of the Lost Ark*, and there was Ford too on another screen seeking the Holy Grail with Sean Connery. A silent film flickered in all shades of ash-silver and gray, biblical-era people dancing on the steps of an impossibly big temple set. On another screen, Jackie Cooper waded ashore from the beached *Hispaniola* onto the sands of Treasure Island, singing Yo Ho Ho and a Bottle of Rum. On yet another screen, Rudolph Valentino rode down the side of a dune.

"That's Pismo Beach, really," Joseph said knowingly.

Lewis turned away from the screens. "Father of Lies," he told Joseph, indignant, though he knew Joseph was right.

"No, I'm the son of lies, and you are too," Joseph replied.

And there was Mendoza, so sad but so beautiful too: she was sleeping in a vault, in a light like blue cellophane, dreaming peacefully, shrouded round in her fiery hair that drifted, drifted. Lewis ran toward the vault.

"What a cheap horror matinee," Joseph said, because a skeleton came flying into Lewis's path, but anyone could have told it was mounted from a boom and jointed together like a puppet. It was a very big skeleton, though, and a strange one. The skull's top had been sawed off and reattached with wire. That was only done during autopsies, though, wasn't it?

Lewis knew whose skeleton it was, hanging there so silly beside Mendoza's vault with its bones still rattling: Edward's. Edward hadn't cheated death, he'd been shot and died in Mendoza's arms. No happy ending. Lewis began to cry. Joseph leaped on the skeleton in a fury, and it fell to the floor, scattering like ivory dice.

"Bastard!" Joseph was screaming. "You got her into this condition, now you'll have to marry her!"

"Aye, but he's dead," Lewis objected.

"But he won't *stay* dead!" Joseph kicked the strange skull across the room, and Lewis realized that his friend had become a werewolf—no, the jackal-headed god Anubis, or was it Imhotep? No, he was only a coyote, after all. He pointed his muzzle at something over Lewis's shoulder, and Lewis turned and caught his breath.

There they were together on the biggest screen of all, Edward and Mendoza, alive. He wore his commander's uniform, she wore a sleeveless gown of beaded peach silk. He had brought her down an aisle of great palm trees to a caravanserai. Sinuous sensual music was playing, a piece Lewis remembered from the late twentieth century called "Mummer's Dance."

He was unable to take his eyes from the romance. Edward led her to a high white room, shutters open to the blue sky. They undressed, smiling, clothes falling effortlessly like dropped scarves, and on a great wide bed of tapestry silk, all dark colors, gold, wine, burnt orange, green, he lay her down. Her arms went around his neck, and they kissed.

Lewis watched everything he'd ever guiltily imagined.

Joseph, behind him, was barking and howling, because they had come for Lewis at last, the little stupid men with his death. It didn't matter. He reached up his arms to the lovers, and the realization came to him: *This is my salvation.* Dissolving in tears, he fell into the moving images and was lost, and it was so peaceful.

But he woke shaking and cold in his cabin. He sat up and turned on the gimbal light: no pale men, only a white dress shirt over the back of a chair and his own pale face reflected in the mirror over the dresser, its round brass frame like a halo. Shivering, he got up and fumbled with the thermostat. He sat huddled in his bed until morning, staring at the wall, and he never got warm.

New Hampshire, 2276

AFTER UNPACKING HIS suitcase and testing the bed, Lewis glanced at his chronometer. Two hours yet until his job, and the cemetery was within walking distance. He adjusted the room's climate control—nothing seemed to warm him these days—and sat down at the courtesy terminal. He tapped in Joseph's code and waited for the screen to clear.

Joseph, mouth ringed in white foam, was brushing his teeth. "Make this quick, okay?" he said. "I'm turning in."

"Are you going on vacation any time soon?"

"Yes, as a matter of fact." Joseph's eyes narrowed. "I just came off a job. I was thinking of San Francisco."

"What a coincidence," Lewis said. "I was going out to the West Coast myself, for a couple of weeks. Why don't we relive our madness in Ghirardelli Square."

"You all right, Lewis?" The green face—this was a cheap hotel and the terminal's color values were abysmal—loomed grotesquely close to the screen in a gigantic parody of concern. "You don't look so good."

"Do I ever?" Lewis said.

"Any more of that trouble?" Joseph held up his hand in a pistol-shooting gesture.

"None whatsoever."

"You realize we can't get any Theobromos at Ghirardelli Square. All those laws the Yanks passed."

Lewis gave a theatrical sigh. "Well then, what about Santa Catalina Island?"

Even with the awful picture resolution, he could see the lightbulb going on above Joseph's head. "Hm," Joseph said. "Independent republic, lots of little loopholes to let people party. We might be able to score a couple of bars at that. I haven't been over there since—when was it? 1923, I think."

"It's settled, then? Where shall we meet?"

"Where are you now?"

"New Hampshire. Little town called Arkham."

"Ah," Joseph said. "I know what you're doing there. You should be done by noon tomorrow. When you finish, book the next flight to Santa Barbara. I'll meet you in the Street of Spain, and we'll drive to the ferry from there. Bring a lot of cash. I hear it's expensive."

"I have cash to burn these days," Lewis said.

"How nice for you. So, you got that?"

"Street of Spain," Lewis said, accessing a map and locating the ancient shopping quarter of the tiny republic. "I expect to be there at twenty hundred hours tomorrow."

"See you. And, Lewis?"

"Yes?"

"Take care of yourself, okay?"

"Always, old boy."

"Good. Mañana."

Lewis signed out, got up and showered, and took some pains combing his hair afterward. He wanted to look his best. A few minutes past twenty-one hundred hours, a yet unknown young Eccentric would limp into the local cemetery with an old pillowcase full of his writing, intent on offering it and himself in a fiery holocaust to shame the philistine world. There the youth would meet a kindly stranger who would talk him out of it, or so his autobiography would later state: a small fair-haired man in an expensive suit who would give him cash for the contents of his pillowcase, enough cash to pay off the writer's debts and buy him that all-important ticket to New York . . .

Avalon

AT LAST, LEWIS said, spotting the old Casino looming white at the entrance to Avalon Bay. "I don't see why we couldn't have taken a ferry from San Pedro."

"Did you really want to drive through Los Angeles?" Joseph asked, and Lewis shuddered.

A little Island Guard cutter sped close and abreast of them for a few miles, scanning the *Catalina Thunderer*. It was doing this primarily for show; on Catalina it was illegal to sell liquor, meat, refined sugar, dairy products, or other proscribed substances, but it was not illegal to *own* them. This careful loophole brought the island a great deal of happy tourist trade. Avalon Harbor was packed with luxury craft at every mooring, and bigger vessels anchored discreetly farther out to sea, sending launches ashore.

"So here we are," Lewis said, looking at the little white town, the steep green mountains rising behind it forested with ironwoods. *This is where Mendoza was, Joseph, all those years, and we never knew. A beautiful place, isn't it?*

A lot better than it was in the twentieth century, Joseph admitted. *I don't remember all these trees.*

The reforestation project has been under way for three centuries now, Lewis said. *I read it in the guidebook. And, look, there's the Hotel Saint Catherine. Remember? Of course, it's been rebuilt, but the book says it's an exact restoration. We can go to the bar where you thought you saw her.*

I don't know if I want to do that, Lewis.

Well, I do.

Joseph leaned on the rail and considered Lewis obliquely. He was more than a little concerned about his friend. He had run a surreptitious scan on him and found no malfunction, though Lewis was manufacturing compounds associated with severe stress. *Lewis still hadn't explained why they were making this trip.*

You really think we'll find her here, Lewis?

I don't know. She might be here.

Then I guess it's worth a look.

That's what I thought. See that little tower, up on the cliff? It's a bell carillon. It used to strike the hours; the islanders disabled it when they adopted the slogan Where Time Has Stood Still. You won't find a public clock anywhere. All the agcars are required by city ordinance to look like early automobiles, and there are never more than fifty allowed on the island at any one time. New buildings have to be as nearly as possible copies of former ones, and there are only two styles permitted: Mission Revival and Victorian.

So . . . it's perpetually 1923 here?

You could say that. To quote the commercial, "Our island throngs with pleasant ghosts: Laurel and Hardy, Charlie Chaplin, John Wayne, and other immortals from Hollywood's Golden Age. When you encounter the costumed actors portraying these celebrities of olden days, feel free to interact with them and ask questions about their lives and films. Each one is a certified historical reenactor capable of providing you with hours of informative conversation."

Jesus. There's retro and then there's retro.

It's a mecca for reenactors, I understand.

I bet. What is this, Disneyland West?

DisneyCorp doesn't own any of it. It's all run by a preservancy, which is run in turn by the Company. They have extensive offices over at the west end.

I'm not surprised the Company's invested in it. You know how Dr. Zeus is about places that don't change.

And this certainly doesn't change, Lewis said as their ferry pulled up to the mole. He turned to contemplate the little front street, and it did indeed look almost exactly as it had during his visits in the 1920s, with the exception of the slightly awkward Model A Fords floating two feet above the quaint old pavement. Yes, and there were a pair of actors portraying Stan Laurel and Oliver Hardy parading along, tipping their hats grandly to the tourists and posing for holocards.

Joseph and Lewis went ashore, and spent an interminable thirty minutes in customs. When at last they passed through the turnstile and onto the old promenade that led into town, the hotel jitneys had long since departed, so they had to walk all the way around Crescent Avenue to the opposite side of the bay, dragging their suitcases. It was a picturesque walk, at least. Bright fish flitted in the clear water, and up every steep street that rose from the bay they caught glimpses of old gardens where clouds of bougainvillea in all its colors grew below steep gabled roofs. Beyond them loomed the jade-green mountains of the interior.

There were inviting streetside bars, where of course you couldn't buy drinks, but you might buy glasses full of ice, and if you poured something you'd brought ashore with you into one such glass, it was nobody's business but your own. Ice came very dear in Avalon. There were amusement arcades, as there always will be in any seaside town. There were adorable little shops full of wildly overpriced clothes. There were elegant old hotel lobbies and the front porches of little flea-bitten hotels. There were terraced restaurants shaded by olive trees, promising (but only promising) an abundance of dishes they could not legally sell, but could, for a nominal charge, prepare and serve to the determined diner who brought his own ingredients. There were stuccoed arches in the Old Spanish Days style and walls faced with Art Deco patterned tiles in soft primary colors. There were tidy beds of bright flowers.

It was impossible to believe that twenty-six miles away, across a cold stretch of deep water, lay the walled gray port of San Pedro, full of machines, and beyond its walls the war-blasted urban desolation of Los Angeles. If you looked closely at the horizon, you could see the alert gunships of the Island Guard making sure that Los Angeles stayed where it was, too.

Neither Joseph nor Lewis looked. They were too intent on the long, long walk to the Hotel Saint Catherine, in neighboring Descanso Bay. At the neck of the rocky peninsula that divided the two bays, Joseph stopped and stared up in awe at the Casino, which sat square on the middle of the peninsula, towering above them like a twelve-story cake.

"*That* wasn't here in 1923," he gasped. "I'd remember something that size."

"No, indeed," Lewis told him. "The guidebook says it was completed in 1929. No one has any idea why it's called the Casino; all it contains is an early-twentieth-century cinema downstairs and the world-famous Avalon Ballroom upstairs. And there are the murals in the lobby arcade by our old friend Beckman. Remember him?"

"I was posted on the Humashup mission with Beckman," said Joseph, staring fixedly at the murals, which featured an undersea garden motif. A narrow-faced mermaid looked askance at him, hair curl-

ing behind her like wet fire. "You know what this looks like? Right
before we went to Humashup, Mendoza and I! The New Year's ball.
Remember the big tent that Houbert put up? It looked like this."

"You're right," said Lewis. "Dear God. That was the last evening
I ever spent with Mendoza. Is this an omen, do you suppose?"

Watch your mouth.

*You know, I think I'm beginning to fail to give a damn what the
Company hears or doesn't hear anymore.*

*Lewis, for Christ's sake, the Company owns this place. What's
wrong with you?*

I don't know, Joseph. I want to find her, that's all. Lewis didn't
add, *And him,* though he might have. For months the images from his
dream had been with him waking and sleeping. He had secretly begun
to entertain the possibility that perhaps Edward hadn't really died, and
that even now in one of these old gardens the lovers might be embracing . . . All that beauty and strength, warm if unattainable.

He sighed and took the pull handle of his baggage again, and so
did Joseph, and they set off along the graceful promenade into Descanso Bay like two old children trundling wagons after themselves.

The Hotel Saint Catherine rose at the end of the promenade in all
her restored glory, early-twentieth-century Moderne at its stately best.
She consisted of a white central building flanked by two white wings,
embracing a green lawn that went down to the sea. The grounds were
shaded by tropical trees; the little strip of shingle beach was clean and
inviting. Even more inviting was the hotel bar on the beach, roofed
with palm fronds in best South Seas tradition, where a white-jacketed
attendant stood on duty shaking a silver canister vigorously. Joseph
and Lewis groaned like sea lions and trundled straight for him.

It turned out he was only mixing soy-milk smoothies, but that was
enough of an excuse to stop. They collapsed into chairs, gulping their
drinks gratefully. You have to be pretty damned hot and thirsty to
enjoy a soy-milk smoothie, but they were, so it was okay.

This might be a good time to tell me what we're doing here, said
Joseph, looking out at the square-rigged cruise ships that moved gracefully into Avalon Bay.

I made a discovery, Lewis said. *In my research. I have a hunch—
actually more than a hunch—that we might find something important
on this island.*

Such as?

Information about what really happened to Edward.

Joseph controlled his temper carefully. *We came all this way to find out something about Mendoza's dead British secret agent boy-friend. Okay.*

It's more than that, Joseph. I can't go into a lot of detail, but . . . you remember when I told you the British were hunting for something mysterious here? I've turned up a clue as to its whereabouts. Lewis's knuckles were white as he held his glass.

Joseph reached out and took it away from him before it shattered. *Aren't you forgetting something? If there's anything valuable hidden on this island, the Company will have taken possession of it long ago.*

Not if it's never been found. And I have reason to believe it hasn't been.

Okay, Lewis, we'll look for it, whatever it is. Do you have any idea where it is?

We need to go over to the windward side of the island. There are hiking trails, aren't there? We could go hiking.

We could go hiking. Joseph swirled the starchy mess in the bottom of his glass and decided not to order another round. *Lewis, how have you been since Eurobase One?*

How have I been? Well, not exactly at my best, but the damage to my hand self-repaired perfectly. I've been a little jittery, I'll admit.

Still having nightmares?

Yes, but now at least I know what's causing them. No more buried memories.

No other signs of the little freaks?

None at all, thank God, though I still expect them at every turn.

They have to be long gone. Anybody with a technology that might put the Company's operation at risk isn't going to get to keep it. You know the way Dr. Zeus defends its interests. Nothing Joseph was saying seemed to be registering with Lewis, so he leaned forward and looked into Lewis's eyes.

Lewis looked back at him. *I don't think the little men are out of the picture, Joseph.*

All right. Look . . . if they ever come after you again, and you can't get in touch with me? Try to contact the North African Section Head, Suleyman. Look up any chapter house of the Compassionates of Allah and leave him a message. It might not do you any good, but who knows? It's always a good idea to jump out of the way of the rooks and the bishops when the game gets hot.

Are we nothing more than pawns, then?

That's all we are, Lewis. Doesn't mean we can't have a nice va-cation, though. Come on, let's go check in. Joseph took up the handle of his carryall.

If you say so. Lewis followed Joseph up the long sloping lawn of the hotel. The wind rolled in over the sea, rustled in the palm fronds that shaded the little bar, went on up across the green lawn, and in through the terrace windows of the restaurant.

The interior of the hotel was all early-twentieth-century charm, spiced up by murals of a certain naughtiness celebrating the first golden era of bootlegging, among other things. The staff were all in twentieth-century costume, too, like a revival cast of *The Cocoanuts:* desk clerks in stiff wing collars and black tailcoats, bellboys in scarlet tunics and pillbox hats. They probably delighted the largely reenactor clientele. Joseph and Lewis, who really had been there during the 1920s, felt disoriented.

After Joseph hung up his shirts and secured his room, he came out to look for Lewis. Sending a faint inquiring signal, he was answered from the hotel's first floor. He hurried down the grand staircase and saw Lewis at the edge of the lobby, peering into the hotel restaurant. He had a sudden mental image of Lewis being wafted out through the terrace door like a blown cobweb. The image quickened his pace as he crossed the lobby and caught Lewis by the arm.

"You want to eat? Let's go into town. There's supposed to be a great dinner buffet at the Metropole. Come on, I'll call us a cab."

Was it here? Were Edward and Mendoza in here? Lewis asked.

Hell, how should I remember? Anyway it's all wrong. The colors are wrong. And it was early afternoon. That bar's in the wrong place, too. The restorers must have been working from a picture off a reversed negative, it's all mirror image—

You must have been right over there. And they must have been sitting at that table over there, by the terrace doors, to slip away so quickly. Lewis's eyes were haunted, intense with what he was seeing. Joseph scowled, trying not to look into the room.

Will you come on? I'm starving, and I don't want to eat here.

Why? Lewis turned to him. *You're afraid you'll see them again, aren't you?*

No. But it gives me the creeps, Lewis. Let's go, please.

Lewis sighed and allowed Joseph to drag him away.

They floated back to town in one of the Model A agcars, piloted by a costumed driver who was doing his best to speak the American of the period, faithfully reproduced from old films.

"Say! Are you guys having a swell time?"

"Yes, thank you," Lewis said.

"Gee, that's swell." The driver peered at them in the mirror.

"Come over here for relaxation, huh? I know a lot of places that deliver the goods, but plenty, if you know what I mean."

"Actually, we were thinking of hiking," Lewis said. "Are there many hiking trails over here?"

"I'll say. Why, people hike up to the old Wrigley place all the time, and what a view, folks, what a view! And how!"

Do I sound like that? Joseph asked, gritting his teeth in silent mortification.

Of course not, Lewis assured him. *Not all the time, at least.* "Yes, I bet that's a great view. What about the interior, though? Are there any trails that go over to the windward side of the island?"

"Say, what would you want to go *there* for? That ain't no fun, chum, there's nothing over there but what belongs to the preservancy. No booze, no dames, and no trespassing." The cabbie shook his head emphatically as he pulled up to the taxi island in front of the Metropole Hotel. "You want a hot tip? Try the old Pilgrim Club up the street. Plenty of action for a couple of guys like you, believe me. But if you run out of steam, just give me a call." He half turned and presented them with a printed card, grinning. "Ask for Johnny."

"Swell," muttered Joseph, tipping him.

The dinner buffet at the Metropole was swell indeed. It seemed that under Catalina's unique interpretation of vegan laws, seafood qualified as a vegetable. Of course, nothing actually looked like what it was—no staring fish eyes or other recognizable parts, that would have been too much for twenty-third-century sensibilities, everything had been chopped/flaked/formed into nice anonymous shapes and baked or steamed healthily—but there was no mistaking it for soy protein.

Having dined well, Joseph and Lewis opted to forgo the delights of the Pilgrim Club and strolled instead along Crescent Avenue, looking at the shops. This year there were a lot of bright silk garments on display, as there was currently a movement to ban silk on behalf of the silkworms and nobody knew how long supplies would last. In one window was a peach-colored silk dress. Lewis paused before it a long moment, long enough for Joseph to start clearing his throat and shuffling his feet.

It was growing dusk, the blue hour when solid things take on a certain transparency and phantoms become palpable. The olive trees on the promenade began to sparkle with little shifting lights. The shop interior was only half lit, and the reflection of the figures passing in the street created the illusion of busy throngs *inside* the window, a whole world silent on the other side of the glass. Suddenly there was a face above the classic neckline of the peach silk dress, an enigmatic smile, and Lewis muttered an exclamation and turned swiftly.

You thought you saw her? Joseph asked. *Lewis, she isn't here.*

You can't know that.

Why would the Company assign anybody to this place? There's nothing to save here. It's all reconstructions of other things, other times.

Only the town. The interior is all forests. Look, look up here. Lewis hurried to the next building, the brightly lit visitors' center. The walls were faced with lit interactive exhibits displaying the island's natural history, its unique endemic flora and fauna. In the middle of the room, however, was a lit dais, and rising from it was a perfect model of the island in holo, just as it would look seen from the air on a bright summer day at noon.

Lewis paused on his way to the reforestation exhibit, struck by the perfection of the model. He walked around it slowly.

"Wow," Joseph said. "Godzilla's-eye view, huh?" He looked down at the little square grid of toy houses, the toy canister of the Casino on its platform of rock.

Lewis did not reply. He had stopped at the southern windward face of the island. Here it dropped away abruptly in high steep cliffs above the sea, a palisaded wall of rock, unassailable from below. There were caves visible. It was directly behind Avalon, perhaps eleven kilometers away in a straight line.

Joseph, I think I've found what I'm looking for.

That'd be nice. Joseph walked around to his vantage point. He frowned. *Nasty cliffs. We don't have to climb those, do we?*

I don't think so. But see the caves above them? We need to investigate there.

I see. And I forgot to pack hiking boots.

Joseph, we have to look!

Okay, we'll look. Joseph peered down at a tiny incongruity in the green wilderness, a stone tower and sweeping battlements embracing a garden. It was about midway between the town and the palisades. "Hey, check this out. This is supposed to be the Wrigley Monument, Library, and Botanical Garden. You want to go see this library tomorrow? It's supposed to be *the* big collection. Most of what they salvaged from the Library of Congress wound up here."

"Great idea," Lewis said, coming around the holo to see. "Oh, yes, we must visit that. I wonder if there's an admission fee?" *It's right on the way. We can scout out the road tomorrow.*

Joseph and Lewis walked out again into the evening and strolled back to the Hotel Saint Catherine. It was warm, with a sky full of stars now that the last glow of sunset had faded, and from every terrace and balcony came music, and the determined laughter of mortals enjoying lost pleasures. As they passed the old Encanto, a man came reeling drunkenly out into the street toward them, the very image of a South Seas derelict in stained tropical whites and a battered hat. They braced themselves as he accosted them; but he turned out to be merely an actor re-creating Charles Laughton's performance in *The Beach-comber*. They tipped him, and he went away.

Back at the hotel, there was a crowd getting very rowdy on Singapore Slings that may or may not have contained authentic gin. A man at a piano was pounding out "The Sheik of Araby." In the old-fashioned cage elevator, the elevator boy in bandbox uniform insinuated he could get Joseph and Lewis the real thing, and how, if they wanted some fun. All they had to do was ring the desk and ask for Johnny.

"Do you suppose he meant liquor or prostitutes?" wondered Lewis as they trudged down the hall to their rooms.

"Liquor, probably," Joseph said wearily. "If you ordered up a whore here, you'd probably get a theater major doing Joan Crawford as Sadie Thompson. I wonder what would happen if I ordered a Hershey bar?" His eyes lit up for a moment. "I wonder what would happen if I ordered a whore *and* a Hershey bar?"

"You'll never know unless you ask," Lewis said.

"How true." Joseph peered back down the hall toward the elevator. "Well. Nighty night, sleep tight, don't let the bedbugs bite, okay, Lewis?"

"Good night," said Lewis, and unlocked his door and stepped inside.

The hotel room was lovingly re-created to look like any one of the dozen hotel rooms he'd lived in during the twentieth century. Of course there was a modern entertainment center in the period-styled armoire, and of course the plumbing and heating were state of the art; but the narrow bed would be authentically empty when he lay him down to sleep.

He went to the window and looked out at the night. Dark branches, rustling in the night wind, and the sigh and crash of breakers on sand. Faint music, laughter, Joseph's door opening and closing, voices. The clink-clink of rigging and blocks on the little pleasure boats rocking at their moorings.

But not *their* voices anywhere, Mendoza's voice shy and young as it must have sounded once, Edward's voice strong and confident.

No, Lewis could fantasize all he liked, but the stony likelihood was that Edward was dead, long dead, and Mendoza was alone, wherever she was. There would never be the ending Lewis hoped for, with the gallant commander somehow claiming his Spanish lady.

I will not be silenced.

Lewis turned, electrified by an idea. It was the same empty room it had been a moment before, but now the air was full of voices. The yellow pool of light around the table lamp was like an island in the night sea, welcoming, full of promise. With trembling hands he pulled his Buke out of its case and set it up in the lamplight. He turned it on and opened a new file.

It asked him for a name. After a moment's hesitation he typed in HAPPY ENDING. Then he paused over the keyboard, biting his lower lip. He'd never read much science fiction; he'd never written any. True, he had seen the classic Hollywood epics . . . But the future hadn't turned out the way they'd imaged it.

"Don't leave me, Captain!" begged Zorn, reaching out a bloody hand.

"He's done for, Hawke," Moxx grunted. "And if we don't get back to the ship soon, O'Grady will take off without us!"

Captain Marshawke Daxon paused to fire another laser blast at the pursuing Company troops before he snapped, "I don't care! I'm not leaving anyone to be interrogated. If they find out about the contraband, we're all done for!"

"I'll put him out of his misery, then—" began Moxx, but scarcely were the words out of his mouth when he found himself staring into Captain Daxon's icy blue eyes, lit with the glare of deadly rage usually reserved for the smuggler chief's worst enemies. He had taken hold of the front of Moxx's spacesuit and hoisted him bodily into the air, and Moxx's jackboots dangled a full twelve uncomfortable inches from the ground.

"You shoot any member of this band, and you'll have me to reckon with, do you understand?" roared Captain Daxon.

"Aye, Captain!" gasped Moxx.

"We haven't got time for this," Berenice reminded them, ducking as a laser beam shattered the top of the rocky outcropping behind which they had taken cover. "They're advancing again, Hawke!"

"Right." Captain Daxon dropped Moxx and turned decisively. He bent swiftly to Zorn and hauled the wounded man over his shoulder. "We'll run for it. Go! Go! I'll keep you covered!"

The smugglers took to their heels, scrambling frantically over the rugged island slopes as laser fire shrieked out on all sides. Over the next ridge they could just glimpse the silver nose of the *Starfire*, with clouds of smoke coiling up around her: O'Grady must have already started up the star drive.

Captain Daxon brought up the rear, a towering figure in black smuggler's leathers, turning frequently to rake the advancing Company troops with withering laser fire as his band ran for their lives. He was slowed only a little by Zorn's considerable weight, but it proved to be, fatally, enough: for as he turned and fled again, leaping skillfully from rock to rock, a blast screamed terribly near and he felt a sudden sickening impact. Zorn stiffened and groaned once; Daxon staggered and nearly fell, then ran on, but was conscious of sticky warmth flooding down his side.

The other smugglers had already vanished over the crest of the hill, and the *Starfire* was now hidden in boiling clouds. O'Grady was going to leave without them!

Cursing under his breath, Daxon ran faster; only at the last moment did he spot the chasm opening in the rock, almost under his boots.

"Hold on for your life, Zorn!" he cried, and vaulted into space. Wide as the chasm was, he could have easily leapt it under ordinary circumstances: for Marshawke Daxon was no ordinary man. Zorn's dead weight worked against him, however, and his fingers clawed desperately at the edge of the abyss a moment before losing their hold. Down, down he fell, as laser fire whistled through the space he'd occupied scant milliseconds before.

Daxon spotted a projecting edge of rock and grabbed for it. He caught it, and the rock held; but to his horror, he felt Zorn slipping, falling free. As he looked over his shoulder he beheld Zorn plummeting down, limp as a broken doll, staring up with wide unseeing eyes. Daxon had been carrying a dead man.

Thief though he was, Daxon felt an involuntary prayer for the man's soul rise to his lips. He looked up at the narrow strip of sky and beheld the *Starfire* rising gracefully against the sun. Had the crew made it aboard? Even as he wondered, laser fire

came from some source too near to allow him time for
reflection. Using the force of will that had made him a legend in
the renegade underworld, Daxon pulled himself up on the edge,
groping for a better handhold.

To his astonishment, his hand seemed to disappear in midair.
Understanding instinctively what he had found, he threw himself
forward at what appeared to be sheer rock wall but was in fact
an illusion, a trick of light to conceal the tunnel mouth that was
really there. Daxon rolled and came up on his feet, staring
around, all his senses sharpened by danger. Slowly, silently he
drew his laser pistol. Beyond the tunnel mouth, outside, the
whine of laser fire was louder; the troops had come up to the
edge of the abyss and were firing down, now, at what must have
been Zorn's just barely visible corpse. Daxon held his breath
and waited for them to stop and move on.

He was in a smooth-walled passage that led into the depths
of the island, but not into darkness; far down its length was an
eerie blue glow. On the wall immediately opposite where he
stood a steel plate was set into the wall, with the words SITE 317
inscribed upon it.

Daxon began to edge his way along the tunnel, moving with
the silence of a great cat. Something about the blue light drew
him, for a reason he was never afterward to explain
satisfactorily. Down he went and down, into the subterranean
lair of . . . what?

After a hundred paces the tunnel opened out into a room, lit
by the blue glow that had become stronger and brighter as he
had descended. Daxon stepped into that room and caught his
breath at what he saw there.

The blue glow was emanating from a great vault made of
what appeared to be transparent glass. Floating within was a girl,
naked, dreaming, and her long hair was the color of fire and
moved like flame in the slow currents of the heavy fluid that
imprisoned her.

Daxon walked like a man in the grip of enchantment. He
knew her: surely he knew her, had always known that graceful
body, that face at once childlike yet possessed of a somber
dignity. He knew that her eyes, when they opened, would be
black as smoldering coals in her pale face; he knew that her hair
was fragrant with myrrh and attar of roses, that he'd buried his
face in its burning waves. When had he done that? How did he
know these things?

Impossible memories rose to assail him, of places he'd never been, in an era long past. Suddenly he remembered the sea, and the man he'd been once, a man with nobler aspirations perhaps than mere smuggling, and the girl's name, which had been . . . Mendoza.

He could not say with any certainty just who he had been, or why he remembered these things; it was enough that he remembered the girl, and knew that she was his true love. This he knew beyond all doubt, as tears streamed down his unshaven face.

Acting on impulse, Daxon aimed his pistol at the imprisoning glass and fired. The whole side of the vat gave way and flooded its contents outward: but he was there to catch her as she was spilled free, and he held her above the glittering blue tide and splashed to a couch at one side of the room which he had not previously noticed.

There he lay her down. She was shivering, trembling with returning life, only barely conscious. He knelt beside her, unable to keep his mouth from hers any longer; and her lips were warm as he kissed her, and opened in surprise as she woke to him.

Yes, that was the mouth that had haunted him in dreams, all the years of his life. He had wanted to kiss that coral mouth, stroke that body of ivory, wind his hands in the copper hair unbound at last for him, for him, she was his now. None of the others had mattered. This was the one he'd searched for, never knowing.

"Mendoza," he gasped. She opened her dark eyes and saw his dear familiar face: her incoherent cry of joy echoed in that cavern.

Lewis got up and stumbled into the bathroom, where he pulled a handful of tissues from the dispenser and dried his streaming tears. Blowing his nose, he sat down again and reached for the keyboard.

They melted into another kiss. Daxon knew that whatever had sundered them in the past, he would never let her slip through his fingers again; somehow he knew that at last, after centuries of heartbreak and false starts, their story was truly beginning.

And though they were going to escape from that dark prison and soar free of the Company, though they were about to go on to a life of wonderful adventures together, this perhaps would be

the moment to wreathe around in flowers as their happy ending:
the ending of their separation and lost years. Love had
triumphed at last.

Lewis read it over, wiping away the tears that still welled in his
eyes. It wasn't good enough, it never was; he couldn't write worth a
damn.

He sagged at the table, looking out from the circle of light into
the shadows of his room. It was late. Almost no sound in the grand
old hotel, where the mortals on night shift leaned half asleep at their
posts. A wind moving through the dark garden. The quiet surge of the
sea. Less quiet surging from Joseph's room, where a certain rhythm
of sounds and voices suggested that Joseph wasn't alone.

Lewis got up and opened the compartment in his suitcase that
concealed the flask. He found a chilled bottle of mineral water in the
minibar and a glass, poured himself a drink, and added gin. He went
back and sat in the circle of lamplight, sipping his drink, reading over
what he'd written.

The bed still waited on the other side of the room, as narrow and
cold as before. He wasn't ready to face it yet.

"You know, guy, you're not getting enough sleep," Joseph remarked at breakfast. "You look like hell."

Lewis shrugged and warmed his hands on a cup of herbal tea.
Bootlegged coffee was harder to come by than gin.

"Maybe we should concentrate on relaxing today. There's a nice
golf course here. You play golf?" Joseph asked.

"From time to time," Lewis said.

"A lot of nice greens." Joseph indicated the brochure he'd picked
up at the front desk. "Oldest miniature golf course in the world. Famous pitch-and-putt course. World-Class Restored Course of the Stars.
That's in Avalon Canyon, here." He opened out the brochure and held
it up so Lewis wouldn't miss the point he was making: Avalon Canyon
pointed straight behind the town, toward the palisades.

"That looks challenging," Lewis said. "Perhaps we can stroll up
there and see."

"We can check it out, anyway. And look, just a little way farther
up the road is that memorial thing, with the library. You wanted to
see that. And it looks like there's some hiking trails behind the library.
Sounds like a great way to spend the day, getting lots of fresh air and
exercise. I bet you sleep tonight." *I've got it all figured out. We walk
up there today, see what the best route is for getting into the interior,
and then come back. Dinner, early bedtime, and as soon as it's dark*

and you're in bed with your eyes shut, you turn on a little device I'm going to slip you. It'll zap the datalink, but if anybody's monitoring you, they won't be able to tell, because you'll have gone to bed so they'll think it's normal to be getting a black screen. Is that subtle or what?

Bravo, Joseph.

Thanks. I have a zapper too. We get dressed again and sneak out, head straight up Avalon Canyon, and you can look for your secret whatever it is all night if you want. As long as we're back in our beds by morning when transmission resumes, nobody will ever know we were up there.

"Yes," Lewis said aloud. "Let's do that. Fresh air and exercise, that's what I need. What a Facilitator you are!"

"Just fulfilling my program," Joseph said, grinning. He looked at Lewis's untouched tofu waffle. "You going to finish that?"

"Be my guest," said Lewis, pushing it across the table to him. "Let's go as soon as you've finished, shall we?"

"Mm," Joseph agreed, mouth full.

It was a bright and hopeful morning, if a rather silent one. In all the terraced restaurants, trays of breakfast were being sent back by disgruntled merrymakers, to be replaced by trays bearing tomato drinks festooned with celery or chaste bottles of mineral water. Even Laurel and Hardy looked a little green around the gills as Joseph and Lewis passed them, though they tipped their derbies gallantly.

At Sumner Avenue the two real immortals turned right and walked in the direction of the interior, through the residential district with its high narrow Victorian houses, and beyond, where they entered Avalon Canyon Road. Once they had passed through the maze of screening pepper trees, they got their first clear view of the long valley that ran back into the interior.

It was surprisingly wild-looking. Great sleek mountains faced one another, ignoring the emerald-green golf course that climbed their lower slopes. The road ran up the right-hand side of the valley, between stone walls that blazed with flowering vines, and a double row of palm trees spread vast fanned crowns over most of its length. Looking up at them, Lewis caught his breath. He remembered Edward and Mendoza walking together here, under these enormous palms. These were the trees in his dream.

"Nice golf course," said Joseph pleasantly. *What's wrong?*

Look at this green valley. Joseph, I think the agricultural station was here. This had to have been Mendoza's prison.

You have some psychic hunch about this, huh?
Call it what you like. She was here.
A hundred and fifty thousand years ago, maybe.
Lewis exhaled sharply. "Yes, this *is* a nice golf course. Let's see more of it, shall we?"
They walked on, and the valley was quiet in the sunlight, and the mountains watched them.
Tell me something, Lewis. We didn't really come here because you had some kind of vision or dream. You turned up some hard evidence about whatever it is we're looking for, didn't you?
Yes. What do you think I am, a complete fool?
Lewis, I wish to God I knew what you are.
Lewis set his chin and marched stubbornly on, so that Joseph had to hurry after him, passing in and out of the shadows cast by the great palms.

In less than an hour they came to the head of the valley, which narrowed gradually beyond the golf course until the road was running up its center, through a green twilight cast by great old mahogany trees that grew down the flanks of the mountains on either side. Here a pair of ornate gateposts rose, supporting between them a wrought-iron arch bearing the words THE WILLIAM K. WRIGLEY MEMORIAL GARDEN AND LIBRARY.

They looked through the arch. There was an open area like an amphitheater, full of sunlight and air, and the paved road gave way to a raked gravel one branching off into neat beds of endemic plants. Looming above the garden, backed into the mountain beyond, was a stone tower seven stories tall, reached by sweeping staircases to the right and left that converged on a terrace at its base.

Joseph and Lewis walked up through the botanical garden, half expecting a familiar figure to rise from her work and look in their direction. Nothing moved but a raven, which swooped down to land on the path and cocked a bright inquisitive eye at them. It did not speak. At the monument they took the left staircase, ascending through figured bronze doors, climbing to the central courtyard with its patterned tile walls, its friezes of pink-and-green stone carved with birds and sea creatures.

It was a tomb fit for a Moorish emperor, not for a chewing gum magnate. His family had thought so too, because they'd had his body removed shortly after his death and reinterred in some sensible little American cemetery on the eastern seaboard. And so the tomb here stood empty, in all its lonely and absurd grandeur, until a certain Kronos Diversified Stock Company offered to excavate the heart of the mountain behind it and put in a library worthy of ancient Alexandria.

This Joseph and Lewis learned from a brass plate set beside the door of the elevator that would have taken them down into the library, had it not been locked. The plate further informed them that actual physical visits to the library were by appointment only, on certain days of the week, to persons with the proper academic credentials.

"Well, that's a sign of the times, I must say," remarked Lewis in disappointment. *The Company again. Good lord, there are probably books I acquired for them in there.*

Joseph shrugged. "Who reads anymore?" *It's very Company, though, isn't it? Collect a huge mass of something really valuable, put it in an unbelievably safe place where the monkeys can't get at it, and sit on it. Nice piece of design. Bet it's safe from electromagnetic pulses and anything else that could happen.*

"What a pity." Lewis put his hands in his pockets and strolled out into the courtyard, looking down the right-hand staircase. "There appears to be a trailhead over there. Do you suppose we could follow it to the other side of the island?"

They could and did, up a steep switchback grade. It brought them, after an hour's steady labor, to the top of the coastal ridge. The view was well worth the climb: sea in all directions dotted with white sails, the long valley opening out to their right with the little white town at its end. To their left, wild canyons descended to the windward shore, beyond a fence posted with the sign NO ADMITTANCE. ENDEMIC SPECIES PRESERVE.

Somewhere down there, transmitted Lewis, staring.

You think so? Joseph pretended to shade his eyes with his hand, scanning intently. He turned this way and that, recording, interpreting, analyzing. *I don't find anything, Lewis. And that's good. I'm picking up definite Company signals off at the other end of the island, and some from the library below; but nothing in this quarter. It's called Silver Canyon on the maps.*

I don't read any trails going in or out, either.

You're sure this is the place?

Joseph, I know it. Standing here, I can almost hear her voice.

Not as bad as I thought. Just a few square miles of wilderness nobody cares about. No alarms, no security techs. I hope you brought working clothes?

Naturally.

And you're not going to die of disappointment if we don't find anything?

We'll find something, Joseph.

Tonight, then. Joseph yawned and stretched. "Some view, huh? I could use a sandwich right about now. Want to head back down?"

Back in town, the very picture of relaxed vacationers, they spent an enjoyable afternoon idling. They ate lunch at one of the terraced restaurants, and played several games of miniature golf on a course set up as an English-style formal garden complete with maze and marjoram knots. They took several tours, including the noted glass-bottomed boat ride. They dressed formally for an early dinner and went to the Avalon Ballroom to hear swing music played by a Benny Goodman reenactor with his reenactor band. Charlie Chaplin wandered over to their table and attempted a conversation in mime. They tipped him, and he went away.

As they walked back to the Hotel Saint Catherine, Joseph lurched a little on the stair and bumped into Lewis. Lewis felt something slipped into the pocket of his dinner jacket.

That's the signal killer?

That's yours. I've been playing around with a model Latif designed. It looks like a class ring. Slip it on. When you're back in your room, go through the whole business of getting undressed, getting into bed, turning off the light, closing your eyes; then activate the ring by turning the bezel mount to the left. It's good for ten hours. Then get up and put your work clothes on. I'll meet you in the hall.

I feel like James Bond.

Cool, huh?

There was nothing remarkable about two gentlemen in formal dinner dress going to their rooms at ten o'clock in the evening. There was nothing remarkable about their reemergence twenty minutes later, dressed in simple exercise suits of dark-gray cotton fleece and dark running shoes. A certain amount of daily exercise was mandated by law in the twenty-third century, and many people preferred to jog in the cool of the evening.

So nobody noticed the two gentlemen as they pounded dutifully along Casino Way and then Crescent Avenue, or as they turned up Sumner. When they neared Avalon Canyon Road, an observer might have found it curious that they were increasing their speed, inasmuch as they were now going uphill. But all the golfers of the day were long since sprawled in front of entertainment centers with drinks in their hands, so there was no observer. Which was a good thing, because just past the pitch-and-putt greens the two gentlemen, shifting into hyperfunction, accelerated into blurs and vanished up the canyon, on the dark road under the white stars.

Where do we start?

Good question. Joseph looked down from the spine of the island, regarding the impenetrable dark mass of trees. He switched to infrared, and it lit up for him. Ordering a topographical analysis, he saw the whole landscape behind his eyes, neatly lined and graded. Beside him, Lewis was doing the same thing.

Let's start with the nearest ridge and work our way along it, scanning downhill as we go, said Joseph.

Good thinking. We're looking for caves and electromagnetic anomalies that would suggest old excavation.

That's what I thought.

They jumped the fence and moved out together, silent in the gigantic silence of that night. Not a bird called, the crickets had fallen still, no wind moved in the trees. Even the surf washing the rocks far below made no perceptible sound.

Here's something. Lewis transmitted.

Joseph whirled to scan. He found the anomaly and analyzed; moved in a little closer for greater detail. *Old mine adit, probably.*

How old is it, do you think?

We'll see.

They worked their way down the hill slowly and found the adit, half collapsed and masked by bushes, invisible to mortal eyes even by daylight. Joseph extended his scan, detected the remains of wooden supports, analyzed the extent of their decay. *I'd have to say 1890s, plus or minus a decade. That doesn't fit, though, does it?*

No. What we're looking for should be much older. Something prior to 1492.

You think your mystery is from a pre-Columbian civilization?

It might be.

Wow. Okay, let's move on.

They went back up the hill and continued along its crest. They found evidence of three more adits, all dating from the same era, then traces of grading that might have been a road for pack horses, also from the late nineteenth century. There were a number of spot anomalies where holes had been. The holes might have been dug for buried treasure or camp latrines, or might have been the work of extraordinarily busy ground squirrels. When they came to the end of one ridge, they made their way down and up the side of the next and began again.

Two hours went by in this way, yielding no caves and nothing else of interest.

In the third hour they entered a region west of their starting point, where even the ground squirrels had never chosen to burrow. Lewis was silent and withdrawn, and Joseph ran a diagnostic on himself for malfunction. It didn't seem possible they'd found a place where *nothing* had ever disturbed the soil.

Then, abruptly, it showed up on both their internal screens at once: an anomaly bigger than any they had seen yet, undoubtedly a cave. There was something else, too.

What the hell is that? Joseph stopped in his tracks.

Is that old aircraft wreckage? And there's . . . some kind of masking wave. It's cloaking most of an acre. To hide the wreckage from discovery, or is this one of your bunkers, Joseph?

No. Joseph was staring hard at the anomaly. *I know where all the bunkers are, and there are none on this island.*

There aren't?

I can tell you one thing for certain: the masking isn't being generated by any Company technology. That's one weird frequency. There's a cave there, all right. I don't know what the wreck is, though. And I'm not picking up any life signs, are you?

No.

But I think there's a dead mortal.

Edward. It must be Edward. Lewis started for the anomaly at a run.

Joseph stood gaping a moment before he ran after him. *Come back here. Are you nuts? Was this what you dragged us up here after? A goddam dead Englishman?*

I thought—Nennius implied—

They skidded to a stop just short of the anomaly. Lewis stared down, white-faced, at the old wreckage: a small Beecraft of the kind that had been popular just before antigravity was patented. Its stubby wings and fuselage had smashed on impact, but the cockpit was intact. A skull grinned through the windshield at Lewis, an ordinary mortal skull, nothing remarkable about its shape.

When did you talk to Nennius? said Joseph, seizing Lewis by the arm.

Last year. He told me about Edward, he said his disappearance might have been connected with a cave up here. Lewis had begun to shake.

Joseph let go his arm and doubled over, as though he was going to be physically ill. *You fool. How could you have been so stupid as to tell Nennius—of all people—about what we've been doing all these years?*

I didn't! It happened by chance. We ran into each other on a cruise, and he told me the story to pass the time.

Then he knew about you, Lewis. The Company finally noticed your prying into old secrets, and they sent him after you. He set a trap, and we've walked right into it. Mendoza's not here, and neither is Edward. We've got to get the hell out before the security techs come for us.

Joseph straightened up and looked around, preparing to run for his life; but it was too late.

"We have weapons," a drippy little voice informed them.

Both turned. There, instead of the phalanx of security techs they expected, stood three small pale men, dressed in what appeared to be golfing ensembles. They did indeed have weapons, and the weapons were trained on Lewis.

"You don't do anything smart, this time," said the foremost of the men. "We wait here until the others come for us. Then we take you home."

Joseph, they're only after me, transmitted Lewis, deadly calm. *You can get away.*

"For Christ's sake!" snarled Joseph, and winked out, to reappear between Lewis and the pale men. "Go, Lewis! Look, you stupid little—Ow!"

Lewis, who had obediently winked out and reappeared thirty yards away, heard Joseph's howl of pain. He saw the pale men firing again, and watched in horror as Joseph fell.

Then he was beside Joseph, caught hold of him, and they were away, this time getting as far as the next canyon before Lewis lost momentum. When they stopped, Joseph tottered a moment and fell again. He struggled to pull himself up but seemed unable to use his left arm and leg.

Lewis crouched over him. *My God, I've killed us both.*

Joseph struggled, making croaking noises. His face was terrifying: the left side slack, the left eye turned up sightless and white. The right eye rolled wildly as he strained to see over Lewis's shoulder. Lewis followed his stare to behold three little globes of light floating over the ridge, coming after them.

Betrayed, said Joseph. *Company told them, deal. Find you. Company let them take—*He went into a seizure.

Lewis, supporting his head, looked across the canyon in quiet despair. The lights came closer. *Can you see, Joseph? Can you hear me?*

Uh.

I'll lead them away from you. I'll go as far as I can. They might forget there were two of us. Try to crawl to cover. If you can make it to morning, most of your systems ought to reset, and you can get away. I am so very sorry about this, Joseph.

Lewis.

But Lewis had winked out, and at the head of the canyon Joseph heard a shout and saw a waving figure, dark against the skyline.

"Here I am! Up here, you wretched imbeciles!" yelled Lewis, and dashed over the top out of sight. The three lights froze and then moved after him with uncanny speed, drifting above the brush like balloons. Joseph was left in darkness. He tried to keep from passing out from the pain, which was unlike anything he'd experienced in his twenty-odd thousand years.

After a moment he was able to coordinate his right arm and leg sufficiently to drag himself backward, half upright in the deeper gloom of an ironwood thicket. Panting, he tried to run a self-diagnostic. As he did so, he heard a distant crashing, a faint shout from Lewis, something Joseph couldn't make out.

There was another light on the ridge across from him.

Right eye widening, Joseph crouched back into the shadows. Someone whined in the darkness beside him. But there was no one beside him. On the opposite ridge a lot of lights now moved fast, all in a line, like ants following ants, following Lewis, up and over the ridge. A torchlight procession. The Hollywood Bowl performance of *Midsummer Night's Dream.* When was that, 1938? Max Reinhardt's stupendous colossal extravaganza. Fairies in the trees with lights. Shine, little glowworm. Joseph went with Lewis, had drinks afterward in the bar at Musso and Frank's, Lewis in his tuxedo elegant and so funny critiquing the show over his martini, acting out the worst moments, Joseph laughing and laughing—

A flare of light in his face, a tremendous vibration. He was flat on his back looking up at the biggest damn full moon he'd ever seen. But the moon didn't notice him, it rose majestically and drifted up over the ridge, following all the little horrible lights. It dipped out of sight on the other side, but he could still see the glow through the trees.

As he was levering himself upright again, with unbelievable effort, he heard far off a long, wavering cry of agony.

Lewis!

He toppled and fell, going into another seizure. When it subsided, he grappled frantically at roots, stones, anything to pull himself along, anything to go in the opposite direction from the monstrous light, scuttling like a crab, blindly going faster and faster, and gravity was helping him now, because he was rolling, tumbling, oh *shit* he'd forgot about the cliffs—

Roaring air for a moment, and then a deafening crash as he hit the water. Darkness and deathly cold. Smashed like a bug. But he wouldn't drown, would he? He was immortal.

He was floating face up when the full moon reappeared, drifting over the top of the cliff. He gasped and flailed, but once again it took no notice of him. It rotated, and he saw it was a beautiful craft really, a glowing drop. It hesitated a moment before moving out to sea, picking up speed as it went but still zigging and wobbling unsteadily, as though piloted by idiots.

He watched it leave. It had no need to come back: it had caught what it had been hunting for so long.

San Pedro

MAN? BOAT? DEAD? *Not dead?*

Joseph was instantly awake, his eye narrowed. He waited until he felt the prodding beak again, nudging his painful ribs.

Not-man? Dead?

Alive! He grappled with his right arm and clung, sinking his teeth into its dorsal fin for good measure as the dolphin screamed and darted under, trying frantically to throw him off. He hung on, through a long icy bubbly ride.

Ow ow! Not-man, off! Not-man, off!

Hear me.

Okay!

Seek boat. You swim me to boat. In boat, I stop bite, you go.

Okay, the dolphin agreed sullenly, and they rose slowly to the surface. The dolphin cast about for a ship, located one, and swam for it awkwardly, still giving a stealthy flip now and then in hopes of dislodging Joseph, who gripped it like grim death.

Not soon enough for either of them, the animal closed with its object, a small craft cutting through the darkness under power. It was towing a dinghy.

Baby boat, Joseph indicated. The dolphin swam to the dinghy. Joseph lunged and got his leg over the side, then his arm. He rolled gasping into the bottom of the dinghy, as the dolphin called him dirty names and swam away.

He looked up at the stars. Late, look how far they'd wheeled across the sky. He closed his eyes for a moment, and when he opened them, the sky was pale, the stars had disappeared. Gray air, stale smells, and suddenly a very large tanker was taking up most of the view. He lurched up on his right elbow. The left side of his body was still dead.

Important things to do right now:

1. Reactivate signal killer.
2. Get out of dinghy before you are noticed.

Joseph groped for his left hand, pulled it into his lap, twisted the bezel on the ring, and felt a comforting little jolt. He writhed around and took his bearings.

He was traveling into San Pedro Harbor courtesy the good ship *Bobbi Jo*, which seemed to be making for a berth near the old Ports O' Call sector. He made a tentative attempt to access a map; he got one! Los Angeles County. In the last moments before the *Bobbi Jo* docked, he scanned the map, made a plan, and rolled over the side into murky water.

Ten minutes later, he was crouched shivering under a boat dock, snarling at the crabs who advanced, intrigued by his condition. Finally he killed a few of them and cracked them open, and sucked the meat out of the pieces of shell.

He stayed there all day, unnoticed by anyone. By nightfall his left leg responded to commands somewhat, though he was still blind and deaf on the left side and unable to use his left arm at all. In the afternoon he reactivated the signal killer.

When the evening grew late and quiet, he crawled out and up to the marina. Filthy, unshaven, staggering, he looked like any of the other zombies who roamed the night. He quickly found the paths they used, the alleyways and ugly places where they passed freely, invisible to others. Before morning he found his way to the city wall. He waited near an access port and watched. At dawn a convoy of transports lined up to exit. He shambled to the last one, swung himself up on its loading step, and hung on for dear life. He didn't worry about being seen. Nobody cared about people going *out* to Los Angeles; it was only the incoming transports that were searched for refugees.

He clung like a limpet as the transport picked up speed, following the route of what used to be the old Harbor Freeway. As it drew near a certain overpass in Compton, he launched himself and fell, rolling and tumbling down the embankment, to come to rest against an ancient chain-link fence in a nest of blown paper and trash. The rest of the world collected its garbage to run fusion plants: not Los Angeles.

He lay there bleeding, running a self-diagnostic. Contusions, minor cuts, no more.

Growling at no one in particular, he dragged himself upright and stumbled along the verge, until he was able to find an offramp. He seemed to have sustained a scalp wound, and now the blood was running down into his good eye. Blinking, he made his way into Watts and shambled down Avalon Boulevard, looking through the ruins for an address.

Nobody bothered him.

The mission was easy to spot. It was the only intact building for blocks, had once been a big rambling private house, and there was a line of people stretching out the door onto the front porch. They looked at him, appalled, except for the young man in some kind of monastic habit who was addressing them, handing each one a form to fill out. Joseph wiped the blood from his eye and read the sign mounted above the porch: THE COMPASSIONATES OF ALLAH. He lurched forward and began to crawl up the stairs.

Somebody finally thought to nudge the brother and tell him there was a white guy getting into line. The young man snapped out: "No whites treated here—" Then he saw Joseph and stopped, gulping. Joseph fixed him with his good eye, which the blood was obscuring again, and tried to form words. He couldn't, quite.

An elderly lady groped in her pocket for a handful of gray paper napkins and held them out to Joseph timidly. He accepted them and wiped his bleeding face. She told the young brother she thought Joseph might be Mexican. He leaned forward and told Joseph, in Spanish, that this was a blacks-only immunization center. Joseph just stared at him, breathing harshly.

"Maybe Filipino?" somebody else suggested.

Joseph raised his hand and made a writing gesture in midair.

The people in the line conferred briefly among themselves and decided that maybe the brother had better take the stranger inside before he died on the porch. Thoroughly unnerved, the young man went to the door and opened it, pointing inside. Why was Joseph moving so slowly? Blood loss. Internal hemorrhaging. Estimate fugue state in four minutes fourteen seconds, if self-repair not initiated prior to that time.

Inside was a waiting room. The young man held open a door marked EMERGENCY CARE for Joseph, waving at him to go in, but Joseph spotted the one marked ADMINISTRATOR and pushed that instead, and went through.

A thin-featured black man in old-fashioned reading glasses was going over forms at a desk. He glanced up in irritation at being interrupted, and his eyes widened at the sight of Joseph. Limping just ahead of the young man, who had run after him, Joseph grabbed a grease pencil from a jar on the desk and got its cap off. On the back of a form he wrote, with infinite care, the word *Suleyman*.

The Administrator looked at him sharply.

That was the last clear impression Joseph had for a while.

He was on a cot in a locked room. Mortals had carried him there. There were compresses on his wounds. It was day. He moved convulsively, twisted the bezel of the ring. Still safe.

It was night. He had a blanket now. Bandages too. The ring, again. Still safe.

Still night, but there were mortals moving around him, cutting away his torn and filthy clothing, washing him, bandaging him again, exclaiming over his bruises. Black men, all in the same monastic robes. They were talking to him, trying to get him upright, into white cotton pajamas. They put shoes on his feet. They pushed his arms through the sleeves of a long coat. Then, thank God, they let him lie down again.

Somebody was feeding him broth. Did he think he could manage with a straw? He tried. He managed, mostly, and somebody wiped away what had run from the slack corner of his mouth. He thought they would let him sleep then, but here were more of them, back with a stretcher. They moved him onto the stretcher and took him out into the night air. It was foul and cold. Old petroleum sump nearby. He was riding in an ambulance—when did that happen? An ambulance but no siren. He remembered the ring again.

They told him to be quiet, that they had to wait for the gate patrolman who knew them.

A shipyard? He had the sudden awful feeling that he was still crouched under the dock, eating crabs, and had only dreamed he made it this far. No, they were explaining that he had no papers, but Suleyman had arranged passage anyway. It was just getting light as he was carried on board the ship, big square freight barge, unlovely thing. Down to a tiny dark closet of a room. The fusion drive boomed steadily somewhere close. They all went away and left him, except the man in the reading glasses. Darkness. The ship was moving out. He could sleep now.

He slept for a long time in the darkness. Brother Ibrahim never left him. He explained about the ring, how it had to be twisted every ten hours. Brother Ibrahim knew. Suleyman had made the ring? Sort of. It was all right.

Day was nearly as dark as night, except for long slanting fingers of sunlight that somehow found their way down into the hold and through his ventilation grate.

He woke weeping, weeping for Lewis, and Brother Ibrahim comforted him. You have no souls, he explained in Arabic, and so need fear no fires of hell. But if your friend was serving Allah's purpose, he died in glory and light, and feels no pain, which is the best that can possibly be hoped for such creatures. Moreover, he is remembered eternally, for God forgets nothing, and surely that is a kind of eternal life.

Joseph agreed hazily. But how had they come to be speaking in seventh-century Arabic?

You spoke first, Brother Ibrahim told him in mild surprise.

Oh, you're a scholar?

Yes, Brother Ibrahim was a scholar.

Sunlight stripes followed by darkness, followed by sunlight. He could see a little out of his left eye now, he could manage the straw better. He could work the thumb on his left hand. Brother Ibrahim told him the wounds were healing.

The smells changed. He could smell land. Then, a flood of air and light, and mortals came in through the doorway. More brothers. Moonlight? Brief muttered conversations in French. Brother Ibrahim was coming with him, must deliver Joseph into Suleyman's hands himself, he had promised to. They reached an agreement, and the stretcher was taken up again. Joseph was carried out into the night, tilting this way, tilting that way, and into the back of a van with Brother Ibrahim crowded in beside him. A long, long drive.

Fez

JOSEPH.

Suleyman was looking into his eyes.

"Joseph, you're not self-repairing fast enough. We're going to help you."

"Will it hurt?"

"We'll have to shut you down to do it."

"That figures," Joseph grumbled, and lost consciousness again.

Silence, incredible silence. He was alone, and damaged.

Well, of course he was damaged. Shot twice by a death ray, fell off a cliff, was half drowned, and jumped from the back of a convoy speeding through Watts.

No, he was *really* damaged.

His eyes were swollen nearly shut, his sinus cavities plugged solid and throbbing. Someone had done maxillofacial surgery on him, broken his nose . . .

His datalink was gone. Not offline, not even temporarily disconnected. Gone. Surgically removed.

Joseph peered around cautiously, and found he had no difficulty turning his head. He lay in a bed, in a pleasant room with windows shaded against the sun.

"Joseph?"

He met Suleyman's somber gaze.

"Tell me what happened to you, Joseph. I need you to tell me as quickly as you can."

Joseph gave him the briefest version of the story, about the stupid little men who'd been after Lewis for years and finally caught up with him. About the weapons they had, that could ruin the biomechanicals on an operative.

Suleyman looked grim. "There's more to the story than that, though, isn't there?"

"Yeah," Joseph replied. "What have you done to me, Suleyman?"

"Modified you. We had no choice. You won't need the signal disrupter anymore, at least. You're officially dead now, Joseph, as far as the Company's concerned. You don't exist. But they may have a problem solver hunting for you anyway, and we can't risk their finding you here."

Joseph lay there blinking, unable to take it in.

Suleyman went to the window, looking down into the street below. "We'll get you back on your feet again, of course, and I can give you a list of contacts. You'd heal faster if we had a regeneration tank, but the closest ones are in that bunker you showed me, and I don't think you want to go there. Once you've recovered, though, you'll need to run. You're a hazard to my people."

Joseph nodded.

"I am truly sorry about this, Joseph, sorrier than you can know. A lot has happened in the last few weeks. When you're well enough, you're going to have to tell me the whole story, from the beginning, no lies, nothing left out. Do you understand? And the others are going to want to talk to you."

"Okay," said Joseph, but was distracted by the echoes that were beginning in his head.

Suleyman scowled at him and crossed swiftly to his bedside. He leaned down and looked hard at Joseph, then straightened up. "Latif!" he shouted.

Joseph didn't know what happened after that.

He wasn't well for a long time, even after they repaired him. The Company wasn't with him anymore. Nobody was watching him, but nobody was watching *over* him either. For some reason his body seemed to believe it was mortal again. Systems faltered or gave out for no apparent reason, and Latif would be suddenly there beside him with a stabilizer cabinet, cursing, pounding on his chest, telling him it was all in his head.

His head wasn't at its best, certainly. He had long periods of clarity, but there were still intervals when the echoes would come, when he had to wait, to listen, trying to unravel them, and he couldn't focus on anything else then. When Joseph was able to think once more, Suleyman would come sit beside him and resume the debriefing. It went on for days. They pried out every detail from his story, going back over the events. Sometimes Suleyman brought in other people, operatives Joseph didn't know, and had them listen.

The more Joseph told the story, the more terrible it seemed to him, until he could scarcely believe what he'd done. There were times when he lay there weeping helplessly, desperate to redeem himself with Dr. Zeus, ready to go crawling to confess everything, excuse anything, if the Company would only take him back. He wanted his old life again. He'd never wanted trouble. He didn't want to be alone, cut off, adrift.

One afternoon he opened his eyes, and Nan was sitting beside him, holding his hand. He smiled.

"Joseph, dear," she said. "We've found out something."

"What?"

"The details of your story are confirmed. You did take a room at the Hotel Saint Catherine on 5 August, and so did Lewis. On 6 August you were both seen in town. On 7 August the maid went to your rooms and found the beds unmade and all your luggage still there, but no sign of either one of you. Three days later, just as the manager was about to call the police, two men representing themselves as your attorneys came to the hotel and removed your personal effects. They paid what you owed and left. The manager was disinclined to pursue the matter further."

"Ah," said Joseph.

"I broke into your personnel file. I examined Lewis's, too. The last entry shows that you were transferred from long-term active duty in Madrid to a location known only as Site 489. Lewis's last entry shows a short-term mission to Arkham, Vermont, following which he too was transferred to Site 489."

"Same place."

"Joseph," she said, squeezing his hand. "Both entries are dated 5 August 2276. The day before the accident happened."

He stared at her as that sank in. "Then the Company did plan it," he whispered.

"Someone planned it," Nan said. "Someone let those creatures know where Lewis was. And you were meant to be taken with him."

"I was right," he said dully. It didn't make him happy.

"Now we know," Nan said, her voice precise and quiet, "that a site number is a designation not of place but of fate. It signifies permanent disposal of some kind, or at least what the Company imagines to be permanent. Lewis has been disposed of. So has Mendoza. So has Kalugin. So have you, as far as they are aware. Why, Joseph?"

"We were poking around. Getting into secrets."

"And my dear Kalugin, who never did anything but follow kind impulses at the wrong moment? Or poor unhappy Mendoza, who loved a mortal man?" Nan's voice hardened. "What happened to them, Joseph? Are they really lost, has the Company found some way to reverse immortality? Or are they hidden away in bunkers, like your friends the old Enforcers?"

"I know what they did to Lewis," said Joseph. "I know what they did to me. If the Company doesn't know how to kill us, the little stupid men do. Maybe. Though I'm not dead. Maybe Lewis isn't dead, either." But it was a mistake to say that, for it brought terrible images to his mind: Lewis alive and unable to die no matter how desperately he wanted to, helpless somewhere. Joseph began to tremble.

Nan held him, but her voice was like steel now. "We really must find out. Don't you agree? Before more of us join the ranks of the disappeared? Because the rate of disappearance has accelerated. In the last week, fifty operatives were transferred to sites designated by numbers. The week before that, it was twenty-seven. How many of them were people we knew, Joseph? Will we be obliged to rebel?"

He closed his eyes. "This is it, isn't it? The pieces are beginning to fall into place for 2355. Infighting and treachery. Is this where the Silence starts?"

"I wish I knew," she replied.

The following day he woke to see Victor standing beside his bed, white-faced with anger but composed. "So it's true?" he said. "They gave Lewis to—those things?"

"Yes," Joseph said. "The little stupid people."

"Worse perversions of humanity than our own damned father Budu, I can tell you. Homo Umbratilis, the Company called them."

Man of the shadows? thought Joseph foggily. He said, "You know something about them?"

"Oh, yes," Victor said, pulling up a chair and sitting down. His fists were clenched on the arms of the chair; Joseph noticed this because Victor was wearing white gloves indoors, which was strange. "Filthy little dwellers under rocks. Idiot craftsmen. Responsible, I daresay, for all the legends of dwarves and kobolds and malevolent fairies. Marginally human, but debased and retarded for all their genius. I don't know what the Company did to earn their hatred; but it seems they set themselves the task of disabling our operatives."

"They got Lewis once before," Joseph said. "But the Company saved him that time."

"I know," said Victor, tight-lipped. "I was there when we revived him. I was his, how would you describe it—? His handler. It was my job to see how fully he recovered, how much he remembered about the incident. And when he did remember, it was my job to see that he forgot again."

Joseph regarded him a long moment. "You've done some dirty work in your day, haven't you?" he said at last.

"Vile things," Victor said. "I marvel I don't leave stains where I walk. Listen to me, Joseph. There was a black project. It was by sheerest accident that Lewis blundered into one of their warrens the first time. When the Company rescued Lewis and saw what the little monsters could do—no operative had ever been so badly disabled—they captured and bred the damned things, to see if such genius could be turned to Dr. Zeus's advantage. But they could never get enough of them, the creatures didn't breed well, the males tended to die young. So Dr. Zeus crossbred them with Homo sapiens, and had slightly better success.

"And then the Company discovered that they were still after Lewis. They can focus on only one idea at a time, but they focus with dreadful intensity, and they never give up. They got it into their heads that they could perfect their weapon against us if they could recapture Lewis and study him.

"Dr. Zeus shipped him off to New World One, out of their reach. I was sent there a while to observe him. His memories hadn't returned, so I reported that he might go back to active duty when the Company had further use for him.

"I thought it was all over. I thought the creatures had all been captured." Victor tugged absently at his gloves. "There were no more reports of fairies in the world. All the old stories were being dismissed as superstition. I didn't know they'd simply got better at hiding themselves. But the Company knew. The Company watched Lewis, waiting to see if the creatures had forgot about him."

"And they hadn't," said Joseph.

"No. They were lurking after one of the Company's half-breeds when he led them to Lewis, quite by chance. And then the hunt was up again. You know what happened after that. Lewis fled to you, after all."

"The Company creamed them again."

"No, as it happened. It would appear that some sort of contact was attempted at that time. The Company wanted to reach an agreement with them."

"Just to get Lewis out of the way?" Joseph was aghast. "What had he done? All we ever did was talk about trying to find Mendoza."

"Oh, you did other things." Victor gave him a shrewd look. "You know that perfectly well. You might have been able to get away with it—you're a Facilitator—but not Lewis. He'd developed a fondness for certain Company secrets, for one thing. And it began to be obvious that his lost memories were returning. But I'm afraid that wasn't the whole reason he was marked for disappearance."

"What?"

"The creatures wanted Lewis for experiments," said Victor, spreading his gloved hands. "Well, the Company decided to let them have him. And if you can't imagine why our masters might want someone, anyone, to devise a weapon against us—but you're not that naive."

Joseph just stared at him.

"Things are rather sticky, just now. Rumors are flying, distrust and paranoia abound, rebellion is in the air. Personally, I can't imagine how the Silence is going to wait until 2355 to fall," he said.

"Me either," Joseph said.

"But it will," Victor mused. "Giving us seventy-four years to prepare ourselves. I can't say I find the prospect of my own death that alarming. I certainly merit capital punishment, several times over, and if you knew the details of my very unpleasant career, you'd agree with me. But Lewis was a gentleman, and he didn't deserve what they did to him." He looked at Joseph with his pale catlike eyes. "Neither did poor old Kalugin. I begin to suspect that even our father wasn't as bad as he seemed, set beside the monsters who created him."

Joseph lay his head back on the pillow, exhausted. "But what do we do?"

"I must go on playing the game for another few decades. I haven't much choice," Victor told him. "You, however, now have a certain freedom denied the rest of us. If you're a clever fellow—and your history persuades me you're very clever indeed—you'll put it to good use. You can go wherever you wish. Set traps for guilty parties. Pursue the truth. I strongly recommend that you begin in San Francisco."

"San Francisco, huh?" Joseph narrowed his eyes.

Victor got up and went to the door. He paused there a moment. "And you might want to take a shovel with you."

Latif disconnected the diagnostic apparatus. "See? Not a damned thing wrong anymore," he told Joseph. "I told you."

"My nose hurts," Joseph complained.

"Psychosomatic. So you weigh an ounce less than you used to. Big Brother won't be in your head, either. No more worrying about making the Company suspicious over those embarrassing little power surges that happen too often."

"Nobody seems to suspect the bunch of you," Joseph grumbled, rising from the chair.

"There's a power station across the street." Latif bared his teeth in a smile. "Neat, huh? All kinds of interference, and there's nothing anybody can do, so it's ignored. Not that anybody would question Suleyman, anyway."

"People have questioned me," Suleyman told him, watching from the sidelines. "Nobody's untouchable, son. Never forget that."

"I'd like to see Dr. Zeus try to doublecross you!" Latif said.

"No, you wouldn't," said Suleyman and Joseph at the same time.

Latif shrugged and went to the weapons cabinet, where he drew out a high-speed ballistic handgun and checked it. "Ready when you are," he told Joseph. "Bunny-slope setting, okay?"

Joseph poised on one of a number of blue circles painted on the floor. Latif took careful aim and fired at him point-blank from a distance of three meters.

Joseph was gone, of course, before the bullet reached him, having winked out to one of the other circles. Latif whirled, though still moving at mere mortal speed, and fired again; Joseph was gone to another circle. His choice of circles was random. Another shot, and another circle, and so on, until the clip was empty.

"Normal response time, normal readout," Suleyman said. "Next level."

Latif reloaded. Joseph took his position on the first circle again, and the game resumed, but with the difference that Latif was now moving at Joseph's speed. The game was over in a few seconds, and Joseph was still unharmed.

"Normal response time, normal readout," repeated Suleyman. "This seems as good a time as any to tell you about the coup attempt. Next level."

"Excuse me?" Joseph looked up from watching Latif's trigger finger. Latif fired anyway, and the game began again, at the same speed, with the variation that Latif was now attempting to anticipate Joseph's next position rather than the one he happened to be occupying at that particular millisecond.

"Normal response time, normal readout. Yes, you remember I mentioned things were getting a little edgy up there? It seems the Plague Club made a premature bid for power. Either that or someone in the ruling cabal finally took notice of my warnings and mounted an operation against them," Suleyman said. "Next level."

Latif reloaded, grinning. The next level was like the previous one, only faster, and utilizing the circles that had been painted on the walls and ceiling also.

"Really?" Joseph said, panting slightly.

"Normal, normal. Yes. Most of the Company personnel will never hear about it, but all the executive operatives had to be informed. Perhaps I should say *explained to*; we couldn't help but notice something was going on. Normal, normal. Next level." Any mortal in the room at this moment would have thought Suleyman was talking to himself, as the other two immortals were moving far too quickly to be seen. Of course, no mortal could have heard what Suleyman was saying over the roar of continuous gunfire.

Suleyman continued: "Quite a few executive assignments of long standing have been unexpectedly reshuffled. One hundred and six operatives of differing grades have been transferred to numbered sites over a period of six weeks. There have been some promotions. There have been three outright arrests, which as you know is extremely rare."

The noise stopped suddenly, and two figures became visible through the clearing gun smoke.

"Damn, this gun's melted," said Latif. Suleyman looked at him in mild reproach.

"So who got arrested?" gasped Joseph, leaning forward and bracing his hands on his knees.

"Nobody you know. They were, however, very high in the Plague Club cabal, subordinates only to Labienus. He didn't get arrested, which I find interesting." Suleyman took the ruined gun from Latif and examined it thoughtfully. "An intercabal purge to free himself of anyone still loyal to Budu, perhaps. Of the operatives who were sent to numbered sites, about half were known members of the Plague Club. Of course, many weren't. Lewis, for example. I'm certain he was never a member. You—" Suleyman sighted along the barrel. "You, I'm giving the benefit of the doubt." He tossed the warped thing away in disgust.

"Thanks so much," Joseph said, mopping his face with a towel.

"You're welcome. And I received a commendation from our masters, in appreciation of my dogged attempts to warn them of this possibility, and their assurances that it has been dealt with. They continue to depend on my unshakable integrity and loyalty. Isn't that nice?"

Joseph rolled his eyes. "If they're throwing around words like *loyalty*, things must have got pretty shaky up there."

"So I guess it will quiet down, now," said Latif.

Suleyman and Joseph looked at each other.

"Maybe," said Suleyman. They walked together out of the diagnostic room. He drew a deep breath. "So, Joseph. You tested out fit and fine. You're completely recovered and ready to be cut loose. You understand."

"I guess." Joseph sighed and flexed his shoulders.

"You are the security risk from hell, man," Latif said.

"He knows that, son. My people have too much at stake. There are mortals who would lose their lives. There are immortals who would lose more. We haven't seen Joseph, haven't heard from him, have no idea what became of him. He is lost and will stay lost. It shouldn't be too hard for a man of his experience."

"I owe you, Suleyman—" Joseph began, but Suleyman held up his hand.

"In return, he will forget anything he saw concerning my immunization program." He looked at Joseph sternly. "To each his own rebellion."

"And if you tell anybody about the program," added Latif, "it won't matter how lost you are—I will come after you and I will find you, man."

That evening a solitary traveler slipped out of a side gate and made his way to a public transport stand. A ticket was purchased, in cash, for the coast. At Casablanca the traveler got out and moved through the darkness to the waterfront, where great cargo ships waited for morning. He found the one he wanted. No mortal security guard saw him run aboard, quicker than a rat and quieter.

The traveler found his way among the shipping containers, seeking one with a broken seal, inching between the stacks in the darkness. When he found the container he needed, he prized it open and slithered in, clambering up through boxes of electronic equipment to the top, where there was a comfortable clearance between the roof of the container and his face. The traveler stretched out and sighed, feeling secure.

No mortal would have been able to bear a stateroom like that, but it had its advantages. Cargo ships were not subjected to the same rigorous security measures air transports were. They were too useful for smuggling, for one thing. The official argument was that terrorists always took planes. In any case the cargo ships traveled so slowly that no mortal who had places to go and things to do would choose one as a method of transport.

Joseph, of course, wasn't mortal, even if he felt not quite as immortal as he had been.

He closed his eyes and set his internal clocks, factoring in emergency protocols. He began to breathe very slowly, and more slowly still. Gradually he slipped into a voluntary fugue state. He was only dimly aware, hours later, when the ship backed ponderously from her berth and made her way out into the Atlantic. By the time she was well out to sea, he had shut down entirely. He rested, waiting, dreaming.

He didn't dream particularly well. The great voice was booming in the darkness, impressively echoing and quite unmistakable. "And when he opened the fifth seal, I saw under the tabernacle, the souls of them that were killed for the word of God, and for the testimony they had, and they cried with a loud voice saying: how long tarriest thou Lord holy and true, to judge and to avenge our blood on them that dwell on the earth? And long white garments were given unto every one of them!"

"Don't you tell *me* about John of Patmos," Joseph heard himself growling. "I knew the guy, okay?"

But the speaker rose from his table and stood, lit only by the single candle that had enabled him to read, and the light fell on the long folds of the scholar's black robe and on the face. The eyes above the wide cheekbones were shadowed, but a spark glinted there, and light glinted on the teeth.

"And it was said unto them that they should rest for a little season until the number of their fellows, and brethren, and of them that should be killed as they were, were fulfilled!" shouted Nicholas Harpole, holding out his hands as though he were about to present Joseph with something. So eloquent was his gesture, so well acted, that Joseph stepped forward half against his will to see what it was, though he knew there was nothing there.

There was something in his hands, after all: a sheet of mirrored glass. Joseph looked at himself and saw a snarling dog face, foam dripping from the jaws. And more: stretching into the darkness behind him, a vaulted bunker with row upon row of open coffins, each containing a figure robed in white. There were too many to count, but Joseph could see the two in the foreground with perfect clarity. Mendoza and Lewis, too pale, too still.

"You bastard," Joseph wept. At least he was weeping inside; the dog's face showed no emotion. "They're your victims, you know that? You got them both. Couldn't stay dead, could you? Reached out of your grave and made them love you, and it destroyed them. Age after age, you come back." Joseph reeled, trying to think what else had

happened, what else he had said and done, in that prison cell so long ago.

Chortling, he drew back his fist, ready to deliver a sound right hook to Nicholas's jaw. Up he soared, into midair, laughing to himself, but he connected with nothing, and after a moment's breathless pause he looked down to find himself hurtling into a red canyon with a tiny ribbon of blue water winding through it, far below.

Down he tumbled, thinking in resignation that this too was déjà vu. Then, crash, he'd made a hole in the ground just his own size and shape, and he knew that the big Englishman would be looking down from his great height at the puff of rising dust and sneering.

And in fact that was what he was doing, as Joseph saw when he dragged himself out of the hole. Sneering down from horseback, no less, as though he wasn't tall enough already, and resplendent in a fine tailored Victorian traveling ensemble.

He made a covert gesture, and Joseph tensed, thinking he was going to draw a hidden weapon. Instead he produced a shovel out of nowhere, and threw it at Joseph's feet. Joseph jumped backward.

"Seek for thy noble father in the dust, Hamlet," said Edward Alton Bell-Fairfax contemptuously, and, turning his horse's head, he galloped away.

"You think you're so smart," Joseph shouted after him. "You quoted it wrong, big shot!"

He turned and looked over his shoulder to avoid falling into the hole again, but to his amazement he saw that the hole had changed: it was no longer the size and shape of his own body but much bigger, as though it had been made by his father.

San Francisco

THE CARGO VESSEL *Hanjin* maneuvered slowly into Island Creek Channel and moored there, dropping anchor. Her captain went ashore to register her arrival with the proper authorities. Her crew were showering, sprucing up for a night on the town.

Joseph, deep in the hold, woke in darkness and listened a long while. He heard the crew leave, all but the night watch. He heard the great city grow quiet as the hours went by. When he judged the time to be right, he crawled from his hiding place and crept up on deck, avoiding the surveillance cameras that swept back and forth relentlessly.

Watching for the proper moment, he dropped over the side and swam ashore. He made his way to Third Street and trudged along it, passing the big ballpark, squelching all the way up to Market. Here he paused a moment before turning left and walking up Market as far as Grant. At Grant he turned right and went into Chinatown.

He walked more slowly now, scanning as he went. He disabled the security system of a small grocery store, broke in, and loaded the pockets of his long coat with fruit, protein bars, bottles of water, and herbal tea. He hurried on from there and sought out an apartment building, an older and less desirable one. Half its units were presently vacant, its security system offline. It still took five minutes' work to persuade the elevator to take him up to the eighth floor, which was completely without tenants.

He broke into one unit and settled himself on the floor, where he gorged on what he'd stolen from the market. His body received it gratefully. He was overwhelmed with the need for real sleep, now, and sprawled in a strategically chosen corner near a window and let himself rest.

It was late afternoon when he awoke. It was later by the time he finally got the elevator down to the street and exited from the building by a service door.

He did not go to Sacramento yet. He walked back to Market Street instead, through the going-home crowds, pacing up its length until he found a major department store. He went in, found a holomap of the store, noted where the hardware and sporting goods departments were, noted moreover what kind of security system protected the store. Then he left and went down to stroll along the Embarcadero, a grubby little man in a long coat.

When it grew dark, he went quietly to the back door of a restaurant and disabled its security system. The cook, bending over the oven to take out a pan of rolls, felt a faint chill. He looked around to see where the draft came from and saw, to his astonishment, that an entire casserole of lasagna had vanished. So had two loaves of fresh-baked bread.

A mile away, Joseph leaned back against a pier piling and ate, watching the lights of Oakland glitter across the water. When he finished, he buried the evidence of his meal and waited until the crowds all went home, the floaters, the cyclists, the performance artists. He waited until the lights in the towers began to wink out. Then he walked back up Market Street and stole a truck.

A City Parks and Recreation Department agvan, to be precise, from a transit yard south of Market. The yard wasn't locked. No point, when vehicles were capable of floating over fences. Car theft was virtually unknown in the twenty-third century anyway, thanks to alarms that could not be disabled by the most determined mortal. Five minutes after Joseph strolled into the transit yard, he was piloting the agvan around the corner of Market and Second to the main entrance of the department store.

No subtle cyborg tricks on the lock this time. He just broke and entered, and went into hyperfunction as soon as he heard the faint high scream of the alarm. The security cameras saw no more than a blur racing up and down the fire stairs and through the departments he needed. Rapidly, things began to appear in the back of the van as though teleported there: three cases of high-energy bars, a crate of bottled water, two tarpaulins, an electronics tool kit, picks and shovels, a sleeping bag, clothing, and, last but not least, a sixty-gallon fusion trash receptacle.

Long before the security officer staggered out to see what was going on, the agvan was roaring away down Grant Avenue.

Joseph slowed as he turned left onto Sacramento, up one of the desperately steep hills that made motoring so memorable in the days of manual transmissions. He climbed slowly, scanning as he went, and passed Waverly Place. On the right-hand side of the street he found what he had been seeking. He had to get out and stare, though, peering through the fence. Why couldn't he be wrong about his worst fears once in a while?

There was no house at that location, above Waverly Place. There was a tiny fenced park, walled around by towering buildings. What Joseph had been seeking registered as ten feet down, under the neat flowerbeds and pristine lawn.

He got the simple lock open and went right to work, draping the fence with tarpaulins to mask his activities. He brought out the tools and the trash receptacle. He walked the length of the little park, scanning again, moving his head this way and that as though listening for something. When he had it pinpointed, he began to dig, quickly.

The first shovel broke after half an hour, when he'd gone down six feet. Then there was a hard impacted layer, clay and ash, tumbled bricks; he used a pick to get through that. It was the stratum from the 1906 earthquake, the truth buried so far under the pretty flowers, the past that the present was built on. When Joseph brought up a piece of human skull, one eye socket hooked on the business end of the pick, he stopped and went in with another shovel, more carefully.

Charred mortal bones, fragments of wood, bits of brass. An opium pipe. A bronze hatchet head. Joseph peered at it and made out the characters that told him it was the property of the Black Dragon Retribution Tong. More bones, more hatchet heads, and something that didn't grate or clank under his shovel. Soft and dull, like leather.

Joseph dropped the shovel at once. He knelt and began to dig with his hands, crying silently, tears running down his face and silvering in his beard.

He found an arm first, fragments of its rotted coat dropping away as he lifted it out: withered sinew, tarry flesh, the leather of the skin strangely supple even so. Bright glint of metal, ferroceramic at the bone end. He lifted it, and it flexed like a snake. Clawlike fingers curled into a fist as he watched. It was a very big arm, wasted and shrunken though it was.

He set it on the edge of the hole and kept searching. Here was a gigantic thigh, still wearing riveted rags: Levi Strauss jeans, for God's sake. The rest of the leg followed, but the foot had been hacked off.

Eventually he found a boot, with a bit of ankle and gimbal joint protruding from its top.

The rest of the body was battered and hewn but in one piece, except for the head. He found it, after a long moment of panicked scrabbling in the hole. You really don't want to know what it looked like.

Joseph crawled out and attempted to fit the body into the trash receptacle. With some effort he got it to flex, and pushed it down. He placed the head in too, more or less in its own lap, and the arm and leg and foot, and closed the lid. He rolled the receptacle awkwardly to the back of the agvan. Having secured it, he got in and drove to Van Ness, took Van Ness to Lombard, and took Lombard to the Golden Gate Bridge, just as mortals had done for the last four centuries.

The bridge had changed. Its scarlet towers were supported now by antigravity banks, and it had twisted and broken and been repaired more times than could be counted. It was still something to make you catch your breath, whether you were mortal or immortal.

The agvan roared across it under the unsleeping lights and disappeared into the wall of fog that was tumbling down the Marin headlands.

Mount Tamalpais

JOSEPH PULLED TO the side of a particular mountain road and got out, sniffing the air. Morning on the wind, even if there was no appreciable light in the sky yet. He scanned and spotted the entrance to the bunker, which, predictably enough, was where he had found it a century earlier. He unloaded the agvan, lugging things up a steep hill, following a deer trail through madrone and manzanita. Last was the trash receptacle, and he blessed its little wheels that allowed him to drag it along the trail.

When he'd secured everything at the bunker's door, he staggered back down and leaned into the cab of the agvan to program its auto-pilot. He backed away and watched as it rose smoothly and rotated. It sped off, back to the distant transport yard in the city. He climbed back up the hill.

Having worked the seal on the door, he went down the long echoing passage, dragging behind him the trash bin full of discarded god.

Abdiel was very old, but he didn't know he was very old. His memory wasn't all that good. Looking in a mirror wouldn't have reminded him: he appeared perpetually twenty, and a young twenty at that, wide dark eyes with a sort of startled Bambi expression, lots of soft curling black hair and a soft dark beard.

He didn't know he'd looked like that for the last thirty thousand years. He wasn't very bright.

But bright enough to do his job, and follow the few simple commandments with which he had been programmed. There are seven holy shrines, he had been told. Thou shalt go from the first to the second, and from the second to the third, and so to the seventh, when thou shalt go back to the first again. At each shrine shalt thou labor, as thou hast been instructed; and when thy labor is done there, thou must bear witness and travel to the next place appointed. Thou shalt not fail in this, neither shalt thou speak of thy task to any mortal thou mayest meet without the shrines.

Nowadays it generally took him about twenty years to make a full circle. When he came back to the first shrine, he was always surprised to see his own handwriting on the chalkboard, because he never realized until that moment that he wasn't arriving there for the first time. The moment he erased the board, it was always as though he'd erased the realization too, for with proof of the past gone, the past ceased to exist for him.

Abdiel was a failed immortal, but if his brain was like a sieve, his body at least was perfectly untiring, ageless, beautiful. Accordingly, the Company had found a use for him, making the most of his plight.

He walked up the side of Mount Tamalpais, keeping to the recreational paths because they were easy, and he liked to follow the line of least resistance. He smiled and stepped aside for every jogger he encountered, keeping his eyes modestly downcast. His clothes were nondescript and a little shabby, though not too shabby, because he didn't like being arrested as a vagrant. It kept him from his duties, and nothing mattered except his duties.

The fog was rolling up the mountain now, drifting like a reverse avalanche from the sea, a torrent of boiling silver in the afternoon light. It floated over the laurel groves and the yellow meadows of autumn, soothing all that dustiness with cool moist air. Abdiel drew it into his lungs gratefully, thanking it for obscuring his way from the mortals. He was invisible in the fog when he sprinted off the path and down through the moss-hung trees to the dark fold in the rock that he'd seen in his dreams.

Yes, there was the doorway to the seventh shrine. He'd completed his pilgrimage at last. He addressed the seal, and it opened for him. He crept in reverently, hurrying down the long tunnel toward the celestial light.

He didn't remember having been here before, so he wasn't as surprised as he might have been to see that there was another person in the shrine, moving about in one of the side chapels. This shrine looked very like the sixth shrine, which he vaguely remembered, because he'd been there most recently: the soft light, the sweet fragrance, and the blessed ones floating in their dreams.

He set down his pack. The motion drew the attention of the other person, who stepped out of the side chapel and looked at him. "I'll bet you're Abdiel," the person said, scanning.

Abdiel nodded. "Are you one of the Masters?" he asked, for the other man wasn't a mortal. The man narrowed his little black eyes and smiled.

"Why, yes," he said. "I am."

As soon as he told Abdiel this, Abdiel knew that it must be so; and though the man looked nothing like the Masters that Abdiel had seen, being grubby and rather small, instantly Abdiel's mental picture of *Master* had reconfigured to resemble the one who stood before him.

"Pleased to meet you," Abdiel said, smiling back.

The Master considered him. "I notice you have no datalink, Abdiel. That must be because your appointed tasks are so top secret and important, right?"

"Yes." Abdiel looked earnest. He wasn't sure why his duties should be top secret, but he certainly knew they were important. "I've found the seventh shrine at last."

"No kidding? Well, good for you. What are you going to do now?"

The Master was testing him! "See that all is clean and in order," Abdiel said fervently. "Check pumps number A3 and C5 in each unit for corrosion. Monitor alkaline balance of regenerative fluids. Check thermocontrols. Check lighting regulators. Check integrity of all seals. Monitor vault integrity and report any cracks, leaks, or evidence of stresses. Bear witness to my labors. Sir!" He saluted snappily.

"Excellent," the Master said, and his smile twisted up into his beard at one side. "Now, you know, of course, that you can't tell anybody you've seen me here? That it's top secret?"

"Oh, yes, sir." Abdiel saluted again.

"Okay, then." The Master rolled up his ragged sleeves. "You run along and do your job, and let me do mine."

"Are you preparing one of the blessed ones for eternal rest?" Abdiel said, looking past him into the side chapel. Something was stretched out on the steel table in there.

"That's right."

"Gee, do you need me to help?" Abdiel looked eager. "I've never done that. I just look after the ones who are resting already."

"You do, eh?" the Master said thoughtfully. "Maybe you can help me. Are you strong?"

"Really strong!" Abdiel held up both arms and made fists to show his muscles.

When the Master led him into the side chamber, Abdiel drew back in horror at what he saw lying on the table there. "Oh. That's one of the evil ones!" he said, averting his eyes.

"Why do you think so?" the Master asked, watching him.

"Well, he's all dirty and horrible and dead-looking, and the blessed ones are never like that," Abdiel said, trying not to see. "The blessed ones are clean and whole and sleep in the heavenly light. The evil ones sleep where it's dark and dirty, and they get all withered and ugly."

The Master took up the bucket of regenerative solution with which he'd been washing the thing on the table. "Do you know why that is, Abdiel?"

"Because—" Abdiel faltered, then remembered that the Master had tested him before. "Because the blessed ones have worked hard for the Masters, and deserve a nice rest in a shrine. But the evil ones disobeyed, so they have to sleep in the other place."

"And where's the other place, Abdiel?" The Master was bathing the blind eye sockets, the great brown snarling teeth.

Abdiel shuddered and looked away again. "Where you got him from."

"Smart boy, Abdiel," the Master said. "Now, I'll let you in on a little secret. We Masters are all-wise and all-merciful. Sometimes we forgive the evil ones their sins and take them out of the other place and put them here instead. That's what I'm doing now. This guy wasn't all bad, you know. Only he's got to be repaired before he can heal in the heavenly light. See?"

"I guess so." Abdiel made himself raise his head and look at the ruined giant on the table. Oh, he needed repairs terribly. Dermal integrity breached in thirty-eight places on ventral surface. Left pedal support structure disarticulated, left foot avulsed. Left leg avulsed at pelvic articulation, femur analogue frame dented at supports 5, 8 and 13. Right arm—Abdiel ran to the sink and threw up.

"That's okay," the Master said cheerfully. "Good thing you got rid of your lunch before we really got to work. Now, blow your nose and come help me. I'm going to need you to hold him still so I can reattach his leg."

It wasn't a very nice experience. Once the leg was reattached, the great body jerked and twisted, and the bright gimbal of the pedal support structure moved unnervingly until they got its horrible black foot on and sutured in place. The arm was even more frightening, but the head was the worst of all. As soon as the Sinclair chain gimbal was reconnected, even before the muscles could be tugged back and sutured into place, the head began to turn, the fearsome jaws to clash. What remained of the structure of its eyes clicked and fluttered as though trying to see. Abdiel had to run for the sink again.

It didn't bother the Master, though. He just kept working away.

"Now, you see why it's so important to obey us Masters and do your job?" he lectured Abdiel. "Wouldn't it be awful to suffer the way this old guy has? You don't ever want this to happen to you."

"Gosh, never ever!" gasped Abdiel, pulling himself upright and wiping his mouth.

"So you will keep the commandment about silence, right? Because it would be just too awful to break it and turn out like *him*." The Master gritted his teeth and reached up into the neck to pull down one end of a severed tendon. He reconnected it and went on. "Now, I've pretty much got the hard parts over with, so you can go on and do your regular work. Run along."

Abdiel was only too glad to go, out into the heavenly light where the blessed ones slept, fresh and clean every one of them. He busied himself with his assigned tasks and soon forgot all about the nastiness in the side chapel, in fact he was quite startled a week later when the Master came walking down an aisle between the vaults, lugging the ugly old man who was all put together now.

"Hi there," the Master said. "Where's an empty vault, Abdiel?"

Abdiel showed him. The Master climbed up nimbly and dropped the body into the regenerant, where it bobbed for a moment before being drawn in. Then it sank, settled, and, seen through the pure blue glow, seemed no longer quite so dead. Was it moving? Were the shriveled limbs stretching out?

"That's a nice sight," said the Master. "Wasn't as hard as I thought, either. I feel like celebrating! You want a granola bar, Abdiel? My treat." He held out a nubbly confection, and Abdiel accepted it thankfully. He hadn't remembered to eat in days, and his own stash of Power Crunchies was back at the entrance in his pack. The Master drew out another bar and unwrapped it, and they stood there chewing companionably, looking up at the floating figure.

"Will he get better now?" Abdiel asked.

"Oh, yeah," the Master said with his mouth full. "Now that he's all put together, his self-repair will take over and the nanobots will bring him up to specs, rebuild anything he's missing, get the organs functioning again. His brain's offline, but that's the protective fugue. It might take years, but one of these days he'll look just like the rest of the people in here. Like the big guys, anyway."

"What about his heavenly crown?" Abdiel asked, indicating the circlet all the other floating figures wore.

"Oh. Well, he was pretty bad, even if he got forgiven, so I don't know if he'll get one of those," the Master said. "We'll see."

Abdiel nodded, feeling compassionate and hoping the old man would merit a crown. The crowns were terribly important, and must never, ever be taken off a sleeper, because they gave the blessed ones good dreams. Evil ones, of course, had nightmares.

The rest of that time the Master walked with Abdiel, observing him at his duties. He was interested in everything Abdiel did, and asked him a lot of questions. He particularly tested Abdiel on the access codes to the terminals that connected the bunker with the Masters in their distant abode of delight. Abdiel passed every test. The Master congratulated him and told him he was a good operative. When at last Abdiel chalked his witness on the board, shouldered his pack, and walked away down the tunnel to the mortal world, he turned and waved at his new friend, buoyed by a pleasant sense of self-worth.

By the time he was walking along Highway 1, however, he'd forgotten the Master ever existed. All his attention was fixed on finding the mysterious first shrine, which he'd heard was off somewhere in a land far away . . .

Joseph in the Darkness

So THERE IT is. So here we are.

You're getting better, father, I can tell. You still look like a murder victim six times over, but at least you don't seem to have been dead quite so long. Some day soon you'll start growing back the soft tissues of your eyes, your liver, your heart, all those things the rats . . .

What if she . . .

I wonder how you got on the wrong side of the Black Dragon Retribution Tong, father, in an opium cellar on Sacramento Street, just minutes before the 1906 earthquake? Must be quite a story. You'll tell me someday. Or maybe Victor will. I have a feeling he knows. He could never have inflicted those hatchet wounds, he's half your size. And yet something happened when he spit on you. I wonder if it has any connection with those gloves he never takes off.

Were the hatchetmen sent later? Were you unconscious then? Did Labienus set you up? Was he power hungry? Were you a little inconvenient to have around with your rigid moral code? If it wasn't your own people, was it the Company? It's just like something the Company would do. I can testify to that.

This is what the Company does to all its operatives, sooner or later, isn't it? None of us actually dead, but we'd be luckier if we were. Those of us who behaved ourselves get to dream away time in a nice warm bath. Those of us who haven't behaved? They find an excuse to lower the boom on us, one day when we least expect it. Then we're abandoned to rot in a grave like you were, or handed over to the enemy like Lewis was, or used and thrown away like Mendoza so nobody would ever discover the truth about her . . .

The Company must have watched us all, weighed every incident, heard every word we said, and waited, keeping score. They could afford to wait years, hundreds of years, thousands of years, and while we worked so faithfully for them, the list of marks against us grew longer.

Maybe I deserved what happened to me, and maybe you did too, father, but Lewis? What harm did he ever do anybody? And yet I can't imagine what he's suffering now, if he's not so damaged he's past suffering. Poor romantic idiot.

Was he in love with Mendoza? Was he in love with the Englishman? With both of them? Did he even know? He never gave up trying to find them. He wasn't a coward, like me.

She's still lost, my little girl, and maybe in some dungeon blacker than the one in Santiago, with hotter coals. What would they do to a Crome generator? Try to disconnect her extra talents? Experiment on her? She's not in here now, I know. I've looked. If there's the least chance she alone can go forward in time, she alone can discover the truth about 2355, the Company will have locked her away some place a lot more secure than this; and they'll never let her out.

I should have gone after her sooner. I should have gone after you sooner, too.

He was right, the goddam Englishman. I screwed up just like Hamlet. You handed me the truth about your betrayal right at the beginning of the play, and I delayed, procrastinated, because I was scared, wasn't sure, didn't want trouble. Now look. I've lost everything I had, and the curtain's coming down on a stage littered with bodies.

But we'll write a new last act, won't we, father? When I get you out of there, we'll make a plan. You were always a lot better at battle strategies than I was. It'll be easy. I still have the Company access codes Lewis downloaded to me, we know where all the bodies are buried, and we have seventy-four years to get ready.

Maybe we'll set all the Old Guard free, and see how they feel about what's been going on. And then! Wouldn't that be great, father? All of us together again, one last time? I couldn't save Lewis, but we can avenge him. Lewis and all the other innocents. Will we go after treacherous bastards like Nennius? Will we hunt down the masters who have lied to us so shamelessly, for so many thousands of mortal lifetimes? Is 2355 payback time? Is it time to sing the Dies Irae?

Yeah! *For behold, the Lord cometh out of his place to punish the inhabitants of the earth for their iniquity: the earth also shall disclose her blood, and shall no more cover her slain. In that day the Lord with his sore and great and strong sword shall punish leviathan the piercing serpent, even leviathan that crooked serpent; and he shall slay the dragon that is in the sea!*

I can quote Scripture too, you know.